THE MIKO

Fawcett Crest Books
by Eric Van Lustbader:

BLACK HEART

THE NINJA

SIRENS

ERIC VAN LUSTBADER

THE MIKO

FAWCETT CREST • NEW YORK

A Fawcett Crest Book
Published by Ballantine Books

Copyright © 1984 by Eric Van Lustbader

All rights reserved under International and Pan-American Copyright Conventions. Published in the United States by Ballantine Books, a division of Random House, Inc., New York, and simultaneously in Canada by Random House of Canada Limited, Toronto.

Library of Congress Catalog Card Number: 84-40057

ISBN 0-449-20596-7

This edition published by arrangement with Villard Books

Grateful acknowledgement is made to Doubleday and Co., Inc., for permission to reprint the haiku by Shiki and Chiyo from *An Introduction to Haiku* by Harold G. Henderson. Copyright © 1958 by Harold G. Henderson. Reprinted by permission of Doubleday & Company, Inc.

Manufactured in the United States of America

First Ballantine Books Edition: August 1985

ACKNOWLEDGEMENTS

No character in *The Miko* bears the slightest resemblance to any actual person, living or dead, save those mentioned as obvious historical figures. Though MITI is real, and though its power and role in the development of the postwar Japanese economy have been accurately portrayed here, certain specific events at the time of its formation as well as the ministers depicted are purely a product of the author's imagination.

Thanks are due to the following people:
Roni Neuer and Herb Libertson, the Ronin Gallery;
Richard Bush, the Asia Society, Washington, D.C.,
for unlocking the riddle of the *Wu-Shing;*
Charlotte Brenneis, assistant to the president,
Asia Society, New York City;
Nancy Lerner;
All at the Grill & Bar, Kapalua,
for helping to make work so pleasurable;
HM, for editorial assistance;
VSL, for editorial assistance and spiritual sustenance; and,
especially, Tomomi Seki, the Ronin Gallery,
for translations, assistance in all things Japanese time and
again, not only for the *The Miko* but for *The Ninja* as well.
Dōmo arigatō, Seki-san.

Tsugi-no ma-no tomoshi
mo kiete
yo-samu kana

The next room's light
that too goes out, and now—
the chill of night

—Shiki (1867–1902)

MRS. DARLING: *George, we must keep Nana.*
I will tell you why. My dear, when I came into
this room to-night I saw a face at the window.

—J. M. Barrie, *Peter Pan*

NARA PREFECTURE, JAPAN

SPRING, PRESENT

Masashigi Kusunoki, the *sensei* of this *dōjō*, was making tea. He knelt on the reed *tatami*; his kimono, light gray on dark gray, swirled around him as if he were the eye of a great dark whirlpool.

He poured steaming hot water into an earthen cup and, as he took up the reed whisk to make the pale green froth, the form of Tsutsumu shadowed the open doorway. Beyond his bent body, the polished wooden floor on the *dōjō* stretched away, gleaming and perfect.

Kusunoki had his back to the doorway. He faced the edge of the *shōji* screen and the large window through which could be seen the cherry trees in full blossom, clouds come to walk the earth, marching up the densely wooded slopes of Yoshino, their oblique branches as green as the hills beyond, covered with ancient moss. The scent of cedar was very strong now, as it almost always was in this section of Nara prefecture, save during those few weeks of winter when the snow lay heavy through the ridges and rises of the terrain.

Kusunoki never tired of that view. It was steeped in the history of Japan. It was here that Minamoto no Yoshitsune sought the shelter of these fortresslike mountains in order to defeat the treachery of the Shōgun, his brother; it was here that the great doomed Emperor Go-Daigo assembled his troops and ended his exile,

1

beginning his attempt to return to the throne; here, too, where Shugendo developed, the way of mountain ascetics, a peculiar fusion of Buddhism and Shinto. Mount Omine was out there and on its slopes congregated the *yamabushi*, the wandering, self-mortifying adherents of this syncretic religion.

He looked now at the tea, its color lightening as the spume rose, and he saw all there was to see beyond that thin pane of glass.

Behind him, Tsutsumu was about to announce himself softly but, seeing the *sensei* kneeling, unaware, froze his tongue. For a long time he contemplated the figure on the *tatami*, and as he did so his muscles began to lose their relaxedness. He had been alert; now he was ready. His mind sought the many pathways toward victory while his eyes drank in the utter stillness in the other. The hands must be moving, Tsutsumu told himself, because I know he is preparing the tea . . . yet he might as well be a statue for all I can see of it.

He knew the time to be right and, unbidden, he rose, unfurling himself like a sail before the wind. Taking two swift, silent strides, he crossed the threshold and was within striking distance. His body torqued with the first onset of intrinsic energy.

At that instant, Kusunoki turned and, extending the hot cup of tea, said, "It is always an honor to invite a pupil so quick to learn into my study."

His eyes locked onto Tsutsumu, and the student felt as if he had hit against an invisible, impenetrable wall. All the fire of the energy he had banked for so long, now at last turned loose, was stifled, held momentarily in thrall, then dissipated.

Tsutsumu shivered involuntarily. He blinked as an owl might in daylight. He felt intensely vulnerable without that which had always been his.

The *sensei* was smiling pleasantly. "Come," he said, and Tsutsumu saw that another cup of tea had somehow materialized. "Let us drink together . . . to show respect and our mutual good intentions."

The student smiled awkwardly and, shakily, sat on the *tatami* facing Kusunoki. Between them was a break in the reed mats that was far more than an architectural or an esthetic delineation. It was the space between host and guest, always observed.

Tsutsumu took the cup and, holding it carefully and correctly in both hands, prepared to drink. The warmth of the tea rushed into his palms. He bowed to his *sensei*, touched the curved rim of the cup to his lips, and drank the intensely bitter beverage. It was very good, and he closed his eyes for an instant, forgetting

2

where he was and, even, who he was, to the extent that that was possible. He tasted the earth of Japan and with it all things Japanese. History and legend, honor and courage, the weight of *kami*, hovering. And, above all, duty. *Giri*.

Then his eyes opened and all was as it had been before. He felt again the uncomfortableness of being so far from home. He was from the north and Nara was an alien place to him; he had never liked it here. Yet he had come and had stayed for two long years. *Giri*.

"Tell me," Kusunoki said, "what is the first thing we assess in combat?"

"Our opponent," Tsutsumu said immediately. "The exchange of attitude and intention tells us where we are and how we are to proceed."

"Indeed," Kusunoki said, as if this were a new concept to him and he was mulling it over in his mind. "So we think of victory."

"No," the student said. "We concern ourselves with not being defeated."

The *sensei* looked at him with his hard black eyes that seemed ripped from a hawk's fierce face. "Good," he said at last. "Very good, indeed."

Tsutsumu, sipping his tea slowly, wondered what this was all about. Words and more words. The *sensei* was asking him questions to which any good pupil must know the answers. Be careful, he cautioned himself, remembering the instantaneous dissolution of his attacking force. Be on guard.

"So here we equate defeat with the end of life."

The student nodded. "In hand-to-hand we are on the death ground, as Sun Tzu has written. We must fight, always."

Now Kusunoki allowed a full smile. "But Sun Tzu has also written, 'To subdue the enemy *without* fighting shows the highest level of skill. Thus, what is supreme is to attack the enemy's strategy.'"

"Pardon me, *sensei*, but it seems to me Sun Tzu was speaking solely about war in that instance."

"Well," Kusunoki said evenly, "isn't that what we are also talking about?"

Tsutsumu felt his heart skip a beat and it was with a great personal effort that he kept himself calm. "War? Forgive me, *sensei*, but I do not understand."

Kusunoki's face was benign as he thought, And Sun Tzu also wrote that those skilled in war can make themselves invincible but cannot cause an enemy to be vulnerable. "There are many faces war may take on, many guises. Is this not so?"

3

"It is, *sensei*," Tsutsumu said, his pulse in his throat.

"We can ask, what war can be made here"—his arm drifted through the air like a cloud, describing an arc toward the wonder and peace of the wooded hillsides visible through the window—"in Yoshino where the history of Japan lives and thrives. One might think war an outmoded concept here among the cherry trees and the cedars."

His great black eyes fixed on Tsutsumu, and the pupil felt a muscle along his inner thigh begin to tremble. "Yet war has come to this indomitable fortress of nature. And thus it must be dealt with."

Now Tsutsumu was truly terrified. This was no ordinary invitation to sit at the *sensei*'s feet and sip tea while speaking of mundane matters, the substance of daily lessons.

"There is a traitor here in Yoshino," Kusunoki said.

"What?"

"Yes, it is true." Kusunoki nodded his head sadly. "You are the first I have spoken to about it. I observe you in class. You are quick, quick and intelligent. Now you will work with me on this matter. You will spy for me among the students. You will begin now. Have you observed anything out of the ordinary that might help us in identifying the spy?"

Tsutsumu thought furiously. He was not unaware of the amazing opportunity being afforded him and was immensely grateful for it. He felt as if a great weight had been taken off his chest. Now he must make the most of this opening. "I seem to remember," he began. "Yes, yes. There is something. The *woman*"—he used a most unflattering inflection—"has been seen here late into the evening hours."

"What has she been doing?" There was no need to name her. The *dōjō* contained only one woman—a choice of the *sensei* that was not popular with his pupils though none dared voice their displeasure where he could hear. Nevertheless, he knew about it.

Tsutsumu shrugged. "Who knows, *sensei*? Certainly she was not practicing."

"I see." Kusunoki seemed engulfed in thought.

Tsutsumu sought to press his advantage. "Of course there has been much talk lately concerning her; a great deal of talk."

"She is not liked."

"No, *sensei*," Tsutsumu confirmed, "most of the students do not feel she has a place here within the sanctity of the *dōjō*. It goes against tradition, they feel. This kind of...ah...training should not be open to a woman, they believe." The student bowed his head as if reluctant to go on. "Forgive me, *sensei*, but there

4

has even been some talk that her presence here was the reason that you left your high position within the Gyokku *ryu*. They say she came to you there, that on her behalf you went to the council of *jonin* and sought their vote for her entry into the *ryu*. They say it is because you could not muster enough votes within your own council that you left." His head raised. "All because of her."

Invincibility lies in the defense, Kusunoki thought. The possibility of victory is attack. To his pupil, he said, "It is true that I was once *jonin* in the Gyokku *ryu*; that much is common knowledge. But the reasons for my departure are my own; no one else knows them, not even the other members of the council. My great-great-grandfather was one of the founders of Gyokku; it took much thought on my part to make the decision. It took much time."

"I understand, *sensei*," Tsutsumu said, thinking that what he had just been told was an utter lie. He was certain within his own heart that Kusunoki had, indeed, jeopardized his entire career for this one woman. Inexplicably.

"Good." Kusunoki nodded. "I thought you might." The black eyes closed for a moment, and the student breathed an inaudible sigh of relief. He felt a trickle of sweat creeping like an insect down the indentation of his spine and he struggled to keep his body still. "Perhaps I have been wrong about her, after all," the *sensei* said. With a great deal of elation, Tsutsumu recognized the sadness in the other's voice. "If what you have gleaned is indeed the truth, then we must deal with her swiftly and ruthlessly."

Tsutsumu's head swung around at the mention of the word *we*. "Yes, *sensei*," he said, thinking, Softly, softly now, knowing he was moving in, trying to keep his jubilation in check. "Any way I may serve you is an honor. That is why I first came here, and I have not wavered in that resolve."

Kusunoki nodded. "It is as I suspected. There are few one can trust even in this day and age. When I ask for your opinions now, when I ask for you to take action, both of these must be given willingly and faithfully."

Tsutsumu could barely contain his euphoria; outwardly he showed nothing. "You have but to ask me," he said.

"*Muhon-nin*," Kusunoki said, leaning forward, "this is all I ask."

The word *traitor* had only begun to register on Tsutsumu's brain when he felt the incredible pain engulf him and, looking down, saw the *sensei*'s hand gripping him just below the collarbone. It was not a strike he had yet mastered and, staring bewilderedly at it, trying to fathom its secrets, he died, a froth of pink saliva bubbling between his trembling lips.

5

Kusunoki, watching life escape like a puff of invisible smoke, took his hand away from the corpse. Without his support, it swayed and fell to one side, the pink drool staining the *tatami* on which Tsutsūmu knelt.

Behind the *sensei* a shadow appeared to move behind the *shōji* and then a figure emerged. Hearing the pad of bare feet, the *sensei* said, "You heard it all?"

"Yes. You were correct all along. He was the traitor." The voice was light, pleasingly modulated. Female.

She wore a dark brown kimono, designed with gray plovers within circles of black. Her gleaming black hair was drawn tightly back from her face.

Kusunoki did not turn around at her silent approach. Instead, he was staring at the rice-paper scroll hung in a niche along one bare wall. Just below it was an earthenware bud vase in which he had placed one perfect day lily. At dawn this morning, as he did every morning of his adult life, he had gone walking in the wilderness, strolling the slopes, through glades still dark and misty with remnants of the night, past rushing streams etched with the last silvered thorns of moonlight, in search of this one flower that would reflect its mood of peace and contemplation all through the day. Plucking it carefully, he had made his way back to the precincts of his *dōjō*.

On the rice-paper scroll a Zen master of the eighteenth century had written in flowing characters: *"Rock and wind/only they remain/through generations."*

"But you allowed him to get so close to you."

Kusunoki smiled up at her and said, "I allowed him the luxury of cutting his own throat. That is all." He watched her as she sank down on her knees. He was conscious of the fact that she chose a spot near his right hand and not directly in front of him. "Often, times dictate that one becomes more intimate with one's enemies than with friends. This is a necessary lesson of life; I urge you to listen well. Friends engender obligations and obligations entangle life. Always remember: complication breeds desperation."

"But what is life without obligation?"

Kusunoki smiled. "That is an enigma even *sensei* may not unravel." He nodded toward the fallen form. "Now we must find the source from which this *muhon-nin* sprang."

"Is that so important?" Her head turned slightly so that the flat curve of her cheek was outlined in the soft light filtered by the *shōji*. "He has been neutralized. We should return to our work."

"You are not yet privileged to all that goes on here," Kusunoki said seriously. "The martial and the military arts are but two. It is *essential* that we discover the source of the infiltration."

"You should not have destroyed him so quickly then."

The *sensei* closed his eyes. "Ah, rash youth!" The voice was soft, almost gentle, but when the eyes snapped open the female felt her insides fluttering involuntarily, drilled by that basilisk gaze. "He was professional. You will learn someday not to waste valuable time on men like him. They must be dispatched as quickly and as efficiently as possible. They are dangerous—highly volatile. And they will not talk.

"Therefore we go onward." His hands folded into his lap. "You must return to the source . . . *his* source. The people who sent him, who trained him, represent a very great threat to Japan." He paused, his nostrils quivering as if he sensed some telltale vibration. When he spoke again, his voice had lost its hard edge; his eyelids drooped. "There is more hot water. Tea is waiting."

Obediently she went past him, grasping the tea pot and pouring while the light went out of the sky and purple clouds obscured the terraced mountains.

Carefully she brought the tiny cups toward him on a black lacquered tray; a small flock of golden herons lifting off from racing water painted there. Delicately, she set the tray down, began to use the whisk with practiced strokes. Her *wa*—her harmony—was very strong, and this was what Kusunoki felt engulfing him. At that moment he was very proud of what he had helped to create.

Six, seven, eight, the female turned the whisk, creating the pale green froth. On the tenth stroke her delicate fingers dropped the whisk and in the same motion were inside the wide sleeve of her kimono. Reversing the motion the short, perfectly honed steel blade flashed upward, biting into the back of Kusunoki's neck. Either her strength was at such a level or the blade was so superb that, seemingly without effort, the steel bit through flesh and bone, severing the spinal column. In a grotesque gesture, the head came forward and down, hanging only by the thin length of skin at the neck, as if the *sensei* was deep in meditational prayer.

Then crimson blood spurted upward from the severed arteries, fountaining the room, spattering the *tatami* where they both knelt. The *sensei*'s torso jerked spasmodically, its legs tangling beneath it as it tried to leap forward like a frog.

The female knelt rooted to the spot. Her eyes never left the body of her teacher. Once, when he lay on his side and one leg spasmed a last time, she felt something inside herself trembling like a leaf before a rising wind and she felt one tear lying hotly along the arch of her cheek. Then she hardened her heart, strengthened her will, and dammed up her emotions.

With that, elation filled her. It works, she thought, feeling her heart thundering within her rib cage. *Jahō*. Without it, she would never have been able to mask her intent from him, she understood that quite clearly.

As she stared down at her handiwork, she thought, It's nothing personal; nothing like what that bastard *muhon-nin* Tsutsumu had in mind. I am no traitor.

But I had to prove myself. I had to know. And therefore I had to take on the best. She got up and, moving like a wraith across the *tatami*, avoiding the spattered stains that had already begun to seep away across the floor onto other *tatami*, went to him.

You *were* the best, she thought, staring down at her mentor. Now I am. She bent and wiped the blood—*his* blood—from her weapon. It left a long scar on the fabric of his kimono.

The last thing she did there was to strip him and reverently fold the precious garment as if it were the national flag. Soon it disappeared into an inner pocket.

Then she was gone; and with her absence came the rain.

BOOK ONE

SHIH

[Force, influence, authority, energy]

NEW YORK/TOKYO/HOKKAIDO
SPRING, PRESENT

Drowsing, Justine Tomkin became aware of the nightblack shadow that slowly pierced the sunlight like the blade of a sword.

Her mouth opened wide and she tried to scream as she saw the face and recognized Saigō: the images of blood and carnage, a deathhunt too frightening to contemplate. The odor of the grave had pervaded this once peaceful room in her father's house on Long Island so full of childhood memories: of a Teddy bear with one eye missing and a plaid gingham giraffe.

Her powerful scream was muffled by the thick wind of Saigō's passage, as if he could control all God's elements with a wave of his hand. His torso expanded, extending through the light streaming down through the great glass dome in the ceiling, an opalescent mist rising about him as if his connection to the earth was not meant for her eyes.

He bent over her prostrate form and while her mind screamed, Wake up! *Wake up!* he slowly began to work his magic on her, the icy menace in his eyes as dead as stones somehow transferring itself into her heart.

She felt the horror squirming there like a palmful of live worms. An unholy bond was forming which she was powerless to deflect. Now she was part of him, she would do his bidding like a servant, take up his fallen *katana* and slay his enemy for him.

She felt the cool haft of the heavy *katana* beneath her curling fingers as she drew it upward off the floor. She wielded it just as Saigō would have had he not been dead.

And before her stood Nicholas, his vulnerable back to her. She raised the *katana*, its shadow already beginning to slice through the sunlight striking his spine. *Nicholas, my one and only love.* Her mind whirled in a sick fury and her last thought before she began the lethal downward strike was not her own: *Ninja, betrayer, this is your death!* . . .

Justine jerked awake. She was in a sweat. Her heart was thumping uncomfortably, as loudly as a blacksmith strikes his anvil. Slowly, she ran a shaking hand through her damp hair, pulling it back, away from her eyes. Then, with a great indrawn breath that halfway through turned into a wracking shudder, she clamped both arms about her body and began to rock back and forth as she had when she had been a child, frightened by dreams welling up from the pitch blackness of the night.

Blindly she reached out to the empty spot beside her in the large double bed, and fear touched her heart anew. It was not the terror of her own private nightmare which reared up at her. This was a new fright and she twisted, grabbing up a pillow from beside her where normally Nicholas would have been and, holding it tightly to her breast, squeezed it as if this gesture might bring him back to her arms, and the safety of America.

For Nicholas was on the other side of the Pacific and Justine was quite certain now: the fear she now felt was for him. What was happening in Japan? What was he doing at this moment? And what danger was amassing itself against him?

In a moment she lunged for the phone, a little cry filling the silence of the room.

"Ladies and gentlemen, we are beginning our descent into Narita Airport. Please make sure your seat back is in the upright position and that your tray table is closed and secured. All hand luggage must be stowed under the seat in front of you. Welcome to Tokyo, Japan."

While the unseen flight attendant repeated her short speech in Japanese, Nicholas Linnear opened his eyes. He had been dreaming of Justine, thinking of yesterday, when they had driven out of the city to get away, as they often did, from the pressurized life they led within the steel and smoked glass canyons of Manhattan. Outside their house in West Bay Bridge they had doffed shoes and socks and despite the early spring chill loped across the white sand.

Running down to the sea after her, the cerulean waves cutting off her feet and ankles in violent foam. Catching up with her, long, dark hair in his face as he turned her around, linking them, a softly feathered wing coming down at the close of night. His hard burnished arm around her, pulling her to him, the feel of her like liquid against flesh heated by the sun and more.

Whisper of the salt wind, "Oh, Nick, I don't think I've ever been happy before; not ever. Because of you I have no more sadness in me."

She was voicing the knowledge that he had saved her from the many demons that life held in its fisted claw, not the least of which was her own masochistic self; an ego robbed—so she said—by the domineering specter of her father.

She put her head on his shoulder, kissing the side of his neck. "I wish you didn't have to go. I wish we could be here in the surf together forever."

"We'd turn blue." He laughed, not wanting to catch her abruptly melancholy mood. He felt his love for her like a gently purling river in the night, hidden from sight yet present nonetheless. "Anyway, don't you think it's better that we're both so busy before the wedding? No time to get cold feet and back out." He was joking again but she lifted her head and he stared into her extraordinary eyes, highly intelligent yet possessing an odd kind of naivete he had found so alluring when he had first met her. He still did. He watched the several crimson motes floating like a hint of her soul in the midst of her left iris. Her eyes were hazel, that day more green than brown, and he found himself feeling grateful that the harrowing events of the past year had not altered the essence of her. For through those eyes he could still see her heart.

"Do you ever dream of it?" he asked. "Do you ever find yourself back in the house with the *dai-katana* in your hands; with Saigō in your mind?"

"You took all that he did—the strange kind of hypnosis—away," she said. "That's what you told me."

He nodded. "That's what I did."

"Well then." She took his hand and led him from the chilly curling wavelets up above the high-tide mark, strewn with the dark wrack of sea grape and odd bits of ashy wood, as perfectly smooth as stones. She turned her face up toward the sun. "I'm glad winter's over; I'm happy to be out here again with everything returning to life."

"Justine," he said seriously, "I just wanted to know whether there had been any—" He broke off, searching for an English equivalent to the Japanese thought. "Any echoes of the incident.

After all, Saigō programmed you to kill me with my own sword. You never speak of it."

"Why should I?" The light turned her eyes dark, concealing all their delicate colors. "There's nothing to say."

There was silence for a time, and they were engulfed by the rhythmic suck and pull of the sea along whose edge they had begun to walk again. Near the flat horizon a trawler hung as if suspended in a gulf of piercing blue.

She was looking out there, as if the ocean's expanse contained within it her future. "I've always known that life isn't safe. But up until the time I met you, I had no reason to care one way or another. It's no secret that I was once as self-destructive as my sister is." Her eyes broke away from the glitter of the horizon. She stared down at her laced fingers. "I wish to God it had never happened. But, oh, it did. He got hold of me. It's like when I had chicken pox as a kid. It was so bad I almost died; it left scars. But I survived. I'll survive now." Her head lifted. "I *must* survive, you see, because there's us to think about."

Nicholas had stared into her eyes. Was she keeping something from him? He could not say, and he did not know why it should worry him.

She laughed suddenly, her face becoming that of a college girl, innocent and carefree, the light dusting of freckles over her creamy skin catching the warming sunlight. She had a pure laugh, untainted by sarcasm or cynicism. There were no danger signs in it as there were in many people.

"I won't have you here beside me tomorrow," she said, "so let's make the most of today." She kissed him tenderly. "Is that very Oriental?"

He laughed. "I think it is, yes."

Her long artist's fingers traced the line of his jaw, pausing at last to touch the tender flesh of his lips. "You're more dear to me than I thought anyone could ever be."

"Justine—"

"If you'd travel to the ends of the earth I'd find you again. That sounds like the unrealistic statement of a little girl, but I mean it."

To his astonishment, he saw that she did. And he saw in her eyes at that moment something he had never seen there before. He recognized the determination of the *samurai* woman that he had encountered years ago in his mother and aunt. It was a peculiar combination of fierceness and loyalty that he thought nearly impossible for the Occidental spirit to attain. He was warmed by how proud of her he felt.

14

He smiled. "I'll only be gone for a short time. Hopefully no more than a month. I'll make sure you don't have to come after me."

Her face had turned serious. "It's no joke, Nick. Japan *is* at the ends of the earth, as far as I'm concerned. That country's terribly alien. Anywhere in Europe I may be somewhat of a foreigner but still and all I can trace my roots back there. There's at least *some* feeling of belonging. Japan's as opaque as a stone. It frightens me."

"I'm half Oriental," he said lightly. "Do I frighten you?"

"I think, yes, at times you used to. But not so much now." Her arms slid around him. "Oh, Nick, everything would be perfect if only you weren't going."

He held her tightly, wordlessly. He wanted to say that he'd never let her go but that would have been a lie because in less than twenty-four hours he would do just that as he boarded the plane bound for Tokyo. Too, his Eastern side—and his training—made him a private man, inward directed, the enigma of the blank wall. Nicholas suspected that his father, the Colonel, had been much the same way though he had been fully Occidental. Both father and son had secrets even from the women they loved the most in life.

He took a deep breath now, felt the change in pressure, the ozoned air, so thin and dry it clung to the back of the nose.

The 747-SP was banking to the left in a slow, lazy arc, chasing the streaking cloud layer until pale green fields, striped with perfectly regimented furrows, began to appear. Then, in the distance, the snow-capped crown of Fuji-yama, majestic and immutable. He was home again.

Then they were into the heavy smog layer, lying like a pall over a festive party, drifting in an ever-widening circle from the intensely industrialized areas of the swarming metropolis.

"Christ," the stocky-muscled man beside him said, craning his neck for a better look, "I should've brought my goddamned gas mask." A pudgy finger stabbed out at what lay beyond the Perspex window. "They've got an inversion layer worse than the San Fernando Valley."

His lined, aggressive face was absorbed in the disappearance of the rising landscape outside. He had the eyes, Nicholas thought, of a seasoned Roman general, canny and weary at the same time. Both were a result of hard-fought experience, battles on two arenas, the huns in front and the political infighting behind.

The man's hair was short cropped, a gunmetal gray; he was dressed in a handmade lightweight business suit of a conservative

15

cut. He was a man who over the years had become accustomed to a measured degree of luxury, but the twist of his nose, the thickness of the lips indicated that such had not always been the case. He had not been born to money, Raphael Tomkin, millionaire industrialist for whom Nicholas now worked. He was the man whom Saigō had been paid to kill; and though Nicholas had protected him, defeating Saigō, this was the same man who, Nicholas was certain, had ordered the death of Detective Lieutenant Lew Croaker, Nicholas' best friend.

Nicholas watched the profile of Tomkin's powerful face without seeming to. American power, Nicholas had come to learn, was often merely skin deep, and for him to incise beneath that layer to the soft interior was not difficult. But Tomkin was atypical of his fellow board chairmen. His *wa* was very strong indeed, proof of his inner determination and rock solidness.

This interested Nicholas intensely because his vow to himself and to the *kami* of his dead friend was to gain access to the interior of this man and, once having possession of that knowledge, sow the seeds of his slow destruction.

He recalled his thoughts on learning that Tomkin had ordered Croaker's seemingly accidental death in a car crash just outside Key West. Croaker had been there on his own time, and only Nicholas also knew that he had been running down the one solid lead in the Angela Didion homicide. She had been a high-fashion model who had once been Raphael Tomkin's mistress.

A modern rendering of a well-known tactic of Ieyasu Tokugawa, greatest of all of Japan's Shōgun, whose family ruled for more than a thousand years, keeping tradition alive, safe from dilution from the West: *To come to know your enemy, first you must become his friend. And once you become his friend, all his defenses come down. Then can you choose the most fitting method of his demise.*

Nicholas' vow of revenge had led him, despite Justine's fervent arguments, to accept Tomkin's offer of employment a year ago. And from the first day on the job, all their energies had been directed toward this moment. Tomkin had been brewing this proposed merger of one of his divisions with that of one of Sato Petrochemicals' *kobun*. Any deal with the Japanese was a difficult enough task, but this kind of complex merger of two highly sophisticated entities was utterly exhausting. Tomkin had admitted that he needed help desperately. And who better than Nicholas Linnear, half-Oriental, born and raised in Japan, to render that assistance.

The wheels bumped briefly against the tarmac and they were

down, feeling the drag as the captain put the four powerful jet engines into reverse thrust.

Now as they unstrapped and began to reach for their coats in the overhead compartment, Nicholas watched Tomkin. Something had happened to him since he had first made his vow. In coming to learn about Raphael Tomkin, in gaining his trust and, thus, his friendship—a gift the industrialist did not give often—Nicholas had come to see him for what he really was.

And it was clear that he was not the ogre that his daughters, Justine and Gelda, were convinced he was. In the beginning he had sought to communicate this new aspect of Tomkin to Justine, but these discussions inevitably ended in bitter fights and at length he gave up trying to convince her of her father's love for her. Too much bad blood had gone on between them for her ever to change her mind about him. She thought he was monstrous.

And in one way at least she was correct, Nicholas thought as they walked off the plane. Though increasingly it had become more difficult for him to believe that Tomkin was capable of murder. Certainly no man in his position got there by turning the other cheek to his enemies or those whom he had to climb over. Broken careers, bankruptcies, the dissolutions of marriages, this was the detritus that such a man as Raphael Tomkin must leave behind him in his wake.

He was smart and most assuredly ruthless. He had done things that Nicholas could never even have contemplated. And yet these seemed a long way from ordering a death in cold blood, a life snuffed out with Olympian disdain. His genuine love for his daughters should have precluded such a psychotic decision.

Yet all the evidence Croaker had unearthed had led directly back to Raphael Tomkin summoning his bodyguard and authorizing him to end Angela Didion's life. Why? What spark had ignited him to do such a desperate thing?

Nicholas still did not know, but he meant to find out before he meted out his revenge on this powerful and complex man. Perhaps this quest for knowledge would delay the time of his vengeance, but that had no real meaning for him. He had taken in with his mother's milk the concept of infinite patience. Time was as the wind to him, passing unseen in a continuous stream, secrets held within its web, enactment inevitable but coming only at the propitious moment, as Musashi wrote, Crossing at a Ford.

Thus he had set for himself the task of first coming to understand his enemy, Raphael Tomkin, to peer into every nook and cranny of his life, stripping away flesh and bone until at length the soul of the man lay revealed to him. Because only in understanding the why of the murder could Nicholas find salvation for himself for what he himself must eventually do.

If he should fail to understand Tomkin, if he should rashly hurl himself down the narrow bloodred path of vengeance, he would be no better than his enemy. He could not do such a thing. His cousin, Saigō, had known just that about Nicholas and, using it, had caused the death of Nicholas' friends. For mad Saigō had no such compunctions concerning murder. He had learned how to destroy life through *Kan-aku na ninjutsu* and, later, through the feared *Kōbudera*. But somewhere along the line the forces he was attempting to tame had taken him over, using him for their own evil designs. Saigō had possessed the power only to become possessed by it. In the end he had been too weak of spirit and it had driven him mad.

Nicholas took a deep breath and shook his head to clear his mind of the past. Saigō was a year dead.

But he was back in Japan and so the past had begun to crowd in on him like a host of *kami* chittering in his ear, all clamoring for attention at once. So many memories, so many sensations. Cheong; the Colonel; Itami, his aunt, whom he knew he must eventually see. And always Yukio, sad doomed Yukio. Beautiful Yukio stunning his adolescent mind when they had first met at the *keiretsu* party. The first contact between them had been electric with sexual promise. Her warm, firm thigh between his legs as they danced through the chandeliered room, staring into each other's eyes, oblivious of the glare the young Saigō leveled at them from his place at his father's side.

Though she be dead at Saigō's hands, still her *kami* continued to haunt him. Though he loved Justine with all his heart, still his spirit danced that first dance with Yukio in a kind of private glowing world where death held no dominion. The mind was an awesomely powerful instrument and if the dead could ever be said to have been resurrected, Nicholas had brought Yukio back from her watery grave with the power of his memories.

And now his feet were back on his native soil for the first time in over ten years. It seemed like centuries. Closer to Yukio now, to all that had happened to him. Dance, Yukio, I'm holding you tight and as long as I do nothing can come between us, nothing can harm you anymore.

"Good afternoon, gentlemen." A young Japanese woman stood, bowing, before them. "Sato Petrochemicals welcomes you to Japan." Just behind her and to the left was a young Japanese male in a dark business suit and wraparound sunglasses. He reached out and took their bag claim checks. They had just cleared Customs and Immigration. "Junior will take care of your luggage." Her smile was sweet. "Won't you follow me, please?"

Nicholas hid his surprise at being met by a woman. Of course he would not tell Tomkin this but it did not bode well for their coming negotiations. He might find this creature charming and Tomkin might not care either way, but to any Japanese this would constitute a serious insult. The more important the emissary of the company who met you, the higher your status in the eyes of that company. In Japan, women were very far down the executive ladder indeed.

She took them through the congested heart of Narita, past scurrying tour groups, their leaders brandishing stiff calligraphied banners to rally them just as generals on the ancient battlefields of Japan had once done with their troops. Past regimented school-children, uniformed and gaping at all the incredibly tall *gaijin* stumbling bewilderedly by them. Around old couples with brown paper shopping bags, sidestepping one brilliantly colored bridal party being seen off on their honeymoon.

Tomkin was huffing by the time the young woman brought them out into the vapid sunshine and across to the waiting lim-ousine.

She paused as she held the back door open for them. "I am Miss Yoshida, Mr. Sato's administrative assistant," she said. "Please forgive the discourtesy of my not introducing myself ear-lier but I felt it prudent to remove all of us from that tumult most expeditiously."

Nicholas smiled inwardly at the endearing awkwardness of her English. He watched her as she bowed again, returning her gesture automatically, murmuring, "There was no discourtesy, Miss Yosh-ida. Both Mr. Tomkin and I appreciate your thoughtfulness," in idiomatic Japanese.

If she was at all startled by his use of her language she gave no outward sign of it. Her eyes were like glass, set in her oval, seamless face. In any other country she might have made millions putting that countenance on display before the camera. But not here. Sato Petrochemicals was her second family, and she owed it all the loyalty she devoted to her blood family, Nicholas knew. What it asked of her she performed flawlessly and without ques-tion. This, too, was tradition handed down from the time of the Tokugawa Shōgunate.

"Won't you please take advantage of the car's comforts?"

"Jesus, I could use some real comfort," Tomkin growled as he ducked his head and entered the black gleaming limo. "That trip's a ball breaker."

Nicholas laughed, pretending it was a mysterious *gaijin* jest, relieving Miss Yoshida of her embarrassment. She laughed lightly in concert with him, her voice musical. She wore a rather severely cut business suit of raw silk, its forest green contrasting nicely with the toffee-colored blouse with its deep maroon string tie at the tiny rounded collar. On one lapel she wore a discreet gold and lacquer pin emblazoned with the feudal design of Sato Petrochemicals. On the lobes of her ears were gleaming emerald studs.

"It must feel good to be home again, Linnear-san," she said, pronouncing it "Rinnearu."

It would not have been good manners for Nicholas to have acknowledged her oblique reference: she had cleverly told him that she had been briefed on his background without ever having said it outright.

He smiled. "The years have melted away," he said. "Now that I am back it seems only moments since I left."

Miss Yoshida turned her beautiful face away from him. Junior was emerging from the terminal, loaded down with their luggage. Her eyes returned to his and her voice lowered, became less formal for an instant. "There will be a car for your use," she said, "should you desire to light joss sticks."

Nicholas struggled to hide his surprise. He now knew the extent of the briefing Miss Yoshida had been given on him. Not only had she said that Sato would provide transportation for him if he chose to visit his parents' graves but also that he would want to light joss sticks on his mother's stone. It was not widely known that Cheong had been at least half Chinese; "joss stick" was a peculiarly Chinese term, though the Japanese, being also Buddhist, lit incense at the graves of family and friends.

Miss Yoshida's eyes lowered. "I know I have no right to offer, but if it will be easier for you to be accompanied on such a journey I would make myself available."

"That is terribly kind," Nicholas said, watching Junior approach out of the corner of his eye, "but I could not ask such an enormous inconvenience of you."

"It is no bother," she said. "I have a husband and a child buried not far away. I would go in any case."

Her eyes met his but he could not say whether she was telling the truth or simply employing a Japanese lie in order to make him feel more comfortable with her offer. In either case he determined he would take her up on it when a lull in the negotiations permitted it.

"I would be honored, Miss Yoshida."

Inside the car, as Junior hurled them into the stifling traffic on the outskirts of the city, Tomkin leaned forward, staring out the gray-tinted windows at the growing expanse of the steel and glass forest rising from the borders of the farmers' green fields. "Jesus," he said, "it's just like New York. When the hell're they gonna stop building? I come twelve thousand miles and I feel like I never left home." He sat back with a sudden lurch, a smirk on his face. "Except, of course, that you and I're the tallest creatures for a thousand miles, eh, Nick?"

Nicholas gave his employer the semblance of a nod and in the same motion said to Miss Yoshida in the front of the car, "*Gaijin* are often rude without meaning to be, eh?" He shrugged his shoulders. "What else can you expect from ill-bred children."

Miss Yoshida covered her bowlike lips with the palm of her hand, but her mirth was obvious in her sparkling eyes.

"What the hell're you two chattering about?" Tomkin growled, feeling left out.

"Just informing the natives that it isn't only height that's outsized on foreign devils," Nicholas lied.

But he'd struck the right chord. "Hah!" Tomkin guffawed. "You're damn straight! Very good, Nicky."

Just over an hour later, the three of them stepped off the high speed elevator at the summit on the triangular Shinjuku Suiryū Building. All of Tokyo lay shimmering like a dusky multifaceted jewel beneath them. Suspended six hundred and sixty feet—fifty-two stories—in the air, Nicholas was amazed at the profusion of ultra-modern skyscrapers that had sprung up in his absence. They shot from the bedrock pavement like a Mandarin's glittering fingernails, lifting the Shinjuku District of downtown Tokyo into the dome of the heavens.

Tomkin grimaced as he stopped them and, pulling Nicholas close beside him, whispered, "Coming here always reminds me of cod liver oil. When I was a kid my father insisted I take two spoonfuls every morning. He kept telling me it was for my own good, just like he did when he beat me if he found me dumping the stuff down the toilet. Then I'd have to gag on that vile stuff anyway." He grunted heavily. "Huh, you can eat your raw fish with these barbarians, Nick. I've still got the taste of cod liver oil in my mouth."

Miss Yoshida led them through a set of wood-paneled doors, the oversized knobs carved into the Sato crest. Down a corridor softly lit by indirect lighting. Edo period *ukiyo-e* prints by Hiroshige, the master of rain, Hokusai, the master of the countryside, and Kuniyoshi, the master of Japanese myth, hung on the walls. A dove gray carpet was beneath their feet, acting as a damper for

21

the bustle of work going on all around them, drifting out from a multitude of office doorways. Teletypes chattered softly, and in another section a battery of electronic typewriters were going full speed.

Miss Yoshida stopped them before another set of doors. These were of thick slabs of ash burl fitted together with wide wooden pegs in the traditional Japanese manner. The handles were of roughly worked black wrought iron, reminding Nicholas of the *riakon*—the inns of the countryside—he had stayed in.

"Mr. Sato knew you would have a strenuous trip," Miss Yoshida said. "Such a journey is fatiguing even to the strongest of constitutions. That is why Junior has gone on to the Okura with your luggage. He will see to your rooms." Her arm raised, her hand held palm upward. It was a simple gesture, yet elegant for all that. "Here you may relax without concern or worry." Now her cherry blossom lips pursed in a smile. "If you will be so kind as to follow me."

Tomkin's angry voice checked her. "What the hell's going on here?" His eyes were belligerent. "I didn't come halfway round the world to scorch my flesh in some sitz bath while the big man goes about his business." He tapped his black crocodile attaché case. "I've got a merger to consummate." He snorted. "This other stuff can wait as far as I'm concerned."

Miss Yoshida's face showed nothing of what she must be feeling. The smile was still on her face and to her credit it had not frozen there. "Mr. Tomkin." she began, "let me assure you that—"

"Sato!" Tomkin's strident voice overrode her quiet controlled tones. "I want to see Sato now. He can't keep me cooling my heels like some goddamned functionary. Raphael Tomkin waits for no one!"

"I assure you, Mr. Tomkin, no disrespect is intended," Miss Yoshida pressed on, struggling to contend with this irrational outburst. "My task is to serve you, to help you relax, to put your mind into the proper frame of—"

"I don't need you or anyone else to tell me what my frame of mind is!" Tomkin thundered, taking a step toward her. "Now you get Sato in here or—"

Nicholas stepped forward, coming between them. He could see that despite herself Miss Yoshida's face had gone ashen beneath the artful cosmetics. Her hands were shaking.

"What d'you think you're doing, Nick?"

Nicholas ignored Tomkin, using his own powerful frame to move his employer back. At the same time he composed his face,

22

smiling easily, projecting his own relaxation in order to short-circuit the woman's obvious alarm.

"Please excuse the *gaijin*," he said in Japanese, not wanting to use Tomkin's name. "He's had a long, uncomfortable trip." He lowered his voice and went on, keeping the pressure on Tomkin as he did so. "The truth is, Miss Yoshida, his piles are bothering him and he's like a dog who's sat on a warrior anthill. He snaps at anyone and everyone." He grinned. "And he hasn't the sense to be cordial to so dutiful a blossom but in his pain seeks out to blindly crush the beauty before him."

Miss Yoshida gave Tomkin a wary look before she bowed, thanking Nicholas. "Sato-san will be with you shortly," she said. "His wish is only for your comfort and ease before the rigors of negotiations begin."

"I understand completely, Yoshida-san," Nicholas said kindly. "It is most thoughtful of Sato-san to be concerned with our total well-being. Please be so kind as to extend our compliments to him." He bumped his muscular shoulder against Tomkin's struggling form. "And as for the *gaijin*, leave him to me."

Miss Yoshida bowed again, relief flooding her face; this time she made no attempt to mask her feelings. "Thank you, Linnear-san. I cannot think what Sato-san would say to me if he knew I had not performed as he had anticipated." Half running, she squeezed by them both and hurried back down the corridor.

Tomkin felt a lessening of the awesome pressure brought to bear on him and broke away. His face flushed. He raised a sausagelike finger. "You owe me an explanation, Nick, and it goddamned well better be a good one or—"

"Shut up."

It was not said particularly loudly, but some hidden tone seemed to strike Tomkin's nervous system. His mouth snapped shut.

"You've done enough damage to us already," Nicholas said, struggling as Miss Yoshida had to keep his emotions under control.

"Damage? What are you—"

"You lost us incalculable face with that woman. We'll both count ourselves lucky if she hasn't gone straight to Sato with the affront." The last was a lie. Miss Yoshida was so frightened of offending the guests she'd do no such thing. But Tomkin would never know that, and some fear was good for him right now.

Nicholas pushed by him. He found himself in a rather small, dimly lighted room with a cedar slat-boarded floor. Along one wall was a row of spacious metal lockers. He went over to one and opened it. Inside he found not only a terry-cloth robe but comb and brush, an entire array of toiletry items. Off to the right

23

an open archway led into a mirrored bathroom with sinks, urinals, and a row of toilet stalls.

Nicholas could hear the muffled sounds of water dripping, as if within the walls. To the left of the row of lockers was a plain wooden door. The baths, he surmised, must be beyond. The air was moist and warm, decidedly inviting. He began to disrobe.

Tomkin came in behind him. He stood rigidly in the middle of the room, glaring at him, willing Nicholas to face him. Nicholas went methodically on with what he was doing, his long, lean muscles rippling, consciously letting Tomkin steam.

After a time, Tomkin said, "Listen, you bastard, don't you ever do that to me again." His voice was thick with pent-up fury. "Are you listening to me?" he said finally.

"Get your clothes off." Nicholas folded his trousers, hung them over the metal hanger. He was naked now, stripped of the layers that civilization dictated he must wear. It was clear he possessed an innate animal quality that was almost frightening. Justine had felt it the first moment she had seen him moving naked across the room like a wraith, a dancer, a nocturnal predator. Even when he made so mundane a move as putting one foot in front of the other, he used his body as an instrument, achieving a confluence of grace and power.

"Answer me civilly, dammit!" Tomkin's voice had risen, a function of not only his anger but his abrupt fear of the man standing in front of him. He was nonplussed. In his world of corporate business, nakedness was a state of vulnerability. Yet looking at Nicholas Linnear now, Tomkin felt only his own vulnerability, so acutely that he was aware of the thunder of his heart pumping, his accelerated pulse.

Nicholas turned to face Tomkin. "You hired me for a specific purpose. Kindly allow me to do my job without interference." There was no anger in his voice now; he had that under control.

"Your job is not to insult me," Tomkin said in a more normal tone of voice as he struggled to control his runaway pulse.

"You're in Japan now," Nicholas said simply. "I'm here to help you stop thinking like a Westerner."

"You mean loss of face again." Tomkin snorted and hooked a spatulate thumb at the closed door. "That was just a girl. What the fuck do I care what she thinks of me."

"She is, in fact, Seiichi Sato's personal representative," Nicholas said in a calming tone. "That makes her important." This lie was essential now to keep Tomkin under control. If he should even suspect the slight that had been dealt them, there would be

24

no stopping him. "As such, here, she is part of Sato himself and therefore no less important."

"You mean I should bow and scrape to her? After Sato didn't even have the courtesy to meet us himself."

"You have been over here many times," Nicholas said evenly. "It astonishes me that you have learned nothing at all about Japanese customs." He gestured. "This treatment is accorded to only the highest dignitaries. Do you have any idea what this setup—the Japanese bath—must cost with space at such a high premium in Tokyo." Nicholas sighed. "Stop thinking with your Western ego and try a little acceptance. That will go a long way here." He reached into his locker, brought out a fluffy white towel embroidered with a dark blue triple wheel, the emblem of Sato Petrochemicals.

Tomkin was silent for a moment. Then, abruptly, he grunted and began to undress. It was as close to an apology as he was going to come. When he, too, was naked, he drew out his towel and the key to the locker.

"Don't use it," Nicholas said.

"Why not?"

They stared at each other for a moment, then Tomkin nodded. "Loss of face, right?"

Nicholas smiled, opening the wooden door beside the bank of lockers. "Come on," he said.

They stepped into a chamber perhaps twenty feet square. The floor was the same cedar slats but here the walls were of gleaming blue tile. The ceiling, of smaller tile, was a mosaic whose center was the interlocking wheel pattern of the company's logo. The room was taken up by two enormous bathtubs both now filled with steaming water. Two young women stood in attendance.

Without hesitation Nicholas stepped in front of them, allowing them to pour scalding water over him, then begin rubbing him down with soapy sponges. After a moment spent taking this in, Tomkin followed him.

"This I understand," he said, allowing the woman to wash him. "First get clean, then let the heat relax you."

They were rinsed off carefully, shampoo provided for them, then, dripping, their flesh steaming, walked to one of the steaming tubs.

Here the water was even hotter, making Tomkin cringe. They discovered niches within the walls of the tub so that they could sit with just their heads out of the water. Tomkin's face was red, beads of sweat rolling freely down his cheeks. He found that if he moved it made the heat intolerable. Nicholas' eyes were closed,

25

his body relaxed. There was no sound save the soft, hypnotic lapping of the wavelets their own bodies created in languid movements within the bath. The tiled walls were stippled with moisture.

Tomkin put his head back against the wood, stared up at the Sato triple wheel. "When I was a kid," he said, "I remember I hated to take a bath. I don't know why. Didn't think it was manly or something. There was a fag kid in school always smelled like he'd come from the bath. Jesus, I hated him. Beat his brains out one day after class." His chest moved up and down slowly with his breath.

"I thought, you know, that it'd make me some kind of hero with the other kids, but it didn't." His voice lapsed for a moment before resuming. The drip of the water was like a metronome. "I remember my father coming after me, throwing me into the tub, scrubbing me with that kind of powdered cleanser—Ajax or something. It hurt like hell, I can tell you. 'Cry,' he said. I can just hear his voice. 'It'll do you a world of good,' he said. 'Tomorrow you'll take a bath on your own so I won't have to clean you this way again.'

"Yes." Tomkin nodded. "My father certainly taught me the wisdom of keeping clean." He closed his eyes for a moment as if picturing the scene all over again.

Nicholas looked at him and thought of his dead friend. Lew Croaker had been so certain that Tomkin had had Angela Didion murdered. That obsession had a peculiarly Japanese flavor to it because it sprang from Croaker's blind obedience to the dictates of the law. "Nick," his friend had once told him, "I don't give a rat's ass what Angela Didion did or what her rep was. She was a human being, just like all us slobs. What I'm doing... Well, I figure it's something she deserves. If she can't get justice, then no one at all deserves it."

What Croaker termed justice Nicholas knew as honor. Croaker knew where his duty lay and he had died in that pursuit. It was a *samurai*'s death, Nicholas knew that very well, but it somehow did not ease the sadness that welled up in him in odd quiet moments or erase the emptiness he felt inside him, as if a vital part of him had been abruptly severed.

"Nick, you and Craig Allonge get along well." Tomkin was speaking of the company's chief financial operations officer. "You know that I rely on him a great deal. Besides me, he knows more about the real running of Tomkin Industries than anyone. He's close to its heart." If Tomkin was trying to make a point, he did not finish. Instead, he seemed to veer onto a tangent. "Craig's going through a particularly hard time now. He's moved out of his house. He and his wife aren't quite seeing eye to eye since she told him about her lover."

Tomkin moved involuntarily and sucked in his breath with the searing heat. "It's a helluva situation. Craig told me he wanted to move into a hotel in town, but I wouldn't hear of it. He's staying with me until he decides what to do. I told him I'd help him with the divorce if that's what he wanted. I'll also pay for a counselor if he thinks there's any chance of a reconciliation." He closed his eyes. "But, more important for the moment, he needs a real friend. I'm his boss; I can't be his friend, too, not in this way. You like him, and I know he thinks the world of you. And you know the real meaning of friendship."

Nicholas settled back in the scalding water, thinking, Westerners are so unpredictable. They bluster one minute, insensitively ignoring civilized courtesies, then the next, show an inordinate amount of insight and caring. "I'll do what I can as soon as we get back," he said.

At length, Tomkin turned his head toward Nicholas, and when he spoke his voice had unaccountably softened.

"Nicky," he said, "are you going to marry my daughter?"

Nicholas, half-dreaming, nevertheless heard the touch of desperation in the other man's voice and wondered at it. "Yes," he said immediately. "Of course. As soon as we get back to the States."

"You've discussed it with Justine?"

He smiled. "You mean have I proposed? Yes." He heard Tomkin exhale deeply and opened his eyes, looked at the other man. "We have your blessing?"

Tomkin's face darkened and he gave a harsh bark that Nicholas recognized as an anguished laugh. "Oh, yes, for all the good it might do you. But don't tell Justine. Christ, she might decide not to marry you just to spite me."

"I think those days are over."

"Oh, you're wrong about that. Nothing will ever be right between me and my daughters again. There's too much bitterness on their part, too much resentment of the way they think I've interfered in their lives. Rightly or wrongly. I'm not even sure I know which now."

Time to break the mood, Nicholas thought, and he clambered slowly out of the tub. Tomkin followed, and they went through another door into a steam room. They sat on hexagonal tiles while the long vertical pipe coughed and belched pockets of water that ran down, gurgling into the drain. Then, with a great gout of

27

sound, the steam began to shout from the open end of the pipe and talk became impossible.

Precisely five minutes after they entered, a warning bell rang. They could no longer see one another though they sat fairly close together. Periodically, the pipe running along the tiled wall to their left screamed like a banshee, delivering forth a new cloud of steam which wrapped itself around their shoulders with a new wave of heat.

Nicholas touched Tomkin on his beefy shoulder, and they went out through the second door set into the far wall.

They were in a fairly large, dimly lighted room that smelled faintly of birch and mentholated camphor. Four long padded tables were aligned along the periphery of the room. Two tables were occupied by dark lumps that they soon could make out as bodies. A young woman stood by each table.

"Gentlemen." A male figure sat up on the table to their right. He bowed slightly. "I trust you are more relaxed than when you entered our doorway."

"Sato," Tomkin said. "It took you—" But feeling the pressure of Nicholas' hand on his arm, he changed in midsentence. "This's a helluva way to greet us. The Okura couldn't've done as well."

"Oh, no, we cannot come up to that standard." But Seiichi Sato nodded his head in acknowledgement of the compliment. "Linnear-san," he said, turning slightly, "it is an honor to meet you at last. I have heard much about you." He swung his legs around, lay back down. "Tell me, are you pleased to be back home?"

"My home is now America, Sato-san," Nicholas said carefully. "Much has changed in Japan since I left, but I trust there is more that has remained the same."

"You missed your calling, Linnear-san," Sato said. "You should have been a politician."

Nicholas wondered who was lying on the table against the far wall.

"Lie down, please, gentlemen," Sato said. "You have not yet completed your course in relaxation."

They did as he bade, and immediately two more young women emerged from the semidarkness. Nicholas felt the splash and roll of oil, then skilled hands kneading his muscles.

"Perhaps you are already wondering why these girls are not Japanese, Linnear-san? Do not think I am not nationalistic. However, I am a realist as well. These girls are from Taiwan." He chuckled. "They're blind, Linnear-san, could you tell that? The prevailing explanation is that their affliction allows them a more

28

sensitive sense of touch. I am inclined to agree. Ever since my first trip to Taiwan in '56, I have dreamed of bringing Taiwan masseuses here to Japan. What do you think, Linnear-san?"

"Superb," Nicholas grunted. The girl was turning his rocklike muscles to butter beneath her talented fingers and palms. He breathed deeply into the expansion, experiencing an almost dizzying sense of exhilaration.

"I was obliged to remain in Taiwan for ten days while we jury-rigged a deal that was falling through. I assure both you gentlemen that the only worthwhile features of that country are its cuisine and its extraordinary blind masseuses."

For a time then there was only the soft somnolent slap of flesh against flesh, the sharp camphor smell of the liniment that somehow increased the overall sense of drowsiness.

Nicholas' mind returned to the mysterious fourth man. He was well acquainted with the convoluted byways of Japanese business structure, so different and alien to Westerners. He knew that despite the fact Sato was this *keiretsu*'s—enterprise group's—president, still there were many layers, many men in power, and there were those in the highest reaches of power in Japan who the outsider and even most Japanese never saw or knew about. Was this one of those men? If so, Nicholas had to believe Tomkin's admonition of extreme care on the long trip across the Pacific. "This deal with Sato Petrochemicals is potentially the biggest I've ever put together, Nick," he had said. "The merging of my Sphynx Silicon division and Sato's Nippon Memory Chip *kobun* is going to bring untold profits over the next twenty years to Tomkin Industries.

"You know American manufacturers; they're so goddamned slow on the uptake. That's why I decided to start up Sphynx two and a half years ago. I got fed up with relying on these bastards. I was always three to six months behind schedule because of them and by the time I got their shipment, the Japs had already come out with something better.

"Like everything else, they've been taking our basic designs and making the product better and at a far lower price. They did it to the Germans with thirty-five-millimeter cameras, they did it to us and the Europeans with cars. Now they're gonna do it to us again with computer chips unless we get off our asses.

"You better than anyone, Nick, know how goddamned hard it is for a foreign company to get a toehold in Japan. But now I've got something they want—want badly enough to allow me fifty-one percent interest in my own company. That's unheard of over there. I mean, they took IBM to the cleaners when they opened up in Tokyo."

Nicholas recalled the incident well. Japan's all-powerful Ministry of International Trade and Industry, known more colloquially as MITI, had sprung up after World War II to essentially help guide Japan's economy back onto sound footing. In the 1950s, MITI's chief minister, Shigeru Sahashi, became the *samurai* bent on discouraging what he saw as a massive invasion of American capital into Japan.

He also saw the enormous potential worldwide market coming for computers. Japan had no computer technology whatsoever at the time. Sahashi used IBM's desire to open up Japan for its trade to effectively create a national computer industry.

MITI already had set policies severely limiting the involvement of foreign companies in Japan's economy. The ministry was so powerful that, in effect, it could exclude all foreign participation without its consent.

Sahashi allowed the formation of IBM-Japan but as soon as the fledgling company was set up, he set about showing them what they had stepped into. IBM, of course, held all the basic patents that Japan required to begin its own homegrown industry.

In a now historic meeting with IBM-Japan, Sahashi told them: "We will take every measure possible to obstruct the success of your business unless you license IBM patents to Japanese firms and charge them no more than a five-percent royalty."

When the understandably appalled IBM officers indignantly accused the Japanese, through him, of having an inflated inferiority complex, Sahashi said, "We do not have an inferiority complex toward you; we only need time and money to compete effectively."

Stunned, the Americans were faced with the difficult choice of having to withdraw IBM completely from a major part of its planned worldwide expansion or capitulating to MITI's total domination.

They chose to submit, and for years afterward Sahashi would proudly recount the details of his triumphant negotiations.

"I learned from that fiasco." Tomkin's voice had brought Nicholas back. "I'm not so greedy that I'll put one foot in the trap before I know what the hell's going on. I'm going to use the Japs, not the other way around.

"I won't spend dollar one on a Japanese company until the deal's set. I've got the patented advance, but there's no way I can manufacture this new-type chip in America without the costs making sales prohibitive. Sato can give me that; he controls Japan's sixth largest *konzern*. He can manufacture this thing cheaply enough to make this venture profitable in a big way."

He laughed. "And I do mean big, Nick. Believe it or not, we're looking at a net profit of a hundred million dollars within two years." His eyes were on fire. "You heard me right. One hundred million!"

Nicholas might have been sleeping when the hands lifted from his muscles. He felt better than he had in years. He heard muffled movement in the room and then Sato's commanding voice. "Now we shower and dress for business. In fifteen minutes Miss Yoshida will fetch you." He stood up, a thick, black shadow. Nicholas twisted his head to try to get a good look at him, but all he could discern was that Sato was not tall by American standards. Behind him, the specter of the fourth man stirred and got to his feet. Nicholas shifted his gaze, but Sato's bulk was between him and the mysterious stranger.

"Very little business," the Japanese industrialist was saying now. "Of course you must still be fatigued by your journey and it is, after all, late in the day. But still"—he bowed formally to them both—"it is Monday and the preliminaries cannot wait. Do you agree, Tomkin-san."

"Let's get on with it, by all means." Even though he was closer to Nicholas, Tomkin's voice sounded odd and muffled.

"Excellent," Sato said shortly. His bullet head nodded. "Until then."

When they were alone, Nicholas sat up, the towel draped across his loins. "You've been very quiet," he said into the gloom.

In the brief pause, the girls shuffled away, rustling like reeds in the wind.

Tomkin slid off the table. "Just getting a feel for the territory." He wrapped himself in his large towel. "Sato seemed busy talking to you; I let him. What's it to me, right? I was thinking about who was with him."

"Any ideas?" Nicholas said as they walked through into the shower room.

Tomkin shook his head. "You know Jap industry. God alone knows how they run things here and it wouldn't surprise me to learn that even He gets confused once in a while." Tomkin shrugged his beefy shoulders. "Whoever he was, he's a big one, to be allowed into Sato's inner sanctum like that."

Seiichi Sato's office was almost entirely Western in aspect—comfortable sofas and chairs grouped around a low black lacquer coffee table with the ubiquitous Sato logo etched into its center,

31

and, farther away toward the sheets of window looking out on Tokyo, a large rosewood and brass desk, low cabinets, all atop deep pile champagne colored carpet. Woodblock prints were on the walls, all, Nicholas saw, from twentieth-century artists.

Yet as he accompanied Tomkin across the expanse of carpet Nicholas noticed a half-open door beyond which he saw a *tokonoma*—a traditional niche into which was placed fresh flowers every day in a small, simple arrangement. Above it on the wall was an old scroll with some of its original gilt powder still on it. Nicholas could not read the inscription as the angle was too acute but he knew it would be a Zen saying, written by an ancient master.

Seiichi Sato came around from behind his desk in quick, confident strides. He was, as Nicholas had gathered, a rather short man though not overly so. Through his Ralph Lauren suit Nicholas could make out the great bulge of muscles across his shoulders and upper arms like a mantle of iron and he thought, The man works out religiously. He searched Sato's face, pockmarked and rather angular, with slab cheeks that rose high into his eye sockets and a wide, sleek forehead topped by coarse, brushcut hair. There was nothing subtle about the man's physiognomy. Nor was he a particularly handsome individual, but what his face lacked in beauty and subtlety it more than made up for by the sheer force of its inner drive and strength of will. His spirit was enormously powerful.

Smiling, Sato held his hand out to each of them in a very American form of greeting. Behind his great looming shoulder Nicholas was amazed to see the summit of Fuji-yama. He knew on clearer days it was visible from the top of the new International Trade Center building at Hamamatsu-chō Station, where the monorail leaves for Haneda. But here in the heart of Shinjuku: fantastic!

"Come," Sato said, gesturing, "the sofa offers more comfort for the weary traveler."

When they were seated, Sato made a small noise in the back of his throat, no more than if he were clearing the passage, but immediately a figure appeared through the half-open door to the *tokonoma*.

The man was fairly tall and rail thin. He had about him the air of the sea, changeless and formidable. He could have been ten years older than Sato, in his sixties, but that was difficult to judge. His hair was graying and wispy, almost frondlike. He wore a neat, immaculately clipped mustache that was yellowed by smoke tar along its lower rim.

He came across to them in jerky, almost somnambulent strides as if he did not quite have total control of all his muscles. As he came close, Nicholas saw that something had been done to his right eye for the lid was permanently locked in a semiopen position and the gleaming orb within, though his own and not a piece of glass, was clouded and milky like a damaged agate.

"Allow me to introduce Mr. Tanzan Nangi." The one-eyed man bowed formally, and Nicholas returned it. He was dressed in a charcoal gray suit with a faint pinstripe, brilliantly white shirt, and a plain gray tie. Nicholas recognized him immediately as one of the old school: conservative and wary of any foreign businessman, perhaps not unlike Sahashi of MITI.

"Nangi-san is chairman of the Daimyō Development Bank." That was all Sato had to say. Both Nicholas and Tomkin knew that almost all multimanufacturing *keiretsu* in Japan were ultimately owned by one bank or another because that was where all the money resided; it was quite logical. The Daimyō Development Bank owned Sato Petrochemical.

Miss Yoshida brought in a tray laden with a steaming porcelain pot and four delicate cups. Carefully, she knelt beside one end of the coffee table and, using a reed whisk, slowly prepared the green tea.

Nicholas watched her, noting the competence, the strength held tightly in check, the grace of the fingers as they handled the implements. When all of the men had been served, she rose and silently left. At no time had she looked directly at anyone.

Nicholas felt Nangi's hard stare and knew he was being sized up. He had no doubt that the bureaucrat knew all about him; he would never come to a meeting such as this without being properly briefed. And Nicholas also knew that if he was indeed as conservative as he appeared outwardly he would hold no love for one such as Nicholas Linnear: half-Oriental, half-English. In Nangi's eyes, he would be below the status of *gaijin*.

Together, as was traditional, they lifted their small cups, brought the pale green froth to their lips, drank contentedly. With amusement, Nicholas saw Tomkin wince slightly at the intensely bitter taste.

"Now," Tomkin said, abruptly setting his cup down and hunching forward as if he were a football lineman ready to leap across the line of scrimmage at the sound of the snap, "let's get down to business."

Nangi, who held his upper torso as stiffly as he used his legs, carefully extracted a filigreed platinum case from his inside breast pocket and, opening it, extracted a cigarette with a pair of thin, pincerlike fingers. Just as carefully, he clicked a matching lighter

33

and inhaled deeply. Smoke hissed from his wide nostrils as he turned his head.

"'Softlee, softlee, catchee monkey.'" He said the words as if they had the bitterest taste on his tongue. "Isn't that how the British often put it out here in the Far East, Mr. Linnear?"

Inwardly appalled, Nicholas nevertheless held his anger in check. There was nothing but the hint of a benign smile on his lips as he said, "I believe some of the old Colonials may have used that phrase borrowed from the Chinese."

"Corrupted," Nangi corrected.

Nicholas nodded his acquiescence; it was quite true. "That was a long time ago, Nangi-san," he continued. "Times have changed and brought with them modern, more enlightened values."

"Indeed." Nangi puffed away, apparently annoyed that he had no ready rejoinder to that.

Sato stepped in to guide the conversation away from the friction. "Mr. Tomkin, you and Mr. Linnear are only just arrived here. Mr. Greydon, your legal counsel, is not due until 11:15 tomorrow morning. Shall we then limit ourselves to agreeing to the outlines of the merger. There is time enough for details. I—"

"The percentage split afforded Nippon Memory in this country is totally unacceptable," Nangi broke in. He ground out the stump of his cigarette, began almost immediately on another one. "It's a case of attempted robbery, pure and simple."

"Considering the revolutionary nature of the new chip Sphynx is bringing to this merger," Nicholas said before Tomkin could open his mouth, "I hardly think a fifty-one–forty-nine split is a high price to pay. Think of the enor—"

"I am a banker, Mr. Linnear." Nangi's clipped voice was as cold as his blinkless stare. "Though our *keiretsu* owns many different kinds of *konzerns*, including trust and insurance companies, trade and real estate associations as well as the Sato Petrochemical group, they are all linked by two factors." He puffed casually at his cigarette, certain he had once again regained control of the conversation.

"One: they are all dependent on the money the Daimyō Development Bank makes for them. Two: they are all based on profitability; when that goes so, too, do they."

"And profitability is precisely what this merger is offering you, Nangi-san."

"It affords us no ready capital and I know nothing of computer chips," Nangi said shortly, as if dismissing the subject.

"To understand the tremendous importance of what we have,"

Nicholas said evenly, "it's essential to get an overview. The computer memory chip is a tiny slice of silicon that, for want of more accurate terminology, is composed of microscopic bins within which are stored bits of information. For instance, the most common chip, a 64K RAM, is composed of sixty-four thousand bins in a space about the same size as your fingertip."

Nangi crossed his legs at the knee and continued to smoke as if he were at a social tea. He said nothing and Nicholas went on. "RAM stands for random access memory. These chips are most often used because they are very fast and when a computer is at work speed is essential. The problem with RAMs is that when power is cut off to them they lose all their memory and they have to be reprogrammed from scratch.

"That's why ROMs were invented. These are read-only memory chips which are totally non-volatile. That means their bins are either filled or empty—permanently. That, of course, is their drawback. They must be taken out of the computer in order to be reprogrammed.

"For years, the computer technician's dream has been for a non-volatile RAM: a speedy, readily reprogrammable chip that won't lose its memory when the power is turned off."

Nicholas looked at everyone before he went on; no one seemed bored. "Recently, the industry has come up with a partial solution to the problem: E-squared PROMs, or electrically erasable programmable read-only memory chips. The problem with them is that they're just too slow to replace RAMs in the heart of a computer.

"Xicor, one of our competitors, has even gone one step further. They're beginning to combine a RAM with an E-squared PROM to allow the RAM to do all the fast calculations, then to transfer its memory to the E-squared PROM just before the power is cut. But they are unwieldy, expensive, and still cannot do a full range of functions. Further, disk or tape data-storage systems, mechanical switches, or just RAMs with battery backups can still do much of what this tandem chip can do."

Nicholas put his hands together and concentrated on the banker. "In other words, Nangi-san, the elusive, non-volatile RAM which will change the face of the computer industry for all time was still not available. Until now." His eyes lit up. "Sphynx has it. Sato-san's own people have validated the test data. There can be no doubt. We have it, and we are offering it to you on an exclusive basis."

Nicholas shrugged his shoulders resignedly. "Naturally, such a monumental discovery cannot remain exclusive for long; imitations will surely come. But in the meantime Sphynx-Sato will have the head start that is essential to cornering the market. Our production plants will already be in full swing filling orders while the other *konzerns* are still scrambling to work out the electronics."

"There is your profitability base," Tomkin said. "Within two years, we should be looking at a combined net profit of one hundred and fifty million dollars. That's—"

"Thirty-six billion, six hundred and sixty million yen," Nangi said. He stubbed out his butt with the formality of an aloof professor confronted by a group of vociferous but inferior pupils. "Do not attempt to teach me about money, Mr. Tomkin. But this is all in the future and these are your figures, not ours. Their astronomical nature is problematical."

Tomkin apparently had had enough. "Now, look, Sato," he said, pointedly ignoring the banker. "I came here in good faith thinking we had a deal to iron out. I am prepared for problems along the way; that's part of all business ventures." He gestured. "But not this nonsense. I'm hearing talk here like I'm in the middle of a MĪTĪ meeting."

"Nangi-san was vice-minister of MĪTĪ," Sato said with a kind of wolfish smile, "until seven years ago when, as a *ronin*, he helped found Daimyō and, quite directly of course, Sato Petrochemicals."

"I'm not surprised," Tomkin said, furious. "But you can tell him for me that this isn't a case of the foreign devil trying to undermine Japan's economic balance. Each've us's got something the other wants—and needs. I've got the goods and you've got the wherewithall to manufacture it at the right price. It's profits for all." He abruptly switched his gaze to the banker's odd mask-like face. "Get it, Nangi-san?"

"I understand quite well," Nangi said, "that you come here wanting a good sized piece of our *keiretsu*'s property in Misawa, land we have already designated for Niwa Mineral Mining's new expansion. Land is at a premium here, the expense unimaginable for such as you who sprawl like hedonists in your multi-acre estates with pools and stables and gatehouses.

"It is what you ask us to give up; it is what you always expect us to give up." His eyes were glittery, as hard as obsidian. "And for what? The technology of the future. But I ask you directly: will this 'new technology' ease the enormous land problem here; will it make Japan more independent of the fuel-rich nations who seek to bleed us dry; will it free us from our heinous obligation to the United States to be its guardpost against the encroachment of Communism in the Far East."

36

He rose up even straighter, an adder about to strike. "Times have indeed changed, as you yourself pointed out. We are no longer your vanquished foe, subject to the blind acceptance of your demands."

"Listen to this," Tomkin said. "I'm bringing you the key to millions and you're preaching reactionary politics at me." His stubby forefinger pointed at his own chest. "I'm non-political, see? I'm a businessman, that's the beginning and the end of it right there. You wanna pull this, I gotta think about going elsewhere. Like to Mitsubishi or Toshiba, for instance."

"What you must try to understand," Sato said calmly, "is that historically it's a difficult position for us to be in. Japan has not nearly the space and, er, elbow room attendant with what the United States has. There is, therefore, quite a different attitude toward foreign companies who want a slice of the Japanese pie."

"But that's just it," Tomkin said angrily. "I'm not interested in Japan. Last year the big three U.S. supercomputer companies sold only two mainframes to Japan out of a total output of sixty-five. It's the *world* market I'm thinking of. And so should you. You're so busy erecting what you call 'safeguards' to your business that you've all got a severe case of tunnel vision.

"These so-called safeguards are nothing more than barriers to international trade." He was just beginning to hit his stride now. "I think it's high time Japan came out of its global infancy and owned up to its responsibilities as a nation of the world."

Nangi appeared unruffled. "If, as you say, these safeguards were precipitously withdrawn, the effect on the Japanese economy would be disastrous. But beyond that, the overall effect on American imports into this country would increase by no more than— uhm—eight hundred million dollars. Even you, Mr. Tomkin, can see that would hardly be a drop in the bucket in solving your country's massive trade deficit."

"I think you guys'd better wise up," Tomkin said, his face beginning to flush around the jowls. "Your reactionary insular trade policies're beginning to isolate you from the rest of the world community. You're much too dependent on foreign energy sources to allow that. Stop flooding our market with your products while hindering our own from sale here, or you're likely to become prosperous orphans in the international arena."

"Why must the Japanese be constantly castigated," Nangi said, "for manufacturing superior products. We have no armhold on your American public; no one has made them buy our products. The simple—and for you sad—fact is we make things better and more cheaply. Americans trust our know-how more than they do the advances of their own companies."

But Tomkin was far from finished. "Right now," he said softly, "Sato Petrochemicals is not one of the six major Japanese computer firms. It is my understanding that you are looking for an entree into that charmed circle.

"Sphynx's non-volatile RAM is your key. My sources tell me that MITI has ordered a project meant for completion by 1990: a machine capable of performing ten billion operations a second, which would make it a hundred times faster than the state-of-the-art supercomputer Cray Research currently has on the market. MITI has allocated up to two hundred million dollars a year for the project."

He paused. Neither of the Japanese had made a move, and Tomkin knew he had scored with them.

"Further," he said, "we know of another ministry-financed project to build a supercomputer capable of understanding human speech, making it incredibly easy to use." He laced his fingers together. "Now let's get down to the bottom line, which is that our non-volatile RAM would give Sato the edge in *both* projects. MITI would be forced to come to you for help, and that would mean the big six over here would become the big seven."

He looked from one foreign face to another; one bleak, forbidding countenance to the next. They're just businessmen, he told himself. Nothing more. Nangi said nothing, which, in Tomkin's opinion, was a giant step forward.

"Proposals and counterproposals must not be made in haste," Sato said. "The war is often lost through the impulsiveness of an intemperate nature. As Sun Tzu so wisely tells us, 'When the strike of a hawk breaks the body of its prey, it is because of timing.'"

He stood up and bowed as Nicholas and Tomkin rose automatically. Nangi rose awkwardly, stood swaying slightly. "At tomorrow afternoon's meeting," Sato continued, "we will discuss this further when associates and legal counsel are all present to add their wisdom to our own. For now, I would hope you will find time to enjoy our city." They murmured their assent and he said, "Good. My car will be at the Okura at two P.M. tomorrow to bring you here."

He bowed again, formally, and Nangi did the same. "Until tomorrow, gentlemen. I wish you a restful evening." Then he took Nangi out of the room before another word could be spoken.

"That goddamned sonuvabitch Nangi." Tomkin paced his hotel room. "Why didn't my people brief me about him?" Back and forth while Nicholas watched. "That bombshell he laid on us about having been a MITI vice-minister, Christ. Do you think he'll actually block the merger?"

Nicholas ignored Tomkin's agitated state.

Tomkin answered his own question. "I know he's for sure gonna try to sweeten their percentage."

Nicholas had picked up a large square buff envelope off the writing desk. He flicked its stiff corner with a fingernail.

"Stop playing and tell me what you think, goddamn it."

Nicholas looked up. "Patience, Tomkin," he said softly. "I told you in the beginning that pulling this merger off would require patience—perhaps more patience than you have."

"Bullshit!" Tomkin came over to where Nicholas was standing. His eyes narrowed. "You saying they're outmaneuvering me?"

Nicholas nodded. "Trying to, at least. The Japanese are never open about negotiation. They won't come to terms until the very last instant because they're looking to see what will happen in the interim. Nine out of ten times, they feel, something will occur to their benefit. So until then, they'll do their best to keep us off balance."

"You mean like Nangi," Tomkin said thoughtfully. "Put a fox in the henhouse."

"And see what evolves." Nicholas nodded again. "Quite right. Perhaps, they reasoned, the friction would bring out your real anxiety in making the deal and they could negotiate better terms tomorrow or Monday." He tapped the envelope against his finger. "The Japanese knew that you never come to a negotiation showing your true nature. To deal effectively with you, they must find this out. It's called To Move the Shade. It's from the warrior Miyamoto Musashi's guide to strategy. He wrote it in 1645 but all good Japanese businessmen apply his principles to their business practices."

"To Move the Shade," Tomkin said thoughtfully. "What is it?"

"When you cannot see your opponent's true spirit, you make a quick decisive feint attack. As Musashi writes, he will then show his long sword—today we can transform that into meaning his negotiation spirit—thinking he has seen your spirit. But you have shown him nothing of value and he has instead revealed his inner strategy to you."

"And that's just what happened a few minutes ago with Sato and Nangi?"

Nicholas shrugged. "That depends on how much they actually drew you out."

Tomkin touched the tips of his fingers to his temple. "Well, it doesn't matter worth a damn," he said a little breathily. "I have you, Nick, and between us we're gonna squeeze these bastards into the box I have waiting for them—Musashi's strategy or not."

"Like the disparity in profit figures?" Nicholas said sardonically. "You told me Sphynx's share would come to a hundred million but the figures you gave Sato indicate that Sphynx and the Sato *kobun* will be splitting a hundred and fifty million between them."

"Ah, what's fifty mil more or less," Tomkin said, massaging his temple with some force. He grimaced. "Goddamn migraines." He looked at Nicholas wearily. "My doctor says it's purely a product of the world I live in." He made a rueful smile. "You know what he prescribed? A permanent Palm Springs vacation. He wants me to rot by the side of a pool like the rest of those flyblown palms." He winced at the pain. "But he ought to know, all right. He's writing a book called *Fifteen Ways to a Migraine-Free Life*. He thinks it's going to be a bestseller. 'Everyone gets migraines these days,' he says. 'God bless stress.'"

Tomkin went and sat down on the edge of the plush sofa. He opened the small refrigerator just beyond, poured himself a drink. "What've you got there?"

"It's a hand-delivered invitation. I got one as well."

Tomkin put down his drink. "Let's see it." He tore open the flap, pulled out a stiff, engraved card. "It's in goddamned *kanji*," he said angrily, pushing it back at Nicholas. "What's it say?"

"You and I, it seems, are invited to Sato's wedding. It's on Saturday."

Tomkin grunted, downed the remainder of his drink in one gulp. "Christ," he murmured, "just what we need now." He looked up as he poured himself another. "How about you?"

Nicholas shook his head and Tomkin shrugged. "Just trying to get your liver in shape. These sonsabitches drink their Suntory Scotch like it was water. You go out with them of an evening, you'd better be prepared for the onslaught."

"I wouldn't worry about that," Nicholas said coldly. "I'm well aware of their habits."

"Sure, sure," Tomkin said. "Just trying to be friendly. You did all right on the battlefield with those two jokers." He gestured with his glass. "You speak to Justine yet?"

Nicholas shook his head. "She didn't want me to take this trip at all."

"Well, that's only natural. I'm sure she's missing you."

Nicholas watched Tomkin wade through his second Scotch on the rocks and wondered if that was an antidote to his migraines.

"It's more than that," he said slowly. "When Saigō got to her he used *saiminjutsu* on her, a little-known art even among ninja."

"A kind of hypnosis, wasn't it?"

"In a way, in Western terms. But it went way beyond that." He sat down next to Tomkin. "She tried to kill me. It was the hypnotic suggestion Saigō planted within her, but still." He shook his head. "My healing broke the *saiminjutsu* spell, but the deep remorse she feels . . . I was not able to erase."

"She blames herself? But it's not her fault!"

"How many times have I assured her of that."

Tomkin swirled the dregs of his drink around and around. "She's a tough one. Take it from me, I know. She'll get over it."

Nicholas was thinking of how badly Justine had taken his decision to work for her father. Her bitterness toward what she saw as her father's manipulation of her life up until just several years ago was understandable to him. They were, he felt, two people unable to communicate with each other. Tomkin had expected certain things from her and, not finding them, had reacted in his typical overbearing manner. Justine simply could not forgive him for his various intrusions into her life.

Repeatedly he had used bribes or threats to discourage a succession of boyfriends. "My father's a master manipulator, Nick," she had told him over and over again. "He's a bastard without a heart or a conscience. He's never cared about anyone but himself, not me, certainly not Gelda; not even my mother."

Yet, Nicholas knew, Justine was blind to the kind of men she had been attracted to. They had been manipulators all—far worse than her father ever had been. No wonder Tomkin had been so hostile toward him when they had first met. He naturally assumed that Nicholas was another in the long line bent on using his daughter.

It was impossible to make Justine see that it was his very love for her that obliged him to interfere in an area that, up until now, she had been unable to handle. This did not absolve Tomkin, but it seemed a realistic starting point for the two of them to come together and possibly understand each other.

The tirade that had followed Nicholas' announcement of his going to work for Tomkin Industries, if only temporarily, had been followed by days of uncomfortable silence; Justine had simply not wanted to talk about it further. But in the last days before his departure it had seemed to Nicholas as if she had relented a bit, and was more at ease with his decision. "After all," she had said as she saw him off, "it's only for a while, isn't it?"

41

"What?" he said now, setting his concern for her back in its niche in the shadows of his mind.

"I asked who Sato's marrying," Tomkin said.

Nicholas looked down at the invitation. "A woman named Akiko Ofuda. Do you know anything about her?"

Tomkin shook his head.

"She's the newest major interest in your partner's life," Nicholas said seriously. "I think it's time you thought about hiring a new team of researchers."

With great difficulty Tanzan Nangi turned fully around. At his back the snow-clad slopes of Fuji-yama were fast disappearing into a vast golden haze the consistency of bisque. Tokyo buzzed at his feet like a giant *pachinko* machine.

"I don't like him," he said, his voice like chalk scraping a blackboard.

"Tomkin?"

Nangi arched an eyebrow as he extracted a cigarette from its case. "You know very well whom I mean."

Sato gave him a benevolent smile. "Of course you don't, my friend. Isn't that why you assigned Miss Yoshida—a *woman*—to meet them at the airport? Tell me which Japanese business associate of ours you would have insulted in that fashion. None, I can tell you! You even disapprove of the amount of responsibility I accord her here because it is, as you say, man's province, and not the traditional way."

"You have always run this *kobun* as you have seen fit. I begrudge you nothing, as you know quite well. But as for these *iteki*, I saw no earthly reason why we should lose valuable manhours by reassigning an upper-echelon executive for their convenience."

"Oh, yes," Sato said. "Tomkin is a *gaijin* and Nicholas Linnear is something far worse to you. He's only half Oriental. And then it has never been determined to anyone's satisfaction how much of that is Japanese."

"Are you saying that I am a racist?" Nangi said, blowing out smoke.

"Not in the least." Sato sat back in his swivel chair. "Merely a patriot." He shrugged. "But in the end what does Cheong Linnear's lineage mean to us?"

"It's a potential lever." Nangi's odd triangular eyes blazed with a dark light. "We are going to need every weapon in our arsenal to bring down these brash *iteki*—these barbarians who think of us as so much rice they can gobble up." Nangi's shoulders quivered at odd moments as if they had a will of their own. "Do you think it means anything to me that his father was Colonel Linnear, the 'round-eyed savior of Japan'?" His face screwed up in contempt. "How could any *iteki* feel for us, Seiichi, tell me that."

"Sit down, old friend," Sato said softly, taking his eyes off the older man to save him face. "You already hurt enough as it is."

Nangi said nothing but, walking awkwardly, managed to sit at right angles to Sato, his back erect, his thin buttocks against the very edge of the chair.

Sato knew that Nangi was lucky to be alive. But of course life was a relative thing and this thorny enigma was never far from his thoughts, even now after thirty-eight years. Did the man tied to the iron lung think life was worthwhile? So, too, Sato sometimes wished to crawl inside his friend's head for just the moment it would take to learn the answer to the riddle. And in those moments shame would suffuse him; precisely the same kind of shame he had felt when his older brother, Gōtarō, had found him sitting, sexually aroused by their father's book of *shunga*, erotic prints.

There was no privacy in Japan, it was often said. The crowding because of the lack of space that had existed for centuries; the building materials—oiled paper and wood—that the islands' frequent and devastating earthquakes, the seasonal typhoons dictated be used in order to facilitate speedy rebuilding: these factors went a long way in guiding the flow of Japanese society.

Because real privacy, as a Westerner understands it, is physically impossible, the Japanese have developed a kind of inner privacy that, outwardly, manifests itself by the many-layered scheme of formality and politeness that each individual lives by because it is his only bulwark against the encroachment of chaos.

That was why the thought of stepping into someone else's mind, especially so close a friend, brought the sweat of shame out on Sato. Now he riffled through the file they had compiled on Tomkin Industries in order to cover his intense discomfort.

"As for Tomkin, we should not underestimate him, Nangi-san," he said now. Nangi looked up as he heard the note of weariness in the younger man's voice.

"How so?"

"His blustering barbarian ways cannot mask for long his keen mind. He hit us squarely when he said that we're much too dependent on foreign energy sources to allow ourselves to become isolated from the rest of the world."

Nangi waved away Sato's words. "A mere stab in the dark. The man's an animal, nothing more."

Sato gave a deep sigh. "And yet he's quite correct. Why else

43

would we be laboring so long and hard on *Tenchi*, eh? It is something that is critically draining our financial resources; it is the most desperate gamble Japan has taken since Pearl Harbor. In many ways it is more crucial to this country's future than the war ever was. We were able to rebound from that defeat." Sato shook his head. "But if *Tenchi* should fail or if—Buddha forbid!—we should be found out, then I fear that there will be nothing left of our beloved islands but atomic ash."

"Tsutsumu's dead, along with Kusunoki." The voice was flat and cold. It might have been conveying the message, "Here are ten pounds of rice."

"Before or after?" By contrast this voice was heavy, thick with foreign inflection. "That is the only thing that matters."

"Before."

There was a muffled curse in a language the first man could not understand. "Are you certain? Absolutely certain?"

"I was thorough enough to do an anal search. He had nothing on him." There was a slight pause. "Do you wish me to withdraw?" Still the voice was emotionless, as if all feeling had been trained out of it.

"Certainly not. Stay just where you are. Any sudden movement on your part could only bring down suspicion and these people are not to be underestimated. They're fanatics; exceptionally dangerous fanatics."

"Yes . . . I know."

"You have your orders; adhere to them. The *dōjō*'s bound to be in turmoil for the next few days at least. Even they need time to gather themselves. They haven't picked Kusunoki's successor yet, have they?"

"There are meetings going on to which I am not privy. As yet there have been no announcements. But tension is high all through the *dōjō*."

"Good. Now is the time to burrow in. Get as close as you dare. Strike in the midst of this confusion; our tactics are more efficient in this atmosphere."

"Kusunoki's death has turned them into alarmists; they see hostiles in the movement of the shadows."

"Then be especially bold."

"The danger has increased."

"And has your dedication to the goals of the Motherland therefore decreased?"

"I will not waver from the cause; you know that."

"Good. Then this conversation is at an end."

44

A light went on atop the scarred metal desk, dim and buzzing, coldly fluorescent, emanating from an ancient khaki gooseneck lamp that had been functionally ugly when new and now was light-years away from that.

This fitful pale mauve illumination revealed a face no more unusual than an accountant's or a professor's. Black eyes above sloped Slavic cheekbones were penetratingly intelligent, to be sure, but his fine, tufted hair, the liver spots high on his domed forehead, and the rather weak chin all combined to paint a portrait of a bland, unremarkable man. Nothing could be further from the truth.

His slender-fingered hand came away from the phone; already his mind was racing. He did not like the sudden murder of the *sensei*; he knew well Kusunoki's power and was astonished that the *sensei* had been overpowered at all. Still, he was trained to use any and all unforeseen circumstance to his benefit, and striking swiftly and surely during times of confusion was standard procedure.

Contrary to what his brethren back home espoused, he enjoyed working with these locals. While he would never invite one to marry his daughter—if he had one—he could admire their expertise, their dogged persistence, and, above all, their rabid fanaticism. This fascinated him; it was also his secret weapon against political assassination back home.

While his position, among all his brethren, was most secure—simply because he fed them a steady diet of fear and secrecy, two elements which never failed to catch their attention—still one found it good practice to keep shuffling the cards, keeping options open, finding the soft spots in one's superiors' private lives that would turn the key in the lock of one's future. That was a lesson he had learned well and hard.

He turned away from the phone, activating the portable but very powerful 512K computer terminal, rechecking the myriad random elements he had thrown at the original program. Still it was holding up.

His grunt in the otherwise silent room told of his satisfaction. With an effort, he rose and lumbered to the door as thick and impenetrable as a bank vault. Dialing the combination, he let himself out.

Nicholas left the dazzling glitter of the enormous hotel behind him, a city within a city, and took the immaculate, silent subway into the Asakusa district. The blank-faced jostling throng who rode along with him with their fashionable clothes and French-style

45

makeup were outwardly very different from the members of the war generation. Yet Nicholas could not forget what happened here—as it did throughout all of Tokyo—on March 9, 1945. The firebombing by American warplanes.

Here in the Asakusa district, people sought the sanctuary of the great and beloved Buddhist temple of Kannon, the goddess of Pity. Built in the seventeenth century, this was thought safe because it had survived all the great fires of Tokyo as well as the most infamous earthquake of 1923. But as hundreds crowded inside, the long, arching timbers, so lovingly wrought by artisans of the fabled past, caught fire. The gray slat roof which had been such a staunch landmark for hundreds of years collapsed inward, crushing the already burning throng. Outside, the ancient stately gingko trees of the surrounding gardens burst into crackling torches, pinwheels of sparks arcing into the howling crimson night, running along street gutters like voracious predators.

Asakusa, like the rest of the city, bore no scars from that time, Nicholas realized. The Japanese had been very careful about that. In this downtown area of Tokyo, more than in any other place in the city, perhaps, the ethos of Japan's splendiferous Edo period still held sway.

Crowds clouded the gates of Kaminarimon, streaking its great two-story vermillion face with their darting shadows. A scarlet and ebon rice-paper lantern of gigantic proportions swung between the two red-faced wooden statues of the gods of wind and thunder, the bodyguards of Kannon, who, though she failed her people once in the incinerator of the war, was worshiped and loved still.

Dodging those Japanese on the run, Nicholas took the stone-paved Nakamise-dōri, passing sweet and souvenir shops piled high with wares.

On impulse he turned down a near side street, strolling slowly through the relative gloom. He stopped abruptly in front of a tiny storefront that spelled out "Yonoya" in *kanji*. Inside, glass shelves were lined with the slightly oily boxwood combs.

Nicholas remembered Yukio slowly, rhythmically stroking her hair with such a comb. How soft and long and shining were those tresses, thick and lustrous. Once he had asked her if all Orientals had such beautiful hair and she had laughed, embarrassed, pushing him from her.

"Only the ones who can afford these," she said, still laughing. She showed him the exquisitely hand-carved implement. "Feel it," she offered.

"Sticky," he said immediately.

"But guaranteed never to tangle your hair, Nicholas," she had said in her singsong voice. "This boxwood is brought all the way from Kyūshū, the southern island. It is cut and steamed to remove any imperfections and then dried for more than a week above a boxwood-shaving fire. Then the lengths are tied together and bamboo hoops slipped over the bundles, and they are left to dry for thirty years to ensure that they are completely dry before being carved.

"In the shop in Asakusa where I buy these, their craftsmen have studied for twenty years. They sit for ten or twelve hours at a time, immobile except for their working hands, to shape these combs." Nicholas had been fascinated then just as he was fascinated now. Even with such an everyday implement as a comb, he thought, we take exceptional care and artistry in its manufacture. Could a Westerner—*any* Westerner—ever fully understand the reasons why. Or would they think us mad to devote such time and intense effort to such a small and seemingly insignificant matter.

Again on impulse, he entered the shop and bought a comb for Justine. As he waited for the saleswoman to reoil the boxwood, carefully wrap it in three separate layers of high-grade rice paper, and then place it into its hand-sanded cedar box, his eyes traced the forms of the combs lying in artistic display. With each meticulously rounded corner, with each matched tooth end, he again saw Yukio in front of the mirror, her pale hand rising and falling like a tide through the river of her dark hair. He saw that ebon cascade highlighted against the snow-white kimono, its crimson edges moving like flowing blood.

He leaned forward and, hands on her delicate shoulders, turned her around, lifting her so that she rose. Soft rustle of silk like the bittersweet drift of heavenly cherry petals in mid-April when, it seemed, the ancient gods of Japan returned, filling the scented air with their ethereal presence.

The feel of her, the sight of her, the scent of her, all combined to transfix him, so that he experienced again his deep-seated fear of what she brought out in him: the intensity of sexual feeling. He was barely eighteen, it was 1963. He had had no experience with women, especially one as powerful as Yukio.

It was as if she held him in a tender spell, and now her palm came up to stroke his cheek and he shuddered at the fiery lick the caress engendered in him.

As was usual with them, she had to take the first few steps, sliding her fingertips back along her own body, pushing the rim of the kimono away from her shoulders. It parted with a rustle,

47

revealing the inside slopes of her hard-nippled breasts. Nicholas' breath caught in his throat and his belly contracted painfully.

With a slither the soft white kimono slid down her arms, the line of crimson along its verge flickering like flame. And now she was bare, the light striping her, throwing into deep shadow the erotic dells of her torso, hiding as it revealed.

Nicholas felt the terror filling him up as, like a sorceress, she moved, freeing his own sexuality, drawing out his own ribboning desire. He could deny her nothing at moments like this.

And yet there was a deeply buried sadness in her as she reached between his thighs, caught gentle hold of him, stroking.

"Is that all you can think of?" he said thickly.

"It's all I have," she said in a moan, guiding him.

Slowly refocusing, Nicholas' gaze lit upon the empty space in the display case caused by the present he had bought Justine. Yukio was gone just as the boxwood comb was gone from the case.

The spotlights' glare was harder in just that spot, magnifying the nothingness. He wondered what had ever become of Yukio's magical boxwood comb. Had Saigō hurled it after her into the Straits of Shimonoseki? Had she been wearing it when he clubbed her, stunning her, then binding her for the long rowboat ride across those haunted waters? Or had some small child found the artifact among her abandoned belongings and was wearing it today?

Nicholas found that his eyes were full of tears. Despite his vow never to relive the moment when his evil cousin had told him of Yukio's death, he had done it. His heart was breaking anew; he felt her loss as keenly this moment as he had a year ago. Perhaps this was one wound that time would never heal.

Blindly he received the exquisitely wrapped package, signed the American Express receipt. It was as if Yukio's *kami* had appeared at his side, linking arms with him, and, standing by his side, was now looking down at the display of boxwood combs with him.

And for that moment it was as if death had been banished from the world of man, as if there was no dark barrier between life and death, the unknown becoming suddenly known and accepted. Did he walk with the dead, or had Yukio crossed over to live again at his side?

With a start, Nicholas found himself alone again in the shop. The saleswoman was looking at him oddly, not certain whether to smile or frown at the peculiar expression on his face.

Back on the Nakamise-dōri, he returned to the precincts of the Sensōji Temple, where rice crackers and tortoiseshell sticks were

48

still sold just as they had been a hundred years before. He wanted to stay immersed in the past, unwilling as yet to let go of the last sweetly painful tendrils of his waking dream. At a streetside stall he paused to buy a confection made of egg and flour poured into a doll-shaped mold before bean jam was squeezed on and the whole was grilled with the deftly economical movements of the ancient vendor.

But, once holding the tiny cake in his hand, he found that he had no taste for food, especially sweets. The past was like the taste of ash in his mouth. He had thought that with Saigō's death the detritus of his earlier life would dry up and blow away like the soft shed skin of a snake. But he saw now on his return to Japan that this was not so. It could not be. There was a certain continuity to life that was not to be denied. As Nicholas' father, the Colonel, had often said: this is the only true lesson of history, and those who do not heed it, perish because of their ignorance.

Now, at the doorway to the Sensōji Temple, he gave the unwanted food to an old man with a back as thin and bent as a sapling's trunk in a high wind. The old man, in a black snapbrim hat and Western dress, nodded his thanks but made no effort to smile.

As Nicholas went into the temple itself, echoes and the ripples of history seemed to reach out from the dim incense-filled interior with its high vaulting ceiling and cool stone floor, to remind him once again of all that he dare not forget.

When he reemerged into the spangled night of *shitamachi*, Tokyo's downtown, the old man was still where Nicholas had left him, one hand curled around the thick copper rim of the huge vessel used to burn incense.

Nicholas had had enough of old Japan and the tangled web of memories it had unearthed in him. He longed for the spark and dazzle of the new Tokyo, the soaring, ugly buildings so new the lacquer had not yet dried in their towering gallerylike lobbies; he longed for the bustle of the young Japanese, so chic and beautiful in their wide-shouldered jackets, their loose blousey shirts, and their high-waisted trousers.

Underground, he took the Ginza Line nine stops, transferring to the Hibiya Line for the short trip to Roppongi. He emerged from the subway exit and went west, toward Shibuya. He took the all glass elevator in the Ishibashi Building to the top floor and entered the ironclad doors of Jan Jan. From its southeasterly facing floor-to-ceiling windows he could make out the floodlit stone walls of the Russian embassy.

The air was alive with the percussive rhythms of rock music:

49

The Yellow Magic Orchestra and an English group called Japan. It was well after midnight and the place was jumping. Cigarette smoke blued the pale walls. The intense spot lighting striking like arrows straight down from the enormously high acoustic baffled ceiling dappled the springy wooden dance floor, turning it into a rippling tiger's pelt.

Around the central dance floor rose three tiers of clear Plexiglas tables and midnight blue velour-covered banquettes. Waitresses moved quickly and efficiently in amongst the crowd. There was movement, heat, sound in crushing waves. The electricity of modern life.

Nicholas' mind was engaged as he moved slowly through the bouncing energetic throng. His eyes roved across the sea of young painted faces, seeing the laughter, the self-engrossment; observing slick-winged hairstyles, arms entangled around waists and buttocks, whirling torsos, dervishes of the night, enraptured by a combination of the musical pulse, the boost of liquor and, perhaps, illicit drugs, and, above all, the narcotizing sense of eternal youth. The concept of mortality had no place here and, if it came, would never be recognized.

For just an instant Nicholas wondered what it was he was searching for. Then he thought of Justine and knew that he would not find it here.

When Akiko Ofuda saw Nicholas walk in through Jan Jan's high Edo period portals she turned her head partly away into the shadows. Her heart was beating fast. Bewildered, she fought to understand the reason for his abrupt appearance. Did he know anything? *Could* he?

But no, she thought, calming herself. It was too early. His presence must be merely a coincidence. A jest of the gods. She rose from where she had been sitting at a table along the second tier and walked slowly, lithely, circling the perimeter of the light-streaked dance floor.

She kept him in sight all the while, watching him clandestinely but carefully. What she saw was a ruggedly angular face that had nothing of the classical beauty about it. It was far too odd and distinctive for that. The long upswept eyes hinted of his Oriental blood, as did his prominent cheekbones. But he had a good solid Anglo-Saxon chin that was as Western as his father.

He was black haired and wide-shouldered, with the odd narrow hips of a dancer and the thickly muscled legs of the serious athlete.

Akiko found herself longing to strip him naked to admire the sight of those overlays of long, sinewy muscle. But other than this, it was difficult to say what she thought of him on first sight. So many conflicting emotions swirled inside her, contending for ascendancy.

How she hated him! She was struck anew by the force of it. Seeing him so abruptly, in so unforeseen a manner brought the full shock of the secret emotions she had been harboring for so long into the forefront. She trembled in rage even while her eyes drank in the emanations of his power. It was evident even from such a distance: the lift of his head, the rolling liquid stride, the minute movements of his shoulders and upper arms. These all spoke of the extreme danger leashed tightly inside this man.

But as she herself moved, keeping pace with him, she felt an odd elation begin to suffuse her and she thought, What extraordinary *karma* I must possess to gain this added advantage over him from the start! Her pulse beat hard within her as her eyes drank him in, noting his strength, the intensity of his spirit. Oh, but she longed for that moment when he first saw her. Unconsciously, her fingers rose to her cheek, softly stroking the taut flesh there. She experienced an almost giddy sensation at the intensity of her longing, and a part of her wanted to draw it out as long as possible. After all this time, she did not want the end to come so soon, certainly not until the time of her own choosing.

Oh, yes, it had been a stroke of genius suggesting to Sato that he invite the *gaijin* to the wedding. "Especially this Linnear," she had whispered in his ear late one night. "We all know his family's history. Think what face it will give you to have him present at such an event!"

Yes, yes, Nicholas, she crooned silently as she stalked him high above his head, the time is coming soon when I will look directly in your eyes and see that strength crumble and fly away like gray ash in the wind.

She felt intoxicated, her throat constricted, the muscles in her thighs trembling with the flutter of her heart as she felt herself drawn inexorably toward him. But she used all her training to restrain herself from destroying in an instant of ecstatic gloating everything she had worked for for so long.

Now she broke away from his orbit, walking more quickly, ignoring the glances of those she passed, the lust of the men, the envy of the women; she had become inured to that. It was time to pick up Yōki; Sato would soon be home from the wars.

Akiko watched Yōki out of the corner of her eye as they sped through the center of Tokyo and out again. She is a magnificent creature, Akiko thought. I have chosen well. She had found Yōki some weeks ago and when she was certain of her choice had struck up a conversation with her. That had led to an odd—at least Akiko saw it as that—kind of friendship. Its borders were the night when, as far as Yōki was concerned, they both emerged like nocturnal birds.

Akiko had once asked Yōki what occupied her during the day. "Oh, on and off, I'm a saleslady," she had said. "You know, door to door. Perfumes and cosmetics. Otherwise I watch television. Not only dramas but programs where I learn calligraphy, flower arranging—even the tea ceremony."

In a culture where 93 percent of the population watched TV at least once a day that was, perhaps, not surprising. Yet it nevertheless chilled Akiko that her country was teaching its population by proxy. She had learned the tea ceremony from her mother, and she remembered watching the older woman's face, listening to the tone of her voice, seeing the patterns on her kimono moving just so here and not at all there, resolving to memorize every detail no matter how tiny for those, her mother had once told her, were all that would be noticed.

Could the emissions of an electronic cathode ray tube provide such teaching? She was sure it could not, and she found herself disgusted when she thought of the number of women being taught in such an impersonal manner.

But outwardly she showed none of this disdain. Yōki was important to her—at least for the next several hours.

The limo pulling up onto the gravel verge of the two-story house pushed her thoughts back to the present. Seiichi Sato lived just north of Ueno Park in Uguisudani in Taitō-Ku. A block and a half to the southwest was wide Kototoi-dōri, the avenue that curled like a serpent around two sides of the park. Beyond, the high tops of the carefully pruned cypress stood stark and utterly black against the faintly pink and yellow glow from the Ginza and Shinjuku nightspots. The trees were the natural markers of the Tokugawa Shōgun graveyard across the myriad railroad tracks in the northern end of Ueno.

Sato's house was large by Tokyo standards, built on the *ken* principle, the standard six-foot unit of construction. It was made of bamboo and cypress; the three-layered roof was of terra cotta tile. The far end of the house contained a great notch to accommodate a more-than-one-hundred-year-old cryptomeria whose boughs overgrew the sheltering eight-foot fence, swaying over the road itself.

The driver came around and opened the rear door for them, and Akiko took her charge inside.

52

Seiichi Sato sipped hot sakē from a tiny porcelain cup and contemplated the Void. He did this, sometimes, in moments of intense stress, to clear his mind. But mainly he used this form of mental exercise when he was impatient. In a land where patience was not merely a virtue but a way of life, Sato had had to teach himself this attitude as if he were some form of alien in his own culture. Yet he had worked diligently, even obsessively at it, and he knew that his patience had won him all that he held dear today.

He was in the six-*tatami* room—space being defined in Japanese houses by the number of reed mats the wood floor could contain—with only a small table, a cotton futon and a drawered *naga-hibachi* of burl paulownia wood dating from the early part of the nineteenth century. A recess in the right top of the long brazier allowed for the heating of sakē as well as food.

Sato wore only a white cotton kimono. Its bold crimson square reproduced the crest of the Danjuro line of *kabuki* actors. He looked calm and assured, his cool eyes staring at a spot not within the realm of the physical world.

A soft knock on the *fusuma* made him blink but otherwise he did not move. Now he unlocked his thoughts and allowed the keen sense of anticipation to enfold him like a cloak on a chill winter's eve.

He reached out and moved the paper door an inch to the right. Just the pronounced curve of the front half of Akiko's eye gazed at him from beneath a half-lowered lid. The sable darkness dusted along the delicate flesh was like the painting of dusk across a changing sky. The coal black iris was like the heart of some deeply buried treasure. Despite himself, Sato felt the quickness of his pulse, the heat of his own breath firing in his throat.

"You are late." His voice was breathy as he began their ritual. "I thought you would not come."

Akiko heard the thickness in his voice and smiled to herself. "I always come," she whispered. "I cannot do otherwise."

"You are free to walk away." Sato's heart constricted as he said those words.

"I give my love to you freely and I am bound by it. I will never leave you."

The script had been developed over a period of months to provide them both with a degree of excitement and intrigue within the carefully prescribed boundaries of societal courtship. Of course, there were aspects about their courtship—minor ones, to be sure—that had Sato's mother been alive she would have disapproved of in the most vociferous language.

Sato bowed his head and, opening the *fusuma* farther, moved back on his knees and shins to allow her entrance. As Akiko entered, the dual *kanji* ideograms for *sōbi* hovered in the center of Sato's being like a feudal *daimyō*'s banner, for she did indeed possess sublime beauty. And, despite their ritualistic dialog, he knew it was he who was bound to her for all time, body and spirit.

For a time they knelt facing one another, Sato's large, capable hands held palms up, Akiko's smaller ones resting lightly in his. Locked, their eyes stared within and through. Sato, contemplating the *karma* that had brought them together, felt the essence of her stirring, a lacquered kite rising above rooftops and rustling crowns of cypress and pine. A strong gust took it suddenly and it shot straight for his heart, lodging there like a broken wing.

"What are you thinking?"

The question startled him. Was it just because of the abrupt sound from out of the silence of the beating of their hearts, he asked himself. From deep within him came a secret fear that somehow, in some unfathomable way, her mind had pierced his flesh, peering into his inviolable thoughts. And in that split instant, a brief shudder contracted the muscles ridged along his gently arched back and he blinked, his eyes searching hers as if she were a stranger.

Then her lips bowed into a smile and her white, even teeth showed. "You are so solemn this night." She laughed, and he saw the play of light along the side of her throat, the small shadow lying in the hollow like a teardrop.

He said nothing, and after studying his granitelike countenance for a moment she made a move to rise. "I will—" But his fingers curled around her wrist stopped her and, perched like a bird, her lips opened. "Sato-san."

Slowly he brought her back down to her knees, then drew himself upward. The fabric of his kimono winked and rippled as his shoulders squared and Akiko was abruptly aware of his strength and, even more, his power.

"This night is special," he said thickly. "There will only be one like it in all our lives." He paused for a moment as if collecting his thoughts. "So our lives will be truly bound by the laws of the Amida Buddha." His eyes raked her face. "Does this mean nothing to you?"

"I have thought of little else all day."

"Then stay." At that moment his fingers let go their grip and her arm, freed, drifted down to her lap. Her perfect, lacquered nails overlapped as her fingers interlaced, a streak of light lying along the gleaming surface of each beyond which he could not see. "On this most special of nights, send my gift away."

Her face, as composed as a porcelain mask, disclosed nothing of her inner feelings. Sato could scarcely discern the rise and fall of her breasts as she breathed. Her *wa* was as unruffled as the still skin of a mountain lake, reflecting rather than revealing.

He was disconcerted. "Surely you must know it is you who I desire."

Akiko turned her head as if he had struck her a physical blow. "Then you hate the gift I bear; you have hated all the gifts that I have brought you since—"

"No!" Trembling, Sato silently railed against the trap he had entered.

"I have dishonored you with my desire to please you." Akiko wrung her hands like an aggrieved little girl.

Sato leaned forward. "I have loved each and every gift; I have treasured the thought behind them." He had regained control of his voice if not his emotions. "There is only honor in what you have brought me, knowing—" His eyes slid away from her, staring fixedly at the *tatami* between them. "Knowing that you have never . . . been with a man, understanding my desires"—he took a deep breath—"and wanting to bring me happiness in this sphere."

Her head lowered. "It is my duty. I—"

But his hand shot out again, covering hers. "But tonight we are so close to being joined. Seeing you and—"

"What you ask—" Her head snapped up. "And then what of our wedding night? Will we make a mockery of tradition? Will we degrade the path that is ours? Do you want that?"

Sato felt her nails digging into his calloused flesh and knew she was right. He grasped at the fluttering of his intense desire for her, choking it off. His head nodded on his thick neck and he whispered through dry lips, "It is your gift that I desire."

Akiko stood by the *naga-hibachi*, feeling its heat suffuse her. She paid only the most minimal attention to the work her hands were doing, cooking the *soba*, the buckwheat noodles, preparing the soy-based sauce in small porcelain cups, pouring the rest into a tiny matching pitcher, setting out the green horseradish and chopped cucumber on a saucerlike plate.

The *soba*, when done, was lifted in tiny portions into rectangular stacking trays of black lacquer. Normally, she would be waited upon as would be Sato. But this was part of her gift to him, and at this time of the night servants were enjoined from this side of the house.

Akiko served the food and more hot sakē. She observed that Sato and Yōki were talking in low, intimate tones. She had prepared the girl well. Yōki knew what to expect and what was expected of her.

Akiko rose and walked silently to the edge of the *fusuma*. She paused with a delicate hand on the light wooden frame. The sound of them washed over her before she slid the paper door shut behind her.

But she did not leave the house. Instead, she moved to the left, entering a smaller, two-*tatami* room. Carefully closing the *fusuma*, she slid across the reed mats on her knees until she reached the *shōji* common with the room within which Sato and Yōki reclined. The screen was actually composed of many long and narrow vertical panels, decorative and pleasing to the eye. Some time ago, just after she had been introduced into the household, Akiko had secretly altered the nature of one of these panels so that it became removable by a subtle manipulation of its thin wooden border.

Through this rift she now gazed upon Sato and Yōki. They had finished their *soba*; the sakē was almost gone. They were very close together. Kneeling at her spyhole, Akiko settled herself for what was to come.

Sato's back was to her. She saw the movement of his arm and then the soft slide of Yōki's kimono—for Akiko knew better than to present the girl to Sato in her Western-style clothes—back and down, exposing one soft white shoulder.

Akiko held her breath as the rich play of the girl's muscles was revealed. Sato's eyes were drawn to Yōki's breasts; the brown and gray kimono lay like wings on the *tatami* on either side of her, her thighs still partially wrapped. Then Sato's head bent down and forward and with a soft cry Yōki's head went back, her fingers caressing his ears as his tongue streaked hotly across her nipples.

Akiko crossed her arms over her own breasts, feeling the hot stiffness there like points of fire. Her mouth was dry and she longed for sakē to slake her thirst.

She had almost given in to Sato tonight. That had shocked her like a lightning bolt out of the blue. It had been relatively easy to keep him at arm's length all these long weeks; she had been disgusted by the lust clouding his eyes. But this night had been different.

Yōki was now completely naked. Sato's open mouth licked and sucked at her flesh with such intensity that Akiko could feel her own flesh heating, tingling just as if it were she he was making love to.

56

Why? What had been different? Akiko searched her mind, analyzing as Sun Hsiung had taught her to do so long ago: quarter your memory, then divide it into eighths, sixteenths, and so on. "Eventually," he had told her, "you will find the detail you have been seeking for your senses are the most sensitive of receptors. They record everything; it is only your conscious mind which filters out what it believes to be all the important data. The lesson you must learn—and it is a most difficult one—is that your conscious mind often makes the wrong choice."

Now, as her eyes drank in the erotic movements unfolding just beyond the aperture in the *shōji*, Akiko began the quartering search of her memory, for she was well attuned to her own emotions as she was to others'.

Tonight, just like all nights, she had sprung the right trap to ensnare Sato so that she could slip away from his advances. She had been filled with elation at the frustration she was causing him. But that feeling had been short-lived. Why?

Rock music's primal pulse so full of anger, aggression, and lust, sizzled in her blood like alcohol; a room blue with smoke, making figures as indistinct as priests inside a temple wreathed in incense lit for the dead. She stalked a tiger there, lithe, full of a terrifying atavistic power. It magnetized her; spooked her.

For now she had traced the loosening of her sexual emotions to the moment when she had been circling Nicholas Linnear like a hungry jackal. Summoning up the image of him within the confines of exotic Jan Jan, she experienced again the triphammer beat of her heart, the tiny trembling of her inner thigh muscles, and the powerful compulsion to approach him.

Again, as they had at the nightclub, her fingers rose up to touch the flushed flesh of her cheek as if to assure herself that it was still there. It had not been that long. She must always keep that in mind. A stranger to herself, she must learn to become her own best friend. She had never been able to do that . . . before. On the advent of her rebirth she had vowed to herself that she would try. But first, unfinished business. And that involved Nicholas Linnear. Oh, yes. Most surely it did!

Akiko's eyes opened wide. Sato and Yōki were entangled on the *futon*. The folds of their kimonos rippled about the edges of their working flesh like the sea's waves upon the shore, concealing and revealing at once.

The panting bellows of their breaths rose toward her like a flock of gulls, pulling her onward as a third member as it fueled the furnace of their passion.

She saw Sato's erection, large and reddish from the stroking ministrations of his partner. Yōki's eyes were fluttered closed in pleasure and her soft breasts heaved into Sato's calloused palms as his head slid down and down until his open mouth touched the insides of her heated thighs.

Unconsciously Akiko strained forward, and when she saw his tongue flick out to caress the flesh there, she gasped silently. A line of warm sweat trickled like a serpent's tail down the deep indentation of her spine, staining her kimono, marking it with her lust. Her palms traced a circular pattern inward across her own spread-apart thighs until, lifting the material of her kimono, she encountered bare flesh.

Now, instead of her own fingertips, she felt Sato's flickering tongue in maddening repetition as it moved across Yōki's damp thighs, his hands behind her knees for an instant, lifting her legs.

Yōki's thighs, Akiko's thighs. There was no difference there to the touch. What had been done to her had not marred the silkiness of the flesh. But, she knew, should Sato see what lay along the inside, hidden skin there he might call off the wedding and that she could not afford. Afterward . . . well, then he would have no choice but to accept her.

Sato's mouth moved upward, covering the curling black hair covering Yōki's high mound. Akiko could see the other girl's hips trembling with excitement and the building of her orgasm. Sato's head burrowed down into the heat and the wet and Yōki threw her head back, the thin cords at the side of her neck standing out, her lips open, her teeth bared. Her thighs trembled uncontrollably.

And all the while, Akiko's deft fingers were opening up her own petals, making gentle circular sweeps in concert with the movements of Sato's head. She felt him but it was not enough; she needed more. The sensations touched her, beading like rain. But what she craved was a torrent, a tidal wave to lift her off her feet and tumble her helter-skelter into the arms of ecstasy.

It would not come, and she increased the pressure of her fingers, beginning to dig into the soft folds, pulling them apart, pressing harder against her clitoris.

Sato's head came up. His chest was heaving like a bull's. His great male form arched itself above Yōki's supple female one, shadowing her from the diffuse light, streaking her face so that she appeared to be wearing some bizarre makeup.

And now she drew him upward, rubbing him against her until she had no other choice but to arch up and impale herself on him, thrusting her hips wildly off the *futon*, the breath whooshing out of her with an audible rush, the mounds of her breasts quivering with the strength of the sensations running rampant through her.

How Akiko longed to feel what she was feeling: the tide gathering, calling, running inward from the vast depths of the sea toward her like a blanket of night, blotting out all thought, all pain, all memories in the shooting inundation of vibrating pleasure.

Sato was stroking down to meet Yōki's frantic thrusting, their hips hot in contact, the warm salty sweat dripping down from Sato's bulging muscles, beading along the girl's rippling skin.

She began to cry out, her arms enfolding him, drawing him all the way down on her, so that to Akiko it seemed as if he was burying her with his mass. The rhythmic grunting picked up in tempo and the motion of their hips became ragged and indistinct.

Yōki was sighing out her passion in great long jets, her face unlined and taut. The heels of her hands jammed against Sato's powerful muscular buttocks, urging him to thrust himself even deeper into her.

"Going, going going . . ." Yōki's voice held the edge of hysteria and something more. Whatever it was, Akiko longed for it just as she longed for the release from the bunched tension ribboning her thighs and stomach. Her muscles were knotted and the pain came roaring at her just as it always did at these sessions. She bit her lower lip in an effort not to cry out. Her heart hammered, threatening to burst its cage of bone and slippery membrane to explode like a sad sun in her constricted throat.

Please, she moaned to herself. Please, please, please. Though initially she had felt more than she ever had before, though she thought she might experience the blessed relief of the clouds and rain, this night was no different from all the rest. She heard Sato's animal grunting as he shot in rapid fire into Yōki's spasming depths.

It was too much for Akiko to bear and she fell back, slamming her shoulder against the floor beneath the *tatami*. Her eyes rolled up in their sockets, she heard the rushing of a sharp wind so briefly she was uncertain of its existence. Pain and a terrible longing transported her to a black plain. She heard Sun Hsiung saying, "There is a way—and if you are patient I will teach it to you— to scrutinize the enemy's external appearance so that you may be able to discern his inner mind."

Then unconsciousness took her.

Nicholas rose promptly just before six A.M., awakened by his own inner clock. He took a quick shower, turning the water on first scaldingly hot, then needle cold. Emerging from the bathroom, his skin glowing from the tough toweling, he folded down into the lotus position, facing the window and Tokyo. He took three long, deep breaths. Then he dissolved into himself. And expanded outward, until his being filled the universe and he was wholly a part of everything.

The discreet knock on the door brought him out of his deep meditation; he had been waiting for it. His eyes focused on the spires of the city and, breathing normally again, he rose. He ate his breakfast of green tea and rice cakes silently. Then, dressed lightly, a small black bag slung over one shoulder, he went out of the hotel. It was just after ten o'clock.

He walked two blocks, east then south, and found himself in Toranomonchō. Past the small, immaculately tended park, on the far side of Sakuradōri he came to *sanchōme*, the third area designation in Toranomon. There were no exact street addresses in Tokyo, a peculiarity that nonplussed all foreign visitors. Rather, the vast city was divided up into, first, *ku* or wards; then zones such as the Ginza; finally, into *chō*. Within *chō* were numbered *chōme* and block designations.

On the odd-shaped thirteenth block, Nicholas found what he was searching for. The building overlooked a small ancient temple and, just beyond, Atago Hill.

Inside, he changed out of his street clothes. Reaching into the black bag he toted, he withdrew a pair of white cotton wide-legged pants. These were kept up by a drawstring. Over this he drew on a loose-fitting jacket of the same color and material. This closed by means of a separate belt of black cotton tied low on the hips. Finally, he stepped into the *hakama*, the traditional black divided skirt worn now only by those who had mastered *kendo, kyudo, sumō* or held *dan*—black belt—ranking in *aikido*. This, too, was tied low on the hips to give a further feeling of centralization, handed down from the time of the *samurai*.

Thus dressed in his *gi*, Nicholas went up a flight of perfectly polished wooden stairs. In his mind he heard the click, clack-click of wooden *bokken* clashing against each other. And it was suddenly last summer. He and Lew Croaker were in a New York *dōjō* and he was watching the look in his friend's eyes as for the first time Croaker saw the flash of *kenjutsu*.

Nicholas had always been slow to find friendship, principally because that concept in its Eastern form meant a great deal more than it did in the West. For him, as for all Orientals, friendship meant duty, the upholding of a friend's honor, bonds of iron no Westerner could fathom. But Lew Croaker, within Nicholas' orbit, had learned those definitions and had chosen to be Nicholas' friend.

They had promised each other that after Croaker returned from Key West and finally wrapped up the Angela Didion murder, they would go fishing for blues or shark off Montauk. Now that would never happen. Croaker was dead, and Nicholas missed him with a fierceness that was almost physical pain.

He knew that he should clear his mind in preparation for what was waiting for him at the top of the stairs but he could not get the memory of his friend out of his mind. What turned out to be their final good-bye was a poignant moment full of the kind of hushed feeling two Japanese friends might express.

They had been at Michita, the Japanese restaurant in midtown Nicholas frequented. Their shoes were just outside the *tatami* room's wooden lintel, Croaker's heavy Western work shoes lined up next to Nicholas' featherlight loafers. They knelt opposite one another. There was steaming tea and hot sakē in tiny earthen cups between them. *Sushi* and *tonkatsu* were coming.

"What time are you leaving?" Nicholas said.

"I'm taking the midnight plane." Croaker grinned lopsidedly. "It's the cheapest flight."

But they both knew that he had wanted to get into Key West under cover of darkness.

The subdued clatter of the restaurant went on around them as if for once it had no power to touch them. They were an island of silence, inviolable.

Abruptly Croaker had looked up. "Nick—"

The food came and he waited until they were alone again. "There isn't much but I've got some stocks, bonds, and such in a safety deposit box." He slid a small key in a brown plastic case across the low table. "You'll take care of things if . . ." He picked up his chopsticks, pushed raw tuna around with the blunt ends as white as bones. "Well, if it all doesn't work out for me down there."

Nicholas took the key; he felt honored. They fell to eating and the atmosphere seemed to clear. When they were through and had ordered more sakē, Nicholas said, "Promise me one thing, Lew. I know how you feel about Tomkin. I think it's a blind spot—"

"I know what I know, Nick. He's a goddamned shark, eating up everything in his path. I mean to stop him and this lead's my only way."

"All I mean is don't let this . . . passion of yours lead you around by the nose. Once you get down there take your time, look around, size up the situation."

"You telling me how to do my job now?"

"Don't be so touchy. I just mean that life's more often shades of gray than it is all black and white. Tomkin's not the Prince of

Evil; that's the role you've assigned him. It's just possible that he *didn't* have Angela Didion murdered."

"Do you believe that?"

"I don't think it matters what *I* believe."

Now Nicholas did not know whether that was true, because he had become involved. He had accepted Croaker's abrupt death so far away in Key West; he was here now in Japan because of it. *Giri.*

"So long, Nick." Croaker had grinned in the multicolored street lights just outside the restaurant. He had half stuck out his hand, then, thinking better of it, had bowed instead. Nicholas returned the gesture and they had both laughed into the night, as if warding off any kind of trepidation.

Their last moments together had been so casual, in the manner of most men parting for a short time. Despite what Croaker had given Nicholas, neither man believed anything would happen to the cop in Florida. And now it seemed to Nicholas that there had been so little time to savor what they had. For one such as Nicholas, so guarded, so hidden within himself, such occurrences were rare indeed. He found now that he liked to remember their times together, running scenes back in his mind's eye as if they were clips from a favorite film.

He shook his head now as he reached the head of the stairs, more certain than ever that the path he had chosen for himself was the right one. He could not allow the murder of his friend to go unavenged. *Giri* bound him; it was, as all who had come before him had discovered, stronger even than life itself.

The *sensei* of this *dōjō* was sitting at the *kamiza*—the upper seat—of the *aikido* mat which was made up of a series of *tatami* of uncovered rice straw padding. He was a man of indeterminate middle years with a dour countenance, a wide slash of a mouth, and cat's eyes. He had burly shoulders and narrow waist and hips. He appeared almost hairless.

His name was Kenzo. This bit of information had been given to Nicholas—along with a letter of introduction—by Fukashigi, Nicholas' *sensei* in New York. "He is a hard one," Fukashigi had said, "but I can think of no other to suit your array of, er, unconventional *bujutsu*." He knew that Nicholas was a ninja just as he knew that there was a whole range of subdisciplines in which Nicholas could be his *sensei*. "Kenzo will not know what you are, Nicholas, but he will understand the scope of your knowledge and he will work with you."

Behind Kenzo, Nicholas saw a raised dais flanked by a pair of seventeenth-century *dai-katana*—the longest and most lethal of the *samurai* swords—a traditional ceremonial drum, and, hanging on the wall between them, a rice-paper scroll that read, *"All things appear but we cannot see the gate from which they come. All men value the knowledge of what they know, but really do not know. Only those who fall back upon what knowledge cannot know really know."* Nicholas recognized the words of Laotse.

Barefooted, he went upon the *tatami*, performing the *ritsurei*, bowing before the *sensei*. Then he presented Fukashigi's letter.

Kenzo seemed to take a long time reading. Not once did he look up at Nicholas. At length, he carefully folded the sheets, returning them to their envelope. He put the packet aside and, placing his hands on the *tatami*, bent forward in the *zarei*, the sitting bow. Folding his legs beneath him, Nicholas returned the salutation.

And just at the far apex of his bow, the short stick came hurtling at him. There was just the hint of a blur at the periphery of his vision and if he had taken the time to think, he would surely have been rendered unconscious.

Instead, his right arm lifted reflexively even as his torso shifted to the right, away from the trajectory of the oncoming attack.

The stick struck the leading edge of his forearm, bouncing end over end like a pinwheel, but already Kenzo had leapt forward, using Nicholas' own anticipated momentum as he swung to the left, using a punishing *shomen uchi*, a straight blow to the head to try to bring Nicholas to the mat.

In so doing Kenzo had grabbed hold of his right wrist and immediately Nicholas used an immobilization—a *yonkyo*—a twist of his own wrist so that now he was gripping the *sensei*'s left forearm. He dug his thumb deeply into the embedded nerve center running up the inside of the arm. But instead of backing away from the pressure, which would have allowed Nicholas to bring the now outstretched arm into alignment, Kenzo moved into the paralyzing hold, sacrificing one arm in order not to lose the contest.

A second short stick appeared from somewhere and he slammed it down hard on Nicholas' shoulder. Nicholas gave up the *yonkyo* but instead of moving into a second immobilization as Kenzo suspected he would, he employed an *atemi*—a percussive—moving out of the *aikido* discipline as the *sensei* already had.

The stiffened fingertips jammed themselves into the space just below Kenzo's collarbone, digging for the nerve juncture there. The *sensei*'s head jerked spastically up and away and Nicholas bore down.

But now the short stick was between their straining bodies, hammering against Nicholas' rib cage. Nicholas moved in even closer, aware that Kenzo was attempting to swing the stick in a short arc in order to assault the muscles directly over the heart. This he must not allow.

He tried two quick dorsal *kites* before switching back to immobilizations. Nothing worked, and slowly the wooden stick began to arc its way closer to the left side of his chest. Power was slipping away from him and he felt his centrism now as a separate entity, far away and almost useless.

He cursed himself, knowing that he would lose. Loss of sleep, the time imbalance had conspired to sap his concentration. What reserves he still possessed were being rapidly depleted by the repeated *tambo* attacks. Blood was singing in his ears, bringing with it the first telltale signs of disorientation. Physical coordination would soon follow, he knew, unless he did something to forestall it.

And then a lesson in *kendo* leapt into his mind and, remembering Musashi's Red Leaves Cut, he set his spirit toward gaining control of Kenzo's stick.

Instead of defending himself, he broke his hands completely free and rushed toward the *tambo* attacks. In a blur he grasped the slippery cylinder, twisting it down and to the left, breaking the set of the *sensei*'s wrist as he did so, disrupting the energy flow long enough to deliver a vicious liver *kite*.

Kenzo rocked back on his knees, swaying, and Nicholas followed through only to come up against the stone wall of the *sensei*'s calloused fist. Pain flamed through him and he gritted his teeth, pulling inward and down, digging the heel of his hand into Kenzo's shoulder, using the other's momentum to rock him off his haunches.

The moment the *sensei*'s shoulder touched the *tatami*, Nicholas broke off. His torso was bathed in sweat, his heart pounded, and with each breath he took, pain etched itself through his tissues.

He thought about how close he had come to defeat.

Ichiro Kagami was in a surly mood. He was a man of unusually calm and controlled disposition, a virtue that had awarded him with the vice presidency of finance for Sato Petrochemicals.

But today he had been unable to concentrate on any of the fine points being hammered out between this *kobun* and the American microchip company. He was enormously grateful when Sato-san had given the attending executives the signal to leave the proceedings before his lack of concentration became a liability.

After almost an hour of staring out the window at the misty rain forming in odd prismatic patterns against the windows behind him, he had had enough. He swiveled around, his fingertip stabbing at the intercom. He told his secretary to cancel all his upcoming appointments for the rest of the day. He told her where he could be found if an unforeseen emergency required Sato to get in touch with him.

Then he got up. Tokyo looked bleak and steel gray, all the gaiety of *hanami* that prevailed throughout the city for the past several days dissipated by the weather. But the cherry blossom viewing had provided no happiness for Kagami this year.

His face was a bleak mask as he walked out of his office. The soft lights, the beautiful *ukiyo-e* prints did not soothe his mind. He came to the iron-clad door and pushed through. Inside, in the locker room, he began to disrobe.

Everything would be fine, Kagami told himself, were it not for his brother, Toshiro. Brother-in-law, really, if the truth be told, he thought sourly. But Kagami's wife was *hera-mochi*, currently enjoying meting out the ordeals she had had to endure from Kagami's mother. She held the pursestrings. Several notches too tightly, he thought, as he padded naked along the wooden slats, into the baths.

While a young woman, her bland, flat face beaded in sweat from the heat and the exertion, cleansed him, Kagami thought about his wife. It was not that she begrudged him his *geisha*. Did not the monthly bills come to her and did she not pay them without a word of protest precisely on the fifteenth of every month? She did all that a wife should. And yet the manner in which she doled out tiny portions of the salary, the *oseibo* and *ochugen*—the year-end and midyear gifts from those in his department currying favor and promotion—left a bad taste in his mouth and, more often than not, sent him scurrying to Anmitsu, where all his favorite women resided.

Yet it was Toshiro even more than his wife who got under his skin, Kagami reflected as he transferred to the second bath.

Alone, Kagami inhaled the steam rising off the surface of the water. It was so hot that when he moved his limbs, even a little, they began to burn.

Toshiro was a farmer and, as such, he was far wealthier than Kagami himself was. Of course he did not have the plethora of benefits that Sato Petrochemicals provided its family of employees. But still. At year's end Toshiro's bank account swelled to unnatural proportions. And it irked Kagami no end that, at least in part, he was subsidizing his brother-in-law.

Kagami thought of the idiocy of it. Japan was no more than 30 percent rural and dropping fast. Yet the farmers still held as much political power as they did just after World War II when the country was 70 percent rural. That was because there had been no electoral redistribution and the Liberal Democratic Party, which had held power almost constantly since then, did all they could to keep the farm vote loyal. That meant subsidizing the inefficient farmers.

Kagami had read in *Time* magazine that the average American farm was 450 acres. By comparison, the average Japanese farm was 2.9 acres. How was that for efficiency? Kagami had to snort in derision.

And as if that weren't enough, there was the rice problem. Japanese farmers produced much more per year than the country could possibly consume. Since this short-grained variety was not favored worldwide and because to export it would require a second subsidy to bring down the price that the first government subsidy raised, the excess went totally to waste.

Kagami knew that the government spent over twenty billion dollars per year on such subsidies. Much of that money came from selling imported wheat to Japanese millers at exorbitant prices. But even that wasn't enough. Tax money as well was used, short-changing housing and much-needed roadwork throughout the country.

And now, the greatest insult of all was that Toshiro had come, hat in hand, for a loan of money. Kagami knew that Toshiro was a profligate. He spent whatever he made and more. It was often said that the Japanese were good savers. One could certainly not judge that by Toshiro's behavior. Women—he was a widower—and gambling had become his passions. He had hired others to run his farms and they had been derelict in their duty.

At least that was how Toshiro had put it. Kagami snorted again. More likely, Toshiro had been remiss in his hiring. It served him right, and Kagami would have derived much clandestine pleasure from his brother-in-law's plight had it not been for the request for the loan.

Of course, there was no question about giving it to him. Kagami's wife had been quite clear about that. "You have no choice," she had stated flatly after Toshiro had left last night. "He is your brother. There are family ties to think of. Duty." Her eyes flashed. "I shouldn't have to remind you of such basic matters."

It was no good telling her that had the situation been reversed they would not have seen one sen from Toshiro, who cared for no one but himself. After all, had he ever sent a gift for Ken's graduation or Tamiko's thirteenth birthday? Oh, the children never knew. Presents arrived for them on the appropriate days, ostensibly

66

from Toshiro. But Kagami knew that his wife secretly traveled to Daimaru to purchase them herself—with his money.

Kagami closed his eyes, felt the heavy pulse of his blood through his veins. It was really too much. It strained the boundaries of duty.

Sighing, he rose and walked, dripping, across the room, down the short hall and into the steam room. He wanted to be quite relaxed before his massage.

As Kagami sat down on the tiled bench and put his head back against the moisture-streaked wall, he thought about a massage he had once gotten in Korea. Business had dictated he travel there in his younger years, but nothing could get him back now. He shuddered inwardly at the recollection of their form of massage. Torture, more like it. He should have known better. The Koreans were barbarians in everything they tried to do. The Tokugawa Shōgun had called them "garlic-eaters." That was in 1605, and they had progressed not at all since then. Except that they had learned how to take graft from the Americans. Dirty people without a sense of honor.

Kagami shook his head, wanting to clear his mind of Koreans and Toshiro and all other negative influences. This had begun as an evil day, but he was determined that it should end otherwise.

The steam pipe to his left hissed and coughed; new mist began to form in the room. The heat rose and Kagami began to sweat. He had forgotten to cool off in the shower before coming in here. He had Toshiro to thank for that as well.

It was just as well. He put his hands on his belly. Too much fat there these days. Maybe his extra sweating would do him some good. His eyes closed. He was completely relaxed.

The door opened. Kagami did not open his eyes but he was aware of a brief lessening of the intense heat, a momentary thinning of the humid atmosphere. Then the swirling clouds of steam enveloped him once more.

He did not wonder who had come in. Members of the upper-echelon management team were in and out of this section of the floor all through the day and even on into the night after the rest of the building was closed and dark. The men rarely spoke to one another here, understanding implicitly the nature of the renewing process that ultimately led to a more productive workday for all of them.

Kagami felt a presence, no more than a shadow perhaps. As it passed, something caused him to open his eyes. He could not immediately say what it was, a premonition perhaps or a subtle change in the environment.

He saw a figure across the room, made indistinct by the steam. Mist seemed to flow around the form, changing its shape even as Kagami looked.

The figure was standing and now it came forward in an odd, gliding gait that seemed all liquid, as if the being before him had no bones or hard muscle. Kagami wiped the sweat from his eyes. He felt the absurd urge to pinch himself to make certain he had not somehow fallen asleep, lulled by the heat and the peacefulness.

For now he could discern much of the figure, and it appeared to him as if it might be female. But surely not! he admonished himself. Even the blind Taiwanese girls were forbidden in the steam room.

Kagami's mouth dropped open and he gasped. Appearing out of the layers of mist was the unmistakable patch of female pubic hair, dark as night, beads of water clinging in its curls like pearls on the bed of the sea. This is monstrous, he thought indignantly. What gross breach of protocol. I must lodge a protest with Sato-san.

The naked hips swung back and forth minutely as the woman came toward him and Kagami felt the first faint stirrings in his lower belly. There was something so intensely sexual, made all the more powerful because there was an absence of flaunting. The sexuality seemed to have an existence all its own, lacing the steamy atmosphere so that, despite himself, Kagami felt the blood pooling in his loins, the telltale thickening of his penis.

And all the while his mind was outraged, for with the excitement came the unmistakable—yet totally unfamiliar—sensation of being goaded into desire against his will.

Now he could see more of the torso, the high cone-shaped breasts, the dark nipples hard and distended, the flat, slightly curved stomach.

He could no longer hide his erection and he put his hands down between his thighs, trying to cover his embarrassment. That was when he first sensed the danger. She stopped in front of him and, standing straight-backed, thrust her legs out. Jeweled water dripped from the fringe of tight curls onto her firm columns of flesh. Kagami found himself straining forward to see the central vertical ribbon, nature's most beautiful route.

He gasped and began to choke on his own saliva. Bile came rushing up from his grinding stomach and his mind, stunned, blanked out. All he could do was stare at the inner flesh of her thighs, slack-jawed, while his erection withered on the vine.

Then, stupefaction still dominant on his face, he raised his gaze upward to the woman's head, saw only a pair of dark enigmatic eyes behind a spread fan of gilt, red and jet.

"Who—" he began, abruptly finding his voice.

But now the fan was moving, coming away, revealing the soft smile on her face. A beautiful face. It made Kagami sigh with its exquisite line and youth. Then, lagging far behind, recognition came, flooding him like a spotlight. And in his mind's eye the oval, high-cheeked face turned into a painted demon's mask.

"You—!" The scream bubbled out of his open mouth like a geyser.

The fan struck him edge on, twisting at the very last instant, wielded by a master. It sliced through sweating skin and warm flesh, scraping most painfully along the cheekbone.

Kagami was slow to recoil. The strike was so unexpected, so skillfully administered and with such a razor sharp edge, that he was barely aware of what had taken place.

Kagami's first thought was to protect his genitals and thus he offered no real resistance. The great gilt fan flicked out again, again, again. He cried out each time he was cut but he steadfastly refused to bring his hands away from between his thighs.

The torso of the woman flowed toward him like smoke borne on the gentle wind of a cloudless summer's day. Her presence seemed to fill the room, blotting out all light, all air. It was as if she were sucking all life into herself, creating only the ultimate blackness of a vacuum before her.

Kagami shrank before her, cowering and trembling, filaments of pain streaking through him like tracers. He was appalled at how much blood was around him, how hard his heart beat in his ears, how small his penis had become cupped in his protective palms.

Then the fan flickered with a brief whistle. Kagami's eyes bulged and his mouth opened wide. He felt the fierce bite of steel across his windpipe, the atlas vertebrae of his neck.

His mind screamed hysterically and at last he understood the ultimate goal of this attack. His hands came up, his fingertips trying desperately to fend off the attack. A fan? his mind gibbered. A fan? His head whipped back and forth and he began to climb up the slick tiles of the wall. Anything to get away, to regain life.

His problems with his wife, with Toshiro now seemed laughable to him. How trivial they were compared to the primeval struggle for life. For life! I will not die! his mind screamed at him. Save me!

Wildly he flung out his fists, trying to strike back at his assailant. But he had no training and the lurid image of what he had seen on the insides of her thighs rose within him and he despaired.

He knew what she was, though all logic, all tradition cried out to him that it could not be so.

Kagami knew what it was that had a grip on him. He felt in the midst of a nightmare from which he would never awake. Yet still he fought on because hope was all he had now, and for a time it sustained him. He clung to life, he held it to him, he exulted in the knowledge of his existence.

Then the forged steel blades struck once more and what little oxygen was seeping through to him, through his strangling windpipe, ceased. Blood rushed to nowhere, lungs heaved fearfully, then fitfully as carbon dioxide filled them and, through their porous fibers, the whole body.

Kagami's eyelids fluttered, his eyes began to cross. He saw her fearful visage before him; his ineffectual fingers slid against her sweat-streaked flesh like a child digging into sand. His mind, the last to go, tried to fight on, not comprehending that the body to which it was still attached was already falling into a dreamless, depthless slumber.

With his last ounce of strength, Kagami stared at that face, projecting his bitter hatred as if that were a physical weapon. And in truth it was a rage of such depth that it convulsed already dying muscles. His fingers clenched, grabbing.

But it was a futile gesture for his lower belly was rippling, his eyes rolling up into his head, blinding him, leaving only the unseeing whites to stare blankly up at the steaming tiles, the drifting mist, the rivulets of blood circling one another, mazelike, as they slowly slid down the drain in the center of the otherwise empty room.

Nangi stood up, walking on his stiff, ungainly legs away from the conference table. It was the signal for a break in the proceedings.

While Tomkin rose heavily and left the room, Nicholas strolled to one of the high windows overlooking Shinjuku. Beads of rain swirled downward upon the sea of umbrellas, taking what was left of the delicate cherry blossoms, strewing them along the gutters or park walkways where they were soon ground to fine dust underfoot.

Nicholas stared blankly at the mist-enshrouded city. For the past three and a half hours they had been locked like deadly combatants on the field of battle: Sato, Nangi, Suzuran, their attorney, Masuto Ishii, vice president of operations and Sato's right-hand man, bolstered by three of Sato's division heads, Tomkin, Greydon, the Tomkin Industries' counsel, and himself. Now it

70

was rush hour with hordes of people racing homeward or to dinner rendezvous along the bright-lit Tokyo side streets.

But up here in Sato's spacious offices there was no movement at all. Inwardly, Nicholas sighed. Sometimes even he found dealing with the Japanese a trying experience Their seeming reluctance to come to any decision, though an obvious negotiating tactic, was often taken to an extreme. Patience was one thing, but Nicholas was often convinced that weeks, even months from now, Sato and Nangi would still be reworking the same points they had all brought up within the first hour and a quarter of this initial agenda.

There had seemed some hope of a break an hour ago when the division heads, Oito, vice president of acquisitions, Kagami, v.p. of finance, and Sosuro, v.p. of research and development, had made their profuse excuses and, with a double round of formal bowing, had taken their leave.

Nicholas had seen the subtle hand sign Sato had given them and had taken heart. His belief then had been that the negotiations were about to reach a level that the Japanese, who were usually more comfortable bolstered by a contingent of executives, thought should be limited strictly to the principals.

But what had followed had been disappointing: yet another one of the seemingly endless discussions batting around the same major areas of difference. One was the monetary split between Sphynx and Nippon Memory. The other was somewhat more bewildering to Nicholas since it was a topic about which he had not been briefed prior to the negotiating session.

This concerned where the Sphynx-Sato manufacturing plant should be built. Apparently Tomkin had done almost eighteen months of cost estimates comparing construction timetables, weather pattern analyses, production and shipping logistics, all of which pointed to building the plant in Misawa, on land owned by the *keiretsu*. The plant's only neighbor in this small town in the extreme northwest of Honshū, Japan's main island, was an American Army base.

But, as Sato had pointed out during the opening negotiations, that piece of land had already been designated for use as an expansion site for the *keiretsu*'s Niwa Mining *kobun*.

Around and around it had gone, with no side gaining or giving any ground. It was maddening, Nicholas thought now. Ordinarily it wouldn't matter much. In different times he was confident that they could outlast Sato and Nangi; Nicholas' own patience would have ensured that.

However, he was recalling the discussion he had had with

71

Tomkin just before they had left the hotel to get into the limo Sato had sent for them.

He had been struck by the paleness of the other man but Tomkin had only dismissed his query disdainfully. "Just a bout with the flu," he had said. "If you'd been up all night with diarrhea, you wouldn't look in the pink either, iron man."

"Just keep calm no matter what happens in there," Nicholas had advised. "They'll do everything they can to slow down the pace, to equivocate while subtly needling us.

"They'll want to get a glimpse inside our guard so they can study our strategy. Also they will need to know just how far they can push us. To go beyond that would lose them great face." He had shrugged. "It's strictly S.O.P."

Tomkin's haggard face leaned into his so that he could smell the other's sour breath, rising from his empty roiling intestines. "Then you do something to shake 'em out of their standard operating procedure, Nick. I don't give a goddamn how you do it, just get it done. I'm not one of those candyasses coming to Japan hat in hand begging for an operating license."

"Fine. Then all we have to do is wait them out. Do I have to tell you again that patience is everything here? It's the one quality they cannot conceive of in a foreign devil. Don't worry. I'll get you what you want from them."

But Tomkin's voice changed and he clung onto Nicholas' arm like a child. "No, no," he breathed, "you don't understand, Nicky. There isn't any time. This deal's got to be set by next week the latest." His brown eyes turned inward. "I . . . I have commitments I can't turn my back on. . . . There're great sums of money dependent on this merger . . . Loans that come due . . . Payments to be made . . . Above all, payments . . . Debts to be fulfilled." Then, refocusing, the eyes came to rest on Nicholas' face. "You won't let me down, Nicky. Not now. Why, you're almost my son-in-law."

Nicholas turned away from the rain-streaked window as he heard Tomkin return. In a moment he felt the big man's presence beside him.

"Now's the time, Nicky," Tomkin whispered. "I almost hit Nangi a couple of minutes ago. They're like goddamned mules."

"It doesn't mean anything," Nicholas began. "They're doing just what I told you they would do. It's only a matter of—"

But Tomkin had him by the coat sleeve. "Now, Nicky. We can't afford to wait. You know that. You've seen the reports, for Christ's sake. We'll be eaten alive back home."

"Then let's give them Misawa. We can build—"

72

"No!" Tomkin's tone was sharp. "Misawa's a non-negotiable point—no matter what, understand?"

Nicholas took a hard look at his boss. "Are you all right? Maybe I should call a doctor."

Tomkin winced. "Goddamned Japanese bug. I'm getting it from the inside as well as the outside." He gave a short bark as if to dispel Nicholas' concern. "Whatsamatter, Linnear, don't you think I know the flu when I got it?"

Nicholas stared hard at him for another minute, then gave a curt nod. "Okay. Sit down at the table. I'll be there in a moment. I want to be the last one. Then shut up and let me do the talking."

"What're you gonna say?"

"Don't you like surprises?"

"Not with a multimillion-dollar merger," Tomkin muttered but did as he was told.

Nicholas turned back to the blurred cityscape and thought of nothing. Behind him silence had settled over the room. He could smell the tobacco from the fresh cigarette Nangi had lit, hear the soft whir of the central air-conditioning. Nothing else.

Strategy. He went back to the master, Musashi. What was called for here was a variation of "Existing Attitude–Nonexisting Attitude." He had been taught that in battle when one takes up the *katana*, whenever one springs, strikes, hits, even parries the enemy's sword, one must cut the enemy in the same movement. If one thinks only of springing, striking, hitting, or parrying without the inner sense of cutting, no damage will be done.

Nicholas took three deep breaths. He turned and went back to the conference table where the other five men were patiently awaiting him. He now knew what he had to do, but he required a clue to the Japanese strategy before he could decide how to do it.

He looked to Nangi, who was in the process of tapping his cigarette on the edge of the ceramic ashtray before him like a conductor bringing the assembled to order.

"Perhaps we have covered as much ground today as it is possible to," he said in a neutral tone of voice. Sato shook his head immediately.

"In my experience, bargaining is often difficult. Pathways are often locked for long periods at a time, then quite suddenly are free. I think we should continue."

Nicholas watched this charade with intense interest. He had encountered this bear and badger strategy before; he knew it well, in fact. When he had been working for Sam Goldman's advertising agency in New York, he had suggested just this line to take on a recalcitrant client. It had worked quite well. Goldman had been

73

the bear on that one—the hard man. That had made the client instinctively want to bring Nicholas into his camp. Nicholas had played the badger—the soft man—to perfection.

Before Tomkin had a chance to respond, Nicholas said, "As far as I can see, we're at a total impasse. I agree with Nangi-san. I don't see where further discussion at this time will do any of us any good."

"You want to break this off?" Sato said somewhat incredulously, so startled that he neglected to use the polite form of address.

Nicholas nodded. "Unless you can come up with a more constructive suggestion, I'd say the best thing for all of us would be to cool off for a while." The thing was to confuse the roles: side with the bear, rebuff the badger.

"My feeling is," Sato said quietly, "that a recess will only solidify our respective positions. The next time we meet, I fear we'll be even further apart, more committed to making a stand."

"None of us, I think, wants a confrontation," Nicholas said carefully. "We've come here to work together for mutual profit." He paused, fully expecting Tomkin to chime in with a statement reiterating the urgency of starting up the chip-manufacturing process. But the other was silent.

"We are all by now aware of the necessity for speed in setting up the Sphynx-Sato *kobun*," Nicholas said. "I must tell you that there has already been a certain amount of, er, clandestine activity around our main Sphynx locations in Connecticut and in Silicon Valley. We are, quite frankly, in a similar situation to the one in which you find yourselves here. We are small with, to be sure, an enormous growth potential. But for today we are overshadowed by the three or four giants who would literally give up half their net profits for the past five years to gain the secrets of the new Sphynx T-PRAM, the totally programmable random access memory chip."

"If you are having security difficulties," Ishii said, rising to the bait, "you surely cannot expect us to lift a hand to help you. Not after the scandals of last year and the year before." He was referring to the members of a number of Japan's most prominent computer companies being caught in their attempts at industrial spying in Silicon Valley.

"You misunderstand me entirely," Nicholas said, his tone as well as his words deliberately abrasive. "What I mean is that if attempts at industrial espionage against us are beginning in America, it is only reasonable and prudent to expect the same situation to arise here. Other than the property in Misawa, which, I think

74

we are all agreed, is perfect for our joint venture—if, of course, you were not already in the process of greatly expanding the Niwa Mineral Mining *kobun*—what is available is a small but adequate tract in the middle of the Keiyō industrial belt in Chiba prefecture."

Ishii nodded. He was a bearlike individual, roughly handsome, with short bristly hair and clever eyes a soft brown color. The muscles of his arms and chest rippled his suit jacket. "There is our perfect site."

Nangi smiled thinly, sensing the corner into which the *gaijin* had painted himself. "Ishii-san is quite correct. As you know, Keiyō is built on landfill reclaimed from Tokyo Bay. It is close to the center of the city, close to Sato Petrochemicals' main offices and plants. The logistics of shipment and transceiving would be greatly simplified and, as such, would more than compensate for the higher real estate cost of the land itself." Nangi sat back, pleased with the way in which the negotiations were progressing.

But only Nicholas could read that subtle display in a face that was in all ways perfectly serene. He allowed a small silence to build before he leaned forward and, directing his words at Nangi in particular, said, "But that is what worries me the most. Keiyō's nearness to Tokyo. That closeness, combined with the fact that our plant would be virtually surrounded by our *larger* and *more powerful* competitors fills me with alarm.

"Sato-san's *konzern* could not employ enough personnel to stave off the inevitable security problems, nor would we want him to. The cost as well as the added activity would surely be counterproductive to the new *kobun*'s best interests. While, by contrast, when we set up shop in Misawa, a small town far to the north of any major industrial center, we would have as neighbors only Niwa and the U.S. Army base, neither of which as far as I can see pose any security threat to the Sphynx T-PRAM secrets."

He glanced down at several sheets of paper before him as if they pertained to what he was about to say. "And, gentlemen, as far as the lost land to Niwa is concerned, I have spoken to Mr. Tomkin and he has agreed—since at the time of our merger Niwa will be one of our sister companies whose welfare we must take partial responsibility for—to finance the purchase of new acreage so that the *kobun*'s plans for immediate expansion will not be delayed in any way."

He spread his hands, watching the awe suffuse the Japanese faces. "Now what could be fairer than—"

A commotion just outside the office door caused him to break off. Several voices had been raised in alarm or anger. Then, riding above these dominantly male voices was a higher-pitched female voice, much closer than the others now. It was laced with an emotion close to hysteria.

In a moment, the door had burst inward and Miss Yoshida half-stumbled in. Strands of black hair had come undone from her perfect coif and now drifted, untended, over her ears and eyes.

Her face was pinched and all color seemed to have faded from her cheeks.

She bent at Sato's ear. At first, Nangi, who was still smarting from Nicholas' remarks, paid her no attention. He was far too angry. But as Miss Yoshida continued with her whispered report, as the sallowness of Sato's skin became more apparent, he turned his withering gaze away.

He said nothing but watched carefully as Miss Yoshida, her tale of woe completed, stood up. Her eyes darted about the room like a pair of frightened plovers, never coming to rest for long, never looking any of the men around the table in the eye.

After a moment, Sato said to Ishii, "Please inform Koten that he is needed." Then, as the executive departed, he leaned over and spoke for a moment into Nangi's ear. The older man's body stiffened and he jerked away from Sato as if the other were giving off an electric shock.

He turned his head. "You will excuse us now, gentlemen. I really must insist. This meeting is at an end. Please see Miss Yoshida on the way out and she will schedule our next session."

But Sato's hand was on his arm. "If you don't mind, Nangi-san, I would like Linnear-san to accompany us."

"What?" Nangi's exclamation, a breach—at least as far as he was concerned—of iron-clad etiquette that history dictated could not be broken, was quickly stifled. He wanted to say that this was none of the *gaijin*'s business, that taking him in on such a matter of utter privacy was dangerous. But he had been taught never to argue with a family member—whether business or blood—in front of outsiders. Thus, despite his bitter opposition, he held his tongue, merely bowed his head curtly.

"Please, Linnear-san," Sato said by way of explanation. "There has been a terrible tragedy. I know of your skills." He held up a hand as Nicholas began to protest. "Denials are really quite unnecessary." He put his palms flat on the conference table. "But before we go I must have your own assurance that what you will see and hear will also be held strictly private."

Nicholas understood the privilege he was being accorded and began to nod his head.

"No member of my company will make such a unilateral promise," Tomkin said abruptly. "What you are asking could ultimately

76

result in actions detrimental to Tomkin Industries. He cannot make such a pledge."

"I can," Nicholas said, "and I do. You have my word, Sato-san, that I will reveal nothing of this to any outside party."

"Does that include the police?"

"What the hell is this?" Tomkin cried. "What're you two trying to pull?" He stood up. "C'mon, Nick, let's get out of here."

Nicholas made no move to rise. His gaze was locked with Sato's. "You ask for a great deal." His voice was soft but nevertheless carried quite distinctly in the room. Miss Yoshida had come out of her anxiety-filled reverie and now stood just behind Sato, staring fixedly at the two of them. Even Tomkin had been silenced.

"Hai." Sato's head nodded. Yes. "But it is no more than any business associate would ask of another. This is family now, you understand."

"Hai." Nicholas' head bobbed as Sato's had a moment before. "My pledge stands. It includes everyone."

"Well," Tomkin began, "I want no part of this. Nick, if you think—" He froze as Nicholas looked up at him, the force of will behind those dark eyes so powerful he sat back down without a word.

When he had done so, Nicholas turned his head back to Sato. "That goes for Tomkin-san as well."

Sato bowed. "Good." He stood up. "Please follow me."

They were met at the elevator by Ishii and another Japanese. This second man was enormous. He was dressed in *montsuki* and *hakama*; his blue-black hair was intricately coiffed in *ichomage*, marking him as *yokozuna*—a *sumō* grand champion. Sato introduced him as Koten. There was no doubt that he was a bodyguard.

Nicholas stopped them in the corridor before the steam room. The steam had been turned off in the room but still Sato suggested they take off their jackets before entering. Miss Yoshida draped each one, carefully folded, over her left arm. She remained outside the door, an odd, glazed-eye guard. No one else was around.

"Jesus Christ," Tomkin said when he saw the body half sprawled across the tile bench.

"Please be careful of the blood," Sato said, and they all stayed on the perimeter of the room. "Kagami-san was found just moments before Miss Yoshida interrupted our meeting."

Nangi, standing, swaying slightly on his walking stick, said nothing.

"Do you see his cheek?" Sato asked. "The left one."

77

Tomkin looked at Sato; he'd had enough of staring at the mess lying across the room. "You sure don't seem broken up."

Sato turned to him. "He is dead, Tomkin-san. *Karma*. There is nothing I can do that will bring him back. But he was with us for many years and I will miss him. The privacy of grief is something that is understood here."

Tomkin turned his head away, put his hands in his pockets.

Sato watched for a time, then slowly redirected his gaze. "Linnear-san?" His voice was quiet.

Nicholas had not moved from the time he had entered the steam room and caught sight of the corpse. His gaze had been immediately drawn to the man's left cheek.

"It looks to me like a character. *Kanji*." Sato's voice floated in the room.

"All I see is blood," Nangi said curtly. "He was cut at least a dozen times."

Without a word, Nicholas went carefully across the wet tile floor. Pink, stringy puddles were everywhere but he moved with such care and grace that they were left undisturbed. Tomkin had seen Nicholas move in such a way before, the night in his office building when Saigō had come to kill him.

With an abrupt movement like the skim of an insect across a still lake, Nicholas removed a handkerchief and carefully wiped away the trickles of semicoagulated blood from Kagami's left cheek.

The breath whistled through Nangi's half open lips. "It *is* a character: Ink."

"What's it mean?" Tomkin asked.

"*Wu-Shing*," Nicholas said. He could not believe what he was seeing. The blood pounded in his temples like a hammer on an anvil. He felt lightheaded, as if reality were slipping away from him.

"That's Chinese, I know," Sato said. "And old Chinese at that. But without seeing the character I don't know what it means."

Nicholas turned around, his face pale. It had been a decided effort to break away from the sight of this bloody crimson character, glowing with evil intent. He looked at all of them. "*Wu-Shing*," he said slowly, "are a series of ritual punishments of Chinese criminal law."

There was silence for a time. Sato looked from Nicholas to the pathetic drained corpse of his employee and friend. When he looked back again, he said, "There's more, isn't there?"

Nicholas nodded. His eyes were sad. He had never thought to say this in his life. He turned back and again gazed at the glyph,

78

etched into human flesh, terrible and mocking. "This is *Mo*," he said. "It means tattooing of the face. And it is the first of the mutilating punishments taught at the Tenshin Shoden Katori." His heart was breaking as he turned back to them; he could look at the glowing character no more. "That is the ninja *ryu* from which I came."

Nicholas was on his way to Tomkin's room when the call came through, that fragile line connecting them so tenuously. Justine's voice, thin and stretched out by the electronics of the medium, made it seem as if he had been away from her for weeks. "I miss you so, Nick. West Bay Bridge isn't the same without you. I'd love to be in a foreign place with you."

"Japan's not foreign," he said without thinking. "It's too much like home."

"Even now? After all this time?"

Belatedly, he heard the terror in her voice, but he could do nothing about it. "My soul is Japanese," he said. "I told you that when we first met. Outwardly, perhaps, I am my father's son. But inside . . . the *kami* of my mother resides. I can no more do anything about it than I can pull the clouds down from the sky. I wouldn't want to."

There was silence for a time, the gentle wheezing of the unquiet wire unable to hide from him the soughing of her breath.

"You won't want to stay, will you?" Her voice as tiny as a child's.

He laughed. "Permanently? Good God, no. Whatever gave you that idea?"

"Please let me come, Nick. I can be on a plane tonight. I promise I won't be in the way. I just want to be near you. To hold you again."

"Justine," he said as gently as he could, "it's just not possible. There's too much to do here. We'd have no time together."

"Not even at night?"

"This isn't a nine-to-five business."

"I think I liked you better when you were doing nothing."

"I'm happier now, Justine."

"Nick, please let me come. I won't be—"

"It's out of the question. I'll be home soon enough."

That singing down the wire, as if *kami*, hovering, were growing restless.

"The truth is, I'm frightened, Nick. I've been having a recurring dream; a kind of . . . premonition. I'm scared something awful is going to happen to you. And I'll be left here—" Her voice choked off abruptly. "Then there'll be no one."

"Justine," he said quietly, "everything's fine and it's going to stay that way. As soon as I get back, we'll get married. Nothing's going to prevent that." Silence. He pushed the thought of the murder out of his mind. "Justine?"

"I heard you." Her voice was so still, he had to strain to hear her.

"I love you," he said, hanging up the phone.

Was there something more he could have said? he wondered. Sometimes her irrationality was impossible to control. Fears in the night. Phobias. The terror of darkness. These were all alien to him and he had difficulty understanding the fixity of their power over others not like him.

"Nick, what the hell's going on here?" Gray-faced, Tomkin hung onto the door frame leading from the bedroom of the suite to the large bath. "I come to Tokyo to negotiate a straight-ahead business merger and suddenly we're involved with a weird cultlike murder. I could've gone to Southern California if I'd wanted that."

Nicholas smiled thinly at the semblance of humor, sat down on the corner of the king-size bed. They were back at the Okura. It was late in the evening and neither had eaten since breakfast which, for Tomkin, had been nothing more than tea and toast, which he had immediately vomited up.

"Let's eat first," Nicholas said. "We'll talk afterwards."

"The hell we will," Tomkin said as he came unsteadily into the bedroom. "You seem to know more about this—what did you call it?"

"Wu-Shing."

"Yeah. You're the expert. Give me an explanation."

Nicholas ran his fingers through his hair. "Traditionally there are five punishments, each one a response to a more serious offense. Therefore each punishment is more severe than the last."

"So what's that got to do with Sato Petrochemicals?"

"I don't know."

For a moment Tomkin peered down at the younger man, then he went slowly to his dresser and pulled on a pair of faded jeans, a blue chambray workshirt. He slipped on a pair of shiny black handstitched moccasins. "I guess you're as hungry as a bear."

Nicholas looked up. "Aren't you?"

"Frankly, the sight of food nauseates me. I'm running a low-grade fever so that doesn't surprise me. I'll let this thing run its

80

course." He paused. "And don't look at me like that. You remind me of my mother when you do. I'm perfectly all right."

The phone rang and Tomkin went to answer it. He spoke in low tones for some time, then cradled the receiver. "That was Greydon. He wanted permission to go up to Misawa to see his son. Apparently the boy's stationed at the air base there. He's a fighter pilot and is scheduled to go up on one of the first test runs of those new F-20s we've just imported. I think Greydon feels there's some danger."

"He's quite right," Nicholas said. "Stationed at Misawa puts those supersonic jets just 375 air miles from the Soviet Union's Pacific coast and Vladivostok."

Tomkin shrugged his shoulders. "So? What harm can they possibly do?"

"Those F-20s have nuclear capacity," Nicholas said. "And the Russians're worried as hell about them. Which is why we've seen an increased Soviet military buildup in the Kuriles over the past year of an alarming size."

"The Kuriles?"

"The Kurile Islands. They're the chain just to the north of Hokkaido, Japan's most northerly island—the one where the winter Olympics were held in 1976. In effect, they connect the southeast of Russia to Japan in a series of stepping-stones.

"The Kuriles had been Japanese territory until they were seized— the Japanese say illegally—in 1945 at the close of the war. Quite naturally, they want them back."

Nicholas got up from the bed. "Recent reports tell us that there are over forty thousand Russian troops currently stationed in the Kuriles. Quite recently they sent in a squadron of twelve supersonic MIG-21 fighter-bombers to replace the subsonic MIG-17s, which they obviously felt were overmatched by the F-20s. They've got an air base on Etorufu, or, as they call it, Iturup."

"You sure seem to know a lot about this."

"It concerns Japan, Tomkin," Nicholas said evenly. "So it concerns me. The situation's serious; Greydon's got every right to be anxious. I hope you gave him the weekend off. We've only got the wedding tomorrow and negotiations won't resume until Monday."

"He's booking his flight now," Tomkin said archly. "That meet with your approval?"

"If Greydon's son doesn't make it back from that flight, you'll be happy you let him see the kid."

There was silence for a time. The phone rang again but neither of them made a move to answer it. In a moment it stopped, and the tiny red light on the base began to wink on and off.

"I told you before," Tomkin said at last, "that my old man was a real sonuvabitch. I can't tell you how much I hated him sometimes." He put his palms together as if he were praying. "But I loved him, too, Nick. No matter what he did to me or my mother. He was my father. . . . Do you understand?" It was a rhetorical question, and Nicholas remained silent.

Tomkin sighed. "I guess in some ways I turned out just like him. Years ago I could not have believed such a thing possible. But the passing time . . ." His voice fell off. "Time has a way of molding people to its own ends. You remember Chris—I know Justine must've told you about him. He was the last of her boyfriends before she met you. He was the biggest bastard of the lot. He was sexy as hell. He seduced her, made her move to San Francisco. She was using her real name, Tomkin, then. She got a monthly stipend from me. It was very generous and she took it all. It—" His eyes slid away for a moment, searching, perhaps, for a place to hide. He took a deep, shuddering breath. "It made me feel better that she took it all. It assuaged my guilt for all the years I'd accepted her presence, her demands on my time, only when it suited me.

"They were fucking like bunnies out there; the relationship was all sex. Or so I thought. Justine wanted more money, then more still. Finally, I hired a team of detectives to find out just what the hell was going on. Two weeks later I took the corporate jet and flew out. I presented my darling daughter with all the evidence. I packed her up and took her home that afternoon before Chris got back."

Tomkin seemed to be having difficulty breathing as the emotions surged within him. "The shit was using my money—" He stopped abruptly, his eyes wide and feverish. "*Justine's* money, to finance an ongoing cocaine deal. He was a user himself, and besides . . . He was unfaithful to her every day of their relationship." He made a disgusted sound.

"She hates me for interfering, though. That's a helluva laugh, isn't it? He was slowly killing her with his infidelities and his craziness. He'd beat her and—" His throat seized up on him. He ran a hand through his damp hair. "But at least she has you now, Nicky. That's the most important thing."

For all this time Tomkin had not taken his eyes off Nicholas. He was a shrewd man with an acute, analytical mind. His intolerance of foreign custom and his lack of patience in no way negated that fact.

"Now it's your turn. You're dragging your feet about something." His voice was quiet with more strength in it than had been apparent for several days. He sounded almost like a father. "I think you'd better tell me what it is because I have a funny feeling in my gut it has to do with that Wo Ching or whatever you call it."

"Tomkin—"

"Nick, you've got a duty to me. You've gotta tell me what you know. All of it."

Nicholas sighed. "I had hoped not to tell you."

"Why, for Christ's sake? I've got a right to know if I'm putting my neck on the chopping block."

Nicholas nodded. "Yes. You do." He looked directly at Tomkin. "But the simple truth is I've got nothing definite, no cold facts and figures like the Soviet buildup in the Kuriles. Here, as happens often in Japan, there is nothing but legend."

"Legend?" Tomkin laughed uneasily. "What is this, the start of a vampire movie?" He cocked an ear. "Jesus, I hear the wolves howling, Nick. It must be a full moon tonight. We'd better stay indoors and hang up all the garlic."

"Stop it," Nicholas said shortly. "This is precisely why I'd hoped not to tell you."

Tomkin proffered an upraised palm. "All right." He crossed back to the bed, sat down. "I promise to be a good boy and listen."

Nicholas stared at him for a moment before beginning. "At the Tenshin Shoden Katori *ryu* where I received my *ninjutsu* training, where the *Wu-Shing* was taught, this legend was told . . . and believed.

"In the old days when only the Ainu inhabited the Nippon Islands and true civilization had not yet spread southeast from China, *ninjutsu* was in its infancy on the Asian continent. It was still too early in the discipline's life for there to have been *sensei*—true masters—or even, as there are now, *jonin*—*ryu* patriarchs—simply because the differentiated schools of *ninjutsu* were barely formed.

"There was much more ritual then, more superstition. The thinking among what *sennin*—adepts—existed was rigid and unyielding, principally because the forces they were working with were still so newly strange and deadly potent. Thus any deviation was summarily condemned wholesale."

Nicholas paused here to pour himself a glass of water. He drank half of it and continued. "As the legend goes, there was one *sennin* more powerful than the rest. His name was Hsing, which has many meanings in *kanji*. His meant 'shape.'

83

"It is said that Hsing walked only in the darkness, that it was his only lover. His devotion to his craft caused him to be celibate. And, also unlike his compatriots, he took only one pupil, a strange wild-haired boy from the steppes far to the north where the Mongols dominated.

"This student of Hsing's, it was whispered, could not speak any civilized dialect, nor could he read Mandarin. Yet he conversed fluently with Hsing. No one knew how.

"Yet the other *sennin* began to suspect that Hsing was slowly expanding his scope of *ninjutsu* knowledge, experimenting in the darker unknown aspects which the others shunned. His power grew even greater and at last in fear—or perhaps simple envy—the other *sennin* massed against him and destroyed him."

Nicholas' eyes were alight and although it was now deepest night outside and though the lamps in the suite were turned low still Tomkin saw him clearly, every detail etched against the light glow. For a moment the bustling modern world had faded and the mist-shrouded Asian past was being recreated before him, plunging him into a world of arcane laws.

"The murderous *sennin*," Nicholas continued, "were content with driving off the wild-haired student, shouting derisively to him that he should return to the northern steppes from whence he had come.

"But they had not reckoned with Hsing's power. Apparently his death had come too late, for he had already created from his pupil *akuma*, what the Japanese call an evil spirit, a demon with *jit suryoku*—superhuman powers."

"Oh, please, Nick, This's—"

"You asked to hear this, Tomkin. Kindly have the courtesy to hear the legend through."

"But this is the stuff of fairy tales."

"Hsing had taught the pupil all he knew about *jahō*," Nicholas said, ignoring him. "A kind of magic. Oh, there's nothing supernatural about this. I'm not speaking now of spells and incantations, demons out of some fictitious hell dreamed up by the mind of man.

"Saigō had studied the *Kōbudera*—that is, *jahō*. He practiced *saiminjutsu* on your daughter; that, too, is a form of *jahō*."

Tomkin nodded. "Okay, I can accept that. But what's all this got to do with the murder?"

Nicholas took a deep breath. "The only recorded instance of death in conjunction with the first four *Wu-Shing*—the fifth ritual punishment *is* death—concerns Hsing's pupil, who began a series of just such murders in Kaifeng. Bloody, horrific, terrifying, they enacted a perverse poetic justice on those who had destroyed his *sennin*.

"He had become *mahō-zukai*. A sorceror."

Akiko Ofuda wore a snow-white kimono, heavy with hand-stitched brocade. Over it she wore a light silk dress the precise shade of the last of the cherry blossoms bobbing in the breeze above her head.

Her hair was hidden beneath the ornate tresses of a gleaming wig. These swirls and complex loops were surmounted by a *Tsu-nokakushi*—the hornhider—a ceremonial white hat with wide brim said to be worn to hide whatever bad parts of a woman existed.

Her eyes were large and clear through the delicate makeup. Her face was very white, her lips a startling splash of crimson. She wore no earrings or other jewelry. In her right hand was clutched a closed fan.

Saturday had dawned bright and clear with just a hint of the crispness of March, the preceding month.

The enormous crimson camphorwood *torii*, symbol of the Shinto shrine, rose over the heads of the still assembling guests who, according to the final count of RSVPs, were going to number over five hundred.

Morning mist still clung to the steep hillsides, feathering the boles of the cedars and fir, obscuring the sapphire glint of the lake far below. At the guests' backs huddled the dense and hazy superstructure of the northwestern edge of Tokyo.

The four buildings of the temple spread out in a rough horseshoe, their cedar-beamed, canted roofs with the raised ribs striping the sunlight into shadow and gloss.

The guests milled about, chattering among themselves, commenting on the fine weather, gossiping about late arrivals or even, in one or two instances, forging the underpinnings of an important deal. A great majority of the country's foremost business and bureaucratic leaders were in attendance.

Seiichi Sato looked from the beautiful face of his bride to the milling throng of guests. As he recognized a face from business he recited to himself the man's name and position, then filled in the appropriate slot on an imaginary pyramid in his mind. The structure he was forming was important to him. The face he gained at this marriage would go a long way toward furthering the prestige of the *keiretsu*. While Akiko's parents were dead, the name Ofuda still ranked as most prestigious, tracing its origins all the way back to the time of Ieyasu Tokugawa.

That first Ofuda—Tatsunosuke was his name—was a great

daimyō, an ingenious tactical commander whose genius for victory on the field of battle was called on many times by Ieyasu.

It pained him to know that Akiko had never known her parents, that she had no relatives, in fact, save the gravely ill aunt whom she visited so frequently in Kyūshū. Sato had a brief somber flash of Gōtarō's broad, smiling face. Sato knew well the grief at a family cut off at the waist.

How Gōtarō would have loved this day! How his smile would have driven the morning mist into the lake. How his great barking laugh, so like a triumphant shout, would have echoed and reechoed through these woods so that even the small creatures in their burrows might know the extraordinary joy of this day.

Sato passed a hand quickly across his eyes, using the pads of his fingers to wipe away the specks of wetness there. Why do this to yourself? he asked silently. Gōtarō is gone.

Kare wa gaikoku ni itte i masu, Sato's mother had said when he brought her the news. *He has gone abroad*. And never said another word. She had already lost her husband. Now the death of her oldest son was too much for her to bear. She did not survive the war, though she was not burned by the bombs. The war had devoured her from within.

No, Sato said to himself now. Do not be like your mother. *Kare wa shinde shimai mashita*. Banish Gōtarō's *kami*. *He is dead and gone*. And he turned to Masuto Ishii, speaking to him of business matters of import to both of them in order to banish his sorrow or, at the very least, to keep it at bay on this happiest of days.

Not far away, Tanzan Nangi stood with his back ramrod straight, his bony knuckles enwrapping the white jade dragon capping his hardwood cane. Pain girdled him from standing so long but he would not move. It had been his duty to be among the first to arrive here; no one else was sitting so he could not either.

Further, he would not lose face to these priests. Nangi would have preferred, of course, for Sato to have had this ceremony in a Christian church. The vestments, the sacraments, the soft Latin litany that he could understand fully and respond to were comforts to him that arcane Shintoism could not be. Ghosts and spirits were not Nangi's way. And spending one's life placating a bewildering variety of *kami* seemed farcical to him. He believed fervently in Christ, the Resurrection, and Holy Salvation.

He was with a younger man, in the eye of one of the main eddies. They enjoyed almost constant attention from both newly arriving guests and those who had been there for some time who, having observed a proper interval, now were returning to seek

86

advice from Nangi or tidbits of news of MITI from Riuichi Yano, the new minister. He was Nangi's protégé, and Nangi's last official act before he left that organization six years ago had been to assure that Yano would succeed him.

As he smiled and spoke, thoughtfully answering all questions as best he could, Nangi kept a sharp eye out for the *gaijin*. He wished to monitor their movements from the time they arrived. One could divine much from observing the enemy at play.

Akiko, too, had one eye out for the *gaijin*. But only for one: Nicholas. This was the moment, and her eyes were like cameras, ready to record the event, to drink in expressions and emotions.

She felt her pulse racing, her heartbeat seemed to flutter her kimono. She used her training to calm herself, to gather her resources for the beginning of her revenge. She forced herself to concentrate on Sato's presence beside her. She looked his way, saw instead Ishii staring at her with hooded eyes. He smiled and nodded, turned back to his murmured conversation with Sato.

There was a rustling through the assembled guests, just the tiniest of ripples but Akiko, her senses finely attuned, shifted her gaze. The mask of a smile was frozen on her intensely crimson lips, her white face perfect as she saw the throng begin to part at its farthest reaches.

"Ah," Sato said, turning, "Tomkin and Linnear are here at last."

Slowly, as if in a dream she had composed innumerable times, Akiko raised one hand, her fingers spreading open her fan of gilt, red, and jet so that only the edge of one eye could be seen. The rest of her face was hidden.

Softly, she thought, softly. Don't give away too much. Not yet. Give him time to approach. Come closer, Nicholas. She willed him drawn to her. Come closer and begin the destruction of your life.

She could distinguish the two *gaijin* now, one broader than the other but both tall, towering above the other guests.

She could pick out Nicholas' features as the *gaijin* continued to make their way through the throng. Tomkin wore a dark pin-stripe with white shirt and rep tie. Nicholas had chosen a less conservative suit of sea green linen, a gray shirt, and a tie as blue as an ocean trough.

His wide-cheeked face was still in shadow as the two passed through the long stand of tall bamboo but Akiko could already discern the odd tilted eyes, neither truly Caucasian nor Oriental. They gave him a quality she could not understand. Once again she felt the same kind of magnetic wave she had experienced in

Jan Jan and she had to will herself to remain where she was at Sato's side.

Now they were very close indeed. Nicholas' face sprang into the sunlight as if abruptly brought into focus in the center of a lens. The gusting wind took a lock of his dark hair, sent it curling down across his forehead. Automatically, his hand came up to push it away, a bar of shadow racing across those strong, confident features.

Not for long, Akiko whispered to herself. The moment was almost at hand, and she knew that she had orchestrated it to perfection. A sense of intense excitement—of ecstasy, almost—gyred within her, fueling her for what was about to happen.

The tiny pink tip of her tongue flicked out to moisten her lip as she watched the litheness with which he moved, the low center of gravity which propelled him with such controlled power—the training of dance or *sumō*. In her mind's eye he became the great tiger, lord of the earth, padding with great stealth and coordination through the dense forest, prepared at any instant to make his prodigious killing leap onto the back of a lesser animal turning to flee his presence.

Now. The moment was here at last. Akiko waited until his gaze slid up, turning from Sato to her. He was understandably curious; he had never seen her before and he must want to know what kind of woman Sato was about to marry.

She felt the intensity of his gaze. He held on her fan, then her eye. Their eyes locked, and for an unfathomable instant Akiko felt suspended in time and space. All the preparations, the arduous years flew by her again in the brilliant flash of a film montage to culminate here. Now.

With a firm hand she lowered her fan, exposing her face.

When Nicholas emerged from the limousine that had brought them out of Tokyo, he was first struck by the natural beauty of the setting. On the way, they had skirted the large lake, moving away from its placid mist-covered surface as they began to wind their way up toward the cliff upon which the Shinto shrine was situated.

It was not surprising to him that the priests had chosen this spot to build their temple. Shintoism was an attuning of the soul toward nature, life's currents. *Karma*. One's life was a part of a much vaster skein in which every living thing, human, animal, vegetable, and mineral, played its role.

Nicholas' spirit expanded outward, his heart soaring, as he put his feet down on the loamy pine-needled earth. The wind was

88

fresh, and warmth was already creeping into the air. Soon the mist would disappear from the boles of the pines and the skin of the lake. The view would be fantastic then.

He was aware of the wings rushing by overhead, the rustling of the great branches, the concerted sway of the stand of bamboo. The buzz of insects was in his ears as the breeze flapped his jacket.

Then, lastly, he recognized the stir within the crowd. It was subtle and he was doubtful whether Tomkin was even aware of it. But Nicholas knew. The *gaijin* were here. Even him. Nangi had made it eminently clear that many did not consider him a Japanese.

As he passed through them, looking from face to face, he wondered what they privately thought of Colonel Linnear, Nicholas' father. Were they proud of how he had helped in the rebuilding of Japan when he was brought in by MacArthur's SCAP forces? Or did they secretly revile his memory because he was a foreign devil at work in Japan? There was no accurate way of knowing, and Nicholas preferred to believe that at least some of them—like Sato—still honored his memory. Nicholas knew that his father had been a great man, that he had fought long and hard against some deadly opposition to create a new and democratic superstructure for the postwar nation to rebuild itself.

"Jesus, these bastards're small," Tomkin whispered to him out of the side of his mouth. "I feel like a bull in a china shop."

They were heading toward Sato. Nicholas could see him clearly, with Koten, the giant *sumō*, looking grotesque in a suit, not far away. And by his side, a slim, elegant woman in the traditional bride's garb. Nicholas tried to get a good look at her but she was holding a ceremonial fan spread across her face. The *Tsunokakushi* hid the top of her head completely.

"If this were any other country," Tomkin said softly, "I wouldn't even be here. I still feel like shit."

"Face," said Nicholas.

"Yeah." Tomkin tried to cover his sour expression with a smile. "Face is gonna kill me one of these days."

Now they had come almost all the way through the mingling guests. Nicholas could see Nangi off to the right, amid a dense swirl of dark-suited men. It looked as if the higher echelons of seven or eight ministries were present.

They stopped a few feet away from Sato and his bride-to-be. Tomkin took one step forward about to greet Sato and congratulate him. Nicholas was gazing at Akiko, wondering what features lay behind the mask of the golden fan. Then, almost magically, in response to his wish, the fan came down, and all the breath left his lungs. He stepped backward a pace as if pushed by an invisible hand. His eyes opened wide and his lips parted.

"No!"

It was a whisper that seemed a shout to him. Blood rushed uncontrollably in his ears and the beating of his heart seemed painful. Tears broke the corners of his long eyes, trembling with the enormous force of his emotions.

The past was rising up like a haunted demon to inexplicably confront him again. But the dead could not rise. Their bodies were laid to rest and were decomposed by the elements: earth, air, fire, water.

She had been murdered by Saigō because she belonged to Nicholas, body and soul, and could never be his. He had drowned her in the Straits of Shimonoseki where the *Kami* of the Heiké clan etched the backs of the crabs into human countenances. She was gone.

And yet here she was standing a foot away from him. It was impossible but true.

Yukio.

MARIANAS ISLANDS, NORTH PACIFIC OCEAN

SPRING, 1944

What Tanzan Nangi remembered most vividly about the war were the red skies. There seemed no gentle color left in the world when the sun rose over the vast heaving bosom of the Pacific; only slashes of fierce orange and crimson like the vast tentacles of some monstrous sea creature emerging from the seabed at the sun's slow dawning.

The long nights of the engines' thrumming, the constant vibration of the mighty screws of the carrier as it plowed southward past the small black humps of the Bonin Islands gave way grudgingly to days filled with blinding light. Cloud cover hung far off and mocking at the edge of the horizon.

They were only a thousand nautical miles from Tokyo yet the weather here was so much different. There was a great deal of speculation on the part of the men as to what their destination would be. They were not part of a fleet; they had no escort. They had even put to sea in the dead of night when only a scattering of bare bulbs burned here and there along the great military harbor, casting hard shadows across the gently rippling water. Hunched guards spoke in whispers and studiously ignored the careful progress of the carrier out into open waters.

They were traveling under sealed orders, that much Captain

Noguchi had told them. He had meant it to squelch rumors but it only had the opposite effect.

Where were they bound?

At night, after all lights had been extinguished, the men huddled in their cramped windowless quarters to discuss issues and destinations.

It had been Gōtarō Sato who had been certain they were bound for the Marianas. Most of the other men found that idea preposterous. The Marianas were far too close to Japan for there to be any fighting and this was most definitely a war mission of the highest priority, as Captain Noguchi had made clear to them in his speech.

But the idea of the Marianas piqued Nangi's imagination and, after the men broke up, he sought Gōtarō out. Gōtarō Sato was a bear of a man, thick-necked and round-faced. He had wide, shrewd eyes that revealed nothing, but, far from emotionless, he was given to wild bursts of great good humor. He had the ability of knowing when a dose of his absurd wit—he was a prankster—would cool tensions or allay fears.

And in those dark days, deep in the final months of the war, there was plenty of both. The Allies had already won two long, extremely hard fought campaigns, the first in the Solomons, late in 1943, and more recently in New Guinea. Everyone knew they were heading inexorably toward Japan, and they looked toward their leaders for a supreme strategy to alter the tide of the bitter conflict.

They went up on deck. Gōtarō took out a cigarette, then thought better of lighting up. The Pacific lay dark and foreboding all around them and, not for the first time, Nangi experienced an eerie chill. He was a brave man and the thought of death in battle—a *samurai*'s proud end—did not disturb him. Yet out here, with only the depths of the sea surrounding him, so very far from any land mass, his stomach was never calm.

"It's the Marianas," Gōtarō said, staring south, the way they were headed, "and I'll tell you why. If the Americans are not already there, they soon will be. We have an air base there. The Islands are no more than fifteen hundred nautical miles from home." His head turned as a sudden gust of wind came up, feathering his short hair. "Can you imagine a better target for the Allies to base and fuel their own planes for bombing runs into Japan? I can't."

There was no humor in him now as he leaned his elbows on the metal bars of the top rail. The sea hissed by far below them.

Despite himself, Nangi felt a terrible despair engulfing him.

"Then there can be no doubt. The war is surely lost, no matter what the Imperial Command tells us."

Gōtarō turned to him, his eyes bright amid the shadows of the carrier's many tiered superstructure. The proximity to so much reinforced metal was chilling, coming as they did from a culture intent on building structures of wood and rice paper. "Have faith."

At first, Nangi was not sure that he had heard the other man correctly. "Faith?" he said after a pause. And when Gōtarō nodded, said, "Faith in what? Our Emperor? The Imperial Command? The *zaibatsu*? Tell me, which of our many traditional icons shall I bow down to tonight?" He heard the bitterness in his voice but he did not care. This night, so far from home, so close to the utter alienness of the battle lines, seemed meant for a venting of emotion long bottled up.

"Greed got us into this mad war," he rushed on before the other could answer his rhetorical questions. "The blind ambition of the *zaibatsu* who persuaded the government that Japan was not a large enough area for their empire. 'Expand, expand, expand,' they counseled, and the war seemed like a superb excuse to carve out the niche we had long been seeking in Asia.

"But, Gōtarō-san, answer me this: Did they attempt to get a sense of our enemy before the attack on Pearl Harbor was ordered?" He shook his head. "Oh, no, no. Not a jot of ink was put to paper, not a moment of research was applied." He smiled grimly. "History, Gōtarō. If they had known—or understood—anything about American history, they would have perhaps been able to anticipate the response to their attack." Nangi's gaze dropped, the fierceness went out of his voice. "Now what will happen to us in the end?"

"Have faith," Gōtarō said again. "Trust in God."

God? Now Nangi began to understand. He turned toward Gōtarō. "You're a Christian, aren't you?"

The big man nodded. "My family does not know. I cannot think that they would understand."

Nangi stared at him for a time. "But why?"

"Because," Gōtarō said softly, "for me there is no more fear."

At 04:15 on the morning of March 13, Nangi was summoned to the captain's cabin for a briefing. Dressed smartly in his pressed uniform, he moved down the silent narrow corridors up the ringing metal companionways. He might have had the entire carrier to himself. The *kami* of the ancient Shōgun seemed to walk with him, a descending line of invincible *samurai* with the wiles of the fox, the strength of the tiger.

That he, of all the men on board, should be summoned seemed

a clear sign of his *karma*. Though he disagreed with the war, his soul still belonged to Japan. Now that they were in the thick of it, what frightened him was the specter of defeat. Perhaps he was to be a part of the new strategy; perhaps the war was not yet lost.

He rapped softly on the captain's white-painted door with his knuckles, then went in. He was surprised to find Gōtarō there as well.

"Please be seated, Major," Captain Noguchi said after the traditional formalities had been dispensed with. Nangi took a chair next to Gōtarō.

"You know Major Sato," Noguchi said in his clipped tones. His bullet head bobbed. "Good." A steward appeared, bringing a tray of sakē. He set it down in the center of Noguchi's desk and departed.

"It is the middle of March in what we all fear may be the last year of the war." Noguchi was quite calm, his eyes boring into first Nangi, then Gōtarō, magnified through the circular lenses of his steel-rimmed spectacles. He was a powerfully built man who emitted confidence and energy. He had intelligent eyes beneath heavy brows, a wide, thick-lipped mouth, and odd, splayed ears that stuck out from his close-cropped head like mushroom caps.

"The European playwright Shakespeare wrote that these days are the Ides, an evil time." Noguchi smiled. "At least they were for Julius Caesar." He spread his long, delicately fingered hands on his desk top. "And perhaps they will be so for the Allies."

He had the habit of looking directly at you when he spoke instead of away as so many of his fellow upper-echelon officers did. Nangi felt instinctively that this was one source of the confidence he instilled in his men.

"Within the month the cherry blossoms will again come to the slopes and valleys of our homeland." His eyes blazed with light. "The enemy threatens the extinction of the cherry blossom as he threatens our very lives." His chest heaved as if he had gotten something hard and ugly off his mind.

"At this very moment, the mechanics are preparing another kind of cherry blossom for you two majors. I see the perplexed look on your faces. I will explain."

He got up from behind his desk and set about pacing back and forth in the small cabin as if he was beginning to generate too much energy to be held to a sitting position. "We have precisely one hundred fifty planes on board. All—save one—are Mitsubishi G4 M.2e bombers. The ones the enemy calls 'Bettys' in an inexplicable form of derision."

His closed fist slammed the desk, making the tiny cups quiver and rock where even the sea could not. "But no more! Not now that we have the Ōka!"

He turned toward them. "One of our Mitsubishis has been modified. Beneath its fuselage is another, smaller craft: a single-seat midwing monoplane of a length of just over nineteen feet and with a wingspan of sixteen feet, fifteen inches.

"The Ōka will be borne aloft by the Mitsubishi mother plane. At an altitude of 27,000 feet the two craft will separate. The Ōka will be able to cruise up to fifty miles at an effective airspeed of two hundred thirty miles per hour. When it comes within sighting distance of its target, the pilot will cut in its three solid-fuel rocket motors. The craft will then be flying at almost six hundred miles per hour."

Noguchi was standing directly in front of them now, his cheeks red from the height of his emotion. "For a period of nine seconds, the Ōka will have a total thrust of 1,764 pounds. A great rush of momentum and then..." His head lifted up and his eyes went opaque as his lenses caught the light, reflecting it back at them in a dazzle. "Then you will become the avenging sword of the Emperor, opening up the side of an American warship."

Nangi remembered this quite clearly. Noguchi did not ask either of them if they understood. But of course they did. The Ōka was a rocket bomb, manned for supreme accuracy.

"*Yamato-dama-shii*," Noguchi said now, returning to his seat behind his desk, "the Japanese spirit will be our bulwark against the superior material force of the Allies. That and the Ōka attacks will quickly demoralize the advancing enemy. We will blunt their coming attack on the Philippines."

Noguchi began to pour the sakē, handed a gleaming porcelain cup to each of them and, lifting his, made this toast: "A man has only one death. That death may be as weighty as Fuji-yama or it may be as light as feather down. It all depends on the way he uses it. It is the nature of every Japanese to love life and hate death, to think of his family and care for his wife and children. Only when a man is moved by higher principles—by *junsuisei*, the purity of resolve—is this not so. Then there are things which he must do."

They all drank together. Nangi saw that there were tears in the corners of Gōtarō's eyes. At the time he supposed they were because of either his Christianity or his ignorance. What Captain Noguchi had used for their fond farewell, masquerading as his own words, Nangi recognized as an excerpt from a letter famous in Chinese history. It had in fact been written in 98 B.C. by Ssu-Ma Ch'ien.

Noguchi put down his cup. "You two are privileged to be the first to war test this new and devastating weapon against the Allies. You are the first two recruits in what will come to be known as *Shimpū Tokubetsu Kōgekitai*: the Divine Wind Special Attack Force.

"This is your opportunity to follow in Major Oda's footsteps, to become a reincarnation of *shimpū*, the divine winds of 1274 and 1281 which drowned the invading Mongol hordes, rescuing Nippon from their destruction."

Both Nangi and Gōtarō—indeed everyone in the Japanese Imperial Navy—had heard the story of the pilot Oda who had taken his Ki-43 fighter into the side of an American B-17 bomber, tearing the larger airship in two, thus saving an entire Japanese convoy. He had been a sergeant then. In death he had been promoted twice.

"Major Sato," Noguchi was saying now, "you have been selected to guide the first Ōka to its flaming destiny. Major Nangi, you will pilot the mother ship." He glanced down at a sheaf of papers. "We have been informed of an Allied sighting: a battleship and a destroyer, the vanguard no doubt of a larger fleet, heading toward the Marianas. The destroyer is your target. The ships are now"—he consulted his dispatches again—"three hundred fifty miles southwest of the island of Guam. When you leave this cabin you will go directly abovedecks. Your flight gear will be waiting for you. You will take off at 05:30. I will be in the conning tower to observe you firsthand."

He stood up. The briefing was over.

The predawn air was chill with a gusting inconstant wind quartering in from the northeast. Nangi and Gōtarō, clad in their flight suits, walked across the vast expanse of the carrier's open deck. Before them loomed the hump-bellied shape of the twin aircraft, as disfigured as a leper.

"I have more flight time than you," Nangi said. "They should have chosen me for the Ōka."

Gōtarō smiled. "There are few like you left, Tanzan. Most of them coming up now are raw recruits with little or no training. With that in mind—with the war having so completely depleted us—do you think it a wise decision to test this flying bomb with a veteran pilot?" He shrugged his shoulders. "What possible good would it do when those who will follow, the true members of *Shimpū Tokubetsu Kōgekitai*, will know nothing." He shook his head. "No, my friend, they have made the correct choice."

He was upwind of Nangi; when he abruptly stopped and turned to face him, his body blocked the fierce bite of the wind from Nangi's face.

Gōtarō produced a white square from a pocket, luminous in the werelight. "Here," he said, "this is for you. A *hachimaki*." He tied it around Nangi's helmet. "There. With that ancient symbol of determination and derring-do you look just like the other meaning of *shimpū*. Do you know it?"

Nangi shook his head.

"In Tokyo these days I've heard the term is used in a humorous way to describe the daredevil taxi drivers. *Kamikaze*." Gōtarō laughed. "I would have called you that in Noguchi's cabin but it is surely too lighthearted a word for him. This is quite a solemn moment for him."

Nangi squinted up at his friend. "And for you, Gōtarō-san, knowing what must be the end of this mission."

"I have faith, my friend," the big man said. "I have no thought but to serve my country."

"They're mad if they think this Ōka will frighten the Americans. More likely—knowing them as I do—they will laugh at it. They have no concept of *seppuku*, the warrior's way of death."

"So much the worse for them," Gōtarō said, "for this has surely been a war of misunderstanding. I cannot think of what will happen to us or what may come after. I have my duty to perform. In all else, I put my trust in God."

The wind was picking up as the high bowl of the heavens began to lighten, pitch black fading to a deep cerulean. Down low in the east, where the sea met the sky, there were already the first fugitive streaks of pink, rising.

Gōtarō reached out. "Listen, my friend, Captain Noguchi was right. We all love life; that, too, is our duty. But there are higher principles than self. That is one of the first teachings of Christianity."

The mechanics took over as they came up on the half-tarpaulined planes. They took them through a brief but explicit tour of the tandem units. There wasn't much to see, actually. The twin-engined Mitsubishi had been stripped down to accommodate the intrusive hump of the stubby Ōka. It had also been converted so that one man—the pilot—could fly it satisfactorily.

Beneath was the *Cherry Blossom*. When Nangi poked his head inside, he was inwardly appalled. It appeared to be nothing more than a flying coffin with almost no equipment. Only a steering mechanism and a speaking tube to allow communication with the pilot of the Mitsubishi.

The mechanics explained that Gōtarō would sit in the larger craft with Nangi until their target was sighted. Then he would slide down through the modified bomb bay doors into the tiny

97

cockpit of the Ōka. All phases of the mission were gone over in detail, and then the two majors were asked to repeat the drill. By that time it was 05:19.

They climbed into the Mitsubishi.

The sea was a sheet of flame, reflecting along its vast, rippling skin the rising of the bloodred sun. For a time all blue was banished from the sky as the lurid tendrils of light floated higher.

For Nangi and Gōtarō there was only the monotonous thrumming of the twin engines, the steady vibration. Now Nangi began to understand the desperation of his country. This was a plane he was quite used to, and the differences in flight were considerable. It had been stripped down in more ways than the mechanics had cared to mention. Of course there was no armament—that had been apparent on the ground at first inspection. But a great deal of the inner insulation of the plane was also gone. Nangi supposed that some of this was essential in order to offset the fully loaded weight—4,700 pounds—of the Ōka; there were over 2,500 pounds of high explosive in its nose.

And yet the farther he flew this "new" plane the more he became convinced that even more than was strictly necessary had been taken out. He thought of what Gōtarō had said about the sad state of Japan's military manpower. Didn't it follow then that the same might hold true for materiel. Were they already down to cannibalizing planes? Would that mean that by year's end untrained teenagers would have rifles shoved into their soft fists and be cast off from the Japanese shore in rowboats to meet the advancing enemy? Nangi shuddered at the thought and made a minor course correction.

Just behind him Gōtarō, acting as navigator for the moment, studied the aerial map of the North Pacific. He glanced at his watch and, leaning forward to make certain Nangi could hear him over the ferocious din of the aircraft engines, said, "We should be sighting them in just under ten minutes, approximately two hundred fifty miles southwest of Guam." He looked at his map again. "That will put them and us almost directly over the Marianas Trench. That is supposed to be the deepest depression on earth."

"I know." Nangi had to yell to be heard. "I'm trying not to think about it. I read somewhere that scientists have guessed it might be more than forty thousand feet deep." He shuddered.

"Don't worry," Gōtarō said lightly, "neither you nor I will touch water on this mission."

Just over six minutes later, Gōtarō touched Nangi's shoulder, pointed south. The unbroken skin of the Pacific seemed placid and so flat it might have been a sheet of gunmetal, solid and unyielding. Then, following the other's finger, Nangi saw the two tiny specks. He made another minor course adjustment.

"Time," Gōtarō said in his ear.

Nangi was trimming airspeed. "Wait!" he called. But when he turned his head, his friend was already gone. Nangi could picture him slithering down the makeshift tunnel into the dark, cramped, coffinlike cockpit.

"Here I am."

Nangi heard Gōtarō's voice emerging through the top end of the speaking tube. He lowered the flaps, and they began their descent. He kept Gōtarō informed every step of the way.

"We're at thirty-five thousand feet. I can just make out some definition in the target."

"I've got the destroyer," Gōtarō said. "Just get me there on time. I'll do the rest."

Nangi's skilled hands were busy bringing the plane down on course. He felt keenly the *hachimaki* wound tightly around his helmet and he said, "Sato-san."

"Yes, my friend."

What was there to say? "Twenty-nine thousand feet and closing. We're right on target." He put his hand up to touch the white cloth fluttering slightly in the chill air.

The sky was enormous. Off to the left, dark cumulus clouds were building along the horizon, and Nangi was mindful of the first abrupt shift in wind direction. Still rich sunlight splattered the target area. The sea stretched away, limitless.

"Twenty-eight thousand," Nangi said and put his hand on the Ōka release lever. "I'll give you a second-by-second countdown."

Gōtarō must have heard something in his voice because he said, "Take it easy now, my friend. Don't worry."

"Unlike you, I have no faith to believe in." Nangi shored up his emotions. The altimeter was hovering near the cutoff point. Soon the Ōka would be but a swiftly falling blossom, dropping toward the bosom of the Pacific. "It is time we said our good-byes."

The droning of the wind and then, drifting up to him from the speaking tube, came Gōtarō's voice, "Today in flower, Tomorrow scattered by the wind—Such is our blossom life. How can we think its fragrance lasts forever?"

There were tears in Nangi's eyes as he pulled the lever. "Good-bye," he whispered.

A moment later the rockets came on. Abruptly, the Mitsubishi canted over horribly. At first Nangi thought they had been hit by

99

enemy fire. But they were still too far away from their target for the ships' guns, and the sky had been clear of enemy aircraft.

Then, with one wingtip pointing toward the roof of the heavens, the nose went almost straight down, and he knew with a sudden chilling certainty what had occurred. The wind was moaning through the stripped down fuselage as he leaned forward, screaming into the speaking tube. "Gōtarō! Gōtarō!"

"I'm stuck in here, still plastered to your underbelly."

"The rockets are misfiring! I can't bring the nose up!" Frantically, he worked at the controls, but it was useless, he knew that. They were not meant to correct for 1,764 pounds of thrust.

They were hurtling out of control, heading toward the flat bed of the sea at a heartstopping six hundred miles an hour. Still Nangi did not give up hope and he did what he could to slow their terrific rate of descent. The rockets cut off after nine seconds, but their tremendous initial thrust had done their damage.

"Get back up here!" Nangi cried as he tried to regain control of the aircraft. "I don't want you in the belly when we hit the water."

There was no answer but Nangi was too busy at the controls to repeat his urgent message. Now that the rockets were off, some semblance of control returned to the plane. But they were dangerously close to the sea and Nangi realized there was no hope of pulling out of the spin. The Mitsubishi's twin engines just could not cope with the powerful thrust of the rockets' misdirected fire.

The airframe was juddering dangerously, and because of the acute horizontal angle with which they were dropping he was afraid a wing would crack off. If that happened, he knew, there would be no chance for them at all. The ungainly craft would plunge like a stone into the wall of the ocean, crushing them instantaneously.

So Nangi abandoned the impossible task of pulling them out of the dive and instead redirected his attention to rectifying the angle. If he could level them off somewhat they would have a chance of survival. The Ōka would be sheared off as they hit, but as long as Gōtarō was out of there that would be all right—the stubby plane would take the brunt of the force.

Out of the windscreen the sky was pinwheeling, merging with the sea, back and forth like a funhouse ride. The fuselage was screaming as the force of gravity applied pressure to the riveted joints. The sea was clear of the enemy and there was nothing on the horizon but the storm piling up, purple and yellow like a bruise.

They were very close to the water now, and Nangi began to hear a high, thin wailing above the rest of the sounds inundating him, and he began to sweat. The top wing had still not come down far enough and now the stress on it was horrendous.

There were only seconds left before he knew it would shear off, plunging them to their death. He did not want to be crushed inside this steel coffin and he worked even more frantically at the controls.

He felt a pressure on his back, then Gōtarō's big hand gripping his shoulder and he thought, It took him long enough. He was angry with himself and with Gōtarō because of the added anxiety it had caused him.

The sea was coming up fast and now he thought, It doesn't matter. If the angle doesn't kill us, the explosives in the nose of the Ōka surely will. But still he worked on, and the upper wing grudgingly began to level off.

They were now no more than five hundred feet off the water and Nangi wondered if he had left it too late because they were falling, falling like a leaf in a storm, the sea coming off its two-dimensional plane, breaking up into light peaks and dark troughs, the dark blue almost black and the last thought whirling around his brain, We're over the Marianas Trench and if we sink we just might go on forever.

Then the Pacific came up and slammed them so hard all the breath went out of Nangi's lungs like a balloon bursting. He heard the shriek of ten thousand demons then a quick searing flash of heat and his tiny world collapsed in on him, bolts of pain imploding, nailing him to a cross of agony.

It must have been Gōtarō who pulled him out of the ruined, twisted cockpit because Nangi never remembered climbing out himself. Many years later he would have recurring nightmares about those few terrible, confused moments, no true images coming, only vague impressions, unease, terror, the sense of suffocation, of immobility.

Then the bright sky was above him, a harsh wind scouring his cheeks and the rocking motion of the waves far out at sea. He opened his eyes to a red haze. Pain lanced through his head, and when he tried to move, he could not.

"Lie still," someone said close beside him. "Lie still, *samurai*."

His breathing was labored and he fought to speak. But something seemed to be clogging his voice box. His throat felt lined in fire and his mouth was full of cotton. He had a sense of heat again, flames running along his cheeks like tears. A great crackling filled his ears and the stench of smoke clogged his nostrils, choking him. He vomited and someone held his head, wiping his mouth with a smudged white cloth unwound from his head.

101

His vision began to clear and he saw, rearing up over them, blotting out everything, what he took to be the black fluke of an immense sea creature. He began to whimper, an irrational fear turning his skin wet and cold. Then his head cleared and he saw it for what it was: the tail section of the Mitsubishi. He closed his eyes and lost consciousness.

When he opened his eyes again, the first thing he noticed was that he had lost some depth perception.

"One eye's out," Gōtarō said from beside him. "And don't try to move. Something's happened to your legs."

Nangi was silent for a time, digesting this. At last he said one word, "Explosives."

Gōtarō smiled at him. "That's what took me so long down in the Ōka. I was working the nose loose. I jettisoned it at about eighteen thousand feet. It made quite a bang."

"Didn't notice."

Gōtarō shook his head. "You were too busy." His smiled washed over Nangi again, easing his pain. "You saved us, you know. The minute those rockets misfired I was certain we were dead. We would have been but for what you did."

Nangi closed his eyes. Saying three words had depleted all the strength that was left him.

When he awoke again, Gōtarō was bent over his legs, trying to do something.

"What's going on?" Nangi said.

Gōtarō turned quickly away from what he was doing. "Just checking on your wounds." His eyes slid away from Nangi's toward the heaving sea.

"No land."

"What?" Gōtarō said. "No. None at all. I thought we might be close enough to one of the Marianas, but I don't think that's the case now."

"Noguchi will find us soon enough."

"Yes," Gōtarō said. "I suppose he will."

"He'll want to know what went wrong. All the vice-admirals and admirals in the Imperial Navy will want to know. They've got to get us back safe and sound."

Gōtarō said nothing, his gaze roving this way and that across the water.

"Where's that storm we saw before?" It was difficult for Nangi to talk and he was monstrously thirsty. But he would not give it up. In the silence the thought of the awesome yawning Trench falling away below them would fill his mind with dark twistings

102

and his stomach would lurch and he would begin to retch in irrational terror.

"The wind hasn't shifted yet," Gōtarō said absently. "It's still hanging in the northwest." Clearly his mind was on other matters. What they were Nangi could not guess. Nor would he ask.

There was a silence between them then. Just the wind whistling, a constant force against them like an invisible wall, and the long up-and-down motion caused by the swell of the sea, sickeningly regular. Nangi longed to see even one gull, pulling and swooping across the barren horizon, harbinger of land.

He was still wet, and the wind crawling through the rents and gaps in his uniform caused his skin to raise itself in gooseflesh. His bladder was uncomfortably full and, grunting with the effort, he turned heavily away from Gōtarō, urinated awkwardly, trusting for the wind and the motion to take it away from them.

It was true, something was wrong with his legs. He willed them to work and they would not. Painfully he raised himself up and grabbed at his flesh. He could feel nothing; his legs might have been made of wood.

To take his mind off the numbing thought of paralysis, he began to look around him. For the first time he noticed what it was they were riding on. It was part of the heavily baffled bulkhead from the Mitsubishi. In this case the modifications had worked to their advantage. All the heavy insulation against ground and air fire which would have pulled them down into the sea had been stripped away, replaced by lightweight baffling that trapped air in its webbing.

Nangi grunted to himself. Noguchi and the admirals would be happy with that knowledge, he thought ironically. Even if their precious *Cherry Blossom* refused to fall.

Exhausted, he lay back down, closing his eyes, but the lurch and drag of the heaving tide was not conducive to rest. He looked at Gōtarō. He was sitting cross-legged, still as a statue. Perhaps he was praying. Perhaps he felt no fear. If that were the case, Nangi envied him.

Fatigue and shock caused his mind to wander. He was no longer aware of whether he was awake or asleep. On the borderline, in twilight cerebration, all the black unnameable fears he had been harboring took hold, gaining ascendancy in his world.

He was aware of his own isolation, of himself as a lone bobbing speck, totally exposed and defenseless. He saw himself on the makeshift raft, felt the pain of his wounds, even the intermittent bursts of warmth amid the otherwise chill of the unforgiving wind.

And abruptly he was no longer alone, for rising like some

demon phantasm from the bottomless depths of the sea below him was a terrifying shape. Oh, and how the waves rose higher all about him as if an invisible storm had come up. Great black pyramids built and crested dangerously high, pulling him downward, spinning him into cavernous troughs as endless as tunnels.

Terrified, he clung to the rough surface of his raft, his heart beating triphammer hard, paining his chest, as he waited for what he knew must come.

And then it did breach the water, a monstrous creature from the lightless ocean depths, so enormous it blotted out the stars in the sky: a kraken with glowing eyes and gaping jaws and long writhing tentacles like cables.

Nangi's eyes bulged and he screamed.

Gōtarō shook him awake. "Tanzan. Tanzan!" he called urgently in his ear. "Wake up! Wake up now!"

Nangi's eyes flew open. He was drenched in sweat which, cooling in the gusting wind, sent chill shivers running through him. It took him several minutes to focus his good eye. Then he saw the look on his friend's face.

"We're in trouble."

"What is it?" Nangi had to talk around his tongue which seemed swollen and recalcitrant. "The enemy?"

"I wish I *had* made a sighting," Gōtarō said. "Anyone." His arms held Nangi close, his warmth calming the other's almost constant shivers. "I held off telling you because I thought I could do something about it. But now . . ." He shrugged. "You have some wounds. How serious they are I cannot tell. But you've been losing some blood."

Of course, Nangi thought, angry that he had not realized it himself. That explained the weakness, the brief periods of warmth he felt.

"I've tried everything I know to staunch the loss of blood. I've brought it down to a trickle but still . . ." His eyes were very sad.

"I don't understand," Nangi said. "Am I dying?"

At that moment their makeshift raft gave a shuddering lurch. Apparently Gōtarō was prepared for it because he grabbed Nangi hard with one arm, held on with the other. Still, such was the force of the jar that they both slewed around on the hard surface of the bulkhead.

Gōtarō's face was very close to Nangi's. Nangi could see the reflection of his own frightened face in the curve of the ebon iris.

"Look out there."

Gōtarō's voice sounded like a death knell to Nangi as his gaze followed his friend's lead.

"No!" His voice was a sharp bark, a terror-filled exhalation. For there just off their starboard flank was the great black triangular fin of a hunting shark. As Nangi watched, bile caught in his throat, the slightly curved fin swung around, and now it headed straight toward them. It loomed large, so large. And Nangi could imagine the size of the beast beneath. Thirty feet, forty. Its gaping jaws . . .

His eyes squeezed shut at the next lurch, his stomach turning over and he was retching again, what little there was left in him spewing up all over himself and Gōtarō.

"No," he moaned. "Oh, no." But he was far too weak to raise his voice. It was his worst nightmare come to life. Death held no terror for him. But this . . .

"That's why I was trying to stop the bleeding so completely. He picked us up over an hour ago, when you were still gushing. I thought if I could stop it in time he'd get tired of hanging around and go after something else. I couldn't."

On the shark's third pass, a section of three tubular baffles, already weakened by the crash, broke away. Something at least ten feet in front of the slashing dorsal fin snapped the baffles in two beneath the unquiet surface of the ocean.

Nangi began to shiver anew, and this time even Gōtarō's human warmth couldn't deflect him. His teeth began to chatter and he felt blood leaking from his ruined eye.

"This is no way for a warrior to die," he whispered. The wind took his words, flung them away from him like a hateful child. He put his weary head against Gōtarō's shoulder and at last broke down fully. "I'm afraid, Sato-san. Not of death itself. But the manner in which it has come. Ever since I was a child the depths of the sea have terrified me. It is an uncontrollable fear."

"Even a warrior must feel fear." Gōtarō's deep rumbling voice filled Nangi's ear. "A *samurai* must have his nemesis, just as he must do battle." His arms closed more tightly about his friend as the bulkhead rocked and shuddered. Metal shrieked and then was silent. The sea climbed around them. The fin moved away from them and swung in a tight arc.

"This nemesis may come in many forms, many guises," Gōtarō continued as if nothing at all had happened. "He may be a human foe of flesh and blood. Or then again he may be the force of an avenging *kami*. Or even a demon."

Light was fast going out of the sky, the encroaching night seemed vast and close at the same time so that one had the uncomfortable sensations of utter isolation and intense claustrophobia at the same time. The clouds were too near for there to be any stars visible. The darkness, when it came, would be absolute.

"The world is full of demons," Gōtarō said, his eyes on the approaching fin, "because life is haunted by creatures who cannot experience it as we can. As their envy turns inevitably to hatred, they gain in evil power." One hand reached out like a bar of iron to grip the bafflings as tightly as he could. "Or so my grandmother would tell me at night. I could never understand whether it was to frighten me or to make me more aware that one must fight in life. Always fight to get what one wants."

It was very bad this time, the bulkhead screaming and canting at an extreme enough angle to allow a wave to wash over them. Nangi felt them sliding sideways, and beside him Gōtarō desperately scrabbling to halt their slide. Nangi, too, did what he could to help. It did not seem much to him.

When they were righted, Gōtarō gathered Nangi back to him, as protectively as a mother will a small child. The raft still shuddered and groaned, complaining in the aftermath.

Gōtarō felt for the rift forming beneath them as he said, "I thank God now that my younger brother, Seiichi, is being taken care of by her. She's very old now but so very wise. I think she's the only one with enough force of will to stop him from illegally enlisting. He's almost sixteen, and God knows the war would chew him up and destroy him utterly."

Abruptly, his voice changed and he said, "Tanzan, you must promise me you will look Seiichi up when you get home. My grandmother's house in Higashiyama-Ku in Kyoto, just off the southern edge of Maruyama Park."

Nangi's vision was going in and out of focus. There was a pain in his head like a steel spike hammered home and it made all coherent thought an effort. "I know it well. The park." He could see the cryptomeria and cherry trees, youthful and vibrant, their myriad leaves shivering in the warm breeze of summer. Bright shirts of the children contrasting with the precise patterns of kimonos and oiled paper parasols. Music drifting over the carefully mowed grass, mingling with the laughter.

"'The Lord is my shepherd, I shall not want.'" Nangi heard the strange litany as if from a great distance yet he felt the vibrations from Gōtarō running through him as if they were connected, and some of his terror abated, knowing that this great bear of a man was here beside him. And he thought, Somehow, some way, we'll make it until Noguchi finds us.

"Pray for me, my friend."

And abruptly Gōtarō was no longer beside him. Nangi felt the chill wind tearing at him mercilessly and he rocked alone on the baffled bulkhead. A muffled splash came to him, and his good

106

eye began to burn as he turned his head this way and that. There was just enough illumination to see the foam from Gōtarō's powerful kicks as he swam away from the rocking raft.

"Come back!" Nangi called. "Oh, Sato-san, please come back!"

Then he gasped, his ragged breath coming like fire, as he spotted the great curved dorsal fin rising out of the water. It drew him as it repulsed him, and the fear and loathing stuck in his throat as if it were a physical thing. He wanted nothing more in the world than to kill the monster and he cried aloud, his fists beating impotently against his useless thighs as he saw the black shape cutting through the crests of the waves.

Gōtarō reared up once as the thing hit, spinning up and around, half out of the water, hurled there by the force of primitive nature.

Nangi's vision blurred with bitter tears and he struck at himself over and over as his head bent, the wind moaning in his ears like the voices of the damned.

After a long, long time he began to pray to a God he did not know or understand but to whom he now turned for solace and the continuation of life.

BOOK  TWO

CHUN HSING

[The shape of the army]

C. Gordon Minck, head of Red Station, sat a dizzying eight feet above floor level, his hydraulic crane-lift chair set at maximum. There was nothing much between him and the fall straight down to the hardwood floor, and that was the way Minck liked it; he thought best and most creatively when there was a sense of danger.

His was the only office in the building—six short blocks from the White House—without wall-to-wall carpeting. That was because Minck wanted nothing in here to dampen sound. He was a fanatic on the keenness of the six senses—had been for years, ever since he had graduated at the top of his unit from the elite Fairchild Academy tucked away in rural Virginia. Most of those who made it through its awesomely grueling curriculum called the place the Bonebreaker.

Minck was continually asked the importance of the sixth sense and his answer was always the same, "Intuition is everything." While many of his fellow station leaders spent more and more time at their increasingly sophisticated computer consoles, Minck spent less and less.

And he could see the difference. These other men were becoming gray worms, their lined, worried faces lit by the green phosphor light, racked by increasingly debilitating headaches until, made aware of the insidiously malignant effects of the consoles,

111

they began to hire assistants to relay the computer information to them. They apparently were not disturbed overmuch by the need to replace these assistants every six months or so, or by the rising budgetary expense of the maximum security sanatorium housing them within a stone's throw of the National Zoo, an enormous sprawling mansion over two hundred years old and designated a National Landmark. Every year the Smithsonian attempted to get it opened to the public, being ignorant of its real purpose, and every year they were denied.

There were no computer terminals anywhere in Minck's offices; they were strictly *verboten*. However, there were a number of printout stations, one of which was in his spacious office. Two of the walls below the sixteen-foot ceiling were given over to enormous rectangular panels that resembled windows more than anything else. This was deliberate. In fact, they were giant projection screens composed of a particular chemical amalgam able to "take" the rear-projected holograms, so that they blossomed to life with an astonishing reality. The holograms, of course, changed from time to time but mostly, as now, they were of two views of Moscow: of Dzerzhinsky Square, to be more accurate, the great, open plaza dotted with bundled, astrakhaned pedestrians and, in the street behind them, one black Zil limousine caught as it entered the black, blobby hole in the forbidding facade of the structure known with fear throughout the world as Lubyanka Prison and headquarters for the KGB.

On the other wall was the second view of the square. Minck knew for a fact that some of the cells within Lubyanka looked out on this other building across the square, where children strolled with their parents, hand in hand, too young yet to know or comprehend how close they really were to the one true embodiment of evil left on earth.

Minck was gazing meditatively now at this second edifice. Once again he opened up his mind, his memories, trying to find any trace of the hatred, the fear he had once experienced upon looking out at this same view. Oh, not so expansive of course. The slitted windows in the outer cells in Lubyanka were not those of a hotel.

But Minck remembered. It had been winter then, the sky grayed with clouds stretched like sinews. Lights were always on in the vast city as night swept in off the frozen steppes to the north for its eighteen-hour stay. And everywhere the noise of the city was muffled by the ubiquitous snow, turning even the most normal of sounds strange and unreal, increasing Minck's sense of disassociation. How he had come to hate the snow, for it had brought him to Lubyanka, his wrists manacled. Snow had hidden the icy patch in the street on which he had skidded. He would have eluded them otherwise without doubt, for they were mathematically minded, drilled to precision, but, as with all KGB underlings, lacking the concept of intuition.

Intuition equaled freedom in Minck's mind. And his intuition would have saved him that chill night in Moscow. Except for the snow. *Snyeg*, the Russians called it. In any language he hated it.

He continued to stare at the building that had been his last look at Moscow before they pulled him from the holding cell and began the "interviews." From then on his home was a windowless space of not more than fifteen square feet, with a plywood cot bolted to the wall and a hole down which to wash his waste products. The stench was appalling, as was the cold. Heat was unheard of in the inner cells.

Sightless, like a rat in the dark, Minck fought to retain his senses against the numbing effects his interviewers were inducing in him. And to that end he conjured up in his mind memories of the view from his holding cell, for a time certain that it was the last sliver of the world he would ever see.

He observed the young Russian couples walking, the families trudging through the last of the spring snows—for these holograms revolved with the seasons—and felt the clear space within him, the embers of passionate hate and terror that consumed him, that, for the instant before he crossed over the border into neutral territory, had caused him to pause, to consider wildly returning and killing them all singlehanded.

And like a careful cowboy on a dry and dusty plain, Minck kicked over these glowing ashes, nurturing the essence of that hate: Protorov. He gave his whole attention to the crenellated building in the hologram that had come to mean even more to him than its sinister sister structure across the square: the Moscow Children's World department store.

His eyes closed in easy meditation. His finger depressed one of a series of studs recessed into the left arm of his chair.

"Tanya," he said softly into the void of the room, "two directives. One: get that Doctor Kidd—what's his Christian name? Timothy?—on the phone. If he's not at the Park Avenue office, try Mount Sinai Hospital. Get him out of rounds."

"What pseudonym shall we use as imprimatur?" The voice that emerged from the hidden speaker system was husky, with just a trace of a foreign slur.

"Oh, let's be ingenious today, shall we? Use the Department of International Export Tariffs."

"Very good."

"Second," Minck said, "since our time seems to be rapidly running out, invade ARRTS and call up the file on Linnear NMN Nicholas."

It was Justine's first day on the job and she was uncomfortable as a cat on a hot tin roof. For more than three years she had been more or less happily ensconced in her own one-woman company, delivering free-lance advertising concepts to medium-range accounts. While she had not amassed a fortune, her talents were such that even in an uncertain economy she had managed to do quite well.

Of course from time to time she had received offers to join agencies, but the comfort of working for herself had always outweighed the increased security that working for someone else would give her.

But meeting Rick Millar had begun to change all that. Just over six weeks ago Mary Kate Sims had phoned Justine in frantic need of a project designer. Mary Kate worked for Millar, Soames & Robberts, one of the newer agencies with a high profile and even higher net yearly bookings. Two of their best designers were down with the flu and would Justine be a dear and fill in on the American Airlines project? It was a rush job, but Mary Kate said she could guarantee Justine a sizable bonus for on-time delivery.

Justine took the project, working on it eighteen hours a day for almost a week. But ten days later, into three or four of her own projects—one of which was giving her fits—she had forgotten all about Mary Kate and her American Airlines package.

Until the call from Rick Millar, the head of the agency. Apparently American had loved Justine's idea so much they were turning what had been a New York regional into a national campaign. The firm of Millar, Soames & Robberts had received a sizable bonus and a long-term contract with American.

Rick said that he had loved Justine's idea before the agency had submitted it to American. Justine did not know whether or not to believe him. He made a lunch date with her.

The following week they met at La Côte Basque, a superb French restaurant that Justine had read about several times in *Gourmet* but had never actually been to.

Yet the delicious food was the least memorable aspect of those several hours because, as it turned out, Millar had more on his mind than just wanting to meet her.

"Justine," he said, over drinks, "I'm basically a people-oriented

114

person in business as well as in my private life. I believe in creating an atmosphere that allows my employees to work at full throttle.

"But more than that, I allow certain individuals to cut across departmental boundaries when their talents warrant it." He took a sip of his bourbon. "I think you're such a person. A job with us wouldn't be all that different for you than having your own business." He grinned. "Except of course that you'd make a ton of money and build your rep among the high-level accounts that much quicker."

Justine put her drink aside for the moment, her heart hammering. "Are you giving me a direct job offer?"

Millar nodded.

"Isn't this supposed to come over the Grand Marnier soufflé or something?"

He laughed. "I'm a maverick in every way."

She watched him for a time. He was fairly young, perhaps just forty. His hair was thick and long enough to reach his collar. Streaked blond, brushed straight back, it could just as easily belong to a surfer from Redondo Beach. He had a good hard face with the hint of crow's feet at the corners of his intelligent, wide set blue-green eyes. He had the kind of nose that made you think of Mercedes, pink gins, and polo along the carefully manicured greensward of the Connecticut shore. He should have had a cable-knit sweater spread on his back. But his manner belied all that.

"I can see the wheels turning in there," he said as they were served the first course of fresh bluepoint oysters. He grinned again, a sunny, somehow reassuring expression that showed good white teeth. "I wasn't born into money. I worked hard to get where I am today."

But she found that she had little appetite, because she knew that she was going to take him up on his offer. Dreams like this one rarely came along in life. Though the idea turned her edgy, she had learned early to grab them before they slipped irretrievably by.

In fact, she had been so keyed up about the job that she had asked Rick if she could start on the following day. Friday, instead of waiting through the weekend. With Nicholas just gone she had had no plans, and three idle days, waiting, was too much for her patience. So it was that she had shown up just past eight—a full hour before she had to—at Madison Avenue and Fifty-fourth Street. The offices of Millar, Soames & Robberts were three glittering twenty-first-century floors of the sleekest furnishings money could buy, with floor-to-ceiling windows in every executive office, and mechanical and production departments that would surely make her work a snap—she had been so used to doing everything herself. Now, as Rick had said to her over lunch, she could concentrate on ideas, allowing others to complete her sketches.

Rick himself introduced Justine to Min, her secretary. She was no more than twenty and, with the patch of green in her dark hair, seemed to be the agency's concession to the post-punk era. But Justine soon found out that beneath the wild hair was a sharp brain that understood all the convoluted workings of the organization.

Justine's office was a floor below Mary Kate's and, because Mary Kate was a vice president, it was somewhat smaller than her friend's. But it was light and airy. A fresh-looking coleus with a pink satin GOOD LUCK ribbon tacked to it sat on a desk otherwise empty save for a phone. The office was sparsely furnished with, it seemed, an agglomeration of cast-offs.

Rick apologized for the state of the office, saying that the company was in the midst of reorganizing departments and that Min would bring her a stack of furnishing and accessory catalogs "so that things can get straightened out in a couple of weeks."

She thanked Rick for the plant and, putting it beside the window, sat behind her new desk. Her first call was to Nicholas, in her excitement forgetting that it was the middle of the night in Tokyo. The hotel balked at putting the call through, the officious operator asking if it was an emergency. When she explained to her what the local time was, Justine settled for leaving a message, not knowing of course that he was out wandering through Jan Jan.

But as she cradled the receiver, she experienced a sharp pang of sadness. She had never felt more acutely Nicholas' absence or her desire for him to return. She had fought with desperation the fear and anxiety welling up inside her when he had told her he was going to work for her father. Were her feelings irrational or real? When it came to her father, she knew that she felt trapped by her emotions. The shape of her life had been dictated by Raphael Tomkin. As a woman in her twenties, she had had love affairs abruptly severed without her knowing; as a teenager, she had seen the devastation his harshness and self-involvement had wreaked on her mother; as a child, she had been rendered fatherless by his business affairs.

Even though Nicholas' new job was temporary, she had been terrified that it would turn out to be a permanent position. She knew only too well how persuasive her father could be when he set his mind to it. She had been terrified too of his going away. So soon after the terrible nightmare with Saigō, who through Justine herself had almost succeeded in killing Nicholas, she felt that being alone was a kind of exquisite agony.

She knew that whatever it was Saigō had done to her had scarred her for life, despite all Nicholas' efforts to exorcise that particular devil from her. True, she was free from Saigō's arcane grip over her, but she could never be free of the memories.

In the deepest shoals of night, when Nicholas lay peacefully sleeping beside her, she would awake with a shivery start, into a nightmare.

I almost murdered him, she found herself repeating to herself as if there were a stranger alive inside her body to whom she must make sense of this. How could I? Another repeating riff, an agonizing counterpoint. I'm not even capable of killing a fish, let alone another human being, my own love.

That, of course, might have been her salvation: the conviction that *she could not kill* and therefore was not responsible. But the nightmare continued to stalk her. Had not Nicholas stopped her, she would most assuredly have killed him. Just as Saigō had programmed her to. She was not concerned with responsibility. Only with a guilt greater than any she had ever known.

But, oh, she ached for him even as she feared for him every moment he was in Japan, every moment he was with her father. For she knew intimately all the myriad ways Raphael Tomkin had of getting what he wanted. He could be bullheaded or subtle, as the occasion warranted. He could get you even when you were certain he wouldn't.

She shuddered now within the confines of her new office. Oh, Nicholas, she thought. If only I had been able to make you see what he's like. I don't want him to steal you away from me.

Because the thought of Nicholas permanently wedded to Tomkin Industries was more than she could bear. She wanted her father out of her life, had struggled all through her formative years for just such an objective, even going so far as to change her last name to Tobin. And she knew that if there was a chance that he would come back into her life she would move heaven and earth to prevent it.

Angry now as well as lonely, she dialed Mary Kate's extension. If Nicholas had phoned at this moment, she would have spat at him for putting her in such an impossible position, for making her fear for him and them both.

Justine was told that her friend was in a meeting, so again she left a message, hoping they could have lunch and celebrate. Then she asked Min to come in. Together they began working out logistics, departmental and otherwise, so that Justine could get on with her first projects for Millar, Soames & Robberts.

* * *

It took all of Nicholas' training to cover his true feelings. The shock had been so great, so totally unexpected that he had taken that one lurching step backward, losing for an instant his centrism, exhibiting a certain paleness of complexion, a momentary flaring of the nostrils as animal instinct threatened ascendancy; he was certain no one had noticed. His face closed down like a steel trap as the soft mix of voices from all around him faded. . . .

And he was back in New York, his long *dai-katana* drawn, its gleaming blade arching away toward Saigō. He took a step forward and his cousin said, "You believe that Yukio is alive, somewhere, and thinking every so often of the old days with you. But, oh no, this is not so!" He laughed as they continued to circle each other with murderous intent. He looked into Nicholas' eyes as he said, "She lies at the bottom of the Straits of Shimonoseki, cousin, precisely where I dumped her.

"She loved you, you know. With every breath she breathed, with every word she spoke. And at last it drove me out of my mind. She was the only woman for me . . . without her there were only men." His eyes blazed like coals, red-rimmed and mad. He was bleeding heavily.

"You made me kill her, Nicholas!" he blurted out in sudden accusation.

For months Nicholas had lived with that pain, a black cyst of torment he rarely let out into the light of day. And now to see . . . It was not as if Akiko Ofuda looked like Yukio: a family resemblance, a sister even. Her face *was* Yukio's. And as for her figure, well, certainly there were differences. But Nicholas had last seen Yukio in the winter of 1963 on that long, terrible journey south to Kumamoto and Saigō. And when he had returned at last to Tokyo, alone and confused, everything had changed. Satsugai, Saigō's father, had been murdered. Then the Colonel, Nicholas' father, died. Shortly thereafter, Cheong, his mother, had committed *seppuku* with her sister-in-law, Itami, as second.

Now, staring hard at Akiko Ofuda, Nicholas wondered wildly whether Saigō had lied that one last time. Was it possible? He was a master of twisted truths. He had been dying when he told Nicholas. What would that have made him do? Lie or tell the truth at last? Whatever would hurt Nicholas the most. Truth or fiction? Nicholas could not tell.

Yet how Akiko had stared at him from the moment he was close enough for her to see him. Though there were more than a hundred people at the affair, her eyes had locked on his. She had created the aura of mystery, hiding her face until he was quite close. She had used her fan deliberately. Why? If she were not

Yukio, why would she have any interest in him? And yet to turn up here as Sato's soon-to-be-wife . . . The wild coincidence did not escape him. Nicholas, quite rightly, did not trust in coincidences as a force of nature.

All through the ceremony, as the traditional sakē cup was being passed from Sato to Akiko, Nicholas' mind was preoccupied by the bizarre puzzle. But the more he thought, the more he seemed to become entangled in a mare's nest of questions without answers. It was clear to him that he would get nowhere until he could speak to Akiko herself. And yet his mind would not stop turning over the possibilities: was she, wasn't she? His eyes stared at her bleakly. That face, her face. It was as if he had suddenly stepped into a haunted house and now, confused, could not find his way out again. It felt precisely as if all solid ground had fled.

Was the ceremony long or short? He could not tell. He was suspended in an agony of not knowing. Hope, fear, anger, and cynicism all mixed inside him. His own thoughts and memories took precedence over outside events. His body went through the proper motions like an automaton.

And always he found her looking at him. Those eyes he had known so well, had loved so desperately, so wildly, so utterly passionately in the dark days of his youth locked with his. He tried to read some kind of emotion there and, because he was a master of this as well as of many other things, he was dismayed to find that he drew a blank. Did he see mockery there or love, desire or betrayal? He found he had no way of knowing and this, too, was as frightening as this *kami* resurrected from his past.

All Nicholas could think of was getting a chance to talk to Akiko. But quickly he saw just how difficult it was going to be to get her alone. With the ceremony's end, clusters of friends immediately gathered around the couple, wishing them well, offering their congratulations.

Others began to drift away down the narrow dirt path toward the edge of the lake below, where striped pavilions had been erected the night before.

There was no space for him. The best he could do was to offer his own congratulations to them both. Sato was smiling hugely, being very American about it, pumping hands just like a canny senator in his re-election bid.

Tomkin grunted at Nicholas' elbow, said, "I'm about ready for him to pass out the cigars." He turned his head away. "You go on to the reception. My gut still hurts; I'm going back to the hotel. I'll send the car back for you."

Alone, Nicholas began to walk down the path circling the cliffs.

Ahead of him he could see Sato and Akiko, still surrounded by well-wishers. There was laughter and gaiety now that the stiff formality of the ceremony had been dispensed with.

He saw her descending through the darkness and light, the moving shadows of the pines painting abstract symbols upon the delicate curve of her back. A slight swaying of the shoulders and hips, appearing and disappearing as he descended behind her.

The wedding, the crowds, the swirling chattering talk faded so that he was alone with her and the elements. He was acutely aware of the sunlight, the shadows, the scents of pine and cedar, incense and wild lemon, but only as they pertained to her.

Her passage was like the return of the plovers after a long, sere winter when the ground was rimed with frost and only the glowing hearths emanated warmth.

Once Nicholas had likened Yukio to the fading pale petals that fall on the last of *hanami*'s three days. Although many said that at *hanami*'s peak, the second day, the cherry blossoms were most beautiful, still, to almost every Japanese the third-day petals were most affecting. For it was on that last day when one truly understood the ineffable nature of beauty's transience.

But now what was he to think? His whole reality had been turned upside down. *Was* Akiko Yukio? How could she still be alive? Had Saigō pulled one last diabolical trick from beyond the grave? Had he kept Nicholas from her all this time when she was alive and . . .

He could not go on with that thought; the idea made him sick to his stomach with the intensity of longing and bitter frustration. Then he managed to get hold of himself. He knew where he was and what he would have to do in order to find the answers to all these questions. He would have to allow his Eastern side complete ascendancy. Time . . . and patience. He knew that he would have to employ them both if he was to successfully break this maddening riddle. Meanwhile he would just have to ignore his breaking heart.

He had been watching Alix Logan for over five months now. Through the sun-drenched streets of Key West, along the narrow, flat beaches, in and out of the small clothing and jewelry boutiques. He had even gone with her when she went to pick up her dog, a large brindled Doberman. He cringed when he saw the neat white and black sign hanging from a crosstree on the lawn: Gold Coast Obedience School, and in smaller letters beneath: Police and Attack Training Our Specialty. And the one thing he had learned from all that time on the job was that there was no conceivable way in to her.

Alix Logan was a looker. She had a slender model's body, long thick hair the color of honey, streaked nicely now by the Florida sun. Her eyes were an intense green. He had seen them only through the compact Nikon 7×20 binoculars, flattened by the lens' prisms into ovoid orbs as large as the sun.

For just over five months she had been his universe, this powerful man with the wide shoulders and the cowboy's pushed-in face. He had dogged her for so long and so intensely that it was as if he were living with her. He knew what she ate, what her tastes in clothes and men were. What she liked, what she didn't like.

Her favorite item was a hot fudge sundae with coffee ice cream and two cherries. What she disliked most were the pair of monsters who shadowed her constantly. At least that was how she thought of them. He had heard her call one just that, "Monster!" as she accosted him on the pier one bright cloudless afternoon, rushing into the shadows to deliver her impassioned message to him directly, using her small fists on his burly chest for emphasis.

The monster stared at her impassively from out of his close-set brown eyes.

"I'm fed up!" she screamed at him. "I can't take it anymore. I thought it'd be all right down here. But it's not. I can't work, I can't sleep, I can't even make love without you monsters breathing fire on my back." Her honey hair whipped in the salt wind. "Please, please, please, just leave me alone!"

The monster turned his face away from her and, crossing his massive arms across his chest, began to whistle something from a Walt Disney movie.

The man with the cowboy's lined face witnessed all this from the small boat he sat in, gently rocking at pierside while he worked on his fishing tackle, a stained canvas hat scrunched down low over his forehead, putting his face in black shadow. They knew him here as Bristol and that was how he liked it. He also responded to "Tex," a rather unimaginative nickname Tony, the dockmaster, had given him, owing to his face.

"Tex" Bristol. If you thought about it for more than a moment, it was idiotic. But then, he thought, this whole scene was something for the books.

He finished his work on his rod and prepared to shove off. On the pier, Alix Logan, tears trembling like diamonds in the corners of her eyes, was stalking stiff-legged away from the monster, toward the gangplank of a pleasure boat.

He cast off, heard the twin screws of the engines thrumming

liquidly behind him. He picked up speed, the thought of marlin in his head.

Far from shore, he had to laugh. For someone dead and buried, he was leading a remarkably action-filled life.

Akiko Ofuda Sato felt the press of her husband's hand in the limo on the way home from the reception. Felt the heat emanating from his body, the pressure of his lustful spirit so close beside her. He made no overt move, but in all other aspects she felt the electricity crackling through him as they drew closer and closer to home.

Multiple images, thronging her mind in such profusion they tumbled end over end over each other, of her voyeuristic nights in the house, of the bodies of all the gifts she had presented him with over the long months, made her gasp inwardly with a manufactured excitement. She squeezed Sato's hand, the edges of her lacquered nails scratching gently along the warm flesh of his palm.

Once inside, she went immediately to the bathroom and, doffing her kimono, removed all her undergarments. Naked, she carefully wrapped her kimono around herself, tying the *obi*, checking her makeup in the mirror. She reapplied eye shadow and lipstick.

The master bedroom was in the *omoya*, far from the six-*tatami* room where he had received his gifts. Those women had never been allowed into this section of the house. They were outsiders, after all, not family.

On a pedestal not far from the generous *futon* bed was a sculpture of Ankoku Doji, scowling fiercely, one leg up in the classic sitting position. He was an aide to the kings of hell and, putting brush to a paper-covered plank, it was his responsibility to annotate the sins of each penitent who entered that unholy court to be tried for his misdeeds on earth.

This particular Ankoku Doji was carved from camphorwood, dated to the thirteenth century.

Akiko hated him. His sculpted eyes seemed to follow her, seemed to know what she planned to do to his owner. As soon as she was well ensconced here she was determined to move him to another place, preferably one she did not visit often.

Sato welcomed her to his *futon*. They drank hot sakē and he made several jokes. She made sure she laughed although she barely heard them.

Was she terrified or revolted at the prospect of being penetrated by her sworn enemy? She used all her prodigious skills to push down the black tide that threatened to engulf her mind. She did not want to think about what Sun Hsiung had said to her, but she had no choice.

Sato touched her and she jumped. Her eyes flew open and she realized they had been squeezed shut as if that physical act could blot out the reverberations filling her mind.

"You are an empty vessel which I will now proceed to fill," Sun Hsiung had said to her. "You came to me of your own volition. You must remember that in the days and weeks and months to come. Your time will be long here. It is not inconceivable that you will feel a desire to leave. I will tell you now that you cannot. That if you harbor any suspicion that you cannot tolerate hardship, pain, arduous labor, then you must leave immediately. Now is the time, the only time. Do I make myself clear?"

And with terror filling her heart like a rush of water, she had nodded, said, "I do," just as if these were marriage vows she was taking.

And, oh, they were, she thought now. They were.

The silk of her kimono was sliding with a whisper across the pale expanse of her shoulder, guided by his deft hand. This close to him, surrounded only by the silence of the empty house—for all servants had been dismissed for the night, to stay free of charge at the city's most plush hotel, Sato's wedding present to them—she felt his male presence much the way a female fox is aware of her mate. There was no more than the acknowledgement of lust, of one brief moment stolen out of the net of time.

What she was about to begin had no more to do with love than a pair of microorganisms coming together. What true feelings she had for him she could not express until the moment of her vengeance was at hand. Her nostrils dilated sharply, scenting his odor.

Her kimono had slipped off both her shoulders and now she pressed her hands across herself as a schoolgirl might, embarrassed by her newly budding breasts.

Sato leaned forward and brushed his lips against her throat. Akiko closed off that private part of her which was most dear to her, accepting what might come.

She felt his hands sliding over her shoulders, and she willed herself out of her stupor, parting his own kimono, the bright red angular pattern breaking up into shards as the folds began to appear.

He was naked long before she was, his flesh warm beneath her probing fingers. He was virtually hairless, his skin smooth and unblemished. She put her cheek against his belly, felt the pulse of his life beating in her ear like the surf along the far shore.

123

This meant nothing to her. It was as if she had put her ear to the bole of a tree.

He lifted her upward and now they lay, body against body. Her legs were closed, his were spread apart. There seemed a second heart down there, pulsing in a rhythm all its own. She felt its insistent push as it grew, insinuating itself between her thighs, another kind of serpent.

She reached her hand down and cupped his scrotum. He groaned and she thought it gave an answering throb. She touched the base of his shaft.

Gently, he began to roll over, to move her onto her back. She had never been so aware of one part of her anatomy before. The insides of her thighs burned as if she had pressed herself against an oven and her flesh there rippled as if in terror.

If he saw too soon, if his love was not enough to dissuade him, he would surely reject her. She saw him throwing her out into the street, saw herself banished from the city as it had been done centuries before when the Shōgun held sway and her kind would not be permitted into the bed of a *samurai*, let alone be his bride.

She understood that at this moment there was absolutely no difference between her and her mother. This terrified her beyond all measure, and she commenced to shake like a leaf. Her husband mistook her fear for passion, and groaned aloud.

He had placed her on her back. She could feel the soft silk of her open kimono on her flesh like a sensuous caress. Sato loomed over her, his muscular body throwing her breasts and belly into shadow.

She raised her arms, her fingers and palms tracing the ridges and bulges of his muscles. She used the pads of her thumbs to press inward.

"You like my arms?" he whispered.

Her eyes, black jade, stared up at him, unblinking, delivering the answer he wished for.

"Ah, yes," he breathed. "Ah, yes."

His head came down and his open lips encompassed a nipple. He moved from one breast to another, nuzzling and licking. Akiko felt nothing. His fingertips rolled one nipple while he sucked on another and now she gasped at the contrast between the warm softness of his mouth and the rough-calloused rubbing of his fingers. She did not know whether to scream or to cry. She did neither, merely bit her lower lip, exhaling sharply. She put her fingers in her mouth, transferred saliva to the spot between her thighs.

Then she felt herself being turned on her side, Sato's heated

124

body behind her. His hand gently lifted her upper leg and centered in on the core of her. She gasped as she felt him between her thighs in the tangled forest of her pubic hair.

His fingers pressed open her lips, and she thought briefly again of all his gifts, the movements of his lovemaking. Then she was opening herself to him, feeling the thick hotness of him like a bar of iron between her legs.

She began to weep. His breath hissed in her ear and she could feel the tightening of his powerful arms about her. Her buttocks were hard against him as he moved around and around at the entrance to her vagina until he could stand it no longer.

With a great groan and a violent heave, he pushed himself all the way into her. Akiko's eyes opened so wide the whites showed all around. An engine of fire started up in her chest so that she could not breathe. She felt a fearful tearing in her loins, a great filling up, a pressure on her entrails as if she had stuffed herself with food.

She was overcome by sensation and she cried out wildly. Sato, misinterpreting her, lunged in even deeper, trying to establish an erotic rhythm.

Akiko's mind was filled with black visions. All the myriad demons of hell seemed to be rising out of their moldy beds to dance in the firelight in her mind's eye. Nights bound in the high-land castle paraded in lurid detail before her like a shameless whore. Her head whipped back and forth, her long unbound hair slapping against Sato, enflaming him all the more.

Kyōki. The *sensei* of darkness.

His name made her moan and bite her lip against the unfurling memories like shrouds for the dead. For that was how she thought of herself now. Dead.

Like ships in the night on a storm-tossed tumultuous sea, they rocked to and fro, Akiko locked inside his embrace, allowing him this cruel dominance. There was foam on her lips, hatred in her heart. She had never before offered up her body unwillingly; she never wanted to again, though she knew that she must to preserve this marriage until its bloody end.

Yet she knew what to do; she could give pleasure without ever receiving it. This too was part of the role she had assigned herself. Weeping still, she reached back between her thighs, grasping his swinging sac. At the same time she clenched her inner muscles, working on the engorged head buried inside her slick channel. Her hips revolved in a rapid corkscrew motion. She squeezed lightly with her hand.

She heard his deep groan, felt his muscles trembling all around her, and knew that his orgasm was imminent. I cannot allow him to do it, she thought wildly. Tomorrow or the night after. But not now.

With a little cry, she pulled herself away from him, turning to slide her open lips over his moist, vibrating shaft, teasing him with the faintest of feathery touches until he grabbed at her flung hair and begged her for sweet release.

It was only then that she began to suck, hollowing her cheeks, urging him onward to completion with her fingers. Her other hand covered her pubic mound as if staunching a wound, her thighs close together.

She held herself all the firmer at the instant of his sexual convulsions, as a child caresses a deep hurt to ease the pain. And then she willed her new husband to sleep, watching him drift off, staring blindly down the lightless corridor of her own past at what she might have been.

Akiko rolled carefully over and silently rose from her nuptial bed. For a moment she stood naked, in utter quietude, staring down at the form of Seiichi Sato, slumbering and sated.

From the enigmatic look on her beautiful face it was impossible to tell what she was feeling. Perhaps it was true what Sun Hsiung had once told her, "You do not fully understand anything that you feel." But if that were so, she told herself, I could never have learned what I have. I could never have gone beyond the *Kuji-kiri* and the *Kōbudera*, the arcane disciplines that Saigō had mastered. And, she thought triumphantly, I never could have killed that clever fox, Masashigi Kusunoki. She had used *jahō* and it had worked, masking the nature of her intent from even such an adept as he.

But her delight was short-lived. Shaking her head, her long unbound hair a blue-black cascade across her shoulder, down her back, she bent and retrieved her multicolored kimono. It was the one she had worn at the wedding reception earlier today.

She drew it about her as a child will wrap a bathrobe warm from the radiator around herself in order to ward off more than the chill of night. She had numbed herself in order to ward off what she thought of as an attack. It had been a time when, she told herself repeatedly, she had to retreat now in order to have her revenge. But there was a vile taste in her mouth, salty-sweet like blood. Her own blood.

Never before had she detested so intensely her *karma*. Her training should have protected her from these feelings, and it surprised and disconcerted her that she should feel so violated by one simple act. That it had been a necessary one did not seem to matter at all. She was weeping again in silent agony.

Barefoot, she left the bedroom, making her way through the dark house until she found the *fusuma* that opened out onto the Zen garden.

It was always peaceful there. Above the one ancient cryptomeria the stars glittered hard and twinkling like the many teeth of some grinning nocturnal predator. For one long moment, she allowed the barriers to fall away from her. Thoughts of Nicholas entered her consciousness, seeping through her like woodsmoke. For just an instant an unfamiliar powerful emotion gyred, filling her up to the bursting point, and, her neck arched, her face turned heavenward, she allowed herself to yearn for surcease. Up there, a million miles from anything known, she could be free. Striding through the utter blackness of space, she might at last rest from the turmoil that beset her.

But the feeling only lasted a moment, then she was earthbound again. Her head came down and her dark eyes contemplated the precise grandeur of the garden. Less was more here, a uniquely Japanese esthetic.

The pebbles which covered the ground were hand picked for their size, shape, and color. They were carefully raked twice a day in order to maintain the precise symmetry the garden's designer had labored so hard to create.

Three black, angular rocks jutted up from different parts of the garden. In contrast to the pebbles, each one was unique unto itself, its ridges and rills affecting the onlooker in varying ways, triggers for the evocation of disparate moods.

The place was tranquil and invigorating at the same time.

Akiko turned her head and sat on the cold stone bench, her legs tucked neatly under her. Her hands were folded in her lap, the fingers relaxed and slightly curved. The attitude was so wholly feminine that it was quite impossible to tell what unimaginable bursts of coordinated energy this body was capable of.

She was acutely aware of the arc of a shadow inside her, a demarcation between light and dark whose edge was as finely honed as the most masterfully forged *katana* blade. From this place of shade she felt the rippling of her hatred, her longing to wreak a horrendous vengeance. Her body trembled in anticipation, there was a low rumbling shaking her brain apart, making her moan as if she were in exquisite pain.

Then she felt a veil of wind caress her cheek, cooling her. Sweat dried along her hairline, the precise symmetry of the garden seized her, and she was altogether calm again. She sighed in the

127

aftermath of a great storm and closed her eyes. Her head felt heavy, and as her pulsebeat slowed, she reviewed the events of the evening.

In the stillness of the Zen pebble garden, Akiko was thankful that she did not have to contend with a mother-in-law. For Sato's mother, like all Japanese mothers, would rule this house. Wasn't that why the central living section was called *omoya* by tradition: mother house. Akiko shuddered inwardly. How would she possibly be able to endure the orders of the *heramochi*, the one with the right to hold the spoon used to serve rice, the head of the household. No. Far better that she was dead and buried along with Sato's war-hero brother.

Alone with only the cryptomeria, blacker even than the surrounding night, with the shadows of the Zen stones striking her in odd rippling patterns, Akiko stood up and, under the scrutiny of the pinpoint uncaring stars, threw off her kimono in one convulsive gesture.

Naked, the hard blue light vying with the pink neon excrescence from Shinjuku and the faraway Ginza, boulevards that never slept, she stepped out onto the precisely raked rows of pebbles. They felt so cold and smooth on her bare soles.

Between two of the jutting black rocks she spread herself, draped on the flat ground, curled and serpentine, half in light, half in shadow, and became one with all that surrounded her.

There was an acute irony in using Tanya against the Russians, an elliptical symmetry that affected Minck in just the same way as did gazing upon one of Thomas Hart Benton's huge canvases: its very existence made life worth living.

After Moscow, Minck had needed elements to demonstrate to him in a direct fashion the nobler, the elegant and uplifting aspects of life. His incarceration had leeched that part of his memory away. In returning to America he had had to learn the positive aspects of the human race all over again.

He looked up now as he sensed Tanya's approach. That was another consequence of his imprisonment. Some unseen layer of his mind had been rubbed away by the constant scrutiny he had been under, and like sandpaper taken to skin, what was revealed underneath was a hypersensitivity to human presence.

Minck stared into those cool blue eyes, dotted with gray. They were large and direct, and they were always the first things he saw when he looked at her. That was his own personal purgatory.

They were the eyes of Mikhail. Her brother's eyes. Mikhail, the dissident, had been the reason for Minck's infiltration into

Moscow in the first place. Mikhail had sent a message into the West: he possessed information vital to the American secret service system. Minck had been chosen by computer—because of his facility with idiomatic Russian as well as his somatic matchup with the Slavic Caucasian type—and they had sent him in to pull Mikhail out or, if that were, as they put it, unfeasible, to extract the information from him.

But in pursuit of that knowledge, he had been traduced. Someone in Mikhail's cell had been turned, and Minck's rdv with the dissident had ended in a hail of submachine-gun fire literally tearing Mikhail in two, in spotlights picking Minck out of the shadows, the snow falling, falling. All sounds muffled, blood in the snow like chips of coal strewn in an explosion of malice, chain-wrapped tires clink-clink-clinking in his ears as he ran from the raised voices, the muzzles spewing red death hidden behind the angry glare of the spotlights. And running through the knifing cold, snowflakes riming his lashes, blinding him, making him think, oddly, of Kathy, his college sweetheart, his wife. How she loved the snow, holding out her delicate hand, laughing in delight as one by one the flakes landed on her flesh, melting only after giving up their secret to her, only her.

Slipping on the patch of ice, undone by the blanket of snow, his ankle wrenching, going down, and then strong arms binding him, lights in his face, the gassy smells of cabbage and borscht invading his nostrils, voices harsh and guttural, *"Gde bumagie! Kak vass zavoot!"* Where are your papers? What is your name? repeated over and over, life already reduced down to one dull fragment. Eight years ago.

"Carroll?"

She was the only one who knew what the C. stood for; the only one who would dare use it if it were known. It was the only outward manifestation he would permit of the powerful bond between them.

"Yes, Tanya."

She glanced down at the brief he had been reading. "Is the file on Nicholas Linnear complete?"

"No file on a human being is ever complete, no matter how up to date it is. I want you to remember that." He said this last needlessly since Tanya remembered everything.

Looking at her again, Minck was struck anew by how much she resembled Mikhail. Both had the finely chiseled, high-cheek-boned face of the purebred White Russian rather than the broad, coarse-structured visage of the Slav. Both had that thick, straight shock of hair, though in latter days Tanya had had hers dyed a deep-burnished blond because, she said, it helped dampen the memories.

After he had broken out of Lubyanka, a colonel's blood on his trembling hands, with all of the considerable might of the *Komitet Gosudarstvennoy Bezopasnost* marshaled against him, with the militia out beating on dissident necks to extract information on his whereabouts, Tanya had led him out of Moscow and, eventually, Russia.

He owed her a lot, and it had incensed him when in the hands of the Family—in those days, of course, there was no Red Station—they had taken her away from him and, in a lightless cell, had begun on her what the KGB had worked on him. He soon put a stop to that, risking his own termination in the process. But that was only his first stumbling step to reclaiming a life that he thought had been cut away from him as surely and as professionally as a surgeon takes a scalpel to flesh.

Because of his incarceration, he was himself suspect at first. But when he delivered Mikhail's information to them they saw reason and no longer suspected him of having been turned. He never let them know, however, that the information had come from Tanya long after Mikhail had died in the bloody Moscow fusillade, torn in frozen chunks from her throat during the long, bitter nights in hiding, so near the encroaching death drawing in all around them. He had had little strength after his ordeal and she had done his fighting for him, rising silently up out of their hiding places in cave or fen to cut down any soldier who strayed too close, a blood-drenched spectral figure returning to him after each lethal foray to lead him onward toward freedom. She was strong and she was hard and she had saved him many times, repaying him for taking her out of Lubyanka with him. And, he had quickly learned, her mind was as quick and powerful as was her body. Her memory had been the repository for all of Mikhail's secrets, he being far too intelligent to commit anything so explosive to paper.

When, three years before, Minck, rising rapidly in the Family, had proposed the creation of the Red Station to deal with all the Russias, their satellites, and their global dealings, he was granted eighteen months in which to deliver what his presentation promised. It had only taken him eighteen weeks, and from then on a burgeoning slice of the Family's annual budget was assured. He negotiated for his section much as a good attorney for a star baseball player will negotiate with a club president. His contract was airtight. If he continued to deliver. And Minck made certain of that.

130

But it was not really of budgets, Tanya, or even the Family that Minck was thinking now. He had sunk deep into an odd kind of reverie that, increasingly, had become his habit over the past several months.

In fact he was wondering how a highly intelligent, well-trained operations officer named Carroll Gordon Minck could find himself in such dire straits.

It was somewhat of a shock to him, because after his nightmare ordeal in Lubyanka he never thought he would feel this way again. In those bleak, bloodfilled days, the memory of Kathy was all that he had allowed himself to dwell on. Anything to do with the Family was strictly no go since at any given moment he could be dragged from his steel cot and shot full of God only knew what new blend of chemicals—psychedelics and neutral stimulators— so that he would be transported and talking before he knew that he had opened his mouth.

The Russians were at last as intimate with Kathy as he had ever been. But they knew no more about the Family than they had the day the snow had worked against him and they had pulled him in. *"Gde bumagie! Kak vass zavoot!"*

When he returned to America, his relationship with Kathy was irreparably damaged. He had shared their most intimate moments with too many people for whom he felt only fear and loathing. It was as if he had sat down to discuss his sex life with the man who had just raped his wife. There had been a silent explosion in his head. He did not love Kathy any less on his return from his own private hell, but he found that he could not touch her without being torn out of time and place back to the dank, fearful cell deep within Moscow. That his mind would not allow, so they remained apart to the night she was killed. And of course by that time he had convinced himself that they had stripped him of his capacity to savor sexual release.

Then this whole godawful mess had begun. But still it was beyond him to understand how he had gotten from there to here, hopelessly in love with a woman whom he should not—*could* not—love. Was it only two weeks ago that he had clandestinely flown down to see her for the weekend? Oh, Christ, but it felt like two years. He stared blindly down at his hands and had to laugh at himself. Needed to do that lest he slit his wrists in utter frustration. What an idiot he was! And yet he could no more stop loving her than he could cease to hate the Russians. What elation filled him when he thought of the gift she had brought him—a simple enough pleasure, but one that he had been certain would never be his again. How could he possibly give that up?

And how he longed to confide in Tanya. He could whisper the secrets of the world into her ear without a qualm . . . but not his. No. This he could not allow her to know.

Because it was a clear sign of weakness in him. Then she would look into his eyes with that stern, Slavic gaze too serious to dismiss and tell him what he ought to do. And Minck knew what he ought to do; knew that he should have done it months ago. The woman he loved had to die, *had* to, for the sake of security. Every day she remained alive, a potentially damaging leak was walking around.

How many times during these past few months had he picked up the phone and begun to dial the coded mobile number? And how many times had the termination order died in his throat, leaving him with the acrid taste of ashes in his mouth. He could not do it. And yet he knew that he must.

"—in here."

His head came up. "I'm sorry; I was—"

"Lost in thought," Tanya said. "Yes, I could see." Her eyes, Mikhail's eyes, held his steadily. "I think it's time for the pool."

He nodded, sighing. She was fond of saying that giving the body a good workout did the same for the mind.

Tanya switched on ARRTS, the Active/Retrieval/Realtime/ System, an advanced network that the Family had had installed for Red Station at the behest of its director. The system would now monitor all incoming and outgoing communication. In this mode it had been programmed by Minck to deal with the first three nominal levels of data on its own. For levels four through seven, it would hold before contacting Minck, wherever he was, for instructions on how to proceed.

They took the lead-lined elevator up three floors to the rec level, passing through two distinct modes of electronic security checks. Stripped down, Minck had a hard, lean body that looked at least ten years younger than it was. It seemed a perfectly normal body until one came close, and then one began to see details forming, the hard rills and scars, the patches of dead white skin, hairless and glossy. Lubyanka had been hard on him.

He hit the water in a quick flat-arced dive, the surface barely rippling at his smooth entrance. In a moment Tanya followed him into the Olympic-size pool. Both wore brief nylon suits. At these, and perhaps other times as well, Minck found himself admiring her lithe, muscular body. He so constantly relied on her steel-trap mind, her unerring cunning at trapping the Russians at their own game, that these infrequent moments always struck him anew like revelations from out of the blue. She had the wide shoulders and narrowish hips of the dedicated female athlete, but there was nothing masculine about her. Just powerful. And Minck never made the typical man's mistake of equating the two.

They kicked full out for ten continuous laps up and back the long pool, using each other's speed and stamina to spur themselves on.

Eventually Tanya won, as she always did, but by less of a margin than she had several months ago.

"Close," he said, between breaths. He wiped the water off his face. "Very damn close."

Tanya smiled. "You've been training harder than I have. I'll have to remember that in future."

Reaching upward, he pulled himself to a sitting position on the tile rim of the pool. Water scrolled off him, and his dark hair was plastered down across his forehead, giving him the look of a Roman senator. His clear gray eyes were unnaturally large in his face. He had recently shaved off his thick handlebar mustache and as a result looked astonishingly boyish for his forty-seven years.

Tanya, still treading water, waited patiently for him to begin. He had had a dour expression on his face ever since he had had the conversation with Dr. Kidd in New York. She had not been privy to the dialog and Minck had been particularly unforthcoming about it. She just hoped that was the only thing weighing on his mind now.

He was a man to whom, in far different circumstances, she could find herself intensely attracted. He had that quality she most admired in people: the expression of intellectualism through his physicality.

"It's this goddamned Nicholas Linnear," Minck was saying now with his characteristic abruptness. "I think we're going to have to deal with him sooner than later."

Now she knew how the conversation with Dr. Kidd had gone, but she said nothing of that.

Minck's gray eyes leveled on her. "I don't for a moment think I'm going to like the bastard; he's too damn independent for his own good. And of course he's monstrously dangerous."

"I've read the file," she said, pulling herself up beside him. "He'd never even contemplate aggression."

"Oh, no," Minck agreed. "Absolutely not. And that's our key to him. He's a naif on our territory. We must therefore make quite certain he stays in our bailiwick so that we can reel him in when he's given us everything we want."

He ran his hands down his nearly hairless thighs. "Because

should he be allowed to return to his own turf, then God help us. We'll lose him, the Russians, and the whole ball of wax."

"Hello?"

"Nick. Nick, where have you been? I've been trying to reach you all day!"

Mumbled something into the receiver. His eyes seemed glued shut.

"Nick?"

Images enwrapped him. He had been dreaming of Yukio. A marriage ceremony before the tomb of the Tokugawa, a black kite wheeling in the sky, gray plovers darting for cover. Yukio in her white kimono with the crimson edging, the two of them facing a Buddhist priest. Low chanting filling the boughs of the pines like snow.

"Nick, are you there?"

Taking her hand, the chanting growing, loudening, her head turning, the shock of a yellowed, drowned skull. Recoiling, stumbling backward, then seeing that it was Akiko . . . Akiko or Yukio. Which one? *Which one?*

"Sorry, Justine. Sato's marriage was yesterday. The reception went on until—"

"Never mind that," she said. "I've got fantastic news." It was only now that he heard the note of excitement like a line of tension feathering her voice.

"What is it?"

"I spoke to Rick Millar the day you left. Remember he'd been romancing me for that dream job? Well I took it! I was so excited I started Friday!"

Nicholas ran a hand through his hair. It was barely light out, dawn was not far away. Still he seemed enmeshed in the events of yesterday much as if a new day were not dawning; he seemed somehow trapped back at that heartstopping moment when Akiko had slowly lowered her fan. That face! He felt haunted, an outcast from time, doomed to relive that terrible moment over and over . . . until he found the answer.

"Nick, have you heard anything I've said?" There was an edge to her voice now, all the elation punctured out.

"I thought you wanted to work for yourself, Justine," he said, his mind still far away. "I can't see why you'd want to tie yourself—"

"Oh, Christ, Nick!" Her voice, sharpened by anger, broke in on him. It was all abruptly too much for her: his taking that loathsome job, his being so far away from her, her fearful lone-

134

liness through the long nights while the deathless ghost of Saigō returned to hover over her, and now his inattention, mirroring her father's self-absorption when she needed him the most. And, oh, she needed Nicholas' support now! "Congratulations. That's what you're supposed to say. I'm happy for you, Justine. Is that so hard to say?"

"Well, I *am* glad, but I thought—"

"Jesus, Nick." It exploded inside her like a burst dam. "Go to hell, will you?"

Nothing at the other end but dead space, and when he tried to dial her number it was busy. Just as well, he thought sadly, slowly. I'm not in much condition to make a success of apologizing.

He lay back in bed, naked on top of the covers, and wondered in how many ways his memories were betraying him.

Miss Yoshida's discreet knock on his hotel room door came at precisely nine A.M. She was right on time.

"Good morning, Linnear-san," she said. "Are you ready to go?"

"*Hai*. But I confess I haven't had time to purchase—"

Her arm came around from behind her back, producing a long, wrapped package. "I took the liberty of bringing you joss sticks. I hope you will not be offended."

"On the contrary," he said. "I'm delighted. *Domo arigato*, Yoshida-san."

It was Sunday. Greydon was up in Misawa visiting his son and Tomkin was in bed trying to shake the fever his flu was gifting him with. Now there was time for family obligations.

In the smoked-glass-windowed limousine, heading out of the city, Nicholas saw that she had changed her makeup. She could have passed for twenty, and he realized that he had no clear idea of her age.

She was very quiet, almost withdrawn. She sat on the other side of the backseat, deliberately leaving a space between them that might as well have been a wall.

Several times Nicholas was about to say something, then seeing the look of concentration on her face, thought better of it. At last Miss Yoshida settled her shoulders and turned to him. Her eyes were very large. She had chosen to wear traditional Japanese attire, and somehow the formal kimono, *obi*, and *geta* served to further transform her, peeling back the years.

"Linnear-san," she began, then, apparently overcome, closed her mouth. He saw her take a deep breath, as if screwing up her courage, in preparation to begin again.

135

"Linnear-san, please forgive what I am about to say, but it is disturbing to me that you use *anata* when you speak to me. I entreat you to use what is proper, *omae*."

Nicholas considered this. What she meant was that no matter how far the emancipation of women had come in Japan—and there was certainly a good degree of lip service, at least, paid to this concession to the changing ways of the modern world—women and men still used different forms when speaking. In effect, men ordered when they spoke, women pleaded.

Anata and *omae* meant the same thing, *you*. Men used *omae* when speaking to those on their level or below. Naturally women fell into that category. Women always used *anata*, the more polite form, when speaking to men. If they were ever allowed to use the less polite form it was invariably the *omae-san* version.

And no matter what anyone said, Nicholas knew, this divergence engendered in women a certain subservient way of thinking.

"It would make me happy, Yoshida-san," he said now, "if we were to both use the same form. Can you deny that you as well as I deserve the same politeness in conversation?"

Miss Yoshida's head was down, her liquid eyes in her lap. The only outward sign of her agitation was the constant twisting of her fingers.

"I beg you, Linnear-san, to reconsider. If you ask this of me I cannot of course refuse. But consider the ramifications. How could I ever explain such an egregious social breach to Sato-san."

"This isn't the feudal past, Yoshida-san," Nicholas said as gently as he could. "Surely Sato-san is enlightened enough to understand."

Her head came up and he saw the tiny sparks that might have been incipient tears at the outside edges of her eyes. "When I joined Sato Petrochemicals, Linnear-san, I was the Office Lady. That was my title, no matter my functions. One of the requirements for Office Lady was that I possess *yoshitanrei*."

"A beautiful appearance? But that was ten years ago. These days I cannot imagine that the same holds true."

"As you say, Linnear-san," she said softly, bobbing her head in obvious acquiescence. She could not have made her point more forcefully.

"All right," Nicholas said, after a time. "We'll settle on a compromise. The *anata* form will just be between us, when we are alone together. No one need hear this blasphemy but us."

A small smile curled at Miss Yoshida's lips and her head bobbed again. "*Hai*. I accept."

After a time, her head turned away, her gaze stretching out to encompass the dimly flowing countryside beyond them. "You are very kind." Her whispered voice was very soft.

Miss Yoshida was a barely seen stick figure in the misty distance.

Nicholas turned and confronted the gravestones of his parents. So many memories, so many terrible deaths. The quick, hard jerk of his mother's shoulders then the short *seppuku* sword did its work. And Itami, Cheong's sister-in-law, dutifully wielding the *katana* that would end his mother's pain forever.

"She was a child of honor," Itami had told him.

Nicholas knelt and began to light the joss sticks, but no prayer came to his mind. He thought he would remember it all against his will and for no discernable purpose. Instead, he was overwhelmed by another set of memories.

As a teenager he walked the steep forested hillside of Yoshino, beloved of all the Tenshin Shoden Katori *ruy's jonin*. There was, he had come to understand, a mystical connection between this land and the men of arcane profession who had made it their home.

Blue mist drifted off the cypress and cryptomeria like veils, the colors of dawn shading in pastels of green, blue, pink, and white like chrysanthemum blossoms dissolving in the distance. A sharp-eyed thrush followed them in intervals, the white blobs on its wingtips flashing now and again like the swift opening and closing of a fan as it flitted from tree to tree, twittering at them.

Nicholas and Akutagawa-san strode side by side, the one in the simple black *gi* of the student, the other the pearlescent gray cotton kimono edged in earth brown of the *jonin sensei*. At their backs, the stone walls and green tiled roofs of the Tenshin Shoden Katori *ryu* sprang into light as the slowly rising sun broke the plane of the horizon.

Oblique strokes of new sunlight broke through the branches, picking out pinecones and brown needles with the delicacy of a master's brushstroke.

Akutagawa-san was still in shadow when he said, "The mistake we all make before we enter here is the notion of civilization. History, ethics, the very concept of law itself depend for their existence on this one crucial underpinning."

Akutagawa-san's long, melancholy face with its wide lips, rather sharp nose, and Mandarinesque eyes, was even more serious than usual. Among the students—who, in the tradition of students the world over, had created nicknames for their *sensei* in order to regain at least a semblance of the control that the *ryu* took from

137

them—he was known as "the smileless man." Perhaps it was not so unusual then for these two to have recognized in one another an aspect of themselves and be thus drawn together.

Both in their own way were outcasts in a *ryu* of outcasts, for the legend of the ninja had it that they had evolved from the *hinin*, the basest level of Japanese society. And, as in many levels of Japanese society, legend often became history. Whether or not those origins were true now seemed irrelevant, since existing ninja had taken that legend and turned it to their advantage, using it to further their mystique among people already steeped in mysticism.

Akutagawa-san was half Chinese, it was rumored among the boys, the initiates always curious about why he was allowed to be a part of such a secret society within a society. Their question was answered when they found out the origins of *aka-i-ninjutsu* were to be found in China.

"The fact is," Nicholas remembered Akutagawa-san saying, emerging into the light, "there is no such thing as civilization. It is a concept the Chinese confected—or, if you prefer the Western mode, the Greeks—simply in order to give a certain moral credence to their attempts at dominion over the other peoples of the world."

Nicholas shook his head. "I don't understand. What about all the minute aspects of Japanese life that set us apart from everyone else: the complexity of the tea ceremony, the arts of *ukiyo-e*, *ikebana, haiku,* the concepts of honor, filial duty, *bushido, giri.* All the things we are."

Akutagawa-san looked in that young open face and sighed. He had had a son once who had died in Manchuria at the hands of the Russians. Every year he made a pilgrimage to China to be closer. To what or to whom he had never been sure. But now he thought he knew.

"What you speak of, Nicholas . . . all these things are an accretion of a *culture*. They have no relation to the word *civilization* save what today's conditioning superimposes on them."

They moved out along the hillside, the thrush keeping a stuttering pace, expecting perhaps that his breakfast might be strewn in the wake of these mighty shadows.

"If a society were truly civilized," Akutagawa-san continued, "there would be no need for the *samurai*; and it would surely not abide warriors such as we. There would simply be no need, do you see? But the concept of civilization is like that of Communism. Pure in the mind, it nevertheless cannot exist in reality. It is too absolute a concept for man. Like the theory of relativity it is best thought of, food for contemplation, for a *civilized* man would

138

harbor no warlike tendencies. He would not spy on another, he would not be an adulterer, a slanderer, a destroyer."

Akutagawa-san put his hand on Nicholas' arm to stop him. Together they stared out at the partially hidden valley, the tops of trees protruding through the sinuously winding mist like the stones on a *Go* board.

"For most people, Nicholas, this is what life consists of: the clear and the hidden, the knowable and the arcane. But for us here, it is different. When we set the concept of civilization aside, we free ourselves.

"And in plunging into the mist, we learn to ride the wind, to walk on water, to hide where there is no hiding place, to see where there is no light and hear when our ears are bound. You will learn that one breath may sustain you for hours, and you will learn how to deal with your enemies.

"None of this is to be taken lightly. You understand this, I know. Yet it must be repeated. For with the knowledge of how to take life comes the responsibility of a god. Control is the essence of it all. Without it there is only chaos, and given a chance, that kind of malignant anarchy will voraciously engulf our culture . . . all culture."

Nicholas was silent, his body still and attuned in his attempt to understand all that Akutagawa-san was saying. Much of it seemed beyond his ken for the moment, larger than life and thus unknowable. But he stored it all in his memory, understanding that if he showed patience all would be made clear to him.

Akutagawa-san stared out at the ancient countryside, inhaling its sharp, clean odors as if they were the mingled perfumes of the country's most accomplished courtesans.

"What you must understand now—now before it is too late, while you still have time to make the decision—is that *aka-i-ninjutsu* is just one form of an entire discipline. And as in all such disciplines, there are the negative aspects." His head turned and his black stone eyes gripped Nicholas'. "In donning our mantle you may also become a target for these negative . . . forces.

"One of the reasons I am here is that I am *sennin* in a number of these. Have you heard of *Kuji-kiri*, the nine-hands cutting?"

Nicholas might have stopped breathing. *Kuji-kiri* was the discipline with which Saigō had defeated him in Kumamoto the year before, defiling him and taking Yukio away from him, then disappearing with her as if the two of them had never existed.

His lips were dry and he had to try twice before he could articulate it successfully. "Yes." It was a harsh sibilant whisper. "I have . . . heard of it."

Akutagawa-san nodded. He was careful not to look directly at Nicholas and thus be exposed to the inner struggle of emotions, causing his student loss of face.

"Fukashigi-san suspected as much. He believes you may need this, er, unorthodox training in order to survive. And survival is what is taught here at the Tenshin Shoden Katori *ryu*."

Akutagawa-san's head turned, hawklike, and his obsidian eyes struck Nicholas with the force of a physical contact. It was not a blow as such, but the electricity of the force behind it caused all of Nicholas' muscles to tense, the reflex of a more primitive and physically aware creature.

Oddly, his mind was at peace, perfectly clear for the first time since he had returned from his journey across the Straits of Shimonoseki, his river Styx, to seek out Saigō in the underworld of *Kan-aku na ninjutsu*.

Akutagawa-san smiled slightly. "There are many Chinese origins here. But you know the Japanese. Everything must be altered, refined to fit their own cultured sensibilities." This would be the only time that the *sennin* would ever speak this way to Nicholas or to anyone, a sign that he recognized their kinship: their mixed heritage.

"You now know the dangers, the risks. Fukashigi-san was quite adamant about giving you these caveats."

"And you were not," Nicholas said, responding to an ephemeral shading in the *sennin*'s tone.

"Do not think that I am not careful. Fukashigi-san and I think alike in many aspects. However, I did not believe you required these warnings."

"You were correct." Nicholas took a deep breath. "I want you to teach me, *sensei*. I am not frightened of the *Kuji-kiri*."

"No," Akutagawa-san said almost sadly, "but in time you will learn to be." He reached out and took Nicholas' hand. "Now come." His voice altered. "Let darkness and death be your middle names forevermore."

They went off the hillside. Soon the mist had swallowed them completely.

The monsters had needed designations. They were never with Alix Logan at the same time but rather spelled each other in twelve-hour shifts. The beefy one was on duty during the days and Bristol thought of him as Red. The other one, the thin, wiry, nocturnal monster with the long neck and beak of a nose, he dubbed Blue.

The first question he had asked himself when he had come upon them was: had they been in the car?

It had been many months since that dark night filled with rain and an evil wind that bent the high, thin palms of Key West almost to the ground. He had been doing forty-five on the highway when they came up on him very fast with their lights out.

He felt the fierce jolt forward, said, "What the hell!" to no one in particular and felt grateful for his seatbelt. They were close, and knowing that instinctively his eyes would move to his rearview mirror after the ram, they turned on their brights.

In that moment of utter dazzle, they moved in for the kill. He knew in that flash just how clever they were, knew also from his years of experience that there would not be time to regain control of the situation: he was not James Bond and this was no movie. So he did the only thing he could. He concentrated on his own survival.

In the brief instant before they struck again, he unlocked the driver's side door and opened it a crack. He unsnapped his seatbelt. He was no longer concerned with what they would do or how they would do it, he only knew that if he did not center all his concern on himself now, they would surely kill him.

When the second ram came, it was at just the right angle. They had hesitated long enough so that both cars were racing around a bend to the right. Beyond the low fence on the left, the land shot down in a sheer drop of perhaps seventy-five feet. The ground was not particularly hard. In fact, the recent rains had made a rather springy mat of it but there was very little purchase. It was a dangerous stretch, particularly in this storm, and every ten feet or so along the side of the road large signs dotted with ruby red reflector buttons flew by.

It was as if an enormous creature had taken a bite out of the car. The back end slewed right around and the wheel flew out of his hands. He let it go, working on keeping his equilibrium. Centrifugal force and the colliding momentums of the vehicles were working against him, and the darkness of the night only added to the sense of intense disorientation.

His hand flew to the partially open door and he had to will himself to stay put through the horrendous sounds of grinding and squealing metal, the frightening, out-of-control movement, and the sure knowledge that he was heading over the edge and down.

If he left the car before it went over, there'd be no point. The other car's headlights would pick him up and they'd run him over while he was helpless.

But now the front end of the car had slammed into the low railing, the shriek of more metal tearing, flinging itself upward, bursting apart, and he lurched forward, having to brace the heels of his hands against the padded dash, remembering to flex his elbows slightly to help cushion the force so that he wouldn't break his arms in half.

Then the nose of the car was thrusting upward, the seat springs rocking crazily. Rain sleeted in the partially open window drenching him, blinding him, and for that instant he felt a rising panic, afraid that they were going to succeed after all.

The car bucked forward as if kicked from behind, the front end lowering, the wheels spinning for purchase and finding none. He had long ago taken his foot off both the gas and the brake pedals. He left the car in gear, though it might have been better to throw it into neutral. He did not want to leave any traces of how he was going about saving himself, to feed to the investigators who would surely come and do their thorough job if the sea didn't claim his coffin.

He wanted to be dead.

Now he began to tumble, leaving behind the short verge beyond the slick road. He heard the tearing of clods of earth above the noise of the engine and the car's back wheels skidded sickeningly, slewing him again so that his shoulder slammed against the door post and he sucked in his breath. Another inch or so forward and he would have tumbled out the unlocked door on his head. All the way down, a broken neck and sightless eyes staring impotently up at the white, peering faces of his murderers.

None of that for him. He held on, and now there was only an eerie kind of silence, rushing in the aftermath of all the frenzy and sound. Wind whistled through the partially opened window and then the car took its first unsteady bump on the side of the sheer cliff. One side hit heavier than the other, and that started the oscillation. Soon, he knew, it would get so great—on the fourth or fifth landing perhaps—that the vehicle would flip over and then he would have no chance at all.

He could see nothing that would help him. He was in the tunnel of the night, a steel coffin, and he knew he must rely totally on sensation, the feeling in his stomach, his hands, his legs, his heart.

It was now or never.

He drew his legs up so that he was kneeling on the seat, so that there was no possibility that his feet would get caught in the well. Quickly now he moved onto his back, feet first toward the swinging door.

Out he went. Watched dizzily, detachedly, the shock and pain turning him into an unconcerned spectator, as the tumbling car hit the churning water hood first and sank into the deep without a trace.

Bristol did not think much about that night now except to speculate on who it was who'd tried to kill him. At first he was certain that it had been Frank, Raphael Tomkin's man. But that was before he had come upon the monsters. Now he was not so sure.

He had come down to Key West to find Alix Logan. Now that he had found that she was already covered, he wondered, Who were they, these monsters who never let her out of their sight? Were they working for Tomkin? Were they all part of the cover-up of Tomkin's murder of Angela Didion? There was no way Bristol could know that until he spoke to Alix Logan. Back in New York, Matty the Mouth had given him her name. Bristol had known there had been a witness to the murder and if he was going to nail Tomkin, he would have to find her. The contact had given him the name and the place for an unconscionably large amount of money. But it had been worth it. Now Bristol knew he was very close, and he had told Matty the Mouth to get out of town for a while. He owed the man that much.

Down in Key West, after his supposed death, after he had recovered from the fractured arm, he had set himself up on watch. He had plenty of idle time when he had nothing to do but wait. Movement or stillness. Dark and light. They were all that existed for him. And Alix Logan.

Staring at her often brought the thought of Gelda to mind but that was, of course, pointless. He could not contact her in any way. He must remain dead in order to stay buried near Alix Logan, undetected and unmolested. It was a difficult enough task to shadow someone; it was all but impossible to do it when someone was trying to ice you.

Bristol. How may times during those long, cramped hours of waiting had he worked the name around on his tongue. His real name had faded out, an image in an old and bleached photo album that was long ago and far away.

He had become "Tex" Bristol and that was how he thought of himself now, just as everyone around him who knew him did. There was only one person in the world who knew he had not died in the flaming car crash that night and she would never tell. He had had just enough money left to get him up to San Antonio. He had known Marie a long time ago in New York. They had been on opposite sides of the law then. Now, he was not so sure of where either of them stood.

But she was smart and tough and she knew everyone. She had provided him with medical service and the paraphernalia of his new identity: birth certificate, social security card, driver's license, even a passport, slightly worn, franked several times for Europe and Asia. He thought that a nice touch even though he didn't think he'd need it. He'd taken the passport anyway, along with thirty thousand in cash.

Marie had asked no questions and when he had offered no explanations she went on to other matters. She even seemed pleased to see him. Back in New York they had worked each other to a Mexican standoff; it had been the first time for each of them and they had learned from it. You could even say they liked each other, after a fashion.

When he left, Bristol knew that he owed her more than he could ever repay.

"Sir?"

The penetrating ebon eyes lifted up into the pale mauve light, and shadows skittered about the bare walls of the room like kittens chasing each other.

"What is it?" The voice was more than brusque; it contained within its guttural growl a definite tinge of disdain that caused the young lieutenant who had come into the room to feel somehow diminished, as if he were in the presence of a being more than human.

It was a calculated tone but no less effective for that. Artifice, thought the man now as he accepted the young lieutenant's presence, nodding him forward, ruled the world. A careful daily grooming of his voice kept things running smoothly at the safe house.

It was his experience that one could many times give the merest outline of fear and one's adversary—whether it be this young lieutenant eager for promotion or one of the old guard back home— supplied all the rest. It left one free to pursue more pressing matters.

"The latest printouts from Sakhov IV, sir," the young uniformed lieutenant said, handing over a sheaf of graph paper.

"And how many passes have we here, Lieutenant?" Viktor Protorov, head of the Ninth Directorate of the KGB, said.

"Just over a half dozen, sir."

"I see." Protorov's gaze lowered to the sheaf. He could feel the slight relaxing of the man in front of him. "And what, if anything, does this mass hold for me, Lieutenant?"

"I don't know, sir."

"Oh, come now." Protorov looked up. He tapped the sheet with a rather long nail. "A new batch of highly classified printouts from Sakhov IV, what our government publicly calls a 'digital imaging reconnaissance satellite," centering on that section of the Pacific Ocean between the Kuriles and where we are in the north of Hokkaido, an area we have been concentrating on for—how many months now?—"

"Seven since we moved from the aerodrome in Iturup."

"—comes in. If you haven't taken a good, hard look at these, Lieutenant, you're either stupid or incompetent." Protorov leaned back in his chair. "Tell me, are you either of these?"

For a moment the young man said nothing; he had begun to sweat beneath his superior's intense gaze and questioning. "You put me in a most untenable position, sir. If I say yes, then my career in the Directorate is finished. If I say no, then it is obvious that I have deliberately lied to my superior."

"Well, Lieutenant, if the day ever comes when you are captured by the Capitalist enemy, then you can be quite certain that they, too, will put you in an untenuous position."

They had been conversing in English. "Excuse me, sir," the young lieutenant said, "but that's 'untenable,' not 'untenuous.'"

"Answer the question," Protorov said, beginning to sift through the visual data provided by Sakhov IV's immensely powerful infrared video equipment. An involuntary chill went through him at the thought that the Americans might have such a potent weapon. He was only slightly cheered by the knowledge that his country's land-based antisatellite lasers could—and had in recent days past— bring down the threat.

He got to the third sheet. "Time's running out. It's a sure bet the Americans won't give you this long."

"You won't find what we've been looking for in those," the lieutenant said at last, as if with one long breath all the air had gone out of his lungs.

Protorov's gaze stripped him bare. "Then you *have* looked at these."

"Sir, security regulations require that the O.D. bring all Passionate documents to me first for verification."

"Passionate" was the rather ironic term Protorov had coined for highest-priority matter circulating within the Directorate. "Sneak peekies, you mean," Protorov grumbled. He lifted a hand. "All right. I hope you do as well with the Americans if your day ever comes."

"I am more frightened of you than of the Americans, sir."

"Then learn to be frightened of them, Lieutenant." His gaze lifted again. "Because they mean to destroy everything you and I hold dear." But he was pleased with the young man; he had seen the only way out of the trap Protorov had set for him. He had even caught Protorov's deliberate usage error.

Once the young man had left, he pored over the computer-generated satellite photos again.

But by the end of his second pass, he had been forced to admit defeat. There was no anomaly of any kind. Again. He did not know of course precisely what he was looking for, only had knowledge of its name: *Tenchi*. It was the Japanese word for "heaven and earth."

Where are you? he thought now, staring impotently at the detailed pictures covering the graphs before him. *What* are you? And why are you so important to the Japanese?

.*Tenchi* had begun as just another routine report crossing his desk back in Moscow. Yet it had tantalized him, and once he had come out here and had immersed himself in the well of rumor, alleged fact, and outrageous fiction, he had found himself totally hooked. Until at this point he was obsessed with finding the answer. From what he had gleaned he was convinced *Tenchi*—even the knowledge of it—would give him the last of the leverage he needed for the coup back home.

How bitter it was to learn that Fedorin—one of the KGB's own—was no better than all the rest of the career diplomats who had populated the Kremlin before him. Oh yes, at first he had seemed to be getting the sluggish leviathan that was Soviet Russia working again. Movement here and there could be discerned.

But in the end it had all been a sham, a self-serving political maneuver whose scope could not long conceal its sole purpose: to rid the Communist hierarchy of all those who might oppose the new premier.

But of course Protorov had held out no real hope that Fedorin—or anyone else in power for that matter—would grasp the one true key to awakening the USSR, the essential nature of the beast: and that was that Russia was not one country but an uneasy amalgam of many different Russias, all fiercely protective of their own part of the mother country. What did an Uzbek or a Kirghiz give a fig what was happening in Moscow anyway? Did a Belorussian or an Azerbaidzhani care how many missiles America had leveled at Vladivostok? And the Lithuanians, Estonians, Georgians—not to mention the non-Slavs such as the Tatars, Bashkirs, Mordvinians, Udmurts, or Komi—did they feel any differently? What was there to bind them together?

Protorov knew the answer to that one. Nothing.

The first step to putting Soviet Russia on the move lay in uniting all its divergent people. Because once that happened, the USSR

146

would be unstoppable. No nation on earth—no coalition of nations—could stop her.

Fedorin had had a chance to get the new revolution underway. But he, like all the bureaucrats who ran the country, lacked the scope of vision necessary to make that one great leap, to cross the Rubicon into dangerous and unknown waters. Thus he had allowed the slothful giant to lapse back into somnolence.

Protorov knew only too well how long a time it could be between Soviet premiers. He was unwilling to wait his turn—or perhaps he was intelligent enough to understand that it might never come on its own. Therefore he had begun his own plans for cutting short the current premier's term in office.

And now he believed that *Tenchi* was the wand of power he needed to persuade the cabal of militant generals and officers in the KGB to exert their influence at once.

A point of ignition had to be reached, Protorov knew. He must be the bridge between the traditionally feuding KGB and GRU. To that end he had spent more than six years cultivating a young GRU colonel. Powerful and ambitious, Yvgeny Mironenko would soon be in a position to also be a bridge between the factions.

For only by uniting these two mailed fists outside the Kremlin could Protorov be certain of the success of his coup. Without them, he was lost. And without him, Russia was lost. He lacked only the one element of power that would bring all of them into his palm.

And that one element was *Tenchi*.

The intercom buzzed on his desk like an angry insect, and for a moment Protorov's attention was deflected. He reached out one long finger. "Yes?"

"The subject is ready."

"Good. Bring him in." He reached out and extinguished the mauve light, plunging the room into utter darkness. There were no windows here and only one egress, its fifteen-inch steel door.

Protorov sat back in his chair and fought the urge to smoke. He compromised his restless hands by lacing his fingers. Presently he heard movement. The thick door sighed open pneumatically as three men crossed the threshold.

For just a moment the heavy light of the hallway streamed across the black rubberized flooring, then as the door swung shut, darkness swallowed the floating ribbons.

Without sight Protorov knew who had entered: the young lieutenant, the doctor, and the subject. Protorov and the doctor, who was a neuropharmacologica expert, had been at work on the subject for almost three days now. The American was a very stubborn

147

man, Protorov had to give him that. He had not broken and, frankly, Protorov did not expect him to. He expected him to die.

In a way Protorov felt sorry for the man as he heard the semi-articulate babbling created by the multitude of sera the doctor had shot into the subject. This was not the way for a modern-day warrior to go, captured by the enemy, forcibly ejected into rapid-paced day-night continua so that weeks became compressed into hours until a state of body vertigo was induced. According to the prevalent theory, the body would do their work for them, breaking down the mind blockages through its own induced trauma.

Protorov believed none of it. These days there were ways to stop a ferret from talking when he did not want to: hypnosis, electronic implants. And if all else failed, he could self-destruct.

Sadness overwhelmed Protorov as the increasingly animated animal noises invaded his ears. This was not the way it should end for any of them. Better by far the fierce hand-to-hand struggle, the rising anima, the primal urges that came in the struggle to avoid death at all costs.

Protorov's mind raced back to the first time he had felt the cold. "To feel the cold" was the KGB wet—meaning active in the field—directorates' phrase for the kill. The first time for Protorov was indelibly etched into a corner of his mind. He had been a raw lieutenant then, well trained from the KGB complex outside Sevastopol. He thought he was a crackerjack, a world-beater. He had not reckoned on the field, which cut all men down to size.

They had sent him to Siberia. A top-secret series of experiments attempting to tap the perpetual gale-force winds in the north had been infiltrated by the Americans.

In Verkhoyansk, the coldest place in the world, he had ferreted out the infiltrator, made him bolt from his hole, and one after the other they had raced across the frozen tundra onto the ice fields. Two utter madmen.

Only the cold could win in Verkhoyansk. Man was nothing, a tiny mote in nature's vast well of snow and ice. The snow. The snow. Always and forever the snow. It was blinding, chilling, numbing. It was death.

But all Protorov could think of was his first assignment. Oh, but he did not understand the meaning. Not at all. Singlemindedly he pursued his quarry, seeking to feel the cold.

Together they tumbled to the ice, skidding and sliding, froths of loose snow fountaining upward as they collided. Stupidly Protorov had decided on a gun with a silencer. But long since the elements, laughing, had frozen all the carefully oiled working parts. Similarly, his knife would not unfold. There was nothing left but his hands.

For almost half an hour they grappled indecisively in the ice and snow. The bulky clothes made hand-to-hand combat clumsy and difficult. Meanwhile the frost was sapping their energies and, later, Protorov would come to understand that it was only his stamina that had allowed him to prevail. He had not been smarter or stronger or quicker, all the things he had been taught to believe he was. Those were lies. He had just outlasted the American.

What little satisfaction he had found in grinding the dark, foreign head into the blood-pink snow while the breath slowed and, at last, stilled, stemmed from the knowledge that he, Protorov, was still alive, chest heaving, mouth dry, pulse thundering, and the bile rushing upward into his throat, bitter and searingly acidic.

All at once his extremities began to shake uncontrollably and all warmth left him. He stared down at the humped thing he straddled and thought, wonderingly, This was once a human being. An enemy of the State, they had told him. Yes, he reiterated, an enemy. An enemy.

". . . time that's left."

With a start that no one could see, Protorov came out of his memories. "What's that?" His voice was sharp, making certain the doctor understood that it was his fault Protorov had not heard what he had said.

"We've used up all the time that's left, Comrade."

"Do we have anything?" Protorov wanted to know. "Anything at all?"

"The tape machines have every word," the doctor said and Protorov thought, I have your number, Comrade.

"There is one positive element."

Protorov turned his attention to the young lieutenant, seeing something of himself in the younger man.

"We now know that the Americans are no closer to *Tenchi* than we are. In fact, I would venture a guess that we have more penetration at this moment."

Protorov considered this. The lieutenant was, of course, correct. But Protorov also knew that there was a second positive element to this, and that was the subject himself. Or, more accurately, who the subject belonged to.

"All right," Protorov said in his dismissive tone, "wrap up the corpse and deliver him back to his kennel on Honshū. I want the Americans made aware of their error immediately."

When he was again alone in the odd windowless room, he

turned on the powerful fans to rid the space of the cloying after-scents of drugs and death. Then he lit up.

Switching on his lamp, he once more pored over the readouts from Sakhov IV. He was closer to *Tenchi* now than he ever had been. He could feel it. His eyes roved the folded sheets. Was it already here? Why couldn't he see it then?

With a deep growl of disgust, he swept the useless sheaf into the hopper beside his desk and turned the shredder to autofeed. The deep whine of scissoring steel teeth filled the air.

Thoughts of feeling the cold and the grisly package that would soon be delivered to the enemy's doorstep led to his concern over Sakhov IV. Even with all its ultrasophisticated equipment, he had found it to be a dismal failure. But then again, it was only a machine; it could only do what men had programmed it to do. Nothing more. Or perhaps there had been a malfunction some-where within the miles of multimillion-dollar circuitry.

No matter. Protorov had his own human satellite, and it was still functioning perfectly.

"Now," Akutagawa-san said from out of the mist, from out of Nicholas' memory, "we will begin."

"But how," Nicholas said. "I can see nothing."

"Did you never in Kansatsu's *ryu* train with the blindfold?"

"Of course. But that was within the boundaries of the *dōjō*. The space was precise and uncluttered with trees, stones, and underbrush the configurations of which I am unfamiliar with."

"This vapor," Akutagawa-san continued as if Nicholas had not spoken, "is like the darkness but far more difficult to negotiate. In the darkness you may be guided by albescence, a sliver of moon, the patch of a household lantern, even the glitter of the stars. But here there is nothing but the mist."

"I cannot even see you."

"But you can hear me."

"Yes. Quite well. You sound as if you are in my left ear but I shall discount the peculiar acoustics."

"Never discount acoustics," Akutagawa-san said. "Rather strive to understand them so that they will become another weapon in your arsenal."

Nicholas said nothing, but tried to concentrate on gaining his bearings in the valley in Yoshino. Finally he decided that were it not for the *jonin*'s comforting presence he would be totally lost.

"You have heard, I imagine, that much of the *Kuji-kiri* derives its power from *jahō*, magic. Tell me, Nicholas, do you believe in 'magic'?"

"I believe in what is, *sensei*, and discount what is not."

For a time there was silence. "That is a very wise answer from such a young man. Now I want you to listen to me closely. There is, in all people, a layer—a middle layer of being—that lies between the conscious and the subconscious. It is a land where the imagination reigns. It is where daydreams originate, where quick, overblown fears are created. It is where day-to-day anxiety is manufactured.

"It is not magic, nor is it an extrasensory layer. Rather, its origins are quite primitive. Our early ancestors required the active assistance of this layer to heighten their perceptions in order for them to survive: against wild animals, marauding bands of other primitive men who sought their women or the shelter of their home caves.

"Oh, yes, caves. That is how far back in time I speak of now. But with the coming of so-called civilization this middle layer's reason for existence slowly atrophied. With houses and apartments locked and bolted, with man's utter dominance over all other life forms on the planet, what use was this layer?

"And yet it refused to die out. Instead it became the creator of small fears: anxieties at work, fear of dismissal, fear of rejection in love, petty jealousies regarding other workers, all blown up out of proportion, meant to keep the organism alert and functioning at peak efficiency for its survival. And yet survival is no longer the issue from day to day. Rather it is betterment. And so the supposed sharpness turns to anxiety, the modern ailment.

"Now I reiterate to you, Nicholas-san, that there is nothing mystic about this layer. It is not meditation. We are not now speaking of the province of the holy man, for you and I are certainly not that. We are both men of the world and have not the time nor the inclination to give up the plethora of worldly appetites the holy man must divest himself of in order to reach these exalted states.

"*Getsumei no michi*, the moonlit path, is open to you now, Nicholas. You must find it and learn to sink into it. I cannot help you in this other than by alerting you to its existence, but it may be of some help to daydream and then follow that daydream home."

"How will I know *getsumei no michi, sensei*?"

"By two things. One is that you will feel all sensation gained in weight and resonance."

"Do you mean that I will hear better?"

"Yes, but only in a certain way. Do not confuse weight with amplification. You will not, as you say, hear any better. You will

151

hear *differently*. The second sensation will be the awareness of light even when there is none in your immediate surroundings."

"Forgive me, *sensei*, but I do not understand that."

"It is not necessary to understand, Nicholas. Merely to remember."

At the last Akutagawa-san's voice had begun to fade, and now Nicholas feared that he was all alone on the lower slope of the hillside. He was a long way from the *ryu* and the mist had damped his usually reliable directional facilities.

He felt the first hard pangs of panic welling up in his chest. He found he had an overpowering urge to cry out to Akutagawa-san but the acute loss of face involved not only for him but, even more importantly, for Kansatsu, his former *sensei* who had guided him here, made him bite his lip instead.

Through the fluttering of his heart he recalled Akutagawa-san's one bit of advice: to take a daydream and ride it home. He sat down on the damp ground in the lotus position and closed his eyes. He struggled to control his breathing, the intense pounding of his blood in his veins. His hands lay open, palms up on his bent knees.

He opened his mind to the first image that swam to the surface. Yukio. Instinctively he clamped down on the image and he thought, No, it's still too painful, I don't want to think about her loss, try something else.

But nothing else would come. Yukio was who he wanted to daydream about, and with a great effort he willed himself to relax and think about her.

Cascade of night-black hair, those heavy-lidded eyes so full of sexual promise. He recalled their first meeting at the military dance, her firm, warm thigh pressed against his leg and then, astoundingly, the erotic feel of her mound rubbing against his crotch, her eyes sparkling with mischief as they danced amid the spinning couples.

He remembered the shower he had taken, the sinewy shadow appearing beyond the glass door, its abrupt opening and Yukio standing beside him, nude. Droplets of water beading along her cool flank, the jut of one dark-nippled breast. His startled sound as she moved against him. The warm friction, the silken embrace, the peach taste of her mouth, the hot swipe of her tongue. And the heated, liquid union, the long ecstatic slide, the engulfment while the silvery sheen of the water spattered their shoulders and necks in a cascade of . . .

Light!

His head came up and his eyes opened. And abruptly he saw

Akutagawa-san standing to the side of him, silent, observing. Nicholas felt a peculiar heaviness in his chest, an oddly sexual feeling. He felt as if he had descended into a depression from which he had the perfect vantage point on the world. He was aware of more even while he saw less in the conventional sense.

He moved his head. Was he actually *seeing* Akutagawa-san or sensing him? He opened his mouth and voiced the question.

"I have no answer to that, Nicholas, save to say that it does not matter. *Getsumei no michi* is there and we use it. But I will tell you this quite important aspect of it. It is body sense rather than ego. It is only your non-Oriental side that seeks an understanding. Your Oriental side allowed you to let go of your ego, something no Westerner could ever do because he is too afraid. He fears a letting go because in the primitive mind it is eternally linked to death. Westerners, as we are aware, seek to understand death because they fear it so. They cannot accept as we do; they have no concept of *karma*, nor can they see what is most apparent to us, that death is part of life."

Akutagawa-san began to move, and as he did so it was Nicholas' impression that his *geta*'d feet did not touch the earth. "Now that you have found the moonlit path, it is time to use the energy there to conjure up the first superficial stages of the *Kuji-kiri*. This alone will take many months and at first it will be bad for you, for here we will manufacture pure terror and before you can inure yourself to its manifestations you must succumb. Nightmares will haunt your sleep as they will your waking hours. You will become sunken-eyed and even at the lowest ebb may wish to commit *seppuku*."

"You do not frighten me, *sensei*."

Akutagawa-san's grim visage did not lighten. "That is good. Now remember well what you have said as we begin our descent into the maelstrom of hell."

The dawning of a dank, drizzly Monday brought everyone back to reality. A smog alert was in effect, and immediately Nicholas stepped out of the hotel entrance he could see why. The air above the slick streets was brownish gray and, as it rose upward, so solid seeming it completely obscured any structure above the twelfth floor. No hope of seeing the crest of Fuji-yama from Sato's office this day.

Tomkin, joining him in the limo for the stop-and-start trip across town to Shinjuku, seemed better, though he was still pale and drawn from his ordeal and he said the smog was giving him a pounding headache.

153

As they left the limo outside Sato's building, Tomkin caught him by the arm and said in a low, gritty voice, "Remember, Nick. This week's our deadline. You've got to make the merger happen now." His eyes still contained a tinge of fever brightness and his breath was as foul as ever.

Miss Yoshida met them at the elevator's summit and ushered them into Sato's enormous office. This high up the windows overlooked darkness; it could have been the middle of the night. All the lights were on as if to dispel this cloud of gloom.

When they were all seated comfortably—save for Ishii, who stood against the wall like a guard—Sato began. "Before we resume our negotiations, I would like to explain why I asked our respective counsels if they would step away for a moment. No disrespect to Greydon-san was intended, but Nangi-san and I both thought it prudent to keep this part of our meeting just between us."

He cleared his throat while Nangi lit a cigarette with careful deliberation. "Tomorrow afternoon's meetings will have to be rescheduled, I am afraid, because we must attend the funeral of our loyal friend, Kagami-san." He paused for a moment as if unsure how to proceed. "It may seem a crass request to make at this time, but we quite naturally feel that some answers must be reached." He leaned slightly forward so that he approached the area where Nicholas and Tomkin were seated side by side on the sofa.

"Linnear-san, I must tell you that we are absolutely mystified by the manner of Kagami-san's death. We know nothing of this *Wu-Shing* that you mentioned on Friday, nor can we think of a reason for murder being committed here.

"In light of all this I trust that you now, having had some small time to marshal your thoughts and surmises, may give us some insight into what happened to our poor colleague and friend."

It was an elegant speech and Nicholas admired it. But he could not rightly say that his mind was fully focused on the murder of Kagami. Truth to tell, since he had seen Akiko at the wedding his mind had been filled with nothing but the burning image of her face and the maddening thought, Is she Yukio?

He felt slightly ashamed now to have been so slavishly self-involved all weekend. It was utterly unlike him and that, above all, worried him.

Now, as he hurriedly recalled the catalog of his observations in and around the blood-splattered steam room, he muscled his own doubts and fears aside.

He laced his fingers together, tapped the thumbs. "Over and

154

above the bizarre appearance of the *Wu-Shing* tattoo on Kagami-san's cheek, there were a number of abnormalities that would, I think, préclude a simple explanation such as assault by a madman, that sort of thing."

"It was premeditated," Ishii broke in. "Is that what you're saying?"

"I am," Nicholas said. "For one thing, the murderer left no discernable footprints outside the door, even though that area's constantly saturated with moisture."

Sato groaned heavily and glanced at Nangi. When the other did not return his gaze, Sato stood up and walked to the bar. Though it was only a little past ten he fixed himself a drink, and it was a measure of his agitation that he forgot his manners completely and failed to offer anyone else a refreshment.

He took a long swallow and, staring at nothing in the mirror behind the bar, cleared his throat. "Linnear-san, you said there were a *number* of abnormalities."

"Why don't you wait for the police?"

A Westerner would have, of course, given an answer. Sato merely stared at Nicholas. And what his eyes said was, That is why you were allowed inside Sato Petrochemicals business, because we want no police intervention.

Nicholas had asked the question because he had to be certain of these people. Why they did not relish the thought of police involvement did not concern him; why they had involved him did.

"I fear Kagami-san was not killed quickly."

"Pardon me, but what do you mean?" Ishii asked.

"He was struck many times," Nicholas said, "by a sharp-bladed weapon."

"Do you know what kind?" Sato asked.

"I'm not certain," Nicholas said. "It could be any number of *shuriken*."

Sato had gone through half his long whiskey. Otherwise there was no outward sign of his agitation. "Linnear-san," he said, "when you first mentioned this *Wu-Shing*, you said it was a series of punishments. May we deduce that because it uses the character *Wu*, there are five of them?"

Nicholas looked uncomfortable. "Yes, that's correct. *Mo* is the first and therefore the least of the punishments."

"What can be more severe than death?" Nangi said somewhat angrily.

"I was referring to *Mo* itself." Nicholas looked at him. "Strictly speaking, it should only have been that: tattooing of the face."

Nangi's cane click-clacking across the short expanse of bare wooden floor that separated Sato's true office space from the informal conference area where the rest of them stood or sat announced his approach. "Then this murdering of the victim as well is unusual." He had pounced on it immediately.

"Highly unusual," Nicholas said. He sat quite still, his hard hands clasped between his knees. He forced an absolute calm onto his face, into every aspect of his physical being. The last thing he wanted was either of them to become aware of his inner feelings. His mind was still reeling from the thought that someone from his own *ryu*, someone steeped in the arcane ways of *aka-i-ninjutsu*, could perpetrate such an act. It was quite unthinkable. And yet it had happened. He had seen the grisly evidence and he knew there could be no doubt at all. Fervently he prayed that no one would ask him the one question that might detonate the whole situation.

"There's something I don't understand," Tomkin said, and Nicholas prepared himself to answer the unanswerable. "This Wo-Ching or however it's pronounced, is Chinese you said. What's with this cross-referencing between Japanese and Chinese? I thought the two cultures were separate and distinct. I thought only ignoramous Westerners say they can't tell one from the other."

The phone rang in the ensuing silence and Ishii launched himself away from the bar to pick it up. They waited while he spoke softly into the receiver. He had left instructions that they not be disturbed.

He punched a button, hung up. "It's a call for you, Nangi-san," he said. What dark emotion swam within his eyes? Nicholas wondered. "Apparently it cannot wait."

Nangi nodded. "I'll take it in the other room." He went back across the office, through the open passageway to the *tokonoma* where Nicholas had first caught sight of him.

The tension in the room was thick and now Nicholas used his training to seek a way of dissipating that high level of energy, as well as diverting interest away from areas he was still reluctant to discuss here. "Why an ancient form of *Chinese* punishment should be taught in an essentially Japanese discipline is simple," he began. "It is said—and not I think without a great deal of merit—that *ninjutsu* had its origins on the Asian continent somewhere, more specifically in northeastern China. Certainly it had existed long before Japan became civilized.

"But then so have many of the more ancient customs and traditions in Japan." He got up and went across the room, his movements pantherlike. He moved like some dancers Tomkin had seen, with a very low center of gravity, as if the floor itself were springy as a mat of dried grass.

Resettling himself on the sofa across from Tomkin, with Sato and Ishii on his left side, he continued. "In fact, China and Japan are more closely bound than either country likes to admit, since the enmity between them is longstanding and quite bitter.

"Nevertheless, you only have to take such a basic of life as language to see what I mean. Chinese and Japanese are virtually interchangeable."

He paused a moment to see if the Japanese were going to protest. "Until the fifth century there was no written Japanese language at all. Rather, they relied on *kataribe*, people trained from birth to be professional memorizers, building up a finely detailed oral history of early Japan. But that, as we know today, is a mark of a primitive civilization. Chinese characters were introduced into Japan in the fifth century, but the practice of using *kataribe* was so firmly entrenched in a culture always reluctant to change that it persisted for at least another three hundred years."

"But there are differences in the two languages," Sato offered. He seemed grayed and defeated. Ishii appeared to be doing nothing at all but breathing.

"Oh, yes," Nicholas said. "Of course there would have to be. Even so far in the past the Japanese were true to their own nature. Never very good at innovation, they nevertheless excel at improving on someone else's basic design.

"The problem with Chinese is its awesome cumbersomeness. It contains many thousands of characters, and since it was used largely for the recordings at the Imperial court and official proceedings, the language was not well suited for everyday use.

"The Japanese therefore began to work on a phonetic syllabary now known as *hiragana* to make the Chinese *kanji* more adaptable as well as to express those matters uniquely Japanese for which there were no Chinese characters at all. And by the middle of the ninth century this had been done. It was, coincidentally, just about the time that the Eastern European countries were developing the Cyrillic alphabet.

"Sometime later, another new syllabary was introduced—*katakana*—to be used for colloquialisms and foreign words being introduced into Japan as an augmentation for the forty-eight-syllable *hiragana*.

"But a curious holdover from Chinese custom was already in effect in Japan. No Chinese woman ever used *kanji* and therefore here too it was considered, well, ungraceful for a Japanese woman to use the language. So they took to *hiragana* and *katakana* and, in the process, created the country's first true written literature,

The Pillow Book of Seishonagon and the classic *Genji Monogatari*, both dating from the beginning of the eleventh century."

Just a wall away, Nangi was sitting at a desk clear of all papers and folders. The cedar gleamed, its high polish giving it an almost mirrorlike surface within which he could see part of his own face.

"Yes?" he said down the open line.

"Nangi-san"—the voice sounded thin and strange, as if the electronic medium had somehow inverted it, pulling out its soul in the process—"this is Anthony Chin."

Chin was the director of the All-Asia Bank of Hong Kong that Nangi had bought into almost seven years ago when, through a combination of fiscal mismanagement and a series of unfortunate market fluctuations within the Crown Colony, it had been on the verge of going under.

Nangi had flown into Hong Kong and had worked out a bail-out scheme within ten days that left his *keiretsu* with a maximum of cash flow after twenty months while providing it with a minimum of risk after the initial year and three quarters. However, beginning in the spring of 1977, a land boom had commenced within the tiny, teeming colony of unheralded proportions.

Anthony Chin had been at the forefront of the boom and with Nangi's consent had invested much of All-Asia's primary capital in real estate. And both he and the *keiretsu* had prospered tremendously as property values rose sharply, until by the end of 1980 they had quadrupled.

But for almost a year before that Chin had counseled expansion. "It's got to just keep going," he had told Nangi in late 1979, "there's just no alternative. There's no room at all left on the Island or across the harbor. There's plans afoot to make Sha Tin in the New Territories the Hong Kong for the new middle class. I've seen plans for sixteen different high-rise complexes all within a mile or two of the race track. If we get in now, we'll double our capital within two years."

But Nangi had opted for caution. After all, he told himself rationally, Britain's ninety-nine-year lease on the New Territories was coming due. Of course, every citizen of the Colony discounted Communist China, reasoning that since Hong Kong and Macao were its only real windows on the west and provided such a lucrative flow of money into Red China, it would be against their own best interests to abrogate the lease or not to renew it at the very least.

But Nangi had had plenty of dealings with the Communist Chinese and he knew how their minds worked. And he thought, near the beginning of 1980, that there might be something else they would be needing more than mere money.

He had successfully predicted the downfall of Mao and, thence, the Gang of Four. This was easy for him since he recognized in modern China precisely the same circumstances that created the overthrow of the three-hundred-year Tokugawa Shōgunate in his own country and had established the Meiji Restoration: in order to survive in modern times, the Chinese leadership had come at last to the painful conclusion that they must open themselves up to the West. They had to pull themselves out of the self-imposed isolationism that Mao had thrust them into, a veritable dark ages since industry atrophied along with culture, commerce, and artistic expression, all for the sake of the Five-Year Plans and intense repression.

Increasingly, Nangi had seen that more than profits, China would need two elements to set her on her lumbering feet, and both inspired within him awe and terror: heavy industry and nuclear capability. China was in need of wholesale transplants and there just was not enough money to pay for them. There was only one other path for them to take: barter. And the only commodity they possessed with which to play for such astronomical stakes was Hong Kong. If they could threaten England with expulsion, a complete breakdown of all that Great Britain had labored so hard and so long for on the tip of the Asian shore—and if they could make it completely believable—then they could extort almost anything they wished from that country. Certainly England possessed all the modern technology China could hope for.

Toward this end, Nangi felt, China would soon be making her first move. That would, no doubt, involve some kind of public statement indicating that the original lease was a document which, for them, had no validity. Then would come their inevitable announcement that at some time in the future—date unspecified, of course—they would begin a reinstitution of Chinese control over the Colony.

Revelations like that, Nangi knew full well, would burst the current real estate boom in a flash. What foreign investor would want to sink his money into that kind of political quicksand? The inevitable result would be that both the Hong Kong real estate and stock markets would take a nose dive. Nangi did not want to be caught in that. So he vetoed all of Anthony Chin's requests for expansion. "Let the others do that," he had said. "We'll sit on our profits."

And events had borne out his worst fears. The Chinese announcements had come late in 1982, bringing Her Majesty Queen

Elizabeth running at full tilt. Her people had set up an extensive round of talks with the Communists, hoping to get the main issues resolved immediately and thus head off the expected downturn in the Colony's economy.

Nangi had had to smile at that, just as he had had to smile at his own perspicacity and caution. The Chinese, now that they had the upper hand, were going to string this out as long as possible, enjoying their dominant position. It was essential to make Britain suffer as long as possible in order to bring home to the dense Westerners the dire straits in which they found themselves.

The talks had broken off inconclusively. And the crash had come to Hong Kong. From a high of 1730 in June of 1981, the Hang Seng—the Colony's stock market—index plummeted to the 740s in December of 1982. In early 1983 some of the smaller property companies began to fail, followed in the third quarter of the year by two or three of the larger ones.

"But," John Bremidge, Hong Kong's Financial Secretary, said, "the real thing to worry about is the financial and banking sector. They're scared at present."

Now, as he took Anthony Chin's call, Nangi again thanked God for his wise course of conservative action. "How are things in the garden spot of China?" It was their own private capitalistic joke, but this time Chin did not respond.

"I'm afraid I have some bad news, Nangi-san."

"If it's another run on the banks, don't concern yourself," Nangi said. "We can weather it. You know how much capital we have."

"That's just it," Chin said. "It's much less than you think. We won't be able to hold against even a minor run."

Nangi consciously slowed his heartbeat, which, for just an instant, had leaped. He fought for calm and, reaching into the nonspace that was the home of the Holy Trinity, he found it. His mind teemed with a thousand questions but before he opened his mouth, he arranged them in order of importance. First things first.

"Where is the money?"

"In six of the Sha Tin developments," Anthony Chin said miserably. "I know what your orders were, but you were not here. I was on top of the situation, day to day. I saw just how much money we stood to make. Now we can't get tenants to move in. Not with the unsettled climate, the fears about the Communists. Everyone is shaken here, all the *tai-pans*. Even—"

"You're fired," Nangi said curtly. "You have ten minutes to be out of the building. After that the security people will have orders to arrest you. They will do the same if you touch or alter any files."

160

He hung up and quickly redialed the bank, asking for Allan Su, All-Asia's statistical vice president. "Mr. Su, this is Tanzan Nangi. Please do not ask any questions. As of this moment, you are president of All-Asia. Anthony Chin no longer works for me. Please give your security people orders to evict him as of now. Have them make certain he takes nothing of the bank's with him. Now, to business . . ."

He would have to take one of them out. Red or Blue, which would it be? Riding the waves, cerulean and a green the shade of translucent jade, Bristol thought it would be Blue.

He sat in a sway-backed canvas director's chair that had seen better days, paying out his line, waiting for something to strike the bait twisting fifteen feet below. Not more than a hundred yards to port, the long sleek twinscrew pleasure boat carrying Alix Logan, a half-dozen of her friends, and the Red Monster, who was doing his level best not to stick out like a sore thumb, sat in the water.

He had gone so far as to take off his shirt, which, Bristol thought, was a mistake because it only emphasized the paleness of the flesh on his chest, back, and upper arms. There was plenty of muscle, though, and Bristol took careful note. He wondered how Alix had introduced him to her friends.

The line went taut and the ratcheting of the set reel began. Bristol watched the end of the rod bending and quivering, and he began the reel-in. If it had been a toss-up he probably would have chosen the Red Monster to take out because he was even bigger than Bristol was, and after all this time Bristol was itching for a fight.

But as it was, there was no contest. In the months of his surveillance, he had come to hate the Blue Monster. For one thing, he had a way of looking at Alix that went beyond a strictly business interest. Somehow, over time, Blue had developed a proprietary absorption.

To the Red Monster she was just another piece of meat, an assignment like many others he had had before and would have again. Isolate and protect; he stuck to the letter of the command he had been given—they had a Laundry List, an accounting of people in her life who had been checked out and were okay for her to associate with.

Blue, the night man, loved to look at her. He was allowed inside her apartment. Not for the entire night, of course, but just long enough when she returned home to check the place out thoroughly. Then the door would slam and he'd saunter down the concrete steps, a wooden toothpick twirling from one corner of his mouth to the other.

He'd cross the street, heading for the chrome and glass box of the fried chicken franchise less than a block away. He'd buy a pail of extra crispy that would feed a family of four and hunker down in an orange plastic seat. His lips full of grease, his cheeks flecked with bits of chicken skin, he'd stare at the lighted window square behind which Alix Logan was undressing for bed and lick his lips. Bristol did not think it had anything at all to do with the food.

A force jolted him, all the way down at the base of the rod, and things began to hot up. He pushed the soles of his worn topsiders against the aft coaming and hauled back mightily on the rod. The force of God was down there, and the answering twist almost pulled him out of his chair. What in Christ's name had he lit onto? His back muscles tensed as he brought all his brawn to bear against the sea creature at the other end of his line.

A hundred yards away, across the diamondlike sparkle of the rolling sea, Alix and her friends were in their suits, their coppery skin shining with suntan oil, faces held up to the streaming sunlight, hair floating in the wind. Tops popped off iced cans of Bud, handed around. Laughter floated across the water.

Bristol fought the fish, even as his eyes were on the activity aboard the pleasure boat, even as his mind still turned over his feelings for the Blue Monster.

His great muscles corded and he felt the adrenaline pumping through him, exulting him. Damn, but it was good to be alive. The terror of the grave Tomkin wanted him in was an inconstant specter inside him. That night, the tumbling car, the uncontrollable motion, the soaring, stomach-wrenching free fall, the ground coming up, the overpowering darkness, the vertigo, the getout, and the searing fireball of his coffin, the triumphant shout of the flames licking near his cheek, and rolling, rolling, looking again and again with each rapid revolution into the face of death.

With a fierce grin, Bristol reeled in the line, feeling with every sense he possessed the skein of life flowing all around him. He felt the rhythmic rocking of the boat as it negotiated the deep sea swells, he breathed deeply of the clean salt air laced with the pungency of marine fuel, felt the hot bite of the sunlight on his arms and shoulders. The colors of the water flashed before him, now deep blue, then aquamarine, turquoise, even, far out, a thin feathery line of pale green.

But mostly, he felt the life at the other end of the line, the fight, the strategy of working the big fish closer, ever closer to the boat's side and the ultimate landing. During New York's long, frigid winters he had dreamed of such moments, and now he was living them.

The fish was close now. He could see its frothy wake every so often as it neared the surface, knew that that was the time to brace himself, to let off the reel's safety and allow the creature its head to plunge downward into the ocean's depths. That would do nothing more than set the hook more firmly in its cheek but it only knew that it must get away, and instinctively it went down.

The reel screamed as the line payed out in a blur and he knew that if he were holding on to the line too tightly, it would snap under the enormous force of the fish's dive.

And now it reached the end and, lifting the rod in a long smooth arc, he began to reel in the line, slowly, steadily, with a great deal of patience. It would be a long afternoon out here and he had nowhere else to go unless the skipper of the nearby pleasure boat decided to move on.

Always he had one eye on the other craft. It was important, he knew, not to become a passive observer. Most likely, you'd be put to sleep and you'd learn nothing. He had been taught to use stakeout time to actively learn about the subject. Moods as well as habits were important, because there would surely come a day when observer and subject would meet and in that confrontation the observer's acquired knowledge often made the difference in establishing a dialogue.

The big fish was tiring, and as Bristol wound the line in more quickly now he saw Alix's tall, lithe form detach itself from the pack and move with surefooted grace up along the deck forward. The Red Monster, drinking a beer, turned his head for a moment, catching the movement. Nothing was happening, so he went back to his quiet drinking.

Alix reached the tubular aluminum railing rising from the prow of the boat and stood leaning, her arms rigid, her long-fingered hands wrapped around the upper bars. For a long time she stared out to sea, at the long unbroken line of the horizon, blue on blue. Then her gaze dropped to the water lapping gently below her. Her eyes were fixed. She seemed mesmerized by something she saw down there in the clear water.

In one last burst of energy, the fish at the other end of Bristol's line dove straight down and for just a moment his entire concentration was directed at not losing the creature.

When he looked up, Alix was gone. Bristol's head whipped around. She was not on deck. Perhaps she had needed to use the head. Or the sun had got to be too much for her.

Bristol had a sinking feeling in his gut. That fixed look in her eyes, that staring. He had seen it before when he had first met Gelda. His gaze was drawn to the sea just in front of the pleasure boat's prow. Caramel hair floating, a golden shoulder bobbing. Was she swimming or drowning?

The Red Monster glanced forward and didn't see her. He put his beer can aside and got up. His mouth opened and he said something to the skipper. The other man shook his head in a negative, pointed toward the forward railing.

The Red Monster sprang upward and Bristol thought, He'd better be quick because Alix was drifting away from the boat and there seemed no doubt now. She was making no effort to stay within range and this far out with the current so strong it was as good as saying, "I give up."

Running along the side deck, Red spotted her and he leaped overboard. His strong confident strokes brought him to her in minutes. On board the pleasure boat, the skipper was breaking out the inflatable rubber dinghy. Several of the oiled men were helping him. The women were gaping.

The skipper lowered the dinghy, and the Red Monster with one capable palm tucked beneath Alix's chin swam slowly toward safety.

They were lifting Alix's body up onto the deck as Bristol's fish broke the surface. It ws a marlin, and by all rights it should have whipped him out of his chair and into the sea during its fight for life.

Bristol watched the long arch of her golden body, raised like a rainbow being lifted into position. Her hair, darkened by the sea, hung down like seagrape, obscuring one shoulder.

Moments later, after the Red Monster had given her mouth-to-mouth, she rolled over. Sea water ran from her mouth in a torrent. Someone came over and put a baseball cap on her head to keep off the sun. The skipper draped a towel across her shoulders, and the Red Monster took her below.

Bristol looked down into the huge, glistening eye of the marlin. Its long body whipped, its tailfin sending a spray of cool water up into his face.

The fish was very close, and as Bristol leaned over the side with his landing hook at the ready he saw the marlin for what it really was: not a game fish, not a trophy stuffed over the mantel in his apartment, but another life.

He thought of the burning car, the fight he had had to put up in order to escape death, and he saw that the marlin's desperate battle had been no different. They were both gallant soldiers, and this creature deserved to die no more than Bristol did.

He stared once more into that round eye, so alien yet for all that so full of life. He could not take that away from the creature. Dropping his landing hook, he dug in his pocket for the knife. He used the blade to slash through the line just beyond the hook.

For just an instant the marlin lay there, close to the boat, floating, its eye on him. Then with a flash of its mighty tail, it leaped away, its blue-green-black body arcing, sunlight spinning off its scales, and then there was only a narrow foaming wake, a tiny incision in the skin of the sea to mark where it had once been.

Tengu was the name his *sensei*, as tradition dictated, had given him. He was another of Viktor Protorov's agents inside the precincts of the Tenshin Shoden Katori *ryu*. As such he walked a fine line, and even his sleep had developed a crack in it upward to the more alert alpha layers so that he might never be caught off guard. As Tsutsumu had.

Always he was conscious of being in a hive filled with buzzing, angry bees. That anger, he knew very well, needed only one word of accusation to be leveled at him. Never had he experienced the kind of conglomerate emotional upheaval that had come from the unexpected and unexplained death of Masashigi Kusunoki, the erstwhile leader of this ninja *ryu*.

Tengu had come from a large rural family in Kyūshū and he remembered the day his father had died. The family reunited silently, moving almost as a single unit. But even that display of togetherness could not compare with the singleminded will which apparently pervaded all levels of the society here. *Jonin*, leader-*sensei*, *chunin*, the tactical unit leaders, and *genin*, as well as the students such as himself were all affected to a frightening degree.

Something was happening within the *dōjō* that Tengu did not understand, some unconscious whirlwind, some spiritual flashpoint of which he was not part. He tried—and pretended to be a part to those around him—but he knew inwardly that it was useless. He was lost here and he could not say why. Had he been able to step outside of himself and observe the totality of the circumstances within which he found himself, he would have seen that he simply lacked the dedication, the intense concentration of energies that would have allowed him to become a part of the mourning, the renewed dedication of spirit that came with Kusunoki's passing.

Tengu developed many fears during these volatile days when he was obliged to expend tremendous amounts of psychic energy in concealing his true mission at the Tenshin Shoden Katori from those about him. But none was as acute or as draining as the fear he developed of Phoenix.

Next to Kusunoki himself, Phoenix was the most powerful of the *jonin*. In fact, to Tengu's way of thinking, Phoenix was more of a threat than Kusunoki ever had been. For one thing, he was younger, his vitality at the peak. For another, he was an explorer of pathways it seemed to Tengu that Kusunoki had long ago turned away from. Foolishly.

Too, Phoenix had always spent more time with the lowly *genin* than Kusunoki ever had, at least during Tengu's tenure at the *dōjō*. The old *sensei* had increasingly seemed to devote himself to quiet contemplation and the instruction of certain favored pupils, among them the lone female, Suijin.

So it was that just before dawn Tengu would slip silently back into his cubicle, exhausted and utterly drained after a night spent alternately hiding and searching, his heart pounding heavily every time he sensed the approach of another.

Terror stalked him. He lived in fear that Phoenix would become aware of his clandestine activities. The thought of coming under the scrutiny of that glowering countenance was too much for him to contemplate for long. Better by far to die by his own hand than to be delivered up to the vengeance of such a one.

To Tengu, who had been brought up with all the superstition and ritualism of country folk, it was like trying to battle a *kami*.

Phoenix was a shade, something that Tengu could not understand. Seeing him, seeing the fiercely visaged tattooed tiger rampant across his shoulder and back, Tengu was gripped by a primal paralysis that he could not break. Therefore, despite what Protorov had advised, he kept his boldness in check, masking himself against discovery while he continued his recreancy.

When Nangi returned to the larger office suite his face was entirely composed. He had done all he could for the moment. It was now up to Allan Su and his staff to go through Anthony Chin's books and ferret out just what had been done to All-Asia, to see if it was still a viable entity. Su had advised that they close their doors until the matter was determined but Nangi, knowing how rumors flew in the Colony, had decided to keep the bank open and to issue an immediate story about Anthony Chin's dismissal for fiduciary improprieties to both the Chinese- and English-language newspapers. He had no compunction about ruining the career of the man who had brought his bank to the brink of financial destruction.

166

The waters in Hong Kong must be muddied, Nangi had told Su. "We must do whatever we can to buy time," he had said. "I do not want to transfer in capital from here to cover a run in an already skittish atmosphere. I will not throw good money after bad. Remember that, Mr. Su. Your job and those of all the others under you is in your hands. Please don't fail."

Running over it all again, he was certain that he had covered everything. Now it was in the hands of God. Let Him decide the fate of All-Asia. Of course he had not told Su that the *keiretsu* could not afford a major transfer of funds. But if the bank could not provide it, capital would have to come from somewhere.

Satisfied for the moment, he turned his full attention to matters within Sato's office. He remembered what he was going to ask Linnear when the phone call had deflected him. He stopped behind the back of the sofa on which Nicholas, Sato, and Ishii were sitting. Tomkin was now sprawled in an oversized chair, facing them.

"Linnear-san," he said, extracting another cigarette and producing his lighter, "before I was inopportunely called away, you said that it was highly unusual for death itself to be associated with this *Mo*."

Nicholas, his face pale, said nothing, and Nangi, staring hard as he lit up, wondered whether he had hit a nerve that would somehow serve him in his quest for dominance of the *gaijin*.

"I wonder," Nangi continued, pouring blue smoke from his half-open mouth, "whether you would be kind enough to tell me the *Wu-Shing*'s purpose."

Now Nicholas had a choice of losing face or possibly causing a panic among the Japanese and thus endangering the negotiations Tomkin had made eminently clear must be completed this week. He had told Tomkin part of it back in the hotel room on Friday, and now he had told them all a little more. But only he, Nicholas, knew it all, and the ramifications were so terrifying that, at least for the moment, he preferred not to think about them. Yet tenacious Nangi, intelligent Nangi was about to force his hand and in so doing wreck how many years of Tomkin's planning?

His mind was racing, working on the problem, when his head turned as if of its own volition. *Haragei*—his peculiar sixth sense— was warning him . . . of what? Tomkin! What was wrong? Nicholas began to move even before fully coherent conclusions had been made.

Raphael Tomkin's brown eyes, usually so full of cunning and impenetrable guile, were now liquid and runny, as if all the color of the irises were drooling out across his lower lids. His pupils were dilated and he seemed to be having trouble focusing.

Nicholas touched him, felt the minute vibration in his torso, arhythmic, fluttery, abnormal.

"Quickly," Nicholas said, "call for a doctor."

"There's one in the building," Sato said, motioning to Ishii, who was already halfway to the door. "He's ours and he's very good."

Tomkin tried to open his mouth and could not speak. His hands grasped at Nicholas' jacket, crumpling the fabric in thick swatches beneath his clawed fingers. Within his eyes jumped the red spark of fear and terror.

"It's all right," Nicholas said, his tone soothing, "there's a doctor on his way." Something was trying to surface within his mind, a half-remembered memory, tiny, fleeting, seemingly insignificant at the time. What was it?

Tomkin's face was mottled and so close to him Nicholas could feel the beat of his pulse like an engine gone wild. He put his forefinger against the underside of the other man's trembling wrist. After a moment, he moved his finger, then again. His mind was numb with disbelief. He could not find a pulse!

Tomkin's mouth was working and he pulled Nicholas toward him wanting, needing perhaps, to whisper. Nicholas put his ear against Tomkin's lips and listened hard. Hard breath like a bellows working overtime and the sickly sweet stench of decay. It brought up the buried memory, but just as he reached for it, he heard Tomkin's voice, sere, fibrous, unearthly.

"Greydon," Nicholas heard between pants. "For. Christ's. Sake. Get. Grey. Don. *Now*."

Pink light reflecting off the *kanzashi* in Miss Yoshida's hair turned the water-soaked stones glistening at the bottom of a pool into gems. She knelt just inside the open *fusuma* on the fiftieth floor of the Shinjuku Suiryū Building, home of Sato Petrochemicals. It had been given over to a master interior architect and then a *sensei* of gardening in order to create a sanctuary of peaceful contemplation in the smoky madhouse of downtown Tokyo.

A whisper of wind came from somewhere in the pearly atmosphere above Miss Yoshida's bowed head. Off to the right rose a stand of willowy green bamboo, tall, youthful, filled with eternal suppleness, that ineffable quality the Japanese so treasure, whose aura can renew the tired spirit.

Miss Yoshida, dressed in a fashionable dark red suit, knelt by the side of the pool. Though she was Sato's administrative assistant, the simple fact was that tradition dictated that she be known as an Office Lady. It was a tag she had been fighting for years without any sign of success. And indeed under other circumstances she would not have been here but would have fulfilled her traditional female duties of being a wife and mother, of keeping her home in perfect order.

But six years ago her husband had been struck by a careening truck as he stepped off a sidewalk jammed with the crush of midday pedestrian traffic. His skull had been crushed instantly. His death had left Miss Yoshida all alone to care for their one son, Kozo, who was then beginning high school, the one linked with prestigious Tōdai. Miss Yoshida and her husband had labored long and hard—she had even appealed to Sato to use his influence in this matter—to get Kozo in. And they had been dismayed at the boy's appalling display of ungratefulness; he seemed totally oblivious to the great step upward to a successful future his parents had wrangled for him.

Miss Yoshida sighed now, her shoulders hunched as if beneath a great weight as she recalled these events.

At first she had tried accepting the invitation to come and live with her mother-in-law. But that had lasted only a few months for Miss Yoshida found that she had merely exchanged one form of hell for another. By living in her mother-in-law's house she put herself under the direct control of the older woman. She was a *hera-mochi* of ferocious intensity, insisting on taking over the guidance of the money in her son's life insurance and multiple bank accounts. And the servitude under which Miss Yoshida was forced to abide became too much for her.

She took Kozo and fled the baleful eye of the *hera-mochi*, returning to the same section of the city she had loved as a child, renting a small apartment there.

And because there was only Kozo left in her life now she became a *Kyoiku mama*, an education mother, constantly working with her son to improve his grades so that he could get into the elite *juku*, the private study groups that gathered on Sundays and on national holidays over and above the 240 days regular classes were in session. Miss Yoshida wanted Kozo to enroll in a *juku* because she knew the level of teaching in the classroom at his school. Because students were not allowed to repeat or skip grades, the level of teaching was geared to the slightly slower students in each class and these, Miss Yoshida had judged, were on a level far below her own son's.

And through her own diligence and Kozo's innate intelligence, he was soon asked to join a particularly prestigious *juku* which rented a classroom at Tōdai.

Miss Yoshida was particularly pleased because she remembered her own schooling. In junior college, where all of her classmates were women, Miss Yoshida was taught how to behave in society, how to treat her prospective mother-in-law, how to raise children, and how to prepare herself for all the myriad vicissitudes of married life. It was no more than a finishing-school education. She had been bitter about that and had vowed that when she had a female baby, that child would have an entirely different form of education.

But her *karma* had lain in another direction, and when her physician had told her that the one child was all she could ever have, she resigned herself to seeing that her son received the finest in Japanese education so that all the great doors to the business world would be open to him. For everyone knew that without an education at only a handful of universities a young man would be cast adrift on a lonely and unproductive sea.

Thus she ignored Kozo's complaints that his teachers at school resented his enrollment in the *juku*. They felt, he told her, that the *juku* undermined their own teaching and they were jealous at the loss of control and thus made life more difficult for him in class.

"Nonsense," Miss Yoshida told him. "That's merely an excuse to shirk your studies. Do you have any idea how much the *juku* costs me each month?" Of course she would not tell him, but privately she was glad that her husband had been such a hoarder; he was a good provider even in death.

Two years ago—has it already been so long? she asked herself—Kozo was ready to graduate high school. All semester long, he had dedicated himself along with his class to studying for the Tōdai entrance examinations. White faced and tense he would leave the apartment every morning, not returning from the library until late in the evening.

Then, in the three weeks after New Year's, with all regular classes dissolved for the year, Kozo began the rigorous around-the-clock cramming that was known as *shiken jigoku*, examination hell. Miss Yoshida shuddered now when she thought of those words.

She arranged for Kozo to have one entire section of the apartment for his intensive studies. And then one morning...

Miss Yoshida's shoulders shook as she sobbed out loud at the verge of the exquisite garden, the rustling of the leaves, the musical notes of the tiny waterfall which flowed over the smooth ochre stones lost on her.

No! a voice within her cried. *Why torture yourself again? Why make yourself remember?*

But all the while she knew why. Penance. Silent tears streamed down her rounded cheeks, staining her silk blouse, beading on her linen suit jacket.

Ah, Buddha! How can I ever forget the moment when I entered his rooms that morning and found him hanging, twisted in his bedsheet, the small stool kicked over on its side. Swinging back and forth like a monstrous metronome and, oh, when he was a child and sleeping peacefully, that small secret smile on his lips, he would twist his sheet around his legs—his legs, not his neck.

Oh, my poor Kozo!

Three months after she had buried him in a plot next to his father's, she had read a newspaper article by Professor Soichi Watanabe of Tokyo's Sophia University. In part, he lamented "the bitterness of educational servitude" young boys were forced to undergo, "a sentence from which no child can escape." And she had wept all over again, appalled at her own lack of understanding or compassion.

From the moment of his birth she had molded Kozo into the conception of what she wanted him to be. She saw now that she had had no clear idea of him as an individual. Rather, he had always been an extension of her. A most important extension, to be sure. But only a part of her for all that.

Now, her head buried in her hands, she rocked softly back and forth on her haunches and wept bitter tears, drenched in longing and spiteful self-pity.

And that was how death found her, falling across her body in shadow, a rippling nightblack finger that seemed to appear out of nowhere, running across her bent back, ribboning along the folds of her linen jacket like a slice of the Void splitting her in two.

Miss Yoshida was aware of nothing but her own pain and sorrow, the more recent trauma of finding Kagami-san in his own blood in the steam room. And the indelible memory of Kozo. Even the foul stench emanating from Tomkin-san, a product, she supposed, of his meat-filled Western diet, was forgotten in the swelling blossom of her utter despair.

Then she felt a gentle hand on her shoulder and a soft woman's voice crooning to her and slowly she unwound, her shoulders lifting, her spine unbending, and her head coming up to see the source of comfort.

She had just time enough to see the colorful kimono, the long gleaming sweep of blue-black hair, marked with the coarse bloody

Xi, in the manner of the *geisha*, before she heard the odd high whistling and the great ruffled blade of the *gunsen* slashed through the bone and cartilage at the base of her nose, severing it.

Miss Yoshida screamed thickly as her raw nerves overcame the shock trauma and pain flashed through her. Blood gushed from the rent in her face, drenching her blouse and jacket. She fell backward with her feet bent under her buttocks. Her eyes opened wide, blinking rapidly in incomprehension, for now she recognized the figure for what it was and her heart contracted in terror.

"I am afraid this is way beyond my ken," the doctor said. He was gray and wan, seeming ten years older than when he had come through the office door. "His only hope now is a hospital." He sighed deeply, pushing his wire-framed glasses up on his glistening forehead, then massaging his eyes with his thumbs. "A thousand pardons. I am afflicted with an almost constant sinus headache these days." He produced a small plastic bottle, detonated squeezes in each nostril. "My doctor says I must soon leave the city for good." He pocketed the bottle. "The pollution, you know."

He was a stooped Japanese of more than middle yeas, with shoulders so thin the blades could be seen beneath his rumpled jacket. He had kind, intelligent eyes. He sighed now as he put the bottle away. "But if you want my opinion, even that won't do much good." He peered around at the anxious faces in the room: Nicholas, Sato, Nangi, then at the form of Tomkin, sprawled on Sato's sofa.

"It's not his heart," the doctor said. "I don't know *what* it is."

"I took his pulse while you were being summoned," Nicholas said. "He didn't have any."

"Quite so." The doctor's eyes blinked owllike behind his thick lenses. "And that is what is so remarkable. He should be dead, you know." He looked over in the direction of the stricken man. "Was he on any special medication, do you know, Linnear-san?"

Nicholas remembered idly picking up the small plastic bottle in Tomkin's hotel suite. "He's been taking Prednisone."

The doctor seemed to stagger backward a pace and Nicholas reached out for him. His face had gone pale but he made no exclamation, only said so low Nicholas had to lean toward him, "Prednisone? Are you absolutely certain it was Prednisone?"

"Yes."

The doctor took off his glasses. "I fear the ambulance will be useless now," he said softly. Carefully he replaced his spectacles and looked at them. Now his face had altered just as if he were a quick-change artist. His eyes were black, a professional veneer like a curtain hanging between him and everything else about him. Nicholas had seen that look many times before in doctors, and in soldiers returning from a war. It was a kind of defense mechanism, a deliberate hardening of the heart to protect it from sorrow's bitter arrows. There was, indeed, nothing the doctor could do, and he hated defeat so much.

"I am afraid Tomkin-san is suffering from the end phase of Takayasu's arterisis, a uniformly malignant and fatal disease. It is also known as pulseless disease. The reason for that is, I think, obvious to all of you."

Miss Yoshida was confident that she was dying. This did not seem to be a terrible occurrence for it would bring an end to her suffering and would hide her shame at being too cowardly to take up her husband's *wakizashi* and, drawing the steel from its scabbard, plunge it into her lower belly.

But the manner in which she was dying—that was another matter entirely. She was dying like a dog, a poor, broken animal in the street, kicked and pummeled, the life escaping from her in short arrhythmic gasps.

Surely this was no way for a *samurai* woman to die, she told herself, her mind already half numb from the painful contact of the needle-sharp ripple blade of the steel fan.

But the sight of the figure looming over her—that painted demon's face, dead white, with bright orange paint in the manner the *kabuki* represented demons in its plays—transfixed her.

It was as if she had been spun down the awful tunnel of legend, as if quotidian Tokyo with its hordes of rushing people, thick pollution, and bright neon lights had disappeared entirely. And in its place were the wood and paper houses, the green, trembling bamboo groves of the Japan of long ago, mist shrouded and mysterious, filled with magic and the feats of heroes.

This was the essence of the visage which was bent over her now, administering a terrible punishment.

But I am samurai! a voice in the back of Miss Yoshida's dazzled mind cried. *If I am to die, at least grant me the nobility of falling in battle.*

And so Miss Yoshida reached up with clawlike talons, shredding first her nails and then her fingertips on the deadly *gunsen* that whistled down at her again and again. She began to inch away from the blows, uncurling herself awkwardly, using forearms and elbows now, the blood running hot and free down her arms and into the drenched sockets of her armpits.

173

But now her lips were drawn back from her clenched teeth in a cross between a grin and a snarl and adrenaline pumped through her and her heart arose from its gray slumber and sang again at the spirits of her *samurai* ancestors who moved her now to her glorious end.

"Confirmed diagnosis has been relatively recent. Early 1979 at the Mayo clinic, I believe."

"There is nothing you can do, Taki-san?" Sato said.

The doctor shrugged his meager shoulders. "I can sedate him; take away the pain. There's nothing else."

"But surely the hospital has facilities that can—"

But Taki was already shaking his head. "It is almost over, Sato-san. He will feel far more pain if we move him. And the hospital . . . well, personally, I would not want to die there had I the choice."

Sato nodded, also admitting defeat.

Nicholas left them, a modern cabal, ineffectual against the primitive, ultimate forces of nature. He knelt beside Tomkin and looked into the pale, pinched face. Once he had seen the power in that face, the lines the burden of command had etched into it, giving it character and substance.

Now it was those lines that had begun to take over, deepening, widening, extending their networks. Time seemed to have closed in on him, aging him ten years in as many minutes. But unlike Taki, he would never bounce back. The regenerative process in him had been destroyed by disease.

It seemed vastly ironic to Nicholas now to be kneeling by the side of this dying man, the same man whom he had vowed to destroy. But he did not question it. Tomkin's *karma* was his own. Nicholas accepted these events as he accepted all else in life, with equanimity and calmness. It was just this unique quality which had allowed him to put away his intense desire to talk with Akiko, his bewilderment at her physicality. It was what allowed him to recover so quickly from the awesome implications of Kagami-san's terrible murder.

He was Eastern in nature, even though there was but a hint of his mother's blood in his face. The Colonel, had he been alive today, would have recognized in the visage of his son an almost exact duplicate of his own youthful self, save that Nicholas' hair was as dark as his mother's and his eyes somehow did not contain the directness of Western culture.

Within Nicholas now swirled many emotions. He recognized the hate for Tomkin which had allowed him to go to work for him, even become his friend in order to be close to him, to sow the seeds of his revenge for his friend's murder at Tomkin's behest. And yet . . . There were qualities about the man that had begun to affect Nicholas. For one thing, he was fiercely loyal. He would try to bring the sun down from the sky for one of his people who was legitimately in trouble. For another, his abiding love for both his daughters, but especially Justine, was touching. It was in the nature of the man that he could not very well express that love. But his understanding of his troubled younger daughter and, just as importantly, his acknowledgement—at least to himself and to Nicholas—of his complicity in her emotional state was laudable.

Though Tomkin could often be loud and crude, these abrasive qualities hid a man of much emotion. Indeed, in private moments, many of which he had chosen to share with Nicholas, when his guard was down and he was relaxed, he could be an engaging, even a charming, companion.

Nicholas looked down at the gray, deflated face. Devoid of animation, Tomkin had the countenance of an overused wax doll. He recalled Tomkin's sadness over Justine's relationships; how he had ached for her when she had been used by Chris; the final anger that had both saved her and caused her to turn away from him.

Nicholas recognized that Justine should be here; perhaps only he knew how much solace her presence would bring to Tomkin now. Ultimately, it was his family that was Tomkin's weak spot. It seemed cruel indeed that he should die here so far from home and his daughters, all that he loved. Facing death, Nicholas felt always slightly diminished. He understood dimly that that was a Western facet of his personality, a legacy from the Colonel. His Eastern half understood fully that death was integrated with life, the two the same, really. If you were one with all things, then death was one of them. That, at least, should be some solace to him now.

Nicholas saw the eyes flutter open, the brown of the irises dirty and almost gray. Breath was an enormous effort, the dry-lipped mouth was half open.

"I called Greydon," he said. "He's just outside."

But there seemed no recognition at all in the eyes as they drifted, drifted across the room. Outside, day had died and the nighttime splendor of Tokyo was a blaze of neon fire, holding back the darkness with its multicolored shell.

Tomkin turned his head, and Nicholas followed his gaze. There was nothing there, a blank wall. What did Tomkin see there that held the last of his attention? Only cats sat and stared at nothing.

Then a shadow passed across the wall, and as if it were some-how connected to him, Tomkin shuddered once and Nicholas said, "Doctor?" though it was merely a formality; he knew death when he saw it.

"Mr. Linnear?"

Nicholas rose slowly and turned to see the worried face of Greydon, Tomkin's attorney.

"How is he?"

"Let the doctor tell you." Nicholas suddenly felt tired.

Taki knelt beside Tomkin's form with his stethoscope, listening intently. After a moment, he pulled the instrument from his ears. "He's expired, I'm afraid." He stood up and began to write in his notepad.

Greydon wiped at his face with a linen handkerchief. "This is so sudden," he said. "I never... well, I never suspected it was so close."

"You knew about Tomkin's illness?" Nicholas said.

Greydon nodded distractedly. "Yes. Dr. Kidd, his personal physician, and I were the only ones." Then his eyes seemed to focus and he looked at Nicholas. "Tomkin had to come to me for the will, you see. I had to know."

He took a deep breath. "Would anyone mind if I had a whiskey and soda?"

"Excuse me," Sato said. "The circumstances..." He went quickly to the bar and made Greydon his drink, gave it to him. He made something for Nangi as well, who was looking very pale.

Greydon took a long pull at his drink and touched Nicholas on the elbow. "Please," he said quietly, "come with me."

Away from the others, Nicholas stopped. "What is it?" he said shortly. His mind was elsewhere.

Greydon snapped open his black lizardskin attaché case. "There are certain matters which must be—"

"Not now," Nicholas said, putting his hand on Greydon's arm. "There'll be plenty of time for formalities later on."

The lawyer looked up at him from his half-bent position. "I'm sorry, Mr. Linnear, but I have explicit instructions. Mr. Tomkin was quite clear on this point." His hand dipped into the case, extracted an oversized buff envelope. Nicholas' name was on the front. The flap was sealed with a blob of red wax. He handed it over. "Mr. Tomkin requested that immediately upon his death you be hand-delivered this envelope and that you read it and sign it in my presence."

Numbly Nicholas looked down at the envelope. "What's in it?"

"It's a codicil."

"A codicil?"

"To Mr. Tomkin's will." Greydon's face was anxious again. He touched Nicholas on the wrist. "You must read it now, Mr. Linnear. It was Mr. Tomkin's express wish." His eyes seemed large and moist. "Please."

Nicholas turned the envelope over, broke the seal. He lifted the flap, took out several sheets of paper. The top one was in Tomkin's unmistakable oversized scrawl. He began to read.

Nicholas,

You are no doubt slightly bewildered by recent events. That is only natural. I must confess to wishing that I knew just what emotions are dominant in you now. I only know that were I there now I would never be able to tell them from your face. In many ways you have been even more of an enigma to me than my daughters. I suppose that is only right, since you have come to seem like a son to me.

Actually I think that is only fitting. Wasn't it Oedipus who wished to kill his father? Oh, yes, I know. Because I have come to know you. I have done many foolish things in my life, things on which I have little desire to dwell.

I had an unquenchable desire for power, and toward that end I destroyed people, whole companies even, to achieve my desires. But, in the end, life has a way of making fools of us all, and why should I be any different?

Meeting you changed my life, I can't deny that. Oh, at first not at all. I was too iron-willed for that. But I remember that long night while both of us waited for Saigō to come. You were there to protect me yet, in my fear and desperation, I spoke to him, offering to sacrifice your life for mine.

It was only later that I realized how foolish I had been. And I suspected that you had overheard me. I'm right, aren't I? Well, it doesn't really matter much to me now. Only to say that after that night I began to understand you. Some quality within you that I am still at a loss to define, began to creep through me like a mist. I'm glad you came to work for me, just as I'm glad you will marry my daughter. That, too, is fitting.

There are, perhaps, many reasons why you would want to kill me. But perhaps the most insistent is for what happened to your friend, Lewis Croaker. He thought I murdered Angela Didion; and you thought I had him killed.

177

You're wrong. And you're right.

I'm truly sorry, but I cannot be more specific. I've perhaps already said more than I should. To business:

On the next sheet of paper you will find a legal document. It assigns you sixty percent of the voting shares for Tomkin Industries. With it you can sit on the board of directors; you may even change its composition. Though Justine and Gelda each retain twenty percent, that will be entirely your prerogative, just as it was mine. Sign it and you will become the president of Tomkin Industries. Don't think too much about it, follow your instincts. But know that this is what I want, Nicky, with all my heart and soul, if such a thing truly exists. Soon you and Justine will marry. I am pleased that you love each other. No one understands better than I how precious such a commodity is these days. You're family now, you see, in all ways.

If you sign you will make me very happy. I'll know that the company is in the right hands. But know this: there is one thing that you must do immediately after the funeral. Greydon, who is no doubt standing by, will tell you what it is.

Good-bye, Nicky. Tell my girls I love them,

Raphael Tomkin

It was witnessed by Greydon, dated June 4, 1983.

Nicholas sat down on the arm of Sato's chair. His head was buzzing and he fought desperately for control. Nothing in his training had prepared him for this.

"Mr. Linnear?"

Slowly Nicholas looked up, becoming aware that Greydon had been trying to get his attention for some time.

"Mr. Linnear, will you sign the codicil?"

There was just too much happening at once. Nicholas felt overwhelmed. Emotion welled up from the Western part of him, while his Eastern half fought desperately to suppress those same emotions which if they surfaced would surely cause loss of face. Nicholas felt in the middle for the first time in his life, at odds with either side of himself. Because he wanted to do both: feel and not feel at the same time. Sato had been quite correct. In this country grief was an extremely private emotion, held back from even those closest to you. And yet, he felt acutely the presence of the Colonel urging him to grieve, telling him that it was all right, that it was a man's prerogative to cry, to feel, to need solace in times of stress; it was what everyone wanted.

And still nothing showed on his face. Perhaps Nangi, the astute master that he was, might have seen the pain flitting like dark darting fish in Nicholas' eyes. But Nangi would never even contemplate such a gross intrusion of privacy. Ever since Tomkin was stricken the Japanese had steadfastly looked only at each other, giving no chance for loss of face.

"Mr. Linnear?"

All at once Nicholas found himself in the first attack position, his muscles corded, his hips and knees already moving on their own, the red killing drive welling up in him and his arm beginning to lift.

"Yes?"

Greydon blinked rapidly behind his glasses, standing immobile and defenseless, and Nicholas thought to himself, What am I doing? appalled at the misdirection of emotion, the readiness of his body to act on his *aka-i-ninjutsu* training. It was as if all his time in America had been shed from him and now, returned to his natural element, he was reverting, cerebration giving way to instinct as he had been taught. For *jahō*, the magic of the ninja *ryu*, required the absolute imprisonment of the laws and strictures of so-called civilization.

But this was not Nara prefecture and he was not within the cool stone walls of the Tenshin Shoden Katori. He was no longer a pupil but a *sensei*. He should know better. But he was not entirely Eastern, no matter how much he tried to convince himself otherwise.

And at precisely this moment, as if a great and towering glacial floe that had blocked his path for ages, reflecting the light in its icy rills and ridges, had cracked asunder, he understood the latent anger he felt toward the Colonel for bearing him, for imbuing him with his Western genes, reactions, instincts—his coarsened method of viewing the world. Nicholas realized that his unfaltering reverence for his father was merely a mask for the resentment that lay smoldering in white heat inside him. And abruptly he knew what he must do.

He relaxed his body, consciously draining it of the adrenaline which, unbidden, had been released in the onset of *kokyū suru*, the attack stance. Handing Greydon the papers, he said, "Give me some time, will you," and went across the room, from island to carpeted island, past the four Japanese, who would not dare look into his face, who spoke in low, quick tones of mundane matters.

Nicholas went around the side of the sofa and Tomkin appeared before him again, already laid out as if on a bier. There was a

179

bitter taste in Nicholas' mouth and a burning behind his eyes. The day the Colonel had died, the Linnears' new gardener, another old man, a Zen master of his leafy domain, to take the beloved Atake's place in the house on the outskirts of Tokyo, had begun to rake the snow. And Nicholas could see again the lines of dark and white, the sight of melancholy winter transmuted by personal tragedy into the embodiment of death.

Nicholas knelt down at right angles to Tomkin's body, bowing his head formally as one does to acknowledge the head of a family. After the revelations of a moment ago there seemed no difference between this corpse and the one he and his mother and Itami had buried with such ceremonial pomp and circumstance so many years ago.

Save that now the ache inside him, unknowable and seemingly absolute, had been dissolved in the knowledge of his view of the Roundeyed Barbarian. Though the Colonel had come to love the East with an unfailing passion, still he had been *gaijin* and throughout all his life growing up in Japan Nicholas had suffered because of it. The blood, the blood. The Japanese could not get over that, could not, in their heart of hearts secreted far away from their public display of affection for him, forgive him for that ultimate transgression.

In Raphael Tomkin Nicholas had perceived, albeit unconsciously, all the traits, though untrue, ascribed to his father. He saw now that part of his hate for Tomkin was his hate for what the Colonel had been, what he could not help being. He was an Easterner trapped in a Westerner's body. *Karma*. But Nicholas understood now that he had never been able to accept that, that he had for so many years unconsciously fought against that *karma*, just as he had steadfastly refused to face his deep and abiding hatred.

Now he could. Tomkin's death had shown him the way, and for that he would be eternally grateful to the man. But he knew as well that he had felt far more than hatred toward Tomkin. He had never truly believed him the monster his daughters claimed he was. Always ruthless, sometimes cruel, he could nevertheless display an astonishingly profound love for his children as well as life. Nicholas felt the sorrow bubbling upward, released at last from the iron restraints of his Eastern heritage.

For while he grieved for Raphael Tomkin, he grieved anew for his father as well. Tears fell like stones from his eyes, neatly aligned pebbles from his own inner Zen garden that had forever been diminished by human loss.

After a time, Nicholas rose. His face was calm, composed,

and his mind felt clear, free of the ropy restraints of a half hour before. He went back to where Greydon was standing patiently holding the documents, and took them from him. He read the letter all over again, fascinated anew by Tomkin's insight; he had obviously understood far more than his ugly American exterior had indicated.

When Nicholas got to the paragraph about Angela Didion, he paused. Was Croaker right or wasn't he? he wondered. How could it be both? Shock after shock. Wheels within wheels. The letter's overall tone was curiously Oriental in its acute introspection, its hints at deeper developments.

For a long time Nicholas stared at the letter. He had long ago ceased to read. His eyes might even have seemed blank to an uninitiated observer. But the fact was he had begun to look beyond the words, to find the Void, and, in that peculiar form of meditation open only to the greatest of the world's warriors of the East, the answer to perhaps the largest change in his life.

Abruptly he looked up, and when his eyes made contact with Greydon's they were focused and sharp. He carefully folded the letter and put it away in his inside jacket pocket. "What happens if I don't sign?" he said quietly.

"It's all in the will," Greydon said. "I cannot tell you the details; that would violate my trust. I am authorized to say only that the board of directors will decide on the new president."

"But who will it be?" Nicholas asked. "Will he be a good man? Will he be in favor of this merger? Will he manage the company as Tomkin wanted?"

Greydon smiled thinly. "What would you have me say, Mr. Linnear? Obviously Mr. Tomkin wanted you to make your decision without such knowledge." He looked at Nicholas for a moment. "However, just by your asking those questions I believe you have already come to a decision." He produced a fountain pen and uncapped it. Its gold nib shone in the light like a sword-blade.

"Tomkin said there was something I must do . . . if I sign. You know what it is."

Greydon nodded. "That's correct. As the new president of Tomkin Industries you are required to seek an interview with a man in Washington. His name is C. Gordon Minck. I am in possession of his private number."

"Who is he?"

"I have no idea." The pen was waiting, hanging in the air. Nicholas took it, noting its weight and balance. He put the codicil down on Sato's desk and wrote his name on the designated line.

Greydon nodded his head. "Good." He took the codicil, waved it about until the ink dried, then folded it away. "You will receive a copy after the will is read." He stuck out his hand. "Good luck, Mr. Linnear." He ducked his head. "Now it's time I notified the company and began to see to funeral arrangements."

"No," Nicholas said, "I'll do that. And, Greydon, please wait until I speak to his daughters before informing the office."

"Of course, Mr. Linnear. As you wish." He left the room.

Nicholas looked across the expanse of Sato's office. The others were discreetly not looking at him.

He went across to them and said, "Sato-san, Nangi-san, Ishii-san," bowing formally, "I have been named to succeed Tomkin. His company is now mine." He lifted his eyes to see their reaction, but they were being very careful and circumspect. Too much had already happened today.

Sato spoke first. "Congratulations, Linnear-san. I am so sorry that your good fortune comes through these tragic circumstances."

"Thank you. Your concern is greatly appreciated."

Ishii also expressed his concern in a manner that managed to be sincere without being inquisitive. Nangi said nothing. That was all right. Now it was time to forge ahead. "Unfortunately, I will be forced to return to the States immediately to see to the last rites. Our discussions must be postponed." They bowed all around.

"*Karma*," Sato said.

"But I have no wish to forestall our merger," Nicholas said. "And I will be returning as soon as is proper. But toward that end, I find I must leave with you some information, bizarre though it may seem to you." Now he had their undivided attention. Good, he thought. Here goes.

"I had decided not to bring it up now because I felt some more evidence was needed. I thought I could be of some help in this. Now, however, circumstances dictate otherwise. Because I am leaving, because I hold sacred our mutual pact and do not want anything to disrupt it, I must now answer Nangi-san's question fully.

"He asked if I had any knowledge of death linked to the *Wu-Shing*. I said truthfully that I had never seen such a thing. And yet I have heard of it."

"In what circumstance?" Sato asked. "What happened to Kagami-san, truly? We must know."

And Nicholas told them the ancient legend he had recounted to Tomkin. Quiet electricity built itself in the air.

"I think it's time for all of us to go," Nangi said from out of the silence.

Uniformed attendants, called by the doctor, had arrived, and now they began to wrap Raphael Tomkin in silver-gray plastic swaddling.

Ishii left. Then Sato and the doctor filed past but Nangi, his face as pale as a geisha's white rice-powdered visage, held back, his dark eyes locked on Nicholas' face.

They stood side by side. "In three days," Nangi said, "the cherry blossom springs to life, blooming like a mystic cloud, heaven come to earth for a brief moment. In its opening we find joy; in its fading we console ourselves with the richness of memories.

"Is that not the way of all life?"

With a dry crinkle, the silver-gray plastic enwrapped Raphael Tomkin's face in its code of eternal silence.

KYOTO/TOKYO
SPRING 1945-AUTUMN 1952

When Tanzan Nangi returned from the consequences of war, released from the military hospital in which he had recovered while his country slowly lost the initiative in its desperate struggle against the West, he tried to go home.

He was set free of his antiseptic bed on March 11, 1945, almost a year to the day since he had been rescued from his makeshift raft. The hospital had claimed him, the surgeon's scalpel probing his flesh time and time again in attempts to repair the nerve and muscle damage done to him. Sight in his damaged eye was totally gone and there was nothing they could do but sew the lids in place to stop the interminable tic that had plagued him.

With his legs it was another matter entirely. Three lengthy operations returned partial use of his limbs to him. He would not, as the doctors had at first feared, be subjected to the indignity of amputation. But, they told him, he would have to learn to walk all over again, and it would be a slow, painful process. Nangi did not care. He was grateful to the God Jesus to whom he had prayed in his darkness and who had seen fit to preserve his life.

Travel in those times was difficult for a civilian, even a hero of the war. If you did not wear a uniform, if you were not on your way to a mobilization center, you were largely ignored.

Japan, in dire straits, had more on its mind. The bureaucratic war machine's hegemony over the country was stronger than ever.

But the spirit of togetherness beneath the billowing clouds of war was everywhere and Nangi found a ride into Tokyo in a farmer's broken-down truck, rattling over bumps and holes in the roads, stopped seemingly at every turn to allow the military traffic its right of way.

As it turned out, he needn't have bothered. The sky was black over Tokyo, a dense, acrid pall in no way related to the rain clouds higher up. Choking ash hung in the air, coating face and hands, lining the mouth and nostrils with grit.

Nangi stood shakily up in the back of the trembling truck as they rolled into the city. It seemed as if there was nothing left. Tokyo had been devastated. The high winds made it difficult to see clearly, and he was obliged to blink constantly to keep his eye free of ash. Not whole buildings, not whole blocks, but entire sections of the city had been incinerated. Where Nangi's family's house had stood there were now squads of sweepers and shovelers clearing their way through the lumps of blackened structures. No one was left alive, he was told. The intense heat of the igniting napalm combined with the high winds—the same winds that had fanned the terrible Tokyo fire of 1920—to roast fully half the city.

There was nowhere left to go but to Kyoto. Nangi had not forgotten the promise he had made to Gōtarō to see to his younger brother, Seiichi.

The ancient capital had been spared much of the devastation that had turned Tokyo into a smoldering blackened skeleton, but food was still scarce and starvation was rampant. Nangi had acquired a small loaf of black bread, a pot of jam, a bit of butter, and six *daikon*—white radishes. These he brought to the Sato house as a gift against the disruption and inconvenience of his visit.

He found only an old woman at home, a straight-backed, stiff-lipped creature with iron gray hair pulled back flat to her skull and the eyes of an inquisitive child behind a face full of wrinkles.

"Hai?" The interrogative was somewhat defensive and Nangi recalled what Gōtarō had said about his grandmother. There had been a great deal of suffering and death in this family, and he could not bring himself to be the bearer of more bad tidings. With the current chaos of the war it was all too likely that news of the death of her grandson would not have reached her.

He bowed politely and, handing her the packet of food, told

her that he had served alongside Gōtarō and that he sent his best respects to her.

She sniffed, her nose lifted slightly, and said, "Gōtarō-chan never paid me any respect while he was living here." But clearly she was pleased with this message and, bowing, she backed away from the doorway to allow him entrance.

It was still difficult for Nangi to negotiate, and she turned away in such a natural and graceful way he could never be certain that she had done it on purpose to avoid him embarrassment.

Obā-chama—for Nangi would know her only as others did, as "Grandma"—went to make him tea, a signal honor in those drear days without hope. They sat on opposite sides of the room with the break in the *tatami* between them as was customary between host and guest, *sensei* and pupil, sipping weak tea, leaves that had obviously been used more than once.

Obā-chama spoke and Nangi listened, at times answering her sharp perceptive questions as best he could, fabricating a skein of lies when it came to Gōtarō's whereabouts.

"The war has destroyed this family," she said, sighing, "just as it is destroying this country. My son-in-law is buried; my daughter in a hospital from which she will never leave. Japan will never be the same no matter what the Americans do to us." Her eyes were hard and glittery and Nangi found the idea of being her enemy frightening. "But it is not the Americans I fear." She sighed again and, shaking her head from side to side, took a delicate sip of her tea.

Just when he believed she had lost her train of thought, she began again, leading him slowly into the rhythm of her life. "The Russians have joined the war." The words had the pronouncement of a death sentence. "They waited until the last moment, until the outcome was clear even to their slow, bearlike brains. Now they have jumped in with their swords rattling and they will want a piece of us, too." Her white hands, with skin as translucent as porcelain, gripped the tiny handleless cups with unnatural tension.

"Do you see these cups, my grandson's friend?" Nangi dutifully looked; they were beautiful, impossibly thin so that light falling through the window penetrated from outside in, turning the material they were made of milky and glowing. Nangi nodded his head.

"They are quite magnificent."

Obā-chama sniffed again. "They were a recent gift. From a distant relative of mine. It was all that was left of his family. He stopped here on his way out of Tokyo to the countryside. He had become *sokaijin*.* I urged him to stay here, but the bombing of Tokyo had been too much for him and he could no longer tolerate being within a city's limits. Any city. Poor thing, he did not even understand the nature of his flight, but at least he was smiling.

" 'Obā-chama,' he said, 'the fire raids on Tokyo have forced me to move four times in the past three months, first out of my house, which is no more, then from temporary shelter to temporary shelter. With each move my priceless collection of T'ang Dynasty antiques was diminished. Fire took some of the scrolls here, a stumble on the street destroyed a vase there.' He handed me these cups. 'Here, Obā-chama, I see that your life is still calm. Please take these. They are the last of my collection. Now I have been freed to start my life anew without dragging my collection behind me like a burdensome hump. The war has made me appreciate other things in life.' "

Obā-chama turned the cup in the light using only her thumb and index finger. "Imagine! It is the T'ang Dynasty I hold in my hand!"

Nangi heard the awe in her voice and was not surprised. He looked anew at his own cup, marveling at its artistry and age. He too felt the common appreciation most Japanese had for this most revered of all the Chinese dynasties.

Obā-chama carefully put down the antique and closed her eyes for a moment. "But of what use is talk of art and antiquity now? The Russians will soon arrive along with the Americans, and then we will truly be undone." Beneath the despair Nangi heard the deep and abiding undercurrent of rage and fear directed at the Soviets. He felt a violent urge to reach out across the intervening space that tradition and courtesy dictated must forever remain and touch her, assure her that everything would be all right. But he could not. The words stuck in his throat like needles in the knowledge that everything would *not* be all right for them.

He was about to open his mouth to say something—anything to break the taut, painful thread of silence—when there came a sharp rapping on the door. Obā-chama's eyes cleared and, bowing, she excused herself.

Nangi sat silently without turning around. His back was to the front door; all he could hear was the soft murmur of voices, a

---

Sokaijin means, literally, "escape to the country." The term was used for the thousands of refugees streaming out of the smoking cities into the rural and therefore safer villages of Japan.

187

short silence, the murmuring beginning again. Then the door closed softly, and he heard nothing until Obā-chama returned to his view.

She sat back down opposite him. Her head was slightly bowed, throwing her eyes into shadow. "I have had news of Gōtarō-chan." Her voice was like a wisp of smoke, gently drifting, a shell only, transparent and empty within. "He will not be coming home."

Perhaps she always spoke of death thus with a poet's poignancy, but Nangi suspected not. Gōtarō had been special to her as, in the brief but incredibly intense time Nangi had known him, Gōtarō had been special to him.

The space between them danced with dust motes twisting in the heat of the sunlight. Their false life only accentuated the emptiness there.

The thin sounds of the uncaring traffic outside came to him remote as the memories brought to life by a faded photograph. An era was passing before them, a slow and heavy cortege filled with black roses. The scent of the past was everywhere, with only the dark uncertainty of the unknowable future to keep it company.

A kind of despair seeped slowly from Obā-chama though she bravely strove to be resolute and inwardly calm.

The helplessness of his situation affected Nangi profoundly as they sat facing each other. Her tissue-paper face had been crumpled by *karma*, and his heart ached with the burden of her newest loss, one in a string of bitter beads.

Then what came into his mind was a poem—not quite a *haiku* but exquisitely moving—by Chiyo, the eighteenth-century poet, considered the greatest of all of Japan's female poets. It was what she wrote after the death of her small son, notable for what it did not say as well as what it expressed.

He spoke it now: "'The dragonfly hunter—today, what place has he/got to, I wonder....'"

Of a sudden, they were both weeping and Obā-chama, appalled at her lack of good manners, turned quickly away so that he could see only her thin shoulders moving. And above, her bowed gray head.

After a time, he said quietly, "Obā-chama, where is Seiichi-san? He should be here with you."

Her eyes scored the nap of the *tatami*, searching perhaps for imperfections. She would not raise them. Then, her body moved, as if she were steeling herself to speak. "He is on his pilgrimage. To the mausoleum of the Tokugawa in Nikkō Park."

Nangi bowed. "Then with your permission, Obā-chama, I will go and fetch him. His place is here; it is a time for family."

Now the old woman raised her head and Nangi became aware

of the tiny nerve tremor that kept it in constant motion. "I would be most . . . grateful to have my other grandson beside me again." The corners of her eyes were diamond bright with the hint of tears she was holding back with a supreme effort of will.

Nangi thought it was time he left her to the privacy of her grief. He bowed to her formally, thanking her for her hospitality in these evil times, and with some difficulty rose to leave.

"Tanzan-san." It was the first time she had spoken his name. "When you return with Seiichi"—her head was held very straight; a tendril of hair swept down across one ear, feathering with her minute temble—"you will stay here with us." Her voice was firm. "Every young man needs a home to return to."

The deep green of the cryptomeria occluded the gray pall that still hovered over burnt-out Tokyo where legions of civilians still picked through the massive tons of rubble and blackened skeletons of the Red Night, urban farmers with ash-covered rakes, unearthing a harvest of despair.

All that remained of the terrible winds of the week before were soft, gusting breezes that bent the tops of the cryptomeria and set up a fibrous rustling whose confluence with the natural buzz of the insects brought about a harmoniousness for which this park was noted.

Nangi crossed to the far side of the stream via a stone footbridge and took a winding hillside path through dense foliage that would lead him to the gold-encrusted Yomei Gate and the tomb of the Tokugawa. He had not told Obā-chama because the timing had not been right but he, too, had spent many happy hours during his schooldays lost in deep reverie at the verge of this final resting place of much that had made Japan great.

That the Shōgunate of Ieyasu Tokugawa began the history of modern Japan Nangi had absolutely no doubt—but it was only in the difficult and feverish years ahead that he was to come to fully appreciate the insight he had forged for himself. This Shōgun was the first of a line stretching over two hundred years who tamed the myriad feuding *daimyō*, the only one with enough strength and cunning to bend these powerful regional lords to his will.

In so doing, of course, Ieyasu created the great two-hundred-year peace and forever changed the path upon which Japan would walk. For in effect he destroyed the *samurai*. Warriors have no place in peacetime for there is nothing for them to do. And in this interregnum the *samurai* metamorphosed slowly into bureaucrats, working in administrative functions, thus becoming no more than a "service nobility."

Nangi had heard it often said in school, where astute minds young enough not to have yet been entirely shorn of the objective view which age and full participation in the system would cut from them, that Japanese government was built on the separation of power and authority.

To understand this Nangi had had to return to his studies of history, reading in areas his professors had apparently ignored in their zeal to complete the semesters' curricula. There, in his books, he found the historical and political imperatives that were his answers.

The twin feudal powers of the Choshū and Satsuma families at last brought to an end the Tokugawa Shōgunate. But the resultant governmental corruption caused such a public outcry that they, in turn, were overthrown by the Meiji oligarchs. And the Restoration began.

What this cabal of leaders arranged was the kind of government similar to that in Bismarck's Germany. That many of these leaders had strong ties into that German government seems partly the answer as to why they chose that particular system. The other reason was that they wished to clandestinely retain their control of a government which, on the surface at least, would appear responsive to the needs of the public at large.

Toward this end they set about creating what they termed a non-political civil bureaucracy. It seems ironic that the Meiji oligarchs, so fearful of the traditional *samurai* that they officially abolished the class, were obliged to seek out for administrators of their newly coined bureaucracy the remnants of the very class they hated.

But it was their determination to have this vast and powerful buffer unit of bureaucrats in place before 1890 when the National Diet, the new parliament, would open and candidates from political parties began campaigning for public support and power.

The Bismarckian system of "monarchic constitutionalism" also served the Meiji oligarchs well since it made the prime minister and the army responsible not to parliament but to the monarch. The interim result was a relatively weak and ineffectual Diet and a powerful bureaucracy laced with supporters of the Meiji oligarchs. Thus was the will of the people carried out.

And yet for all its subterfuge and illicit lines of power, the growth of the non-political bureaucracy as the center of the government found great favor among the Japanese, for the corrosive memory of the privilege accorded the two families, Satsuma and Choshū, still burned like a fire within them. What they appreciated about the formation of the bureaucracy was that it was open to all men who had trained diligently and well and who displayed the proper aptitude and fortitude in scoring highly in examinations which could not be more impersonal and thus impartial.

And yet the ultimate result was never perhaps anticipated by the Meiji oligarchs. For with the solidification of the bureaucracy's power as the center of the new government, and with, at last, the passing of the last of the oligarchs, the true power within the government devolved entirely into bureaucratic hands both civilian and, just as importantly, military.

And all this, truly, was the legacy of the Tokugawa. An important lesson, especially for a young man wandering the land of a soon-to-be-defeated country who must think toward the highly uncertain and volatile future.

Change was coming, and the sight of the Tokugawa mausoleum breaking through the stairway of trees between which he had been walking brought home to Nangi just how much he wanted to be part of that change. Because the alternative was too horrendous to contemplate: to be swallowed whole in the inevitable war crimes tribunal of the occupation forces.

Nangi paused, looked quickly around him. He appeared to be alone. He turned and stepped off the path, moving quietly into the protection of the trees. In a tiny clearing he knelt down and, removing his army uniform from the small bag he was carrying that contained all his possessions, he rolled it into a rough ball and lit a match to it. It took some time until it was all gone. At last he stood creakily and ground the ashes into gray dust.

That done, he returned to the path to search out Seiichi Sato and bring him home.

Seiichi was not at all like his fallen brother. For one thing, he lacked the wild sense of of humor that made Gōtarō so easy to be with. For another, he was not a Christian. Seiichi was a swiftly maturing boy with a serious outlook on life.

On the other hand, Nangi found him to be supremely quick witted and a man—it was impossible to think of him as a boy— open to new and unusual ways of thinking. Primarily because of this quality—fully as unusual as wild, gusting humor—the two formed a solid core of confidence and trust in and for one another.

As for Seiichi, he took the news of his older brother's death well. Nangi had first caught sight of him as a black silhouette within the gloom of the mausoleum doorway. He had introduced himself and they had spoken for a long time.

Then, in the intuitive way some younger people have, Seiichi's eyes shifted and he said, "You have come to tell me Gōtarō-san has been killed."

"He died a *samurai*'s death," Nangi said.

Seiichi looked at him peculiarly. "That might not have made him as happy as it makes me."

"He was Japanese, after all," Nangi said. "His . . . faith in another God did not enter into it at all." He turned as if changing the subject. "He saved my life, you know."

Ultimately what bound them was their mutual desire not to die at war's end. Neither were soldiers of the Emperor; they certainly did not think of themselves as *kamikaze*, falling like cherry petals on the third day of their brief bloom. Yet, for all that, they were patriots. And it was this very love of country which spurred them on. Nangi was farsighted enough to want to see Japan rise from the rubble this stupid and ineptly fought war had reduced it to; Seiichi was young enough to still believe in the idealism of the world. Together, Nangi thought, they just might be unbeatable.

To this end, he began Seiichi's education in *kanryōdō*, the modern Japanese's *bushido*, the way of the bureaucrat, while Seiichi was finishing his last year at Kyoto University. Nangi thought that he would need a particularly salient example to hook Seiichi into this new way of thinking. He asked Seiichi if he knew the best route to political power in Japan.

Seiichi shrugged his shoulders. "The National Diet, of course," he said with the absolute surety of youth. "Isn't that where all politicians gain their experience?"

Nangi shook his head. "Listen to me, Seiichi-san: not one of Tōjō's cabinet ministers ever served in the parliament. All were former bureaucrats. Any time you feel your interest flagging, I urge you to remember that."

"But I have no desire to become a civil servant," Seiichi complained. "And I can't understand your desire to become one."

"Have you ever heard the phrase *tennō no kanri*? No? It is the definition of the Japanese bureaucrat, an official of the Emperor. Imperial appointment gives to them the status of *kan*, a word of Chinese origin that meant, in those faraway days, the home of a mandarin who presided over a city. *Kan* is power, Seiichi, believe me. And no matter what the American occupation forces do to us, in the end, *kan* will rule Japan and make it great once again."

Of course history proved the veracity of Nangi's words. Though General MacArthur's SCAP, the occupation authorities, changed the bureaucracy drastically from 1945 onward for seven years, they

192

did not and indeed could not eliminate it. In fact, they unwittingly strengthened one area: the economic ministries.

SCAP did away with the military completely. This they were compelled to do, but not understanding the fundamental nature of Japanese government, they failed to see the ramifications of their action. For the military had been the chief rival of the economic ministries.

But now the war crimes tribunal set in sights further afield and began calling in certain influential members of the *zaibatsu*, the great family-run industrial combines whose might had propelled Japan into the war in the first place.

With the transformation of the *zaibatsu* and the inevitable weakening of their influence as the tribunal's dedicated officers sifted through the rosters seeking out more war criminals in hiding, a power vacuum was created, into which the economic ministries again stepped.

Shortly after the Ministry of Commerce and Industry was purged of forty-two members—among the lowest percentage found within the government—Tanzan Nangi achieved a position in *kōsan kyoku*, the Minerals Bureau. This was in June of 1946 and Shinzō Okuda, the current vice-minister, was glad to have him. Nangi had gone to the right schools and, just as importantly, came to the ministry without taint as far as the war was concerned. He had never achieved a high enough rank or the kind of notoriety for him to have come under the scrutiny of the SCAP tribunal. He had also worked at the Industrial Facilities Corporation, a bureaucratic management foundation or *eidan*, shortly before the war broke out and he was called into service.

It did not take him long to catch on. Because MacArthur had been advised to choose an indirect occupation—that is, working through the existing Japanese government instead of doing away with it entirely—the shrewd ministers of the bureaucracy found a way to protect themselves: *menjū fukuhai*. Okuda explained this to Nangi soon after he had been on the job long enough to have impressed his superiors with his skills and to have gained their trust.

"What we continue to do each day," the vice-minister said, standing in the center of his small office, "is to follow the American orders so long as they are looking, then *reversing them in the belly* when they can no longer see what we do."

And, as Okuda told Nangi, the bureaucracy had already passed its first crisis point. "One day Minister Hoshijima called me into his office. You could see just how agitated he was. He was pacing back and forth, back and forth. 'Okuda-san,' he said to me,

193

'MacArthur is threatening to go to the people and have them ratify this new foreign document—what the Americans call a constitution.' He turned to look at me. 'Do you know what that would mean? We cannot allow the public direct participation in government if we are to keep our absolute power. A plebiscite would be the beginning of the end for us. We must all gather our power now and push for an immediate acceptance of the MacArthur constitution.'"

Okuda was smiling now. "And it was done, Nangi-san, in just this way."

In the months ahead, it became plain to Nangi that the fate of Japanese bureaucracy had been set forever. For one thing, the country's desperate need for economic recovery made it imperative that the legion of bureaucrats be expanded. For another, the political leaders who filtered through SCAP's erratic and, to the Japanese anyway, illogical system were totally incompetent. The occupation forces had returned to power many politicians who had not worked in over twenty years. Time and again, Nangi would confront cabinet ministers who were forced to bring with them their vice-ministers, whom they turned to for answers to almost every question put to them.

Too, it became manifestly clear to him just how little power resided in the Diet. It was at Nangi's own ministry where policy was hammered out and only then presented to the legislature for ratification.

In his new position Nangi was put in charge of carrying out many of MCI's policies that his vice-minister was far too busy to oversee himself. One of these was mining manufacturing.

Morozumi Mining was only one of many fledgling companies in need of total restructuring that came under his purview. Almost all the senior executives had been purged and subsequently tried as class A war criminals since Morozumi had been revamped during the mid forties, becoming one of the leading producers of tri-nitrotoluene for the war effort. Its then standing director had been awarded several medals in 1944 from Tōjō himself for the company's high levels of production.

But Morozumi was too well run to destroy entirely, and after the SCAP tribunal stripped the tree of all its boughs, it asked MCI to restaff the *konzern*. This Nangi was delighted to do since he was able to install Seiichi as production chief, a job which, in better times, might have been suspect for a young man just turned eighteen. But Seiichi was exceptionally bright and well schooled. Further, instinct had taught him how to act with men his elder, and thus his appointment passed without a ripple of protest from the vice-minister's office.

With the money they had received from the T'ang Dynasty cups Obā-chama had given them—even in the worst of times there are those enterprising few on the lookout for treasures—the two men had managed to rent a fair-sized apartment in Tokyo. Sato knew that his friend hated to give up such treasures; Nangi had fallen in love with the antique cups at the moment Obā-chama had first shown them to him. But they had had no choice.

As soon as they had a little money, Nangi had sent Seiichi to fetch Obā-chama. Her daughter had died shortly after Nangi had brought Sato home. And though she loved her little house in quiet Kyoto, age was making a solitary life more and more difficult for her.

One evening early in 1949 Nangi returned to the apartment somewhat early. As always, Obā-chama opened the door. She hurried to make tea, ignoring his protestations. With the tiny cups she brought out three freshly made rice cakes, a special treat in those times.

Nangi watched her distractedly as she went through the delicate tea ceremony, and when the pale green froth was at just the right thickness she withdrew the whisk and offered him the cup. When she had made her own and had taken her first sip, she judged the silence to have proceeded long enough without her intervention.

"If you have pain in your legs I will get your pills." Age had made her more outspoken. In any case she saw no shame in soothing away hurts inflicted by the war. She was grateful that he, at least, had been spared as her Gōtarō-chan, her daughter, and her son-in-law had not.

"My legs are no better or worse, Obā-chama."

Outside, the sounds of traffic ebbed and flowed as the convoys of military transports supervised by the Occupation Forces ran true to schedule.

"Then what is troubling you, my son?"

Nangi looked up at her. "It's the ministry. I work very hard, and I know my ideas are forward thinking and innovative. And yet there seems no hope of advancement. Obi-san, who is younger than I am by more than a year and is nowhere near as quick and knowledgeable, has already been promoted to bureau chief. His *sotomawari*, his going around the track, as these series of postings are called, has already begun on the elite course."

Nangi closed his eyes in an attempt to hold back the tears pearling there. "It is unfair, Obā-chama. I work longer hours than most. I come up with the solutions to problems. The vice-minister uses me when he's stuck for an answer but he never invites me out to drink after work, he never confides in me. I am an outcast in my own bureau."

"This Obi-san," the old woman said, sitting like a Buddha, "he graduated from Tōdai as did your vice-minister, is that correct?"

Nangi nodded his head.

"And you, my son, what university did you graduate from?"

"Keiō, Obā-chama."

"Ah." Obā-chama nodded as if he had provided her with the key to the Rosetta Stone. "That explains it then. You are not of their faction. Do you so soon forget the history, of which my grandson is never loathe to tell me you are a *sensei*? Always the *samurai*-bureaucrat's position depended on Imperial appointment, not on performance." She took another sip of her tea. "Why should it be any different today? Do you think any *iteki*—barbarian—interference can change us that much?"

She snorted in derision. "But you, my son, must learn to work within the system."

"I'm doing the best I can," Nangi said with an edge to his voice. "But I cannot swim against a tide. Keiō is not a well-known university. I know of only one other man in the ministry from there. He's a junior and not a classmate, so he's no use at all."

"Oh, stop sniveling, Nangi," Obā-chama snapped. "You sound like a baby. I'll not have such a demeaning display in this house, is that clear?"

Nangi wiped at his eyes. "Yes, Obā-chama. I apologize. For a moment my frustration seemed too much to bear."

Obā-chama snorted again and Nangi winced, now the object of her derision. "What do you know of the capacity to bear pain, disappointment, and suffering? You are only twenty-nine. When you get to be my age you might have some inkling although, Buddha protect you, I hope not."

She squared her shoulders. "Now. We do what must be done. And that does not include crying over the inequity of a system which all young men must abide by. Obviously *gakubatsu*,* the first and, at least as far as the ministers are concerned, the strongest of the factions that will help you in your life, is of no use to you here. But there are others. We may rule out *zaibatsu* as well, since that bond is based on money and you have very little at this moment.

_____
*The bond between school and university classmates.

"That leaves *keibatsu* and *kyōdobatsu*. Of the first, as far as you have told me you are not related by blood or marriage to any minister or vice-minister and the chances of you marrying into such a family at any time in the near future seems nil. Am I correct?"

"Yes, Obā-chama," Nangi said softly. The bursting of his months-long frustration had brought no relief. Rather it had given rise to a feeling of dull depression.

"Lift your head up, Tanzan-chan," the old woman said. "I want to look in your eyes when I speak to you." Nangi did as he was told. "You look as if all is lost, my son. It is not." Her tone had changed, softening just a bit. "You speak to me of how ingenious your thinking is at the ministry. It is time to bring some of that home, to guide yourself.

"It is my understanding that in order to receive promotions each junior bureaucrat must have a senior to champion him. Tell me, my son, who is your *sempai*?"

"I have none, as yet, Obā-chama."

"Ah." The old woman put down her cup and folded her mottled hands in her lap. "Now we come to the root of the problem. You must have a *sempai*." She knitted her brows together, her eyes crossed in concentration, the stylized *mie* used in the *kabuki* theater and in art. "The first three factions have been put aside, but what about *kyōdobatsu*. Have we, by chance, a vice-minister who comes, as you do, from Yamaguchi prefecture?"

Nangi thought for a moment. "The only bureaucrat of such senior position is Yoichirō Makita. He was born in Yamaguchi just down the road from me."

"Well, then."

"Obā-chama, Makita-san was minister of the Munitions Ministry during the war. He is now a class A criminal serving time in Sugamo Prison."

Now Obā-chama smiled. "You have been so busy working away at your ministry you have no time to read the newspapers. Your Makita-san has been in the news lately. You know that as well as being munitions minister, Makita-san had also been granted cabinet minister status by Tōjō." Nangi stared at her clear-eyed. It seemed as if he had suddenly awakened from a dream. What was in Obā-chama's mind?

"When the Americans captured Saipan in 1944, Makita-san publicly expressed his belief that the war was over for Japan and that we should throw up our arms in surrender.

"Tōjō was outraged. Well, who can blame him, really. In those days the word 'surrender' had been struck from the language, and

197

rightly so, in the spirit of the intense patriotism we all rallied around."

"But Makita-san was right," Nangi said.

"Oh, yes." She nodded her gray head. "Just so. But Tōjō called him to task. Cabinet minister or no he would have no more of this defeatist talk. As the head of the *Kempeitai** he could have had Makita-san executed. But he did not. As it happened the minister had a number of influential friends in the Imperial Household, the Diet, even the bureaucracy, and they were strong enough to stay Tōjō's hand."

Obā-chama picked up her tiny cup, poured herself more tea. "These facts have just come to light. Last week, Makita-san's status was changed to unindicted class A war criminal and the machinery is currently under way to depurge him." Those dark eyes watched Nangi carefully over the rim of the delicate tea cup. She swallowed and said, "You know, my son, Makita-san served as vice-minister of commerce and industry under three cabinets and as minister under a fourth. That would certainly make him *sempai*, would it not?"

"*Hai.*"

Obā-chama smiled charmingly. "Now eat your rice cakes, my son. I baked them especially for you."

Sugamo Prison was a depressing place. It had nothing to do with the physical aspect of the place, which was altogether ordinary. In fact, in those areas not given over to cells, it might have been the repository for any one of the myriad ministerial bureaus housed across the city.

The indifference of those who ran Sugamo appalled Nangi more than anything else. Yes, there were *iteki*—as Obā-chama would call them—always present. But it seemed to Nangi as if the everyday administration of the prison had been given over to the Japanese, and it was the behavior of these people that affected Nangi so intensely. To a man they exuded the shame and indignity the SCAP forces had put them through incarcerating their own people. The daily horror of feeding, exercising, observing, and, most of all, punishing these war criminals was tattooed on their faces as clearly as if they were the inky artwork covering Yakuza flesh.

It took Nangi three weeks to burrow through the labyrinth of red tape guarding the entrance to Sugamo like a Gordian knot. His vice-minister was of some help, though the man himself was

*The military, then secret police.

unaware that his signature on a form in triplicate helped Nangi open the steel-clad doors of the prison.

The scent of defeat rather than despair perfumed the atmosphere inside Sugamo. Bars were everywhere in evidence, and during his hours there the resulting striped sunlight gradually came to seem normal to Nangi.

Because Makita-san had been declassified and was in the process of being depurged, they allowed him to sit across from Nangi without the usual steel net screen between them.

Nangi could remember having seen Yoichirō Makita only once—in a photograph in the newspaper announcing his appointment as munitions minister. That man had been hearty and as rotund as a Chinese, with a fine, wide face and broad, heroic shoulders. The Makita who now appeared before him had another appearance entirely. His body had lost most of its weight. Because one could now see that he was a relatively large-boned man, his undermuscled flesh appeared as thin as the skin over it. He had an unhealthy pallor that made him appear almost jaundiced.

But oddest of all, his face had lost none of its roundness. If anything, that moonlike quality had inexplicably increased, bloating his features. All save his eyes, which seemed sunken in soft folds of meaty flesh.

Nangi expressed none of his dismay in either tone or movement, merely bowed formally as he introduced himself.

Makita nodded absently, said, "Good of you to come," as if he knew precisely why Nangi had shown up. "It is time for my exercise." He waved a hand in an aimless gesture. "I hope it will not inconvenience you overmuch if you accompany me outside."

Sugamo's version of "outside" was a narrow strip of courtyard between two buildings that rose up, bricked and barred, on either side of the lane. At one end was a brick wall much too high for any human being to climb but crowned with corkscrews of barbed wire all the same. At the other end was a glassed-in guard tower. The tarmac on which they walked was hard and unyielding.

"Please excuse my silences," Makita said. "I am no longer used to talking except to myself." He walked with his hands clasped behind the small of his back, his enormous head down. Already he evinced the shuffle of an old man.

Nangi was no longer certain of his course. Could this burned-out husk of a man actually become his *sempai*? It seemed unlikely now that he had come in physical contact with him. It seemed as if his best days were behind him. Nangi was about to excuse himself, saying it was all a mistake, and accept his loss of face as *karma*, when Makita turned to him.

"So what is it about me that has caused you to seek me out here in the depths of the netherworld, young man?"

"Kanryōdō." Nangi said it automatically, without thinking. "I am seeking my way in the new Japan."

"Indeed." Makita said nothing more for the moment, but his head had come up. They commenced walking again.

"You work for which ministry?"

"MCI, Makita-san, in the Minerals Bureau."

"Uhm." Makita seemed lost in thought, but Nangi noticed that he was no longer the shuffling old man he had been at the outset of the walk. "I'll tell you what is most interesting to me, Nangi-san. The Americans are now more interested in the burgeoning worldwide Communist threat than they are in us as a defeated power.

"When SCAP first set up shop here they were adamant about one point. They claimed that since we had brought on our own economic woes, the Allies were not going to be responsible for setting us back on our feet, so to speak.

"Interesting, Nangi-san, because as soon as they found out that due to the complete collapse of our international trade that tack would only ensure a Communist revolution here, they switched one hundred eighty degrees and insisted that the state take complete control of all economic measures.

"Good for us who practice *kanryōdō*. But even better, they removed the largest thorn in our side, the *zaibatsu*. As you know, Nangi-san, these giant cartels were our biggest rivals before and during the war. They snatched economic power from us bureaucrats as often as they could. But by doing this they ensured their own destruction. SCAP rightfully decided that the *zaibatsu* were responsible for our wartime economy, and they have been banned. The ministries have their power now, and it must be like having stepped into the promised land.

"Now Japan is perceived as a bulwark for America against the further spread of Communism in this part of the world. As such it has come to my attention that SCAP's first priority is to make our postwar economy viable." Makita stopped and turned to Nangi. "And do you know how they propose to do that, young man?"

"I'm afraid I don't, sir."

"International trade, of course." They began walking again, up and down beneath the gaze of the guards and the fulminating sky. "And that being the case, it seems obvious to me that the Ministry of Commerce and Industry has outlived its usefulness."

There was silence for a time. It seemed to Nangi that outside the prison walls the wind had picked up, but it was difficult to tell. Certainly the sun had been occluded by dense, dark gray clouds. He swallowed, aware that the barometer was falling. A storm was coming.

"Everyone at MCI is split into two camps," Nangi said. "Half believe in the *seisan fukkō setsu*, reconstruction through production, and the commitment to heavy industry buildup; the other half are advocates of the *tsūka kaikaku setsu*, the control of inflation and a commitment to light industries that would take immediate advantage of our cheap and large labor pool."

Makita laughed. "And which side do you adhere to, my advocate of *kanryōdō*?"

"Actually to neither side."

"Eh?" Makita stopped and peered at Nangi in the gathering gloom. "Explain yourself, young man."

Nangi steeled himself. This was just one of the ideas he had been formulating that he could not articulate to anyone at the ministry. Now he would see if Obā-chama had been right in guiding him to Makita.

"It seems to me that we must devote ourselves to the expansion of heavy industry, if only for the greater value of the finished products. But to ignore currency reform would, in my opinion, be a grave error, for if inflation is allowed to spread out of control it won't matter what kind of industry we are beginning to build. It will all collapse like a house in an earthquake."

Makita stood up straight, and Nangi got the impression that the other man was looking at him as if for the first time. In the ensuing silence, a rumble of thunder could just be discerned, muffled as it was by the high walls. Once trapped in there, however, it reverberated in blurred overlapping waves like the echo of a temple gong, calling the gods for supplication. It was very dark now, a premature evening or the first slide into an eclipse. Nevertheless, Makita's eyes glittered fiercely like diamonds at the bottom of a well.

"An interesting theory, Nangi-san. Yes. But to carry it out we would need a ministry that went beyond MCI, the Board of Trade, or any other now in existence, do you not agree?" Nangi nodded. "We would need a ministry with broader powers. A large ministry whose primary function was the manipulation of international trade." His head came around like that of a great predator. "Do you see that, Nangi-san?"

"*Hai. So desū.*"

"Why?"

"Because of the Americans," Nangi said immediately. "If they are suddenly in such desperate need for us to become a viable

201

country again—to protect their Far East flank—then it will be their international trade which must pull us up. Nothing else will work as quickly or as completely."

"Yes, Nangi-san. It is the Americans we must make our closest, though unwitting, allies in this venture. For SCAP will help us create a ministry able to wield *denka no hōtō*, the *samurai* sword. That status accorded us will bend both government and industry to our will."

Then rain came with a great surge of moisture and almost no wind because of the narrowness of the space. Within moments they were drenched, but neither seemed to mind.

Makita came closer to Nangi and said, "We are from the same prefecture, Nangi-san. That is as good as a blood bond. No, better. If I cannot trust you then I can trust no one, not even my wife, for her second cousin married one of my chief rivals not more than two weeks ago." He huffed. "So much for loyalty among family." The rain pattered against the tarmac, soaking their socks and making their shoes squeak when they moved.

"Now, there are two immediate problems. One is that as long as I am in here I am not as well informed as I might be. Go back to your job at MCI, Nangi-san, and in your spare time gather dossiers of as many of the ministers and vice-ministers as you can. I know where you work and you are only down the hall from the central file.

"The second problem is mine as well. I am being depurged by a most difficult man, a high member of the SCAP team, a British colonel by the name of Linnear. He is a very thorough fellow, and his annoying attention to detail is holding up my release."

Makita smiled. "But I will make him pay for prolonging my incarceration." He put a hand on Nangi's arm for a moment, an unusual gesture. "When finally I am released, rest assured that this *iteki* shall hand over to me the information we will need to complete our files and begin our own *mabiki*, our weeding-out process."

The Board of Trade that Makita had mentioned was a fascinating institution. Because of the terms of the Potsdam Declaration which Japan had accepted as part of its surrender, no private Japanese could engage in international trade. Everything had to go through SCAP.

Therefore the Occupation Forces created a Japanese organization in charge of accounting for and distributing imports brought in by SCAP and handing over to SCAP exports manufactured by local manufacturers.

Nangi had never had much to do with the BOT, and Makita's mention of it was in fact the first time he had thought of that bureau in quite some time. However, when he returned to work at MCI, the Board of Trade was to become a major force in his life.

As it happened, Prime Minister Yoshida, a long-time enemy of MCI's since he had a distinct distaste for their linkage to the old wartime ministries, had appointed his administrative advisor Torazō Ōda to head the BOT three months ago in December of 1948.

As Ōda began to clean house at BOT under the guise of removing some improprieties he was purported to have discovered there, it began to circulate that Yoshida planned to elevate the status of several ministries under his direct control to help decrease MCI's power.

This the powerful ministers at MCI would not tolerate, and on the same day that Nangi was out of the office interviewing Makita in Sugamo Prison, there was an emergency high-level meeting at MCI.

The ministers decided that they needed to forestall Ōda and Yoshida, who they knew were working in concert against them. To this end they were in agreement that they needed to put one of their own inside BOT to keep an eye on Ōda and report back to them his every move. That way, they felt, they would always be one step ahead of him and therefore could deflect him.

There were few candidates to choose from, principally because the list of qualities this man must have was so unusual. He must be highly intelligent, with a quick mind. But just as important, they knew he had to be someone relatively young and without the usual *gakubatsu* connection that would inevitably bring him under Ōda's scrutiny as a possible rival. In short, the candidate had to pass through BOT virtually unnoticed.

They came up with only one name: Tanzan Nangi.

When Nangi was summoned to Vice-Minister Hiroshi Shimada's office, he was in the middle of amassing his *mabiki* file. In fact he had just unearthed several interesting tidbits about the newly appointed vice-minister's wartime activities at precisely the moment the summons came.

He listened blank-faced as Shimada's proposal was given. There was really no question of not accepting. For the bureaucrat as well as for the common worker *Aisha seishin*, devotion to the company, obtained. It was an essential part of *kanryōdō*. Yet even if Nangi had had an actual choice to make, he would have leapt at this opportunity, for he immediately saw in this what Sun Tzu called

203

k'ai ho, to open the leaf of a door. Thus he determined to swiftly enter this gap afforded him, his eagerness masked by humbleness and his evinced dedication to serve to the best of his abilities Vice-Minister Shimada and his bureau.

But in truth it was Yoichirō Makita whom Nangi was sworn to serve. The way of *kanryōdō* was paramount with Nangi just as it was with Makita. Each recognized in the other that which was inside himself: the spirit of the direct descendants of the Tokugawa Shōgunate elite warrior caste, the true *samurai*-bureaucrat.

Nangi's subsequent appointment as chief of the Trade Section of the Bureau of Trade did not long deter him from continuing with his compilation of dossiers. In fact it provided him with a new source of confidential information. So that by the time Makita was depurged, he had a four-inch-thick stack of folders within which were revealed the peccadillos, petty and not so petty, thievery, connivery, and outright bribery by perhaps two dozen bureaucrats of the first and second *dan*.

On the day after Makita became a free man, before he and Nangi had a chance to review this parade of malfeasances, Nangi was summoned to the office of Torazō Ōda. What the minister of BOT had on his mind came as a total shock to Nangi.

Tea was served on a polished tray of filigreed European silver, in cups of bone china, poured from a tall acid-etched silver pot with curling feet. The set seemed grotesque and immensely overstated to Nangi, as all things European appeared to him, yet he smiled like a monkey and heartily complimented the senior bureaucrat on his exquisite taste, though the words threatened to stick in his throat and make him gag. The tea, too, was not to his liking. It was an execrable and ill-advised combination of several teas, dominated by Orange Pekoe, that somehow managed to cancel each other's aromas. He might have been drinking used dishwater.

When he complimented Ōda on the tea, the older man told him it was an American import called Lipton.

"The importance of America cannot be overemphasized, Nangi-san," Ōda said. He was a heavyset man with the overbearing paunch of a *sumō*. He was impeccably dressed in a three-piece pinstripe suit hand-tailored for him on Saville Row. His black wingtip shoes shone like mirrors. "It is time for us to put away our kimono and *geta*, time for the Rat's Head, Ox's Neck, time for us to begin thinking about more than our gardens and the perfection of the tea ceremony."

He watched Nangi for a moment as if gauging his response to this speech. "We have a job to do here, and since the *gaijin* Joseph

204

Dodge has stopped our runaway inflation with his extensive reduction of demand, we have only the future to think about again. And our future, Nangi-san, the salvation of the new Japan, lies in one area: international trade. *Tsūshō daiichi-shugi*, trade number one-ism."

He paused for a moment to sip some of the unpalatable tea. "Tell me, Nangi-san, do you speak English?"

"No, sir."

"Then I think it high time that you learn. The Prime Minister has created a number of courses for bureau personnel. He recommends joining, and so do I."

"I'll look into it immediately, sir."

"Good." Ōda seemed genuinely pleased. "My secretary will provide you with all the information you need on your way out." He sipped at his tea again. He had ceased to watch Nangi with such scrutiny and, in fact, had turned partially away from him to watch the busy streets through the window behind his desk.

"Tsūshō daiichi-shugi." He said it softly, almost as if he had forgotten Nangi's presence. "An admirable goal . . . and a necessary one. But, really, it seems to me that in this new atmosphere of what we must term high-speed growth we will require an entirely new ministry." He spun around to face Nangi suddenly, his eyes dark and penetrating. "What do you think of that idea, Nangi-san?"

"I . . . would have to hear more about it, sir," Nangi said, to cover his shock.

Ōda waved a meaty hand. "Oh, you know, a ministry whose primary function was to oversee and control all foreign trade, technology. It would have the power to dispense preferential financing to those industries the government had chosen for development, and to grant those industries tax breaks to make their growth easier and speedier." Ōda was back to his careful inspection of Nangi. "Does this kind of ministry sound feasible to you, Nangi-san?"

Nangi was caught between a rock and a hard place. How should he answer? Was Ōda-san friend or foe? Certainly he was an enemy of Nangi's superiors at MCI, but that was not really the issue at hand because from the moment he and Makita had formulated their long-range plans in the prison courtyard, Nangi had for all intents and purposes ceased to work for MCI. At least in his heart.

The issue now was whether or not Ōda was inimical to their plans. He could be an enormous aid to Nangi and Makita if he agreed with their theories. However, if Nangi leaked any part of the plan to this man and Ōda turned out to be antagonistic to it, he would certainly destroy the nascent plot immediately.

What to do?

"It seems clear to me," Nangi said cautiously, "that until the Occupation Forces leave Japan we are bound to them hand and foot. However, I have heard rumblings from Korea. If the Communists there carry out their threats to reclaim all of their country, I believe America will drag us into that conflict with them."

"Oh?" Ōda's eyes were heavy-lidded and the overhead lighting made it impossible now to see them clearly. Nangi made a mental note to remember the effect. "How so?"

"I think they will have no choice, sir. Obviously they will need all the paraphernalia of war: uniforms, vehicles, communication equipment, ammunition, and so forth. Korea is a long way from America. We are close. It is my opinion that they will use our economy and put it to work for them."

"That will be good for us."

"Yes and no," Nangi said, knowing he was taking a chance.

"What do you mean?" Ōda's face was absolutely impenetrable, and Nangi cursed the lighting.

"Precisely this, sir: of course the business we will get will be good for our economy because there will be a high degree of turnover and therefore profits will blossom like cherry petals in April. However, there is a danger inherent in the very speed required. Our companies are all undercapitalized, and it seems to me that even a six months' delay in payment will be enough to send them into bankruptcy. The business could kill us."

"More tea?" Ōda was refilling his own cup. Nangi shook his head; he had already done his duty on that score.

Ōda slowly stirred his tea with a tiny filigreed spoon. "How would you avoid the, er, negative aspects of this situation, Nangi-san?"

"Your new ministry would do nicely, sir." There, it was done, Nangi thought, willing himself not to sweat. It had been said yet not been said. Now it was Ōda-san's move, and depending on what it was, Nangi would have his answer.

"You know, young man, that your own Vice-Minister Shimada would oppose the creation of a new ministry."

"He is no longer my vice-minister, sir," Nangi said, neatly sidestepping the trap.

"Ah, yes." Ōda put down his cup. "Of course that is true. It had slipped my mind for the moment."

And now Nangi had his answer and his heart soared. Carefully he kept his surging emotions off his face. "The ministers of MCI struck me as perhaps a trifle overzealous in their protection of their own power."

"Perhaps they have a right to be, Nangi-san. Those most afraid of losing their power are always the most, er, sensitive about supposed threats to its security."

He and Yoshida are thinking of closing down MCI! Nangi thought. It was the only possible explanation for the line of this conversation.

"If you were in my shoes, Nangi-san," Ōda said, his voice neutral, "who would you choose to be the chief of this new ministry dealing with international trade?"

Now Nangi had to make his decision. He had to decide for himself whether Ōda was friend or foe, for he knew that once he answered the question there would be no turning back.

Nangi knew that there was no one in MCI he could turn to; knew, too, that as many friends as Makita had, their influence would not be enough to project him into the center of this new ministry without the blessing of Ōda and Yoshida.

All of a sudden he felt released, his decision made for him. "My choice would be Yoichirō Makita," he said without hesitation.

For a time there was silence in the office. Ōda tapped the bottom of the spoon against his pursed lips. At last he said, "Vice-Minister Shimada would never stand for such a thing."

"He won't be happy about the formation of the new ministry, either," Nangi pointed out.

"Oh, but this is different, Nangi-san. Shimada and Makita are bitter enemies. Creating the new ministry is one thing. Installing Makita at its center is quite another."

"May I inquire, sir, as to whether Makita-san would meet with your approval."

"Well, it hardly matters, Nangi-san, you can see that. There are things we all would wish for but cannot have. One must learn to flow with the tide lest one be pulled out to sea and become lost to land."

In the gathering gloom of the late afternoon outside, Nangi thought of his *mabiki* file and the list of incriminating evidence he had amassed against Shimada. "Correct me if I am wrong, sir, but in *kanryōdō* there is a continual weeding-out process."

"At the lower levels, yes, of course," Ōda said. "The outgoing vice-minister selects his replacement, and all others at the ministry from the new man's university class resign in order to give him a clear field of unquestioned authority."

"And yet," Nangi said carefully, "at the upper echelons there is, from time to time, also *mabiki*."

"Oh, yes," Ōda said, "but there we are generally talking of a scandal of some major proportions. I can recall a time when those things could be manufactured . . ." A small smile creased his face. "There were artists for everything in those days." His expression sobered and he shrugged. "But in the present there is always the Occupation Forces, and like hawks in the sun they are ever over our left shoulders, hovering, scrutinizing." He shuffled some papers. "In any event, all the old artisans are gone."

"If I understand you correctly," Nangi said, his pulse racing wildly as he approached the heart of the matter, "you are speaking now of *manufacturing* a scandal out of smoke and pine needles."

"Poetically put, Nangi-san. And essentially correct."

"I take it, then," Nangi said, keeping the tremor he felt inside out of his voice, "that the Occupation Forces would give us no trouble over a quite *real* scandal."

A telephone rang somewhere in an adjacent office, muted voices could be heard for a moment just beyond the closed door. Minister Ōda's almond eyes glittered like dark gems behind the round lenses of his spectacles.

The stillness in the room was so palpable that Nangi felt as if he was swathed in blankets. Now every motion, ever word, every look became a clue to the outcome of this meeting.

"Scandal, it seems to me, Nangi-san, can mean many things to many people. I think it imperative that one comes to some clearcut understanding of, er, definition."

Nangi locked his eyes with the minister's and said, "Disgrace for our enemies."

After a time, Ōda reached downward, producing a bottle half full of amber liquid. "May I offer you a brandy?"

Nangi nodded his assent, and there was silence in the room while they both drank. Outside, a typewriter had begun, working at a fast-clipped pace.

Carefully, Ōda put down his cup. "It seems to me, Nangi-san," he said, "that Shimada-san was most generous in transferring you into my purview."

"Perhaps, but he was also stupid," Nangi said with uncharacteristic candor.

Ōda shrugged his shoulders. "It is said that the Chinese cannot believe that a foreigner can speak their language so that on those occasions when one does, he is not heard. Vice-Minister Shimada reminds me of the Chinese." He refilled their cups. "He may not have acute insight but he has many friends and allies."

Nangi knew what his minister was obliquely implying. "None

of them have enough power to save him from his own blunders. Hiroshi Shimada has been a very greedy bureaucrat."

"Not the American way."

"Oh, no," Nangi said, getting into the spirit of the play. "Not in the least."

"Good. Perhaps we may even experience some help from that quarter." Torazō Ōda rubbed his hands together. "As for the, er, business aspects, I trust we have come to a mutually satisfactory agreement."

"Pardon me, sir, but I believe we have one more matter to decide."

Ōda, in the midst of rising preparatory to dismissing Nangi, paused. His face was calm. "And what might that be? You have my permission to continue."

"With all due respect, sir, my own position has yet to be worked out."

Ōda laughed as he sat back down, his great belly shaking as if with convulsions. Behind him the first gusts of rain began to bead the windowpane, obscuring the hurrying pedestrians far below. "Young man, I do believe I have the measure of you now." He chuckled. "I shall not underestimate you again. Let's see." He tapped a pudgy forefinger against his pursed lips. "It is clear that you are far too clever to remain here at the BOT.

"You will be my eyes and ears at the new ministry. Makita-san will appoint you chief of the Secretariat. There you will weed through all of the applicants to the new ministry, approving those who are loyal to Makita-san's—and my—policies.

"Slowly we will transform the face of the entire bureaucracy. Slowly we will melt away those who oppose us, those who do not understand the nature of trade number one-ism. It will be the two-hundred-year Tokugawa Shōgunate reborn!"

Nangi recognized the fierce, cold light of the fanatic turning the minister's eyes into beacons, and he found himself wondering what it was Ōda had occupied himself with during the war.

Makita-san and I will have to treat this one carefully, he thought as he rose and bowed formally. "Thank you, sir." He turned to leave, but Ōda-san's voice stayed him.

"Nangi-san, you were quite correct about Vice-Minister Shimada. He was twice a fool. Once to underutilize that fine brain of yours. Second to send you of all people to spy on me."

MCI did not disappear as Nangi had suggested, but the Ministry of International Trade and Industry's creation did sound its death knell.

Nangi and Makita pored over the *mabiki* file and, as had been planned, Makita took Nangi's information officially to Ōda. Because Shimada was a vice-minister and this did have at first whiff the scent of a major scandal, Ōda felt obliged to pass on all the damning evidence to the Prime Minister. Six days after Yoshida received the documentation of Shimada's transgressions, which included manipulation of ministry funds, use of ministry classified information to obtain jobs for several of his family, and the unearthing of a mistress, a *geisha*, as well as a wife, he was forced to dismiss the vice-minister and make the circumstances of his firing public. SCAP demanded such a procedure in order to ensure continued public support for the government and in order to bring home to the Japanese populace at large that they were indeed living in a democracy where nothing was concealed.

Yoshida was, of course, against such a public humiliation and fought it, knowing what the end result would have to be. He was overruled by members of the Occupation Forces, and at last, after stalling long enough to return to him most of his lost face, he released the documents to the press.

Less than twenty-four hours later, Hiroshi Shimada, kneeling on a fibrous *tatami*, clad in a kimono of ash gray field and smoke wheels, directed his *wakizashi* toward the muscled ridge of his lower belly, slashing left to right, then upward, his body quivering with effort, control, and face. His wife, Kaziko, was found by his side, pools of their already browning blood amassed and mingled, their last and only testament.

"I wonder how much Colonel Linnear hated Shimada." Yoichirō Makita knelt on the *tatami* while across from him Nangi reclined in a minimum of pain, his spine against a folded *futon*.

Nangi was surprised. "You mean the *gaijin* who depurged you? How is he involved?"

Makita looked far better than he had in Sugamo. His body had begun to fill out, while his face had most of its former bloat. He now appeared much as he had in the newspaper photograph Nangi had seen years ago, a figure of almost iconic proportions, an aggressive and powerful *samurai*-bureaucrat.

"During my long weeks with the English Colonel he revealed much to me," Makita said thoughtfully, "though far less than many other *gaijin* would. He has the gift of patience, that man."

"You sound as if you admire him."

Makita smiled. "Oh, nothing so strong as that, surely. But still ... for a *gaijin* ..." His voice trailed off for a moment, and his gaze retreated to an inner stare.

"You think he knew Shimada personally," Nangi asked after a time, "as you did?"

Makita's eyes snapped back into focus and he was with Nangi again. "Oh, there was something between them, all right. I have no doubt about that. Colonel Linnear was the man on MacArthur's staff who most vociferously fought to have the facts in the scandal made public knowledge."

"Just like a *gaijin*."

"On the contrary, Nangi-san. Just like a Japanese."

Nangi shifted position to ease the stiffness coming into his muscles. "I don't understand."

"Unlike most of the *iteki* in SCAP, who had no concept of the lethal consequences of their planned public humiliation—for they saw it only as a revealing of the truth—Colonel Linnear knew what Shimada must do. Oh, yes, Nangi-san, he wanted Shimada dead almost as badly as I did."

"What is another Japanese life to an *iteki*?"

Makita heard the bitterness in his friend's voice and wondered at the innumerable kinds of rationalization the human mind could unearth in order to protect itself from psychic trauma. It was apparently easy for Nangi to believe someone like Colonel Linnear would engineer the death of a Japanese merely because he was a barbarian. Did it occur to Nangi that he himself was the minister of justice in this case, meting out Shimada's death sentence in order to help speed Japan's high growth through the direct control of MITI. Now who is rationalizing? Makita asked himself.

He had no doubt about Nangi's brilliance, however. The man had been dead right with his prediction of the Korean War. America had put Japan on a war-materiel manufacturing blitz, and many of the nascent companies dragooned into gearing up were helplessly undercapitalized.

SCAP saw this immediately and allowed the Bank of Japan to step up its loan rate to the twelve city banks, who then passed the money on to the companies in need. For weeks Makita had been thinking of a way to capitalize on this development, for he saw that a lack of adequate financing would leave many companies open to foreign takeover. This he felt quite strongly must never be allowed to occur, and he was in the process of extending MITI's power in this area so that all foreign investors would have to come to MITI to seek permission to approach a company.

"How is our friend Sato-san making out?" he asked.

"Quite well," Nangi said, reaching for one of the *mochi*, concentrated rice cakes that Obā-chama had baked for them. They were three days into 1951 and these were traditional new year's

211

fare. "He has managed to rise to the vice presidency of his mining *konzern*, overseeing all coal operations."

Makita grunted. "Take care you drink plenty of water with those," he observed. "My brother was a doctor and he used to dread the first two weeks of every new year because he was constantly running from patient to patient, trying to unblock intestines clogged with indigestible *mochi*."

"I wouldn't let Obā-chama hear you say that," Nangi said, taking another bite. "But just to be on the safe side, I think I'll have some more tea." He leaned forward.

"She misses him, you know," Makita said after they had drained their cups. "Sato-san. He's making a great deal of money and a solid name for himself. But he's up north and he rarely gets a chance to see Obā-chama. Now if only his *konzern* had an office here in Tokyo. But they're much too small on their own. It wouldn't be profitable. Only the city bank that subsidizes them is located here."

A warning bell went off in Nangi's mind. On the surface there seemed no relation to what Makita had just said and the problem he had been working on. And yet he trusted his senses enough to know that if he took the time to probe beneath the surface, he would find the link.

The problem revolved around money and who had money other than banks. For a moment Nangi's mind was blank, and then the meshing of ideas hit him with such dazzling force that he was rocked back on his buttocks. Yes, of course!

His eyes cleared. "Makita-san," he said softly. "May I have your assistance?"

"You have it gladly. You have only to ask."

"Here is what we must do, Makita-san. MITI must resurrect the *zaibatsu*."

"But they were our enemy. At every turn they sought to draw power away from the ministries. And in any event the Occupation Forces have banned *zaibatsu* forever."

"Yes," Nangi said excitedly, "the *old zaibatsu*. But what I am speaking of now is something new, *kin-yū keiretsu*, financial linkages. As a base, we will take a bank because only a bank has enough capital to finance such a setup. Its capital will finance several industrial firms, oh, say, steel, electronics, and mining, and a general trading company. In times of expansion, as we have now, the bank will be able to underwrite its own companies and, conversely, during times of economic recession, which must surely hit us, Makita-san, the trading company will be able to import raw materials on credit and promote the *keiretsu*'s products overseas, thus avoiding any stockpiling in a contracting domestic market."

Makita's eyes were shining and he rubbed the palms of his hands together. "Call Sato-san immediately. We'll start with the bank underwriting his company. We'll elevate him and in the process bring him home.

"Oh, this is brilliant, Nangi-san. Brilliant! By next year SCAP will be gone and MITI can do whatever it feels is necessary to propel Japan to the forefront of international trade."

"What about control?" Nangi asked. "We must ensure that what happened with the *zaibatsu* never happens with these new *keiretsu*. We must bind them to the ministries as part of their charter."

Makita smiled. "And so we shall, Nangi-san. Because MITI directs policy, because we can issue write-offs in certain areas and not in others, because we can authorize sizable payouts as insurance against bad debt trade contracts, we can totally control the trading companies. And without the trading companies the *keiretsu* is useless. Any bank will see that reasoning."

"Ah, even the Prime Minister will see the pureness of the *keiretsu*, since it is a perfect way to direct what capital is available into the right economic channels." They were like two children wonderingly examining a marvelous new toy. "It's the perfect long-range plan. Because the individual companies within each *keiretsu* are totally financed by the bank, they can concentrate on market penetration, developing the best possible product, and not on shareholders' demands for short-term profitability."

Makita sprang up. "This calls for a celebration, my young friend! Tomorrow is soon enough to speak to Sato-san. Tonight, we are off to a place I know in *karyukai*. A night in the willow world will do us both a great deal of good. Come, we are off to *Fuyajo*, the Castle That Knows No Night, where the sakē flows until dawn and we will lie on pillows that breathe with infinite softness and create patterns of eternal delight!"

An exaltation of larks clung to the flame-decorated branches of the stately maple that grew on one side of the garden that had originally attracted Nangi and Sato to this house near Ueno Park. Brisk October winds had scoured the sky, vaporizing the stringy clouds near the horizon and turning the air to crystal.

As Nangi watched, clad in a padded kimono, a black field with a pewter design, the larks burst from the maple in a fine spray as if he were on the bow of a ship churning through the Pacific. Then, like the Occupation Forces, they were gone, swallowed up in the enormous cerulean sky, the color as translucent as the finest Chinese porcelain.

Though this was the end of 1952 and Japan was once again a free country, purged of *iteki*, there was no joy in Nangi's heart. He knelt by the open *fusuma*, his hands folded in his lap, gazing with blind eyes out at the near-perfect beauty of the garden. It would never be perfect, of course. As the nature of Zen dictated, one must spend one's life searching for that perfection.

Behind him Nangi could hear the soft voices of Makita, Sato, and his new wife, Mariko, a gentle doll-like woman with a core of courage and an open soul Nangi could admire. She had been good for Sato, fulfilling a void in him that had been apparent to Nangi almost since the two had first met.

It was Nangi who mourned Obā-chama's passing the longest. Makita, of course, knew her only peripherally. To Sato, she had been mother and father both, and he had been unwell for almost a week following her funeral.

But Obā-chama had died more than a month ago and Nangi still felt the absence of her spirit like a void in his own soul. She had been more than mother to him, she had been his confidant, his *sensei* even when he needed it. They had shared the joys of his successes, the bitter sorrows of disappointments. She had counseled him wisely in perilous times and had had enough strength to kick him when he thought he had no more stamina to press onward.

She had been old, ancient even. And Nangi knew all things must eventually turn to dust from whence they first came. But his spirit was bitter and sere without Obā-chama's bright eyes and chirrupy voice.

Though he could not understand it fully then, Obā-chama's death sealed his fate, or a good part of it at least. After Gōtarō's death Nangi had made an unconscious pact with himself never to allow that degree of openness—and therefore vulnerability—to spring up between him and anyone else. But somehow Obā-chama had charmed him out of that pact, with this inevitable result.

Though Nangi was to sleep with many women in his time, he would feel nothing for them in his heart. The double deaths from his past were like eternal *kami* hovering in his mind, reminding him of how evil and unfair life could be. These, of course, were very Western concepts, but Nangi could never admit such anathema to himself. Thus his *karma* was complete. This struggle between his Japanese nationalism and what a tiny part of him might suspect was his ultimate reason for turning to Christianity would plague him to the end of his days, an eternal punishment perhaps for submitting to Gōtarō's sacrifice, for lacking the courage to overcome his terror and do for his friend what Gōtarō had finally done for him.

The birds were gone now, but the splendor of the autumnal foliage crowned the maple with a mantle of searing colors. Voices drifted over Nangi like *kami*. Mariko was busy preparing the traditional gifts of foodstuff for tonight's *tsukimi*—the moon-viewing ritual of contemplation and peace.

Nangi's gaze moved over the top of the swaying maple to the brilliant sky swept new by the gathering winds swirling aloft. Soon the moon would rise, showering this small space with silver and blue light. And through the open *fusuma* the chill of night would slowly creep in.

K'AI HO

[1. A gap; an opportunity presents itself,
enter swiftly 2. Spies]

His heart leapt when he saw her. She broke through the cordon of milling people, her long legs pumping, and raced into his arms.

"Oh, Nick," she cried into his chest, "I thought you were never coming home."

He lifted her head up so he could drink in the colors of her large eyes, the swirled sienna and bottle green that could have been hazel but was not. The bright crimson motes danced in her left iris. He saw that she had been crying.

"Justine."

His sigh set her off again, and he felt the slow crawl of her hot tears as their lips crushed together and her mouth opened under his, her sweet warm breath mingling with his, and he thought, It's good to be home.

"I'm sorry about how that call ended," she said. People were shouldering roughly past them and he became aware that they were blocking the egress from the incoming flight. He moved them quickly off to the side.

"So am I," he said. "I was distracted—there was so much to do over there and not enough time to do it in."

She had done something to her hair, he saw. It was as tangly and wild as a lion's mane. Too, there were garnet highlights here and there as the overhead lights spun off it.

"I like it," he said, his arm still around her.

She looked at him. "What?"

"Your hair."

She smiled as they began to walk toward the glass doors. "All that matters is that you're home safe and sound." She put her head against his shoulder, forcing him to shift his bags to a more comfortable position.

He found it odd and somehow unsettling that she had said nothing at all about her father. But, considering what was ahead, he did not think this the best time to question her. Instead, he said, "Tell me about your new job. Are you happy there?"

"Oh, yes," she said and immediately launched into a description of the three major projects Rick Millar had her working on. In so doing she was transformed again into the exuberant little girl she often could be. It was interesting how all shyness evaporated from her at these times. She seemed supremely self-confident and mature. Nicholas found himself wondering how a job could have changed her in so short a time.

But when she was finished, the self-consciousness returned. She could do more things with eyes than anyone else he knew, and now as she lifted her head and stared at him, he saw the shyness and the need for his approval. There was that peculiar coolness swirling in the depths that he recalled vividly from their first meetings that was far better than a verbal warning to keep him at arm's length.

He swept her up, laughing. "But of course I think it's wonderful! It's about time you came out of your shell."

"Now, listen, Nick, I didn't say I'd keep at it or—"

He set her down. "But you said that you enjoy it."

She abruptly had an air about her so fragile and insubstantial that he hugged her to him as if she were a lost child.

There was a gleaming silver limousine waiting for them as they emerged from the swinging glass doors. Nicholas stopped, but Justine tugged at the crook of his arm.

"Oh, come on," she said. "I decided to splurge part of my new salary. Indulge me."

Reluctantly, Nicholas gave his bags over to the uniformed chauffeur and, ducking his head, slid into the plush back seat next to Justine. She gave instructions to the driver and they slid out into the slow-moving traffic on their way to the Long Island Expressway.

"I see Gelda decided not to meet her father."

Justine looked away from him. "You didn't hear my asking to look at the coffin."

"That was all taken care of ahead of time. There was no reason for us to be there." Silence in the car, like a beaded curtain between them. "Your father—"

"Don't start this again, Nicky," she said sharply. Her head turned and he saw the anger in her eyes. "I never for a moment understood why you went to work for him. My father, of all people! He was such a despicable man."

"He loved his daughters."

"He didn't love himself; he didn't know how to love anyone else."

Nicholas put his hands between his knees and clasped his fingers. This might be a bad time to tell her, he thought. But he could think of no good time. She had a right to know; he wasn't that Eastern that he could keep this from her.

"Your father gave me complete control of the company."

Thrumming of the powerful engine, deep and rich, the slide of Queens' semi-urban sprawl drifting by them. And a feeling of helplessness.

"That's a bad joke, Nick," she said. "Don't even make it."

Mentally he sighed, steeling himself for the storm. "It's no joke, Justine. He wrote a codicil to his will six months ago. His sixty percent of the voting shares makes me the new president of Tomkin Industries. Bill Greydon was a witness, and he witnessed my signing the codicil in Tokyo."

"You *signed* the bloody thing?" She was twisted around on the seat, her back stiff, pressed tightly into the opposing corner. "You agreed to that . . . !" She shook her head in disbelief, for the moment words failing her. "Oh, Christ but it's madness." Her voice had turned throaty as if her throttled emotions were aswim in her words.

She put her hand up to her face as if to block out the image of him sitting so close to her, as if that would erase what he had revealed to her. "Oh, God, no. No, it can't be." She tore her hand away from her eyes and glared at him, her chest heaving with her rage.

"I thought it was finally over. I thought my father's death would once and for all put an end to it, that it would sever me wholly from how he had chosen to live his life. Because as sure as we're both sitting here, Nick, Tomkin Industries was built on the blood and bile of everyone my father felt he had to defeat in his climb up to the top." She gave a small, bitter laugh and looked as if she were going to spit. "The top of what? Can you tell me that, Nicky? What was it that was so important that he treated my mother and Gelda and me as . . . *things*, useful to him when he needed us but

221

beneath his notice when he was otherwise occupied—by getting to the top."

Nicholas said nothing, knowing that his best bet was to allow her to run her course.

"And now"—that laugh came again so chill that it seemed to border on hysteria—"now when I'm finally about to get my life into some kind of order, you tell me that I'm again bound to Tomkin Industries *body and soul*."

"I only said that I had signed the codicil."

"And of course that has nothing to do with me," she cried. "We're going to be married in a month, or has going *home* made you forget so soon?"

"Justine, for God's sake—"

"No, no. This involves me as well as you. But bastard that you are, that never occurred to you, did it? Admit it, damnit!" Her eyes were fiery and her cheeks were pink and burning with her anger. "You know how I felt about my father; you knew how I felt about his company. I thought that you working for him would be temporary. I thought...Oh, Christ!" She put her head in her hands, her rage dissolving into tears of helplessness. "Oh, how I hate you! Look what you've done to us!"

Nicholas put his head back against the plush velvet, closed his eyes. "It *was* supposed to be temporary, Justine." His voice was soft, gentle, assuring as he used the opposite side of *kiai* to manipulate his tone. "But life is fluid, events cause us to change our plans. There's a flow to—"

"Oh, don't you dare start with your idea of *karma*," she snapped. "I don't want to hear any of that obscure mumbo jumbo. Try it out on your Japanese friends, not me!"

"Justine," he said simply, "we're both exhausted. A great deal of thought went into my decision and I—"

"But not about me, not about how *I* felt!"

"There's more to it than what you want, Justine," he said, abruptly angry.

"Now you listen to me. I spent all my life listening to what my father *told* me, listening to what a long succession of boyfriends *told* me. And I obeyed them all just like a good little girl should. But that's all over and done with. Because, you see, there *isn't* more than what *I* want. I've never in my life had what *I* wanted; I was always afraid to try for it because of what my father *told* me, what my boyfriends *told* me; how to behave, what to do, what not to say.

"Now it's me and only me. I control my own life; I control

222

my own destiny, not my father, not anyone else. Not even you, Nicholas."

She leaned toward him, moving out from her corner of the seat. Her skin was red, her normally full sensual lips pulled taut and thin. "At last I'm free, and no one is putting me back in my cage again. I won't be chained to anything, *especially* something so heinous as Tomkin Industries."

"Then we have something of an impasse," Nicholas said.

But Justine was already shaking his head. "Oh, no, Nick. That's your definition of this situation. But the truth is this: as long as you're involved with my father's company I don't want to see you, I don't want to talk to you. I don't want to know you exist."

In the great spacious hall of martial arts on the thirty-eighth floor of the Shinjuku Suiryū Building, Masuto Ishii was working up quite a sweat. While others spent their lunch hours over *soba* and Suntory Scotch, Ishii used that time to give his physical self a workout.

Three times a week he rose before dawn to run ten miles along twilit streets before returning to his tiny bachelor's apartment in the Ryogoku district, showering, and dressing in impeccable dark suits for work. The other four days he spent the early-morning hours in this same gymnasium. Since he allotted his section chiefs forty-five minutes for lunch, he felt a duty to conform to the same spartan schedule. That was too little time for a whole panoply of exercises, so midday he confined himself to the repetition of one or two difficult maneuvers culled from the various disciplines with which he was conversant.

Thus when Akiko found him he was in the midst of the *irimi* variations of *jo-waza*, stave *aikido*. There was no one else about, the vast Sato staff emptying out of the building like locusts upon the gleaming field of Shinjuku at precisely twelve-thirty. For a time she watched him intently.

Long muscles rippling, filmed with a light sheen of sweat that lay on his chest like mineral oil, his oval head down, the bull-like chest barely moving as his concentration deepened. She remembered the long, lingering look he had given her on her wedding day. She had seen the veiled lust in his eyes then and had wondered: had it been her he had wanted to get at, or was it the symbol of what his superior was about to possess? For Akiko sensed Ishii's adoration of power as strongly as if it were animal spoor. Not for him the quiet contentment of home and family, of his secure position as number-two man at Sato Petrochemicals.

In his heart he was no man's right hand but, rather, wished only to select his own line of command from top to bottom.

This was in her mind as she came across the polished floor-boards, feeling their supple springiness beneath her white socks. She had left sandals and cloak at the door, after first locking it from the inside. No one else was here, no one would come; there was only the two of them now.

Ishii became aware of her only when she was very close. The particular *irimi* he was working on had been one whose perfect execution had eluded him even after months of the most diligent practice. Still, he was not frustrated, nor was he angry at himself. He had just come to a decision to pass on to another variation when his break in concentration revealed Akiko.

His head came up, sweat sparkling like dew across his black, close-cropped hair. He bowed immediately, voicing the traditional greeting, *"Ikagadesuka*, Oku-san."

Somewhat distantly, Akiko returned it. *"Hai. Okagesamade. Arigatogozaimasu."* It was schoolgirl's rote, that was all. "Tell me," she said, "are you as assiduous in your work on the merger as you are at *aikido*?"

"I do what is asked of me, Oku-san."

Akiko gave the top of his head a bleak smile. She could see his scalp, burnished as brass. "And that is all that you do?"

At the last upward inflection, Ishii's head lifted and his de-ceptively soft brown eyes gathered her in. For an instant Akiko felt like an image upon a plate, developing. Then he blinked and the sense was gone. "I am not a robot, if that is your meaning," he said deliberately. "I create for the company as well as serve it."

"In what way?"

"With my mind."

"You are an impudent man," she said coldly.

"My apologies, Oku-san." He bowed again. "Please forgive me."

Her lips curled upward and she held out a hand, closing her fingers around the stave. She pulled, and he took a halting step closer to her. She made him aware of her as a woman in the way she stood, in the attitude of her head; her expression recalled the moment of his searching look on her wedding day. She melted into him.

"This is what you want, isn't it," she whispered into his ear.

She felt how startled he was at her aggressive stance and laughed to herself. He was pulled by the conventions of his mind, drawn by her heat. It was his moment of indecision.

224

Using that, she broke the stave across his right shoulder with a variation of the *iai* draw, too swift to see clearly. His mind was stunned, his body immobilized at the same time.

Now a part of her felt sorry for him. Kneeling, bent and broken before her, without even uttering one animal mewl of protest, where was his maleness, his traditional superiority? He was nothing now: not an image or an icon, not a protector or a provider; he was, she saw, not even an enemy. He was merely a means to an end.

His face was raised toward her. His skin was covered in pristine beads: the sweat of pain. His ragged breath broke from his partly open mouth like the sigh of an engine winding down.

For a long time Akiko stared down at him while all manner of thought flung itself like rain in her mind. Then she withdrew her blade, seeing its long, gleaming length mirrored in his eyes. She felt his terror and thought, There are no more warriors left in the world.

Then, with neat precise swipes of her *katana*, she cut off his feet.

When the long black Mercedes slid to a halt, the driver came around, opened the rear door, and Seiichi Sato emerged into a morning sparkling with dew. There were two other men with him besides the chauffeur; as was the custom with all VIPs in Japan, he never went anywhere without them. This time, though, he bade them stay where they were inside the car.

Alone, he walked slowly up the pine-needle-strewn path into the precincts of the Shinto shrine where he had gotten married. This was part of his weekly pilgrimage. If he was in Tokyo, no matter the weather, he would make the trek to the lakeside.

Far below him he could see the bright white dazzle of sunlight off the water through the thick stands of pines and cryptomeria.

On his way up to the inner sanctuary Sato passed beneath the crimson-lacquered *Myōjin torii* gate and, just beyond, paused to drop something in the offering box. Reaching just above it, he pulled the rope that rang the sacred bell which would awaken the resting *kami* who dwelled in this place and alert them of the presence of the arriving supplicant.

Inside the main sanctuary building, Sato knelt before the tables laden with offerings. Grouped around the tables were carved figures of sitting archers, spearmen, *samurai* wielding *katana*.

Before the closed doors of the inner chamber wherein the *kami* resided stood the *Gohei*, a wooden wand with bits of folded paper hanging in zigzag fashion from it. Beside it was the *Haraigushi*, the purification wand, a small branch from the sacred *sakaki* tree.

Above, banners depicting the clouds and the moon hung, indicating the presence of the *kami*. Draped from one of the standards which held the banners was a brocaded cloth in which were hung the sword and jewels as well as the shield and halberd of the shrine. These were symbols both of the power of the *kami* in matters of wisdom and justice, and of protection against evil.

Centered directly below the banners on the table was the sacred mirror which was perhaps the most important and certainly the most mysterious element in the Shinto religion. It was thought to reflect the cleanest light, to be able to reflect everything as it truly is and not how we would wish it to be.

Did not the *Jinno Shōtōki* say that "the mirror hides nothing. It shines without a selfish mind. Everything good and bad, right and wrong, is reflected without fail." Was not the Sun Goddess's divine spirit captured in just such a mirror hung outside her cave.

Now Sato knelt before the mirror and, peering into its keen eye, was bathed in its clear light. And as he did so he wished for peace of mind and spirit, he wished for the deep and abiding sanctuary of thought symbolized by the gleaming lake far below. He summoned up the *kami*.

In moments, a peculiar kind of peacefulness stole over him that he had become accustomed to from his earliest days. And he felt as if a connective bridge had been spun out of the ether between his essence and that of his honored father. The elder Sato had come to this shrine almost every day of his life, and when Seiichi was old enough to walk his father had taken him, along with Gōtarō.

Even as a young child Seiichi had been enraptured by this place. While his older brother had fidgeted and yawned by his side, Seiichi had begun to feel the presence of the place steal over him like a mantle of refracted light from the mirror.

And when his honored father had died, he had made his own pilgrimage after the funeral rites here, down the narrow rocky path which he and all the guests at his second wedding descended many years later, to the shore of the lake. Mist was still rising off it then so that it appeared as it must have eons ago at the dawn of Japanese history, prehistoric and pure.

It was only as he stared at the gently rippling skin of the lake that Seiichi had reconnected with his father's *kami*. And so he came here regularly to be as close as he could come to the history of his family.

He needed all their accumulated wisdom now to see him through this maelstrom. It seemed as if all his world were collapsing around him. Thirty-seven years to create, and then in the span of little over a year they were on the verge of ruin. How had it happened? He could not say, even with the supposed help of aftersight. Perhaps they should never have become involved in *Tenchi* in the first place. But the government had made manifestly clear the potential rewards if the project were successful. With the *keiretsu* in the position it was in, just outside the charmed circle of Japan's top seven companies, we could not resist, Sato thought now.

But even though the government was pouring the country's money into *Tenchi*, still there were an enormous number of peripheral costs that the *keiretsu* was expected to absorb. It was their duty, and there was simply no question of charging them back to the government. Over sixty million dollars had been out-layed by the *keiretsu* in the space of fourteen months, a terrible drain on any corporation, no matter how large.

Tenchi, Sato supposed, was one of the major reasons Nangi had allowed their expansion into international banking in Hong Kong. Actually, Sato had been against such a move from the start. The thought of the vagaries of the Crown Colony's financial fortunes filled him with trepidation. It was tantamount to putting your foot in a bear trap and waiting for it to spring shut.

But Nangi had insisted, and Sato had felt compelled to acquiesce to his will. After all, they did need an immediate infusion of money, both for *Tenchi* and to offset the loss of capital from their steel works. So many idle hands and nothing to do with them but pay them their wages and their benefits while the plant ran at 70 percent capacity. Now Sato was close to a deal to sell off the *kobun*. The price would give them only the most modest of profits, but at least they would be out from under that saddle.

But that might not be enough now. The Tomkin deal was in limbo until Linnear returned, and Sato had had the most awful feeling in the pit of his stomach ever since Nangi had gotten that call from the All-Asia Bank in Hong Kong. He had been most unforthcoming about the nature of the call, but his hurried trip to the Crown Colony boded ill.

Sato read the papers, he knew what the Communist Chinese's repudiation of the treaty with Great Britain had meant to the Colony, and he had gritted his teeth as, day by day, his worst fears were borne out. Real estate and banking were the two mainstays of Hong Kong's economy, and he knew once the first went, it was merely a matter of time before cracks began to show in the other.

Just how deeply has Tony Chin sunk us? he asked himself.

Oh, Amida! I pray he has a cautious nature. I pray we are not caught in the bear trap.

But Sato knew that he and Nangi were already in one kind of trap and it was closing inexorably about them with frightening rapidity. What Linnear-san had called the *Wu-Shing*. Sato shuddered inwardly. Three deaths. Kagami-san, *Mo*, the tattoo; Yoshida-san, *Yi*, cutting off the nose; and now Masuto Ishii, found in the gymnasium with his feet cut off. Sato strained to recall. With a sickening lurch that set his gorge to rising, it came to him: *Yueh*. The ideogram was a merging of those of knife and foot.

What was happening to the *kobun*? The company was dying around him, and unless Linnear-san found a way to stop these murders he and Nangi would be finished. For there were two more murders left in the *Wu-Shing* ritual, and it did not take a genius to determine who the final targets would be.

Who wished to punish them, and why? Abruptly, within this place of moving shadows and ancient *kami*, Sato had the growing intuition that their past—his and Nangi's—had somehow been resurrected and a shambling reanimated corpse, trailing rotting flesh in its wake, was making its relentless way toward them. Soon they would have no structure from which to carry out the final stages of *Tenchi*. What would happen then? He bent his head and prayed fervently for salvation or, at the very least, surcease from this terrible nightmare that had grown up around them, destroying the *kobun*'s most efficient executives, the very heart of the empire that he and Nangi had struggled for so long to achieve. He must not allow that to happen. Nothing must be allowed to delay *Tenchi*. Nothing. But there was a cold hand clenched around his heart, squeezing until his eyes filled with tears and the pain was hot in his mouth.

And he thought, Punish us for what? What have we done?

Viktor Protorov should have been in the Middle East. Three weeks ago his presence had been required in Southern Lebanon to put a stop to a dispute that had been going on so long now that it had taken on all the characteristics of a feud.

Yet he had not moved from Hokkaido, from the safe house he had spent four years creating for himself. When he was here no one in the Soviet Union knew where he was or could trace him. Protorov was quite certain of that. He had several of his best apparatchiks tunneled securely into the heirarchies of all eight other Directorates. They had tried numerous times at the behest of their respective leaders. All drew blanks.

As for the men of the Ninth Directorate who manned this safe house, Protorov was just as certain of them. They were, to a man, loyal to him first, the Directorate second, and Mother Russia third. Of course he did not leave such vital matters to chance. Once every two weeks the staff—as well as the operatives alive within the Japanese islands—were obliquely vetted in an ongoing program to ensure that the safe house was absolutely sterile.

Only one man was not thus spied upon by his own people, and that was because he was in such an enormously sensitive position. For him alone Protorov wished to see in person, to ensure his own safety and that the reports he was receiving were pure white. "White reports" were those containing highly sensitive information as well as being entirely free of disinformation.

In point of fact, white reports were rare. Protorov had been in the business of deception long enough to take for granted that a majority of all reports were to some degree gray. That is, they contained some disinformation. And it was for him to determine the wheat from the chaff, discarding the lies to uncover the truth. This was only one of his many specialized talents.

Japan was an exception that proved the rule. Many of the Ninth Directorate's operatives were of such a fanatic nature that they invariably turned in white reports. The man Protorov was going to see now was one of those.

But the problems in Southern Lebanon had not gone away, and just this morning Protorov had dispatched one of his most trusted lieutenants to take care of the feud for him. *Tenchi* was too much a part of him now. As yet a nebulous concept, still, its siren song lured him onward with the promise of awesome reward.

But if the truth be known Protorov had not wanted to return to the baking dusty climate of Southern Lebanon. Always the stink of camel dung and heated machine oil was in the air. And how he had come to despise the Arabs! Oh yes, he had no doubt as to their usefulness to the Soviet Union. But their gullibility—their stupidity, really—the key to their usefulness—was what he could no longer tolerate. They were obscene barbarians, and he was far better off pursuing the specter of *Tenchi* than having to mediate a dispute between Arab and Russian.

Arrogance, Protorov thought now, was a quality the White Russians suffered from; hence their downfall. But the damnable Arabs had it as well. He was well away from them; he had been months getting the sand out of his clothes.

Koten's great bulk descended off Shinjuku. Sato's weekly pilgrimage had given him some free time. Shrines were no place for violence, Sato felt, and therefore would not allow Koten to accompany him.

The *sumō* took the green line four stops, where he changed for the blue line at Kudanshita, riding that to the huge Nihon-bashi station. He was stared at openly in the subways but he was used to that. Outwardly he ignored the attention even while his spirit expanded with pride. He had worked hard to move up the *dan*, and even though he no longer performed in public, still he spent a great deal of time staying in shape and even, from time to time, engaging in exhibition bouts. He had not been defeated in these five years.

He emerged on Eit-dōri and turned right. The avenue was crowded with shoppers. Along the next block he waited for the light, then crossed the avenue and entered the Tokyū department store.

Inside, the place was as enormous and as varied as a city. One of his friends had gotten married here, another had purchased burial plots for himself and his family. But Koten was interested in neither of these services.

A white-gloved female attendant waved him onto the down escalator. He stared openly at her heavily made-up face until she turned her head away beneath the scrutiny.

In the basement, he idly watched cakes being prepared, *sushi* being rolled, tofu being fermented, bean paste being mixed and sugared. He made his lunch from the numerous free sample trays on the glass counters he passed.

When he had judged that he had eaten enough, he moved away toward the up escalator. Still there was an emptiness within his capacious stomach.

He ascended past myriad floors of designer clothing, housewares, furniture, toys and games, theaters, medical and dental clinics, galleries filled with paintings and sculptures, classes on how to wear a kimono, how to serve tea, how to arrange flowers, and in between a plethora of restaurants.

There was a teahouse in the roof garden with red, black, and white rice-paper lanterns on wires dancing in the light wind. Amid the carefully manicured shrubbery was a small zoo attended by flocks of children, some of whose mothers were busy downstairs shopping.

Koten waded in among this lot to get a better look at the baboons and gibbons. Some distance away there were the smallish monkeys from the northern alps around Nagano. Koten edged closer to these though they were less exotic and therefore had less of an audience. Koten was from Nagano, and the sight of these symbols of home abruptly made him conscious of the fact that he had not been back for more than ten years.

"See something of interest?"

He did not need to turn his head to take in the small accountant's body, the undistinguished face.

"These little ones chatter of home to me," he said.

"Ah," the drab man said. "The mountains. Those of us who were born in the mountains never fully adjust to being parted from them."

Koten nodded slowly and made his report. When he was finished, he dutifully answered the drab man's questions to the best of his ability.

"I have to get back," he said. "Sato-san will be returning from his prayers soon."

"Prayers," said Viktor Protorov disdainfully, "are for the already vanquished."

Three times "Tex" Bristol had had to abandon his plans to take out the Blue Monster, and it had more to do with Alix Logan than it did with her nocturnal guardian. After her suicide attempt the Blue Monster wasn't taking any chances, and he had moved in with her at night.

Now the lights never went out in Alix's apartment during the long nights as her keeper kept vigil with the most obvious tool. Light.

And light in the dead of night was not something Bristol had counted on. There was an element of surprise that was needed. It had come to his attention that Alix Logan's monsters were not themselves ex-cops; they were far smarter than that. And they had a manner about them that was, well, almost military. Bristol had spent long hours baking in the sun, doing nothing more than watching Alix Logan from afar, except to wonder where the monsters got their training. Had Tomkin become smarter in his old age? Had he begun hiring a higher grade of gorilla to do his dirty work? That was the only explanation.

After the third aborted attempt to steal into Alix Logan's apartment at night, Bristol reluctantly abandoned his first plan. You had to be plenty flexible in situations like these, he told himself continually. Every plan had to have a backup, and each backup had to have its own backup. That was the only way to be successful, because no situation involving people was ever static. You make that assumption and you might as well go into some other line of work.

So Bristol put into effect a plan he had hoped never to use. He

231

loved to fish, he loved being on the water. But being *in* it, far out at sea, was something else again.

Still, he had rented the scuba equipment, had himself checked out by a pimply boy of no more than eighteen, the shop's pro. He was a mite rusty—it had been some five years since he'd learned his diving—but the basics one never forgot, and after two hours of intensive work in the pink-tiled swimming pool of the beachfront hotel down the street from the shop, the pimply boy tapped him on the shoulder and gave him the thumbs-up signal.

Now Bristol had taken his gear onto his boat, which lay rocking in the oily swells dockside. He double-checked all his gear as he had been trained to do and was bent over fiddling with the regulator when he spied Alix out of the corner of his eye coming down the dock with the Red Monster just behind her.

Bristol's heart beat faster as he saw her turn in toward her small boat. No pleasure cruise this afternoon with the same round of vacuous friends. It was just her and Red.

The Red Monster freed the aft and bow lines and stepped quickly into the rocking boat, his topsiders squeaking. Alix already had the engine throttled, blue haze of fumes rising from the bubbling aft pipe. She turned the wheel over hard, and they began to glide out of the harbor.

Bristol, his pulse still racing, waited patiently before firing his own engine. He tugged at the bill of his beaten-up cap and headed out after them, squinted his eyes against the fierce glare of sunlight dancing off the water. With his free hand he strung up a pair of dark glasses, wrapping the curled ends of the wire temples around his ears.

This plan was far simpler than his first one but it was also far more terrifying to him. It had taken him six months to work up the courage to take his first scuba lessons and finally only direct orders from above had set him in motion. He was a brave man in most respects. But not this.

His hands shook so much that he dropped the speargun twice after he had unwrapped it from its concealing cocoon. This was not an item he had rented. In fact, he had made a point of telling the salesman at the scuba shop that he had an abhorrence of such things when the man had asked if there was any other item he wanted to rent.

Bristol had bought the speargun in a shop in Boca Chica early one morning while Alix Logan still tossed in her bed. He paid cash, dressed in a ridiculous seersucker suit with an old-fashioned straw hat atop his head and a pair of dimestore glasses with mirror lenses masking his face nicely, blending right in with the bushy mustache he had glued on for the occasion.

On his way back south he had his pick of three chemical plants, most engaged in retrieving nitrates from guano, and choosing one, he broke in easily and took what he needed. He spent the rest of the day on his boat in distant view of the long pleasure craft Alix had chosen to climb aboard that day, working out the rest of his plan.

And now that it was time to implement it, he was as nervous as a rookie on his first day in the business. It didn't look good, and with the bulk of the tanks settled between his shoulder blades, he paused, feet planted and spread on the rolling deck, trying to slow his breathing and calm his racing pulse.

But all the time his gaze ran away with him, slipping like an uncontrollable kid over the side, drinking in the long, deep swells and the infinite depth through which he would soon have to navigate. He put his hands out in front of him, saw the tremor there, and said, "The hell with it!" out loud as if he were blowing carbon dioxide from his system. He bent and retrieved the speargun, carefully examining the wickedly barbed flechette at its tip.

He stuck two sticks of shark repellent into his weighted belt, double-checked his wrist compass, working out the realignment of vectors now that Alix's small boat had drifted a bit. He'd have to remember that and not rely solely on the compass.

He went to the railing of his boat and slipped on his powerful fiberglass fins. Then, bringing his regulator over his head and up to his mouth, he made certain the line was absolutely clear. Mentally he ticked off the list of items the pimply kid had gone over with him, partly for safety and partly to keep his mind occupied and off the abyss already lapping at his ankles.

He reached for his mask, washed it with sea water, and then spat heavily into it, smearing the liquid around so that the mask would not cloud up. Fitting it over his face, grabbing the faceplate, his mind a frozen blank, he slid over the side.

The coolness of the sea engulfed him. Even through the protection of the blue rubber scuba suit he could feel the suck of the cold, rising from the ocean's depths like a physical creature.

Steady, schmuck, he told himself. The last thing you need now is for your imagination to run away with you. You're safe and warm in your booties and mommie's coming soon to tuck you in.

Bristol hung in the blue-green depths, going nowhere until he had settled his breathing and had gotten used again to the peculiar form of breathing one was obliged to use underwater.

Strands of sunlight filtered obliquely down from above, giving

233

him the odd sensation of being in a cathedral, and he thought of the old days in Hell's Kitchen before his father had been slaughtered in the filth and darkness of a neighborhood alleyway.

Then he made the mistake of looking down where the bands of light faded out and could not penetrate, blacker than anything he had ever seen and he realized what was below him, down, down, down.

Convulsively, he made himself look at his compass and orienting himself, he set off in the direction of Alix Logan's boat. He swam slowly, almost lazily, but that appearance was deceiving for his enormous fins propelled him through the water in great long kicks. He was in excellent shape and he had no trouble, even with the tidal surge that could potentially become a diver's worst enemy, creating a nausea so strong it could turn even the strongest diver into a mewling baby.

A third of the way there he forced himself toward the surface in order to take a visual fix. He did it in less than three seconds, up and down again into the depths. Checking his compass again, he saw that he was six or seven degrees off and adjusted his course. He plowed on, using the half-leg kick the pimply kid had told him was more economical and less taxing over a long haul than the one he had been originally taught.

He had just come down from his second visual and had again corrected his course slightly when his peripheral vision picked up the shadow almost directly below him. Immediately he ceased his kicking and hung motionless in the water. If it was a shark he did not want its acute vibrational sense picking him up.

But now ahead of him he could dimly make out the bulk of the underside of Alix's boat and below that the taut fishing line. In reality he could not actually see the line but he was certain it was there. The Red Monster had caught a big one. And that was what Bristol saw.

The fish was hooked solidly, its body whipsawing back and forth. And that was the reason for the shadow cruising below him.

Silently, Bristol cursed the Red Monster. But now, as he glanced back downward, he saw how close the shark was to him. He was no expert but he knew a basking shark from a blue, a nurse from a tiger.

This one was about twelve feet long and, from its marking, was surely a tiger shark, one of the flesh eaters. It was there now because it could sense the blood drooling from the fish fighting the line more than a hundred yards away.

Bristol watched the spotted light play along the rough prehistoric hide of the creature as it wound its way upward. He could not tell whether the thing had sensed him or not but he did his best to parallel its course, keeping on top of it. At a certain point that would have to end and then he would have to see what the shark did.

The tiger rose lazily, almost indifferently, moving so slowly Bristol could make out the score lines crisscrossing its flank. Then, abruptly, it veered to port, launching itself through the green void like a missile. It turned, and now Bristol had no doubt. It had seen him.

His heart pounding painfully in his chest, he willed his body to be still. He hung, suspended, watching the tiny green plankton drift by him in oblique sheets. A strand of seaweed.

Food's in the other direction, asshole. He spoke silently to the primitive creature. You don't want any part of me. I'll just bash your pea brain back into your spine.

The tiger was now turned so that it was head on to him and they faced each other like a pair of gladiators in a vast, surging arena filled with awful silence. The lens of the sea turned it monstrously large.

Against all logic, it moved toward him. Not swiftly as it had when it had sensed him, but cautiously. After all, this was not a creature in distress, its senses informed it. Yet there was distress and blood in the immediate vicinity and the shark wanted to feed unmolested.

Though Bristol was carrying two sticks of shark repellent he had little faith in the chemicals. Still, he inched his right hand down toward his belt. Fleetingly he thought of the speargun but quickly rejected that course of action. He had seen too many shots of sharks with spears through their brains still alive and attacking and he wanted no part of that. He only had one spear.

The tiger was very close now and Bristol could see the wicked sickle-shaped mouth below the wide apart pig eyes. Pink plankton clung to its bottle-shaped snout and three ramoras, two above and one below, mimicked its every twist and turn.

It was still coming on and Bristol gripped one of the sticks with a gloved hand and gently drew it out. He was sweating. Christ, he thought, this bastard's gonna come all the way in.

Bristol rode with the tidal surge four fathoms down and gripped the stick with a viselike grip. Come on, old buddy, he whispered inside his head. Have I got a surprise for you.

The tiger's ugly snout nosed in and Bristol abruptly came to life, lifting the stick and slamming it as hard as he could against the shark's snout.

The creature bucked hard, almost standing vertically on its tail.

Then it twisted so quickly it left two of the ramoras temporarily behind and fled into the green depths with a great double wave of its long powerful tail.

For a time, Bristol just hung as he had, feeling the cold sweat drying on his skin beneath his rubber cocoon. Then, replacing the shark repellent in his belt, he got a fix on the boat and moved off toward it.

Twenty-four feet above where Bristol swam and perhaps seventy-five yards distant, Jack Kenneally was having the devil's own time landing his catch. The Red Monster was no professional fisherman but he originally came from Florida and he had done a lot of deep-sea stuff as a teenager. Now his job was to go after bigger game, and he bitterly resented this half-assed babysitting assignment.

Kenneally spat over the side with disgust. He had saved her tan ass once from oblivion and he wondered just how many times he would have to repeat the feat before this shithouse assignment would end. Privately he wondered whose instep he had trod on to be handed this one. He was top echelon and he chafed to be out and setting prey in the sights of the long gun and not at the end of a fishing line.

He glanced over at Alix Logan stretched out in the skimpiest of bikinis, her burnished skin shining with oil, and cursed softly. Who the hell was she anyway, he asked himself, that I gotta risk my neck to keep her alive and separated from the rest of the world?

Kenneally never did get an answer to that question for, at that moment, light danced off a surfacing faceplate and, in the midst of reeling in his catch, the Red Monster said, "What the fuck—!" and reached for his .357 Magnum, got off a shot just before he heard the plangent *twang!*, the bright rush of wind, the ballooning black object, and then the burning pain in the center of his chest.

"Aggh!" he cried as he staggered back under the shock of force, the rod spinning out of his hands and disappearing beneath the waves. He clutched at the fire burning inside him, trying to rip the flechette from his flesh, but that only caused the curved barbs to bite deeper into him.

His chest was expanding and from his vantage point on the deck he looked up into the burning sun. The slim silhouette of Alix Logan stood over him, her hand to her mouth covering the great O her lips were making. Her beautiful eyes were open wide and Kenneally was suddenly struck by how much those eyes reminded him of his daughter's. Now why hadn't he seen that before?

Fingers like swollen sausages and a terrible paralysis beginning

236

to suffuse him, stiffening his limbs, fevering his mind, Kenneally saw the great shade looming up over the side of the boat, flicking sea water from its slick blue skin.

Then his eyes were bulging outward unnaturally and blood ran from his nose, mouth, and ears in bright crimson trickles and his body convulsed twice as the autonomic system shut down for good.

Climbing over the side of the boat, Bristol ripped off his heavy fins, pushed his mask up onto the top of his head, and said, "Alix Logan, I'm Detective Lewis Jeffrey Croaker of the New York City Police Department and to tell you the truth I've had the goddamndest time getting to see you."

Then he vomited all over the running deck.

Justine was numb. The funeral progressed around her like some vast charade which she was fated to witness yet not participate in. The hordes of people from her father's firm flown in from all parts of the world bewildered her. Their assumedly sincere murmurs of condolence slid off her like rainwater. At times she had no idea what they were talking about.

Her mind was otherwise occupied, but when the clouds lifted far enough for her to think of her father's passing, it was only with a sense of profound relief.

At some point she became aware that a male presence was close beside her. Looking up, her heart beating fast, thinking that it might, despite what she herself had said, have been Nicholas, she was surprised to see Rick Millar. He smiled and took her hand. Justine might have asked him where Mary Kate was, but if he replied she did not hear him.

She seemed dead to the world. Not even the beautiful setting beside the great beach house on Gin Lane just east of Southampton where she and Gelda had grown up seemed to affect her. She was as anesthetized in her own way as her older sister was in hers, lying almost insensate in her Sutton Place apartment, having consumed God only knew how many quarts of vodka this last year following the death of Lew Croaker. He had been the only man able to get through her tough exterior, leaving her so very vulnerable. Now that he was gone, Justine had just about given up on her sister. Only a miracle could save her, and Justine had none up her sleeve. She couldn't even manage her own life, let alone Gelda's.

Oh, but how she felt betrayed! As if the solid-seeming earth beneath her feet had abruptly split apart, hurling her downward into a pit of nothingness. Now that Nicholas had done this to her, now that he had become another in the long line of men who ultimately betrayed her, she felt only despair. Even rage was denied her. It was as if some vital spark had gone out within her.

Her head came down, her mane of hair falling over her face. Those assembled studiously looked away from her grief, not understanding its source at all.

Nicholas felt a longing to return to Japan that was so intense even had he not received Sato's disturbing telegram he would in any case have been on the next flight out following Raphael Tomkin's funeral.

He put one hand in his trousers pocket and felt again the flimsy sheet of yellow paper. He did not need to bring it out in order to recall its contents: LINNEAR-SAN. V.P. OF OPERATIONS, MASUTO ISHII, THIRD VICTIM OF WU-SHING. FEET SEVERED. CHEEK TATTOOED WITH IDEOGRAM: YUEH. KOBUN IN GRAVE JEOPARDY. WE SEEK YOUR AID. SATO.

Yes, Nicholas thought now, there was no doubt. *Yueh* was the third of the *Wu-Shing* punishments. Only two remained. And Nicholas feared that he knew who the next two victims would be.

Now it was more imperative than ever for him to return to Tokyo. Tomkin's last wish was to have the Sphynx merger consummated—and as quickly as possible. That Nicholas knew he would accomplish. But first he had to deal with the creature enacting this deadly ritual, for he saw that there would be no merger without the cessation of this danger. He had his duty to Tomkin to perform and he saw now what must have been inevitable since the advent of the *Wu-Shing*. That he must stand against it.

The black day had come that Akutagawa-san had both feared and foreseen when he had begun Nicholas' training in the dark side of *ninjutsu*. And he knew instinctively that he would need to use everything he had learned over the years just to survive.

He spent almost all the time before the ceremony meeting the assembled executives from Tomkin Industries' far-flung offices. Bill Greydon had taken care of those Telexes so they had been prepared and were ready to meet their new president.

Only once did Nicholas think of Justine and that was when he caught a glimpse of her with a handsome, blond-haired man who seemed to have stepped off a fashion layout page. That would be Rick Millar, her new boss. Nicholas made this observation with an odd kind of detachment. He knew that he was now so caught up in the people and events on the other side of the world that he had, in a very real sense, cut himself off from Justine. His feelings toward her were like fish in a tank; he watched them with cool curiosity, removed from their heat.

There had been no question of him dropping Tomkin Industries. He could do that for no one person. His mother, Cheong, would certainly have understood that. And so would the Colonel. There was always *giri* to perform in life. And the debt of honor outweighed all other considerations . . . even one's own life.

It did not seem at all odd to him that only six months ago he had wished to wreak vengeance on the man for whom he now felt *giri*. The forces of life were constantly in flux, and woe unto the man who stood fixed and unyielding in his attitudes.

Tomkin had been responsible for Croaker's death . . . and he hadn't. What did that mean? Nicholas had no idea as yet, but one thing was clear to him now. Whatever Tomkin had done in that regard did not have the mark of a personal vendetta. At least in that Croaker had been mistaken. But where was the truth in this whirlpool?

Executives from Silicon Valley, San Diego, Montana, Pennsylvania, upstate New York, Connecticut, Manila, Amsterdam, Singapore, Berne—there was even one diminutive silver-haired gentleman from Burma, where the company was involved in hardwood foresting—spoke with him in seemingly endless array. All were friendly, all were unknown to him.

Until Craig Allonge, the chief financial operations officer in New York, came up to him.

"Thank God for a friendly face," Nicholas said. "Stay here and don't move. I've got a job for you when this is all over."

In the limo returning to Manhattan Nicholas dialed the Washington number Greydon had given him. He spoke for several moments, then replaced the receiver. He turned to Allonge. "First stop is the office," he said. "Give me a quick course in how to pull information out of the computer, then leave me alone. Get your passport—I assume your Japanese visa's up to date? Good. Pack a small bag. I need you to go over the last five years of this company's life with me so don't plan to sleep on the plane."

But Nicholas was quicker by far than Allonge was, and while the lanky Texan frantically sorted through his files as they began their takeoff four hours later, he sank into *getsumei no michi*, his eyes closed to exclude all distractions.

In the middle level of consciousness that was fully as much feeling as it was cerebration, intuitive expansion was paramount.

He bypassed the enormous inflow of cataclysmic events during the past several days. Deep within the moonlit path he began to explore the center of his dilemma. His Eastern side, so much more dominant these days, had conveniently broken it off from the mainstream of his thoughts, carefully surrounding it with opaque

239

walls so that no feelings could seep out from it . . . or seep in. Thus could he continue with the multitudinous decisions of daily life without his judgment being affected or colored by unwanted emotion.

And finally on the horizon of his imagination he came to the citadel of the unnameable emotion that had been haunting him from the moment Akiko Ofuda Sato slipped her fan away from her face and revealed herself to him. True consciousness had not been able to bring him here, nor could his dreams. It was only *getsumei no michi*, the riverbed of all emotions, that had fetched him up on this far shore.

He felt fully the trepidation he had put away and, yes, the fear like a great funnel of forces trying to wrest control from him. For just an instant he was quite certain that, like staring at Medusa's face, he would be paralyzed if he allowed himself to recognize what was within the citadel.

Then, recalling one of his most basic lessons in the mists of Yoshino, he penetrated that fear. He went completely through it.

And on the other side discovered that his love for Yukio had never really died at all.

Just before sunset, Sato was sitting cross-legged in his study. The *fusuma* were pulled back, revealing a small moss garden that was carefully nurtured through the seasons. There existed more than a hundred varieties of moss; here were represented a score.

Pale light, golden and flickering as the sun descended through the broad-boughed trees, touched the mossed rocks here and there, giving the garden a soft-spectral quality.

He heard movement behind him but he did not stir.

"Sir?"

It was Koten's oddly high-pitched voice. There was no one else in the house. Akiko had gone south to visit her ailing aunt, who had not been able to make the trek north for the wedding, and Nangi was home preparing for his Hong Kong trip. Both he and Nangi had been filled with foreboding at the discovered death of Ishii-san just hours after Nicholas Linnear had taken off for America. As if the gods had been made angry at his departure.

Sato had tried to bring himself to articulate to his long-time friend some of the fears that had overwhelmed him at the shrine, but Nangi was Sato's *sempai* just as Makita-san had been Nangi's, and there were some matters one did not bring up with elders.

"Sir?"

"Ah, yes, Koten-san," he said shortly. "What is it?"

"A phone call, sir."

"I don't want to be disturbed."

"Excuse me, sir, but the gentleman said it was urgent."

Sato thought a moment. Perhaps it was that young Chinese he had hired in Hong Kong to "oversee" Nangi-san's movements. Since Nangi-san was determined not to speak of the situation, Sato had found it prudent to take his own measures to discover what had gone wrong in the Crown Colony.

He rose, nodding to Koten, and walked out of the room. The study was for contemplation and as such it had no telephone. Entering his office, he went around to the side of the desk and picked up the receiver.

"Yes? This is Seiichi Sato."

"It is Phoenix, Sato-san."

"Ah." Sato's heartbeat picked up considerably. "Just a moment." He put down the phone and padded silently to the doorway to his office. Taking a quick look around the hallway, he closed the door, then returned to the receiver.

"What have you to report?"

"I'm afraid the news is not good."

Sato's stomach contracted. First the All-Asia Bank and now this. Big risk, big reward. Both he and Nangi had known this going in. And *Tenchi* would provide them with the biggest reward imaginable. But the downside was rushing to meet them with hellish speed.

"Kusunoki was murdered."

"I already know that." Sato was impatient; the risk he was taking made him so. And the thought of failure.

"But did you know that it was done by one of his own pupils?"

The line between Sato and Phoenix seemed to groan in agony as if many conversations were vying for control.

"I think you'd better tell me all of it," Sato said, gritting his teeth in anticipation.

"Naturally, the *muhon-nin* found with him had been suspected of killing the *jonin*. It has now been determined that he did not. The Soviet spy lacked the prowess to accomplish such an unthinkable deed."

"Then who *did* kill him?"

From out of the silence Phoenix said, "If we knew that, he would already be undergoing punishment."

"Then it is likely that there is another . . . Soviet infiltrator."

"I admit the possibility exists."

Sato was abruptly furious. "You are the best there is. That is why I hired you to guard the secrets of *Tenchi*. If I wanted unthinking thugs I could have pulled them in from the Yakuza clan across town. Amida, what are you doing down there?"

"Have faith," Phoenix said. "All is well. I am assigning myself to this matter personally."

Phoenix, like Kusunoki, was a ninja *sensei*. Sato was mollified. "You *will* keep in touch."

"Each day at this time I will call you at this number."

"Excellent. I'll make certain I am here."

Sato replaced the receiver and, on the other side of the house, the miniature voice-activated tape machine connected to the listening device Koten had secreted in Sato's office turned itself off, its store of information increased.

Nicholas and Allonge deplaned at Dulles International in Washington.

"Mr. Linnear?"

A handsome blonde with the slender spread-legged stance of an athlete.

"You *are* Nicholas Linnear?"

She had a European accent that should have been spiky but was not. She had somehow managed to soften the vowels, clear up the guttural slurring that would have been normal. He thought she must have gone to school for that.

"Yes." The accent was definitely Eastern European, and immediately he began to catalog her facial structure.

She reached inside her Burberry, opened up a black lizard card case. "Would you come with me, please?"

"Was it your mother or father who came from Belorussiya?"

He saw that her eyes were sky blue, azure, really. They were quite intelligent. And she was superb at hiding things. He found that despite the inconvenience she was causing him he liked her.

He took her opened card case from her hand and peered down at it. "*Gospadja* Tanya Vladimova, *vstraychayetzye* Craig Allonge. *On rabotayet dla Tomkina Industrii.*"

The shock registered on her face even as she nodded at the mystified Allonge in response to the introduction. She brushed her thick hair back from the side of her face and he saw that her nails were square cut and clear lacquered. Obviously she worked with her hands, and this interested him.

"It was my father who was born in Belorussiya," she said in the same language.

"Do you take after him in more ways than just looks?"

"He was a very dedicated man," she said. "Extremely dogged

242

when the occasion called for it. He was a rural policeman. My mother was from Birobidzhan."

There was an immediate flash in her eyes, a kind of challenge and a hint of something more. Nicholas knew how it must have been for her family inside Russia. What with a White Russian for a father and a Russian Jew for a mother there must not have been many options open to them. Her father had taken one obvious one; had others in the family taken the other?

"How many of you were dissidents?" he said softly.

She gave him an odd searching look for a moment and he was made peculiarly uncomfortable. Then it was gone, her face had cleared, and like the blank face of a computer terminal, she began again. "Enough so that my father had a great deal of time to grieve."

"Excuse me," Craig Allonge interjected in English. "Nick, what's going on?"

Nicholas smiled. "Nothing, really. Miss Vladimova is merely seeing that I fulfill a clause in Tomkin's will before we jet off to Japan." He put his hand on the other man's shoulder and squeezed. "Take a break at the airport. Stretch your legs, get something real to eat. I'll be back as quickly as I can."

"Mr. Linnear," C. Gordon Minck said forty-five minutes later in a clear, crisp voice, "it's good of you to come on such short notice. I know that you must have a great deal on your mind at the moment."

Nicholas had been taken into a building along F Street, not far from the Virginia Avenue underpass. A private elevator had taken them up to a four-story-high arboretum. Nicholas had successfully hidden his surprise. A cubistic whitewashed brick structure crouched in the center of this unnatural indoor forest. Tanya had taken him inside with a complete absence of self-consciousness for this stagy and, to Nicholas' way of thinking, needlessly indulgent construct.

"Tomkin's will was quite specific on the matter."

"Nevertheless, I'm delighted to see you."

Nicholas smiled and the two men shook hands.

They went through the building, past numerous rooms, all with tile or wood floors. There were no carpets at all, and Nicholas was aware of the sounds they made when they moved.

"I've never heard of the Department of International Export Tariffs," he said. "What do you do here?"

Minck laughed. "I'd be surprised if you *had* heard of us." He shrugged. "We're a bureaucratic backwater that Congress, in its infinite wisdom, has somehow seen fit to keep going." He gave

Nicholas a genuine smile. "We issue overseas licenses and, in some isolated instances, revoke them."

Nicholas realized that Minck had responded to his queries without actually answering them.

He was led out onto a glassed-in patio. Tanya was already there, pouring freshly squeezed orange juice into crystal stemware. Minck waved Nicholas into one of the comfortable-looking rattan chairs covered in Haitian batik. Potted palms, deep green sword plants, and dwarf palms were scattered about.

"This is an odd environment for a government bureau," Nicholas said.

Minck lifted an arm. "Oh, this is nothing but a set. We get a lot of foreign dignitaries in here." He smiled. "We like to make them feel at home."

"Is that so?" Nicholas stood up. He watched Tanya and Minck as he moved about the patio. "It's almost midnight, yet this building is as busy as if it were ten in the morning. I think if this department were what you claimed it was you'd be sitting behind a metal desk in a cubicle filled with fluorescent lighting. I think at this time of the night you'd be tucked safely into your bed. I'd like to know who you two are, where I really am, and what it is I'm doing here."

Minck nodded. "All understandable concerns, Nicholas. May I call you Nicholas, by the way? Good."

A phone rang, the sound muffled through the walls, and Tanya excused herself.

"Please sit down." Minck unbuttoned his seersucker jacket. "This department—it goes by many names; the Department of International Export Tariffs is just one of them—costs about as much as an AWAC to build and maintain. That's considerably less than the cost of a B-1 bomber. Still, it took me six months of memo wars and threats to get this set built." He smiled again. "Bureaucratic minds cannot conceive of such a necessity as this, but I can and do. This is the first sight a Russian defector sees after the wrapping comes off."

"Spies?" Nicholas said, slightly incredulously. "Raphael Tomkin was involved with spies? I don't believe it."

"Why not?" Minck shrugged. "He was a patriot. And he was a close friend of my father's." He poured more juice for them both. "Let me explain. My father was one of the founders of the OSS. Tomkin was an explosives expert—learned his trade in the Marines, where the two of them met. He could take the wing off a finch without ruffling a feather on its breast.

"My father used him on several rather delicate, high-risk forays toward the end of the European campaign. Things were a bit desperate by then; a lot of last-ditch Nazi plots to contend with, along with clandestine work keeping the Russians in line. Anyway, this one mission was a real balls-up. From what I have been able to gather it was Tomkin's fault, although my father would never say a bad word against him. The man simply lost his nerve and broke under the pressure. Three of the unit were inadvertently blown up when the packet detonated prematurely."

Minck drained his glass. "Your ex-boss was a highly honorable man. I guess he blamed himself and, though my father erased him from the field roster, he remained tied to the, er, organization. My father did not want his friend shamed for what he considered a human error and Tomkin, I suppose, did not want to make the break."

"So you inherited him."

"So to speak." Minck cleared his throat. "I'm not callous. In this regard, knowing the circumstances, I gave Tomkin the choice after my father died."

There was a question that needed voicing before they went any further. "Tell me," Nicholas said carefully, "was Tomkin Industries built with OSS money?"

"Good God, no." Minck seemed genuinely shocked. "We have no stake in the corporation whatsoever. You can set your mind at ease on that score."

Nicholas nodded and rose again. He went to the window-door, looked out. Because he was becoming increasingly uneasy about why Tomkin had insisted he come here, he was reluctant to pursue a direct course.

"What happens when they see this place?" he said. "The Russians, I mean."

"They're disoriented," Minck replied. "You'd be surprised at how much current Western fiction they manage to read. Most of them expect to be taken to a colonial mansion somewhere out in the wilds of Virginia." He laughed. "They seem disappointed when they're not interviewed by Alec Guinness or what they perceive as his American equivalent."

Minck stood up. So much for the easy part, he thought.

"The reason you're here now," he said, "has to do with your merger with Sato Petrochemicals."

"Oh?" Nicholas turned to face him. "In what way?"

"It's a matter," Minck said, "of national security."

Akiko had not slept since Nicholas had departed. There was a rhythm to her life, to all her actions, a rhythm that Kyōki had taught her to search for and to use, one that increased her power a thousandfold.

What was she to do now that Nicholas had returned to America? There were three possibilities but only one option because the first, to break off her plan entirely, was unthinkable, and because the second, to follow him to America, would be to put herself at the same disadvantage that Saigō had labored under.

She rolled over on the single *futon*. There were no intricately patterned coverlets here, no luxurious appointments. She might have been in a barracks in the seventeenth century save that there was no one else in the small room. Contrary to what she had told Sato, she had not gone to visit her aunt. That would have been an impossibility; she had no living relative.

Slowly she rose and, stretching, began her morning exercise ritual. Forty minutes later, after toweling off the running sweat, taking a quick cold shower to close the pores of her skin, she returned to her cubicle and commenced the slow, studied ritual of the tea ceremony.

This she did in solitary reflection each morning no matter where she was. It remained in her memory the only link with her mother; the only physical thing the woman had taught her. Akiko's mother had been a *chano-yu sensei*.

There was an almost religious fervor to the tiny, practiced movements. The element of perfection before the Void brought the concept of Zen concentration to the art of preparing tea as it did to many daily Japanese preparations, transforming them, lifting them from the mundane onto the plane of art, involving the spirit as well as the mind and the hand.

With the pale green tea a froth in the small handleless cup, Akiko arose and slid open the *fusuma*. Beyond the wide veranda was the reflection garden, its pure white pebbles dazzling in all light, its three black igneous rocks set in harmonious confluence along the perimeter.

And just to the right of center rose the branched trunk of the giant cedar. As Akiko slowly sipped her stingingly bitter tea, she allowed her eyes to pass over the fluted configurations of light and dark, shadow and sunlight dappling the textured needles. She was so long at it that when at last she returned to her starting point, the shapes had changed subtly with the angle of the sun.

Thus lost in the Void, her mind heard again the plangent double notes of the bamboo flute, elongated and sorrowful. This was the only music she heard—save for the birdsongs which accompanied the changing of the seasons—for all the long years of her stay with Kyōki.

246

The bittersweet song began at noontime just as she was serving Kyōki his tea, abasing herself before him, kowtowing in the ancient Chinese tradition on which he insisted. She could feel anew the chill of the stone flooring against her slightly parted lips—there were no *tatami* in the ancient castle.

Often, in the afternoon, between studies, she would peer through the heavy latticework of greenery beyond the slit windows carved into the thick stone walls on the off chance that she would catch a glimpse of the player. He was a *komuso*, a follower of the Fuke sect of Buddhism. He would have a straw basket upturned over his head, garbed in a simple striped robe, wooden *geta* on his feet. A musician of such consummate skill that often she would find herself weeping for no discernable reason other than the tender cruelty of the notes, dropping one by one through the atmosphere like dissolving snowflakes.

Clever girl that she was, she never allowed Kyōki to see her tears. Had he suspected her of weeping he would surely have punished her. That was Kyōki's way: the battle commander.

High on the castle's ramparts flapped the *sashimono*—the ancient battle standard—that he had fashioned. As tradition dictated it was dominated by the commander's seal, in this case a depiction of a stylized *mempo*—a battle mask of hinged steel. They came in many styles and shapes. Kyōki's was the most feared, the *akuryo*: an evil demon's visage on a black field.

During the day, Kyōki always positioned Akiko so that the *sashimono* was in her line of vision. She was never free from it, for at night she could hear the heavy snap of the cloth in the wind even in her sleep.

And terror rode on her back for so long that she secretly suspected that Kyōki had stolen into her chamber while she slumbered, sectioned out her heart, and, with the dust of some arcane spell, had replaced it with an organ of crystal into which he could peer whenever it pleased him.

Akiko's eyes snapped open and she looked downward at the cup she held tightly in both hands. Tears had stirred the dregs of the leaves, whorling them into new patterns.

She blinked heavily and exhaled a long stream of carbon dioxide she had been unconsciously holding in her lungs. Beyond the opened *fusuma*, beyond the pebble garden where the spreading pine swayed in a gathering wind, she could see the gray wall past which lay the lushly wooded slopes and mist-filled valleys of Yoshino.

* * *

247

Alix was moving away from him. Her green eyes were opened wide so that he could see the whites all around. Her hands were up in front of her in a defensive gesture, and when the backs of her legs hit the gunwale she was so startled he thought she was going to tumble over backward into the ocean.

He made a lunge toward her and she screamed, twisting away from him, slipping on the deck in the process, skinning her knee.

"Get away from me!" she cried. There was a tinge of hysteria in her voice. "Who in the name of Christ are you?"

"I already told you." There was a weariness to his voice he did not bother to hide. "Lewis Croaker, NYPD." He sat on the opposite gunwale, his stomach quietening.

"You threw up all over my boat." And then as if it were an afterthought, "You killed a man."

He looked at her as if she were crazy. "He would have killed me first if I'd given him the chance." He pointed at a spot on the deck somewhere between them. The Red Monster's pistol lay there like a gleaming fish. "He wanted to blow my brains out."

"The smell's terrible," she said, turning away.

"Death's like that," Croaker said archly, but he reached for the bailing bucket and washed his vomit down the scuppers with sea water. Then he picked up the .357 Magnum and studied it. There were no markings and the serial number had been filed off. It was virgin and therefore untraceable.

She began to shiver now, her arms crossed over her breasts, her fingers clutching her shoulders with such force they turned white. Her lips were working as if she might be praying.

He dropped his mask and flippers on deck, got out of his gear, resting the heavy air tank against the railing. "What are you going to do now that you're free?" he said softly.

Alix was still shivering. "What—" She seemed to choke on her words and, swallowing hard, had to begin again. "What are you going to do with him?" She inclined her head but did not look at the corpse.

"He's going down with the boat." And when she gave him a sharp look, he nodded. "The boat's a write-off now, there's no other way."

"There's still the other one." Her voice was very small.

Croaker knew she was talking about the Blue Monster. "The sinking'll throw him off long enough for you to get out of the state."

It was obvious that she had been listening closely because she turned around now and looked him full in the face. "You said 'me' not 'we.'" He nodded. "How come?"

"You've already been in prison long enough. I'm not going to extend your stay."

"But you want something from me, that's simple enough to figure out. It's why I'm here with . . . them. It's why you came after me." Her eyes watched his face.

Croaker looked away. "You know who these two are?" She shook her head silently. "Where they're from?" She shook her head. "Who's protecting you?"

"No."

"But you *do* know what it is you're not supposed to divulge." There was that acid tone again. He grunted when he got no response, and went through the boat very methodically. When he came back on deck, she had not moved.

He pointed to the Red Monster. "This guy's got no name, no ID, no nothing. He's as clean as a pig in shit." He looked at her for any kind of reaction. Then, reaching down for one of the Red Monster's hands, said, "Except for this."

Alix gave a little scream as he peeled what looked like an oval of skin from the man's fingertip. He repeated this process nine more times then held the small pile in his palm.

"Know what these are, Alix?" She shook her head wildly. "They're Idiots. Idiots are print changers. Very sophisticated stuff. I mean your average hood on the street's light-years away from this kind of equipment." He did not show it but his stomach had contracted painfully when his keen eye had spotted the one Idiot beginning to flake off. At first he could not believe it, but now he was coming to understand that that was because he had not wanted to believe it.

Entering into a red sector with preconceived notions was just about the worst of the cardinal sins a detective could commit. And Croaker had to admit that that was what he had done from the outset. His mind had been so set on Tomkin being the villain that no other possibility had entered his mind.

But now with the evidence of the Idiots, the lack of other ID, added to the methodology these two jailers had been using, Croaker saw another possibility forming and he did not like the look of it at all.

"They're disgusting," Alix said. "Take them away, they look like slugs."

He folded the Idiots away, came across the deck toward her. "Alix, who the hell are these guys?"

"I—I don't know. I'm not—" She turned her head. "I'm confused. I don't know what's right and what's wrong anymore."

He saw the fear and shock in her eyes and he decided not to

pursue it at once. It wasn't doing her much good to be so close to the stiff. He weighed anchor, started up the engine, and swung the boat to starboard, heading in a flat arc back toward his own craft.

Once there, he set the engine in neutral, slung the anchor onto his boat to keep the two craft linked, and climbed over the rail after it. He turned and offered Alix his hand.

Slowly she unwound and as if in a trance came aboard his own boat. "Why don't you go below and lie down," he said, gently guiding her to the companionway. "Just relax for a bit."

After she had disappeared he went to work, transferring the half-gallon plastic container of gas to Alix's boat, going below-decks with it. When he returned, he took the Red Monster's corpse and, using his fishing knife, cut out the barbed flechette of the spear. This he threw overboard. Then, manhandling the body, he draped it over the wheel.

Lastly, he took the fallen Magnum and returned belowdecks. There he fired three shots downward through the hull. Sea water began to ooze up through the rents. Then he uncapped the plastic container and drenched the cabin. He went back to the compan-ionway and lit a match, barely escaping the sudden whoosh of the flames greedily eating up the oxygen.

Quickly he scrambled up onto the deck and drew the anchor back on board, wound the chain around the Red Monster's ankles. He set the engine at full throttle, the rudder at a straight course, and, the container in one hand, jumped overboard.

It was an easy swim back to his own boat and, climbing on board, he stowed his scuba outfit along with the empty plastic container. Then he went belowdecks.

Alix was lying on one narrow berth, her right arm flung across her eyes. She heard his approach and her lips moved slightly. "I heard noises. They sounded a little like shots."

"Your engine was backfiring." There was no point in telling her any of it, and some danger in it as well.

"It's gone." She said it like a little girl of her favorite Teddy bear.

"It was part of the price of your freedom."

Her arm came away from her face and she looked up at him. "Well, I never paid for it. It wasn't mine anyway, I suppose."

Croaker nodded and came to sit down beside her on the op-posing bunk. "It's about your friend, Angela Didion."

"Yes." Alix seemed to sigh. "It's always about Angela."

"I caught the squeal," Croaker said. "I found her dead. And I want her killer."

Alix's eyes blinked. "Is that all there is to it?"

"Someone doesn't want me to find the murderer. Bad." He hesitated now, on the brink of the question that had haunted him for over a year, the question that had sent him to Matty the Mouth for information, the question that had led him down to Key West when he had been warned off the case by his captain.

His throat was dry and he felt as if his vocal chords were in spasm. So long a time on this one, such a dogged determination. And now the answers staring at him out of jade green eyes right in front of his face.

"Was it Raphael Tomkin who killed her?" It sounded like another's voice but he knew it was his.

"Tomkin was there."

"That's not an answer."

For a long time she stared at him, trying to make up her mind. The boat rocked gently beneath them in the swells and the vague scent of dried fish, weeks old, still lingered over the swabbed decks. At last she stirred, moving to a sitting position. "We'll make a deal," she whispered. "You get me out of Florida, you get me to a place where I know I'll be safe—" She paused as if quivering on the last threshold. "And I'll tell you everything I know about Angela Didion's death."

If Minck expected a reaction from his guest, he was sorely disappointed. Instead, Nicholas said, "This department is concerned with Soviet Russia. How does it come to be entangled with the Japanese?"

"It will come as no surprise to you that Japan has been our major bulwark against Communism in the Far East ever since the end of the war. We have been putting enormous amounts of pressure on them for years to increase their defense budget, which, I might add, they have been doing slowly but surely." He shrugged. "That's something. And this year they have agreed to allow us to install a hundred and fifty of our newest supersonic F-20 Tigershark jet fighters at the naval base at Misawa."

This conversation had begun to have echoes of the one Nicholas had had with Tomkin last week.

"Our latest intelligence puts each of the Kuriles in the hands of a minimum of two divisions of mechanized Soviet infantry apiece. Twenty-eight thousand troops. And on one of them lies a Soviet command post capable of coordinating the activity of an entire army corps."

Minck sat forward. "There's been a great deal of coordinated activity going on there ever since the new MIGs arrived. But, personally, I don't think it's related to the supersonics. Those were merely brought in as defense against our F-20s.

"No, if our growing file of intelligence is correct, it's far more serious than that. What our probing suggests is a confirmation of what a number of the more militant Joint Chiefs have been concerned about for a while."

Minck took a sip of his drink. "We now feel that this troop buildup is part of a specific program to create a military curtain in that part of the globe behind which Russian submarines carrying long-range ballistic missiles with nuclear warheads capable of reaching the American mainland can operate without fear of intervention."

Nicholas felt chilled despite himself. "What you're talking about is madness. Global madness. We would all die in an instant without any recognition. Three-fourths of the human race gone." He shook his head. "I can't believe it. Even the dinosaurs did better than that."

"The dinosaurs weren't smart enough to split the atom," Minck said ironically. "So you'd better begin believing it." Nicholas could discern a spark of fire in his eyes now. "Because that's precisely what our information indicates is happening."

For a time Nicholas said nothing. The whir of the automatic sprinklers could be heard, doing the rain's work.

"Surely this is 'Eyes Only' material," he said, after a time. "Yet you've revealed it all to me, a civilian. Why?"

Minck rose, his legs unfolding like a crane's. He stood next to a pair of the window doors, his hand on the white wood pillar separating them. His concentration seemed lost in the foliage.

"The Soviet Union's Committee for State Security, known familiarly as the KGB, is comprised of nine directorates," he began. His voice had changed timbre and Nicholas had the impression that his thoughts were still far away. "Each directorate serves its own purpose in the overall schemata. For instance, the First Directorate is in charge of internal affairs. If you're ever inside Russia and picked up, it is to members of this directorate that you will be turned over once you reach the yellow brick building on Dzerzhinsky Square." Here Minck paused as if he were a captive of his own thoughts. With an obvious effort, he continued.

"On the other hand, the Fourth Directorate handles all operations in Western Europe; the Sixth, North America; the Seventh, Asia." He turned around abruptly. "I'm sure you get the picture.

"The Kuriles, with their close proximity to Japan, are and always have been under the control of the Seventh Directorate."

Minck returned across the room to stand in front of Nicholas.

There was too much tension now in his frame to allow him to sit down. "Not more than ten days ago one of my young cryptographic geniuses broke one of the Soviet's new random access Alpha-three ciphers. They're changed weekly so its usefulness is limited. Still, he works on the Alpha-threes exclusively because only the highest priority signaling is done through them."

Minck stuffed his hands in his trousers pockets as if he had no idea what else to do with them. "Before I tell you what that signal contained, I must explain that for the past nine months we have been extending our best efforts in trying to determine who was running the Kuriles operation.

"It should have been Rullchek, Anatoly Rullchek, the head of the Seventh Directorate. And indeed we put a finger on his movements in and out of the Kurile Island command post three or four times during that span.

"But frankly, something smelled. There was just too much GRU movement over there at the same time. Rullchek I know well and he hates the GRU with the fierce fanaticism of the old regime. Too, I kept getting reports of a certain Colonel Mironenko who was gradually assuming command while Rullchek was home in Moscow seeing to his bureaucratic flank. What was going on there that no one knew about? I began to ask myself.

"Was *Gospadin* Rullchek really running the ops, and if so, why would he cede even partial control to the GRU? Because, Nicholas, I will tell you quite truthfully that the idea of a united KGB and GRU fills me with a deep sense of foreboding.

"But then again the alternative, that Colonel Mironenko was running the show, seemed even more farfetched. Surely the Kuriles ops was far too crucial to entrust to a young colonel.

"So then what was the truth?"

Minck now folded himself, perching on the arm of a white rattan chair. One leg swung back and forth like a metronome as he spoke. "Now we return to the intercepted signal. It speaks of someone known as Miira. It tells us that Miira is in place and is feeding regularly. Which makes Control grow richer."

Minck withdrew his hands and pressed the palms together. Nicholas noticed that they were sweating lightly. "This signal was sent from somewhere in the north of Hokkaido and was received by the Soviet Kuriles command post. This was at a time when Colonel Mironenko, *not Gospadin* Rullchek, was presiding."

Nicholas thought it high time he added to the proceedings. "And was this signal signed?"

Minck's leg ceased its hypnotic arc for a moment and he nodded his head as if he were a professor approving of a pupil's question.

"Oh, yes, indeed. But we'll come to that in a moment. First would you be so kind as to tell me if this word *Miira* means anything to you."

Nicholas thought a moment. "It would help if I saw the *kanji* character in order to be certain of which meaning was being employed. But guessing just by the context, I would say it was Japanese for mummy."

"Uhm. Mummy." Minck appeared to mull this over as if it were all new to him. "A mummy, you say."

There was no point in answering.

Minck lifted his head. "I'd say it was more like Dig Dug."

"Dig Dug?"

Minck seemed pleased to be able to explain something again. "An arcade game. We keep a large supply two floors down to increase eye-hand coordination in stationary personnel. The object of Dig Dug is to have your man burrow, burrow, burrow through the earth in order to score points."

"You're saying that the person referred to as Miira is a mole?"

"In effect, yes. The text makes sense taken in that light, doesn't it? Miira is in place and is feeding—insert information there—regularly. Of course Control grows richer."

"But where is this mole?" Nicholas asked. "Did the signal give you a clue?"

Instead of answering, Minck stood up. He brushed down his trousers with his hands. "Tell me, did you ever wonder why Mr. Tomkin was so insistent on the site of your proposed Sphynx plant being at Misawa?"

Nicholas nodded. "Of course. Especially when it became a source of contention in the negotiations. I advised him to drop the idea; it was holding up consummation of the merger. Then he gave me the facts and figures as to why we had to have the Misawa site."

"Bullshit," Minck said blandly.

"What?"

"What he gave you—and Sato's people—is bullshit." Minck lifted a hand. "Oh, the cost ratio study was done all right and all the figures're real. That's just not the real reason for Tomkin's insistence on Misawa."

"I don't understand."

"Tomkin's insistence on Misawa stemmed from the same source that caused Sato to resist giving it to you. The company is involved in an operation of its own. We don't know what it is, only its name: *Tenchi*. By its name alone, Heaven and Earth, we know it must be incredibly important."

254

"And whatever *Tenchi* is, it's being done in Misawa?"

"We believe that to be so, yes. Although the *keiretsu* maintains offices for a mining *konzern* in Misawa, we have confirmed information that there is not enough actual mining being done to warrant all the activity there." Minck, the master of his profession, allowed that innocuous remark to hang before adding, "It's my opinion that the Russians also have this information."

Nicholas was instantly alert. "Miira?"

"Right now there's no way for us to know." Minck stared directly into Nicholas' eyes and there was no mistaking his intent.

"Oh, no," Nicholas said. "That's not my line of work."

"On the contrary." Minck's eyes would not let him go.

"But you have men trained for this. Use them."

"I have," Minck said simply. "For nine months. The last one was sent back in appalling disrepair. There's no point in sending another of mine in; I've run out of cover. Besides, my time's just about run out."

Nicholas thought about that for a moment. "Are you convinced that Miira is placed within the *keiretsu*?"

"Where else would the Soviets place Dig Dug to extract maximum information about *Tenchi*?"

"It's likely then that they're further along in solving the mystery than you are."

The ensuing pause was more forceful than anything Minck could have said.

"Do you know anything else about the mummy?" Nicholas asked, knowing that he was one step closer to doing what Minck desperately wanted him to do.

"Unfortunately, no."

"Jesus, why don't you try blindfolding me, putting the donkey's tail in my hand, and spinning me around."

Minck stared at his polished nails. "I've heard it said that ninja—true ninja, that is—can kill people blindfolded, in the dark. I've heard that they can infiltrate the most heavily guarded areas; appear and disappear at will into the night. Disguise themselves in the most remarkable ways."

"All of that's true," Nicholas said. "But I won't do it for you."

"Oh, it's not for me that you'll do it, Nicholas. Not at all. There is, as you call it, *giri*. Tomkin passed on responsibility to you. I think you owe *him* that. I know that he would ask it of you if he were here. Besides, the merger will be meaningless if the Soviets succeed in penetrating *Tenchi*."

Now, Nicholas knew, nothing mattered. What he thought of Minck or what Minck wanted him to do. There was *giri*. And

255

without duty, life would become a meaningless jumble of unrelated noise and action. When he had walked in here an hour or so ago he had had no intention of being coerced into a situation he had no interest in. But Minck had very cleverly robbed him of that option. There was *giri*. Nicholas owed Minck nothing and Minck knew it. But Tomkin was another matter entirely.

Now, in the light of all this new information, what was Nicholas to make of the three murders at Sato Petrochemicals? Could they possibly be the handiwork of Miira? He thought it unlikely, since *Miira*'s job entailed anonymity and quiet, and therefore decided not to bring it up to Minck. Besides, he had given his word to Sato not to talk of them with anyone. Technically, of course, that referred to only the first murder.

"What do you know about *Tenchi*?" he asked after a time.

"Four hundred billion yen, that's what the Japanese government has already poured into the project, and there's no end in sight."

"Christ, what the hell is it?"

"Your guess will probably be as good as mine."

"Oh, God."

Minck stood up. "There is no one else, and that's no lie." He walked back to the windows. The sprinklers had begun again, their sprays beading the glass at the beginning of each pass.

"And now, I suppose, we come to the person who signed the intercepted signal."

Minck's back stiffened just as if he had scented the enemy. "Oh, yes. That. You've got a good memory. It was signed, 'Protorov.'"

Minck turned around, the light streaming in behind him, shadowing his face. "Viktor Protorov, my friend, is the head of the KGB's Ninth Directorate."

"What's their field of expertise?"

"It varies with whom you speak to. Some say the Ninth is the KGB's overlord, their own private watchdog. But that seems to me to be overly redundant even for the Russians. Besides, that would be just the thing the GRU would agitate for, so I'd discount it."

"Well, then."

"My own theory is that the Ninth controls and regulates the worldwide terrorist network the Soviets train and, in some cases at least, control."

"A very dangerous man, this *Gospadin* Protorov." He was watching Minck carefully because he suspected that they had come to the heart of the matter.

With barely a flicker of his eyelids Minck said, "Extremely

dangerous. He's exceptionally militant. Exceptionally bright. But even worse for us, he's no bureaucrat."

"They'll purge him in the end, then," Nicholas observed. "They'll take care of him for you."

"I suppose they'll try."

"Meaning?"

Minck came away from the windows. "For years Protorov was head of the First Directorate. Then about six years ago he was elevated. I rather think that this particular *Gospadin* has already amassed too much power for that."

"I'll have to remember to use extreme caution, then."

"Ah," Minck said. He watched Nicholas. "I'd be, er, grateful if you did. Protorov has a nasty habit of bringing ferrets in and playing around with them."

"Is that what I am now? A ferret?"

"Sato Petrochemicals is the tunnel I'm putting you down," Minck said, taking Nicholas' hand. "Mind you only light the lamps as you go."

They went back through the odd house. "Tanya will give you an access code that will tie you in to the network twenty-four hours a day. You can always get either one of us." He smiled at last, perhaps out of relief. "And, Nicholas, I'd appreciate it if you'd memorize the thing."

Dusk was gathering when Tengu decided it was time to take his leave of the *dōjō*. Ever since his brother in arms, Tsutsumu, had been found slain at the feet of the *sensei*, Kusunoki, he had become increasingly ill at ease in this walled castle that had been his home now for more than a year.

How had Tsutsumu been discovered? He had begun asking himself that terrifying question as soon as he had heard the news. If Tsutsumu, then why not him?

In the time he had been here he had come to understand that there were more forces in the world than he had ever dreamed could exist. He had witnessed feats he had previously thought impossible and to this day could not fathom. All these and more could be his if he stayed on and worked diligently. But that was not to be.

The signal from Control had assured that. Tengu now wondered who he was more afraid of, Control or these strange folk all around him. Though he had lived with them, he was intelligent enough to know that he was not part of them. He floated outside their orbit as a cold moon does a sun, soaking up what energy it could through the vastness of the gulf between them.

Part of him was loathe to leave, but that area could stand little scrutiny, Tengu knew, and he forcibly pushed his thoughts in another direction.

Even so he would not be preparing to depart now had he not found the safe. It was an accident and, afterward, Tengu realized that that would have been the only way anyone would have stumbled upon such a cleverly concealed cache.

All the novices took turns picking the day lilies that, dew laden, lined the slopes of the Yoshino foothills beyond the walled compound. Today had been his turn and just before dawn—as Kusunoki had done when he was alive—Tengu climbed the slopes in search of the most esthetically pleasing blooms.

Returning to the *dōjō*, he went to the *sensei*'s study. It was deserted. As was the custom at the *dōjō*, this room would never again be used save for studied contemplation of the spirit of the master, which was the spirit of all that was taught here.

Tengu knelt before the earthenware vase which stood atop the raised platform of the *tokonoma*, the contemplative alcove within Masashigi Kusunoki's study. Pouring fresh spring water into the narrow neck of the vase, he began to carefully arrange the lilies.

In truth his mind was far away. Instead of concentrating on the spirit of the flowers in his hands, his mind was recalling all that he had done during the past week to discover the *sensei*'s secret. What it had to do with he did not know—and it was not for him to know.

Of course his search was hampered by how circumspect he needed to be around these highly dangerous people. But at that moment he was engrossed with wondering where he had been remiss.

And because his mind was wandering in the Zen sense, he became clumsy. But, ironically, it was just this clumsiness that led to his discovery. As he was arranging the lilies, several drops of water fell onto the highly polished wooden surface. As he moved to wipe them off with the edge of his sleeve, he perceived the barest hairline shadow.

At first he thought it to be a natural fracture of the grain caused by the expansion and contraction with changing temperature. But his concentration returned and he then observed that the line ran straight as an arrow's shaft for perhaps five inches. At that point he saw another hairline connecting with the first at right angles. His pulse began to jump and he looked around, fearful that he might be observed. All was quiet.

Now as he craned his neck he could see that the porcelain vase was at the very center of what could only be a secret door. He

258

jammed the flowers into the vase and carefully lifted it away, putting it to one side.

He produced a blade so thin it appeared no wider than a filament of wire. The point of this he slowly lowered to the hairline shadow, probing with the utmost caution for should he slip or in any way mark this polished, smooth surface, he would be undone. Already his brother in arms had been discovered, by what method he could not guess, and destroyed. There must not be the slightest hint that another traitor existed within the *dōjō*.

His ears attuned for the slightest alteration in the quiet background sounds from within the buildings, he worked his blade surely and methodically, rejoicing at the slightest movement of the wood panel, content to be patient.

And at last he was rewarded. There was no hinge; the piece just lifted out. Tengu nodded to himself. Considering the nature of the hiding place it was a far securer system, for the *sensei* was sure to see any signs of tampering with such a tight fit.

Beneath the panel was a drop of perhaps three inches, then a horizontal metal door with a spring lock. Again, using his multipurpose knife, the man popped the lock. Inside he found papers. It was these he had come here to search for. Quickly now, he stuffed the wad of rice paper into his loose cotton jacket. He could feel their frail fluttering like a trapped bird against his bare skin. Then he set about returning the double-lidded safe to its original position.

Concentrating fiercely, he spent an extra few minutes arranging the day lilies in the simplest yet most sublime arrangement. His *ikebana sensei* would have approved.

Now, in the failing light, he finished packing up his meager belongings in a cotton roll sack that fitted across his shoulders and, touching the packet of papers held fast by his belt against one side of his lower belly, he emerged from his room into the empty corridor.

Swiftly, yet with no hurrying of his spirit, he went through the maze of the *dōjō*, passing without incident through the ancient stone gates. He skirted the red lacquer *torii* which stood guard over the grounds and took the high, winding path that would lead him through the foothills of the thickly wooded slopes of the Yoshino mountains. Rising stands of cypress, cedar, and fir, rendering the air heady with their scents, swept away almost to the apex of the vault of the heavens, standing black and impenetrable against the last fiery glow of sunset.

Already, to the east, a few first-magnitude stars could be seen dimpling the oncoming bowl of night. Swallows and gray plovers darted through the rustling edges of the fields below him, on their way home before the keen-eyed predators of the dark roused themselves and took wing.

Behind him, lights were already lit within the walled fortress of the *dōjō*, wavering and hazy. He was well quit of them. It took all of his concentration to keep his thoughts utterly disciplined every moment he was there. It was an exhausting business even for one such as he, for he knew by observing carefully that this particular *dōjō* specialized not only in a myriad of arcane *bujutsu* subdisciplines involving the body but a number involving the mind as well.

As he pushed onward up the twisting woody slope, Tengu contemplated this. He was somewhat acquainted with the dark side of *ninjutsu*. But here in Yoshino he had begun to enter into areas in which even he did not feel entirely comfortable.

Rounding a long, sweeping bend, he lost sight at last of the bastion which had been his home for so long. He felt as if some obscure weight which had been crushing his heart had been lifted from him. And, like the horned owl, who, bloody clawed and bloody beaked, lifts it prey up into the night, he felt a kind of eerie elation that seemed to fizz the blood in his veins.

And with it came a curiosity he could not control. Searching for a slight break in the underbrush on the upward slope to his left, he struck off from the path in an oblique angle. Now, hidden within the sheltering cedars, he sat cross-legged on a moss-encrusted rock. He chose it because it had the appearance of Tokubei, the great mythic fire-breathing toad.

Mounting it made him feel more keenly the hero that he was. He reached into the crossed opening of his jacket.

He looked up and outward past the barely discernable mountain path to the wide valley beyond, dotted here and there by glowing lights from small houses and farms. He caught the pungent scent of a fire and he thought of the hearth, a steaming bowl of miso soup piled high with noodles. Then he shook himself and, producing a plastic-sheathed pencil flash, unfolded the sheets of rice paper he had stolen from Kusunoki's safe.

With a curt nod he set himself to reading the vertical lines of ideograms. Why not? He had certainly earned the privilege. For fully half an hour he pored over the text, substituting *kanji* for the *ryu*'s complex ciphers, and as he did so his heart began to pound within his chest, his pulse rate shot up, and he found he had to fight to control his breathing. Buddha! he thought. What have I stumbled onto? His fingers trembled when he thought of the overriding implications for Japan.

260

And so engrossed was he in his reading that he did not notice until it was very close a small bobbing light flitting like a will-o'-the-wisp through the trunks of the cedars. Immediately, he doused the pencil flash, but it was already too late. The light had stopped its rhythmic movement and now shone still and fierce at a spot on the path directly below where he sat.

Cursing the excitement that had narrowed his normally keen senses, he refolded the papers, stuffing them back into his jacket. He hid the flash and, climbing down off the rock, moved slowly off the slope. Far better, he felt, to emerge himself from the forest than to have the source of the light come up to find him. Especially if it was one of the *sensei* from the *dōjō*. Tengu girded himself for such an eventuality, bringing his *ki* up to a sufficient level so that he could call upon its power at a split second's notice.

But as he emerged onto the serpentine pathway he saw that it was no *sensei* who had inadvertently seen his light but merely a young girl.

She was dressed in a gray and green kimono, rope *geta* on her otherwise bare feet. She carried a small kerosene lantern in one hand, a *janomegasa*, a brightly colored rice-paper parasol, in the other.

Moisture beaded his face and he became aware of the soft pattering of the rain. He had not felt it at all within the sheltering arbor of the forest. He saw the rain in beads, sliding down the oiled rice-paper *janomegasa*, dripping dolefully into the earth.

"Pardon me, madam," he said, bowing mainly to hide the flood of relief in his eyes. "I hope my light did not frighten you. I was out collecting wild mushrooms when I—eh—?"

She had taken a quick step toward him, raising the level of the lantern so that its compact glow spread upward across her face.

With a quick painful lurch of his heart he recognized her. It was Suijin, the female student from the *dōjō*. What was she doing here? he wondered even as his small blade snickered out into his right palm.

But the lantern was already falling, Suijin's now free hand gripping the bottom of the *janomegasa*'s lacquered bamboo haft, pulling it down and away from the spread top in a blurry glitter.

His eyes only had time enough to register the transformation from harmless bamboo to thousand-layered steel edge before the foot-long blade pierced his chest and, slashing downward, rent his heart in two.

Suijin watched only his face as component by component it fell apart and his hot, pumping blood spilled. His eyes showed bewilderment, rage, shame; then they crossed and all human emotion was wiped from the slate of his face. Like the small and defenseless warrior she had as a child once made out of mud, twigs, and lichen, he flopped this way and that, without coordination, without the divine spark. Now, as then, she placed the flat of her hand across the tautness of her lower belly, wondering what magic lay within her womb, the anvil of creation.

Now there was only a twisted mass at her feet, a waxy parody of what had once been alive. She stuck the point of the blade into the wet earth to free her hands as well as to clean the gleaming surface, black with blood.

Raindrops pattered all about her as she dropped down. Her nostrils dilated as she caught the freshening scent of the wood, the spoor of animal life. The rain fell heavier, turning the traitor's cheeks to putty.

She had suspected that there might be another one, even at the moment of Tsutsumu's death. Strictly speaking, it should have been none of her business at that point. Her mastery over her *sensei*, Masashigi Kusunoki, had been her graduation from the *dōjō*, and if experience had taught her anything, it was never to look back. Accomplishments were strictly the province of the present. Those who sat back to gloat over their achievements often died with those thoughts.

And yet despite this knowledge, she had returned. Studying the contents of the traitor's pockets and experiencing again the feeling of outrage that had fired through her breast when she had observed him this morning rifling the *sensei*'s most closely guarded secrets, she knew that somehow Kusunoki had been different. He had gotten to her in some way she was at a loss to explain. She felt keenly his loss, and all at once in the midst of this vast mountainous forest he had loved so dearly, with only the gusting wind and the swirling rain for companions, she was weeping silent tears, her chest constricted and her heart full of an unnameable anguish, a burden abruptly too terrible to bear.

When the spasm subsided—for that was how she thought of it the next day—she completed her meticulous search of the corpse. She found the sheaf of papers half stuck to the traitor's hip and she had to be extremely careful in peeling the top sheet away from the damp skin.

Quickly now, protecting the papers from the wet, she refolded them, put them away in a dry place within her kimono. Kusunoki's violation had become her own. She did not look at the papers; she had no interest in them. They were the property of her *sensei*, and whether he was dead or alive their place was still where he had put them.

She stood and pulled her blade from the earth. It was clean and shining again. She reattached it to the top of the *janomegasa* and with it disappeared into the wood above to change into her student's *gi* for the last time. The glowing lights of the *dōjō* beckoned her; or was it Kusunoki's *kami*? She did not know. The papers were safe with her, and soon they would be back in their rightful place.

Justine had a surprise waiting for her at Millar, Soames & Robberts when she returned there the morning after the funeral. Mary Kate Sims was no longer in her large corner office. In fact, Mary Kate Sims was no longer a vice president at the advertising firm.

She was about to go and see Rick Millar to get an explanation—neither Min nor anyone else she knew at all seemed to be around—when he strode into her bare office.

"I'd heard you just came in," he said, a concerned look on his face. "I thought I told you to take a couple of days off. There's no need for you to—"

"Work's the best tonic for me right now," she cut in. "I hate hanging around the house staring at shadows. I'm always afraid I'll turn into a cat."

Rick nodded his head deferentially. "Okay. It's just as well you're here anyway. I've got something to show you." He began to propel her out the door.

"Just a minute," she began, "there's something—"

"Later," he said, taking her down the hall toward the elevators. "This's more important."

A floor above, he led the way around a turning. "Here it is. What d'you think?"

Oh, holy Jesus, Justine thought. It can't be. "What the hell is my name doing on Mary Kate's door?"

"Your office now, Justine. That spare office downstairs was just temporary. Surely you knew that."

She turned on him, flaring. "Temporary until you got rid of Mary Kate."

"Absolutely not. She left of her own accord. She tendered her resignation at closing yesterday."

"I don't believe you," Justine said hotly. "If she were thinking of leaving she'd've told me. We're friends, remember?"

"Let's go into the office, shall we?" Rick prompted. He closed the door after them.

"You'll damn well tell me the truth or I'll walk out of here right now!" Justine shouted. On top of what had happened to her

263

father, what had happened with Nicholas, this was just too much to take. It was all piling up like the weight of the world. Her head was spinning and she found herself holding onto the edge of the knurled wooden desk with white knuckles.

"The truth is Mary Kate wasn't, er, well, working out. She had gotten into a number of scraps with the senior executives. I had spoken to her, of course... more than once. But"—he shrugged—"Well, you know Mary Kate."

"I know she wouldn't take too much of your bullshit, Rick." Justine shook her head. "I don't believe this. What you're telling me is that you had every intention of firing her when we had lunch together. You were interviewing me for her job!"

Rick shrugged again. "It happens all the time, Justine. And, anyway, what're you so steamed about? The better girl won. You can run rings around Mary Kate. You should be—"

"What a bastard you are to do that to me!" She stepped up to him and slapped him across the face. "To us!" She gathered up her things. "You'd better find someone else to do this kind of shit, because it's not going to be me!"

"Nice touch," Rick said, smiling. "If you're angling for more money, I'll go along with it. I'll have to twist some arms but there won't be any—"

"Are you out of your mind?" Justine backed away from him, heading toward the door. "I don't want one dollar from your firm. Get the hell out of my life!"

Downstairs on the milling sidewalk, she realized that she had nowhere to go. She couldn't face the apartment, empty and lonely, most of all couldn't face the clothes, the belongings, the photos of Nicholas there. She could not think of going to Gelda's; that kind of depression would put her over the edge. And as for returning to her own free-lance business, the idea of starting up again seemed beyond her at the moment.

Confused, she crossed the avenue and went into a coffee shop. She could not taste the coffee set before her, which was perhaps just as well. Tears slid down her cheeks as she stared at the blurs of color hurrying by outside. I've got to do *something*, she told herself.

She went to the closest branch of her bank and withdrew five thousand dollars. She kept half as cash, the rest she converted into traveler's checks. She did some clothes shopping after that, stopping into a luggage store to buy a lightweight suitcase. She charged everything. Cosmetics were no problem, but by the time she did that number she realized that she would have to go back to the apartment after all for some essentials she just could not buy duplicates of. She made it as quick a stop as she could. But still she was struck by the difference. It no longer felt like home. Everything seemed out of place or missing. The comfortable had become disquieting and sad. She wiped the tears away and got out of there, locking up as if she were going away forever.

It was only when she was already airborne, on her way to Honolulu and thence Maui, that she realized that, indeed, one item had been missing from the apartment.

The long black lacquer scabbard that sheathed Nicholas' prized *dai-katana*, the supreme long sword, was gone from its spot on the bedroom wall. So, of course, was the deadly weapon.

Instinctively, something inside her began to wail.

Minck saw the concern on Tanya's face as she returned from putting Linnear back on his flight east. She had heard and seen everything, secreted behind the panel of the mirror that was, in the adjoining room, a rectangle of one-way glass.

"Carroll, I don't understand what you're doing," she said. "You've as good as killed him, sending him against Protorov like that. That wasn't the plan . . . unless I missed something."

Minck was not in a good mood, despite his success with Nicholas. "Come with me," he said brusquely. He led her through to the opposite end of the rambling house. Here, in an area that was restricted even to some of his own staff, Minck took her through several windowless laboratories and into a steel-walled cubicle. It was very cold in there.

He flipped on the fluorescent overhead light. Tanya squinted in the harsh purple-blue illumination. Still, she saw the draped corpse immediately. It would have been hard to miss since its bulk dominated the small room.

Carefully she strode over to the head and pulled back the white muslin cloth. "Oh, God," she whispered. "It's Tanker." That was not his real name. She turned to Minck. "When did he come in?"

"While you were out."

She came away from the blued body. "I wondered why you created that 'signature.' Anyone with a knowledge of how it all works would have known that in signals only code names are used, not real ones."

"Then let's be thankful that that's one area in which our Mr. Linnear is ignorant," he said acidly. "Because of this beauteous package dropped on our doorstep in Honshū I now have to deal with our brother services who were obliged to transfer Tanker here."

They stood in the dim hallway with the door closed at their

backs. "We now know that Croesus is Protorov's code name, however."

"Tanker was the only one close," she said.

"Obviously he got too close." Minck closed his eyes. "Now, like it or not, we must make do with Mr. Linnear."

"Do you think that's wise?"

"That remains to be seen. But wise or not, our time has run out. I'm afraid that were we not to send Mr. Linnear into the lion's den, the lion would eat us all for supper."

"He may still do that."

For a time Minck was silent. "I take it, then, that you disapprove of my improvisation."

Tanya knew that she was on thin ice here and she thought her words out carefully. "I think he's an amateur. Amateurs have proven in the past to be highly unreliable as well as disconcertingly unpredictable. They're not under discipline."

"Uhm. True enough. But that's also one of his great advantages. Protorov cannot connect him with us as he did Tanker or as he would you." Minck had the manner of a country yokel, sitting on his back porch of a Sunday, sleepily passing the time with a neighbor. It was as if nothing of moment was in the air. "And after all, he's quite frightening, you know." He seemed to be musing. "Up close like that I believe he'd frighten the devil himself." His eyes opened and he looked at her. "Even kill him if he was given just cause. If he or those around him—those he cared about—were put in jeopardy. Mr. Linnear strikes me as an extremely loyal fellow as well as a deadly one."

"You think he'll be provoked enough to bring Protorov down." It occurred to Tanya that this had been his goal all along.

"Yes," Minck said. "I have sent our Mr. Linnear out, rather cleverly I might add, to bring me Viktor Protorov's head; to end our feud once and for all. I don't like this KGB connection with Colonel Mironenko. In fact, it scares me like a rattling skeleton at my door. I begin to imagine the connection between Protorov and Mironenko as being highly significant. The paranoid in me sketches out a scenario wherein the KGB and the GRU would somehow unite."

"Impossible!" Tanya exploded, but her ashen face betrayed her own fright. "There are too many points of contention, far too much bad blood between the two."

"Yes, yes, Tanya, my dear. We're all well acquainted with that line of thought." Minck seemed inordinately pleased with himself. "Still I can imagine the attempt being made; I can especially imagine Viktor Protorov spearheading that attempt. He's

266

got a vicious mind; he's not a bureaucrat. That's a particularly noxious combination in an enemy."

He stirred. "In any case—whether this is all imagination or frightening reality—the time has come for Protorov to die. Mr. Linnear will be my terrible swift sword. I have quite a bit of faith in him even if you do not."

"I didn't say that."

"Not in so many words, no." He contemplated her as if she were an entrée set before him. He rose. "But just in case you're right in your assessment, I'll be sending you after him in a few days' time. Timing's crucial so you'll have to be ready immediately. The beeper'll signal you if you're out of the building. Tickets will be waiting at Pan Am; the rest's standard procedure."

"What about Linnear?"

Minck looked at her cynically. "The first priority—*absolutely the first*—is Protorov. If you and Mr. Linnear can come to terms and team up, so much the better."

"And if not?"

"If not," Minck said, moving away, "if Linnear becomes a hindrance, you'll just have to dispose of him."

Seiichi Sato possessed big *hara*.

Kneeling across the low lacquer table from Nicholas, he had already taken the top off one of the small dishes and with artful dexterity was using his chopsticks to serve his honored guest.

Hara, strictly speaking, was the Japanese word for stomach, but it was also the symbol of a man being well integrated with all the aspects of life.

One of the primary lessons of all martial arts required the student to find that deep well of reserves of inner strength that resided in everyone just below the navel. It was known as *tan tien* by the Chinese and *tanden* by the Japanese.

Both physical and spiritual power dwelled there. A man with big *hara* was centered within himself, grounded to the elements of nature. Japanese often observed that Westerners "bounced along" as they walked, evidence that they were centered only in their minds and therefore not attuned at all to the world around them. Japanese, on the other hand, walked with a heavier stride, their gait flowing smoothly from hips and pelvis, a certain sign that they possessed *hara*.

Nicholas was intrigued by Sato's big *hara*; it was a great compliment to pay any Japanese. He had flown the trail of "the endless night," as the Japanese call it, chasing the darkness for twenty-one hours, leaving Washington at night, arriving at Narita the same night, one day later.

Mr. Sabayama, one of Sato's many minions, had been waiting, bleary-eyed, for hours at the airport. He murmured away Nicholas' apologies and, taking their bags, led them through the terminal to the waiting car. Nicholas asked Mr. Sabayama if he would take care of Craig Allonge at the Okura. Mr. Sabayama assured Nicholas that there was someone already at the hotel to see to all their needs; he would accompany Nicholas out to Sato-san's house on the edge of Tokyo.

Outside the hotel Nicholas spoke quietly to Allonge. "I may be out of touch for several days, Craig. Even as much as a week. I want you to stay in touch with New York and keep things running smoothly. We've already had enough of a shakeup."

Now Nicholas could hear the boughs of the boxwood scraping against the side of the wood and tile house. The air outside was clean and clear. On the rain-soaked streets, the pedestrians bowed before the wind, only partially protected by their *ama-gasa*. Briefly he saw the high arc of the Nihon-bashi as they crossed the river that flowed into the wider Sumida. Parasols over the span reminded him of Hiroshige's prints, the great artist's images speaking to him from another age.

The summons to Sato's house came as no surprise to Nicholas considering the high-pitched tone of the Telex he had received from the man. Three murders, unexplained and bizarre, were more than enough reason for this late-night rendezvous. The Japanese were a practical people and in times of emergency even politeness might be bypassed for efficiency's sake.

But for Nicholas the summons held other echoes, ones that Sato could not know about or understand. Being at the industrialist's home meant that Nicholas would see Akiko again and if his luck held even get to speak to her.

He remembered the gilt and crimson fan trembling like a flower in that extended split second just before she began to lower it and changed his life forever. For it seemed clear to him now that everything he had done after seeing Akiko's face, every decision he had made, had been so that he could see her again.

He was drawn to her as a moth is to a flame, without reason or logic, with even some atavistic knowledge that the journey might end in destruction.

Nicholas was no longer the person he had once been when he and Yukio had been so madly in love. Yet there was a piece of that madness still burning within him. And he knew that he could not get on with his life, could not fulfill his *karma*, without first investigating this last blind spot within himself. His entire life had been spent in the pursuit of pushing back the darkness. He had found that he could control the chaos of life through the mastery of the martial arts. Through that powerful conduit he had not only learned how to channel the natural forces which he had hitherto found frightening—for they were the forces which had robbed him of his father and mother—but also the spiritual forces whirling within himself.

Yukio's power over him was obvious. She had spoken to his spirit before he had even known fully of its existence. Her attraction had bypassed his conscious mind, the rational decision-making sector on which he had come to rely so heavily. He was drawn to her and he did not know why. He had become frightened of her and of himself. Oddly, this had served only to deepen his love, to etch it on his heart like a black tattoo that could never be erased.

As he raced through the rain-filled Tokyo night, spangled with pink and orange neon, he was conscious only of nearing Yukio again. Impossible but true. Which was the dream and which reality? His body had quivered with the certain knowledge that soon he would find out.

But to his bitter disappointment Sato had told him in response to his query that Akiko was still away in Kyūshū, visiting her infirm aunt. He saw only Koten, the *sumō* bodyguard, lurking in the background like a well-trained Doberman.

Drinks first, then food. At night tea was subordinate to liquor for the modern Japanese. For this, too, they had the West to thank.

Nicholas thought Suntory Scotch vile but he drank it anyway, grateful that Allonge, half Scotch, was not here to witness firsthand what had been done to his nation's most treasured asset.

As was the habit of the Japanese, they spoke of everything but what was on their minds. That would come later. Sato mentioned that Nangi-san was on his way to Hong Kong to close an important business deal.

"Would you consider it impolite," Nicholas inquired, "if I told you that my opinion is that Nangi-san does not see this merger in a favorable light?"

"Certainly not," Sato said. "We are drinking together, Linnear-san. This makes us friends. This binds us more than our business ever will. Businesses are not like marriages, you know. They rise and fall of their own accord. The whims of the market. Economic factors that have nothing to do with us."

Sato paused for a moment. "But you must try to understand Nangi-san. The war left its imprint on him like a tiger's clawing.

269

Each day he wakes he cannot forget that we live with the atomic sunshine. You understand me. The fallout's effects seem never-ending. He is childless and therefore without any true family but me because of it."

"I am sorry, Sato-san," Nicholas said. "Truly."

Sato eyed him, his wooden chopsticks suspended above the steaming food, three kinds of cooked fish, *sashimi*, glass noodles, steamed rice, cucumber, and sea urchin in sweet rice vinegar.

"Yes, I'm sure you are," he said at last. "I see quite a bit of your father in you. But then there is the other side. That part I do not know." He resumed serving his guest.

For a time they ate in silence, with rapid, economical movements. Sato drank more than he ate and he ate quite a bit. It was obvious he wanted to talk openly and without restraint. That was quite impossible to do for a Japanese under normal circumstances. Once drunk, all actions, all words were immediately excusable and allowable. Therefore Nicholas drank with him. There would be no point to the session if only Sato drank and, besides, that would be insulting, as if Nicholas was saying, I don't want to be friends.

He perceived from the moment Sato himself had met him at the door to the house that the older man needed his friendship and support. Whatever was behind the *Wu-Shing* slayings was far more important to him than holding pat in resisting the merger as originally outlined by Tomkin. Whatever fear had erupted in Sato and Nangi of the ritual punishments overrode their normal caution and preference for hard dealing.

And within this softening of his stance Nicholas, trained to dissect every situation in evaluating the elements which created it, perceived a weakness.

It did not make him feel particularly noble or honorable to use this weakness to gain the advantage, yet he desperately needed an opening into *Tenchi*. He knew quite well that under almost any other circumstance he would have come up against a stone wall where *Tenchi* was concerned. However, in this instance the *kei-retsu*'s secret work made them vulnerable to outside scrutiny. Sato had made it clear that no police were to be involved. Nicholas was the only person who could conceivably break the chain of the *Wu-Shing*, thus he had a powerful bargaining point from which to open the negotiations.

"Fah!" Sato exclaimed, focusing Nicholas' attention. He threw his cup to the floor. He was wearing a kimono composed of the flaming colors of autumn. He had generously offered one of his own—the one with the angular *Nōh* pattern that he had been

270

wearing the night Akiko had brought him his last gift before they were married—and Nicholas was now wearing it. Dregs of the brown liquor flew up the sleeve, lying in beads like decoration. "This Scotch is no true liquor at all." He turned red-rimmed eyes on his guest. "Linnear-san, you pick our drink for the evening."

"Thank you, Sato-san." Nicholas bowed. "I'd very much like some sakē. Hot, if that's possible."

"Possible!" Sato exploded. "Why, it's the only way to drink it!" He lurched heavily to his feet, padded in his low white socks to the bar against the longer of the two inner walls of the room. It was fairly large by Japanese standards, sixteen-*tatami*. The wet bar also contained a black iron-and-boxwood *naga-hibachi*, smaller than the one in the other side of the house. This one was never touched by the women of the household but was reserved expressly for the use of the host.

As he went about heating the rice wine, Sato hummed quietly to himself an ancient folk tune his Obā-chama had crooned to him when he and Gōtarō were children. It seemed to fill the house with a warmth that was not exactly physical, as if he had summoned up the attention of good *kami*.

But when he returned to the low lacquer table with the sakē, his face was set into somber lines. "I fear we have fallen on evil times, Linnear-san," he said as he poured. "This *Wu-Shing* . . ." He shuddered. "I am *samurai* but this . . . this is simply barbaric. I am not at all surprised that its origins are Chinese. How very indiscriminate we Japanese are, eh, to take the worst from them along with the best. The Yakuza are nothing more than glorified Triads; and the ninja have their origins there as well."

His eyes crossed for a moment as if he had just forgotten something important, and then his head went down. "Forgive me, Linnear-san. An old man's tongue runs on and on late at night."

Nicholas lifted his left arm as if to make a gesture and in so doing caught the hem of his sleeve on the lip of the delicate porcelain sakē pitcher. It made a tiny sound as it shattered. Clear liquid ran across the table.

Nicholas jumped up. "A thousand pardons, Sato-san. Please forgive my Western clumsiness."

Sato calmly wiped away the liquor and quickly gathered up the shards of porcelain. "There is nothing to forgive, my friend. Akiko is not here to serve us from the best porcelain. This was an old and timeworn piece that needed throwing out. In fact it is only my laziness which had precluded me from disposing of the pitcher myself."

Thus did Nicholas cleverly negate his host's acute embarrass-

271

ment, gaining enormous face in Sato's eyes while saving face for his host.

When Sato returned from heating more sakē, there was new respect in his eyes. He bowed as he pushed the filled cup across the table.

"*Domo arigato.*" Nicholas returned the bow.

Sato downed more sakē before he spoke again. "It is my opinion, Linnear-san, that the *Wu-Shing* is being directed at us—that is, Nangi-san and myself—even though the three deaths have seriously undermined the effectiveness of the *konzern*. There is something personal in the manner of the deaths. With each one, Kagami-san, Yoshida-san, Ishii-san, we come closer and closer to the core of the company. The path is indeed terrifying to contemplate."

He stared down at his empty cup, and Nicholas realized that even with so much alcohol inside him this was a difficult moment. All Nicholas could do was to remain silent.

"I have thought much about these ritual punishments." Sato's head came up. "And I now believe that we are being stalked by our past. Can you understand that? Yes, I thought so. You of all people."

"Have you and Nangi-san discussed the possible . . . origins of these punishments."

"No. Nangi-san is *sempai*."

"Yes. I see."

"Besides," Sato admitted, "Nangi-san is no good when it comes to the past. There are many things that he would rather forget, some because they are too hateful, others because they are just too full of intimate emotion. You may think Nangi-san cold and heartless but this is not true. No, no. On the contrary, emotion is quite dear to him.

"He wept bitterly when my Obā-chama died. He was heartsick at having to sell a pair of her T'ang Dynasty cups. Sadly, we were forced to do so in order to come to Tokyo and begin our careers just after the war ended.

"These cups, you know, were superb examples of the genius of those faraway Chinese artisans, as limpid as a mountain stream. But beyond their undeniable aesthetic value I believe a component of Nangi-san's attachment to them stemmed from the poignant circumstances under which my Obā-chama received them." He told Nicholas the story of his grandmother's distant relative fleeing the firebombing of Tokyo. "I think for Nangi-san this incident more than any other exemplified the useless cruelty of the war.

The past is dear to him, and I think you can understand why he would not wish to speak of it."

Sato shook his head. "I'm afraid he cannot be counted on, there. Memory is an affliction with him. He will not speak of the past, even with me."

"Then it must be up to you, Sato-san."

"I know," the older man said miserably, "but up to now I have been able to remember nothing out of the ordinary. You know what it was like here after the war. Those were extraordinary times. More often than not survival called for taking extraordinary measures. Regimes came and went. Alliances were hastily formed and just as hastily dissolved." Sato poured them both more wine.

"I understand. Many enemies could have been made then, as well as friends."

Sato nodded. "Those were pressurized times. I often think that decades were compressed into years, years into months. We accomplished so much in such a small amount of time, coming back from the abyss of defeat, regaining our self-confidence. It was as if we had to begin all over again. The holocaust purged us in a way of many of the worst elements we had allowed to run our society.

"Like the contents of Noah's Ark, we stepped ashore on Mount Ararat prepared to begin a new society. And we did just that. We overcame runaway inflation, we directed the growth of our industry through MITI and allowed picked sections to enjoy the most high speed growth known in the world."

He looked at Nicholas and smiled. "We were even successful at turning the slogan 'Made in Japan' from a derogation into a status symbol.

"None of this was an accident; none of it was luck. Our *karma* is great, and we continue to thrive though we sometimes experience growing pains."

He poured more saké, slopping some onto the lacquer. "But do you know the one thing we still cannot tolerate, Linnear-san? It is the knowledge that even in times of an oil glut there is what amounts to a caravan of tankers arriving and departing Japan, day and night, dotting the Pacific in an endless stream.

"The world must feed us in order for us to survive. Like a mewling infant who cannot make his own food, we are stuck on these beautiful islands, on rock devoid of all fossil fuels.

"Can you understand how galling that is for us, Linnear-san?" He nodded sagely. "But of course you can. You are part of us, after all. I can see that even if others cannot. And you know there is truth to the saying that misfortune never lasts a lifetime."

He sighed heavily. "But I tell you that sometimes I am not certain." His hair hung lankly on his head and his kimono had come partly unwrapped so that Nicholas could see a broad section of his hairless chest and the edge of one dark nipple.

"The truth is," he said, his voice slurring slightly, "that there are times when I miss my wife. Oh, not Akiko. No, no. I was married before. Mariko was her name. Beautiful Mariko. She was very young when we met." He smiled again and Nicholas could discern a light, boyish quality pushing through the years of accumulated sorrow. "And I? Well, I was a good deal younger, too.

"Nangi-san and I already knew each other. He was in MITI and I was in business. I had several *kobun* in those days and all were successful. In some matters I relied on Mariko's judgment. It was she who had recommended that I buy the Ikiru Cosmetics Company. This was in 1976. Ikiru manufactured face creams and astringents, and when I purchased it the Japanese cosmetics boom was just beginning its sharp upswing.

"The investment was fantastic. In the first year of acquisition alone the *keiretsu* made back its purchase price and even showed a small profit from Ikiru. The future looked bright indeed for the second year.

"As part of her familial duty Mariko began to use Ikiru's products herself, rationalizing that she certainly could not expect all her friends to use Ikiru's products if she herself did not.

"Because her perfect porcelain skin was her pride she used the face cream and astringent twice a day as she had with her former brands. Several months later she began complaining of headaches of migraine intensity. These would often last several days. She would become alarmingly dizzy on and off during that time.

"I took her to a doctor. He could find nothing wrong with her and suggested a week at a spa for relaxation. Dutifully following his advice, I packed her off to the peaceful countryside. But at the spa Mariko became ill with a fever that went well above 103. When another physician was summoned by the worried proprietors, he found her heartbeat irregular and far too rapid.

"At their urging, he phoned me. I went immediately and fetched her. In Tokyo, she was referred to a specialist, who after administering a battery of tests informed her that she was having trouble with her gall bladder. He prescribed some medicine.

"But the fevers persisted and now she began to feel that the flesh of her face was sticky beneath the glossy skin, so she used the astringent even more religiously after each application of the face cream.

"Until one morning she woke up to discover that the skin all

274

over her body was as slick and smooth as that of her face. Running her hand down her leg, it seemed more the appendage of a wax doll than that of a human being.

"More upset than ever, she returned to the specialist, who subjected her to yet another battery of tests. This time he assured her it was her pancreas. More medicine was prescribed and dutifully consumed.

"A week later Mariko awoke in a sweat. She sat up with a start, her heart beating like a triphammer. She had been dreaming. Blood in her dreams. And now looking down at her pillow she saw a reddish brown stain there.

"Automatically she put her palm up to her cheek. It came away smeared with blood and some other discharge she could not name. Hysterical now, she called out for me, and this time I insisted she be admitted to the hospital.

"She had lost a lot of weight and now she had trouble breathing. Yet the doctors could detect nothing wrong with her lungs or indeed her respiratory system. Matter continued to ooze from her pores and Mariko had to be restrained lest the incessant itching cause her to lacerate her skin. She continued to insist that something was under her skin.

"The matter she exuded was sent to the hospital's toxicological lab for analysis but the technicians were overworked, and in any event testing takes time.

"In the interim, Mariko went on continuous IV, unable to eat. Slowly she slipped away from me, submerged in a coma that was as inexplicable to the physicians as were all of her other symptoms.

"She died less than a week later, drifting from the twilight of coma, from half-death to the full measure of sleep, without ever having regained consciousness. I cannot remember having said good-bye to her or even that I loved her during those long days and even longer nights."

There was no more food and even the wine was gone. Empty plates stared at them from the litter of the table.

"It was only some consolation," Sato said, "when the toxicological lab finally worked out the problem. It seemed that the face cream she had been using contained a paraffinlike polymer, similar to one used in the manufacture of enamel paint. The astringent dissolved that particular polymer, thus allowing it to be absorbed by her bloodstream. It had blocked the pores of her skin, suffocating her by minute degrees, and had affected a number of her internal organs, including her gall bladder and pancreas.

"At once thunderstruck and heartsick, I immediately took steps to alter the formulas of Ikiru's products and, that done, began to

275

list all the ingredients in Ikiru products on their containers. But it was not until 1979 that the Japanese Ministry of Health and Welfare, acting on the prolonged outcry not only from me but from the thousands who had suffered from the less than fatal *kokuhisho*, black skin syndrome, from the inclusion of Red 219, a coal tar dye, in some creams, established the act requiring the listing of all cosmetic ingredients.

"Six months after Mariko's death, when I could think clearly again, I founded *Keshohinkogai higaisha no kai*, the Organization of Cosmetic Victims, using profits from Ikiru."

There was pain in Nicholas' heart at the enormity of what Sato had to bear. Mariko had not been the sole victim of *kokuhisho*. Other victims' suffering and death could be only slightly less painful to Sato. And atonement, as Nicholas knew well, was not the same as never having sinned at all.

Sato turned his cup over and placed his palm across it. "Tell me, Linnear-san, have you ever felt anything other than pleasure at being in love?" His damp head bobbed. "Ah, yes, Buddha knows there is pain and suffering sometimes when there are arguments, when animosity lingers, perhaps, for a day or so. But that is a temporary thing, surely. It fades like the snow each winter and when the sun shines, the blossoms open up again.

"I am speaking of something entirely different now." His head was weaving, sunk down as it was onto his broad shoulders. "Experience means nothing in this realm. Have you ever felt imprisoned by your love, Linnear-san? As if you love despite yourself rather than because you wish to. No, no, you *must*, do you see?" His hand came away, and Nicholas could see that the tiny porcelain cup that had lain beneath was now gone. "As if some cruel heart had cast a spell over you?"

In the gloaming at the end of the day Lew Croaker sat slumped in the car that had taken them up the east coast of Florida. Traffic rushed by him, the procession of crimson taillights like searching eyes. Alix had just gone to the bathroom in one of the highway cafeterias. He felt the vibrations of the road as if they had become a part of him.

Just behind him was the Savannah River. Up ahead stretched Georgia, then South Carolina, North Carolina, and so on as I95 snaked its way northeast. They had not eaten since Jacksonville; there was no point in stopping in small towns along the way, leaving footprints for anyone to follow. Big cities had a habit of swallowing new arrivals and transients; no one paid attention.

Alix had wanted him to slow down as soon as they had crossed the Florida border, but Croaker had kept his foot on the accelerator. She thought he was being stubborn, but he didn't want to tell her what he had found in the Red Monster's Ford sedan. It was a Phonix cipher transmitter/receiver that he had read about. The sight of it had sent chills down his spine. He did not think that anyone Raphael Tomkin would hire would know what to do with a Phonix let alone have one in his car.

The Phonix was a relatively new instrument that automatically turned the spoken word into a preset cipher. It was the code alone that was broadcast between units, so that rapid transmission was virtually indecipherable to an eavesdropper.

Now, alone in the gathering Georgia night with the endless miles of dazed flight still thrumming through him, Croaker wondered again where his obsession with Angela Didion's murder was taking him. He had forsaken his job, his friends . . . and a woman he was just beginning to know and fall in love with. His entire existence had been turned inside out, upside down. And for what?

Vengeance against Raphael Tomkin. For despite the gathering evidence, Croaker was still convinced that the industrialist had murdered Angela Didion. How and why still had to be determined. But he had his key now. Alix Logan was the sole witness, and against all probabilities she was still alive. And again he asked himself, Why?

With a shiver, he went over it again. By all rights she should be deader than a doornail now. He saw her emerging from the lit doorway and gunned the engine. She was alive. And being kept that way by a brace of very deadly creatures. Why? And why in one place? Surely they could have moved her anywhere. Who were they protecting her from? Croaker? But "Croaker" was dead, drowned and crushed beyond recognition when his car went off the road in Key West. Who had instigated that? Tomkin?

With a start, Croaker remembered Matty the Mouth. He had been the fly on the wall who had delivered Alix Logan's name and address to him. For a usurious price to be sure, but what the hell, he had come through, hadn't he?

"Stay here," Croaker said to Alix as he sprinted toward the cafeteria. Inside, he dug out some change and made a long-distance call. A woman answered. At first she professed to never having heard of Matty the Mouth. Croaker did some first-class persuasion. Matty was out, the voice didn't know where, didn't know when he'd be back. Since he got back from Aruba Matty'd gone low profile. Croaker said he understood, it was the same with him. He had no number to leave with her and under the circumstances wouldn't've left one if he had. Said he'd call back.

"Let's go," he said as he slid behind the wheel and nosed the car out into traffic.

"I'm tired," Alix said, golden girl beside him. She curled into a ball.

It was like having a dream come to life, sitting at his elbow. Lithe, blond, beautiful. Croaker had only seen women like this from afar. This close, he had expected her to turn to garbage at any minute. When she hadn't, he was startled. It wasn't that he lusted after her precisely as the Blue Monster had, although he had to admit there was an element of sexuality about how he felt.

Rather there was this protectiveness thing. Having her safe and with him made him feel warm and somehow more alive. He did not want to take her to bed, but as a father will with his daughter when she comes of age he longed to see her nakedness, to caress her with his eyes. It was as if the presence of her nude in front of him, that acquiescence of vulnerability, would increase his feelings, fulfill them, even.

But this night his thoughts were not of the golden girl lying like a cat curled on the seat against his hip. Rather his thoughts retraced the moment when he had first seen the Phonix and had broken out into a cold sweat.

The ultimate purpose of a Japanese drunk such as this one was reciprocity. While it was true that the freedom the Japanese found in drunkenness allowed them to unburden their spirit, that could not be accomplished alone. A mutual unburdening, a clasping of warm hands, was what really mattered.

Nicholas knew that Sato was waiting. This was a crucial moment between them; much would depend on what Nicholas next said. If he lied now—for whatever reason, not trusting Sato being just one of them—there could never be anything between them. Despite what Sato said before about their being friends. Those were just words and the Japanese did not take much stock in words. What mattered to them most, what they truly revered above all else, was action. Because actions never lied.

For better or for worse, Nicholas suspected, he and Sato had to trust each other now. They were in deep water with nothing but an abyss below them. If there was no trust between them, then their enemies had already won.

"I think, Sato-san, that in some ways we are the same. Perhaps that is the reason why Nangi-san dislikes me. Perhaps he has already sensed this bond.

"When I was a young man . . . young and foolish"—the two men grinned hugely at each other—"I met a woman. She was old beyond her years; certainly beyond *my* years. But then my, er, studies precluded my early initiation into certain basic worldly matters."

Sato, both fists against his rather flushed cheeks, was rapt; he was obviously enjoying himself immensely.

"She possessed a power I could not explain—I still can't, though I think I understand it better. But it was as you have so eloquently said. It was as if some cruel heart had cast a spell over me. I was powerless before her.

"She was a purely sexual animal, Sato-san. I still cannot fully believe that such a creature could exist. And yet I must confess that it was precisely this quality which drew me to her. You can see that she could not possibly be a happy person. How could she? If she were not making love there was a nothingness for her. Oh, not the Void. You and I know that there is power in the Void, and an essential kind of peace that causes a completeness of the spirit.

"But Yukio's was diminished when we were not at sexual play. I did not think on this part of her at all until one day in April we were walking through Jindaiji. I favored that place above all others in Tokyo because my father had always taken me there rather than Ueno. I suppose he liked it better because it was a botanical park.

"The *bonbori* were hung on the trees though the time of the *someiyoshino* had already passed. It was late into *hanami*, the third of the traditional days when the cherry blossoms fall. We had meant to go the day before when the petals were at their height but Yukio had felt ill and we had stayed in, watching old movies on TV.

"We walked through the winding pathways of Jindaiji on that third day, and it felt to me as if we were high on the slopes of Mount Yoshino with one hundred thousand cherry trees whispering in the wind about us.

"I had never before wept at *hanami*, though certainly my mother had many times and, once, I had seen tears in my father's eyes. That time, as well, it had been on the third day, and I had wondered why he might be so moved since it was obvious to me that the blossoms had been more beautiful the day before.

"Now I wept, understanding what it was my father had seen that as a child I had not. Though, indeed, the *sakura* were past their peak, as they fell this day one knew that there was no tomorrow, that this was the last leavetaking, and their beauty seemed enhanced, deepened, even, by this knowledge. The ineffable sadness inherent in the moment was palpable. And for the first time I found myself understanding in a purely visceral way the mystique

279

known as the nobility of failure which we, as Japanese, revere so highly. For I saw that the sorrow of the moment caused the *effort* to be truly heroic."

Nicholas paused for a moment. He had become as rapt as Sato at the return of those long-ago memories. He was transported by the opportunity to unburden himself.

"Then something odd happened. I turned and looked at Yukio. Her beautiful head was raised toward the pink-white cloud of the descending blossoms. I could clearly see the line of her long neck, the hollow between the collarbones. Two pale *sakura* clung to her silk blouse as if they belonged to her.

"And I saw that somehow they were the same, these last, most precious of the cherry petals and Yukio. That she possessed that same quality that made them so special. It was not a nothingness that possessed her when she was not making love but rather a terrible, aching, unassuageable sadness that went beyond anything I had encountered.

"And all these years later I find myself wondering whether that was why I loved her, cherished her above all others. Because somehow I knew that, given time, I was the only one who could remove that sadness from her."

"You speak of her in the past only, my friend."

"She died in the winter of 1963. Drowned in the Straits of Shimonoseki."

"Ah," Sato murmured. "So young. How sad. But she is with the Heiké. The *kami* of that doomed clan will care for her." He turned his gaze downward, wiped at the remnants of spilled saké on the lacquer with the hem of his kimono sleeve.

Sato's large frame seemed as hulking and hunched as a brown Hokkaido bear's. There was an unbreachable gulf between them but at the same time they were closer now than many men ever got in their lives. For they were bound by a common sadness that drew them together like blood brothers. Twined as much by what had been left unspoken as by what had been said.

"Linnear-san." When he spoke again, his voice was soft. A hint of the paternal tinged it. "Did it ever occur to you that perhaps you would no longer have loved her had she lost that ineffable sadness? That, indeed, she herself might not have survived in this world without it? Perhaps it will help when next you think of her."

But Nicholas was not thinking of that. He knew that the next logical step in this unburdening process was to tell Sato of Akiko's uncanny twinness to Yukio. Indeed, he tried several times to get out the words. But nothing came. It was as if his throat had become paralyzed.

280

A shadow passed across the open doorway to the room and Nicholas saw Koten's bulk for a moment. Just checking up on his boss, Nicholas thought. See that I haven't strangled him yet, carved an ancient Chinese character into his cheek. He shuddered inwardly, returning fully to the present. For a blessed time they had both dwelled in a world free of revenge and bizarre murder.

Across from him Sato lurched to his feet. "Come, my friend." He beckoned with a hand and, stumbling across the *tatami*, fumbled open a *fusuma* at the far end of the room.

The night breeze stole in. Following him, Nicholas found himself a step down, on a smooth pebble path that seemed luminous in the moonlight. Around him shivered dark peonies, releasing the scent of roses, clumps of iris and hollyhock. Farther away he made out the shape of chrysanthemums beside the bole of the boxwood tree.

Sato stood in the center of his garden, his chest expanding as he breathed in the fresh air. The storm had scoured away the last of the pollution, at least for the several hours left before dawn. Low in the distance, beyond the boxwood, the sky was pink and yellow, tattooed with the pigment of Shinjuku's neon.

"Life is good, Linnear-san." Sato's eyes glowed, reflected in a combination of cool moonlight and the warmer light streaming out to them through the open *fusuma*. "It is a rich and varied tapestry. And I do not want to prematurely leave it." His eyes blinked heavily in the manner of the drunk. "You are a magician, Linnear-san. You have come into our lives most fortuitously. One learns one cannot turn away from *karma*, eh?"

He hugged himself. "Tell me, Linnear-san, are you a student of history?"

"My father, the Colonel, was," Nicholas replied, "and he taught me to be as well."

"Then surely you remember the Emperor Go-Daigo who in the early fourteenth century sought to break away from the Hōjō regime. Soon it became clear to him that the only way to do this was to utterly destroy the 'eastern savages,' as he called them.

"Yet he had no clear plan and he, himself, was no military commander. He did not know what to do. Until one night he dreamt of standing near the boughs of a great spreading pine tree, more ancient than any he had ever seen before. There were three ministers of state sitting beneath the boughs, each facing a different direction. On the south side of the tree was a pile of mats. It was the seat of the highest rank.

"Two children appeared before Go-Daigo and told him that

281

nowhere in the land would his safety be assured for long. Yet they bade him sit beneath the tree for a time in the Seat of State.

"When the Emperor awoke, he perceived that the Bodhisattvas Nikkō and Gakkō were attempting to give him a message through the dream. It occurred to him that if he put the character for 'south' next to the one for 'tree' it created 'camphor tree.'

"Therefore he called to his Master of Discipline and asked if there were any master warriors close by with the surname of Kusunoki, 'camphor tree.' The priest replied that the only warrior Kusunoki that he knew of dwelled in the province of Kawachi in the west."

"His name was Masashigi Kusunoki, who could trace his ancestral line back to Minister Lord Tachibana no Moroe," Nicholas said. "The Emperor summoned him and Kusunoki came at once. He became Go-Daigo's tactical commander and his staunchest supporter. He led the losing side in the Battle of Minato River in 1333, approximately where Kobe is today. At the conclusion of the terrible seven-hour battle he left the field and committed *seppuku* inside a neighboring farmhouse."

"The nobility of failure, eh, my friend?" Sato sat down on a round stone seat with no back. "But it is incidents such as these—*men* such as Kusunoki—that make up the warp that is the tapestry of our history."

Sato leaned forward as a bit of wind stirred the folds of his kimono. "Linnear-san, I dreamt last night of the camphorwood tree. The Bodhisattvas were not present but two figures, shrouded in shadow, were there nonetheless. Can you tell me the meaning of this dream, my friend?"

"These are indeed evil times, Sato-san," Nicholas said carefully. Sato was giving him the opening he needed. But was there a catch? He reviewed the situation once more before continuing. "We—and I include myself because with this merger I have become a part of the *keiretsu* family and, therefore, partly responsible for its survival and prosperity—are beset from within and without."

Sato nodded. "Yes. The wielder of the *Wu-Shing* and those who would try to wrest the secret of the T-PRAM chip away from you."

Nicholas waited a beat. "Not quite. In fact, there are just as serious breaches which are right now threatening our merger and the continued stability of the *keiretsu*."

Noting that Nicholas had not said, *"Your keiretsu,"* Sato said, "Then you must possess knowledge picked up on your brief trip back to America."

"Yes." Nicholas nodded. "To put it simply, Sato-san, there is a *muhonnin*, a traitor, within the *keiretsu*."

Sato went very still. His eyes were steely. They had lost the unfocused glaze from the sakē. "So. And which of your competitors does this *muhonnin* work for?"

"None," Nicholas said. "Rather the traitor is in the employ of one of *your*, er, competitors. The KGB."

For once Nicholas could see a distinct reaction play itself across that broad Japanese countenance. Sato lost all color in his face. His hands began to shake so uncontrollably that he was obliged to lace his fingers together.

"The Russians." His voice was a whisper. But what emotion it contained! "Yes, I see. The Russians would love to get their hands on a T-PRAM prototype."

"Or then again," Nicholas said, watching the older man closely, "it could be something else entirely they're after."

Sato shrugged his shoulders. "Such as?" Nicholas had his undivided attention.

"Kusunoki was a loyalist. As am I. His emperor asked a great deal of him yet he did it unhesitatingly." Nicholas was beginning his bargaining. He was not about to release his last bit of information without obtaining the guarantees he needed. "The *Wu-Shing* is a matter of life and death. And as you have said, Sato-san, life is good. I, too, have no wish to see you leave it prematurely."

He turned and opened the scarred wooden case he had brought with him. Opening the three latches he produced the *dai-katana*, his great longsword, forged almost two hundred years ago. It was thirty inches long.

When Sato saw what was inside his eyes opened wide, moving from the black lacquer scabbard to Nicholas' face. Silently, then, he slipped off his perch to kneel on the stones before Nicholas. He bowed so low that his forehead touched the ground.

Nicholas returned the honored gesture, said, "My father named this blade *Iss-hōgai*, 'for life.' It is, as you know, the soul of the *samurai*."

Carefully, Nicholas picked up the sheathed blade and placed it between them. "My *kami* resides here, Sato-san." He did not have to tell the older man why he had brought the *dai-katana* back to Japan with him; it was not for show but to use it. "And while the *Wu-Shing* is life and death, this merger between our *kobun* is no less important for the future. I beg you to—"

"The merger! The merger!" Sato exploded. "I am sick to death of thinking about the merger. You have my word that when Nangi-san returns from Hong Kong the merger will be immediately consummated according to the agreement already outlined."

For a moment Nicholas was so stunned that he forgot what he was about to say next. He had been prepared for debate, not capitulation.

"Then it is settled between us." Nicholas found that his mouth was dry. "By deed as well as by word."

Sato unhesitatingly held out his right hand. Nicholas did the same with his left and, using his free hand, tied a length of cord around their wrists. Thus bound together, they put the palms of their free hands over the sword.

Nicholas unbound them. In a moment, Sato said, "Some moments ago you were about to tell me what, other than the Sphynx T-PRAM, this KGB traitor would be after. Or was it merely a ploy with no documentation to back it up?"

"The KGB involvement is real enough," Nicholas said. "I have firsthand information that cannot be disputed."

"What do they want then?" Sato said, a bit sharply.

"Tenchi."

At that moment they both heard movement from inside the house and, turning their heads, saw Akiko, haloed by the inner room light, step down onto the smooth pebbles of the garden in which they knelt.

Returning from her mission in Yoshino to fulfill her last promise to Masashigi Kusunoki, Akiko felt the thrill of fear race through her like a shock of freezing water.

She had been caught totally unaware; no one had seen fit to tell her that Nicholas Linnear was returning so quickly, and now she cursed Koten for not having the common courtesy to tell her that Sato was entertaining a guest.

"Akiko!" Sato jumped up like a puppy seeking its master's lap. "I did not expect you back until tomorrow afternoon."

"Auntie was feeling poorly," she said by rote. "There was no point in my staying longer."

"You remember Linnear-san. You met at the wedding."

Akiko lowered her eyes as she advanced across the shining moonlit pebbles. They were so white against the darkness of her shadow as she passed over them. "Of course. I am so sorry about the passing of Tomkin-san. Please accept my condolences."

For the longest time it seemed as if she did nothing but stare into his shadowed face. She barely paid attention to Sato's fussing as to drinks and something to eat for her after her long and tiring journey. It occurred to her that her husband wanted to be rid of her; she wondered what it was the two men had been discussing when she had broken in on them.

To Sato's ire, she sat down on the stone perch he had used earlier in the evening. She wore a brocaded traveling kimono with flights of white herons crossing its dark blue background. Japanese invariably wore their best clothes while traveling. She held the bone handle of a rice-paper *janomegasa* with its point down against the pebbles.

Sato was doing all the talking but it was as if an aura surrounded her and Nicholas, as if they were the only two people left on earth. And inside the overlapping field of their powerful *wa* something was happening, something Akiko could never have anticipated.

She felt giddy, lighter than air. All *hara* seemed to have left her; she could not ground herself and without that centering she was utterly powerless.

She felt the first painful flutterings of panic take wing inside her and decided that she must do something immediately to forestall this loss of the Void. What was happening to her?

The more she stared into that face she had come to know so well, to hate with an almost inhuman passion, the greater her sense of helplessness became. She was spinning out of control. Why? What was he doing to her?

Dizzily she downed the hot sakē Sato had brought her, heard herself ask for another in a thin, strangled voice she could barely recognize. This too she tumbled down her throat, almost choking on it.

Yet she went on watching him, tracing each contour of his head and face as if she were touching him physically. She felt as if she were being embraced and she felt her thighs tremble, her throat constrict. She felt a tingling at the back of her neck as if she were being caressed there and the fine hairs were raised like the whiskers of an animal.

She closed her eyes in an effort to steady herself, but found, instead, that she was compelled to see him again. Her eyes snapped open. He was still there. Sato was still prattling on about Buddha only knew what.

Years raced before her opened eyes like veils parting before a freshening wind. Years of laborious training, obsessive dedication. A heart filled with burned love and from those bitter ashes a thirst for revenge that smoldered and, fanned by hate, had burst into full flame. *Vengeance will be mine.* How often during the painful years of growing up had that one phrase given her the courage to close her eyes and sleep so that she could live another day. Without

285

that phrase to hold to her like a blanket on a frosty night, she might never have survived unto this day.

To become aware of this moment, an arrow piercing her heart. Dear Amida! she cried silently. Now she began to tremble in earnest with the knowledge of what Nicholas Linnear was engendering in her. Wildly her mind sought this avenue and that in order to avoid what she already suspected was an inescapable truth.

Oh, Buddha, she thought, I want him. I want him so much I can't see straight.

Ikan lived within the pale green and caramel walls of *Fuyajo*. The Castle That Knows No Night had been her home ever since she was eight years old.

That year, so long ago now, had been a time of ill omens and poor crops throughout the countryside. Bow-backed farmers had no money and little hope of making it through to the end of the year.

It is said in Japan that hard times are the best friend of tradition for it is during these periods that the people fall back most heavily on the ways of their ancestors.

And so it was with Ikan's family that year. Her father's crops were no better than those of his neighbors, which was to say no good at all. It was as if the earth refused to release its nutriments that year.

The first Ikan suspected something serious was amiss was when she returned from the fields with a handful of reeds and saw her mother weeping.

The next morning Ikan was driven from the farm in a dusty, backfiring truck that smelled of cabbage and tomatoes, a small bag filled with the pitifully tiny pile of her possessions, the savior of her family destined for the precincts of the *Yoshiwara*.

Like many young girls throughout the ages before her, Ikan

287

was to be sold into prostitution by her family in order to retrieve them from the indignity of bankruptcy.

Yet unlike the Western view, the Japanese view of prostitution was filled with nobility mixed with an odd poignancy. As he did with many other institutions, the Shōgun Ieyasu Tokugawa created the legitimate need for *baishun*, the selling of, as it is known in Japan, spring.

Because he was obsessed with his own power—the only force able to tame the multiple feuds of the regional *daimyō* that had kept feudal Japan in a constant state of civil war for years before his ascendancy—he required that each *daimyō* make a pilgrimage to Edo, now Tokyo, every other year, along with his *samurai*, where they would stay for a year. This *sankinkotaiseido* served two purposes. First, it cut into the *daimyō*'s solidification of his own power in his native *ryochi* and second, the long, often arduous trip helped deplete his coffers of accumulated wealth.

The *daimyō* and the wealthier *samurai* were able to avail themselves of the services of their mistresses. But the poorer *samurai* were forced to turn to prostitutes for, as Ieyasu himself said, prostitution was needed in order to negate the possibility of adultery.

In 1617, a year after the Shōgun's death, a feudal lord in Edo petitioned the Tokugawa government to allow him to create a sanctioned area within the city for *baishun*. He found a desolate field filled with reeds, hence the name *Yoshiwara*. In the succeeding years, a different character was substituted for "reedy," and the *Yoshiwara* became known as the happy field.

The original red-light sector was destroyed in a fire and in 1656 was rebuilt in the Asakusa district of Edo, where it remained until April of 1958.

In 1649, Ikan subsequently was taught by her *sensei*, the government declared that all rice grown was subject to confiscation by the Imperial *samurai*. In its place farmers were told they had to subsist on millet.

Stricken, farmers were forced to put their wives to work sewing or weaving and to send their young children to toil in the city. Yet even this was not enough, and so often one female child was selected to be sold to the brothels in order for her family to survive.

There was no loss of face in this. On the contrary, these young girls were looked upon with a mixture of great respect—for submitting to their *giri* of filial piety—and pity, for it was generally known that while a prostitute might on a very rare occasion become the mistress of a wealthy *samurai*, once she crossed the moat that surrounded the *Yoshiwara* she surrendered all hope of becoming a wife and creating her own home. So there was always an air of mystery tinged by the purity of sadness that drew men into the arms of *geisha* in the same way it drew them to Ueno each spring to view the cherry blossoms.

Ikan began life at *Fuyajo*, the most ancient of such establishments in the *Yoshiwara*, as a *kamuro*, a kind of apprentice who fetched for the *oiran*, the higher-level prostitutes, when she was not busy cleaning and polishing.

In this capacity she was constantly busy yet she always found time to observe and to learn from her observations, often imitating the motions and delicate swirls of the *oiran* early in the mornings before, exhausted, she fell on her *futon*.

When she was twelve, Ikan took a strenuous examination and passed on to the level of *shinzo*, where she began her courses in the study of *baishun*. These included singing, the difficult art of *haiku, ikebana, chano-yu*, dancing, a study of literature, and, of course, lovemaking.

Her training took five years, at the end of which she was required to take another exam. This was the crucial one for, if she failed to pass it, she would return to the level of *kamuro* and spend the rest of her days at *Fuyajo* doing nothing more than taking out the garbage.

She had no serious trouble and, at the age of seventeen, rose to the exalted station of *oiran*. For four years she plied her difficult and complex trade diligently and well, her open, inquisitive mind allowing her to absorb the best from the more experienced women around her, her innate sensitivity to creating all forms of pleasure in a man, intellectual, esthetic, as well as physical, creating an ever-expanding world that she alone could explore.

And on the day of her birth, twenty-one years after she was born, Ikan became *tayu*, the loftiest of the three stations of *oiran*. Never in the history of the Castle That Knows No Night had there been a *tayu* of such tender years, and a celebration was thrown in her honor.

And it was in that most festive of atmospheres, when the sakē was flowing freely and the *samisen* spangled webs of music in the steamy air, that Ikan first encountered Hiroshi Shimada.

He was a man of quiet intensity, not a handsome man by any but the broadest of standards, yet possessed of a strength of spirit that she found most attractive.

For his part, Shimada had singled her out almost at once. His eyes fell upon her stately alabaster beauty and his heart turned to water. He felt a great cry rising up from within him, and for a

289

moment he had to put a hand out to grasp the knurled wooden stairpost for support. When his knees stopped shaking, he began to breathe again. His head felt light, as if he had been drinking saké long into the night; there was an odd metallic taste in his mouth as if he had bitten down into a piece of tinfoil.

It never occurred to him that he might be falling in love. One did not fall in love with a *geisha*, one came to her for comfort, relaxation, and a night of total enjoyment. And yet at the moment he first saw Ikan, her awesome physicality struck from his consciousness any thought he might have held of any other woman, his wife included.

There was an aura about Ikan that was undeniable. Even the other *oiran* whispered of it in clandestinely envious tones among themselves. For she had achieved what all members of the floating world aspire to: that ineffable merging of the ethereal and the animal that unfailingly set men under its almost magic spell; an aphrodisiac for all the senses, all the pleasures. For her clients loved her just as strongly when she was reading to them from *Genji Monogatari*, when she arranged day lilies just for them or wrote a *haiku* in their honor, as when she bedded them.

Thus Shimada found himself drawn to Ikan's side, his gaze lovingly caressing each elegant fold of her glittering kimono, the three translucent tortoiseshell *kanzashi* angled through the gleaming black pile of her hair, the *kushi*, the simple traditional comb of *tsuge* wood at the back of her head.

And when he spoke his first word to her through cracked lips, merely the gesture of her turning her head in his direction sent flutters of desire through his chest.

There was, of course, no chance for them to be alone at the party and, in any event, a proper assignation had not been arranged beforehand as was the strict policy at *Fuyajo*. But the next week, when Shimada could take time out from his busy schedule, he returned to the *Yoshiwara*.

On the threshold of the pale green and caramel structure he paused, trembling. Rain pattered on the conical shelter of his *amagasa* and he looked up, watching it drip off the eaves just beneath the curved tiles of the roof. As the *samurai* in olden days had done he had disguised himself somewhat before setting out on his trek to the red-light district.

It was not that he was ashamed of coming here or that he wished to hide his presence at *Fuyajo* from his wife. On the contrary, it was to her that the Castle That Knows No Night sent the bills for his sojourns of pleasure.

Rather it was the unsettling political and economic climate

290

within the bureaucracy that caused him to act with caution. As vice-minister of MCI he had many enemies and he had no wish to present his ill-wishers with fodder for his political demise.

A chill gust of wind bowled down the street, making him shiver and pull his long capelike raincoat closer about him. That SCAP hound, Colonel Linnear, was already sniffing around for incriminating bones and though Shimada was quite certain he had buried his deeply and well, he nevertheless refused to relax his vigilance, for he knew that in the wake of the war's end he could not rely on his Prime Minister for refuge if the truth were to come out. In fact, knowing Yoshida, he would be among the first to deliver Shimada up as a sacrificial lamb to the *gaijin* war crimes tribunal.

War. The thought made Shimada shiver. Always it came back to the war. How he wished now that Japan had taken another course. In retrospect, he saw his own rabid ideas of expansionism, his close ties to those warmongers in the *zaibatsu* as tantamount to slashing open his own belly. And yet there was no dignity in the association. His hands were soiled by the clandestine work he had done for his friends in the *zaibatsu* both before the war and during it. Shimada had been a key figure within the Ministry of Munitions and had been saved from the war crimes tribunal by a mixture of his own cunning in hiding his past and the decision of his superior to break apart the ministry at the last moment, turning it into the Ministry of Commerce and Industry before SCAP had set itself up and begun its own purge.

Shimada looked down at his hands. His palms were slick with sweat. He took a deep breath, calming himself. He resolved to stop by the Shinto shrine on his way home and petition the gods and *kami* for the gift of confidence and the blessing of forgetfulness. If not for the *gaijin* Linnear, all would be peaceful, he knew.

Abruptly, the door to *Fuyajo* opened and cool illumination flooded over him like a spotlight. Shimada hurried inside.

At first he wanted nothing more from her than for her to serve him tea. The complex ritual of *chano-yu* was as soothing as a massage or a soak in a steaming tub.

Watching Ikan perform the ceremony just for him caused all the problems, fears, and doubts that snapped at his heels in the world beyond the happy field to dissolve like tears in a pool. In their stead he found himself filling up with a delicious contentment, a clarity of mind he had thought he could never achieve.

And because every movement Ikan made no matter how minute or trivial—turning a teacup or touching a wisp of her hair—was the epitome of grace and fluidity, he found his enjoyment multiplying geometrically as he unraveled each layer of meaning from what she did or spoke. For her words were never trivial or mundane. She made no small talk. Rather, each question she asked or each answer she gave to his questions were both fascinating and eloquent.

In the world beyond *Fuyajo* memories transformed Shimada like a growing cancer into a man old beyond his years. But here, Ikan had the ability to banish that haunted quality of his life and, like a serpent shedding its skin, he was reborn in her presence as he was enchanted by her awesome ethereal prowess.

For her part, Ikan never saw the man that Shimada was in the outside world for with her he had no need of scheming, he had no need of fiercely keeping his enemies at bay. She saw, rather, the man he might have been in another time, another place.

He was gentle with her, and warmhearted. And his obvious delight at all she did warmed her. She recognized in him a deep need to be nurtured and loved, and since it was her belief that all men were at their core nothing more than infants, she felt no need to probe too deeply into the source of this need.

But, it must be said that another factor entered into this self-deceit. Ikan knew there was something special about Shimada when on his second visit he brought her a set of old traditional *kanzashi* made of *tsuge* wood in a similar design as her *kushi*. Now she had a complete set for her hair.

Her manner was calm, her smile sweet, small, and proper, her eyes properly downcast, her murmur of thanks soft and brief as he presented her with the magnificent gift. But inside her heart was pounding and she could feel her blood singing through her veins. This was a completely new feeling for her and she was inwardly bewildered.

But later than night, when she lay entwined with him on the lushly fabricked *futon*, as their sweat commingled, as she felt the double-beat pulse of his heart close to hers, as he gently entered her after the careful and delightful hours of sensuous preparations, Ikan knew what that feeling was. She was in love.

The decision to have the baby was entirely hers. It was her privilege as *tayu*—at least that was the custom established years ago by those who ran *Fuyajo*. The decision had been an entirely pragmatic one. Like champion racehorses who are put out to stud, it was felt that many of the *tayu*'s unique qualities were innate, needing only the proper training to emerge and be enhanced.

But this usually happened somewhat further on in a *tayu*'s career because there was fear of markings or disfigurement from the rigors of childbirth as well as the months of enforced idleness and thus lost revenue to think of. However, Ikan was of such stellar quality that the greed of those who ran *Fuyajo* eventually overcame their initial doubts.

Ikan was certain that she wanted to bear Shimada's child. Already he insisted that she see no one else and paid for the privilege of her exclusivity through the nose. He did not care, although what his wife thought of the increasing level of the bills was quite another matter.

But Shimada's wife was someone Ikan never thought of. Why should she? That woman was part of another world, a world in which Ikan could never participate. What use such thoughts? Too, she was acutely aware of how she affected Shimada, and she suspected that after the birth of their son—for she had no doubts that she would bear him a son—his elation would be so extraordinary that he would grant her any wish. And she had only one: to become his mistress. He would have to buy her freedom, of course, but he could well afford the price.

It never occurred to Ikan that she would bear a daughter who would bind her to *Fuyajo* forever, and who would herself be bound to the Castle That Knows No Night.

And yet it was a female child to which she gave birth, a squalling, hairless infant with nothing between its legs but a slit.

For three days Ikan wept on her *futon*, her dreams of a glorious future destroyed in an instant. She saw no one, spoke to no one, ignored all the notes sent up to her by a worried Shimada. These last she burned instantly as if by handling them she could be contaminated.

During this time she did not sleep. Rather, she lay curled on her left side, her face to the wall. Her shame was overwhelming, and her face burned with it. At first her hatred for her daughter was overwhelming, so powerful that she shuddered to its bitter taste in her mouth. And this, too, caused her to decline all food, wanting perversely to subsist wholly on her hate.

But by the middle of the second day, she found that she could no longer sustain such a harsh and cruel emotion. It went against all her training and, after all, the child was so helpless and alone.

She was weeping again, hot, bitter tears that swept down her cheeks, depleting her strength. For she began to understand—as one begins to see a red, swollen sun appear after a long, debilitating storm—that her hatred was for herself. A terrible despair began to engulf her, and with that awful feeling rose the shame, a black, baleful raven in her tortured mind.

Oh, how her love had warped her, how her own selfish desires

293

had driven her to this shameful reality. For in her egotism she had been confident of bearing a male child—had she not spent two hours every day at the Shinto shrine two blocks away, propitiating the gods, seeking their aid?—and had thrust to the dark back recesses of her mind the consequences of bearing a daughter. For all female offspring of *tayu* became the property of *Fuyajo*, to train when they came of age to replace their mothers as new *oiran* and, if the gods favored them, eventually *tayu*.

She spent all of the third day contemplating this, taking a little food now when it was offered to her but still wanting to see no one. And at the end of that time, after she had lit incense and prayed to the Amida Buddha for guidance, she asked to see her baby.

"There is no name as yet for this little one, lady," the old woman who cooked for them and took care of them when they were ill said as she transferred the tiny bundle into Ikan's trembling arms. "It is bad luck," she added needlessly.

Ikan dropped her gaze to the tiny face of her daughter, still wrinkly and red skinned.

"Reiko, one of the *kamuro* who failed her examination, has been nursing her," the old woman said softly as she gazed up into the troubled face of her lady. "This is a hungry little one." The old woman giggled, hoping to break through the oppressive atmosphere she had sensed when she entered this chamber.

Ikan nodded absently. It did not really matter who nursed the baby; she would not be allowed to.

"I have lit many sticks of incense," the old woman went on. "I have done what I could to protect this innocent from bad *karma*. But, lady, forgive me, she must have a name."

Ikan heard, but it was impossible to say what was going on in her mind. She felt enwrapped by her guilt. And now, face to face with the tiny creature she had borne, knowing what kind of a life her unthinking actions had condemned it to, she felt sick at heart.

Her pale lips opened and she whispered, "Yes, old one. A name. I will give you a name." There was a sighing in the room as if the autumn wind outside had somehow crept through a crack in the window sash and now swirled around them.

Ikan's eyes were filled with tears so that the tiny face blurred and became indistinct. Her whisper could barely be heard. "Call her Akiko."

She was an exceptionally healthy child, strong and fully as robust as a boy. She was up and walking early, as if somehow even at that early age she suspected she would need to rely on her own resources to survive. And for all that Ikan grew to love the child, she showed very little overt emotion. Rather she left the supervision of the infant to the old cook and the other girls, all of whom were enchanted with the new baby.

She hung back as if she were afraid of the child, especially during those times when those who ran *Fuyajo* congregated in the infant's room, leaving their gifts near the sleeping form.

Often Shimada would come to the Castle That Knew No Night and, as before, he would spend the long, languorous nights with Ikan. But the one request she continually denied him was to look at his daughter, to hold her, to speak his first words to her so that she would know that he was her father.

She took exceptional pleasure in keeping Akiko from him. Outwardly she would be attentive, responsive to his every wish, often without his having to utter a word of direction—that was a courtesan's greatest skill, after all. But all the while she would be gloating inwardly at the unique kind of pain she brought him, and like sadist and masochist, this became a kind of bond between them that somehow brought them closer together—or at least afforded them a more intimate understanding of the essence of one another.

Akiko recalled meeting her father only once, and that was on an unseasonably warm spring day when she was midway between her third and fourth birthdays. She had been playing with Yumi, the old cook, and had returned to her mother's room as she always did at this time of the day. But instead of her mother waiting for her to comb her hair, she found a man in a chocolate brown suit. He had slightly stooped shoulders, thick features, a grayish mustache no thicker than a pencil, thick, tufty eyebrows like clouds. He smiled when he saw her and she saw his slightly yellowed teeth.

"Akiko-chan," he said, bowing.

She returned the gesture. She was close enough to smell the halo of cigarette smoke that seemed to envelop him. She wrinkled up her nose and rubbed it with her finger.

"I've brought you a present, Akiko-chan." He bent toward her and held out his hand. Nestled within his palm was an exquisitely carved *netsuke* of a horse with its head down, its forelegs raised as if set for flight or to ward off some unseen advance. It was made of tulipwood.

Akiko stared at it but made no move to take it.

"It's for you. Don't you want it?"

"Yes," she whispered.

So he reached out and, taking her hand, deposited the *netsuke* into her small fist, curling up the fingers around its cool girth. "Now this is just from me to you. Our secret."

She nodded. *"Domo arigato."*

He smiled down at her and took her other hand. "Now we have the entire afternoon to ourselves."

It was the time of *hanami* and he took her by train to a small park on the outskirts of the city with gently sloping contours dressed with lines of old cherry trees.

She remembered the smell of the train, an agglomeration of luncheon foods, and could still feel after all those years the tightly packed claustrophobic sensation of being pressed in with so many people. Shimada held her hand tightly but still she was uncomfortable and began to weep silent tears until he picked her up in his arms and held her rocking gently with the motion of the train against his chest.

In the park they stopped in front of a cart selling sweet jellied tofu and he purchased small paper cones filled with the confection for both of them.

The sky was clear and sparkling, so hard seeming that it reminded Akiko of a piece of green glass she had found by the seashore, its edges rounded and smoothed by the constant immersion at the verge of the tidal pull.

Shimada pointed upward, showing her the orange and green box kite with a fierce tiger's head. Akiko laughed as it dipped and swooped in the wind.

She ate her tofu hungrily and Shimada wiped her cheeks with his snow-white handkerchief. It felt very soft against her skin.

But most of all she remembered the cherry blossoms. It was so quiet here that Akiko thought she could hear the drift of the light pink petals through the clear air and they seemed suspended in time, all motion attenuated, all the world attuned to their drift.

Lifting up her head, she laughed out loud with delight, skipping away from Shimada and back again, grabbing onto his trousers' leg, pulling him forward, wanting in her own inarticulate way for him to dance too.

She never saw Shimada again, and it was a long time before she understood why. During her time with him she had no inkling that he was her father. Certainly he had never even broached the subject. But yet when she thought back on it through the prism of time, she saw that she had known immediately that he was unlike all the other men she had met in her short life and would meet in the passing years. Shimada was special, just as that memory, piercing the veil of time with such pristine clarity, was special.

What she had not been able to understand was why he had

taken his life not more than twenty-four hours after he had watched her, smiling, as she capered through the last hours of the cherry blossoms. She thought she could never forgive him for that and then, upon learning the terrible truth, thought she could never forgive herself.

As for Ikan, she was never the same after Shimada's death. Like a blossom at *hanami* she had reached her peak of beauty and, having slid past it, could never go back. An intense form of melancholia stole over her like a shroud, etching lines into a face that had been filled with perfection. She drank copious quantities of sakē, often passing out insensate in the middle of an assignation as if the mere state of consciousness was too much for her.

Those who ran *Fuyajo* were understandably perturbed and then, as Ikan's state declined rapidly, filled with anger. She had many more years left in her and, they felt, after she had passed beyond the barriers where sexual union was paramount, she could still fulfill her potential as the house's finest *sensei*, training the younger women.

But such was not to be. In the spring of 1958, when Akiko was thirteen, Ikan could not be roused from her *futon*. Fright flew through *Fuyajo* like an evil *kami*, turning the girls nervous and short-tempered. All conversation dropped to a whisper as the doctor arrived and took the long, slow climb up to her room. Akiko was kept with a group of the girls and they forcibly restrained her from ascending.

There was no life left within Ikan's glorious husk. The old physician shook his head from side to side and clucked his tongue against the roof of his mouth. He sat on the edge of her *futon* and stared down upon the pale face and thought that he had never seen such magnificent human beauty in his life.

By her side he found an empty bottle of sakē and a small vial. This, too, was empty, save for a light dusting of white powder along its curved inside. The doctor dipped his little finger and touched the white tip to his tongue. His head nodded again, his tongue continued its clucking.

He heard movement behind him and he quickly pocketed the vial. Perhaps there was something for him to do here, he thought. For when those who ran *Fuyajo* asked him the cause of death, he lifted his shoulders, let them fall resignedly, and told them she had died of heart failure, which in a sense was true.

He felt no compunction about lying to them or even falsifying the death certificate. In fact he felt ennobled by the deed. He had read the papers concerning Vice-Minister Shimada's shocking suicide and in its aftermath the unraveling of the evidence against

297

him. This woman had endured enough, he thought. Let her death be a peaceful, natural one; a death that will cause no further ripples of evil talk.

Those who ran *Fuyajo* wasted no time in explaining to Akiko what had happened. And at last it dawned on her what the composition of her life would be from this moment on until the day she died, perhaps in precisely the same manner that her mother had expired. And that knowledge was totally unacceptable to her.

That night she gathered up her belongings, much as Ikan had done the night before her departure from her family's farm deep in the countryside, and several items of her mother's that she loved and did not want to leave to the scavengers at *Fuyajo*. Stuffing these, too, into a small, battered bamboo suitcase, she stole out of the building in the dead of night. The height of the varied activities served to shield her from discovery.

Soon she was crossing the narrow street and, turning a corner, hurried down a dark alley, moving quickly and surely until she had left the *Yoshiwara* far behind her. She never once looked back, and she never returned.

They came after her, of course. They had every right to. She was an enormously valuable commodity and they had a great many years invested in her. There were no *Yakuza* involved in running *Fuyajo* and the *Boryokudan* held no piece of it. Still, those who had founded the Castle That Knows No Night were hard businessmen and their descendants to whom the running of the brothel now devolved were much like their ancestors. And though the Occupation Forces had begun to disband the *Yoshiwara*, and *Fuyajo* was thus forced to move, they did not take kindly to Akiko's defection. In fact, they wished to put an end to it as swiftly as possible. To that end they dispatched two thugs to return her to her proper home and, if that were not practical, to exact from her the highest possible penalty for her treacherous deed.

The first Akiko suspected that she was being followed was when she saw two shadows moving at once, one slightly ahead of her and one perhaps two blocks behind her. She would never have seen the shadows at all—for they were absolutely silent—had it not been for the cat. Four tiny kittens had been suckling at the cat's distended teats when Akiko stumbled into her territory and, startled, she had arisen and, arching her back, hissed at the intruding shape, baring her teeth and glaring carnelian eyes into the wan light.

Akiko gasped, her heart pounding painfully in her chest, and she skidded to one side, her head and shoulders moving away from the angered cat even as her feet and legs were still sliding along the pavement toward it. That's when she saw the twin movements, and her eyes went wide.

She pressed herself against a cool wall, looked to front and back. Now there was nothing. Silence. The absence of traffic was eerie and not even a *kōban*, a police call box, around.

She was still in the Asakusa district, filled with the old traditional ways, Tokyo's last remnants from ages gone by. The buildings here were small and low, of wood and oiled paper as they once had been throughout Japan, no steel and glass towers as in other sectors of the city.

Akiko, her heart still in her throat, sidled away from the bristling cat, certain now that the long arm of *Fuyajo* was stalking her. But there was no way they were going to bring her back to that hated place, she decided. She would die first. And not before she hurt someone badly.

A red rage beat through her like a tide, an accumulated sizzling she was still only dimly aware of. Quickly she knelt down and as she did so, a dark flicker came to the corner of her eye, a swift blur like a racing cloud obscuring for a moment the face of the moon.

Unhesitatingly she opened her bamboo suitcase and took out the pistol. It was fairly small, a pearl-handled .22 caliber, well oiled and in good operating condition. It was fully loaded, she had double-checked that before she had removed it from its hiding place beneath her mother's *futon*. Why Ikan would have such an implement in her possession Akiko could not fathom, but the day she had discovered it more than a year ago she had had enough sense not to tell anyone, not even her mother, what she had found. And tonight she had not wanted to leave it behind. Now she knew why.

They were closing in. Akiko swiftly closed her suitcase and stood calmly, the pistol hidden behind her. Curiously, she felt no fear. She had been born into the night, and darkness held none of the primitive terror it did for many people. She was at home in its furtive light and rather enjoyed the anonymity its shadows afforded her. Night at *Fuyajo* would find her rising from her *futon* to roam the many rooms at will, honing her instincts and her hand-eye coordination, stealthily climbing back stairs and crawling through vent passageways in order to observe the myriad couples.

One came. Lithe and slender, he blended into the darkness so that he was almost upon her before she became aware of his presence. She turned her head, startled despite herself, giving a strangled little cry, angry with herself for not sensing him sooner.

"What do you want?" Her voice was a husky whisper, little more than the night wind which rustled the leaves of the cypress above her head.

Sound, too, could betray him, so he remained silent. And now, unbidden, Akiko felt fear flutter her heart. Her eyes were open wide, the pupils dilated to their maximum as she peered into the blackness in order to pick out some tiny gleam that would make of him something more than a wraith.

"I know you're there," she said softly, willing her voice not to tremble. "If you come near me, I'll kill you." But despite her bravado, she began to tremble. She felt chilled to the bone and everything around her seemed strange and forbidding.

On the verge of tears, Akiko made a decision. She knew that the longer she waited the more certain it was that she would lose her nerve. Already tremors coursed through her tightly coiled muscles, wracking her like ague. It was now or never, and she would just have to trust her eyes. She had not seen him move from the patch of shadow so close to her so that must mean that he had not. Visions of ghosts and shape-changing creatures were for children.

I am afraid, she told herself in the calmest inner voice she could summon up. But he'll kill me if I let him or, at the very least, drag me back to *Fuyajo*, which would certainly be worse than death.

She was just bringing the pistol out from behind her when she felt the presence to her left and thought, The second one! She felt pressure on her larynx and, of course, reflexively tried to breathe. When she could not, panic rose within her and she cried out, bringing the pistol up in a blur, her forefinger already squeezing, squeezing, anything to get oxygen into her straining lungs.

The roar of the discharge caused her to scream in rage and fear. Concussion struck her eardrums like a physical blow and she staggered, already retching from the intense stench of the cordite and the heat, searing and instantaneous, that had brushed by her like the hand of death.

Light blinded her and she fetched up against a wooden wall, sliding down it as her legs gave out. Something was in her eyes and she put her free hand up, wiping at her forehead. Her hair was matted and wet, filled with grit that rolled slickly through her fingers.

Blood black on the night, its coppery stench filling her nostrils, making her gag all over again, making her wipe again and again at her face, crying now in great gulping sobs.

A shadow looming over her and instinctively she brought the

300

pistol upward, almost all control gone now so that the barrel weaved back and forth. She tried to get at the trigger again but her finger wouldn't respond to her commands and then the gun was gone from her weakened grasp and she was broken, sobbing still, whispering through it, "Don't take me back, I don't want to go back."

Lifted bodily off the street, a breeze against her hot, streaked cheek for an instant and then a creak, a slam, the noises of a bolt being shot home and the warmth of a house, stealing over her, a place unfamiliar but only one fact surfacing: it was not *Fuyajo*.

Her head went down . . .

A face swam into view, like the man in the moon, pockmarked and huge, descending through a network of sere branches as spiky as a stag's antlers.

Akiko cried out, tried to throw her arms across her face to protect it. She had the sensation of falling and shooting forward at the same time, spinning like a leaf in the wind, toppling from the safety of . . . what?

The man in the moon lifted away, and it was like a weight being pulled off her chest.

"Is this better?" The voice was soft and lilting, a country accent.

"I can't . . . breathe." Her voice was like a rodent's squeak and she realized that her mouth and throat were so parched that she could not summon up saliva.

"In time you will be able to do everything." The man in the moon smiled, or so it seemed to Akiko. She still had trouble seeing as if she were peering through a windowpane streaked with running rainwater.

"You look blurry," she whispered through cracked lips.

"When you stop crying," the gentle voice told her, "you will no longer have that problem."

She slept for a time after that, sliding down into a vertiginous whirlpool, a troubled slumber in which her fear, brought to the surface, would not allow her to slip deeply into unconsciousness.

Rather, she fought in a series of battle-scarred dreams, on the cusp of sleep, her eyelids fluttering constantly, her limbs thrashing and twitching like a dog's.

When, at last, she awoke it was near night again and it was as if no time had passed though, in reality, more than eighteen hours had elapsed from her ordeal in the street.

"Where did you get this weapon?"

It was the first question he asked her. She knew the answer of course, but the effort required in opening her mouth and translating thought into speech seemed beyond her.

He put an enormous lopsided wooden bowl of *larmen dosanko* in front of her and, sitting cross-legged on the *tatami* beside the *futon* on which she lay, laced his fingers beneath his chin and contemplated her silently.

Akiko rose to her haunches. The scent of the steaming noodle soup was overpowering, blotting out all other sensation or thought. Only when she was finished eating did she notice the sleek metal and pearl of the pistol lying by his side. It was this he was referring to when he had asked her the question.

She looked back at the rumpled *futon*. Its fabric was light but in spots deep, rust-colored stains had turned the beautiful cotton leathery and stiff. The sight set Akiko's heart to hammering again, and something must have showed in her eyes because the man sitting across from her smiled and said, "You have nothing to fear from me, Kodomo-gunjin."

Akiko put her fingertips up to the right side of her forehead, near her hairline. A cessation of hunger had made her aware of a painful pulsing there. She felt the bulge of a bandage. "Why do you call me Little Soldier?"

"Perhaps," he said softly, leaning forward to push the pistol across the *tatami* toward her, "for the same reason you carry this weapon."

He cocked his head. It was no wonder she had first thought of him as the man in the moon for his face was as round as a full moon's, with pockmarked cheeks and a flat Chinese nose. He had a long, wispy mustache drooping down around the corners of his mouth but little other hair. Overall his face seemed as soft as raw dough.

He bowed now. "I am Sun Hsiung. How may I call you?"

"You have already named me, haven't you? Kodomo-gunjin."

He nodded. "As you wish."

She leaned forward and took the pistol off the *tatami*. It seemed quite heavy to her now. She did not look at him when she spoke next. "What happened . . . last night?"

Sun Hsiung put his forearms on the points of his knees. "You shot the . . . man who was holding you. You discharged one bullet, which entered his skull through the socket of his left eye. It splintered the ridge of bone just above and lodged in his brain."

"He's . . . dead?"

"Quite."

She swallowed hard. "And the other one?"

302

"He was coming for you when I arrived on the scene. He was going to kill you, I believe. I had to stop him."

Akiko opened her mouth to ask another question but immediately thought better of it. "They may send more."

Sun Hsiung shrugged. "Perhaps."

She put her finger around the trigger and hefted the pistol. "I'll shoot them, too."

Sun Hsiung considered her for a moment. He had not asked her who it was who might send more thugs after her or even why these had been dispatched. "That would be most unwise, I think."

Her look was defiant. "Why? It saved my life." He rose, leaving her there in silence to learn her first lesson.

It was not the pistol that had saved Akiko's life but the advent of Sun Hsiung's intervention. When she had worked that through sufficiently so that she could see the ramifications, she unwound from her sitting position and went to him.

He was outside, in back, tending to his tiny, exquisite bonsai garden. Akiko stood at the edge of it, a giant blundering into a minute world.

"I want to learn," she said softly.

The rice-paper lantern swung from its black iron hook, its light falling across Sun Hsiung's shoulders as he toiled. He did not turn around or make any motion that he had heard her or, indeed, was aware of her presence at all.

"I want you to teach me what you know."

She looked down at the weapon she was still holding in her hand. There was an odd kind of security in its heft and warmth in her hand. And it was something of her mother's.

Slowly, carefully, she made her way through the tiny sculptured trees to where he was working on hands and knees.

"Please," she whispered, kneeling down as best she could in the narrow stone path and bending far forward in a kowtow. She extended the firearm in her open palm. "Take this as payment. It is all I have."

Sun Hsiung set his gleaming tools aside and slowly turned around. He bowed to her and, lifting the pistol from her open hand, murmured, "*Dōmo arigatō*, Kodomo-gunjin."

She had almost killed herself that night as well as the thug. That was why her forehead was bandaged, why, when she finally removed it, there was a reddish weal that gradually metamorphosed into a small white furrow of puckered skin. The bullet that eventually killed her assailant had nicked her as well. Too close. She was glad she had given the pistol to Sun Hsiung.

303

The beginnings of her training surprised her. Days commenced at five in the morning. Pupil and *sensei* began their exercises in the dark, building wind, the cardiovascular system. In the pale light of dawn they were into *Tai Chi Chuan*, slow, languorous movements that increased a sense of balance and limb coordination not unlike ballet.

From midmorning to midafternoon Sun Hsiung left her alone in the house to read selections of certain books he would provide for her. Akiko was an excellent reader, with superb retention and a large vocabulary. She was diligent in her studies, at times even rapt.

When Sun Hsiung returned from his daily errands abroad they would retire to the bonsai garden and the variables of the weather, each with a rice-paper pad, a small sable brush, and a pot of ink. At first Akiko was nonplussed. Her heart was burning with fury and often she shook from an excess of released adrenaline. Her head buzzed with swirling emotions and she would call up those memories from that night, all fear leeched from her, instead, a cold, calculating hatred growing wildly like a weed in an untended garden.

So she balked at the idea of painting. She could put up with the rather gentle *Tai Chi*, the long hours of studious repose but this . . . this was just too much.

The first time she was handed the pad and brush, she said as much. Sun Hsiung looked down at her and said, "Kodomo-gunjin, I fear that I have named you too well. You must learn peace before you can be taught the ways of war."

"But *painting* . . ." Her tone made the word synonymous with garbage collection.

Silently, Sun Hsiung considered whether he had made a mistake. He wondered if this wild young thing could be taught the most difficult lesson of patience. He shrugged inwardly. Her own *karma* would determine that; it was his *karma* to teach her. After that . . .

"Before we can start on the *protective* aspects of your training, your heart must be purged of hatred," he said. "To do that you will require a conduit. I place the leech on the inside of your arm and blood is drained from you."

"But they will not wait long to come after me again."

"You are no longer alone in the world, Kodomo-gunjin," he said, placing the pot of ink beside her.

Her eyes swung away from him and contemplated the vast, snowy expanse of the paper lying on her lap. "But I don't know how to paint," she said in a plaintive voice.

Sun Hsiung smiled down at her. "Then let us begin with the fundamentals."

Over the succeeding months painting became her favorite part of the day, and she came to cherish the sound of her *sensei*'s key in the lock at precisely the same time each day. Lifting her head up, she would look out the window to see the sun striking the bamboo wall of the tiny garden and recognize the light for the finest of the day. Eagerly, then, she would close her books and gather up their painting materials, meeting him at the *fusuma* out to the garden, her mind quivering in anticipation of the new lesson.

Too, at first, the advent of afternoon rain would depress her, for that certain light would not be present and they would forsake their painting and turn to other lessons. But later on, when she became more adept, she would look forward to the rain for then they would sit just inside the open *fusuma* where it was warm and dry and begin to use the diffuse light, the oblique intermittent lines of the rain as the basis for their paintings.

How could Akiko have ever thought that she would be so elated by foul weather? When others were slowly wending their way home through the slicked streets, bent over beneath their *amagasa* against the rain and wind, shivering and damp, she would be busy dipping her brush in ink, putting it to paper.

And, so gradually that she was not at first aware of it, the hatred did indeed fade from her heart, flowing out through the creative conduit Sun Hsiung intuited was right for her. Her paintings softened, flowing more easily over the paper, gaining a kind of organic power that gathered in her lines and spaces, impressing even the *sensei* who had spent so long at this pursuit.

Thus there came a time when Sun Hsiung judged it right for her to begin the more difficult aspects of her training. On a day when the snow had fallen heavily, a sere blanket covering the greens and browns of Japan, he kept her up all night, beginning the long process. He did this with full knowledge of what this might do to her and to him. For in truth he had never before had a female pupil and had he been of another temperament he would have felt a certain trepidation.

In fact, he recognized that on some level it was odd that he had accepted her sex so readily. His native China was so different in its concept of women. Sun Hsiung knew that his father found intelligent women who showed any kind of talent troublesome. "Sooner or later," he would tell his son, "they will open their mouths and talk back to you, and then what use is their talent?"

In Japan as well as in China a woman was expected to follow

305

the dictates of her father until she was married. Then she was required to obey her husband and, in the event of his death, her eldest son.

The worst sin a wife could commit was to fail to bear children. In that event, according to certain ancient codes, she was expected to leave. In some cases she could choose to accept her husband's siring a child via a mistress or, failing that, adopting a child of one of her husband's relatives.

A wife's adultery caused her to be immediately divorced, but a man could have as many mistresses as he chose. In fact, a law enacted in 1870 in Japan established kinship between parent and child to be in the first degree and kinship between a man and his mistress to be in the second degree. Although this was rescinded ten years later, the custom of taking mistresses continued unabated.

When the emperor Mutsuhito ended his reign in 1912 it was rumored that the son who succeeded him as the emperor Taisho had been borne not by Mutsuhito's wife but by his mistress. Taisho's reign was brief; in 1926 he was succeeded by his own son, Hirohito.

In recalling all this history Sun Hsiung again reminded himself what a renegade he had been and still was. He had fled mainland China many years before because of the oppressive nature of the society. The fact was that he did not find subservience in anyone attractive, particularly in a mate. He had, consciously or no, dedicated his life to the pursuit of strength, and he differed markedly from the feudal Japanese *samurai* who fed on strength by day and by night wished only for the obeisance of gentle women.

He looked at his Little Soldier's working body now in the coppery lamplight, a thin sheen of sweat turning her pale skin glowing and burnished.

He asked himself whether he would look upon a male body with the same set of conflicting emotions which seemed to plague him. Would he be so acutely aware of the play of her back muscles, the rippling of her thighs as she stretched and twisted in the *Tai Chi*? She performed it with such startling skill and agility, it was difficult for Sun Hsiung to believe she had been at it for six months rather than six years.

His eyes stole down to the workings of her buttocks as she lifted one leg and spun, and he was profoundly ashamed of the instincts which rose within him. And yet he could not help them.

He was a man who had always dealt with his desire in precisely the same way he did all his other requirements: when he felt the need for it he entered the new *karyukai* district and slaked his thirst. Yet those times had all been of his own choosing and his iron control had dictated the nights he would perform those erotic exercises to the delight of not only himself but his partner as well.

Now, for the first time since he was a young, untrained lad, his desire rose unbidden, a deceitful serpent twining about him, enlacing him within its languorous coils. Angry, he steeled his mind against the onslaught, but his mind had nothing to do with it. He was a man, after all, who was in touch with the totality of his being, and he knew full well that only modern man chose to live completely within his mind.

And it was Sun Hsiung's body that was speaking now and he knew deep down where his essence resided that he must respond to its calling in some manner.

That morning, while his pupil still slept off the night's lessons, he stole from the house and availed himself of the pleasures of the willow world. But now, though he felt the pleasure rippling through him at what was being done to him, though he shot his seed twice within the span of time he was with the *tayu*, these were only surface sensations and while the storm raged, in the depths there was only motionlessness and silence.

He could not say that he had not enjoyed his stay within the precincts of the happy field. He had felt the clouds and rain but yet his spirit was roaming restless. Though his member was for the moment satiated, still the core of him remained unfulfilled.

Sun Hsiung wondered at this all the way back to his house and, turning the key in the lock and entering once again the sanctum of his domain, he at once understood the nature of his agitation.

For as he went through the silent rooms, he came upon his pupil's sleeping quarters. The *fusuma* was partly open, as it always was, and Sun Hsiung paused to check on her. She was still asleep, her face turned to the side, toward him. She was on her back, one leg stuck straight out, the other bent sharply at the knee so that she had the electric appearance of leaping even in repose.

And like the clean edge of a gleaming knife Sun Hsiung felt the flick of his emotions flutter his heart as his eyes drank in the sight of her.

What mysterious essence could a woman of her young years possess to affect him thusly? It was a question that he could not possibly answer for it belied the use of years and experience, the commodities with which he was most familiar.

And as Sun Hsiung knelt just outside the threshold to her room, enrapt by the serenity of her *wa*, he felt a pulsing in the nether reaches of his lower belly, a kind of tidal pull that the Awabi divers spoke of where in a lake none should be.

307

So, too, now with Sun Hsiung. And he craned his neck, staring hard at her sleeping face to make certain. For it seemed to him that something was reaching out across the brief gulf that separated them and was massaging him internally. It was not that he thought of this feat as impossible. He knew too much of *jahō* to rule such a thing out. But from such a one as his Little Soldier? Why, she had had no training.

And yet he could not dispute what was occurring inside his body. He looked around. The day was almost done. Long shadows stretched through the house like animate pets, and the light was fast failing. Night was coming on.

So near him Akiko stirred, both legs extending, arms raised over her head as she, too, stretched like some great cat. Her eyelids fluttered open and her irises were upon him as if in her slumber, through the membrane of her lids, she had been watching him all the time.

"Come here," she murmured in a totally undisciplined voice. And when Sun Hsiung made no move, said no word, her lids pulsed and he felt the kneading in his lower belly increase, radiating downward to the base of his member. All at once his testicles began to tingle and it was as if a silken hand had grasped him about the base of his penis. He began to stiffen and grow.

No! a voice inside his head shouted, but he had no recourse. As if he were a dreamer immersed in water, he swam lazily across the threshold of her room, felt her arms come up and like oiled serpents slide across his muscled shoulders. The long fingers caressed the nape of his neck and the base of his skull.

Sun Hsiung could no longer feel his hands or his feet. He was aware only of an inordinate pleasure pooling in his loins.

Magically, majestically, she parted his kimono, her left hand tracing circles across his chest, belly, nipples. Her eyes, still heavylidded with sleep and perhaps something more, stared up at him, their pupils dilated so completely there seemed no iris at all. Her lips had softened, becoming sensuous, parted slightly so that he could scent her sweet breath.

There was a part of him that did not want to see her naked. But another side, the one she had provoked, would not be denied. And slowly, softly, he pulled apart her thin cotton kimono so that inch by inch her glowing flesh was revealed to him, at first the sections he had already glimpsed, areas in their tempting proximity to the more intimate parts that had already begun to inflame him.

Then, when all of those had been revealed to him, he held his breath as first one breast then the other slid out from beneath the concealing shadows of the kimono. They swelled into the light, capped with nipples and areola as dark as the encroaching night. If Fuji-san was the most perfect mountain in the world then surely these must be the most perfect breasts.

A tiny cry escaped Sun Hsiung's lips as he bent his head in worship. And Akiko, closing her eyes in rapture as she felt his lips encompassing first one nipple then the other, stroked the back of his neck in the expert manner she had observed for so long in *Fuyajo*, sensing now with her own newly learned knowledge the proper nerve bundles and, running her fingertips down their buried lengths, how to keep them burning with electric energy or to calm them into a euphoric stupor.

And yet it was not enough; she was impatient and her right hand snaked between their bodies, seeking to grasp in physical substance what she had reached out for during the last rising moments of sleep when something inside her had become aware of a presence beside her, then sensing that it was Sun Hsiung, and, lastly, picking up the intensely sexual emanations emerging from him. Thus she had reached out for him while still in the beta level of twilight cerebration and, on the cusp of consciousness, she had moved her *wa* across the infinity of space between them.

Now she had in her hand what her mind had touched, and she cupped his heavy scrotum in her palm while her fingers gently probed the soft skin just beneath, midway to his anus.

Sun Hsiung, who had been involved with the pristine symmetry of her breasts, abruptly felt the exquisite invasion of her fingers and thought he was going to perish with joy. She was moving to the core of him, accelerating his pulse rate. He felt inordinately heavy and ponderous, a human put into a sun bear's shaggy body. His mind no longer worked correctly, all the crystal passageways that had led him so successfully through the labyrinth of logic had crumbled. He felt caught up in a power beyond his imagining.

Involuntarily he groaned as her astounding ministrations accelerated his passion further. With a low growl, he finished stripping them both of the robes. Swinging her around on the *futon*, he put his calloused palms flat on her thighs, moving them slowly inward along the incredibly soft flesh there. With infinite slowness he parted the stems of her legs and gazed lovingly down at the moist petals of the flower thus revealed.

His nostrils quivered at her musky scent. He felt his erection leap in her hands, the crown expanding, straining for release. It was as if she possessed a natural aphrodisiac that turned the air heady and thick as honey.

Her soft, high mount was within reach of his lips. Never had he hungered for another with such profound desire. Every fiber of his being was concentrated on these next few moments.

Her hair, just beginning to come in, grew only along the center strip of her pubic mound, leaving the sides as smooth and bare as a small child's gully. This only increased his ardor since he had before him both woman and girl. Without another moment of hesitation, he pulled apart her shining lips with his thumbs.

When Akiko felt the heated stab of his tongue in her core, she arched up with her hips, crying out in inarticulate delight. She felt as if the sun had detached itself from the heavens and had been pressed up between her thighs. Too, she found that if she worked on him at the same time, her pleasure was increased tenfold.

She moved upward slightly on him, craning her long neck until she could press her lips to the skin just behind his scrotum. She felt the heavy trembling of his member as she did so and she began a low vibratory growl in her throat, pressing more directly against him in order to pass on the sensation.

Above her, his nose and tongue gliding along her slippery surfaces, Sun Hsiung's eyes almost crossed with the intensity of the ecstasy he was experiencing. It was as if he had not just recently been drained twice by the *tayu* in the *koryukai*; it was as if he had not had sex in many years.

His tongue laved her from crown to stem and back again as if he could not get enough of her taste. Soon he felt the quivering of her powerful muscles high up along the insides of her thighs and he concentrated feverishly on the core of her, now expanded and pulsing in delicious surrender. He heard her gurgle and gasp beneath him, felt the electric swipe of her pointed nipples against his belly as she worked busily on him.

He wanted to give her her first real orgasm but he did not know how long he could hold out. She had not directly touched the crown of his erection yet he knew that soon he must jet his seed even with no direct touch.

Part of him marveled at this feat as he continued with his erotic stimulation. And now she was in spasm, the ridged muscles rippling just below the surface of her skin, her thighs pulled wide apart and her buttocks as hard as rocks. He could feel the ultimate vibrations beginning inside her.

And then, unexpectedly, he felt her insinuate herself out from beneath him, felt himself turned on his back, watched, wide-eyed, as she mounted him, inserting just the tip of him inside her.

He gasped, and involuntarily his hips lept upward off the *futon* as the liquid electric first contact threatened to overwhelm him.

Her hips moved back and forth, stimulating the crown of his penis, first the top then the underside, back and forth in a rhythm that took his breath away. Then she was sliding down farther and he had to put his hands on her waist, her own over his, pushing, helping himself through the natural barrier of tissue.

And then like the burst of a cannon's fusillade he was through, his shaft sliding all the way up her. He felt her puffed-out lips against his scrotum and then, as she reached around, her fingers caressing him there, urging him onward.

She crouched over him, sliding her breasts and nipples hard against his flesh, her small, white teeth bared slightly as she worked her hips against him, building an irreversible tension within him.

Sun Hsiung gritted his teeth, the cords at the sides of his neck standing out like steel cables. He grunted continuously, all the way inside her now, but his eyes were open, staring up at her face, wanting to wait for her.

And the trembling came to her again, this time in great wracking pulses, shivering her hot sheath around him. It was the last straw and he felt himself melting, all his energy, all his reserves of strength flowing down the ribboning muscles of his thighs to his loins, pooling like quicksilver in his scrotum. As her cupping palm urged him onward, as her sheath fluttered around his expanding penis, he felt a great series of throbs, an unutterably delicious warmth overpowering him combined with an enormous desire to penetrate her farther than he had any other woman.

Then she was crying out as her hips blurred, as she worked herself on him, rubbing and stroking, her sweet breath with a hint of his own musk in his face, her damp unbound hair a tender veil across his eyes. A heavy undulation across her abdomen and belly, her muscles fluting in spasm, and he felt silken fingers grasping him, stroking him anew with such tenderness that, miraculously, he felt a return of his waning orgasm, gathering once again in him as if he were a female, regenerating another form of pleasure entirely, one of which he had been ignorant all his life.

Something inside her—that same thing that had reached out to him in slumber and caressed him—lifted him up with her so that they experienced her orgasm together, united in a kind of spirit dance Sun Hsiung had previously only experienced at the very height of the highest level of combat, when lives hung in the balance and death hung by his side.

Shaken like a leaf in a tempest, Sun Hsiung allowed the full force of her marvelous power to blast through him. He rose with

311

her on wings of ecstasy and, his renewed erection quivering, shot again within her dripping sex all that he could muster.

Years later, the memory of that evening remained fresh inside him. And so it was that she came before him, now fully a woman, and said to him, bowing as she did so, "*Sensei*, I wish to learn one more thing." Sun Hsiung's belly contracted and his heart went cold, for he had known of this moment almost from the first. And dreading its coming, he had erased its specter from his mind. Until now. For now was the time.

"And what is that?" he inquired, his voice faint in the flickering lamplight which served to illuminate one small patch of the surrounding darkness.

Akiko's forehead was against the *tatami*. Her shining black hair was pulled tightly back from her exquisite face, tied in a long ponytail—a Chinese fashion unknown to her but pleasing to Sun Hsiung—that lay curled across one shoulder and her upper back. She wore a kimono of crimsons, golds, and flame oranges, a match for the autumnal foliage beyond their front door.

"I wish to learn how to disguise my *wa*." Her voice was calm and free of excess emotion. She had proved to be an enormously gifted pupil. "Ever since I discovered the talent in me, I have longed to know this."

"Why is that, Kodomo-gunjin?"

"Because I feel somehow incomplete without it."

Sun Hsiung nodded once. "I understand." He thought about saying more.

"There is no need to warn me, *sensei*," she said, catching the essence of his emanation.

"It is more dangerous than even you can suspect." Their eyes locked, Akiko submitted entirely to his will now, her whole being attuned to his words, sensing their import beyond the fact that nothing could dissuade her from her *karma*.

"I am not afraid of death or dying," she said softly.

"Corporeal death is far from the worst eventuality." Abruptly the room seemed webbed with bioluminescent strands, the building of their spirits, pulsing with vitality, making of this place a power spot. "These forces you seek are beyond even our understanding; they are so elemental that they may only be controlled partially. And in those other moments they may change you; they may corrupt all that you have learned here."

Within the echoing silence that engulfed them both, Akiko bowed her head. "I understand. I will guard myself carefully against just such corruption."

312

"Then this is where you must go," Sun Hsiung said, sliding a folded slip of paper across the *tatami* to her.

The next morning, as she finished her packing, he took her painting pad and brush from her. "You cannot take these where you are going, Little Soldier."

And for the first time Akiko had a sense of the depth of the darkness into which she was descending. "This saddens me, *sensei*."

Those were the last words Sun Hsiung heard her utter. They drank one last cup of tea together. Moments later she hefted her bags and, bowing formally, left him.

It was the first time that she had performed *chano-yu* for him, the pupil serving the *sensei* as new *sensei*. For a long time after that Sun Hsiung sat before his tiny cold teacup, the dark green leaves clinging tenaciously to its bottom like a vine refusing to die.

Then, slowly and carefully, as if he were made of delicate crystal, he crawled across the *tatami* to where her painting pad with its black finger of the sable brush lay.

He reached out and picked up the pad, drawing it toward him as his eyes studied the calming confluence of forces within the bonsai garden. He heard the plaintive call of a plover through the partially open *fusuma*; he was quite unaware of the coolness in the room.

And with the pad pressed tightly against his chest, he began a slow rocking on his haunches.

At last one salty tear slid down his weathered cheek, to drop silently on the edge of the pad, immediately absorbed by the sheets of paper, gone forever.

BOOK FOUR

FA CHI

[Release the trigger]

HONG KONG/WASHINGTON/TOKYO/
MAUI/RALEIGH/HOKKAIDO
SPRING, PRESENT

"I am afraid, Mr. Nangi, that the news is a good deal worse than either you or I first imagined."

Tanzan Nangi sat sipping his pale gold jasmine tea, staring out the set of windows that faced the Botanical Gardens on Hong Kong Island's Mid-Levels. Just beyond was Victoria Gap, high up on the Peak.

He was high up above the Central District in the All-Asia Bank's executive offices, a glass and steel tower in the middle of Des Voeux Road Central.

"Go on," Nangi said placidly as he tapped the ash from his cigarette into a crystal ashtray on the desk in front of him.

Allan Su glanced briefly down at the oversized buff folder he was clutching although it was apparent that he hardly needed to do that. He wiped at his upper lip, then ran his fingers through his hair. He was a small, compact Chinese of Shanghainese extraction who was normally calm and clear headed. Now his obvious anxiety filled the room like a strange perfume.

He began to pace back and forth over the antique Bhokara. "To give you an example, we have three-quarters interest in the Wan Fa housing project in the New Territories in Tai Po Kau.

The first mortgage has already been refinanced once and is on the verge of being so again. That would necessitate a second mortgage, which we cannot afford.

"We need an occupancy rate of seventy-six percent to break even at this point. The units should be renting for sixteen thousand Hong Kong dollars a month; we're lucky if we get five thousand now. Since the announcement by the Communists no one wants to live in such an 'unstable' area that 'could be overrun at any moment.'"

Allan Su stopped his pacing long enough to slam the folder down on the polished teak desktop on a pile of other such folders. "The list is almost endless." There was true disgust in his voice. "Anthony Chin could not have done us more damage were he secretly working for one of our competitors."

"Was he?" Nangi inquired.

"In this city, who knows?" Su's shoulders lifted and fell. "But I doubt it. Several of the other banks were caught the same as us, though none to such a degree." He shook his head. "No, I think Mr. Chin was merely greedy, and greed, Mr. Nangi, is the worst enemy of good judgment."

Nangi bent forward and poured more tea. Then he settled himself more comfortably in Allan Su's high-backed leather chair and contemplated the terraced network of white and pale ochre high rises that sprouted from the slopes of Victoria Peak, a forest of concrete.

"Tell me, Mr. Su, when was your last severe earthquake?"

Momentarily nonplussed by the question, Allan Su blinked his eyes behind his wire-rimmed spectacles. "Why, it's been almost two years now, I believe."

"Uhm." Nangi's attention was still firmly on the thicket of skyscrapers. "A bad one, inopportunely placed, would do many of those in, don't you agree? They'd all fall apart like a jumble of children's building blocks. Many lives would be lost, many family lines would abruptly come to a halt, many fortunes would be destroyed."

He turned his head to face Allan Su fully. "And who else do *you* work for, Mr. Su?"

"I . . . Pardon me, Mr. Nangi, but I do not understand what you are talking about."

"Oh, come, come," Nangi said, thinking that all Chinese were alike, "there's no room here for coyness. *Everyone* in Hong Kong holds down more than one job; it's far more profitable."

He paused to pour tea into a second cup. "Now take Anthony Chin, for instance. He was not only the president of the All-Asia

318

Bank of Hong Kong but he was also a lieutenant in the Red Chinese Army." He pushed the cup across the desk.

"Impossible!" Allan Su had ceased his pacing. "I've known him for years. Our wives shopped together once a week."

"Then you must have known of all this fiscal impropriety," Nangi said blandly, indicating the pile of folders filled with their damning evidence. The investigation team he had hired had done their work well.

"I knew nothing of the sort!" Su proclaimed hotly.

Nangi nodded his head. "Just as you knew nothing of his true affiliation."

Allan Su stared at Nangi for a moment, trying to force down his instinctive hatred of the Japanese and see this man for what he really was. He knew that that clarity was all that could save him now. "Then it follows that you also suspect me of being a Communist."

"Oh, you may rest easy on that score," Nangi said. He smiled. "Come, Mr. Su, will you drink with me?"

His heart hammering in his throat, Allan Su did as he was bade. "I should no longer be surprised at the outcome of events here." He gulped at his tea, which had already grown cold, then used the cup to gesture out the expanse of sparkling glass toward the slender fingers of the Mid-Levels. "Take those high rises, for instance. It would take far less than a major earthquake to send them tumbling. More than likely they've been built with a gross insufficiency of supporting iron rods in the concrete. The favorite trick is to set a half dozen in the poured cement—which, by the way will have twice as much sand in it as it should—while the building inspector watches. Then, as he moves on, those same six rods will be removed from the setting cement and used in the next section the inspector is looking at. After he's gone, they'll be removed once more and used at the next building site.

"It's a game, really, because the inspector has already been paid off by the builders not to search through the site too thoroughly."

Nangi frowned. "That's nothing to play a game over: lives. And millions of dollars."

Su shrugged. "If I can buy a twelve-year-old virgin down in Wan Chai, why then should I not be able to buy a building inspector as well?"

"The difference there," Nangi said dryly, "is that the twelve-year-old virgin you've paid your hard-earned dollars for could probably screw rings around your wife."

"Then my lust—and that's a form of greed—has blinded my good judgment."

Nangi stood up abruptly. "How much is the Royal Albert Bank paying you a month, Mr. Su?"

Allan Su almost dropped his porcelain cup. But not quite. He heard the yammering of his pulse in his ears like the screaming of all his ancestors and he thought, Great Buddha, what will happen to my family now? No work and ruined in the midst of the Colony's worst recession in three decades.

Nangi was seeming to slip in and out of focus, and with the exaggerated slowness and care of a habitual drunk he placed the empty cup on the desk top next to the pile of buff folders.

"Come, come," Nangi said. "It's a simple enough question."

"But the answer's a difficult one. I beg to—"

"I do not," Nangi interrupted him, leaning forward with his rigid arms on the teak, "wish to hear explanations, Mr. Su. I require someone here whom I can trust completely. Either you can do it or you can't."

Nangi held his eyes. "You know what will happen to you, Mr. Su, if you can't do it."

Allan Su shuddered, saying nothing.

He stood very straight though his knees felt weak. Of course he could walk out of here now, tendering his resignation. But where would that get him? Had he any assurance that the Royal Albert would hire him? The job market had narrowed considerably in many fields—banking high among them—since the damnable Communists made their accursed announcement. He thought about his wife, his six children, aunt, and two uncles, one widowed—and how many cousins on his wife's side—whose welfare he was responsible for.

Of course he could always try to brazen it out. But he suspected that would be an unwise course for him to take, the result being the same as if he walked out. Nangi was hard. And he was Japanese. But if he were fair he could make a satisfactory employer.

Su decided to tell the truth. "The Royal Albert has been paying me ten thousand Hong Kong dollars a month to keep them informed of all All-Asia transactions." He held his breath. He could hear his accelerated heartbeat like surf in his inner ear.

"I see." Nangi tapped the eraser end of a new pencil on Su's desk top. Then he looked up. "As of now, Mr. Su, your salary is doubled." Great gods of the west wind, Su thought. A thin line of sweat broke out at his hairline. "In six months we'll review the matter and, based on the bank's overall position, it will be reevaluated upward . . . or downward. The same will hold true a year

320

from now." His eyes were searching Su's face. "If, at that time, the bank has performed up to a schedule of profit I shall work up for you before I depart, you will receive a ten percent stock equity in All-Asia pursuant to your signing a lifetime contract."

Nangi saw with satisfaction that all color had drained from Su's broad face.

"I will immediately sever all ties with the Royal Albert." Su's voice was thin and reedy. His eyes seemed glassy.

"You'll do nothing of the kind," Nangi said. "You'll take your ten thousand a month and within sixty days ask for a raise. God knows, you've earned it."

Su's face clouded. "Sir. I don't think I understand." Relief was flooding through him like a spring torrent, muddying his thoughts.

"From today on, Mr. Su, you will provide the Royal Albert with precisely the information I feed you. At the same time you will relay to me just what is going on at our competition. I will want to know every major and minor deal on their boards. I will want to know their capital outlay, their spread, and their investment goals for one year, five years, and ten years." He cocked his head. "Are you getting all this, Mr. Su?"

Su had recovered sufficiently to smile. Oh, gods of all four quarters, he prayed silently, tonight I will offer a feast to each and every one of you. "I'm with you, Nangi-san," he said in his best idiomatic English. "This is sounding more and more like a task I will enjoy immensely."

Then concern flooded his face again. "But I cannot be expected to achieve these great gains with the depletion of capital that currently plagues us. The bank is on the verge of insolvency if we were to have to redeem on any kind of an extended run. And even if the run does not materialize—may all the gods hear and make it so!—it would take more than twelve months for us to recover sufficiently from these setbacks so that I can make even a semblance of headway."

"Two items will help us here," Nangi said, unruffled. "First, we will have additional capital available to us within seventy-two hours."

"May I ask the source of this capital?" Su interjected.

"Just be prepared to invest part of it wisely for a maximum return with a minimum of time factor."

Su was already shaking his head. "Big risk in that. Too much for us in our current position."

"Not with the information you're going to be getting from the Royal Albert." Nangi was smiling now as he rose. "Ride their back, Mr. Su, as the temple dog rides the great dragon. Let *them* take all the risks, do all the work while you make our money grow for us risk free." He nodded his head.

"Congratulations! This is a big day for you. Shall we go and celebrate?"

Tanya was manning the ARRTS terminal when the cipher came in. That was luck, pure and simple. But if someone else had been on, which had been far more likely, he or she would have merely starred the unreadable entry and she would have been flagged down immediately on her return.

The "Spearfish" situation, as she had somewhat ironically designated it, was her baby. She was its monitor principally because it was a personal matter of Minck's and not business.

Well, that was not strictly true. "Spearfish" *had* been business up until perhaps a year ago. It should have been terminated then, as Tanya had argued. In fact, as far as anyone else in Red Section or anywhere else in the Family was concerned, it was terminated. Only Minck and Tanya knew otherwise.

The moment Tanya became aware that "Spearfish" had crossed the line it never should have, into the personal sector, she had come alert. One of her jobs, unspoken and all the more crucial for that, was to protect Minck. In her judgment he had picked a particularly dangerous time to pull something like this, though she knew when personal feelings were allowed to interfere with business there was no good time for it.

Thus she became "Spearfish"'s guardian while acknowledging the foolhardiness of the enterprise. Some things could be kept in cold storage better than others. But nothing could be well kept for long out in the open.

When she knew that Minck would not go for the termination she had switched tactics, arguing for a closed shop. That was out of the question as well, he said. "Spearfish" could not be penned up.

Then she had gone for the box, eight men in two shifts. But Minck had said "Spearfish" would find that distasteful as well. It limited freedom, he said. Tanya had kept her mouth shut, knowing that that was precisely the purpose of the box. It was normally used on more serious tags but it could work just as well on friendlies such as "Spearfish."

Finally, she did what he had asked her to do in the first place: put two men on it. But she would not let it go at that. She kept in constant touch. "Spearfish" was highly volatile and she wanted no mistakes made. The only time she laid off was when Minck

322

himself went down. He thought that even she did not know. But she did.

Now she watched the glowing green letters springing up on the terminal screen, marching across in dedicated rows. When the message had ended, she watched the pulsing letters hanging there for a moment before she pushed the decode button. The word "REALLY?" came up and she hit a six-digit key ultimate access sequence. Now the decoded message wrote itself across the screen. Now she had one minute, no more, no less, to digest the message. If she did not depress the "print" key by that time to get a hard copy, ARRTS would dissolve the cipher as if it had never existed.

She went pale as she read the terse message, so stunned that she had made no conscious decision whether or not to print before her time ran out and the message disappeared from the screen. That did not matter much since it still glowed behind her eyes.

Silently she cursed Minck and his personal problems. Because the cipher had turned "Spearfish" from a potential problem into an active one. She depressed the "send" key, composing her reply as she did so. When only the date appeared, she was reminded that codes were changed weekly and this was the day to get a new one. That meant Tony Theerson.

She got up and went down two floors. The Boy Wonder had his digs in an otherwise unused corner of the floor. His only companions were the jumble of cardboard and wooden crates, shipping labels, and huge rolls of brown wrapping papers. And his cipher machines.

Though Minck had Theerson working on the Soviet Alpha-three ciphers almost around the clock, it was also his devilish little brain that composed the Red Section's own codes. He said they were unbreakable; Tanya believed him.

When she came in on him he was sitting up on the Army cot he had asked be installed in his work space. Tanya suspected that the Boy Wonder had no private life whatsoever; he certainly slept in the building enough. Also, because of the time differential between Washington and the areas he monitored, primarily Russia and Asia, he tended to have odd sleep-wake patterns.

"Hey," he said in his laconic way.

"Want some coffee?"

He offered up his bare arm; he was dressed in a T-shirt with "Dépêche Mode" written on it and a pair of faded blue jeans. "Just slip the needle in this vein, Doctor."

Tanya laughed as she crossed to the coffee machine and filled two mugs. She gave him one. "Had a hard night?"

He sipped at the strong French roast and groaned, his eyes

closing in ecstasy. "Food of the gods." He downed more coffee. "I'm having a bitch of a time breaking this new one." He meant the Alpha-three. He put the empty cup aside. "Frankly, I don't think I'm going to get it." He rose and stretched, yawning widely.

"It's that time again, I'm afraid," Tanya said. She had hardly touched her coffee, preferring tea. But she had not wanted to appear unfriendly.

The Boy Wonder groaned again. "You mean another week's slid by? Oh, God." He ran his fingers through his hair. "I need a shower."

"Business first, personal hygiene later," Tanya said, putting down her cup. "I'm on an open line."

"Gotcha." Theerson poked through a box of floppy disks. He pulled one out, gave it to her. "This one's a doozy."

"They all are," she said, heading for the door. "Good luck."

He grunted sourly. "With this monster I'm gonna need it."

The last she saw of him he was putting on his Walkman headphones as he sat down to work. With the Boy Wonder, business came before anything. Tanya decided to draft a memo to Minck suggesting he give Theerson some enforced vacation time.

Back at the ARRTS console two floors up, she inserted the floppy Theerson had given her and punched the "enter" button. The word "FILE:" came up and she typed in, "SPEARFISH." She waited for the cycle to complete, then entered her reply. The machine would automatically use the new cipher, ARRTS having replaced the old code with the new one in the receiver.

TRANSMIT HOURLY UPDATES. WILL BE MOBILE SOON. WILL GIVE BACKUP WITHIN THIRTY-SIX HOURS. TERMINATE 'SPEARFISH' WHEN SITUATION STABILIZES AND YOU ARE CERTAIN OF TARGET VISIBILITY.

Then she went away to make her report.

Nicholas sat on the backless stone seat in Sato's garden. He had been there for perhaps an hour, ever since his hosts had retired. He had made a show of going to his room so that they would not be obliged to share his insomnia. But he hadn't even bothered to undress, merely waited fifteen minutes before returning to the now deserted garden.

With infinitesimal slowness, light came into the garden. In a way it was a shame, since before only cold moonglow had distinguished shadow and illumination, causing the flower scents to dominate. Now as vision took hold, the perfumes seemed to fade.

Nicholas became aware of the presence behind him the moment it crossed the threshold of Sato's study and stepped down onto the glowing pebbles. The predawn atmosphere was aqueous with white mist. There was no sound save the waking of the birds.

He knew that it was Akiko without having to turn around or hear her voice. Their *wa* had locked hours before and that had been enough to mark her in his mind. The system was as primitive as it was sophisticated. As Akutagawa-san had said, urban life had bred it out of modern human beings.

Because of this, too, he knew that she was dangerous. He did not know in precisely what way or even if it was to him in particular. He knew she was *sensei*. Very few individuals would have been able to make that determination from mere visual observation and the imprint of her spirit—even other *sensei* without all of Nicholas' skills and ability. But he was different.

"Nicholas-san."

Her low voice shivered him and he willed himself to remain calm. Still his pulse beat hard in his temples and he felt a sudden rush of blood to his head.

"Where is your husband?"

"Snoring on his princely pallet."

What was in her voice? Nicholas strained to hear all of the echoes and nuances, even those she might not know were present. Had he found derision there?

"Isn't your place beside him?" It was the petulant comment of a jealous lover, and he cursed himself.

"My place," she replied as if she heard no overtones, "is where I choose to be." She paused as if uncertain whether to go on. "Do you think that unJapanese of me?"

He shook his head. "Untraditional, perhaps, but not unJapanese."

In the ensuing silence she said, "Won't you turn around and face me? Am I so difficult to look at?"

Her words stirred the hair at the base of his neck and he wondered how carefully she had chosen them. Slowly, his heart beating faster than he would have wished, he turned toward her. He melted inside.

Just the first hint of dawn blushed her face in radiant light. She had changed into a pale yellow kimono with ice green and silver thread embroidered in the shape of stands of pine trees. A lone golden heron flew at full wing over her left breast. Her hair was down, a gleaming blueblack cascade stretching straight down her back. She wore no jewelry whatsoever. Her nails shone with clear lacquer but were cut short as would befit one of her training. He thought he could discern the slightest tremor in her face, a fleeting tic along the upper lid of one eye. Then both were gone and she was in control again.

"Was that so hard?" she breathed into the soft wind. Mist swirled at her back, danced around his shoulders.

"You are beautiful to look at, Akiko." He had not meant to make any such admission. Immediately he felt as if he had lost a battle.

She came toward him, gliding along the pebble path. She seemed to him to be emerging from out of the ending of the night. "Why do I feel as if I have been with you before?"

What she said startled them both. It was as if, naked, they were embracing and Sato had walked in on them. Blood flooded Akiko's face and her eyes flicked away from his face. The tremble was back within her.

All sense of reality had slipped from Nicholas' mind. Lost within the white mist, he saw only her. Yukio rose before him, a *kami* who had been granted a second life. Then he, too, reached out for the stability of the Void, seeking an answer to the unanswerable. As if in a dream, he rose from the hard stone seat and came toward her until they were but a hand's breadth apart. He fought with himself to say the words that had been roiling through his consciousness ever since she had slipped the fan from in front of her face. They were words he longed to say, words that would free him, perhaps, from his inner torment but which would also certainly make him vulnerable to her.

What to do? The moment was here. In Japanese society one had very few moments alone with another man's wife. This moment would never have come but for Akiko. What did she want of him? Was she Yukio? Did she want to hear him call her name? If so, why was she torturing him so? He was assailed by questions which led to riddles which in turn brought him to enigmas. It seemed to him now that all his life had been an enigma, a fitfully understood succession of events from which he had constantly turned away.

"Who are you?" he said hoarsely. "I must know."

Her eyes searched his. "Who do you think I am?" There was no coyness; rather he sensed a deeply buried desperation he could put no name to.

"I don't know."

Somehow the distance between them was closing. There seemed to be no conscious volition on either of their parts.

"Tell me," she whispered. "Tell me."

He could feel her breath on him, smell the scent of her, feel the heat of her flesh from beneath the silk kimono. Her eyes were half shut, her lips partly open as if some emotion inside her was on a runaway tear.

"Yukio . . ." Her name was torn from his heart like a tattered battle pennant. It was irrational that he should utter her name, irrational that he should think this was who stood before him. Yet he said it again, "Yukio, Yukio . . . ," seeing her eyes flutter closed as if in thrall, felt the melting of her upper body in against his, her head coming back, the long arch of her neck merging with the image, the memory he had carried with him for so many years.

There was a burning inside him as he reached for her, to embrace her or to stop her from falling he did not know. All his organs had turned to water and were boiling up. There was a fever in his brain. There was no control.

His lips came down over hers and he tasted her essence as he felt the dart of her tongue inside him.

For the first time in her life Akiko was open to the universe. Nothing in all her long, arduous training had caused this ignition inside of her.

She was so dizzy that she was doubly grateful for his strong arms about her. All breath had left her as he had uttered her name. And it *was* her name! How was that possible? But, oh, he tasted wonderful and, oh, how she ached for him! Her thighs were like water, unable to support her. She felt a kind of ecstasy at his touch she thought only possible in orgasm.

What was happening to her? Swept away, still a dark part of her mind yammered to be heard. What strange force had invaded her mind? What had turned her plans of vengeance inside out? What made her feel this way about a hated enemy? And why had she lied to him? She was not Yukio; she was Akiko.

And then with the power of his *wa* surrounding her, with her heart beating in her inner ear like thunder, with the press of his hard chest against her breasts, the answer exploded in her mind with the force of fireworks.

As Akiko she was nothing. She had come from nothing and nothing was her future. As Yukio she was someone. Here there was more for her than *kyomu*, that which Kyōki preached: nihility.

From the moment she had left Sun Hsiung's loving tutelage she had felt herself to be *doshi gatai*, beyond salvation. Without any other anchor in her life what else could she expect?

Now, abruptly, with Nicholas Linnear's appearance, Yukio had

327

become a reality. She was no more idea, no more means to an end, no more two-dimensional schemata. She lived.

The force of Nicholas Linnear's love for her had brought her back from the dead.

Justine saw him on her second day at the hotel. The first time was near the pool bar in the shade of the overhang and she thought that she must be mistaken. But the second time was at the crescent beach while she was wading out into the jade ocean, snorkel and mask in one hand, black fins on her feet. This time there was no doubt. It was Rick Millar.

At first she couldn't believe it. After all, she was six thousand miles from New York on a rambling world-class resort in the midst of a 23,000-acre pineapple plantation. She was in West Maui, in one of the most remote areas on the island, far from the strip of high-rise hotels at Kaanipali where most tourists to this paradisical spot stayed.

She watched, transfixed, the tide lapping around her waist as he headed into the surf toward her. His body was lean and trim, with narrow hips and wide shoulders. He did not have the wrist and chest development nor the overall muscle definition that Nicholas had. But then Rick was a tennis player, not a human killing machine.

Tears erupted through her quivering lids, stinging her eyes, and she turned away, out to sea and the hazy outline of Molokai.

"Justine—"

"You've got some helluva nerve coming here."

"I'd only heard about the famous Tobin temper before. Everything they said was an understatement to the real thing." His voice was deliberately light, bantering.

"Did you give Mary Kate back her job?" She felt the pumping of her heart like a weight of granite hanging inside her.

"It wasn't her job to give back, Justine." He was closer to her than she wanted him to be. "I told you I had found the better person to fill it."

She whirled on him, her eyes blazing. "You used me, you bastard!"

He remained calm. "You know, the trouble with you is that you're a scared child in a woman's body. Come off it, Justine. I didn't use you any more than I'd use anyone else. It's the wrong term. Mary Kate wasn't working out. In the adult business world you don't fire an executive—at any level—until you've hired his or her replacement. I'd be remiss in my duty to the company if I'd gone about it in any other way."

328

"But we're friends."

"That's incidental. But if it means anything to you, I'm sorry that had to enter into it." He smiled, testing the waters. "There was nothing sinister in it, I assure you. I'd seen some of your free-lance work, I spoke to several of my executives who'd used you over the past year. They all thought you were great." He smiled again. "All of them warned me about your temper, by the way."

"I see that didn't deter you." She wished now that she hadn't been crying when he came up.

"I liked your work too much. You've got a singular mind when it comes to advertising concepts. That's an invaluable quality." He looked away for a moment and his expression gave him the appearance of a little boy. "Anyway, I thought I could tame you. I saw it as a challenge." His eyes swung back. "I'd give anything if we could start over from the beginning."

"Is that why you followed me?"

He shook his head, standing his ground as a large wave made it through the coral reef out at the headland to the crescent bay, began to surge toward them. "Not really. I found that the office seemed very empty without you."

When the wave hit, it rose the water up to chin level, knocking them sideways, forcing them together.

Nangi put his ruined legs up on the chaise as he settled back and stared out at the South China Sea as it ran up onto the pale yellow beach at Shek-O. He was on the south side of Hong Kong Island, nearer to Aberdeen than he was to Central District, the "downtown" and financial hub of the Crown Colony.

Shek-O was one of the four or five areas within Hong Kong reserved for the truly wealthy in this teeming city of enormous wealth and abject poverty.

But things had changed in the year and a half since he had been here.

For one, the beautiful old hotel at Repulse Bay had been torn down in order to erect another group of high-rise houses. It was not solely that Nangi had spent many a glorious sun-spangled afternoon at tea, doing business on the expansive Colonial porch of that hotel, that he mourned its passing. It was just as much the thought of the old ways passing, the sunny, serene days transplanted by the lust for profits that the building boom had created during five or six years of the Crown Colony's high-speed growth in the middle and late seventies.

That was what had ultimately brought him here. The collapse

of that real estate boom. And in that light the destruction of the Repulse Bay Hotel was even more bitter.

Now Nangi was alone in the tile and stucco villa watching a young nubile Chinese girl brave the pollution of the South China Sea as she ran down the beach and into the mild surf. No one else was about although a pitcher of iced tea and two tall glasses sat on a pebble glass-topped table at Nangi's left elbow.

He saw the girl's bobbing head in the water. She had not bothered to tie up her hair or to wear a cap. The dark tail of hair flung down her naked back, spreading out in the water like a sea anemone, tendrils waving on the tide.

Wu-Shing. The words kept intruding on his conscious thoughts and that was a problem. Three deaths; three questions to be answered. Nangi wondered what connection there could be between the *Wu-Shing* murders and *Tenchi*.

These days, when anything unexplainable occurred he immediately thought of *Tenchi*. That was logical enough. He knew the Russians would stop at nothing to wrest *Tenchi* from Japan . . . if they knew what *Tenchi* was. As for the Americans, he could imagine them attempting to sabotage the operation. Ever since the end of the war America had been dependent upon Japan to be its anti-Communist watchdog in the East. But America wanted Japan subservient so that, like a willow, it would bend to the will of the victorious country. And it was true that Japan was dependent on America.

But *Tenchi* would change all that. Nangi feared that if the Americans got wind of the operation they would move as quickly as the Soviets to short-circuit it. This could not be allowed.

For the first time in many decades Japan found itself totally alone and, oddly enough, it was a frightening experience. He was becoming increasingly aware that he could no longer cling to his dreams of what Japan had once been. All that was gone now, wiped out by the atomic sunshine and the period of high-speed growth in which he had played such a crucial role.

He closed his eyes, knowing that there were no easy answers in life, nothing was so neat in reality as it was in fiction. One problem at a time, he thought. I must surmount the Chinese obstacle before I again think about ancient and arcane punishments.

Though he had been alone in the villa when he had arrived, he now heard the soft footfalls, opening and closing of doors that foretold the commencement of his assignation.

He reached for the pitcher of iced tea and poured himself a glass. It was bracing and delicious, just the tonic for this already steamy day.

Nangi did not turn his head as his keen ears picked up another's approach but remained where he was, sipping his drink, staring out at the girl now emerging like a water nymph from the rolling South China Sea.

"Good afternoon, Mr. Nangi."

By mutual agreement they spoke only English here. It was foreign to both of them but at least they hated it with an equal passion.

"Mr. Liu." Nangi nodded his head to no one in particular. He heard the creak of the chaise beside him, the musical clink of ice against glass and only then turned his head.

Once this man's ancestors must have been purebred Manchu, for he had the long, high-domed skull structure peculiar to them. He was tall for an Oriental; he knew it and used this advantage as an intimidating tool even when he was seated.

Liu was smiling now as he sipped at his drink. He put his head back against the chaise. "And how is the business climate in Japan these days, Mr. Nangi?" Liu had the habit of beginning topics as if they had been spoken about previously.

"Very strong," Nangi said shortly, thinking, I'll give him nothing to chew on until I'm ready. "The forecast is formidable."

"Ah," the Chinese said, moving his head. "Then your, ah, *keiretsu* is not so much involved in the heavy industries that began your country's great economic leap forward." He put down his sweating glass, laced his fingers across his small potbelly. "It is my understanding that these industries such as steel manufacturing—long the very core of your economic progress—are in serious financial straits in these days of worldwide recession."

Nangi said nothing for a moment, wondering just how well this man was informed. He might know the worst of it or again he might be fishing in order to corroborate unconfirmed reports. It was essential that Nangi answer him without giving anything away.

"There is no problem with our steel *kobun*," he said carefully. "We have seen nothing but profits from it."

"Indeed." With that one word Liu made it clear that he did not believe Nangi's statement. "And what of coal mining? Textile manufacturing? Petrochemicals, hm?"

"This topic is of no interest to me."

Liu turned his high head like a dog on point. "And yet, Mr. Nangi, it is of interest to me why you would wish to sell a division of your organization that in your words has only made profits for you."

"We are no longer interested in manufacturing steel." Perhaps

331

he had said it a shade too quickly. But at least now he knew the extent of the Chinese's knowledge. It was formidable and he was even more on his guard now.

"The real problem for Japan has, I think, just begun," Liu said much as an instructor will inform a pupil. "Your golden age of unlimited global economic expansion has come to an end. In years gone by you could export your finished product into foreign markets where they were snapped up immediately over their domestic competition. It gave you not only profits, of course, but an ever-expanding level of employment in your own country.

"But now times have changed." Liu's fingers unlaced, spread like a starfish, and closed down again, settling back on his stomach. "Let us take as our example one of your greatest successes: automobiles. Your invasion of the United States' domestic auto market has caused a spate of unemployment in that country and not long ago forced one of its giant corporations to the brink of financial dissolution.

"You know as well as I do how slow the Americans are to take the initiative." He smiled thinly. "But sooner or later the deepest sleeper must awake, and when his strength is as vast as is America's, the awakening can be quite rude. Repeatedly now you have been slapped with import quotas from the U.S. government.

"Now you are beginning to understand what it is like to fence in the international arena. In order to survive you must export capital and technology, building new Nissan plants in Tennessee instead of in Kanda. That means less Japanese employment; less profits. Your era of free trade has ended."

Despite the truth in what Liu was saying Nangi detected a strong streak of jealousy in the other man's words. Wouldn't the Chinese love to be in our economic position, he thought dryly.

"And then there is Yawata," Liu continued. He was referring to Japan's magnificent Yawata Steel Works, the oldest and largest of the country's coastal mills, which began manufacturing in 1901. "Curious, I think. It is an historic relic of other times yet since 1973 your government has shoveled more than three billion dollars into updating and refining Yawata's technology. And what has it availed them? Today Yawata is in far worse shape than it was after the oil shock of 1973. At least then the government could take economizing measures, streamlining operations, severely rationing fuel consumption. All those steps allowed Yawata's operations to continue unabated.

"But today those measures are still in effect, and because the worldwide market has shrunk so significantly, Yawata's work force has dropped from sixty-one thousand in 1969 to less than twenty-four thousand today. Three of Nippon Steel's blast furnaces are currently idle and a number of their subsidiary plants have closed down.

"The American steel industry would, I think, be delighted to return to the seventy percent capacity Yawata is currently running at. But Japan is simply not geared for such reductions. And what can you do? In America Bethlehem can lay off their workers; in your country your political and social structure does not allow you to fire your employees."

Liu paused here as if he expected Nangi to make some kind of comment. When he did not, Liu seemed slightly put out and his tone when he spoke again was rather more sharp. "The end result of this little talk," he said crisply, "is that your *keiretsu*, like most others, is currently going through an organizational upheaval. And that, as we both know, takes capital. With cash flow weakened you have been dipping rather heavily into your reserves."

"We are quite solid."

"Solid perhaps." Liu shrugged. "But I am doubtful that you have enough reserves now to save the All-Asia Bank."

If he is going to offer me aid from the other side I shall have to strike him across his head with my stick, Nangi thought.

"What do the Communists want with the All-Asia Bank?"

"Oh, we don't want any part of it," Liu said conversationally. "Rather, we wish a piece of your *keiretsu*."

Nangi, despite having extended all his feelers for clues, was thunderstruck.

"Oh, we're willing to pay a high premium for the privilege," Liu said into the silence, privately hating the necessity for observing the niceties of conversation among equals just as if he were not face to face with a barbarian. "An *extremely* high premium. It is clear that the *keiretsu* needs to be underwritten; we will provide the new infusion of capital."

"I'm not interested," Nangi said, almost strangling on his hatred for this man and all he stood for.

"Please be kind enough to allow me to complete my offer before hastily setting it aside," Liu forced his lips into the configuration of a smile. Well, he thought, what can you expect from the Japanese. They do not have our long centuries of breeding; they merely appropriated from our culture that which they required in order to raise themselves up from the level of the slavering beast. But, oh, Buddha, they have not come far!

"Our offer is this," he said. "You relinquish to us one-third interest in your *keiretsu* and we will deliver to you, divided into

333

six semi-yearly payments, the sum of five hundred million dollars."

At first Nangi was not at all certain that he had heard correctly. But, staring into that long Manchu face, he had no doubts. Five hundred million dollars! His mind immediately embraced all the things made possible by such an incredible infusion of capital. My God, he thought wildly, we could leap to the top if we are careful and courageous and, yes, just a bit lucky.

This was much more money than he could ever hope to get out of Tomkin Industries should their merger go through. It was more capital than he could hope to get from any other source. He was absolutely certain Liu knew this. Too, only the Chinese could come up with enough ready capital to see the All-Asia through the immediate crisis of the bank run. That above all else must be his primary concern. If the All-Asia went he knew the entire *keiretsu* would soon follow. *Tenchi* had put him in a delicate and severely undercapitalized position. Anthony Chin's treachery might be the final straw that broke the whole business empire apart. For that Nangi would curse him and all his progeny to the end of his days.

But Nangi had to ask himself what the Chinese really wanted out of this deal. They did not easily part with such tremendous amounts of money. Profits, yes. But they could get profits in a number of different areas and with a much smaller outlay. Nangi's mind raced to find the answer to a question he knew Liu would never willingly provide him with. But there were other answers which the Chinese would have to give him and perhaps if he asked the right questions Liu would give him the solution without knowing it.

"Tell me, Mr. Liu," he said now, "what do your people propose to do with your one-third interest?"

"Do?" he said, shifting in his chaise. "I do not follow you."

The young Chinese girl had been joined by another and Nangi was hard put to discern which one was wearing the skimpier suit. A wicker basket now sat between them, a treasure chest on the sand from which one took a bottle of wine, pouring them both half tumblers of the pale gold liquid. As they lay back on their blankets he could see the soft, succulent swells of their breasts.

"It's quite simple," Nangi said without taking his eyes off the girls; they were a good deal more pleasant to look at than the man reclining beside him. "Before I even consider allowing an outside, er, firm access to the *keiretsu*—no matter the price—I need to know what it intends to do with its investment."

334

"Why, make money, of course," Liu said. "What other possible reason could we have?"

Nangi smiled thinly as he spread his hands. "You may be able to understand my caution. I have had little contact with members of . . . your firm."

"Perfectly understandable," Liu said a bit more amiably; he had begun to sense a thaw. "I would suspect your own motives if I did not detect your caution. This is, after all, not the sort of business deal one puts together every day. In some ways we are a very young country, Mr. Nangi. The world outside the Divine Kingdom is new to us. Very simply put, there are those currently in power in Peking who wish to probe the beginnings of an Oriental Alliance. They feel a business partnership—strictly business—is a sensible way in which to, er, get the ball rolling."

As if on cue, the two Chinese girls were packing up their belongings. The sun seemed very hot even here in the protection of the veranda—while they talked all the ice had melted in the pitcher of tea—and the dazzle of the water was blinding, like strips of endless gold.

"Though this is an extraordinary opportunity," Liu continued as he mopped his forehead with a handkerchief, "time is of the essence and once you leave China"—he shrugged—"I fear it will no longer obtain."

"Surely you cannot expect me to make such a monumental judgment concerning my *keiretsu* in the blink of an eye?" Nangi said, turning his head toward Liu and away from the girls, who were busy brushing sand from their sleek, oiled thighs.

"On the contrary, Mr. Nangi," Liu said, tapping a long-nailed finger against a portion of his silk suit directly over his heart, "I expect nothing. Rather it is you who must deal—and deal quickly—with the All-Asia's unfortunate difficulties. Bank runs are like wildfire here, Mr. Nangi. Once the Chinese get something into their heads it is often an astoundingly short time before matters get out of control. The Royal Hong Kong Police are well aware of this peculiarity and thus seek to thwart congregating masses. A flame in and of itself is not a particularly dangerous element. But lit at a gas station, well . . ." Liu's hands spread.

"So you may take all the time you wish, Mr. Nangi. Please do not feel any pressure from this quarter to come to a decision." He reached into an inside pocket of his jacket. "However, in a friendly effort, to, er, provide you with some assistance, I have taken the liberty of having the papers drawn up."

"I see." Nangi thought about the implications of this for quite some time.

Liu could not quite keep the smug smile off his face. "Despite some curious Western depictions we run quite a well-oiled machine."

"Yes," Nangi said, hating this man with a much more detached passion now, "I can see that."

"Oh, no, Mr. Nangi. You will pardon me for saying so, but you do not see it at all." Liu paused as the two Chinese girls, coming in off the beach, wiped their sandy feet on the lowest step of the veranda. His deep avian eyes studied the face of one—the tall one who had been on the beach when Nangi had first arrived—as if his gaze could penetrate the shadows as well as the cascade of thick hair that fell across one shoulder. In a moment they were gone, stepping silently past the two men into the interior of the villa.

"We shall have dinner soon," Liu said. "Local langoustes and garoupa, as well as braised sun bear paw, quite the delicacy here." His attitude had altered somewhat at the approach of the women and Nangi struggled with that fleeting change, trying to divine its essence.

"But, back to the topic at hand," Liu continued somewhat more briskly. "We are very well coordinated in Hong Kong; far better and more extensively than the British would dare consider." His shoulders lifted and fell. "And why not? Hong Kong is our property, after all. The true Government of China has never recognized a treaty signed under duress, when a different age caused men to act dishonorably. We tolerate the British rule because it is useful to us. I would not deny how lucrative it is for us. That would be foolish." Liu stood up abruptly. "But I'll let you in on a little secret." He reached into his inside jacket pocket and revealed a multipage document folded twice on itself. Carefully, he placed the document on the small table between them before continuing.

His eyes seemed to glow with an inner light. "The recent land boom is ours." His head bobbed. "Yes, it is true, Mr. Nangi. The recent six-year real estate spiral was instigated by us. You see, we had planned all along to make our announcement repudiating the Crown Colony's right to govern here. But first we had to bring home to them the true import of the situation within which they would one day find themselves."

Liu was smiling now with an evil triumph. "Nowadays, you see, it is we who are the master. We say 'Jump!' and the Queen jumps. The whole world saw it. Her Majesty's loss of face was enormous in hastening here and abasing herself at our feet in order to ensure her country's continued interests in this quarter of the world.

336

"But that humiliation would not have been so great, Britain's situation quite so dire without the illustration of how, with a few well-chosen words, we are able to shake the Western economy of this Colony, of how we are able to affect the finances of so many."

Liu's fingers were clasped behind his back. "Even you, Mr. Nangi, must admit that our latest five-year plan is a brilliant one; the only way to gain our goal: the eventual total control of the vast monetary flow in and out of Hong Kong."

Nangi reached for the folded document and began to read it assiduously in order to calm himself. God in heaven, he thought. If the Crown's authorities ever got wind of this they'd have a collective stroke at the very least. Surely the Colony's chief of police and internal security would be given the ax. How could this kind of manipulation have gone on right under their noses? It must have been vast! Ah, Madonna, they're all fools here! My own people were totally foxed. And I was convinced they were well informed. Why should the officials here be any different?

But debating unanswered questions was a waste of time and he quickly turned his mind to other matters. First and foremost, the contract. On initial reading it appeared to be hardnosed but essentially fair. There were no hidden strings, no floating clauses that Liu had not brought up.

Nangi raised his head for a moment, coming up for air. "I see here on page three that the first inflow of capital doesn't commence until ninety days after the signing of this contract."

Liu nodded, delighted they had gotten this far. "That is correct. There are a number of, er, realistic entanglements at gathering and transshipping that large an amount of money."

"Gold."

"If that is your wish. It will be handled via the Sun Wa Trading Company."

"But surely your . . . ah . . . firm is of a sufficient size to begin payment on signing."

Now Liu's long face looked pained. His hands, coming around from behind his back, were like prehensile hooks. "Regrettably, accelerating the timetable of payments is impossible. My firm has a number of prior commitments that it must see to concluding first. There just isn't enough capital for another ninety days or so."

Nangi sat up, grasping the white jade dragon head of his walking stick. Now we come to the nub of it all, he thought. I must outmaneuver him here or not at all. "Mr. Liu, as you yourself have said, my situation vis-à-vis the All-Asia Bank is critical. If I am forced to wait three months for your money, I will lose that

337

part of my *keiretsu*. That would not be in either of our interests."
And Nangi thought desperately, How I wish we were already one
with the American company so that I could call down their capital.
But he saw the impossibility of the situation. Even had Sato's
kobun merged with Sphynx he did not believe that the company
could have provided enough money within the deadline period.
Maddeningly, Liu was right. He had to stave off the run before
it became a stampede. Otherwise no amount of infused capital
would save the bank.

Liu said nothing, tapped his fingertips together to an odd internal rhythm.

"Time is of the essence for me as well as for you," Nangi said,
carefully feeding emotion into his voice. "If I decide to sign—
and as you have said that must be before I leave Hong Kong—
then there must be a rider that specifies delivery of enough capital
to cover the anticipated run and the short-term obligations—say
the next six months—the bank is required to pay." Nangi, concealing all emotion from his face and voice, took a mental deep
breath. It was sink or swim now, he knew. "Thirty-five million
dollars, U.S., payable no later than twelve hours after signing."

Liu was silent for a moment. Beneath the sounds of the quiet
surf they could hear the small, comforting clinks as the women
worked in the kitchen. Liu required of all his women that they be
able to cook, and cook well. He tapped the side of a nail against
his pursed lips.

"You drive a hard bargain. That is a not inconsiderable sum."

"You ought to know," Nangi said, gambling. "You're the one
who got me into this."

Liu managed a smile. Nangi took that as a sign that the Chinese
could not contain his pride and he thought, I'm leading him in
the right direction.

"Perhaps, after all, something of the sort could be arranged."
Liu nodded as if in final decision. "Yes. I believe that we might
be able to deduct that much from the first of the payments to the
keiretsu."

Oh, no, you don't, Nangi thought. "The thirty-five million is
over and above the purchase price, totally independent and non-
recoverable. I don't want the bank's financial operations tied to
the *keiretsu* in any way. Ultimately that would hamper our profit
potential here, as well you know."

Nangi's heart thudded wildly as Liu considered the proposition.
His hooded eyes revealed nothing. Nangi knew that this was his
chance: an immediate bailout, an infusion of desperately needed
capital in exchange for a third interest in the *keiretsu*. Troublesome

338

but not crucial. Between them, he and Sato could veto anything the Communists wanted that they did not. Besides, working with and not against the Communists in their own country would bring its own rewards.

Liu, for his part, was taking somewhat longer than Nangi judged he needed to make the decision. He was as still as a statue, his parchmentlike skin glowing in the light. At length he stirred, as a constrictor will when it has roused itself from a long somnolence and is preparing itself to feed again.

"It can be done," Liu said. "In that event, however, we would require that you sign over to us a somewhat larger portion of your *keiretsu*. Fifty-one percent."

Nangi showed none of the terror that gripped his heart in that terrible frozen moment. Fifty-one percent! Jesus, Joseph, and Mary, he thought. Sato and I will lose control of our own company!

"I should not be making this offer at all, you know." Liu's voice had turned plummy. "My government does not easily cast that much money on the, er, international waters." He leaned forward. "But I see that you are much like your company and that pleases me. Together we can make a fortune here and in your country." He stood up. "It has been a long day for us both. I trust you are as famished as I am."

He smiled down at Nangi. "This offer is one of a kind. I would caution you about that. Six P.M. tomorrow is the deadline. And that is absolute." He lifted a hand, the perfect host. "And now to the food."

During dinner Nangi spent more time watching Liu's woman than he did his host. Liu took this as a good sign. It signified to him that Nangi was a first-class lecher and he giggled to himself, made secure.

"Let's go inside."

She shook her head, her long dark hair straying across his cheek and shoulder. "I want to be out here. We're elementals now. It's where we belong."

Nicholas felt her soft and yielding against him; his mind was numb with disbelief. She was someone else's wife. And that someone else was his friend. They had shared drunkenness, secrets; they had sworn to be bound together. That part of his mind—the rational part—quailed as her naked flesh slid over him. And what of Justine? Wasn't there a matter of honor where she was concerned? He knew that his love for her was undiminished, untouched by this moment and what it held. An internal shudder wracked his soul. He should stop this, rise up and walk away into

339

the sanctuary of Sato's house. But he did nothing of the kind. Justine was a faraway flame, bending in the windstorm of his current emotions. He breathed a prayer to her even as he drew this creature more tightly to him.

He could not help himself. His body yearned for Akiko as if she were food, drink, oxygen to fill his lungs. He could no more disentangle himself from her than he could still his pulse.

Akiko's yellow and green kimono lay behind her buttocks in hills and valleys of its own, the folds holding deep shadows as if they were secrets. Both of them were enfolded within his kimono—Sato's kimono.

Her flesh was hot and moist. Her nails clawed at him, her small white teeth bit at his hard flesh as if that, too, were a sexual act. Neither of them wanted it ever to end and so their feverishness was tempered with an almost painful holding back.

Their restraint caused Akiko to whimper and moan. He felt her smaller body trembling uncontrollably against him; when his hand first made contact with the already soaking mount of her sex, her hips convulsed inward again and again, her eyes closed, and she gripped him until her fingers went white.

Around them the mist seemed to congeal and darken. The sky could no longer be seen and the air had grown heavy and dank as if with the incipience of a storm. Abruptly, thunder rumbled brokenly, and early morning seemed to turn into dusk.

Akiko was arched against him, trembling, her thighs open, her hands stroking lovingly his back and buttocks. Her tongue licked the hollow at the side of his neck.

Then an animal cry broke from her and she moaned, "I must . . . I must . . ." Twisting herself around until her hot mouth engulfed him, inching down him until her lips enclosed the very root. He wanted to do the same to her, but even with pinpoints of ecstasy sweeping through her she had the presence of mind to deflect him, keeping the insides of her thighs away from his eyes. She could not afford to let him see what lay there, grinning with power. For that would end it all. Yukio would be gone forever and nothing either of them could do would bring her back again. He would know . . . and he would try to destroy her.

So she sucked more heavily on him, reaching up to enclose the totality of his sex, using every technique she had learned to bring him pleasure. He gave up his grip on her, surrendering.

But, oh, how she longed to feel his lips and tongue on her as she was on him. In her mind's eye she imagined it and shivered. Then she felt his fingers returning to the core of her and she sighed inwardly, feeling her sex like the heavy pulse of a second heart.

It began to rain as she reluctantly let him go. Immediately he moved atop her, his wet sex grazing her thigh and belly as he did so. Gently she took hold of him, guiding him. His mouth came down over one dark nipple, then another, back and forth. She could not slow her breathing.

Thunder cracked overhead, approaching, and the rain picked up. There was virtually no wind and the rain came almost straight down, striking the smooth pebbles all around them in a muted roar. They could see nothing clearly but themselves.

Akiko rubbed him against her wet opening with the delicacy of a courtesan. She begged him not to tease her, yet her hands continued to tease them both, increasing the tension and the pleasure until it became unbearable for them.

With a burst of exhaled breath Nicholas tore himself from her gentle grasp and slowly moved into her. Akiko gasped and, shaking uncontrollably, arced herself up against him. She rubbed her wet flesh against his, reveling in the scrub of his hair against her body.

He hilted her and she felt connected to the universe. She felt all weight leave her heart, all hate melt like snow in the burgeoning heat of the first spring day, all blackness disappear from her sight.

She floated in the rain and the thunder like a slender reed on the riverside. Birds flew, calling, above her, the wind rippled all about her, the rain struck her and she bent willingly before its force. Water rushed by beneath her and small burrowing insects tickled her roots. She was part of the river, the forest, the sea shore, the depths of the world.

She plummeted and rose at the same time, night became day, then reversed itself. The cosmic clock beat in her ear, turning seconds into centuries, minutes into eons. Her breathing was the growth of bedrock, the metamorphosis of carbon into diamond, of fossil detritus into fuel.

She sighed and the seasons changed, she shuddered and new islands sprang into being across the bosom of the Pacific. She convulsed, crying out wildly as he shot and shot into her, as their loins ground together, as orgasm followed orgasm, and the world winked out in the blink of an eye.

The Blue Monster had changed cars three times on his way up north. The first time had been in Miami when Route 1 became I95. The second time had been in Savannah when the bastard and Alix Logan stopped to get a bite to eat. The third time had been just outside Beaufort, South Carolina. The Phonix cipher machine was on a locking slide mount and was easy to move from vehicle to vehicle. Right now the Blue Monster would have felt naked without it.

The bastard drove like a sonuvabitch and the Blue Monster had to be doubly careful because this was strictly solo and there was absolutely no margin for error. If he lost them now it was all over for him; he knew that neither he nor anyone else would be able to find them quickly again.

He bided his time. He smoked unfiltered Camels and was patient, allowing the harsh tobacco bite to keep him awake. He took no pills.

The Blue Monster was far better than Croaker had anticipated and he arrived outside the hotel four-and-a-half minutes after Croaker and Alix Logan had disappeared inside the stone and glass lobby. It was an eastern chain hotel just outside Raleigh with an enormous tri-level shopping arcade across the six-lane highway off which its drive curled in a macadamed crescent.

Jesse James, the Blue Monster, pulled his cream-colored Aries K car off Highway 70.

He had spotted what he suspected was their car—a late-model maroon Ford four-door—and had made the turn from the middle lane, causing both voiced ire and the screeching of brakes and horns from those vehicles to the left of him as he slid across their bows, speeding toward the egress.

He lofted a rigid middle finger in their direction. After the incident five miles back he had no patience for any of these southern North Carolina hicks. The goddamned pimply kid in the dusty pickup with the straw cowboy hat and denim jacket, James thought as he rolled up into the parking lot. Probably wasn't even seventeen and sure as shit didn't know how to drive.

James spat out his open window. The kid was how he had come to lose the maroon Ford. Imagine. To come all this way on that bastard's tail only to lose him at a goddamned stoplight because a candy-assed kid wouldn't pull over to let me pass. James still seethed inside at the thought.

Then his keen eye had picked out the maroon Ford sitting in the hotel's parking lot and he had made his move. He pulled into a space three cars down from the Ford and ambled out, stretching his legs. No point in hurrying now, he told himself pragmatically. Either this was their vehicle or he had lost them for sure.

His pulse rose as he saw the license plates. Florida. He came and stood next to the car, put the flat of his hand on the hood. Still warm. It was them all right.

He knelt down as if tying a shoelace and wiped the accumulation of mud that wily bastard had smeared across the plates, making a note of the letter-number combination. Then he rose and went up the stepped concrete path toward the hotel's side entrance.

The young lieutenant's name was Russilov, and the more Protorov saw of him the better he liked him. The man had initiative. The problem with most of the soldiers coming up through the strictly controlled Soviet system, Protorov thought, was that they lacked just that. Initiative.

They were all right if you gave them a blueprint. They'd follow it down to the letter or die trying. You couldn't fault that kind of dedication. Unless you were in Viktor Protorov's line of work. Then that kind of robotic thinking could blow a network, destroy a potential defector coming over from the other side, or expose the mouse in someone else's house. Protorov had too many mice in other people's houses to be satisfied with the grade of soldier that would normally be assigned to him. Bureaucrats were, of course, out altogether.

It galled him that he had to take this raw and basically unthinking talent and make it over. Beneath his skillful hands the clay of Mother Russia was reformed into individuals useful to the Ninth Directorate.

To that end he was headmaster of a school in the Urals. It was much smaller than the one the KGB itself ran—the one filled with American streets, American money, milk shakes and hot dogs, talk of the Yankees and the Dodgers, the Giants and the Dallas Cowboys. That was fairytale stuff and, besides, it had proven to be potentially dangerous. Too many Russian sleepers assimilated into American life via that school had failed to respond to their wakeup call. Life in the West presented a siren call apparently too seductive to resist for all but the most hardened personality.

Protorov preferred to keep the Soviet ethos very much alive at his academy while he expanded the minds of his pupils, broadened their outlook. In short, taught them to think independently.

The old bureaucrats in the Kremlin, had they known what he was up to, would no doubt have closed him down summarily. But the truth was they were afraid of the Ninth Directorate and afraid, especially, of Viktor Protorov. Besides, he brought them too many third world victories. It was too convenient for them to swell upon his most recent successes in Argentina, snaring England into an idiotic and draining war; and in El Salvador, egging the hawkish American administration on into what could easily become another Vietnam. They were not adept at examining their fears, anyway.

Pyotr Alexandrovitch Russilov was a graduate from Protorov's Ural academy. But he was special in many ways. For one, he had

343

graduated at the top of his class. For another, he had adapted superbly to the field. Protorov had found through bitter experience that academic life had little in common with the awesome pressures at work in the field. Many graduates did not make the adjustment and were "retired" to the Ninth's bureaucratic section, where they never again came into direct contact with Protorov.

But *Gospadin* Russilov was different in another way. He was an orphan. Early on the State—or, more properly, Protorov—had taken him over. He was a reclamation project of the first rank.

Because Protorov was married to his job, and also perhaps because sex had never meant that much to him, there had only been one woman in his life. She was someone he would have preferred to forget but could not. Alena was the wife of a Jewish dissident. After Protorov, then head of the First Directorate, had sent Alena's husband off to a gulag, he took her to bed. It had been far more pleasurable for him than he had ever imagined.

Whether it was because of the peculiar circumstances surrounding the incident or whether it was something within Alena herself Protorov could not say. He thought of himself as a basically dispassionate man, able to see clearly and objectively all situations. Yet he had never been able to fathom this one. It remained like a great ice floe, hidden beneath arctic waters, mocking him with its opacity.

But like it or not, Alena was all he had, in reality, and then, after he had her sent down in Lubyanka, in his memory. Until Russilov. Without quite knowing how it had happened Protorov had come to look upon his protégé as family. Son was not too strong a word to use. When Protorov retired from the Ninth, which would not be very long now, he knew that Russilov would run it well.

Now that he had received the signal from Colonel Mironenko that the KGB-GRU summit was scheduled for a week away, his time at the Ninth was coming to an end. But he had to have penetrated *Tenchi* by then. Tengu, his second agent inside the Tenshin Shoden Katori *ryu*, had been mysteriously murdered as he was escaping with the prize that Protorov had been seeking since he had received the information that that particular ninja *ryu* was safeguarding *Tenchi*'s written records. It was a frustrating setback, Protorov thought now. But not a fatal one by any means.

"Sir?"

Protorov looked up, his train of thought disturbed. "Yes, Lieutenant Russilov." He liked the way the young man addressed him as "Sir" and not "Comrade." Rank was important in the Ninth

344

Directorate and, unlike the hypocrisy running rampant in the Kremlin, Protorov made no bones about it.

Russilov entered the soundproofed chamber through the vault-like door. He held a sheaf of computer printouts in his hands. "I believe Sakhov IV has given us a clue after all."

Immediately Protorov cleared his desk of paper, stacking files. Russilov set the sheaf down in the open space. It was open to the fourth page. Both men stared hard at the readout broadcast from the tracking satellite's onboard computer. It showed a gridform geographical tableau approximately 150 by 200 kilometers. The land-sea area was quite familiar to the Russians. It was the section of sea between the northerly end of Hokkaido and the most southerly of the Kuriles, Kunashir. Part of that area was Japanese territory; part was a Soviet possession.

The young lieutenant's finger stabbed out. "You see here, sir"—the pad of the finger roamed across the Nemuro Straits—"there is nothing. Absolutely nothing out of the ordinary.

"Now"—he reached up and flipped to the next page—"just here." His finger hovered over one small point in the Straits.

"What is it?" Protorov asked, knowing quite well what it was. He did not want to deprive Russilov of the fruits of his victory. That would have been unfair.

"An emanation of heat," Russilov said. Protorov looked up at him for a moment. He had to give the young man credit. There was no triumph in his voice, though surely he must be feeling it. "Very strong."

"Volcanic action," Protorov offered. It was the most plausible explanation.

"Oh, this is much too localized for that. Besides, the known northerly fault is here." His finger moved off to the southeast.

"I see." Protorov sat back.

"What is it, then?"

"*Tenchi.*"

Oh yes, Protorov thought. That's precisely what it was. Because they knew from reliable sources that *Tenchi* was some form of monumental industrial or resource project. What Protorov and his unit had been searching for all this time was some discrepancy. Now Protorov felt it was here. Then, as he glanced down at the readout, something else caught his eye. He did some rapid mental calculations, then mulled it over for a time before saying anything.

"Lieutenant," he said meditatively, "this intense heat activity. Where would you place it, exactly?"

"That's difficult to say, sir." Russilov bent over the readout.

"As you know, this comes from a long way up. And, of course, our technicians have had to piece it together to get the whole."

"Nevertheless," Protorov pursued, "I want your best guess."

Russilov took his time, producing a jeweler's loupe with which he routinely scanned the readout. At length he stood up, dropping the magnifier into his cupped palm.

"If I were put to it, sir," he began, "I would have to say that part of the activity is coming from Japanese territory."

Protorov's pulse picked up a beat. "And the other part?"

"The other part, it seems to me, is coming from Russian sovereign territory."

Alix Logan was in the shower. Croaker sat in an easy chair in the large, neatly furnished room. He was sipping a bourbon and water that room service had brought up.

He was tired and he let his head fall back against the chair, closing his eyes. He still felt the slight motion vertigo from having been in the car eighteen straight hours. He would have preferred to fly out of Key West but that would have been suicidal, like putting a "Come Follow Me" sign on their backs.

No, all things considered, a car had been best. At the least it afforded them the option of changing destinations any time they pleased.

Dimly he heard the shower running. He thought again of what it had felt like to have Alix Logan sitting beside him for all that uninterrupted time. The sun-streaked hair falling now and again on his shoulder, those piercing green eyes, the model's lithe, taut-fleshed body, the skin tanned and smooth as cream.

And that led him to thoughts of Angela Didion, the other model and Alix Logan's best friend. But none of the fame Angela Didion had amassed, none of the myriad rumors about her mattered a damn at the moment Croaker had entered her apartment and found her sprawled across her bed, naked save for a thin gold chain around her waist, and very dead.

She was no beauty queen then, no superbly madeup sex goddess, the vision of every man's fantasy. Stripped so harshly of life she was merely a young girl, pathetic in her ultimate vulnerability. And she had moved Croaker more then than she ever had in life.

He remembered that moment well. How he had wanted more than anything else to wave some magic wand and resurrect her. Not for himself. Just for her. In death she was only a human being and therefore far more than she ever had been as a cover girl for

346

Vogue and *Cosmopolitan*, where she had been drenched in two-dimensional unreality.

In one sense that seemed a very little thing to set him on this long, torturous quest. A tiny thing over which to lose one's own life. But when one thought of it another way, it was the only truly honorable thing to do. And Lew Croaker had learned about the importance of honor from his best friend, Nicholas Linnear.

Now Alix opened the door to the steamy bathroom and emerged with a thick towel wrapped around her, another, smaller one wrapped as a turban around her hair.

Croaker's eyes snapped open and for a moment he saw not her but Angela Didion and he found renewed determination not to let Alix Logan die, which she surely would if the Blue Monster ever caught wind of their whereabouts.

"You're next," she said, giving him that direct, disconcerting look that seemed to penetrate his skull. "You look like death warmed over."

Croaker grunted and finished off his drink. "Funny. I feel worse than that."

She sat down on one of the double beds, her hands in her lap. "Why are you doing this? That's what I'd like to know. They'll kill you if they catch you. You know that, don't you."

"It's because of Angela."

"You didn't even know her," Alix said. "You were in love with that face just like everyone else."

"You don't get it at all," he said, shifting in his seat.

"And I never will," she said archly, "unless you explain it to me."

"She died on my turf." He swirled the ice around the empty glass, staring at the cubes but looking at nothing at all. "Someone did her in; I want to find out who. Because she was a person just like anyone else. She deserved that much, at least."

Alix gave a short laugh. "I'm in a better position to know what she deserved." She paused for a moment as if gathering herself. "She was a bitch, Lew. She was mean, vindictive, insanely jealous, and absolutely venal."

Croaker looked up at her. "None of that matters. To me she was no better or worse than anyone else."

Alix poured herself a drink from the bottle of Old Grand-Dad. "You should've spent some time with her," she said, taking a swallow neat. "A couple've days, that's all it would've taken."

Croaker took the glass out of her hand, finished what she had in there. "Were you in love with her?"

"That's none of your goddamned business!" she flared at him.

Her hands clenched into whitened fists and her lips compressed into a thin unattractive line. Then her face began to break apart a small piece at a time.

"Just because you saved my life, what makes you think you can expect answers like that out of me?" By then she was weeping, her sun-baked shoulders heaving, her hands covering her face.

Croaker watched her for a time, suppressing the urge to reach out for her and comfort her; he knew her well enough now to know she would pull back from such a gesture.

After a while her hands came down and she wiped at her eyes. She seemed a great deal calmer. "The truth is," she said softly, "Angela was in love with me." She ran long fingers through her wet hair after unwinding the towel. She began to rub it through her hair. "I could never remember my mother, and Angela was strong. I guess there was a lot of the male in her. Not that she was masculine. It wasn't that at all. I'm talking about something inside. Her personality or whatever.

"She caught me. I honestly don't know how else to put it. I knew she was a bitch from working with her. And I knew she was into drugs: opium and coke. Nice combo, huh? But I thought . . . Oh, I don't know what I thought. I suppose I blinded myself to all those things because I needed a mother; someone to show me the ropes and protect me."

Alix stopped fussing with her hair, sat again with her hands in her lap, so that she appeared very young, almost a little girl, innocent, made of spun pink candy. "We fought all the time. In many ways she made my life hell."

"You could have walked out," Croaker pointed out.

But Alix was already shaking her head. "Like I said, you didn't know Angela. What she wanted, she kept until she was tired of it. She would have ruined me professionally if I'd tried to leave. She could have done it easily; she was quite the expert at it. I saw her do it once to a young model coming up who said the wrong thing to her one day. Angela made one phone call and no one in the business even spoke that girl's name again. Angela had the power of a pharaoh."

Her head came down so far that Croaker could see the soft bit of light down at the nape of her neck. "But the truth is, I didn't have the strength to leave her. She . . . frightened me and, oddly I suppose, within the power of her manipulation I felt more secure than I had outside on my own in the world."

There was a silence that stretched itself, filling the room with an odd kind of chill.

"Then what happened?" Croaker prompted.

"Then everything changed," Alix said, her voice so soft Croaker had to lean forward to hear her properly. "Angela met Raphael Tomkin."

Jesse James had picked up the bastard's name, Tex Bristol, from the harbormaster at the Key West marina when the man and several others who had been on the dock at the time had noticed his boat leaving its slip just after Alix Logan's had.

James did not know who the bastard really was, but he promised himself he would soon find out. He had asked for Bristol by name at the front desk, figuring the bastard wouldn't see any reason to change the alias at this stage, but he had been wrong. He had been told that no Bristol with the first name of Tex or with any other first name had registered that day.

The Blue Monster had launched into explanation C, going the full route, showing a badge. He was a private detective, a case of adultery, here are the descriptions of the pair, nothing to get het up about, just serving divorce papers, et cetera. He got their room number. One room. Very cosy, James thought. What does this bastard have that I don't? He took the elevator up.

The doors opened and Jesse James emerged onto the third floor of the hotel.

Croaker had just come out of the shower. He felt thirty years better. Toweling himself dry, he put on the lightweight slacks, dark blue T-shirt with "KEY WEST IS BEST" stenciled in green across the chest, and his tattered topsiders that he had brought with him into the bathroom.

Alix wore a pair of cutoff jeans and a pink cap-sleeve silk shirt. Her bare toes curled on the bedspread. She was sitting up, her back against a pair of pillows, reading a paperback book she had picked up at the place along the highway where they had stopped for lunch.

"This thing's as bad as the food we had this afternoon," she said, throwing the book away from her. "Vampire's in the bayous. Who's kidding who?"

That was when the door to the hall burst open with a crack like a rifle shot.

Sato found his guest in the garden. In the rain.

"My dear friend," he called from the dry sanctuary of his study, "you'll catch your death of cold out there."

Nicholas did not answer at once. His shoulders were slumped as he sat on the stone seat, facing the swaying branches of the

349

boxwood. There was a fat gray plover strutting impatiently back and forth along a dry patch near the wide bole. Every so often it cocked its head upward, its glaring eye seeming to curse the foul elements.

As for Nicholas, he barely noticed the wetness. The kimono was soaked through and there was not a part of him that was dry. It did not matter. He knew now that Akiko and Yukio were two separate entities.

Deceit could only be taken so far. A face could lie, for instance, whispered words, even a knowing glance. But a body was different. Response to an intimate touch, the softening, the opening, all these were unique. They could not be counterfeited.

An unutterable sadness filled him at the thought that he had lost her all over again. Of course it had been an impossibility that she should be alive. Logic dictated that she had died by Saigō's hand just as he had described it to Nicholas, savoring each word's effect on his hated cousin.

Yet Nicholas, for the first time in his life perhaps, had not heeded logic. He had thrown a lifetime of training and understanding out for the possibility of one desperate hope. It was laughable and sad at the same time.

And he despised himself for the enjoyment he took from the adulterous joining. Though Akiko was not Yukio, still, he had made love to her with more than his body. Who she was and why she looked like his lost love became secondary to the knowledge that his heart was open to her. If she were not Yukio, could he love her anyway? By what magic was that possible? Or had some vital piece of Yukio's somehow lodged in Akiko's soul? In any case, he felt tainted, an outcast from himself. His misdeed had lost him his centricity, and without that he was powerless in a world gone mad.

"Linnear-san." He could hear Sato's voice raised above the racket of downpour. Then the older man was beside him, draping a clear plastic wrap across his shoulders. "Contemplation must conform to the elements which it honors," he said softly. "I will leave you alone."

"No, Sato-san. Please stay." Abruptly, Nicholas did not want to be alone. He already felt too isolated, bereft almost. All his youthful dreams were gone. In the space of a thunderclap, wild hope had died. But what, he thought, is a human being without hope.

"This garden is most calming at all times of the day." Sato moved beside him. He opened his mouth to continue, closed it as a crack of thunder rolled across the sky. "I've often thought that

350

it is the shouting of the gods," he said. "Thunder. I was awakened early this morning by the storm. I drowsed, listening to its cries. Almost human, don't you think?"

"Very human, indeed," Nicholas said. I must confess, he thought. I must return harmony to my spirit. "Sato-san—"

"The Chinese taught our forefathers geomancy," Sato said, forestalling Nicholas, "so that we might forever remain in harmony with the forces of nature. We are not tigers, though we may strive to be. There is a perfection in that lesser state to which we human beings can only aspire."

His eyes were liquid and soft as he looked down at Nicholas. And, quite startlingly, he put his hand on Nicholas' shoulder. "Won't you come inside now," he said, "and allow me to brew you tea?"

Watching Russilov's ramrod-straight back disappear out the steel door, Protorov thought about how, after struggling for so many years to devote himself to the service of ideology, his life had taken on a personal cast. Not creating a family for himself he certainly saw as proof of his overriding dedication to the eventual worldwide triumph of Soviet ideals.

But now he had Russilov. How had that happened? His intense feeling for the young man caused him to feel vulnerable. And being vulnerable made him feel afraid.

Viktor Protorov had not been afraid for eight years. Not since the death of his older—and only—brother. At that time Protorov was head of the First Directorate, responsible for Russian internal security. Creating an unassailable kingdom for himself within the Ninth Directorate, a bastion from which to strike outward at the right time, to lead the motherland onward to global victory, was just dawning on him.

In the winter of that year—a particularly bitter one, filled with day after day of heavy snow—he had many missions running. All were important. In those days he lacked the internal clout to request more men for his understaffed directorate. He had learned to make do. But because of the acute manpower shortage and the inclemency of the weather he was forced to physically oversee more missions than he should have.

Consequently he had been outside Moscow, far to the north, when they had brought in Minck. Protorov had known of his presence inside Russia and had wanted him, badly. A fluke had landed him early, and he was inside Lubyanka when Protorov's brother, of junior rank—a lieutenant—though he was three years older, learned of his presence.

Protorov had always done better than Lev, academically and socially. Protorov knew how to speak to people, knew how to take exams, knew in his own mind what he wanted to be. Lev was always the dreamer, unsure of which fork to take in a road, in which direction to turn his life. He had always been afraid of making a mistake.

He had made a mistake that dark, snowfilled afternoon. Even while notification of Minck's capture was being relayed to Protorov by the despicably unreliable wire system, Lev went into Lubyanka to interrogate the spy himself. He wanted, no doubt, to prove to his younger brother that there was something he could do as well—and on his own.

He failed. Somehow Minck was able to overpower him and, using him as hostage, break free. Then he killed Lev, slaughtered him in the snow like a butcher.

They left him there in the storm, terrified to touch him before Protorov arrived. There was little blood for him to see when, hours later, he returned to Moscow; the cold had congealed it, cauterizing the wound. Still there was a gaping hole in Lev's left temple where the bullet had torn through the skull. Protorov did not want to look at the damage inflicted on the back of the head, knowing that the devastation would be far worse at the egress point. Quite deliberately he turned Lev's body over and stared at the carnage. Snowflakes caught on his lids making vision difficult. Still he persevered even as he ordered the manhunt for Minck and his fellow escapee, Tanya Vladimova.

Perhaps it was then that Protorov thought for the first time that there was too much pain to be borne in having a family. Perhaps it was at that moment that he decided not to have one of his own. For the sense of utter isolation, of a terrible vulnerability, was overwhelming. He found himself hating the American named Minck far more than he had ever thought he could hate another human being.

Six months later he had awakened an important sleeper in order to kill Minck's wife, sleeping alone and vulnerable in their bed in rural Maryland. One shot from a pistol Protorov—and Minck—knew well at close range through the left temple.

Still it had not been enough. So the war went on. And on.

Protorov sighed now, alone in his inner sanctum. He pushed his glasses up onto the dome of his forehead, scrubbed at his face with a palm. He found that he had been sweating. Though Tengu, his second agent within the Tenshin Shoden Katori *ryu*, had been killed, his backup—the last agent Protorov had in that field—was making progress.

At that moment, the compact cipher machine began to buzz, preparatory to decoding an Alpha-three. His satellite was about to whisper in his ear once again.

Croaker grabbed Alix's slim wrist and jerked hard, hearing her short, high scream of surprise and pain as he used his strength to roll her across to the far side of the bed and out of harm's way.

At the same time, his hand snaked beneath the bed to where the gun lay and, without aiming fully, shot out the lamplight in the room.

Now only the oblong of illumination filtering in through the open doorway to the hall pushed back the darkness. And in its midst, the shadow rushed into the room.

He's a goddamned bull, Croaker thought, as he pushed Alix's inquisitive head down to the carpeting and rose at the instant he felt the shadow at its closest.

He lifted his arm, brought the muzzle of the pistol down in a vicious slash across the shadow's cheekbone, felt the contact with pleasure, the split of skin, flesh, and the pressured scrape against bone.

But despite the blow, the shadow's momentum was enough to keep him coming on. And such was his strength that he slammed full tilt into Croaker, knocking the pistol from his grip. It skidded across the floor in the darkness, lost.

Oh, Christ, Croaker thought, we're in for it now. He felt a heavy blow land on his shoulder, twisting him, and blindly he kicked upward, missing once, his knee connecting with the shadow's thigh bone, adjusting his aim accordingly and plowing into the shadow's groin.

He heard the whoosh of air and a groan, and the weight and pressure on him eased sufficiently for him to squirm out from under.

"Come on!" he yelled at Alix, fumbling for her hand and half dragging her from the room, down the blindingly lit hallway to the exit door and the stairs.

Down the metal and concrete staircase they ran until at last they burst out into the soft-skinned night. The car would have been the best bet, but Croaker had left the keys back in the room.

He took a quick look around. There were few people about except at the entrance of the hotel where locals were drawing up as they went into the disco in the lobby, one of the only nightspots in the area. Croaker took them that way though they were certainly not dressed for the occasion. People in dinner dress watched their approach with more amusement than alarm. But he saw it was

353

going to be no go right away. They stood out like beggars at a masked ball, so he veered them away, rushing down the sloped scimitar drive toward Highway 70, dodging the slowly approaching line of cars, pushing Alix out of the illumination of the headlights.

He did not turn his head to see if the Blue Monster was after them; he assumed the worst. If he had been dogged enough—and, Croaker had to admit to himself, smart enough—to follow them all the way from Key West, he wouldn't be so stupid as to lose them now.

He rushed them across the six-lane highway on the amber with the traffic already beginning to pile up and move, jockeying for position for turns.

"Christ!" Alix breathed. "Where are we going?"

Croaker made no reply. He thought it wiser to let her believe that he knew what he was doing. Ahead of them loomed the darkened mass of the shopping mall, all angles and black shadows, a silent, deserted city in the heart of the darkness.

Croaker took them down an exit ramp and they were plunged into the wide, spotless avenues of the arcades. Their footfalls made no sound on the stone flooring and Croaker was grateful at least that he had his topsiders on. But Alix was barefoot and though from an aural point of view that was good, still with all the running they were doing he was fearful of sharp objects she might inadvertently step on. Well, he thought, there's no help for it now. We have to go on.

Deep inside the mall he stopped them. Though they were both in reasonably good shape, a breather was nevertheless called for. Alix's chest heaved with exertion and fear. She stared around her, wide-eyed. Shoe stores, clothing boutiques, a local Sears, endless rows of glass-paneled windows featuring a bewildering variety of wares crouched on either side of them, closed and unhelpful.

"What are we go—"

Croaker put his palm quickly over her mouth and said in her ear, "No, talking. The sound will carry and bring him to us like a beacon. Okay?" She nodded her head vigorously and he took his hand away.

He wiped the sweat from his face with his shirtsleeve, straining his ears for some semblance of sound, but he heard nothing above the soft susurrus of the faraway traffic on Highway 70.

Dim light filtered across their shoulders in thick swatches from the interiors of the shops along the arcade. But patches of deep shadow remained all about them like impenetrable stands of trees. They were in a forest of metal and glass.

354

Alix grabbed his shoulder and leaned her lips against his ear. "What are we waiting here for?" she whispered. "Let's go out of here before he finds us."

Croaker debated with himself whether to tell her the truth. He knew it would probably be better to keep her in the dark as long as possible. But on the other hand she was in this as deeply as he was and it was unfair to keep her ignorant about such a thing. Besides, if she did not know, she might do something stupid at the last minute and screw things up.

He put his mouth to her ear and said softly, "I've got news for you. Your former keeper's followed us this far, he's not gonna stop now. Even assuming we could find a car and I could boost it, we wouldn't lose him. Not now."

Her large clear eyes stared into his for the moment it took her to put it together. "No!" she said. "There's been one killing already."

"Yeah," Croaker sighed, "and there'll be a lot more unless he's stopped." He looked at her. "It has to be done, Alix. You know it does."

After a time her eyes slid away from him. Her cheeks were wet and he heard her whisper, "I wish now he'd never saved me. I wish I'd drowned that day in Key West."

"You don't mean that," he said automatically.

"The hell I don't!" she flared, her eyes bright. "What kind of life is this I'm living? Can you tell me th—"

Croaker shoved her hard, sending her spinning flat on her back across the cool stone flooring as the whine turned into the *spang!* of a ricochet. He saw the place where the bullet had gouged out chips of stone and dived after her, pulling her up onto her knees, then to her feet, dragging her after him down the arcade, turning right, then right again, pushing her into a darkened doorway where they both crouched. Alix was sweating and shivering all at once.

Croaker looked both ways before he reached again for her hand. But Alix was shaking her head. "No," she said, "I can't go on. It's useless. Like you said, wherever we run, he'll find us."

"Get up!" he said fiercely.

She shook her head again, her spun-gold hair obscuring her face. "It's no good. I haven't got the strength."

"Well, for the love of God find some!" he hissed at her, bending over and hauling her to her feet.

"I'm tired, Lew." Her eyes were hooded. "I just want to sleep."

He saw the lassitude flooding her body and wondered if this was how she had felt in the moments before she had hurled her body into the turquoise ocean that day aboard her boat.

355

He grabbed her cheeks in the pincer of his thumb and massed fingers. "Listen, you," he said, his face close to hers, "you'll sleep when I tell you to and not a minute before.."

"Christ!" she cried, teary-eyed, "you're a goddamned knight without a lady. Can't you see that I just don't care anymore?"

"But I do!" He jerked at her. "Now come on!" He skidded them to the left as another bullet whined into the stone just behind them and to the right.

"What's the use," she said as they ran. "He's got the gun."

"Yeah, I noticed that."

"I hate guns," she said.

And Croaker had to laugh. "Yeah," he said. "Me, too. Especially when I don't have one." But the fact was that she was right. The Blue Monster had an edge Croaker could not possibly overcome. A gun against nothing, not a particularly fair fight. But then nothing much was fair in life anyway.

As he ran he recalled Nicholas telling him that he had never used a gun. Yet Croaker knew his friend to be one of the most dangerous men on earth. What, then, was his secret? When he had asked Nicholas that question he had merely smiled enigmatically and said, "There are ways."

Now what the hell did he mean by that? Croaker wondered. I sure could use one of those secrets now. As the third shot rang out, barely missing him, he berated himself, Think! Use the brain your old man bequeathed you!

There was nothing around them but stone, metal, and glass. What could he...Ah! He had it! There was no time to think of whether or not it was a good idea; it was the only one he had and the Blue Monster was right behind them, closing in for the kill.

He ducked them around a corner, dropped Alix's hand, and sprinted ahead. Just around another right-angle turn, he slid to a stop and pulled his shirt over his head. Wrapping it around his left hand, he shot the swathed fist forward into a sheet of glass.

Alix gasped at the sound as she came hurtling around the corner. "What the hell are you doing?"

"Get back there!" he said, waving her behind him. "As far as you can without losing sight of me." Alix did as she was bade and he knelt down, searching among the glitter of glass shards. Somewhere in the dim recesses of the store a ringing was sounding and he knew that this was strictly shut-ended now because as soon as he had tripped the alarm by breaking the window, a new element had been added: the police. And he had as much stake in keeping them out of this as the Blue Monster had.

Croaker found what he needed, both pieces, one a narrow, long strip, the second a shorter, jagged one. With extreme care, he placed the smaller piece in his right hand, keeping the razor-sharp edges away from the web of his hand. Now he took up the larger piece in his wrapped left hand.

He moved to the inner edge of the corner, keeping his body flat against the column and away from the bright fingers of shattered glass still in the windowframe.

Now came the moment of truth. He could stick his head out to see where the Blue Monster was like all the cops on TV did. But then he'd probably get his head shot off; the Blue Monster wasn't firing blanks. Real life presented problems Hollywood scriptwriters never seemed to address.

"Hey, buddy!" he called from his place of concealment. "It's all over. The cops'll be here any minute! You'd better be six miles away from here by then!"

"You 'n' me both," came the voice from around the corner and Croaker thought, I've got him!, using the aural fix and bringing his left hand back in a tensed arc, the muscles quivering with the strain of anticipating the hairtrigger release, the forebrain acknowledging the existence of only one chance.

Then Croaker was holding his breath, striding his left leg forward in a blur, shooting his upper torso forward, closing his mind to the thought of himself as a target and the forearm already coming forward with rocketing speed, the swathed fingers releasing their burden at the far apex of the arc when momentum combined with Croaker's own strength to turn the shard of glass into a glittering missile.

"That's what you think, buddy!" Let it all out in a harsh rush, providing twin stimuli for the Blue Monster's brain to chew on during this moment of extreme stress.

He saw a blurred glimpse of the Blue Monster jerking back at the sight and sound, the glass shard already upon him, cracking in two across the bridge of his nose.

Croaker had no time to wish that his aim had been more accurate. Blood was streaming from the Blue Monster's face and both his hands were up, trying to free his vision.

But there was nothing at all wrong with his hearing and his gun hand leveled on Croaker's stomach as he heard his adversary coming on. He squeezed off one shot, two, then swung the barrel of the gun into the oncoming head.

It was a lucky blow, coming in blind as it did, landing just behind Croaker's left ear. Croaker staggered, off balance from having swerved away from the gunshots, in the midst of transferring the smaller shard of glass from his right hand to his left, missing the first stab. Now at close range with the Blue Monster's sight back he could imagine the hole the .357 slug would tear into him. There wouldn't be much left of his insides.

And as the Blue Monster's finger began to squeeze the trigger Croaker put aside the pain flashing through his head and through sheer force of will made his motor functions return to life, swinging his left arm in a shallow arc inside the muzzle of the pistol, stabbing inward and up with all his might.

He gave a mighty groan at the pain that shot through him and dimly he felt flesh and sinew giving way beneath the pressure he was exerting as he jammed the glass shard into the Blue Monster's chest. Blood flowed from his own palm, mingling with that of the Blue Monster.

He pushed at the body as the gun went off in reflexive response, scattering plaster off the ceiling high above. Croaker became aware of something pulling at his arm, soft breath on his cheek, and a voice, as insistent as a bee, in his ear.

"Come on!" Alix begged him, pulling at him desperately. "Oh, God, Lew, they'll be here any second!"

He rolled heavily, only dimly aware of who she was and why she was bothering him now when he was so tired and only wanted to close his eyes and . . . Get up! his mind screamed at him. Get her out of here before it's too late! Too late for what . . . Just want to turn over and close my eyes and . . . For God's sake stay awake!

On his hands and knees now, bleeding all over the clean, shiny surface of the arcade floor, Alix tugging at his arm, pulling hm dizzily upward, the corridor beginning to be bathed in pulsing crimson light, the sounds of sirens blossoming in his ears. He turned with her now, allowing her to head him out of the labyrinth, loping, willing his stiff legs to work, trying to ignore the pounding in his head, the roar of his own pulse, the acrid coppery taste in his mouth making him want to gag.

Red, black, red, the illumination revolving, until gradually the red began to grow dimmer and then he felt the cool incredibly soft night breeze on his hot cheeks and he had the presence of mind to tell her, "Keys. Alix, get the goddamned car keys!"

Nangi turned his torso over in the bed, ignoring his useless legs. He reached out in the darkness and touched the slim shoulder of the second Chinese girl on the beach. Nangi shook her with some power. He leaned his head in toward the curtain of night-black hair and said, "Wake up, sleepy one," directly into the hollow of her ear. He was greeted with nothing more articulate than a snore.

He rolled away from her and sat up. Good. The bit of white powder, tasteless and odorless, he had put in her champagne had done its work nicely. Now it was time to go to work.

The villa was silent as he quickly dressed in shirt and trousers. He left off his shoes and socks, transferring several small objects from a deep pouch hidden within the silk folds of the lining of his suit jacket into his trousers' pocket.

Across the room, ribboned in bluish shadow, he took up his walking stick and carefully opened the door. The hallway was dark and silent and slowly he crept awkwardly along it, turning his mind from thoughts of powerful athlete's legs, which in this situation would have served him in good stead.

When he reached the closed door behind which Liu and the tall girl had disappeared not more than fifteen minutes ago, he paused. Unscrewing the white jade dragon at the head of his walking stick, he inserted one of the small objects in his pocket. He pressed a stud, peered at the inside mechanism, satisfying himself as to its working order, and slowly, using infinite care, turned the knob on the door before him. He froze as a sliver of pink lamplight slithered out the tiny crack between door and frame.

When nothing further occurred, he continued pushing the door inward. It was time to see if the sensation he had picked up from Liu at the moment he watched the tall girl earlier on the veranda had any validity. Now he could discern the faint, floating lilt of the Chinese. Surprisingly, it was not Cantonese. Nangi had enough ongoing business in Hong Kong so that he had made himself learn the language because he never quite felt secure leaving his business fate to interpreters. But this was a dialect he was not familiar with.

It was not so much that Liu would be speaking it. He was a Communist Chinese from the mainland, where Cantonese was certainly not the lingua franca. But these two beach girls—surely they were local. Of course they could be Chiu Chow or originally from any number of other provinces. But still . . .

Nangi set his walking stick, point first, along the carpeted floor and slowly slid it through the gap in the door, extending it to its full length. Then he settled himself to listen. After a long while he picked up a word he knew and his heart began to race. But cautious man that he was, he waited for another word or phrase that would give him confirmation.

When it finally came, he gave a tiny inward sigh. They were speaking Mandarin, there was no doubt of it. It was extremely unlikely that Liu would find a street girl in the Crown Colony whose native tongue was the same as his own.

Nangi, crouched uncomfortably in the hallway, waited patiently

359

through the grunting coupling and the languid aftermath when the conversation picked up again. When at last he heard the soft slide of bedsheets, he withdrew his walking stick. The barely discernable pad of bare feet came to him as he was closing the door, forcing himself to do it slowly, a millimeter at a time, lest either of the occupants discover the movement.

At last he rose and went down the corridor to the back of the villa. There he opened the door and went out. Earlier in the evening the stars had been visible but now the clouds had come, occluding all light. The air was heavy with incipient rain as he took out a cigarette and lit it. He took the smoke deep into his lungs, let it out with a long, satisfied sigh. Then he threw the thing into the sand and went down the stone steps and across the winding road.

Within the deep shadows along the far verge he found the small red Alfa run up beneath a pair of enormous leafy trees.

"You're going to catch your death of cold," he said in idiomatic Cantonese.

"Eh?" The driver of the car turned his head as if he was only now aware of Nangi's presence.

"It's going to rain in a moment," Nangi went on. He gestured toward the car. "You'd better get the top up."

They watched each other for a moment, a pair of wary animals about to enter into a contest of territory.

"I fear you've picked the wrong car to follow anybody in."

"I don't know what you're talking about," the man said, using the most abusive inflection.

Nangi bent down so fast the other man had no time to react. They were face to face. "I know who you are," Nangi said in a rush, "or, rather, *what* you are. Either the Communists hired you—"

"I spit on the Communists," the man broke in.

"Then you're working for Sato."

"Never heard of him."

"I'm the one who'll pay you, eventually."

The whites of the man's eyes took on a slight sheen as they shifted toward Nangi. "Are you telling me he won't come through with the rest?"

"What I'm saying is this. You do what I tell you from now on and I won't inform Mr. Sato of your clumsiness."

"What are you talking about?" the man protested. "D'you think those sea snakes know I'm here? They damn well don't."

"But I do," Nangi said. "And you were hired to follow me."

"What if I was?"

"Let's see if you're really any good," Nangi said, unscrewing the head of his walking stick. He extracted a small plastic cassette and held it in his palm like a priceless jewel. "Can you speak Mandarin?"

The man looked up at him. "No sweat."

"'No sweat'? What books have you been into?"

"I read Raymond Chandler."

Oh, Madonna! Nangi thought. He probably thinks of himself as a private eye. He gave the man a judicious look, wondering whether or not he could trust him.

"Listen," the man said, shifting uncomfortably in his leather bucket seat. "Give me the tape, I'll get it done. You want it first thing in the morning, that's exactly when you'll get it." He glanced upward. "The gods assure it. Look. It hasn't rained here in three weeks. Now the heavens are about to open. Guaranteed."

"All right," Nangi said, making his decision. He didn't see that he had much choice. He did not want to involve Allan Su at this stage and there seemed to be no other alternative. He dropped the microcassette into the other man's palm. "Bring it to my room at the Mandarin at seven A.M. That give you enough time?"

The man nodded. Then as an afterthought he said, "Hey, Mr. Nangi, my name's Fortuitous Chiu." The whites of his eyes showed again. "I'm Shanghainese. My family owns one-third of the go-downs in Sam Ka Tsuen and Kwun Tong. We're into restaurants and tourist cabarets—you know, the high-class topless places outside of Wan Chai. We trade in carpets, diamonds, jade. If I don't show on time you go to my father, Pak Tai Chiu. He lives in the villa with the jade green tiled roof up on Belleview Road overlooking Repulse Bay."

Nangi knew enough about the ways of these people to understand how much of himself Fortuitous Chiu was revealing. "You come to room 911 this morning, Fortuitous Chiu," he said as the first warm drops of rain began to fall, "and I'll have more for you to do." He pointed. "Right now you'd better get your top up or you'll drown in the next five minutes."

The ringing of the phone, although muted from inside the house, disturbed the contemplation that the tea ceremony brought them.

For a time there had been perfect harmony in the room. The two men kneeling on the greenish-yellow reed *tatami*, both in flowing kimono. Between them were the carefully placed implements of the *chano-yu*: porcelain kettle with a pair of matching cups, whisk. At right angles to this display was the hardwood case within which reposed Nicholas' *dai-katana*, *Iss-hōgai*.

Also between the men, and above them to the right, was Sato's *tokonoma*. The slender, translucent vase contained two pure white peonies—flowers that Sato knew Nicholas loved. Above the froth of the blossoms was the scroll on which had been hand-lettered this phrase, *"Be intent on loyalty/While others aspire to perform meritorious services/Concentrate on purity of intent/While those around you are beset by egoism."*

Nothing else was of import within the study. The confluence of forces from these entities and objects created the aura of harmoniousness that is so rare in life and toward which each individual strives. The momentousness of the moment was lost on neither man.

After the ringing came Koten. He bowed deeply, waiting for his master to become aware of his powerful spirit, an intrusion and, thus, an end to harmony.

Sato's head came up, his eyes refocusing slowly. He and Nicholas had been at the Void, together, as very few men in this imperfect world had been during the long, burning pages of history. His heartbeat, as well as his breathing, were still abnormally slow. He might have been in a trance of a mystical state well known in the Far East, and highly prized.

"A thousand pardons, Sato-san." Koten's voice, high-pitched and slightly comical emanating from that vast, rumbling body, never ceased to amuse Sato. "The man who will not leave his name has called. He must speak with you."

"Yes." Sato's voice was slightly thick. Nicholas had made no move, and Sato envied him. He rose and followed Koten out of his study.

During the time when he was alone, Nicholas slowly pulled himself back from the Void. It took him longer than it otherwise might because part of him did not wish to leave. The vast harmony that he had just been a part of still hovered like an afterglow in the study. After a time, he lifted his head and studied the words on the *tokonoma* scroll.

They were oddly unpoetic, yet very much in keeping with the kind of man Nicholas had come to know Sato was. He was a *kanryōdō sensei*, one of the last true *samurai*-bureaucrats. Soon, sadly, there would be no place for him in the world. As Japan moved fully into the modern world, the last of the *kanryōdō sensei* would die out. And in their place would come the new breed: the Westernized entrepreneurs who understood world economics, no longer true Japanese at all but world citizens. Japan would need them in the coming decades, these far-thinking, trend-analyzing dealers, if it was to survive past its difficult adolescence. These were the men who would remember the policies of Reagan and Mitterand long after they had forgotten those of Ieyasu Tokugawa.

Without having seen him, Nicholas knew that Koten, the giant *sumō*, had entered the study.

"Are you any closer to finding the murderer?"

He had an odd, direct style of speech that, outside the *dohyo* at least, was stripped of politeness and the traditional niceties.

"Unless Sato-san can summon up the past wholesale," Nicholas said, "all I can do is protect him and Nangi-san."

Koten said nothing. Nicholas turned, saw that the giant was glaring at him. He laughed. "Don't worry, you'll get in your licks." It was somewhat of a relief to be able to speak freely again.

"If you're good," Koten said, "we'll work together. No one will get past us."

Nicholas said nothing; an American here would have boasted about his prowess.

"No one will get past us," Koten repeated. Then, as he heard Sato returning, he retired to the hallway.

The older man's demeanor had altered considerably when he reentered the study. All languorousness had melted away. In its stead was a high degree of excitement held tightly in check.

He came swiftly across the room and sat close to Nicholas, breaking the host-guest barrier. "I have had some news." His voice was very soft but urgent. "Concerning *Tenchi*. Of course the *kei-retsu* has official protection from the government concerning the project.

"But privately I enlisted the aid of several members of the Tenshin Shoden Katori *ryu*. Ninja such as yourself to safeguard our secret." He paused for a moment, looking around. He nodded his head and rose.

Together they went through the open *fusuma*, into the garden. The bees were out, descending on the peonies. The gray plover was long gone from his spot beneath the boxwood tree. The sun wove in and out from behind silver and purple clouds.

"A *sensei* was killed there not long ago, along with a student. Now my contact—whose *ryu* name is Phoenix—informs me that a second student was killed only yesterday. It now appears from what this man tells me that the *ryu* has been infiltrated."

"Infiltrated?" Nicholas echoed. "The Tenshin Shoden Katori? Are you certain?"

Sato nodded. "But Phoenix was not calling from Yoshino. He's in the north. In Hokkaido." Sato's face was grave. "I fear our last stand against the Russians has begun, Linnear-san. You were quite right about their involvement. It took Phoenix some time to evaluate his situation. The death of the *jonin*; he was their spiritual leader." He cocked his head. "Did you know him? By the purest chance he had the same name as the hero we were discussing once, Masashigi Kusunoki."

"It's been many years since I've been at the Tenshin Shoden Katori," Nicholas said.

Sato looked at him oddly for a moment, then shrugged. "His death was totally unexpected, and they were thrown into chaos for a time. It took all of Phoenix's skill to return absolute order in such a short time. Meanwhile, it seems the Soviet agents were doing their work."

His beefy shoulders were bent as with an incalculable weight. "We cannot allow *Tenchi* to be infiltrated, Nicholas-san. The knowledge that the Russians are so close fills me with dread. They have the power to destroy us—all of us—if they discover *Tenchi*."

"What has happened?" Nicholas said in a voice a good deal calmer than he felt.

"Phoenix is pursuing one of their agents—the last remaining one within the *ryu*. The man has fled north with a top-secret profile of *Tenchi*. He is now on Hokkaido. Phoenix has allowed him to go even though the man murdered one of his students in the process. He believes the agent will lead him to the Soviet local control. But you cannot imagine just how dangerous this maneuver is. This agent *must* be stopped by any means before he can pass on that profile."

Viktor Protorov, Nicholas thought. I must be at this Phoenix's side when he infiltrates the Russian's base. Sato will have his secrets back and I will have Protorov. "Where is Phoenix now, precisely?"

Sato glanced at him. "I fathom your intent. But if you go, I must also."

"That is impossible," Nicholas said sharply. "Purely from a tactical point—"

Sato raised his hand. "My friend," he said softly. "There has already been too much murder here for me to allow it to go on. Three human beings—people I counted as friends as well as valued work colleagues and indispensable parts of my *kobun*—have ceased to exist because of me. That is a heavy burden for anyone to bear.

"While you were gone, funerals for all of them were held, as well as temporary burials. Miss Yoshida had no family, so it was not so bad in her case. But the others—Kagami-san and Ishii-san—both did. They will of course obey my orders to keep the

364

police out of it. We do not need the *Kempeitai* in here, stomping around in their efforts at investigation.

"But I do not like it. I want these people to have proper burials in their family plots. Can their *kami* be at rest until then?"

Nicholas thought of the afternoon with Miss Yoshida, the sight of her kneeling within a long stone's throw of where his own mother and father were buried. He resolved to be at her final burial, to light joss sticks before her gravestone, and to say the prayers of reverence for the safekeeping of her spirit.

"I know where this is all leading," Nicholas said, "and I cannot allow it. You'll stay here where it's safe."

Sato's laugh was hollow and without humor. "Have you so soon forgotten the *Wu-Shing*, my friend?"

"That's what Koten is here for," Nicholas said stubbornly. "Do you doubt that he can do the job?"

"This has nothing to do with Koten or anyone else."

"I am responsible for your safety, Sato-san. This is what you wanted; it is what we have sworn to."

Sato nodded gravely. "What you say is true, Nicholas-san. You are sworn to protect me and I am sworn to consummate the merger of our *kobun* without difficulties. But this oath only goes so far. I am the final arbiter of my life and death. You must accede to this. You know you must."

There was a silence for some time. A brace of plovers broke cover past Sato's left shoulder, racing into the clouds. The wind was picking up and a heaviness was returning to the air. Unless the wind direction changed abruptly there would be rain again, a good deal of it.

"Then the oath that binds us is severed." It was a desperate ploy. One which Nicholas feared would not work.

"Are you free to walk away then?" Sato smiled. "By all means do so. I will not think ill of you."

"I can force you to stay here."

"And where would you go, my friend? Only I know where Phoenix would meet us. You could roam all of Hokkaido without ever finding either him or the Soviet agent."

There was a deliberate silence.

"Then you'll still join me."

"I seem to have no choice in the matter."

"Good. We will take Koten and fly to the north island. From there a rented car will take us to our final destination."

"Which is?" Nicholas said warily.

"A *rotenburo*—an outdoor hot bath—my friend." Sato smiled

365

with real warmth. "And why not? You appear to be in need of some relaxation!"

In the middle of the night the phone sang shrilly in her ear. Justine, who had had trouble falling asleep, started awake. Her mouth was dry and her throat sore, as if she had been straining for something or constantly calling out in her dreams.

She brushed her hand out to the receiver to stop the racket, picked up her watch off the nighttable. Just after three-thirty. Jesus! She heard squawking from the phone, picked it up as if it were alive.

"Justine?"

"Rick, what're you—"

"Don't tell me you forgot."

She put her hand to her head. "I don't—"

"Haleakala. The dormant volcano. You promised I could take you up there."

"But it's three-thirty in the morning. For God's sake, Rick—"

"If we leave now we'll make it in time for the sunrise. That's the time to be up at the crater."

"But I don't want to see the sunrise. I—"

"You'll never know until you're there. Come on now, we're wasting precious time. We've got to be there by five-thirty."

Justine was about to protest some more but suddenly she felt too tired to try. It seemed easier just to go along with him. Besides, she thought wanly, maybe it will be fun.

It certainly proved to be nothing she had expected. For one thing, just the drive up the winding slope of the volcano was fascinating. The summit was two miles up, and she could see the terrain changing before her eyes as they ascended. Rick had cautioned her to dress warmly in slacks and sweater, a jacket as well if she had one. Walking out to the car in the cool but balmy night air she had felt faintly ridiculous being so overdressed. It seemed inconceivable to her that there could be any place on this tropical paradise where the temperature was hovering at thirty-five degrees Fahrenheit.

But as they rose, as the terrain metamorphosed from palm tree laden, to the dominance of spiky desert cactus, to long stands of stately pine trees more appropriate to Maine or Vermont, she was obliged to roll up her window and don her jacket.

Near the crater itself, Rick switched on the heater. They had already passed the tree line, and now she looked out on black desolation. Long ago, massive lava slides, spewed up from the depths of the earth, had rolled slowly downward, inundating all in their paths. Now hardy grasses peeped up here and there through the dark mounded lava. But otherwise there was nothing. As the car made one switchback after another, Justine glanced back over her shoulder. From this vantage point she could look across the vast undulating slopes of Haleakala's base, down to the shoreline, the crescent beach just beginning to glimmer with an odd kind of phosphorescence and the utterly black feathery silhouettes of the slender-boled palms.

She had said not a word to Rick on the long drive up, huddled on her side of the front seat as if she expected him to deliver a blow to her face. She was shivering by the time he pulled the car into the wide blacktopped parking lot. She put it down to the unnatural cold.

As they got out she could see the looming spectral shapes, spiderweb gantries, towers, and electronic equipment belonging to various institutions from both the military and the private sectors, used for ongoing weather and seismographic study.

Signs bade them to walk slowly, cautioning those with heart conditions not to come up this high at all. And indeed as they began to walk Justine felt a lightness in her head, a certain feeling that her lungs were not getting their quota of oxygen. A fierce wind tore at them, sent paper flapping, making breathing that much more difficult.

She was grateful when they reached the shelter at the top of the wide stairs. This was a stone and masonry edifice whose entire eastern face was composed of large panes of glass.

From this eyrielike observation post they stared out on the blasted landscape of Haleakala's craters. The area resembled photographs Justine had seen of the moon's surface more than it did anything she had come to associate with her own planet. With no visual fix, distances were impossible to judge. Five miles looked more like five thousands yards. It was fantastic.

People gathered in this small place just as the ancient Hawaiians had centuries before to watch the rising of the sun. It was on this very spot, legend had it, that the sun was caught and held hostage, released only when it promised to move more slowly over the Hawaiian Islands to fill them to the brim with its light.

There was nothing in the sky but darkness. There was no hint of change, of the ending of night. But the sun was coming. They all could feel it like a shiver down their spines.

And then like a foundry being fired, one bright red spark speared upward over the intervening rim of Haleakala's crater. There came an exhalation in concert from the assembled as light came into the world, clear and direct and adamantine.

It was a color that had no earthly analog; it took Justine's breath away. She felt as if all gravity were gone and, unmoored, she was about to float away.

Pale fire crept across the blasted plain of the crater. Long, sweeping shadows, impossibly black, scored the face of the lava like newly etched cracks. There was no gray, only the darkness and the light.

Then, without any of them knowing quite when it happened, the multifaceted illumination they had all been born into and knew well returned to Haleakala and, just as if it had been some man-made show, the event was over.

"Now will you forgive me for dragging you out of bed?"

Justine and Rick leaned on the wooden railing, the last two still inside the observation post. Behind them they could hear the muffled cough of engines as cars started back down the serpentine drive to warm sea breezes.

"I'm tired," she said. "Take me back."

Outside, she saw a lone couple at the rim of the crater. Their arms were around one another's waists, their bodies glued together. Justine stopped to watch them, her attention caught. The woman was tall and slim, her copper red hair pulled back in a long ponytail. The man was dark haired and large; muscular even through his windbreaker. When the woman moved she did so with the fluid grace of a dancer. The man had somewhat of the same quality, but Justine had lived with Nicholas Linnear long enough to be able to identify another of his dangerous breed.

"What are you staring at?" Rick followed her gaze and his head went down, his gaze swinging away.

I want that, Justine said to herself, still staring at the lovers moving, embracing above the jagged lava cliffs. Sunlight bathed them as if they were gods. Tears burned behind her lids and she thought, I will not cry in front of him. I will not!

She turned away from the lovers and from him, walking quickly down the stairs so that she was gasping for breath by the time she reached the asphalt parking lot. By comparison, everything here looked banal and uninteresting. She got into the car and leaned her head against the window, closing her eyes. Just below the level of the lot, Rick stopped the car and got out. "These are silverswords," he told her. "They only grow upcountry." He pointed to a fenced-off patch of ground where two or three vertical plants soared from the dark earth. True to their name, their spiky leaves were a peculiar silvery gray. "It's said that they take twenty years to bloom and then once they do, they die."

Justine was staring at the beautiful plants when Rick said this, and despite her resolve she abruptly dissolved into tears. Great wracking sobs broke from her trembling lips and she sat down hard on the path, her head in her lap.

"Justine. Justine."

She did not hear him. She was thinking of how sad life was for the silversword and, then, of course how ridiculous that notion was. No. Life was sad for her. At her father's funeral she had felt only relief, had thought she was reveling in that relief.

But now she knew the truth. She missed him. He was the only father she would ever have. He raised her and in his own way, she supposed, even loved her. Now he was gone without mourning or a sense of the diminishing of the quality of life. Or so she had thought. She was so smart. Oh, yes. The truth was that she was a moron. She could no more understand her own emotions than she could anyone else's. That's why she was useless to Gelda. Useless as well to Nicholas.

But now was not a time to think of that. Not yet. This was her time to grieve, as a little girl who missed her daddy, who had always missed him, and who could never now say to him how sorry she was that they had not had their time together as was right and fair.

Life was unfair, and now she knew it to her roots. She could not stop weeping. She did not want to. Her mourning was long in coming, for her father as well as for the confused and vulnerable young girl she had been up until this moment. Her rite of passage was upon her, and at long last she was making her torturous way through the thorns and nettles that separated childhood from adulthood.

Slowly, as she allowed her long pent-up grief to flow through her, as she allowed her entire being to feel it, wracked with a pain that was almost physical, Justine began to grow up.

Nangi lay atop his bed in room 911 at the Mandarin Hotel. He was on the Island. From his sparkling windows he could see Victoria Harbor and just beyond the clock tower of the Star Ferry terminal, the very southern tip of Kowloon and the Asian shore. Somewhere far to the north, ultimately in Peking, no doubt, Liu's masters lived. They—as well as he—would have to be dealt with judiciously.

The main problem, Nangi thought, was time. He did not have very much of it, and as long as the Communists believed that to be the truth they would sink their teeth into him and never let go.

What they, through Liu, were asking was patently impossible. To give up control of his own *keiretsu* was unthinkable. He had struggled all his adult life, conquered innumerable threats, neutralized many competitors, sent many an enemy to his grave to get to this exalted state.

Yet if there were any other way out for him but to sign that paper he was not aware of it. Either way he would lose the *keiretsu*, for he knew his company could not long weather the set of pyramiding losses and future pledges in which the accursed Anthony Chin had enmeshed the All-Asia Bank.

For all this, Nangi was calm. Life had taught him patience. He had that rare ability known to the Japanese as *nariyuki no matsu*, to wait for the turn of events. He believed in Christ and, He, surely was a miracle. If he were to lose the *keiretsu*, that was *karma*, his penance for his sins in a previous life. For there was nothing Tanzan Nangi held more dear than his company.

And yet he was absolutely certain that he would not lose it. As had Gōtarō on their makeshift raft so long ago, Nangi had faith. His agile mind and his faith would see him through this as they had all the other crises in his life.

Nariyuki no matsu.

A knock on the door. Did he feel the tides turning? Or would they continue to run against him until they pushed him far out to sea?

"Come in," he said. "It's open."

Fortuitous Chiu appeared, closing the door behind him. He wore an oyster gray raw silk suit. In the light of day he appeared trim and hard muscled. He had a handsome, rather narrow face with keen, intelligent eyes. All in all, Nangi thought, Sato had chosen well.

"It's seven o'clock on the button," Fortuitous Chiu said. He stood by the door. "I am anxious to make a good impression...after last night."

"Did you finish the translation?"

Fortuitous Chiu nodded. "Yes, sir. It was only difficult in parts because, as you no doubt already know, inflection is infinitely more important than the word itself in Chinese."

"You needn't be so formal," Nangi said.

Fortuitous Chiu nodded, came across the room, grinning. "There was a great deal on the tape that was wordless. Someday, if the gods permit, I would meet this woman. She must have been born under a lucky star if her manipulation of this foul-smelling Communist son of a diseased dog is any indication."

"I've taken the liberty of ordering breakfast for us both," Nangi said, swinging his legs off the bed with the aid of one hand. "Sit down and join me, will you." He began pulling small plates out of the food warmer, piling them on the table.

"Dim sum," Fortuitous Chiu murmured. Nangi saw that he was impressed, being served a traditional Chinese breakfast by a Japanese. The young man sat down in one of the satin-covered chairs next to the table and took up his chopsticks.

While they ate, Fortuitous Chiu spoke of what the tape had revealed to him. "First, I don't know how much information you have on our *Comrade* Liu."

Nangi shrugged. "The basics, I suppose. I'm no newcomer to Hong Kong but I have been unable to call upon the knowledge of my bank president, Allan Su. He is not privy to what we do here. I don't want him involved until the very last instant." Nangi paused for a moment, marshaling his thoughts. "Liu's a member in good standing of the Crown Colony. His varied businesses on the Island and in Kowloon have brought a great deal of money into Hong Kong: shipping, banking, printing . . . I believe one of his companies owns a majority of the go-downs in Kwun Tong."

Shoveling a shrimp ball into his mouth, Fortuitous Chiu nodded. He munched with the quick, short bites of the Chinese. "Indeed, yes. But did you also know that he is the head of the syndicate that owns the Frantan?"

"The gambling casino in Macao?"

"The same," Fortuitous Chiu said, consuming a dough-wrapped quail egg. "The Communists find it most convenient to wash money in and out through the Frantan because it allows them to convert bullion into any currency they choose without embarrassing questions being asked. Some of the *ta-pans* here do the same thing, though not at the Frantan."

Nangi's mind was working furiously, considering the possibilities. He had begun to get an inkling of the tides turning.

"Comrade Liu and this woman—Succulent Pien—are long-time lovers, that much is clear." Fortuitous Chiu stuffed a pork roll into his cheek, chewing contentedly while he continued to talk. "The slime-ridden sea slug has thought up so many ornate endearments for her it made my head swim. He is quite ardent."

"And she?" Nangi inquired.

"Ah, women," Fortuitous Chiu said as if that covered it all. He stacked the empty plates to one side, brought other laden ones before him. Grabbing the soy sauce, he shook the bottle vigorously over the dumplings before him. Then he reached for the fiery chili paste, red as blood. "It has been my experience that one can never tell about women. They are born with deceit as a deer is with a cloven hoof. They cultivate it like they do a current hairstyle. Is this not your experience as well?"

Nangi said nothing, wondering what the young man was getting at.

"Well, it has been mine," Fortuitous Chiu said, just as if Nangi had interjected a comment. "And this one is no exception."

"Does she love the Communist?"

"Oh, yes. I think she does. Though what she could find of sufficient promise in that lice-ridden motherless goat I cannot imagine. But what she feels for him is, I believe, irrelevant." He cleared another plate, pulled another toward him. On went the soy sauce and the chili paste. "That is because it is clear to me that she loves money much more."

"Ah," said Nangi. He sensed the tides rolling back. "And where does she assuage this burning desire? From friend Liu?"

"Yes, indeed." Fortuitous Chiu nodded. He had worked up quite a sweat eating. "The pox-infested dog enjoys giving her presents. But I fear that he is not as generous as our Succulent Pien would wish."

"Thus she wanders afield."

"So I have been told."

Nangi was quick to anger; he was walking a fine line here. "Who knows what you do?"

"No one but you." At last Fortuitous Chiu was finished. He pushed the last plate away from him. His face was shiny with grease and sweat. "But something she said to Liu caused me to make enquiries. Succulent Pien lives in the Mid-Levels, on Po Shan Road. That territory belongs to the Green Pang Triad." He produced a white silk handkerchief and carefully wiped his face. He grinned. "It just so happens that my Number Three Cousin is 438 of the Green Pang."

"I don't want to owe anyone in a Triad a favor," Nangi said.

"No sweat." Fortuitous Chiu washed away his words. "Number Three Cousin owes his rise in the Green Pang to my father. He's delighted to help. No strings attached."

Nangi thought he could go into culture shock talking to this one. "Go on," he said.

"It seems that someone else is plowing the same fragrant harbor that Comrade Liu is."

"And who might that be?"

"I'm not a miracle worker. I need some time to find out. They've been very careful to cover their tracks." He leered at Nangi. "Number Three Cousin and I may have to do some on-site inspection during the night."

"Does the Green Pang have to be involved?"

"I've got no choice. It's their turf. I can't make a bowel movement over at the Mid-Levels without letting them in on it."

Nangi nodded. He knew well the power of the Triads in Hong Kong. "What did Succulent Pien say to get you started on this?"

"Redman," Fortuitous Chiu said. "Charles Percy Redman. She used his name. Know him?"

Nangi thought for a moment. "Shipping *tai-pan*, yes? British fellow. Family goes way back in Hong Kong."

"That's Redman," Fortuitous Chiu acknowledged. "But what almost no one else knows is that he's an agent for Her Majesty's Government."

"Redman a spy? Madonna!" Nangi was genuinely shocked. "But what's his connection to Succulent Pien? Is she somehow raiding him?"

"Looks that way, doesn't it?"

This is all very interesting, Nangi thought. But how does any of it help me with the Communists? My time is running out. If I don't give Liu an affirmative by phone by six tonight, the deal's off. I've got no capital, the All-Asia will fail and, eventually, so will the *keiretsu*.

"Is there more?" he asked.

"Not until I climb into bed with Succulent Pien and see what she's got between her thighs."

"It's a pillow like all the rest," Nangi observed tartly. "I need something before six."

"This evening?" Fortuitous Chiu's eyes opened wide. "No way, José. She's home and not going anywhere. She had her amah go shopping for her. I think she's whipping up a midnight snack for a friend. Early tomorrow morning's the best I can do. I'm sorry."

Nangi sighed deeply. "Not nearly as much, I'm afraid, as I am."

Night. The drip-drop of rain pattering all around them. The sky was black and impenetrable save for a tiny patch, a nacreous gray behind which the full moon rode as ghostly as the face of a former lover. The warm water moved in minute wavelets up to their bare flesh, reflections of the swinging yellow lanterns in the trees behind them in a white spangle, diffused and softened to a rich glow by the stream rising all about them.

A double strand of manmade lights, curved like a string of lustrous pearls around the neck of an exotic African princess, showed the way toward a black humpbacked shadow rising out

373

of the undulating land. And behind its bulk must be the sea, for Nicholas could already scent the salt tang.

Sato stirred beside Nicholas, sending soft ripples away from them both. "Out there," he said softly, "tell me that sight is not one of the most beautiful in the world, a sight that makes Japan unique."

Nicholas followed the direction, saw the steep falloff of the cliffs down to the Pacific and on its heaving bosom the rhythmic bobbing of tiny orange lanterns hung from the prows and the sterns of the squid boats as their masters and crews bent to their task.

"They seem as small and fleeting as fireflies," Nicholas said. His eyes were somnolent. It had been a long, hard day full of anxiety and fear for his friend's life. And now the hot water was working its magic on his tensed body, loosening his knotted muscles, the cords in his neck and shoulders relaxing, the day's accumulated tension leeching away from him.

It was not that his anxiety about allowing Sato to come had disappeared entirely. But with him here and Koten guarding the front of the *rotenburo*, he felt more confident than he had at the outset.

Sato luxuriated in feeling good. He stretched his long legs outward into the gently swirling water, sighing deeply with the sense of well-being this spa engendered in him.

It was then he felt something against his left calf, soft and warm, bumping, bumping, bumping with an odd kind of insistence.

Languidly, he leaned forward, imagining himself a crane gliding through the currents of a narrow inlet to the sea. His searching fingers grasped what felt at first like a bed of seaweed. Curious, Sato drew it upward slowly. It had great weight.

The rain let up. Racing clouds became visible as the lanterns' glow illuminated their billowing undersides. Now they slid apart and the cool, opalescent light of the pocked moon crowned the silhouette of what he dragged upward from the steaming water.

Sato's muscles bulged with the effort and he was obliged to use his hands even with Nicholas helping him, struggling with the monstrously heavy thing that now fell across his legs beneath the water.

Slowly it rose like a specter out of the deep, and Nicholas made a sharp movement beside him, grunting.

"Oh, Buddha!" Sato whispered. His hands shook so much that droplets flew from the thing like rain, off the great tiger curving around one shoulder, flung down the muscular back, the extended talons of the rear paws indented along the buckled ridge of the spine. Movement as if the colored tattoo had come alive. "Oh, what have they done to you, Phoenix?" Sato cried softly.

Those eyes, milky and unseeing in death, fixed him as the bloated face rose, glittering in the moonlight, the teeth clamped together in pain and determination.

Akiko was thinking about the promise she had made to Saigō. Or, more precisely, to Saigō's *kami*.

She rolled over on her *futon*, passing an arm across her eyes. Red light blotted out the darkness. *Giri*. It bound her like steel manacles. Not for the first time, she found herself wishing that she had not been born Japanese. How free it must be to be American or English, and not feel *giri*. Because Akiko knew that if she did not feel *giri* she would not be bound by it. But she was Japanese. *Samurai* blood flowed through her veins. Oh, not the blood of the famed Ofuda. She had chosen that name upon her majority for much the same reason that Justine had chosen to call herself Tobin instead of Tomkin; she wished to conceal her past.

But had there ever been a time when she had thought of herself as Akiko Shimada? She did not even know her mother's last name. In *Fuyajo* only given names were used, and oftentimes those were not real ones. Ikan. Had her mother been born with that name? Had she taken it inside *Fuyajo*? Or, what was just as likely, had those who ran the Castle That Knows No Night assigned it to her?

She put her hands down between her thighs, cupping herself. She could still feel the aftertremors, the expansion of her inner flesh that Nicholas' stroking had caused. She would never be the same now. And, terrifyingly, was not sure that she wanted to be.

Then what of her vow? Revenge had shaped so much of her life, had given her purpose when she thought that she had none. Without the solace of revenge to warm her soul, she might have withered and died. Those who had driven her out of *Fuyajo* were long dead, put to endless sleep as she hovered over them in the night. But they were old men, and that was not true justice as she saw it. She could do nothing about their longevity; to her way of thinking they had seen the procession of too many days. Still she had avenged herself.

Life must have a shape. Revenge was her destiny. She must have been someone evil in a previous life, she had thought, for her *karma* in this one to be so unremitting.

Now Nicholas Linnear threatened that dark harmony. She supposed that she had known it from the moment she had first seen him in person at Jan Jan. He had melted a heart she had thought

375

made of granite and ice. She thought in her arrogance that she was beyond love.

She was wrong.

As she wept on her *futon* in the otherwise deserted house of her husband and her prey, she beseeched the Amida Buddha only for absolution and death. For the thought—oh, Buddha! the knowledge—that she could love just like any other mortal sent waves of panic through her. She had set her life on a certain course, believing specific things about herself.

But now the ache she felt through to the core of her spirit whenever she thought of Nicholas Linnear—which was to say all the time—blasted her in the furnace of revelation. For she was sworn to destroy him.

She thought about turning away from her vow, of letting peace flow down around her. She dreamed of surcease.

But then she parted her naked thighs and stared down at the delicate flesh of their insides. On each writhed a flaming horned dragon, multicolored tattoos of fantastic workmanship.

And she knew that peace was not for her; or love either. For Kyōki had marked her soul just as surely as he had her flesh. There was no hope of surcease.

She had had her respite, the one lull in the storm, and for that time had reveled in the joy of another life. *Giri* bound her, heart and spirit. What had begun must be seen to its final conclusion.

She thought of Saigō again, standing strong and handsome in the forest glade in Kyūshū, the sunlight striking his shoulders, silvering his hair. How his presence had altered her life!

She rose and went through the silent house. It already seemed dead and buried, the thick bars of sunlight beating against the closed panes of glass, seeking entry. But this was a house of the dead; the sun no longer held any dominion here.

Akiko glided from room to room as if fixing each space, each object in her mind for the last time. She touched everything; she moved everything. In this manner she came upon the mini tape recorder by which Koten had been eavesdropping on her husband.

When she rewound the tape and pressed "Play," she heard all that Phoenix had said to Sato.

Rain puckered the skin of the *rotenburo*, splashing against their shoulders, beating against the tops of their heads. Neither of them felt a drop.

In the distance the beckoning amber lights of the squid boats winked on and off through the downpour as Nicholas and Sato hauled on Phoenix's corpse, pulling it slowly out of the heated water.

"Amida!" Sato whispered through the sibilance of the rain, and scrambled hastily out of the pool, holding the small patch of cloth over his groin while he searched in the wetness and the dark for another one.

He returned as quickly as he could to where the ninja was stretched out by the side of the *rotenburo*, his legs crossed at the ankles, his arms spread wide. Sato placed the small square over Phoenix's private parts.

"The indignity of it," he murmured as he hunkered down beside Nicholas. There was no one else about; the rain had seen to that. "This is no way to die."

"It was not how he would choose to go," Nicholas said, and pointed. "Look here." A hole, black and gaping, disfigured the back of Phoenix's head. "This was done by no *samurai*."

Sato looked sadly down at the corpse, white and bloated, spat upon by the storm. "It could be a KGB execution." His voice was a trifle unsteady. "I had a cousin once in the *Kempeitai*. He knew all about such things and he told me. A bullet through the brain, that's the Russian style."

"Whoever did it," Nicholas observed, "had to be very good indeed. This man was ninja *sensei*."

Sato put his head in his hands. "He had information for us. Perhaps he got careless. He was certain that the Soviets had no knowledge of his pursuit."

"He had to have been surprised here. He would never have died otherwise. This could not have happened in a pitched battle. They were here, waiting for him."

Sato lifted his head. His eyes were red rimmed and perplexed. "But how?"

Nicholas did not like the answer he was about to give. "If there's a traitor in the *keiretsu*, perhaps he is closer than that. Inside your *kobun*."

"Nonsense," Sato said. "No one from my *kobun*—absolutely *no one*—knew where I was going. Phoenix's call came to the house. Only you were there. Akiko—"

"And Koten."

"Koten?" Sato's eyes were wide all around. "Oh, Buddha, no!" Then he considered. "He has been with me the last three or four times Phoenix phoned." He shook his head. "But even so, I took great pains to make certain I was alone when we spoke."

"You mean it was impossible for him to eavesdrop."

"Well, no. I mean—" Sato slammed fist into palm. "Koten

is *sensei* of *sumai*, the most ancient form of his art: combat *sumō*. *Phoenix* knew him, trusted him." He looked to the sky. *"Muhon-nin!"* he cried.

Between them steam rose slowly from Phoenix's cooling body and it seemed as if the twisted, multicolored tattoo that covered his shoulder and back was rising with the mist, the only part of him still alive.

"He must pay!" Sato said. "He knows where Phoenix would have led us. And I'll make him tell us!"

He was up and running before Nicholas could stop him. Beyond the *rotenburo*'s terraced tract, the lights of the squid fleet had disappeared and now only swirling darkness sought to engulf them. The lights of the swinging lanterns in the trees surrounding the pool were smeared by the slanting rain; some of them had already gone out, felled by the strengthening wind.

"Sato-san!" Nicholas called as he ran. But it was useless. The wind tore his words from his lips and, in any case, Sato was not about to listen to reason. *Tenchi* was far too important to him and there was no time for caution.

Nicholas raced across the open expanse between the camphor trees that lined the walkways to the pool. There was no sound but the moaning of the wind and the heavy beating rain.

Nicholas' concentration narrowed as he slewed into the dimly lit locker room. Koten, master of *sumō* and the more deadly *sumai*, would need less than three seconds with Sato to put him away, and thus Nicholas' anxiety level was high.

That was the only explanation as to why he did not sense the surreptitious sound until quite late, and then it was actually the movement of shadow on the periphery of his vision that alerted him.

He whirled just in time to duck away, swivel to his right. Heard the whirr as of a bright insect, the brief puff of wind at its passage. The soft *thunk* just behind and to the left of him indicated the position of the thrown *shuriken*. Ninja! That meant that Phoenix's quarry, the *muhon-nin* who had fled the Tenshin Shoden Katori, was still here. Then there was still a chance to keep *Tenchi* alive and out of reach of the Russians!

Nicholas followed his instincts. His working muscles gleaming with beaded water and sweat, he set off after his adversary. He wanted to come to close quarters with him as quickly as possible in order to negate the advantage of the long-range *shuriken*.

He twisted and turned through the tunnellike labyrinth of the *rotenburo*'s corridors, sliding and sometimes crawling on his belly, always mindful of breaking up any rhythm to his movements.

378

Twice he heard the buzzing passage of *shuriken* quite near him and he redoubled his efforts, knowing from the sounds that he was closing in.

But it was a bad situation and growing worse all the time. Where was Sato? His absence was a constant distraction and any kind of distraction was dangerous in battle.

He skidded around the end of a row of metal lockers thinking about getting to his locker and his *dai-katana*, and felt a blow strike his shoulder, numbing it momentarily. He cursed himself mightily as he slid forward, seeming to skid out of control on the damp floor. The bulk of the oncoming shadow careened past him, just above.

Nicholas torqued his torso, lifting his right arm in a blur, the elbow locked, the heel of his hand leading, crashing into flesh and bone. He heard a heavy grunt and, simultaneously, felt the crash of a weight to his left. He twisted, using his knees and ankles, using the chrysanthemum to bring power back into his frame. He rained blows onto the form which crouched in the darkness in the lee of the lockers.

He felt the satisfying smack of flesh against flesh and began a series of interlocking strikes. Abruptly there was a blow to the side of his head and when he reached out again, the form was gone.

He rose to his feet, swaying, his senses questing. Went instinctively into *getsumei no michi* and found the spirit of the ninja. He was moving *away* from Nicholas. Why?

Then he had the answer and his heart constricted in anxiety. Loosing the *kiai* shout that rocked the walls of the *rotenburo*, Nicholas raced through the darkened interior, tearing after terror.

Sato had found the interior of the *rotenburo* deserted. Where was Koten? Where was the *muhon-nin*? Anger burned through him like a sun. He gritted his teeth, the deep feeling of betrayal powering him, feeding adrenaline into him.

He burst out into the night filled with swirling rain. No one was about, not even the proprietors. Koten! he wanted to cry out. I'm going to kill you; slowly so that I can watch your face as life ebbs out of you.

Into the parking lot he ran. Two or three cars remained beneath the lights. He wiped at his eyes to clear them. All the cars were empty. Then his gaze came to rest on the rented vehicle they had used to drive here from the airport.

Koten!

Sitting in kingly silence, dry beneath the opening heavens.

Unthinking, Sato ran toward the car, skidding once on the slick tarmac, almost wrenching his back. All breath went out of him for a moment. Then, with a grunt, he lifted himself off one knee and loped the rest of the way to the dripping car.

Now he shouted. "Koten!" Reaching for the chrome handle, wrenching the door open. There was a sharp click, as distinct as a dry twig cracking on a forest floor, and the night erupted into a fireball of orange and crimson flames. The car ballooned outward, coming apart in hot, twisting shards of metal and pinpoint fragments of sprayed safety glass. The ignition instantly disintegrated the rubberized mannikin in the front seat.

A sharp report like a cannon shot and then a trailer of dense black smoke, oily and twisting, ascending into the full force of the storm.

The body looked enormous, a lumped animal, throwing a deep shadow across the surrounding stone. All about it shards of glass glittered like stars, arcing tiny rainbows into the cold overhead illumination.

Three uniformed men from the Raleigh City Police stood around taking notes while the fourth, half in, half out of one of the squad cars, was on the two-way radio.

A pair of backup units squealed to a halt beside him and the cops inside emerged and began to set up sawhorse barriers against the growing knots of curious onlookers.

Harry Saunders, the sergeant on the two-way, wrapped up his conversation with his captain and threw the mike on the car seat as he backed out of the unit. His face was set in hard lines as he ambled slowly back to his three buddies.

"Might as well burn those pads," he told them as he approached. "Ain't gonna be any use, those notes."

"How d'you mean?" Bob Santini said, still scribbling in his flip-up pad.

"Someone coming any minute now to take over. Captain says this isn't any've our business now."

Santini's head came up and he glowered at Saunders. "You mean a man is killed and we just walk away from it?"

Saunders shrugged. "Funny you should say that, 'cause I asked the Captain the self-same question." He screwed up his face. "Know what he told me? Wouldn't do no good no matter *what* we did." His finger stabbed out in the general direction of the corpse. "This poor sumbitch's got no prints, got no history at all. He's a nothing, a big, fat zero."

"A spook," Ed Baine said. "Now that's interesting."

"Well, you just take your interest somewhere else," Saunders said, "'cause after we beak up here not even our wives or, in your case, Baine, your g.f., are supposed to know anything that went on here."

"Oh, shit," Spinelli said with mock disgust, "no pillow talk. Now what'm I supposed to do afterwards?"

"Do what you always do, shithead," Baine said. "Roll over and go to sleep."

Saunders' head turned. "Sit on it, your clowns," he said *sotto voce*, "we got company."

They all turned their heads, saw a trenchcoated figure coming down the corridor. None of them liked what they saw.

"Oh, holy Christ," Spinelli said under his breath, "it's a fuckin' woman."

"Gentlemen," she said as she came up, "who's in charge here?"

"Detective Sergeant Harry Saunders, ma'am," Saunders said, taking a step forward.

"At ease, Sergeant," she said with a straight face, "I'm not about to make a grab for your clusters." She took a quick look around. "Anything been touched here?"

"No, ma'am."

"He's just as you found him? Exactly?"

Saunders nodded and then swallowed, angry at himself for being dry-mouthed in front of this woman. "Can I ask what your, er, affiliation is?"

She turned away from him, running her gaze carefully across the area immediately surrounding the body. "You may ask your captain that, Sergeant Saunders. He may be more willing to assuage your curiosity."

Saunders clenched his teeth, biting back a sour comment while Spinelli smirked at him from a distance.

"Sergeant." She was kneeling down now beside the corpse. "I won't need your help anymore. Why don't you and your men retire to the barricades and assist with crowd control. I'll call you if I need you."

"Yes, ma'am," Saunders said with exaggerated politeness and, turning sharply, jerked his head at the other three, who followed him silently down the faintly echoing corridor of the mall to where their units, red lights flashing, were parked.

When they were gone, Tanya Vladimova confirmed her initial I.D. The body was, indeed, that of Jesse James. Quickly, she opened up a small kit and set about taking a set of prints off the bloody glass shard that still pierced James' chest. For the first time she allowed herself to think of what had gone wrong. But she knew the answer without having to go through any process at all.

It had been foolish to allow Alix Logan to live. Foolish and, from a security point of view, sloppy. But men were weak, she thought now, even a man as powerful and intelligent as C. Gordon Minck, It had been Minch, after all, who had insisted she be kept alive, over Tanya's vigorous protests.

And not for any humanitarian reasons, but because he had been making love to her on a regular basis, flying into Key West on clandestine weekends when he was supposed to be sailing his boat on the Chesapeake. Like Scheherazade, Alix Logan had wrapped Minck up and in so doing had stayed the date of her execution.

"Pajalsta zameretse no myeste, Gospadin Linnear." Please stay where you are, Mr. Linnear.

He saw the gun muzzle looming dark and impossibly large.

"If you make a move I will shoot you dead."

Nicholas was not giving away any knowledge he had of the language so he took a step in the direction of the gun. The night exploded for a second time and a clot of asphalt screamed upward, erupting in flying fragments so close they stung his ankles and calves.

"I know you can understand me, *Gospadin* Linnear. The next shot will take off the top of your head."

To his left the twisted remains of the rental car lay partially on its side. Smoke coiled about its stark sculpture like a loosed cage of serpents.

Nicholas' body had twitched when he had heard the muffled explosion, the reaction of an animal in flight for its life. Skidding out into the night, he had confronted the dying flames of the initial fireball. Blackened parts of Seiichi Sato lay smoldering in three separate spots on the tarmac. Rain pounded it all—charred flesh and scorched metal—into rivulets black against the black of the parking lot.

Immediately he had ducked back into the concealing shadows of the *rotenburo*'s cedar eaves. The Russian, with a sharp eye and even sharper ear, had found him anyway. Nicholas suspected that this had been the one who had executed Phoenix after Koten had incapacitated him.

He was carrying one of the newest of the Kalishnikovs, the AKL-1000, a short doublebarreled shotgun that threw anti-personnel projectiles. It was so compact it could be used with one hand. There was absolutely nothing Nicholas could do against it.

So he came out into the night and was pelted by the rain.

"That's better," the voice said, still speaking Russian. "Now I don't have to guess where you are."

"With that thing all you need is a guess," Nicholas said.

"Precisely."

Nicholas could see him now, a tall square-shouldered man—most probably a soldier, judging by his bearing and gait—in a long, black-belted raincoat. He wore no hat and Nicholas could see his face clearly in the harsh spill of the overhead lights: beak of a nose below brows that would in middle age become beetling and would dominate his rather handsome face. Now that face was dominated by wide-apart pale blue eyes.

The Russian smiled thinly. "I am interested in intelligent men . . . no matter what their ideological perversion." His head gave a formal nod. "Pyotr Alexandrovitch Russilov."

"I was expecting Protorov." He had only words to work with at the moment and he intended to make the most of them.

Russilov's face closed down, his amiable expression wiped away. "What do you know of Protorov?"

"How did you know I spoke Russian?" Nicholas countered. "Let's have an exchange of information."

The Russian spat, gestured with the AKL-1000. "You're in no position to bargain. Move out farther into the light."

Nicholas did as he was told. He sensed movement behind him in the doorway to the building, and a moment later Koten emerged. He looked transformed. In the bad light it appeared as if his already considerable girth had been added to, his shoulders enormously wide, humped with unnatural muscle. Then, as he came out from beneath the dripping eaves, Nicholas saw that he had a body slung across his shoulders.

Using a short stepping trot he moved easily with his burden, keeping away from Russilov's line of sight, finally depositing the body at the Russian's feet like a retriever.

"The ninja is beyond reclamation." It was odd to hear him speaking Russian. "That one"—he shrugged in Nicholas' direction—"hit him once too often."

Russilov did not even glance downward. "Did you find it?"

Koten held up a tightly rolled oilskin pouch. It looked minuscule in his huge fist. "It came out of him when he died." And then he laughed, a high-pitched squeak, seeing the Russian's hesitation. "Go on, take it." He proffered the thing in his open palm. It looked no less tiny. "The rain's washed it clean."

Quickly, with his free hand, Russilov pocketed the cylinder. And there goes *Tenchi*, Nicholas thought. He remembered Sato's words, *They have the power to destroy us—all of us—if they discover* Tenchi. What *was Tenchi* that its infiltration by a foreign power could ignite a world war? Nicholas knew that he must find out. And soon.

Koten's dark eyes slid toward Nicholas. "Shall I take care of him now?"

"Keep away from him," Russilov said sharply. Koten glowered at him.

"You've just lost him face, Pyotr Alexandrovitch," Nicholas said.

"The two of you are far too dangerous to pit one against the other."

"Really?" This exchange was beginning to interest him. How in the world did this KGB operative know so much about him? "Surely you can't have a file on me. I'm a private citizen."

"Oh?" Russilov's dark eyebrows lifted. "Then what are you doing here?"

"Sato-san and I are—were—friends as well as business partners."

"And that's all." The Russian's voice was brimming with irony.

There was no point in keeping things at this level. "That car bomb couldn't've been meant only for Sato. There's no way you could have been certain that just he would be at the car when he opened the door."

"If you went, so much the better. As long as we got this"—he patted the pocket where he had dropped the packet—"we didn't need either of you. If our agent had been intercepted—"

"By Phoenix or myself."

"Oh, I believe Koten here would have found some way to deter you. But as I was saying, had our agent been intercepted, we would have brought you in."

"If you want to live," Nicholas observed, "you'd do well to shoot me now."

"I plan to."

"Then you'll never know the modifications we recently made in *Tenchi*."

"We?" For the first time Russilov seemed uncertain.

"Why do you think Tomkin Industries is merging one of its companies with Sato Petrochemicals? Not for the sheer pleasure of it, I assure you."

"You're lying," the Russian said. "I don't know anything about this."

Of course you don't, Nicholas thought. But you can't be sure. And if you don't get me to Protorov it might be a grave error. Time is short; this is no time to blunder.

"Well there *is* something you don't know then." Part of his training had been in speaking. Just as *kiai* was used as a war shout to terrify and, in some cases, paralyze one's opponent, so there was a more subtle offshoot, *ichi*. In this case it meant "position" because of what the wielder could accomplish with inflection and intonation. It was immensely difficult to master. This, combined with the fact that *ichi* was often affected by outside factors beyond the wielder's control, made it virtually a lost art. Akutagawa-san had, among other things, been an *ichi sensei* and he had seen in Nicholas an apt and willing pupil. "I was beginning to think of *Gospadin* Protorov as omniscient." He thought that *ichi* just might save his life now.

"Kill him," Koten growled. "Shoot him now or I will kill him for you."

"Quiet, you," Russilov said. He had not taken his eyes off Nicholas during the entire exchange. He cocked his head. "Come here, Comrade Linnear," he said as thunder rumbled east to west above their heads. The rain beat down on them, silvered as it spun through the lights. "You are going to get your wish, after all."

And Nicholas thought, Protorov!

KUMAMOTO/ASAMA KOGEN/SWITZERLAND
AUTUMN–WINTER 1963-SPRING 198?

This is how Akiko came to save Saigō's life and how he paid her back in kind. The autumn of 1963 was a cold and dismal one, filled with an inordinate amount of rain, sleet, and even snow, premature and the color of silver, dying upon the ground like stranded carp.

Already, in Kyūshū, where Sun Hsiung sent Akiko for the next phase of her training, the farmers were hard at work atop stained wooden ladders, spinning delicate cocoons of retted linen gauze over their precious trees to keep them from winter's harsh hand.

It was unusual to see them at this so relatively early in the year, and like the unpredictable inclement weather it boded ill for the coming winter, whose expected virulence had been spoken of in hushed whispers throughout the countryside ever since summer evaporated overnight like woodsmoke.

Mist shrouded this part of Kyūshū so thoroughly that upon her arrival Akiko could discern neither Mount Aso nor the giant smokestacks of the vast industrial complex sprawled through the valley to the northwest of the city.

She hated Kumamoto immediately. Once in feudal times perhaps it had possessed a certain charm, but in these days of Japan's mighty economic leap forward the blued patina of industrial wastes coating the old buildings were merely a reminder of how tiny a backwater Kumamoto really was.

Nevertheless Akiko had resigned herself to be here at the *Kanaka na ninjutsu ryu*. Its symbol was a circle within which were nine black diamonds. Within the open heart of them was the *kanji* ideogram *komuso*. And when she saw it she knew: the *Kuji-kiri*. Black *ninjutsu*.

There was difficulty, even with Sun Hsiung's personal chop affixed to her letter of introduction. The *sennin*, an ax-faced individual who appeared to be almost unhealthily thin, let her cool her heels for fully half a day before he summoned her within his chamber.

Then he was most effusive in his apologies. In his eyes Akiko could discover nothing, not even the basic spark that distinguished human beings from the less sentient creatures of the earth. And alone, kneeling before him on a bare reed *tatami*, she began to feel at last a sadness she needed some time to identify. At length she was surprised to discover that she missed Sun Hsiung, and part of her wished that she had never left his warm and comfortable house.

And yet there was a stronger, more urgent desire which had driven her from comfort and warmth. It was her *karma* to be here now, she knew that as well, and did not question it. Acceptance was all she had of her own now.

For his part, the *sennin* despised her on sight and silently cursed her former *sensei* for evoking his right of privilege here. There was absolutely no question of sending her away though the *sennin* wished most fervently for such an occurrence.

His only hope, he correctly detected, was if the training here—and the life—were too rigorous, too taxing both emotionally and physically for this woman. He shuddered inwardly and tried not to think about her presence here, the inevitable disruption of discipline and ritual her *wa* would cause.

Even now he could sense the peculiarly female flux of her spirit, experiencing it almost as a painful interruption in the confluence of forces he and those beneath him had labored so long and hard to perfect.

Therefore he smiled as benignly as he was able and with an inward exclamation of delight consigned her into the care of the one pupil who, at the very least, would drive her out of Kumamoto.

The *sennin* watched unblinking as she bowed formally and rose. As he watched her retreating back he smiled to himself, his thoughts on the best of possibilities regarding his newest student's fate: that Saigō would destroy her.

387

Not literally, of course, for had that occurred the *sennin* would have lost enormous face with Sun Hsiung and that he could not have tolerated. No, no. If he knew anything about his pupils, he had chosen correctly. There was a peculiar and somewhat frightening demon which rode Saigō's back, its talons sunk so deeply that the *sennin* had given up trying to exorcise its presence.

Let the Haunted One, as Saigō was known privately by a number of the *sennin*, drive the unwanted female out; let it be her choice. That way face was saved all around. The *sennin* could take no blame from Sun Hsiung and the female could return with honor to the areas for which she was best suited: the tea ceremony and, perhaps, flower arranging.

The moment Akiko came up to him in the *dōjō*, and told him of his assignment, Saigō knew the low regard in which he must be held by the *sennin*. This was an outcast's work, he thought darkly, holding the hand of a *female* student. He glared at her as anger and resentment welled up in him.

For her part, Akiko sensed immediately that she had been directed into the tiger's den. Her *wa* contracted at the icy contact with Saigō's hostile emanations and she knew that in order for her to survive here she must first win him over and then, one by one, do the same with every individual at the *ryu*.

Akiko spent more of her time that afternoon observing him as he took her on a tour of the *ryu*, which was in effect a world within a world, a secret *dōjō* in the middle of a basically industrial town, wrapped in the trappings of a drab and windowless warehouse.

There were no other students or *sennin* about when they completed their rounds.

"I want you to stay here," he told her, "while I go out on an errand." She nodded in acquiescence. "Make no sound while I am gone and, especially, when I return."

"What is happening?"

Without warning he hit her a heavy blow on the side of the face. Akiko staggered backward and fell on one hip. Saigō stood over her, his feet apart, his body totally relaxed.

"Do you wish to ask a question?" His voice was mocking, possessing an edge to it that caused Akiko to shudder inwardly. She made no sound or movement.

Grunting in some satisfaction, Saigō turned and departed.

When she was alone Akiko sank immediately into *shinki*. This involved keeping her *tanden*, that part of her called the second brain by some *sensei*, the reflex control center, immobile. In this way she detached a part of herself from the area where she burned.

388

After a moment of intense concentration, she felt no more pain. Slowly she rose, staring at the door through which he had departed.

Of course she had felt the spit of his spirit microseconds before that vicious emanation had been transmogrified into physical action. She could have easily dodged the blow. But what good would that have done? Saigō's anger would have been further fueled and he would have come after her with more serious intent.

Besides, she sensed that he was a man so unsure of his own masculinity that he needed to physically dominate those people around him, men and women alike. If she was ever to find an accommodation with him, she must first allow his natural tendencies to be made manifest to her. Only then could she choose her own strategy, and then could she tame him.

Saigō was gone several hours. During that time all light left the sky; the day burned out like the dregs of a Roman candle. It was dinnertime and Akiko found herself hungry. Since there was no food here she padded silently into the *dōjō* and, opening her bag, dressed in her all-black *gi*. She did forty minutes of centristic meditation leading ultimately to *shinki kiitsu*, the unity of soul, mind, and body that is so essential to reaching the very apex of all martial arts. She felt the weight of the universe collecting in her lower abdomen. *Shitahara*.

She breathed. In: *jitsu*: fullness. Out: *kyo*: emptiness. *Strike at the precise moment you feel* kyo *in your enemy*, Sun Hsiung had said. *Strike at the precise moment you feel* jitsu *in yourself. Thus will victory be assured*.

Yet, he had told her over and over, *if you are so foolish and full of ego that you allow yourself to think of victory then you are undone. Attach your awareness on* saika tanden, *the breath of the Void. From that central nothingness all strategies may be observed and formulated*.

She did ninety minutes of formal exercise, increasing in difficulty until she was sweating profusely, working on her quickness and her timing, coordinating the two: alternating them and then combining them in sets of three, then six, then nine rapid-fire attacks and defenses.

Then, because she was still a student, still learning, because some essentials still had to be thought about consciously rather than accomplished as second nature without any volition at all, she returned to *saika tanden*.

From her bag she unfurled a length of strong cotton—it was Sun Hsiung's only gift to her—which she folded twice and wrapped with deft economical movements about her abdomen so that the upper edge just touched the bottom ribs on either side. It was very

389

tight; it was a cincture, a constraint. She worked on inhaling as deeply as she could down into her bowels. She sat cross-legged, her body soft and pliable, her shoulders curved and relaxed, her torso bent well forward so that the tip of her nose hung approximately over her navel. *Saika tanden*. Every breath she takes.

And breathing was what consumed her still when her keen hearing detected soft padding outside the metal door. In a moment the grate of the padlock could be heard.

Jitsu; kyo. Fullness; emptiness. In and out.

She heard Saigō in the *dōjō* and her head came up. She focused fully on him.

"Get up," he whispered. "Come here." He stood just inside the closed door.

She did just as she was told, rising and unwrapping the cloth she treasured though it was quite plain and could be bought at any neighborhood store. Folding it reverently, she place it inside her loose black cotton blouse and moved to stand beside Saigō.

"Listen," he said. His voice was as indistinct as the buzz of a mosquito in the distance. They both stood quite still. She would have known not to utter a sound even had he not cautioned her against doing so hours before.

There was nothing but the slight tickle of sawdust, a remnant of the original use to which this old building had been put. No sounds from the streets three stories below made it through the thick walls and massive floorboards. It was as silent as a tomb.

Someone coughed. And again. Akiko heard soft footfalls from behind the door. She glanced at Saigō, whose entire being was focused at the closed door and what lay beyond.

Who was there? Akiko wondered. She listened.

"What is it? Where are we?" A female voice, whispered.

"Come on." Male voice. Then more insistently though no more loudly, *"Come on!"* Presence faded but Akiko had at least a semblance of the two spirits. Male and female. Yin and Yang.

Hate burned itself across Saigō's face, turning him into a gargoyle. So much hate twisting him, she thought. Eating him up inside. Hate was an emotion that she could understand.

Perhaps it was at this moment that she saw them as soulmates: Akiko and Saigō. They were meant for each other, weren't they?

After a while the chalkiness flushed from his face and he was about to speak again. But strangely, he said nothing further of the incident.

"You waited," he said.

"Isn't that what you wanted me to do?" She watched his eyes, which were like dead stones at the bottom of a silkskinned lake.

390

If it were true that the eyes were windows to the soul then Saigō had surely been born without one. She saw no anima there, only the gyring of emotions, dead weight like a corpse at the gibbet.

He nodded and she saw that he was pleased. He felt, wrongly, that his physical strike had caused her to acquiesce. Someone else of his personality type would have relaxed then, but he did not. Akiko noted that.

"It's late," he said. "Time to leave. Get dressed."

He did not turn away as she got out of her *gi*. She felt his stony gaze on her at every moment, as she peeled down. She had never felt the intense sense of embarrassment about her naked body that most Japanese apparently did. Yet she was acutely conscious of Saigō's presence, his scrutiny.

It was not prurience she felt from him, exactly, at least not in the sense of simple lust. That she would have had no trouble understanding. On the other hand, there was no sense of a cold, calculating inventory of all her parts being made. That too would have made some sense to her. He was of another type entirely, one with which she had had no prior experience.

When she was fully undressed and toweling herself off, she confronted him, turning to him face to face. "What is it here that fascinates you so?" As she said this she twisted the towel back over her shoulder so there was nothing for him to miss.

"If it's sex you're talking about," he said, "I've had my share of it." He seemed to be staring at a point below her navel. Perhaps at the spot where her curling glossy pubic hair began.

"I don't give it that freely," she said simply. "What makes you think I'd give it to you."

"You're naked, aren't you? You barely know me."

"If I was like this and I did know you well," she observed, "there'd be far more of a chance."

"You mean this isn't an invitation?"

"If you want me, that's your problem," she said beginning to pull on her clothes. "It was you who did not allow me the privacy to undress."

He watched her for a moment, then abruptly swung away. Striding to the metal door he unlocked it and busied himself with unfastening the square symbol of the *ryu* from the door. He put it aside and began to work on the crimson lacquer so that no marks of its presence remained.

Akiko was curious but knew better than to ask him why he was going to the trouble of erasing all evidence of the *ryu*'s presence in the warehouse. Since this third-floor door was the only one that led out to a landing and the outside, it was the only one that concerned him.

Dressed, Akiko picked up her bag and went out past him. She watched him carefully padlock the door.

"I have no place to stay," she said.

He gave her a key out of his pocket. "There's a spare bedroom," he said. "Don't touch anything else in the house." He wrote a street address down for her. "Wait for me," he said. "I don't know when I'll be back."

Three weeks later they were in the countryside, surrounded by Mandarin orange groves. Much of the southern island was still rural, retaining a high degree of the old ways. Saigō said he liked that.

Even this far south the snow lay heavily banked, glossy on its surface, crackling underfoot with the thinnest crust of ice, as delicate as Ming porcelain. In the moonlight it was luminescent, pushing back the spectral darkness.

Their breath hung in the air, their words made visible in albescent puffs, as connected as an island chain.

Much had changed in Akiko's life in this time, and she wondered if the same could be so for him. With almost any other person she would have known the answer.

It had begun three weeks ago when he had come back deep into the night, opening the house door with absolute silence. Akiko had been dreaming, but even so his spirit obtruded into the beta level in which her mind drifted while her consciousness slept.

She opened her eyes and was fully awake. This had never surprised her because she had been born with the ability but it confounded others.

Saigō, standing in the shadows just inside the doorway, said, "Were you asleep?"

If he were any good at all, he would know the answer to that, so she said, "No. You wanted me to wait for you. I did."

He came into the room on the balls of his feet and she felt the spitting of his spirit again, the anarchic emanations of a spiteful child. She did not flinch from him or give any sign, no matter how remote, that she knew of his intent. To do so would remove her greatest power over him. Also, it would frighten him and she could not afford that.

After he had hit her and assuaged his own weaknesses, he said, "There is a package outside. Go and fetch it." His voice was absolutely normal.

Akiko got up and went past him. As she did so she felt the

dullness of his spirit like a sated serpent, dozing. On the stoop she found, to her surprise, a young girl of her own age. She was leaning against the doorframe and she was shivering. Putting one arm around her, Akiko took her inside.

The young girl stumbled over the doorjamb and fell heavily against Akiko, who was obliged to support her entirely for three or four steps. The young girl was late in recovering, and in the warm lamplight inside Akiko looked at her.

Her face was beautiful but as dulled as Saigō's spirit. The pupils of her large eyes were heavily dilated and there was a subtle musk emanating from between her half open lips.

"She is drugged," Akiko said.

"Indeed." His reaction was no more than if she had said, She's Japanese. "Put her to bed," he said a trifle wearily. "She will share your room."

Without another word, Akiko did as he ordered her. When she had put the young girl to sleep on the one cotton *futon*, wrapping her carefully in wool blankets, she returned to the living room. She watched Saigō. He had sunk onto the *tatami*, his snow-covered coat crumpled around him like a frozen lily. His chin was on his chest and his head was nodding. His eyes were not quite closed.

For a moment Akiko wondered what would happen if she took him now; she knew that she could do it and if that were to be her strategy she would find no better time. He was at full *kyo*.

But at that moment his head snapped up and he glared at her like a viper poised to strike. Immediately, sensing the acute danger, she washed her mind of taking the offensive, and sinking down, knelt before him, her hands open and in her lap.

His eyes became hooded and at last he had fallen asleep. Akiko dozed as well. But once she awoke just before dawn, her attention focused. Across from her Saigō still slept, his breathing deep and regular and slow. Still she could not rid herself of the feeling that he continued to watch her.

Work at the *dōjō* was difficult in the extreme. All life there appeared to come to a stop when she approached. All were polite to her, but there was no harmony when she was about, and no one was more aware of this than she.

She felt that the *sensei* distrusted her and the students disliked her. There was no help they would give her if it were not a matter of face that they do so. She had never felt so alone, adrift, absolutely cut off from everything and everyone. It was as if she were an iceberg in the tropics that the sun refused to melt. If she existed at all for them it was as a wound which refused to heal.

They wished her gone and she knew it. Still she refused to

knuckle under the force of their combined will. Men had never dictated the course of her life and she was not about to allow them to now. She had fought against that, perhaps, from the moment of her birth. Her will was cast in the terrible shades of steel—a thousandfold—that went into the creation of the *katana*, the sword of honor. Did they actually think that they could break her?

But, oh, how they tried! For a start, the *sensei* put her in with the slowest group of students, those young men who, Akiko judged, would be forced to leave the *ryu* within six months. Inside an hour she had made an astoundingly accurate assessment of their abilities. All were at a lower level than she was. It was a deliberate slap in the face, but rather than allow herself to feel humiliation she resolved to use this maneuver to her own advantage.

As any student new to a particular *ryu* will do, she sat silent and rapt during the *sensei*'s lessons, watching with concentration the exercises and, later, the strike-defense combinations being illustrated.

All of this was material that Sun Hsiung had taught her and which she had mastered years ago. Her mien was that of the learning student attempting to absorb the new and complicated. For the moment she was content to give them what they expected.

When it came her time to practice the moves, the *sensei* gave way to one of the students in the class. Another deliberate slap in the face, for all who had gone before her had worked directly with the *sensei*.

She was given a polished wooden pole perhaps half the thickness of a *bokken*—the wooden *kendo* practice sword—and three times as long. She arranged herself on the polished wooden floorboards, encompassed by wood. She did not ignore this aspect of her surroundings, taking her cue from the qualities of hardwood that the Japanese most prized: flexibility and durability.

Went into *shinki kiitsu* and, lifting her pole at the last possible instant, she easily knocked the student off his feet as he attacked.

Within the silence surrounding the class, the *sensei* sent the next boy at her. The result was the same, though she varied her response to his attack.

Now the *sensei* sent two of his pupils at her at once. Akiko still knelt staring straight ahead. She did not have to turn her head in order to know where the second student was or what he was doing. *Shinki kiitsu* revealed his strategy to her. Both her fists gripped the wooden pole lightly yet firmly at its exact center; this was essential because she was employing the fulcrum concept and balance was crucial.

She kept her place, at a disadvantage because she did not have her feet. But there was a lot she could do with her upper torso.

Concentrating on the Void, she felt the advancement from behind her. She torqued her shoulders, dipping her right side and bringing it up to increase momentum and thus power. The pole whistled through the air, slammed into the student's rib cage, sending him flying.

The opposite end of the pole—now the lower end—began its upward swing at just that moment, its rounded end jamming lightly into the oncoming second student's throat. He sat down hard on his buttocks, a stunned look on his face.

It was only then, as her concentration broke its intense focus, that she became aware of the interest from other quarters of the *dōjō*. What she had thought to be an isolated incident had been observed by fully three-quarters of the *ryu*.

But if she suspected that the *sensei* of her class would now accord her the honor of performing against him, she was mistaken. Again the school sought to subtly humiliate her. The *sensei* bade her rise. Taking the pole from her, he led her across the *dōjō* floor to where Saigō's class was working. He left her in care of another *sensei*, a dour-faced individual with severe pockmarks across his cheeks and chin.

He bowed formally to her. "Welcome," he said, though he did not for a moment mean it. It was as if she were a *gaijin* in her own country.

His hard-calloused hand, as yellow as tallow, extended. "Please be kind enough to assume *kokyū suru.*" *Kokyū suru* was an attack stance but as with all Japanese words and phrases it had another meaning; it also meant, "breathe."

"Jin-san."

The student he had named stepped forward, bowing toward his *sensei*. "Hai."

"It seems that Ofuda-san has been inadvertently put in the wrong class through an administrative oversight. We do not wish for such an occurrence to happen again. Would you be so kind as to convince us that with us she has found her proper place." So saying he retreated to the edge of the circle formed by the rest of the class.

Out of the corner of her eye Akiko could see Saigō standing relaxed and calm. Was he curious about how she would fare in his more advanced class? Was he wishing that it were he instead of Jin-san who had been chosen to test her?

There was no bowing done within this *dōjō* circle as there would be in any other form of martial discipline in Japan. They were ninja here; the code of *bushido*—the creed of the *samurai*—was meaningless to them. Though honor was not.

Jin-san stood facing her, his feet apart to about the width of his shoulders. His fisted hands were held before him at waist height, the left cupped over the right.

There was something disturbing in this stance that Akiko could not quite put her finger on. Then he moved and were it not for the fact that she could read his spirit, anticipating his physical strike, she would have been finished even before she had a chance to parry.

As it was, she barely made it. Her foreknowledge allowed her to both prepare her spirit and focus her attention on the unknown. Therefore she saw the glint of the *manrikigusari*—literally "the chain with the strength of ten thousand men"—consisting of two feet of hand-forged iron chain with three-and-one-half-inch blunt-ended weights attached to each end.

And now she knew what had disturbed her about Jin-san's stance: it was *goho-no-kamae*, one of the openings or *kamae* in spike and chain fighting.

Jin-san was already halfway toward her, his arms spread so that the *manrikigusari* hung in a loose arc between his fists. He would seek *makiotoshi*, she knew, winding the chain about her neck, because not only was it essential that he defeat her but also that he do so quickly and decisively.

She did not make the mistake of trying to grab for the chain. She knew that she could expect only a weight in her eye for her trouble or, if she were foolish enough to manage a two-handed grasp, crushed knuckles.

Therefore she sought to ignore the *manrikigusari* entirely as a target. She bent her torso only slightly—and to the side, not, as he had expected, away from the attack. This allowed some of her own momentum to build up while she came inside the attack, using her left side as a wedge combined with his own forward momentum to strike at *ekika*, a vital spot just beneath the armpits. The *ate* broke both Jin-san's rhythm and his concentration. Thus cut off from the Void, he was easy to take down.

The pockmarked *sensei* said nothing as Jin-san got shakily to his feet and returned to the sanctuary of the circle's edge. But Akiko could feel a great leap in the onlookers' tension.

In her memory there was something absolutely otherworldly in the next several minutes. How many times had she relived the *sensei*'s next movements, watching as if in slow motion as he turned toward the press of his students and uttered the word, "Saigō-san."

There was no hesitation, no eye contact, nothing at all in Saigō's demeanor to tell her what was in his mind. But she knew that in the next instant, as they came at each other, the fate of their relationship, present and future, would be spelled out.

She also knew that both their fates were completely in her hands. In his own mind he had already conquered her, so he held none of the dominance-anxiety for her that he might male rivals of his here. He would simply do what his *sensei* asked of him: that is, defeat her as convincingly as possible. Humiliate her in public.

It was up to Akiko, therefore, to divine the twining of their *karma*—if there was to be any at all—and to use this moment to defuse the deep well of hatred that seethed like a volcano inside of him. He was very dangerous, and she never lost sight of that. He could very easily hurt her seriously if she allowed that well to come uncapped. She did not believe the *sensei* would be able to sense it soon enough and intervene in time. Saigō might easily kill her, gripped in the heat of his own energies, without even knowing it.

All this flashed through her mind as Saigō entered the inner circle where moments before Jin-san had gone down before her. Seeing his tense, hot face, she knew that he had vowed not to allow the same indignity to happen to him.

He took three minutes to defeat her, but in that time an eternity of knowledge seethed back and forth between them in microcosm. The employment of strategies revealed the layers of the spirit; there was nothing behind which to hide. They became more intimate than lovers, sharing more, even, than twins. The Void connected them in its wholeness as they maneuvered, as they stared down the dark tunnels of each other's souls.

"Yes," the pockmarked *sensei* said with no hint of the disappointment he felt at the defeat of even one of his pupils at her hand. "You'll do here, Ofuda-san."

Afterward, Saigō suggested that they go out to dinner. The slumbering young woman who he had brought home the night before had been transferred to his *futon*. Akiko had made no comment about that nor about the fact that she never ate and barely opened her eyes during the daylight hours. Drugged she had been and drugged she stayed.

Saigō said nothing at the restaurant, picking disinterestedly at his yellowfin *sashimi* and *daikon* salad for the longest time. Life went on around them in a dizzying explosion of drinking and forced gaiety, as if these people who worked so hard and long during the day at the giant factories just beyond the town felt

compelled to cram a week's worth of carousing into a sin
evening.

Akiko saw many women who were in the same profession
her mother had been in. These were of a different level, of cour
but the end remained the same. Observing them made her f
odd, as if she were back in *Fuyajo*, peeking through gaps
bedroom walls during the endless nights.

Yet she felt as if she had changed, for it occurred to her t
her mother's utter refinement was but a facade, that in so
unfathomable way she was no better than these women here w
lacked status, dignity, and, ultimately, that most precious of
Japanese commodities, honor.

Ikan had had no family, no ancestors she wished to honor,
husband to protect her, through whom she could guide her o
destiny and that of her progeny. She had only Akiko, and t
responsibility had been too great for her.

For she, like these women now, lacked a future into whic
child could grow, prosper, and find herself.

"Akiko-san."

She shifted her attention back to him. *"Hai?"*

"Why didn't you do it?"

She knew what he was talking about but perhaps it would
good for him to say it. "I don't know what you mean, Saigō-sar

He thought about that for a moment. "You could have defea
me in our confrontation at the *dōjō*. Yet you chose not to."

She shook her head. "Please believe me. I could not sta
against you."

"I felt it."

Her dark eyes held his shadowed ones. "What you felt, perha
Saigō-san, was your intense anxiety not to be defeated in front
your peers. Honor rules you; it is your weapon and your fe
How could I possibly strip you of either?"

Now, three weeks later, trodding the snow strewn aisles k
tween rows of dreaming orange trees awaiting next year's su
Akiko knew that she had taken the right path.

Michi. It was the Japanese word for path; but it could a
mean a journey, as well as duty, the unknown, a stranger.

Akiko abruptly felt that she must be the first person on ea
to have come upon a situation in which all of the word's meanir
were in play simultaneously. For her life with Saigō was ting
with all these things, and it was impossible for her to say whe
one left off and the other began.

Silently they passed a stand of tall, whipthin bamboo. A bran
of one older tree was heavily laden with ice-crusted snow. Sure

398

at any moment it must break beneath its burden. But no. The gusting wind caused the branch to bob up and down and such was the resilient nature of the wood that at length the branch sprang upward and like the finest of bows loosed its charge. Snow in a fine spray dusted the cold air, powdering down upon them in bracing fashion. And in its wake they saw the branch of the bamboo now free of excess weight.

They passed on, shoulders hunched, bunched hands in the pockets of their coats while the wind continued to whistle by overhead.

Within the shelter of a dense copse of pines Saigō stopped them. A river sang merrily to their left and below them. From this interior space it was impossible to see either the industrial sprawl beyond Kumamoto or even the looming presence of Mount Aso with its plume of pumice and hot ash. It was possible to believe for a moment that one could be divorced from such things, that the heavily layered structuralism of life had momentarily disappeared.

Turning his back to the gnarled trunk of one great grandfather tree, Saigō slid down until he was on his haunches. Akiko knelt beside him at right angles. He did not turn toward her but continued to stare straight ahead at the puzzle of crisscrossing branches, white with snow and ice.

Akiko stared at his proud profile. In many ways he was still an enigma to her. But then she suspected that he was even more of an enigma to himself. Though he was inordinately introspective for a young man, it was not self-examination that occupied him. The eternal flame of his hate had to be nurtured and, on occasion, fanned. Akiko suspected quite rightly that with the cessation of his hatred Saigō would perish. It was his primary nourishment; mother's milk to his spirit.

Already she suspected that he was wholly evil. Yet she was drawn to him. Was it despite this knowledge or because of it? She felt frightened when she was near him, as if the blight eating away at his soul was contagious. But at the same time she felt a distinct lessening of the anomie which at times buffeted her spirit with the viciousness of a riptide.

With Saigō she felt that she belonged. Time and place coalesced into meaning, for he had the spirit of the outlaw not the outcast, which she had always assumed herself to be. An outcast had no status, no dignity, no honor. She recalled her feelings that night in the restaurant when she saw the *geisha* with their snapping black teeth and faces coated with white rice flour.

It occurred to her then that she thought about Ikan infrequently;

and then it was with a painful lurch as if she were fighting to disengage herself from a particularly loathsome creature. Ikan had no status save that of *tayu oiran*, which, of course, was meaningless outside the *Yoshiwara*. Ever since Akiko had escaped from there, her contempt for courtesans was boundless.

Had not Ikan been sold into what was, effectively, slavery? Had not the very fact that she had worked in the happy field rendered her undesirable as a wife? Where was the dignity in this way of life? Where was the honor?

Akiko could not even summon up anger at her mother; her emotions had gone beyond the stage where she resented Ikan's inability to accept her. She felt only contempt for what her mother had been, what she had done.

Ikan had been an outcast, and without even knowing it Akiko had cast herself in the same mold. But now Saigō had shown her that there was another path she could take. For an outlaw possessed status, dignity, and honor. Japan's ancient tradition of the nobility of failure—the triumph of ideals over actions—proved this beyond any doubt.

Beside her, Saigō felt a spasm grip him. He felt as if something inside him were being pulled in opposite directions. Spite surged within him, and a fulminating desire to hurt her. "There must be an ending," he said.

The wind snatched at his words, sent them hurtling among the snow laden pines. Still he did not turn toward her. There was a minute trembling to his head and she felt the tension in his frame.

"You may have wondered at the identity of the girl I brought home some weeks ago." His head lowered until his chin almost touched his chest. "She is the one that I love." Akiko felt the knife in her ribs, turning slowly, as he had wished. "Her name is Yukio and she has betrayed me. Betrayed me to my cousin; to a *gaijin*! *Iteki!*" The last two epithets were spat with such vehemence that Akiko was obliged to close her eyes against the force of the rage.

Saigō's lips curled back in the semblance of a smile that was more a snarl. "You may well ask yourself how a *gaijin* came to be a cousin of mine. Well, my mother, Itami, had a brother, a fierce and loyal man of great *samurai* blood. His name was Tsūkō and in the winter of 1943, following the death of his superior, he was given command of the garrison at Singapore.

"There he served his Emperor long and well until September of 1945 when, outnumbered, he tried to hold the city against the advancing British forces. His men were surrounded. They died defending the honor of Japan as befits true *samurai*. Tsūkō was the last to perish, shot many times by *iteki* while he slashed their

400

limbs and heads with his *katana*. The British, like all barbarians, have no concept of honor.

"At the time of his death my uncle was married to a woman who was quite beautiful but of dubious parentage. That is to say it was suspected that she was at least part Chinese. She must have bewitched Tsūkō, for he apparently ignored these rumors.

"I know that she could not have been Japanese. No *samurai* blood runs in the veins of a woman who will not avenge the murder of her husband. This Cheong, instead, married the man who commanded the enemy's attack on Singapore. Perhaps he himself fired one of the bullets that fatally wounded my uncle. She did not care."

Saigō's head lifted. "The offspring of Cheong and this barbarian Colonel is Nicholas Linnear." With that one last foreign word Akiko felt a prescient thrill shoot up her spine. Could it be so, she asked herself. Could the wheel of life have brought her to the one person on earth who could truly help her. For it had been this same Colonel Linnear, this *iteki*, as Saigō called him, who had pressed for public disclosure of Akiko's father's so-called indiscretions, thereby murdering him. She concentrated further, anxious now to absorb it all.

"It was he who came to the precincts of our *ryu*, hand and hand with his lover, Yukio," Saigō continued. "She and I were lovers before he met her. Like his halfbreed mother did to Tsūkō, Nicholas has somehow seduced Yukio's spirit. Now I must drug her or she would seek to escape and fly to him. Now only I have her."

"You make love to her . . . still?"

Saigō's head whipped around and his dead eyes glared at her, challenging her. "I take her whenever I choose to do so." He turned again to stare out at the crosshatch of branches. "She betrayed me; she deserves no less."

Akiko remembered his words from before, *There must be an ending*. "Now you wish to kill her."

Saigō said nothing for a time. Then, "I wish for revenge. For myself; for my mother. Most of all, for Tsūkō."

And she thought, *K'ai ho*. I see a gap; I must enter swiftly. But softly she said, "Two weeks ago you left abruptly. I did not see you at home or in the *dōjō* for four days."

"In Tokyo," he said, "I attended the funeral of my father." He closed his eyes. "I wished to take you but I could not."

She bowed to him. "I am honored."

"He was a great man." Again tension gripped him. "But eventually he was destroyed by the invading barbarians . . . by Colonel

401

Linnear. The *iteki* garrotted him. Now I have begun my reven[g]
I have administered a poison to the Colonel. It is absorbed throu[gh]
the pores of the skin and is untraceable. It is slow acting, creati[ng]
a deadly accretion day by day."

"And then?"

He nodded his head. "You are right. Yukio must die. But t[he]
fact must not reach my cousin, Nicholas. He must wonder . . . a[nd]
wait until the time is right. Then I will confront him and j[ust]
before I deliver the death blow I will tell him of his belove[d]
fate. Thus will all the unquiet *kami* who hover about me, [de]
manding retribution and rest, be assuaged."

Death, death, and more death. It surrounded them as if th[ey]
were adrift in a sea of skulls. The *giri* Saigō bore seemed a burd[en]
of unconscionable weight to Akiko. No wonder his spirit w[as]
being trampled into dust. How well she saw now the twining [of]
their *karma*.

Without thinking she reached out, her fingers sliding up [his]
arm. His head whipped around, that red challenge back in [his]
eyes, and she said, "Let me banish your *kami* . . . if just for [a]
moment."

Something seemed to melt inside him, a barrier swinging dow[n]
and the proud warrior collapsed into her embrace, a child at [his]
mother's comforting breast.

The cold was no deterrent to their fire, and for the first ti[me]
in his life Saigō felt the hot surge of blood into his penis a[t a]
woman's touch. Always, before, there had been a certain violen[ce]
to his coupling with Yukio—and more often than not he wou[ld]
take her from behind as he did with his young men lovers, so t[hat]
there was nothing about it that could be termed lovemaking.

But with Akiko it was different. Perhaps it was because he h[ad]
allowed Akiko to melt him, to take the lead. It was he who n[ow]
acquiesced to her lovemaking, responding as she led, using har[d]
calloused hands given to inflicting pain and death in long lega[to]
caresses across the snowy contours of her steaming body.

The moment he felt the movement of her moist lips benea[th]
his, the moment he became aware of her tongue emerging, pro[b]
ing, he was as hard as a rock and as ecstatically eager as a virgi[n].

And in regard to lovemaking he *was* a virgin. Tenderness a[nd]
compassion held no domain inside him. Love was unknown. *M[u]
chi*.

Her breasts swelled to his touch, sensation buzzing from h[er]
erect nipples. He wanted to enter her almost immediately, su[ch]
was his excitement. But Akiko persuaded him otherwise with h[er]

lips, her deft, knowing hands, and the clamp of her trembling thighs.

Near the end she held the base of his erection as tightly as she dared so that he would not ejaculate before either of them wanted him to. Meanwhile she teased his nipples with the tip of her tongue, his scrotum with a wave of her fingers, the head of his penis with the tender flesh of her inner thighs.

She rolled him around and around in that pliant grip until the friction became unbearable and he was so engorged that she took pity on them both and placed him at the font of her vagina.

With a long drawn-out groan he pushed into her, his eyelids fluttering, his chest heaving, until his slender hips crashed into hers and he was fully hilted.

She would not let him move, fearful that just one bull thrust would send his twanging emotions over the edge. Instead, she cupped her hands against his buttocks, fitting her to him as closely as possible. Then she commenced to squeeze and relax her inner muscles. The resulting contractions caused far less friction than if he were stroking into her. He would last longer though he was on the verge of orgasm when he entered her.

Akiko watched his face, feeling her emotions soaring not only from the liquid erotic contact but from what was written across his features. She reveled in the pleasure she was giving him; the banishment at least temporarily of the *kami* that haunted him day and night.

Sweat froze along their backs, riming them, making them into creatures of the winter countryside. Where they made contact their bodies were slick with juices as if hot oil had been poured between them.

Akiko's eyes lost focus and she found her mind wandering as if in a dream. She was close herself. She made herself focus on Saigō. He was past seeing or hearing anything. His hard, lean body surged continually against her in minute ripples. Cords stood out along the sides of his neck and his teeth were gritted hard in his effort to continue the ecstasy. But he could not.

"Ohh, yes!" she cried, beside herself, biting his neck as she, too, lost herself in pleasure.

For a long time afterward he did not seem his old self. Remnants of what he had been, lost in her embrace, continued to hold sway like beautifully architectured ruins on a bloody battlefield.

He continued to cling to her, his breathing taking an unaccountably long time to return to normal. Even when they both became chilly and were forced to don clothing he did not wish to be apart.

Once, he began to weep silent tears. When she asked him what troubled him, he said, "I was remembering that bamboo we passed earlier. Oh, how I wish I could be like that tree, so resilient, so able to free itself of the greatest burden!"

But then, slowly, he returned to the Saigō she had known and, at length, they sat apart, not even their shoulders or hands touching. It seemed to Akiko that in some strange way he had become embarrassed by what they had done here, as if he had allowed himself to transgress against internal rules only he was aware of. She wished she could say that it was only the tears of which he was ashamed, but she feared that was not so.

It seemed to her that he was regretting the fact that he possessed emotions and needs just like every other human being. Akiko had been around him long enough to understand that Saigō had built for himself the concept of his own separatism from the entire human race.

If he believed in a god at all, it was this one. For his separation gave him power as the Void gave most others power. It allowed him to accept all that he did as necessary and right. Without that belief he—like a priest without Buddha—would be bereft.

But in this one instance, this turning away had hurt her terribly and she could not hold her tongue. Watching his face, she said, "You did not enjoy our joining, Saigō-san? You did not feel the outpouring of love as I did?"

His face screwed up derisively. "Love! Pah! There is no such thing!"

"Yet, before, you told me that you love Yukio," Akiko persevered, though she felt a foreboding building inside her.

"What I feel for Yukio is none of your concern," he snapped. "As for what I said, I used an equivalent word. What I feel for her is inexpressible in language. But certainly it is not love."

"And for me?" She knew it would come to this, but her fear of what he might or might not say was insufficient for her to hold onto her words. "What do you feel for me, Saigō-san? Is it, too, inexpressible?"

"Questions, questions, and more questions. Why is it that all women know how to do is ask questions?" He lurched drunkenly to his feet. His breath was a steamy cloud before his lips. He was fully the warrior again. "I find questions insupportable, Akiko-san. You already know that about me yet you persist in asking them."

"I am only human," she said sadly. "Unlike you, *oyabun*."

He laughed then, a low guttural sound. "*Oyabun*, eh? That is good, Akiko-san. Very, very good. You see me as your mentor,

404

your overlord. Well, I'll say this for you, you certainly know how to keep me in good humor."

But already he suspected that the supposedly immutable continents of his being were shifting off their divine axis. Now with a brilliant flash daylight had begun to pour in through the resulting rent, flooding his world, scoring demarkations to a landscape alien to him. And in the shadowed recesses, flickering fires licked, funeral pyres to what had once been.

Looking at her now, it seemed abruptly clear to him that he, indeed, had never loved Yukio; had, in fact, not understood that feeling could be warm as well as cold.

As his eyes drank Akiko in he felt a return of the deep sexual throbbing she had elicited from him. He felt none of the aggressive rage toward her that he had felt toward Yukio or his many male lovers. He was astonished to find that with Akiko there was no anger at all, only this warmth that, belatedly, he could identify as comfort. And now he knew that all that he had said to her today was not as he had thought, to hurt her, but to unburden himself.

The sky had grown dark with low, surging clouds. The air was damp and leaden. It would rain or snow soon, depending on the balance of the temperature. A premature twilight was coming on, as purple as a new bruise.

"Storm coming from the northwest," he said. "Time to go." He wanted to pull his eyes away from her but he was like a child who had discovered his love of sweets; once in the shop he was reluctant to depart.

Yet at the same time he felt a need to break the tenuous connection that still linked them like a length of twined silk. It was important for him to regain a sense of himself, to know that all of him had not been transformed by this new feeling; that the iron warrior still beat strongly within him.

Thus he began without her, walking as if he had forgotten her existence. Then, as Akiko rose to follow him, she saw that something that was hidden from her vantage point had caught his attention. She watched as he turned off the path, heading into the pines on his left.

In a moment he was back. In his left hand he held a squirming ball of gray fur by the scruff of its neck.

"Eeya! Akiko-san, see what I've found! A wolf cub!"

Smiling, Akiko came toward him down the path. For just an instant he had the happy, carefree aspect of a little boy. It was so good to see that spark in him, she thought. If only this time could be extended.

At that moment, she became aware of a blur hurtling through

the air toward him. She opened her mouth to scream a warning but it was already too late.

The great gray thing was already atop Saigō, snarling and clawing. Saigō staggered and fell sideways beneath the fury of the onslaught. Instinctively he dropped the cub but the mother was oblivious, attacking him with insane ferocity.

Akiko ran up, saw them twisting back and forth on the snowy ground. She bent down, trying to grab the wolf behind its neck in order to pull it off him.

But Saigō must have hit a patch of ice for he spun beneath her and, tumbling head over heels, man and beast flew over the embankment, down twenty feet to the riverbank.

Akiko, running to the edge, saw Saigō's back arch, agony contorting his face. Then she was half sliding, half scrambling down the rock-strewn embankment. Landing on her buttocks, she lashed out with her foot, catching the wolf on the snout with the toe of her boot.

The animal leaped high into the air, yelping, and when it landed, turned and loped upward into the rising copse of pine where its cub still wandered, lost and bewildered.

Akiko knelt beside Saigō. His face, shoulder, and forearms were a mass of slashes. She saw a set of teeth marks just above his left wrist. All these were minor. But his spine was canted at an unnatural angle and his rolling, dilated pupils showed how much pain he was in.

With the utmost care she turned him onto his stomach. It was immediately clear to her that in his fall he had smashed part of his upper spine against the outcroppings of rock spiking the embankment.

Delicately she ran her fingertips, as a surgeon might, along the ragged, jutting spine. At least three vertebrae were involved, perhaps four.

She took a deep breath. Among other things Sun Hsiung had been a *koppo sensei*. With two fingers he could break any bone in the body of his enemy. That was *koppo*'s most commonplace and well known expertise. But Sun Hsiung had taught her the other aspect of *koppo*: *katsu*. It was a form of deep resuscitation.

Once she had seen him use *seikotsu*, an adjunct to *katsu*, and had begged him to teach her this more esoteric and difficult art. It was a form of bone-setting.

She slowed her breathing, knowing that if she began the process and failed, she would most likely doom Saigō to a life of partial paralysis. For him that would surely be a death sentence. But what was the alternative? She could not move him. She could not leave him for the time it would take her to search out a telephone. He was already in shock and unconscious. She could not ask his permission, and if she did not act swiftly the cold would infiltrate his natural defenses and kill him.

Without another thought, she put her fears aside and went to work on him. For twenty minutes she labored with only one brief interruption. As she had suspected, a fourth vertebra was involved, lower down than the others. She did not know if any of the *seikotsu aiki* would work here. She did not know whether to proceed.

Then she closed her eyes and sought the no-thought that was the Void. Here, instinct—and something more—guided her: a sense of cosmic harmony. Using both thumbs at *kyusho*—vital spots—on either side of the unaligned bone, she pressed inward and apart. Heard the pop like a cork coming out of a bottle of champagne and thanked Buddha for strength and courage.

For a time after that, she knelt over him, slumped with fatigue and relief, her hot breath keeping the ice from forming on his naked back.

Then, gathering herself for the ordeal, she slung Saigō's still unconscious form across her shoulders, settling his weight as comfortably as she could. As a weight lifter will, she rose with her burden and started off home.

"And that is how you came here," he said.

Akiko nodded. "It was Saigō who told me of you; it was he who suggested that I seek entrance where he could not."

"I consider that presumptuous of him," he observed. "But hardly surprising. He was not fit to stay here. I do not believe that he is fit to stay anywhere for very long."

She resented his words bitterly, knowing that Saigō had deliberately paved the path for her that he had sought for himself but had been denied.

Kyōki broke into her thoughts. "What is it that you seek here, Akiko-san? What do you believe I can provide you that others cannot?"

"I want to learn how to hide my spirit," she said. "To exhibit perfect *wa* even when I am about to strike down my enemy."

Kyōki poured them both more tea. He commenced to sip his. They sat cross-legged facing each other across the flagged stone floor. The castle in which they sat, he had told her, had been built by Ieyasu Tokugawa sometime during the first decade of the seventeenth century for a woman who was half-Portuguese and half-Japanese. A very special woman, Akiko had thought.

407

Outside, a *komuso* with a reed basket over his head played his bamboo flute in plangent fashion.

"Tell me," he said after a time, "how a young girl comes to have so many deadly enemies."

There was no recourse but to tell him all of it: of Ikan and *Fuyajo*, of Shimada, her father, and those who had set the *wak-izashi* in his hands, guiding it in two powerful lifedenying strokes into his lower abdomen, destroying his *hara*. His life. *Seppuku*.

Kyōki closed his diamond-shaped eyes. "It is gratifying to see such an unwavering expression of filial piety in one so young." He took up the goldthread fan lying beside him and began a soft, fluttering motion at his cheek. It was feminine and, Akiko felt, unflattering.

Immediately Kyōki ceased this motion. His eyes pierced her, penetrating her thoroughly. The fan was a stilled butterfly at the side of his head. "Does my use of the fan disturb you, Akiko-san?"

She had to stifle the urge to lie to him. Saigō had cautioned her against this. *Kyōki-san will know*, he told her, *and at once you will be asked to leave*.

The truth shamed Akiko and she felt blood rush into her cheeks. "The fan seems unbecoming to a great warrior such as yourself."

"Or yourself."

"I am no great warrior, *sensei*."

"But you aspire to be."

"*Hai*."

"Then you spurn the fan."

"As a woman I—"

She watched, openmouthed, as the fan hummed through the air, embedding itself in the exact center of a camphorwood chest across the expanse of the room.

"Not as a woman," Kyōki said, "but as a warrior." Unconcernedly, he sipped more tea. "Please retrieve my weapon," he said when he had put down his porcelain cup.

Akiko rose and went across the room. She reached up and as she touched the thing, spread like the hand of Buddha, spearing the wood, he said, "This is no *ōgi*, no mere fan, you pull from my chest, Akiko-san. It is *gunsen*, a weapon of battle."

As she brought it back to him, he said, "All ten ribs are of hand-forged steel, the fan itself a membrane of steel mesh that can slice through skin, flesh, viscera . . . even bone, with the proper strike."

In his hands again the *gunsen* fluttered back and forth at his cheek, the docile butterfly returned to its chrysalis.

408

"Your room is on the second floor," he said. "Directly below mine."

"I have no parents; I make the heavens and the earth my parents. I have no home; I make *saika tanden* my home. I have no body; I make stoicism my body. I have no eyes; I make the flash of lightning my eyes. I have no strategy; I make *sakkatsu jizai** my strategy. I have no designs; I make *kisan*** my designs. I have no principles; I make *rinkiohen**** my principles."

Akiko, alone in the Room of All Shadows, knelt before the double line of joss sticks and long white tapers. Both were lit and the resulting scents pervaded the chamber. The atmosphere seemed to absorb her prayers as if it were listening.

Kyōki's castle lay nestled in a glen shaggy with white birch and larch, acres of bright, blooming giant azaleas and stands of peach trees, one thousand meters above sea level in Asama *kogen*. These were the highlands—cool in summer, frosted in winter— just over 130 kilometers from Tokyo, northeast of the sprawling, jammed supertropolis, almost squarely in the center of Honshū, Japan's main island.

The *kogen* were dominated by 2,500-meter Asama-yama, an active volcano whose upper slopes were kept sere and utterly barren by frequent eruptions.

On the opposite side of the highlands from where Kyōki's castle stood, sweeping northeast off Asama-yama's skirt, was Onioshidashi, a black, blasted lavascape aptly named after the monstrous outpouring of the earth's depths in 1783; "The Devil's Discharge."

Parkland and villas of the rich were strewn all about here but none within seeing distance of the castle, named *Yami Doko*— Kite in the Darkness—by Kyōki soon after he came to live here.

Akiko had as little an idea when that was as she had about anything else in the *sensei*'s background. With her eyes alone she could tell that he was at least part Mongol: the slant to his eyes, the width and flatness of his cheekbones, as well as the hue of his skin. She could envision his ancestors, wrapped in wolf skins and beaten metal corselets, descending on horseback from the Chinese steppes, snowy wind at their backs, to raid the villages of the plains.

They worked within a rigidly formulaic framework that was

---

*Free to kill and to restore life.
**Taking opportunity by the forelock.
***Adaptability to all circumstances.

without even the most minute deviation. This was in direct couterpart to her two years at the *ryu* in Kumamoto. Every momof Akiko's time in Asama was mapped out and had to be assuously accounted for. A blank spot was cause for punishme. Excuses of any kind were not tolerated. Neither was illness, wh was treated by Kyōki with various natural poultices and her combinations. He was a gifted *yogen*—chemist—and Akiko, w was rarely sick in any case, inevitably found herself recove within ten hours. Meanwhile her studies—even the most tax physical exercises—were performed uninterrupted.

For weeks at a time they lived in the wilderness, leaving castle far behind. Often this occurred during inclement weather in the dead of winter or during late summer and early autu when successions of typhoons lashed the island's southern coa sending dark, whipping squalls into the interior like a drago raking claws.

This was purposeful. He taught her how to use the eleme and even, in many cases, to tame them. With them they took o *rokugu*, the ninja's "six tools for traveling." Five were all c tained within the sixth, *uchitake*, a three-meter length of hollow out bamboo. Inside was stored medicine, a stone pencil, tow hat, and *musubinawa*, an eight-meter coil of rope made out women's hair, lighter than regular rope and stronger.

They lived in trees and in the bush, by low-lying alpine strea on rock outcroppings along Shiraito Falls, a staggeringly beauti network of narrow water chutes climbing up a sheer, folia encrusted cliff face.

Tsuchigumo was a technique that Kyōki claimed had been pas down to him through his father from Jinnai Ukifune, an assas in the service of Nobunaga Oda, powerful feudal *daimyō*, uni among all ninja because he was a dwarf.

Tsuchigumo was, as Kyōki put it, "bat in the rafters." He tau her to cling to the tops of rooms where crossbeams and such co be employed with the aid of *nekode*, cat's claws of forged ste Hour after hour they hung in the darkness of the night, us arcane breath-control techniques to slow their metabolisms a therefore remain motionless until just before dawn.

At that time they would drop lithely and silently down o the stone flooring, free of muscle knots and cramps, ready— this were a real situation—to deliver a lethal blow to an uns pecting enemy.

One evening, perhaps a year and a half after she had first entered the castle, Kyōki summoned her to a room which she had never seen before. It was large and had an arching ceiling so high its upper reaches were lost in gloom. It was divided by an odd-looking doorway that had the aspect of a Chinese moon gate, almost circular in nature.

There were *tatami*, the first she had seen at *Yami Doko*. Kyōki knelt on one of these just beyond the arc of the moon gate. Before him was a lacquer tea service, a small plate piled with rice cakes.

Akiko bowed low and, doffing her boots, knelt opposite him. The moon gate rose above them and between them, the demarkation between *sensei* and pupil.

All was quiet in the room, all was serene. Akiko, questing as he had taught her to do, felt only the harmony of his *wa*. She watched him prepare the green tea; she had not known that he had these skills. She was mesmerized by the movements. She felt languid and calm. Almost at peace.

Kyōki put aside the whisk and, turning the porcelain cup one half a revolution, presented her with the steaming tea. He bowed low to her and she followed suit, extending her torso forward. Her forehead touched the *tatami* on the other side of the moon gate.

Whisper, as of silk against flesh or . . .

Galvanized, her adrenals pumping furiously, she tucked her head under and launched herself forward, rolling, ball-like, forward across the *tatami*.

Behind her the metal blade hurtled downward from the apex of the moon gate arc, slicing through the reed mat at the precise spot where the exposed back of her neck had been a split second before, burying itself in the floor beneath.

Akiko bounded to her knees and stared wide-eyed at her *sensei*, who was calmly sipping at his tea.

"How?" she said wonderingly. "I felt not even the tiniest ripple in your *wa*. There was nothing . . . nothing at all."

"This is why you are here," Kyōki said simply. "*Jahō* masks my *wa*."

"*Jahō*," Akiko echoed. "Magic?"

The *sensei* shrugged. "Call it what you will. It goes by many names. Which one you use is unimportant."

"It exists."

"Were you aware of my intentions?"

"I might have died. Would you really have allowed that?"

"Once the blade is released I can no longer control it," he said. "As always, you were the master of your own fate. And I am

411

pleased to see you here beside me. You are not the first woman who has ever come here seeking that which was meant for man. Women, traditionally, seek to *control* power and in that way possess it. It is an oblique strategy; a *female* stratagem. In this way in our society a mother controls her son, a wife controls her husband. It is rare indeed for the woman to seek a more *direct* means; to possess absolute dominion over men through her own strength.

"As I have indicated, several have tried. All have failed. Perhaps, now, you will be the first *miko*." He rose, held out his hand palm up. "Come. It is time we begin your true education."

He was a face in the rain. She saw him and did not see him. He was there beside her and he was not. Quick as a *kami*, he flickered, a blazing light, and then was gone.

Though she had spent years with him, though he had held the key to her world, and had passed it on to her, there came a time when she began to doubt that she had ever been to *Yami Doko*.

The Swiss Alps rose all about the vast chalet in which she lay swathed in pure white bandages. She could not see and most of the time there was nothing of interest to hear. She fed off her memories.

Kyōki became a dream, as insubstantial as smoke rising from a forest floor. But not what she had absorbed from him.

Every day white-suited nurses wheeled her outside into the thin sunshine for exactly forty minutes. The Swiss were as precise as the Japanese about some things. Schedules were one of them.

She remembered the moment the wild boar came crashing out of the underbrush to confront them. She stood her ground as the snorting creature bore down upon her. She was aware of the boar's tusks, rough textured and oily looking, curving outward from that lowered jaw, set to impale her.

She made no move, however. Her spirit was like an untroubled lake. She opened her mouth. From it emanated a *kiai* known as *toate-no-ate*, the distant strike.

The boar spun in the air, emitting a high-pitched squeal, quickly cut off as if a powerful grip had been put on its throat. It fell heavily on its side and was still until, as Kyōki had taught her, she chose to end her shout.

She remembered the touch of Kyōki's kimono against the back of her hand. The passage of his presence during long afternoons of sleep, when he seemed to stalk her dreams, as if even her sleep at *Yami Doko* was part of her training.

She longed for his lessons the way a young man longs for sex,

412

aches for it, dreams about it, becomes, at length, obsessed with it.

There was a chasteness to their relationship which she could never remember having with a man before. He was not saintly; but she did not desire him. Because she lusted after what he possessed more. He had *jahō*, and she longed for that until it became her lover.

She remembered their parting. She had been with him seven years, which was a significant number to both of them; a magic number. It was time to return to the world and claim her revenge.

A face in the rain, flickering.

Behind her, she half suspected the castle to fall into ruin, disappearing amid new foliage magically springing up. Rain beat down on her shoulders in rhythm with the *komuso*'s melody. Before her, rabbits skittered out of her way and a lone hawk flew over the treetops, searching while it rode the inconstant currents.

Coming down off the frosty Asama *kogen*, mingling with tourists and Tokyo residents alike in the rolling parklands, it occurred to her that the person she missed most was Saigō, that Kyōki's lessons had been her lover for seven years because Saigō could not be. She had deliberately put the thought of him aside so as not to torture herself.

He was no longer in Kumamoto, she was told by telephone, so she traveled to the outskirts of Tokyo, where he had told her his family lived.

She had had no contact with him in seven years, yet as the gleaming railroad took her toward her destination, it seemed to her no more than seven minutes. One inhalation of time. There was no space between them, no sense of change or alienation.

Occasionally, Saigō had spoken of his parents—and of course she had seen the devastation written across his face when he spoke of his father's death—but nothing he had said prepared her for the splendor of that house.

For one thing it was large—a rare quality in Japanese homes; for another, it was surrounded by the most beautiful gardens and orchards. Space was so highly prized that Akiko was slightly stunned to see so much in the hands of one family.

Deeper was her surprise when she found that the "family" now consisted of Saigō's mother and a dozen servants. No brothers or sisters, no other family members.

She was a diminutive woman with delicate bones and the beautiful commanding face of a *samurai* lady. Tradition meant a great deal to her.

As a welcomed traveler, Akiko was met at the door by a servant

413

and escorted to a room where another servant unpacked her bags while a third led her to the bath. Afterward, she was fed broiled fluke fin in soy sauce, a superb cold seaweed salad, chicken *yakitori*, rice, and a pale gold tea the taste of which was unfamiliar to her.

By this time it was late in the evening. A fourth servant appeared when she was finished, led her back to her room, where her *futon* had been prepared for sleep. Thus she spent her first sixteen hours in the house without ever meeting her hostess.

The next morning Akiko arose and dressed in her best kimono, which, she observed sadly as she saw herself in the mirror, was not very fine at all. Her life up until now had left precious little room for her to be concerned with the niceties of being a woman.

The hems of both sleeves were threadbare, and the silk of which it was made was hardly of the finest quality.

By contrast, Itami was splendidly attired. But then, Akiko thought, she would be so even in the company of the greatest ladies in Japan.

They met in one of the sixteen-*tatami* rooms where Akiko was led as soon as she was dressed and properly coiffed. The young woman who had first seen her to her room had knocked quietly and politely on the *shōji*, entering only when she was bade, to kneel behind Akiko, spending almost an hour brushing, combing, and putting up her hair with the implements Akiko had handed her: the *tsuge* wood *kushi* that had been Ikan's, the matching set of *kanzashi* that had been presented to her by Shimada.

Handed the mirror by the servant, Akiko was struck by how much she resembled her mother. How many years had it been since she had had her hair like this? She could not remember, could not even say whether she liked herself this way.

A tea set separated them, of superb workmanship and material of equal quality: the porcelain was translucent and as thin as skin. The intricacies of the ceremony Itami was performing with the tea served a dual purpose. It alleviated the tension and uncomfortableness strangers inevitably feel when first they meet. It also served to focus their attention on Zen, on the formation of harmony.

At the end of the ceremony, if they were not exactly friends, neither were they strangers.

"It pleases me that you have come," Itami said. She had a pleasant, well-modulated voice and her manner, though formal in the sense of ancient tradition, was nevertheless fueled by a genuine warmth that served to put Akiko at her ease. "My son has spoken of you several times." There was more that she wanted to say on this score, Akiko sensed.

"You have arrived at a fortuitous time," Itami continued, "for while Saigō is not here, he is scheduled to arrive in a week's time. You will stay, of course."

"I could not think of intruding for so long," Akiko said. "But I thank you for your offer."

"An offer is nothing unless it is accepted," Itami replied. "As you can see, this house is large—some might say overlarge for one woman. My days are sometimes lonely; one's life can be filled with too much contemplation. It would please me greatly to have a companion. Will you favor me?"

"If you wish it, of course. I have never seen such a beautiful house. It is exhilarating to be here."

"Now you are exaggerating," Itami said, but Akiko could see that she was pleased by the genuine compliment.

Late in the afternoon of the next day, Itami said, "After poor Yukio's untimely death, I was afraid that Saigō had turned his heart away from women. He loved her so; his spirit was crushed by her death. Of course, it came on top of my husband's death and, well . . . he and Saigō were always very close." And Akiko thought, Filial piety binds us all, twisting us to its will.

She found herself liking the older woman immensely. She had contrived to make Akiko at home without voicing the usual battery of questions directed at the woman to whom a son is attracted: What is your family? Where do you come from? What is your father's station? And his father's? So on. Rather, Itami seemed content to accept Akiko at face value, and this touched Akiko deeply.

"Today," Itami said, "all things are different. The time when the immutability of Japan was assured is gone. Modern times have assured that it will never come again."

There was a silence then as the two women walked side by side through the groves of lemon and plum trees. Pink and white chrysanthemum bobbed their heads like a Greek chorus in the following breeze. Overhead, white clouds drifted, below which slate gray plovers swooped. The sun felt warm and comforting on their backs.

"Tomorrow my son comes home." Itami had stopped to peer at a lizard basking on a rock. Akiko paused beside her. "Perhaps it would be best if you left early in the morning."

Akiko studied the words as if she were an archaeologist who had stumbled over what might possibly be an important find. "I care about Saigō," she said after a time. "Very much."

415

"Yes," Itami said. "I know. Still, I think best if you were not here when he arrived."

"Why is that, Itami-san?"

The older woman turned to face her. "My son is evil, Akiko-san. Sometimes I think that it was a blessing that Yukio-san died so early, so tragically. I did not wish her involved with my son. When she met Nicholas Linnear I hoped that would be the end of it. But, like you, she came back to Saigō. I do not want the same mistake to be made twice."

"Do you fear for my life, lady?"

Itami stared hard into Akiko's face. "No, Akiko-san. I fear for your soul. My son is the bitterest of fruit; with his ideas he is a poisoner and it is best to stay away from him lest you, too, be poisoned."

"It has not hurt me so far," Akiko said lightly.

"It would be a mistake to make a joke of this, my dear." Itami began to walk again. "If you decide to stay I will not seek to stop you. I have learned that nothing ever changes in this regard and that it is folly to attempt to turn the will of another. I could not do it with my husband or my son or even my sister-in-law. I have not the power, certainly, to do it to you. Still I speak from the heart and ask you to at least listen."

Silence once again engulfed them, eventually to be broken by Akiko's words. "Itami-san, I wish to see him."

The older woman's head bowed. "Of course you do, my child."

Only the four of them were at the wedding: Saigō and Akiko, hand in hand, Itami, and the Shinto priest, who presided. The ceremony took place in the north garden, amid the scents of lemon and rose. The day was clear and bright as crystal. The sun was strong overhead, its warmth pouring down over them like a benediction.

Then Saigō took her away to Tokyo and she saw Itami only infrequently. She could not be at the funeral, when the body was shipped back from America in a sealed coffin that Itami did not want opened after she heard the account of how he died. But Itami wrote her, saying all she wanted now was to have him buried deep, next to his father who had loved him in a way that she could not, who had twisted his spirit in a way she could not forgive him for.

As for Akiko, there was no question but that she do what Saigō had asked of her before he departed for America. Even had he not talked with her, she would have known what to do.

"I know how to do it," she had told him triumphantly, on a day just shy of their eighth anniversary. "It will mean change for me. Total change." And she held up the photograph for him to see.

For a long time he said nothing, merely looked from her to the photo and back again. "It will destroy him," he said. "Utterly and completely. Should I not come back." His face creased. "But I will."

Akiko knew better. Saigō was dead the moment he boarded the JAL flight for America for his final confrontation with his cousin, Nicholas Linnear. But this knowledge did not allow her to stop him or even hint to him of his fate. He was a warrior, and to deny him battle was to destroy him on the spot.

When the news reached her, she was already five weeks in Switzerland. She grieved even as she worked out the details of the revenge he would have wished.

She wanted to exercise during her long internment in the Swiss clinic but she was forbidden to do so at least for the first week. After that it was at her own discretion, they said, believing that she could do nothing while the swath of bandages blinded her. They were wrong, but then the Swiss are a peculiarly insular people.

Guided to the gym each day just before lunchtime, Akiko performed ninety minutes of hard physical exercise to keep her superb body in shape. In the late afternoon she did the same. And because she was used to the night, she arose by herself and, using her hearing, guided herself away from the nurses, back into the gym for further work.

She was desperate for physicality, throwing her entire being into it. For one thing, it took her mind off the consequences of what she had done. If the doctors had not been successful here, she would be lost. They had assured her of their talent and she had seen examples of their handiwork herself. Rationally she had been satisfied. But now that it had been done, now that there was no turning back, now that the Akiko she had known all her life was gone, doubts returned to plague her. What if . . . ? What if . . . ? What if . . . ?

So she toiled hard in the garden of mind and spirit, building on the foundations with which Kyōki had provided her, that Sun Hsiung had drilled into her. Now that Saigō had been killed, there was nothing else for her.

And at last there came a morning when darkness began to lift. Layer by layer, searchlights turned black into shades of gray, lightening from charcoal to slate to dove.

Hazily the room appeared, its shape and character emerging

slowly from behind gauzy veils. The shapes had been drawn, the overhead light extinguished. Only a small lamp was on, its soft glow fiery to her eyes, unused to light for six weeks. It hurt to see and she was forced to blink rapidly, bringing some of the darkness back so that she would not be overwhelmed by the candle-power.

Everything appeared strange and different. Distant, as well, as if she were a new arrival from another planet. She took the mirror that had been placed in her hand by one of the nurses and shone it on herself.

What she saw there was no face in the rain but the first true blossom of her vengeance.

She saw Yukio staring back at her, blinking furiously in the first light of a new day.

BOOK FIVE

THE MIKO

[1. A sorceress 2. A maiden in the service
of a shrine]

NEW YORK CITY/HONG KONG/HOKKAIDO/
MAUI/WASHINGTON/TOKYO

SPRING, PRESENT

"Hello, Matty?"

"Who wants to know?"

"Croaker, Detective Lieutenant, NYPD."

"Nah. He's deader than a doornail."

"Then you're speaking to the grave. This is your lucky day, Matty."

"Who the hell is this, anyway?"

"Matty, I got the dame we spoke about last year. Remember the conversation? Alix Logan. Key West."

"I don't—"

"You said the situation'd gotten hotter than Lucifer's hind tit."

There was a sharp inhalation. "Christ on a crutch, it *is* you, Lieutenant! You ain't dead. I went to Saint Luke's to light a candle."

"I appreciate that, Matty. Really I do."

"Where the hell are you, Lieutenant?"

"Information, Matty," Croaker said into the phone. "I need information like a junkie needs his fix. I'm pulling in my markers—all of them. After this we start clean."

Matty the Mouth, Croaker's main snitch, thought about this for a minimum amount of time. "It could get me killed."

"It almost did me, Ace. You'll be protected. I'll make sure Tomkin's people won't get near you."

"It ain't Tomkin I'm worried about, Lieutenant. That bastard deep-sixed almost a week ago."

"What?"

"Whassamatter, don't you read the papes or nuthin'?"

"I've been avoiding them like the plague. I even told Alix the radio in the car was busted. We got into a mess in North Carolina. I didn't want her to know how bad it was."

"Ain't heard nuthin' about nuthin' in N.C."

"In Raleigh."

"Nada, Lieutenant. And I'd know."

Croaker turned his head, watched Alix in the car by the side of the highway. They were very near the Lincoln Tunnel, almost back in New York. "What happened with Tomkin?"

"Croaked from some mysterious disease. Taka-something. Japanese sounding."

"That's very funny."

"It is? I don't get it."

"Never mind. Private joke." The recorded message cut in and Croaker fed the box with some more change. "About the Raleigh incident."

"Total blackout."

"Yah."

"I ain't surprised, Lieutenant. Tomkin was just the tip of the shit pile in this one." Noise came through the line. "Hold on a minute, will you?" Muffled, Croaker could hear him say to someone else in the room, "Do like I tell you, for Chrissakes, and go to a fuckin' movie or somethin'."

In a moment he was back on the line. "Sorry. Wanted to clear the room. This's risky enough as it is." He coughed. "Told you I'd do some more nosing around, and I did. What I found I didn't like. In fact, I was sorry as hell I'd given you the Key West info. When the papes reported you'd bought it, I thought sure as hell it was my fault so I went straight to Saint Luke's."

"And all that time I thought it was friendship, pure and simple, Matty."

"Life ain't that way, Lieutenant. You know that's well as me."

Croaker could not help thinking of Nicholas Linnear and the friendship he had with the man. Were there any of the usual strings attached to the relationship? He was sure there were not. That was part of what made their friendship so special, so binding.

Fleetingly, he wondered where Nicholas was now and what he was doing. The last he'd heard of him he was back in West Bay Bridge. Probably off on his honeymoon now, he thought. Croaker knew that he would have tracked his friend down long ago were it not for the fact that he wanted this danger kept away from Nicholas—at least until he could define it.

He refocused his attention. "You'd better give me all of it, Matty."

"What I got ain't good. The government's involved."

For a moment Croaker thought someone had lobbed a grenade in his direction. Stupidly, in shock, he said, "Which government?"

"Ours. Jesus, who else's?"

"I don't get it."

"You think I do? All I know is that this's gone way beyond you or me."

Croaker's mind was spinning furiously. "Now I see why you weren't surprised about the blackout in Raleigh. Only the government'd have that kind of clout. D'you know who in the government?"

"Know a character, Minck by name?"

"Never heard of him."

"Neither had I until I did some heavyweight snooping. He runs what's called a 'closed shop' in the trade."

"And what trade might that be?"

"Why, spying, of course, Lieutenant."

"What the hell's this got to do with Tomkin and Angela Didion's murder?"

"You said you'd got the dame with you. Ask her. She was a witness. The only one."

"Yeah? Then why's she still walking around, safe and sound?"

"She alone in Key West?" Matty asked shrewdly.

"No. They had a bracket on her. But it was to keep her safe."

"You know that for a fact?"

"As a matter of fact, I do," Croaker said. "She tried to off herself one afternoon. One of 'em stopped her. I saw the whole thing."

"Something doesn't make sense," Matty conceded. "But I'll be damned if I know what it is."

"You give me all of it?" Croaker asked, feeding his last quarter into the slot.

"One other thing. It's not the same topic, but since you been on the moon for a while I thought I'd pass it on. Your buddy Linnear's been named head of Tomkin Industries."

"You're kidding."

"Why would I do that? He's in Tokyo now—you know, Japan—finishing off some big business Tomkin had going with a company called Sato Petrochemicals."

Jesus, Croaker thought. What's happening here? The whole world's turning upside down.

He cleared his mind, fast. "Do me one more favor, will you?"

"Now it'll cost you, Lieutenant. We're all square, like you said. What's the deal?"

"I need a place for me and girl to flop. Your place."

"Thousand a week or any fraction thereof."

"You're getting to be a wise guy, Matty. This's an emergency."

"I kinda understand that, Lieutenant, but you gotta see things from my point of view, too. Times're tight. I gotta live just like anybody else."

"You forget I'm not on the payroll right now."

"I'll take your marker."

"You sonuvabitch."

Croaker could feel his smile through the phone. "Yeah," Matty the Mouth said. "I know."

At precisely six P.M. Hong Kong time, Tanzan Nangi, sitting high up in the offices of the All-Asia Bank, picked up the telephone and dialed the number Liu had given him at the end of their first meeting.

All afternoon he had glumly watched the ants far below queuing up before the entrance to the All-Asia's Central District branch in order to withdraw their life's savings. Suddenly the All-Asia was poison; it would swallow their money whole. The Chinese were pulling out.

The mechanism by which such enormous masses of people were so instantly galvanized was a mystery to Nangi, but he had no doubt as to who was behind the run. The Communists were turning the screws.

"How long can we expect to hold out?" Nangi had asked Allan Su just after the doors were closed at three. Police had been called to disperse the mob who had been on line when the bank was closed.

"At this rate," Su said, "no more than forty-eight hours. I've just been on the phone with our other branches in Wan Chai, Tsim Sha Tsui, Aberdeen, and Stanley. It's the same all over, more or less. We'll have to go to the vault tonight."

"Don't do anything yet," Nangi said, fist against his cheek. "Not until I give you the word."

"Yes?" The female voice was quiet and well modulated.

"Mr. Liu, please," Nangi said, hating this moment, hating the Communists more now than he ever had.

"Whom shall I say is calling?"

At seven-fifteen that evening, Nangi's car pulled up in front of the Sun Wa Trading Company on Sai Ping Shan Street in Sheung Wan. It was a long store front painted a garish glossy vermillion. The Chinese, Nangi reflected, did not comprehend the subtlety of pastel shades. Instead they surrounded themselves with childlike primaries. They were as superstitious about color as they were about everything else.

He stepped out into the crowded street, inhaling the scents of five-spice powder, star anise, dried fish, soy, and chili. They made him long for home with an intensity that was almost painful. But he knew that part of the pain was from the knowledge of what he was about to do.

Squaring his shoulders, he concentrated on walking as normally as possible so that he would not be further shamed in front of his enemies.

Inside, the atmosphere was gritty with spice powder residues, bringing a tickle to his nostrils. At first the place seemed deserted; it was past the time when the regular employees had gone home.

Nangi paused in the dimness and looked around without seeming to. He spotted a shadow amid other shadows, moving slightly.

"I have brewed fresh tea especially for this occasion." It was unmistakably Liu's voice.

Nangi moved in his direction, mindful of the crates and cartons scattered about. He sat down on a plain wooden chair opposite the Chinese. A scarred table was between them. On it were only two items: a pair of identical documents. Nangi did not have to touch them to know what they were.

"Tea first," Liu said amiably. "I want this to be as painless as possible." He was positively exuding good fellowship now that his triumph was imminent.

They both drank. "Black Tiger tea," Liu said. "From Peking. Only a very small quantity is produced each year. Do you like it?"

"Very much," Nangi said, almost choking on the brew.

Liu inclined his head slightly. "I am honored." He continued to sip. "I understand that there was a disturbance in front of the All-Asia this afternoon," he said conversationally.

Nangi decided to test him. "It was nothing at all."

"Enough for the police to be called in, yes?"

"Traditionally the police are summoned when more than a score of Chinese assemble in one place in the Crown Colony," Nangi observed blandly. "It gives Her Majesty's Government something to do."

"Even the voracious crow knows when to quit the corner field, Mr. Nangi."

This all had the appearance of an elaborate charade. It was as if Liu felt compelled to drag out the hoary cliché of the aphoristic Chinese. But why? Surely he knew that it would not impress a Japanese. Then it occurred to Nangi that charades were never acted out unless there was an audience.

Shadows wreathed the rafters inside the Sun Wa Trading Company. Outside, the light had failed, so that even the skylight far above had turned opaque and impenetrable. Sawdust on the floor, the spices rich and pungent. If there was movement in the darkness, Nangi could not detect it. Yet his sense that he and Liu were not alone was inescapable.

"How bad was the run, Mr. Nangi?" Liu was pouring more tea. It seemed he was bent on carefully delineating the boundaries of his superiority.

"I am certain that you already know that, Mr. Liu," Nangi said carefully. "All runs are bad in and of themselves. That's obvious."

"What is obvious to me, Mr. Nangi," Liu said, sipping his tea again, "is that you will not make it without our direct intervention."

"That occurred to me as well. That is why I called."

Perhaps this was all Liu had wanted in the first place: a humbling by verbal admission, for he nodded now as if accepting a compliment. He inclined his head toward the contract. "I trust you will find each clause you required satisfactorily rendered." He spoke as if it had been he who had made all the negotiating concessions; as if it were he who were under the gun and not Nangi.

For a moment Nangi did nothing. To make an immediate move would have cost him too much face, and he had already given up more than he could spare by agreeing to this meeting. After a suitable amount of time had elapsed, he took up the document and commenced to read. Every sentence froze his spirit, every clause to which he was being forced to sign his name made him sick at heart. The moment he touched pen to paper, effective control of his *keiretsu* would be transferred to Liu's masters in Peking.

The Chinese had placed an old-fashioned fountain pen squarely in the middle of the tabletop. Nangi would be obliged to reach for it.

"We plan no immediate intervention or policy change," Liu said. "There is absolutely no cause for alarm."

"I was thinking of the thirty-five million dollars," Nangi said. "It must be delivered by eight A.M. tomorrow morning."

Liu nodded, unperturbed. Where were his "firm's" prior commitments now? "If you would ask Mr. Su and whichever other bank officers you designate to appear at the All-Asia Bank's main vault in Central, that sum will be handed over to them."

Oh, yes, Nangi thought. I'm certain you're quite familiar with our vaults, thanks to Comrade Chin. But what he said was, "That will be entirely satisfactory."

And then, deliberately ignoring the fountain pen Liu had set on the table, Nangi extracted a pen of his own and signed the last page of both sets of contracts. Retrieving his pen, Liu did the same. He pushed the top copy back to Nangi's side.

"A little more tea, perhaps?" His eyes danced in the darkness.

Nangi declined. Folding away the document, which felt hot and unclean to his hands, he was about to rise when Liu's motion stayed him.

From within the Chinese's breast pocket a shiny red envelope appeared. Liu handed it to Nangi without a word.

Nangi looked at him enquiringly.

"We Chinese have a custom, Mr. Nangi. It is most civilized. The sum inside that envelope is payment for transfer; transfer of ownership, of power, call it what you will. With the physical transfer there can be no loss of face because there has been an exchange, one for the other."

Nangi nodded respectfully, as if they were two men exchanging pleasantries on a park bench. But in his heart he seethed, the anger crackling through him, making his pulse skip a beat. Nothing in his outward manner conveyed his inner resolve. To Liu and whoever else might be watching, concealed in the shadows, he was a clever businessman at the crevasse of defeat.

Carefully, Nangi slid the red envelope away next to the document that lay like a lead weight against his heart. He pushed away from the table and, taking up his cane, rose and walked awkwardly out of the Sun Wa Trading Company to where his chauffeured car was waiting for him.

There was no aspect of nightlife that interested him so he went directly back to the hotel. Food tasted like ash and stuck in his throat as if it were the contract itself that Liu and his masters had coerced him into signing. Stoically he went on eating until his plate was clean, and then could not remember what it was that he had ordered. It did not matter.

Undressed, he lay atop his bed and stared up at the ceiling, at the river of the past. As always, *kanryōdō* consumed him. Once a warrior, always a warrior, he thought. It was impossible to hang up your *katana*, even if, as in his case, it was figurative rather than literal.

The face of Makita, his *sempai*, floated through the clouds of his memory as it often did. Rather than allow them to take out his diseased stomach, he had committed *seppuku*. He had asked Nangi to be his second and, acquiescing, Nangi had taken up his mentor's long sword and with one swift overhand strike had ended the excruciating pain of the two *wakizashi* slashes, the first lateral, the second vertical, that Makita had managed to inflict himself.

And though it had been the honorable thing to do, though Nangi had had no choice but to comply with his *sempai*'s wishes, still he was ashen as he stared at the bloody blade, his friend and surrogate father's head on the *tatami*; he shook all over as if he had contracted ague. His skin felt feverish and dry and there was no saliva with which to swallow.

Surely, Nangi had thought, Christ could not have wished such a thing. And he had fled to church where, in the Confessional, he had spewed out what he had done in rapid-fire bursts like retching. But even that could not cleanse him and he spent the next six hours on his knees before the image of Christ on the Cross, praying for forgiveness.

It had been Sato who had come for him, persuading him to leave that sanctuary where the real world could not intrude. "My friend," Sato had said softly, "you cannot possibly blame yourself. You did what had to be done, what any *samurai* would do. You stood by your friend when he needed you the most. What more can you ask of yourself? It was *giri*."

Nangi's eyes had been full of pain and self-loathing. "It was not the Christian thing to do, Seiichi-san."

To which Sato had had no reply but to get Nangi out of there.

Thoughts of Makita inevitably led Nangi back to *mabiki*, the decades-long weeding-out process he had performed at MITI for his *sempai*. How many had he "slain" in this way, destroying any chance they had for advancement in Japanese bureaucracy? Always he asked himself that question, because always he was uneasy with what he had done.

Shimada had been the first one; Shimada had been the beginning of *mabiki*. He had paid for his greed and his shortsightedness. He could not see change coming, and thus Nangi had doomed him to humiliation or death. Shimada had chosen the honorable path and had committed *seppuku*, opening the way for Makita's immediate appointment as first vice-minister of MITI.

Shimada had been the hardest one. After that, the *mabiki* was easier to handle, the concept easier for Nangi to accept. *Kanryō-dō*'s precepts had hardened his heart.

Now, sweating in a hotel room in a foreign colony clinging with the tenaciousness of woodbine to the very tip of the Asian continent, his great dream lost to him, he wondered piteously whether he had murdered in the name of Christ.

He was never quite certain whether the ringing of the telephone had roused him out of slumber or deep thought. In any case, he rolled over and grabbed for the instrument. The glowing dial of his wristwatch told him that it was thirteen minutes before four A.M. A Chinese might have found this an inauspicious numerical combination; Nangi did not care.

"Yes?"

"It's Fortuitous Chiu," came the thin voice down the wire. "I'm on Po Shan Road, a block from Succulent Pien's flat." He sounded a bit out of breath.

Nangi sat up. "Haven't you been able to find a way in yet?"

"Been in and out already." Now Nangi recognized the excitement in the other's voice. "I think you'd better get down here pronto."

"What is it?"

"Forgive my bluntness, sir, but I don't think you'd believe me if I told you outright. If you see for yourself, that'll be another story."

"I'm on my way," Nangi said, his heart beginning to beat fast. The sweat had dried on his skin. Swinging his legs over the side of the bed, he reached for his cane.

The vault was as airless as it was lightless. Behind him Nicholas could hear the circular door through which he had stepped sighing closed. He heard the pneumatics and was not cheered.

Alone and in total darkness, he moved to where his *haragei* told him was the center of the vault. Then he stood still, his senses questing. A desk and several chairs, a lamp unlit, some machinery which it was beyond him to identify in the absence of visuals. A kind of wooden scaffolding whose purpose was also a mystery to him.

Took stock. He was on Hokkaido but he did not know where since Koten had blindfolded him after binding him hand and foot. He had then been carried to what he could only guess was the trunk of the Soviets' car and locked in. They had driven for just under an hour. Giving the car an average speed of forty-five m.p.h. put him in a radius of approximately thirty-five to forty miles from the *rotenburo*. He knew that was not good enough.

429

Humming invading the void of darkness in which he stood, broke through his thoughts. It was subtle, might not have been discerned by a normal man.

Immediately Nicholas went toward the sound, sniffing like an animal, quick, shallow breaths. Scented it when he was fifteen feet away from the vent high up in the wall and turned away, getting away from that side of the room. It would only prolong the time that he had left before the chloroform derivative took effect on him. But he needed all the time he could get now.

"I don't see why we're waiting so long," the doctor said pointedly. "It only takes the gas three-and-a-half minutes to fully permeate the vault space." He waggled the wrist on which his chronometer was fastened so that those around him would not miss the fact that it had been almost fifteen minutes since the gas—an interesting mixture of a soporific in the chloroform group and a powerful peyote concentrate, altered to be effective when inhaled rather than ingested—had been pumped into the room.

"Patience, Doctor," Viktor Protorov said calmly. "I fully appreciate your enthusiasm to sink your spikes into a new client, but I think I know what is best in this case."

The doctor shrugged his shoulders, began a ragged rendition of "The Czarist and the Revolutionary," a folk song his grandmother had taught him when he was a child, just to show these others that he was not the total Protorov puppet that they were.

With the doctor and Protorov were Pyotr Alexandrovitch Russilov, Koten, and a pair of junior lieutenants under Russilov's direct command. The most recent Alpha-three codes had brought Protorov word that Yvgeny Mironenko, the GRU colonel, had received enough vouchers from his compatriots for Protorov to hold a special session of the General Staff. All the senior generals would be in attendance. All that was required now, Mironenko's most recent communiqué had said, was for Protorov to bring the generals proof of his power.

Proof of my power, Protorov thought now. *Tenchi!* Then, for the first time in history, the GRU and the KGB will be united in a common cause. The Kremlin will shake to the sound of our bootsteps, the old men will fall before us like stalks of wheat; the day of the bureaucrat will be a memory; all the Russians will be on the march. The day of the Second Revolution will have dawned!

With great difficulty he kept his elation concealed; not even Russilov must suspect the vast changes forming on the horizon. Not yet. He will have his hands full running the Ninth, Protorov thought. I do not want to give him too much, too soon.

"All right, clear the vault," he ordered.

One of the junior lieutenants, responding to a hand sign from Russilov, shut one valve, opened another. A pair of 150 h.p. suction fans drew the noxious fumes out of the room. When the red light ceased to glow, replaced by the green one, Protorov ordered the vault door unsealed.

Koten went first, then Russilov and the two junior lieutenants. The doctor and Protorov brought up the rear. Inside, they could smell nothing. The air was pure and clean again.

The men fanned out into the vault as if they were a line of gentlemen on the hunt: arrogant in the knowledge of their elite status, yet wary of a new and extremely dangerous prey.

"He seems quiescent enough," the doctor said, pushing his glasses back up the bridge of his nose. "I don't think there is going to be anything different about him."

Thinking him a fool, Protorov signed to Koten. As the enormous *sumō* moved across the room, Protorov paced him at a tangent that took him to a spot directly in front of where Nicholas lay on his left side.

"Breathing is deep and regular," the doctor said, circling the fallen figure "No eyelid flicker; pulse is slowed, skin color is consistent with deep delta unconscious state." He recited these medical observations like a litany against that which he did not understand and therefore could not control.

From his position, Protorov signed to Russilov to move into position just behind Nicholas. "All right," he told Koten.

Nicholas launched himself feet first at the oncoming hulk. It had not been difficult for him to cease to breathe a sufficient amount of the gas to put him under. At least eight separate forms of *ninjutsu* discipline had as their bases the breath and autonomic system regulation that Tibetan Yogi practiced. This extended to body temperature control as well.

The doctor yelped, skittering away as Nicholas careened into the oncoming *sumō*, the heels of his feet directed at Koten's knees not, as someone unfamiliar with a *sumō*'s strength would have done, at his vast stomach.

Koten was incredibly quick and he almost regained the angle he needed to deflect Nicholas' strike. But not quite. As it was, he saved himself from a pair of broken joints, moving slightly into the line of attack and thus canceling a measure of its force. He went down anyway.

Nicholas was aware of Protorov shouting orders, the doctor retreating past the fringes of the melee, two younger soldiers moving in. He was certain that he could handle them all. Yet some unbalanced equation stirred the periphery of his mind. He was busy with Koten and most of his consciousness was taken up with constantly shifting stratagems against four enemies.

Four!

It was his last coherent thought before Russilov plunged the six-inch needle into the meaty part of his upper arm. Too late, he lashed out. Five black spots swirled before his eyes; he saw five of each individual, closing in on him, felt Koten's blow on the side of his head five times.

The five spots expanded into five black wells down which he plummeted. From a long way off echoes came to him, words without meaning, questions without answers. Then the powerful drug hit his cortex and he passed into unconsciousness.

"Good work," Protorov said to Russilov. "You see, Doctor," he went on, "contrary to what your book may tell you, we are *not* dealing with an ordinary human being. This man could reach out with one finger and destroy you."

The doctor said nothing; he was quietly shaking, thinking, I do not understand this at all. He should have been unconscious long before this. "Perhaps he is faking yet again."

Protorov snorted. "I think not. He has no power to counter injections into his bloodstream."

He nodded toward the wooden scaffolding set against part of the back wall. "All right, Koten," he said softly. "String him up."

You must return to the source . . . his *source.* Masashigi Kusunoki's words rose up from her unconscious, penetrating the dialogue between Sato and Phoenix. Akiko had played and replayed that section of tape as if this might give her some further insight, turning an artifact over and over again in a vain attempt to divine its secret.

She sat in Koten's room, her forehead against her drawn-up knees, her arms girdling her shins. She was naked, and in the lamplight her skin gleamed as if oiled. Shadows rilled her even as light revealed her. Hidden and open, she was a physical paradigm of the riddle inside herself.

The people who sent him, who trained him represent a very great threat to Japan. Masashigi-san's words.

Masashigi. What had possessed her to go to the Gyokku *ryu* in the first place? She did not know or could not recall. She remembered the first moment she had seen Masashigi Kusunoki, though. It was as if she had found a connection with her past—*some* past. As she belonged with Saigō in her private life, so she seemed to belong with Masashigi in her martial one. She had been married to Saigō for three weeks, gone from Kyōki's castle for six.

The Gyokku was where Masashigi-san had made his first stand for her. Together they had left when the other *sennin* of the *ryu* rose up and dissented; they would not allow her—a woman—to stay.

Together they had gone to the Tenshin Shoden Katori in Yoshino.

Why had he done this for her? What was it that the *sensei* had seen in her? What made her so special? And how wrong he had been! All his loyalty had brought him was death; death by the hands of the one he had defended.

Akiko remembered the smile that wreathed his face like lilies at the moment he passed from life into death. Why? Why would anyone smile at that instant? Sadness had no place in Masashigi-san's life. He was attuned to the universe, at peace with himself and the cosmos. He could not have welcomed death. He was, at least in Akiko's mind, somewhat of a holy man. That was another reason why she had chosen him as her first victim. If the masking of her *wa* that Kyōki had taught her would work with such a one, it would work on anyone.

There was something in the air—a spice perhaps—that Akiko could not define. Her head came up and she looked around as if she suspected that she was not alone. For a moment the air shimmered before a half-open *fusuma*. Papers stirred on the desk farther into the room. But it was only the wind, wasn't it?

Akiko shivered slightly. Why was she dredging all this up now? *The people who sent him, who trained him represent a great threat to Japan.* Masashigi-san had been speaking of the *muhon-nin* Tsuts-umu. She herself had slain the second *muhon-nin*, Tengu, returning that which he had stolen to the *ryu*.

Now she knew that there had been a third traitor within the Tenshin Shoden Katori. Masashigi Kusunoki rose up like a specter before her and bade her do what he had trained her to do; to fulfill the promise he alone had seen in her. She thought of Sato, Phoenix, and Nicholas in the north, in Hokkaido. Especially Nicholas.

She rose and went into the bedroom. From the bottom of a low drawer where Sato would never look she drew out a kimono, light gray on dark gray. The top half of one side was stained a dark brown where some of the *sensei*'s fountaining blood had spattered.

Slowly, reverently, she drew it on. Within moments she was ready. She headed north.

When Nicholas awoke, he found himself on a wheel. He rose out of unconsciousness rapidly but did not open his eyes, change his breathing pattern, or in any other way give those who he assumed to be in the vault with him any indication that he was now conscious.

Whatever they had pumped him with was very powerful for its effects were not yet gone. His head felt light, he felt a touch of vertigo; he was not at all sure that he could fully trust his senses. Still, logic dictated that he attempt to assess his current situation.

He was bound by fingers, wrists, waist, thighs, and ankles with leather straps. He was suspended off the floor. He recalled the dim outline of the scaffolding.

But what worried him most was Protorov. He was smart enough to understand what kind of creature Nicholas was. He alone among the Russians had suspected that Nicholas' training would keep him from succumbing to the ambient gas. He had set Nicholas up superbly, distracting him with Koten—the obvious main threat—while he kept within Nicholas' sight. Only the young officer who had been in charge of the *rotenburo*, Russilov, had been missing. Not missing but behind Nicholas. And no time for even *haragei* to work. The stress factor had been too high. Nicholas reflected that perhaps he was getting too old for this. He should have felt Russilov's presence. He had underestimated the Soviets—Protorov in particular—and had paid the price.

Opened his eyes.

"Ah," Viktor Protorov said amiably, "did you enjoy your rest?"

How does he know so much about me? Nicholas asked himself as he tried to flex his fingers. The straps would not allow it. Interesting, Nicholas thought. He had this ready for me; surely this would be unnecessary for a prisoner without my skills.

Nicholas was aware of how many people were in the room—two besides himself and Protorov: Russilov and the doctor—as well as where they were. Russilov stood just behind and to the right of his directorate chief; the doctor was near Nicholas' left shoulder, a hypodermic and medical kit on a stool beside him.

Protorov was not interested in a reply. Instead, he unfolded a long sheaf of computer printout which then trailed down behind him like a tail. He held one page up in front of Nicholas' face. Nicholas stared at the markings, trying to focus his brain. He thought he had seen something quite like this in several magazines such as *Scientific American* and *Smithsonian*, detailing passes of various NASA satellites across the face of the Earth.

"Does this area appear familiar to you, *Gospadin* Linnear?" So far Protorov had used nothing but Russian with him. "It should. It is the northern half of Honshū, the whole of Hokkaido, the Nemuro Straits, the southerly end of the Kuriles."

Protorov had not taken his eyes off Nicholas. "Here," he said, stabbing at one of several red-marked spots, "offshore, is a crack between two geological plates. Here and here, on Honshū itself, are where earthquakes of sizable magnitude—over seven points on the Richter Scale—will occur within the next week. Already an onset trembler has been felt here, just to the northwest of Tokyo."

Protorov snapped his fingers and Russilov, like a prestidigitator's assistant, replaced the exhibited item. In this frame the magnitude had been increased so that a detailed section of the topography from the first page was reproduced.

"Now here," Protorov continued, pointing again, "is another hot spot. But lo and behold, it is not at any previously known geological fault. Rather it is at a precise spot where nothing had shown before. There is no *natural* reason for its existence."

The paper rustled like anxious insects. "What do you make of that, *Gospadin* Linnear?"

"What the hell am I looking at, anyway?"

Protorov clucked his tongue against the roof of his mouth. "Now that would be telling."

During his adolescence Nicholas could recall coming in contact with a number of Japanese nuns. To him the sight had been incongruous. The Japanese spirit had come to be synonymous with acquiescing to nature, the elements of the cosmos. To him, Christianity preached a divine order that had been meted out by man himself, though its adherents professed otherwise. The history of the Roman Catholic Church was a bloodstained banner lifted to the concept of domination.

All Catholics, he had found, were arrogant, and none more so than nuns or priests. It was their utter faith in a narrow spectrum morality that took into account absolutely no natural factors. Man's nature as well as that of his environment held no interest for the Church's hierarchy. Their moral rectitude rendered them deaf, dumb, and blind.

It occurred to Nicholas now that, though he might howl in rage at the comparison, Viktor Protorov possessed those same hideous qualities espoused so righteously by the Church. He was not so far from priestly, though in a manner he could never comprehend; Communism was as blind in its moral rectitude as was Catholicism.

"If you don't tell me, *Gospadin* Protorov," Nicholas said, "I can provide you with no coherent answer."

"Can you tell me that you do not recognize these contours as they might appear from afar?" Protorov brandished the sheets, flailing his tail behind him. "Say, 35,888 kilometers above the earth's surface. That would give it a synchronous orbit, keep it stationary over this one spot in the Pacific."

Protorov stepped closer. "Do you see this, *Gospadin* Linnear? The Straits of Nemuro. An international boundary between Japan and the Soviet Union." His eyes were fever bright. "And do you further see the area marked in red? It is at the bottom of the Straits, in Japanese territory . . . and in ours!"

He gave a nod and Nicholas knew what was coming. There was nothing he could do for his body now, but his mind was another matter. The gleaming steel needle entered his upper arm a scant centimeter from where the first shot had been administered. His skin ballooned outward, fluid swamping the bellows of his lungs. He was drowning; it made him want to cry out. His heartbeat accelerated wildly.

Discipline.

He took his consciousness by the hand as a father will his frightened child, and entered a place that held no fear. *Getsumei no michi.*

Somewhere outside of him Protorov called in a voice turned aqueous. "What do you know of *Tenchi*? How much does Minck know? You will tell me that, *Gospadin* Linnear. Before you die you *will* tell me that much!"

"Will you tell me now why you really followed me all the way to Hawaii?"

Rick Millar sat at one end of the clear plastic raft they had rented at the hotel beach shack. His long, tanned legs dangled in the water. He wore a surfer's brief bathing suit he had bought in Lahaina. "I think you already know the answer."

Justine smiled. Her heart felt lighter than it had in many months. "I'm flattered that you wanted to seduce me."

Millar laughed good-naturedly. "It wasn't *all* lust, you know. I do want you back at the firm no matter what happens between us."

"It's already happened," she said. "I'm glad you came, actually."

He watched a school of small golden fish race by just above the reef over which they bobbed. "You must love him a great deal for you to be so loyal."

What Justine thought about most now, what she held most closely to her, was the memory of waking in the middle of the night, anxious and afraid, and being able to reach out to touch Nicholas' hand. It was a hand like no other she had ever encountered; she would lie there stroking its bottom edge, hard with cast-iron callus. Like hugging a Teddy bear, the motion would calm her and soon she would slip back to sleep.

But those were the old days and that was the old Justine. She did not believe that fear and anxiety would be a part of her life any longer.

Staring out over the sun-drenched Molokai Channel where the humpback whales broke the surface of the water in white and black splendor, she saw her immaturity as if it were part of another person: clearly, objectively. It was already separate from her.

She supposed now that she had always been afraid of love . . . true love such as she felt for Nicholas. Her entire adult life had been a series of encounters with males who could not possibly give her the stability of a twined life. Rather she had been attracted to men lusting to use her, to leave her, to, in effect, return her to a lone state where she felt more secure, more the little girl, and where—this being the most astonishing revelation of all—she would be assured of her father's intervention, his protection, and, yes, a manifestation of his love for her.

It occurred to her that she herself had provoked what she had deluded herself into thinking was his meddling in her life. She understood now that this very meddling had served as an assurance to the little girl inside her that he still loved her, that he cared enough to break away from his all-consuming work to do something for her.

Stunned, she sat in the Hawaiian sunshine, staring blindly at the island that formerly had been a home for lepers. It seemed ironic and somehow proper that she should have come all this way to be near Molokai. Of course she was aware now of just why she had come here. She ws six thousand miles from home, give or take a couple; three thousand miles into the Pacific. She was that much closer to Japan, and Nicholas.

"Would you like to go for a swim?" Millar asked gently.

Justine reached out and squeezed his arm. "You go if you've a mind to. I'll join you in a minute or two."

He nodded and slipped over the raft's side, moving in a slow, easy crawl away from her, all his muscles working in concert.

She watched him idly with the kind of detached contentment she had never before thought she could feel. He was a handsome man, desirable in all ways. How many of her women friends, unattached or otherwise, would have given their eyeteeth to be in her position now. She laughed out loud. It felt good to be wanted by such a man. But it felt even better to revel in the completeness of her love for Nicholas, for she sensed with a wonderful intensity Nicholas' spirit, as if it were he who swam so near her.

Their fight now seemed trivial and ridiculous to her, whereas before it had taken on the titanic proportions of an Olympian struggle. That was because she had not been battling Nicholas at all, but herself. From a distance she recognized the panic with which she had greeted his announcement because she had been quite certain at that moment that the man she was going to marry would be a reincarnation of her father.

Now she understood that she had feared that only because an unconscious part of her had wanted it. But Nicholas was not her father; what he would do with his life had only to do with himself . . . and now Justine. They had their own lives to lead. How would Nicholas put it? They had their own *karma*. She smiled again at that. Yes, *karma*.

And her *karma* dictated that she be at his side, whether it be as the head of Tomkin Industries or anywhere else. She was no longer afraid of giving her heart away to another human being, she was no longer afraid of spending her life with someone. In fact she knew that that was precisely what she did want.

In the water she stroked easily toward where Rick was floating as he watched the antics of the leviathans far out in the channel.

"Finished cogitating?" he said lightly.

"Cogitating." She laughed joyfully. "That's an adult activity, isn't it? I've got a lot of catching up to do."

He eyed her warily, as if she had changed from a puppy into a Doberman instantaneously. "Will you come back and be my creative design v.p.?"

Justine sobered. "Rick, I've got to have some reassurances from you before I make any decision."

He nodded. "Whatever I can do, I will."

"Good." She watched him speculatively. "I dashed away so fast that I didn't have the time to connect with Mary Kate, though I left a message with her service. That means, for the moment at least, I'm going to have to trust you." She paused deliberately to see if he would defend himself, but when he said nothing she went on. "If you summarily dismissed her against her will; if you leveraged me into her spot before that happened, as I told you before, I want nothing to do with the job. That's absolutely final."

"Okay, granted. I've received your message loud and clear. Mary Kate wasn't happy with us, and the reverse was true. We were coming to a mutual parting of the ways when I met with you. I tried to help her, Justine. I wanted her to work out. But the truth is, she didn't. She was smart enough to see it, that's all."

"So you and she had spoken about her leaving before you had that first lunch with me."

"Yes."

"Rick, this is extremely important to me so I don't want any mistake made about it. One call to Mary Kate is all it'll take."

"Then I think you should call her, Justine. I'd like you to trust what I'm telling you, but I can understand that you might have doubts. There's nothing your friend will tell you that I haven't. Period."

It was time to break the tension, Justine decided. She smiled and splashed water on him. "Then I think I'll take your offer." They bobbed together like a pair of corks as the wild tide rushed at the coral reef like an enemy on the march, dissipating itself along the spiky ridge. "But right now I'm going to Japan."

He knew what that meant. She had told him about Nicholas, about where he was and what had happened between them. He smiled, and there might have been a trace of wistfulness to it. It was the kind of smile a fine fisherman will give a valiant marlin that outfought him, snapping the cable at the end. He might rue not making the catch but he admired the creature that had deprived him; might even be glad that independence had won that day.

"You know," he said, "I've been envious of the Japanese's advertising methods for years. I hope you'll come back with a portfolio full of their trade secrets."

They both laughed at that.

Fortuitous Chiu made no answer but to put his forefinger up against his lips and sign for Nangi to follow him. A block up Po Shan Road, the highrise housing structures of the Mid-Levels, built for Hong Kong's wealthy, loomed all about them, giving the impression that they were moving through some enormous spectral forest.

Mist hung heavy in the air and there were no stars or moon to be seen. Nangi was grateful for this; he did not think that he wanted to be spotted prowling around the Colony at four in the morning.

Fortuitous Chiu took them quickly off the sidewalk as they approached one towering structure. Silently the two of them moved down a narrow, shadow-shrouded alleyway, filled with garbage cans and other refuse.

Down a short flight of concrete steps and through a metal-paneled door. They were inside the building, in the basement. Light came from the low-wattage bare bulbs strung from flex along the concrete ceiling. Two young Chinese were playing Fan Tan in the corridor. They looked up, apparently recognized Fortuitous Chiu, and went back to their game. Not a word was uttered by anyone. Nangi did not have to ask his companion who the youths were. Green Pang. Soon, Nangi knew, they must meet Third Cousin Tok, the 438, who must still be secreted in Succulent Pien's apartment.

The Triads, who had effectively infiltrated most of the Chinese-dominated Crown Colony—and this included the corruption-riddled Royal Hong Kong Police force—were a partial acronym for *San Ho Hiu*, Three Harmonies Association. This had once been the most powerful of the original Chinese secret societies. They had been founded by fiercely patriotic men to fight an ongoing guerrilla campaign against the invading Manchus who overthrew the traditional Ming Dynasty in 1644.

Now they battled one another through the narrow streets of Hong Kong with cleaver and ax for the right of jurisdiction. It was the spread of voracious urbanism which had broken down the Chinese family unit so successfully. That and the too-rapid industrialization of a predominantly agricultural people. Now the Triads offered a surrogate family, and with more prestige than running a cutter which turned out three thousand blue jean legs a shift ever could.

These were pathetic reasons to become a street fighter for the Green Pang or the 14K, the Cantonese equivalent, Nangi thought.

They got off the elevator on the fourteenth floor, and Fortuitous Chiu led the way down the hall. He stopped in front of a door and, extracting a set of picks from his trousers' pocket, set to work on the lock. It popped within seconds.

An apartment laid out in pinks and warm yellows. The color combination made Nangi bilious. It was a spacious two-bedroom affair and he was led into one of these.

Saw the glint of reflection off an eyeball and this was his silent greeting with Third Cousin Tok. He was a wide-shouldered man, younger than Nangi had surmised for someone of his exalted rank, with a scarred, dangerous face. Nangi saw no resemblance whatsoever between the cousins.

Crouching down, they approached Third Cousin Tok, who, when they were near, moved away. Nangi saw that he clutched a black-bodied Nikon with a 135mm lens.

There was a door between the bedrooms and it was open just

440

a sliver. Nangi could make out whisperings and, peering over Fortuitous Chiu's shoulder, eyed the next bedroom.

He saw a slice of window, the shoulder of a teak dresser laden on top with small crystal perfume bottles, several lipstick canisters. A frame was on the wall, the print or picture itself out of his line of sight.

A bed with pink satin covers, yellow sheets. Piles of pillows. And two bodies. Both were quite naked. They contrasted badly in the same way the color scheme did. Succulent Pien lying languorously with her yellow-toned flesh gleaming in the shaded lamplight.

Beside her, appearing enormous and grossly overwhelming, was the pinkish flesh, hairy in some places, ruddy in others, hairy *and* ruddy in still others, of a Westerner's body.

It was not Liu at all sharing her bed but a Caucasian well over six feet, Nangi judged, with thick ginger-colored hair, a rather high forehead, neat mustache, and clear, intelligent blue eyes.

Now where have I seen that face before? Nangi asked himself. At the moment, no one else could supply the needed information. He settled down to watch and listen. They were speaking in English.

"They will be bringing three-quarters of a ton across next Tuesday," Succulent Pien was saying. "As usual, it will be Liu's task to guide the property through into the Colony."

"Can we intercept it?" the ginger-haired man said. "It's only been six weeks since the last raid."

"There is more than bullion on this one." Succulent Pien's eyes were sparkling. "Information is to be relayed as well. Very secret information."

"What on?"

She giggled and stroked his hairy thigh. "How badly would you like to know?"

"Me? I don't care one way or another." It dawned on Nangi that the man spoke with a decidedly Scottish burr.

"Then it doesn't matter that I cannot tell you." Succulent Pien's voice was a rich purr now as her fingers moved down off the muscled ridge of his bare thigh. She cupped him in the palm of her hand. "I am sworn to secrecy."

The ginger-haired man's eyes were half closed. "Though I don't care a fig, my darling, Her Majesty's Government might have some small interest in this very secret information."

Her fingers were stroking lightly. "But what am I to do, stuck on the horns of dilemma this way? I cannot betray a trust."

The ginger-haired man gave a low groan. "Since you've sought my help, my darling, I think you should tell me," he said through teeth gritted in pleasure.

"It's so big." Succulent Pien's gaze had dropped. "It constantly amazes me how big you get." Her head came up. "Because this is so, I will tell you."

Nangi saw that this was all a sexual game between them. She had every intention of telling him from the outset. So this was how Succulent Pien supplemented her income, he thought. A confidante of the most powerful Communist Chinese in the Crown Colony, she then selectively betrayed him to the other side.

She was stroking more strongly now. Her eyes never left her work. "The information contains new assignments for over half of the upper-echelon Communist operatives secreted within the Crown Colony's government, police department, and security services."

"God in Heaven!"

It was unclear to Nangi whether the ginger-haired man was reacting to the news or to Succulent Pien's ministrations. He was beginning to understand the reason for her name.

With a throaty laugh, the Chinese girl swung herself atop the prone figure, inserting his rigid length into her with one swift movement. Closing her eyes, she pushed herself against his pubic mound, shuddering deeply at the contact.

"Pull on my nipples," she gasped. "I love it when you do that."

His hands raised obediently and she cried out shrilly. Meanwhile, in the adjoining room, Third Cousin Tok was snapping away with the black-bodied Nikon, the telephoto lens ensuring him of clear and exacting shots of the participants' faces as well as their joined sweating bodies. Beside him, Fortuitous Chiu raised the volume on the micro tape recorder with its extended narrow-dispersion microphone.

On the pink and yellow bed the ginger-haired man's buttocks were bucking upward in a ragged rhythm as if he wished to dislodge his rider, which he most assuredly did not. But he was not yet far enough gone to lose track of priorities. "I don't want to compromise Liu. You understand that."

Succulent Pien was gasping and moaning. "I know it . . . Ohhh! . . . and he knows it as well. He has arranged everything perfectly." Her voice rose to a scream. "Oh, now, now, now, my great stallion! Fill me all up!"

Gradually, after that, Nangi and Fortuitous Chiu crept away, back the way they had come. In the hallway of the basement the same two Green Pang were deep into their Fan Tan.

Outside, in the filthy alleyway, Nangi wiped his brow with a handkerchief. "It's not her at all," he said. "It's Liu himself! He's working both sides of the street. Madonna, he's sure to get himself killed!"

"He hasn't so far." Fortuitous Chiu grinned hugely. "He's a very smart man . . . as well as being a very nasty one."

Nangi was doing his best to keep the elation he was feeling out of his mind; it was far too busy for such an extraneous and potentially dangerous emotion.

He sensed the tides turning for real now and he was thinking furiously. He had to be certain, and he needed help for that. "Fortuitous Chiu," he said, "how can we be certain that what the woman fed this man is not Communist disinformation?"

"Normally there would be no way," the young Chinese said. "Certainly my sources among the Communists are not good, and you can imagine that Third Cousin Tok might fare no better on that avenue." He was grinning again and Nangi wondered what it was that was so hilarious. He was about to find out.

"But in this case we need no outside verification," the young man went on. "Because, you see, the foreign devil locked in the embrace of Succulent Pien is Charles Percy Redman himself. And no one in Hong Kong, least of all Succulent Pien, would dare risk feeding him false information of this sort. He's so well plugged in he'd know in a shot and she would never see the light of dawn."

Nangi, his hand in his breast pocket, touched the glossy surface of the red envelope Liu had given him, thus causing him to lose enormous face. Now he allowed his elation full rein.

"What do you mean you can't read it?"

"Just that, Protorov-san," Koten said.

"It's Japanese, isn't it?" Protorov, who had never bothered to learn the difficult and time-consuming Japanese language, could nevertheless not understand that failing in anyone else.

"It is and it isn't."

"I don't pay you to give me riddles."

"I did what I was ordered," the immense *sumō* champion said. "I infiltrated Sato's *kobun*, I worked with your Lieutenant Russilov at the *rotenburo*, and as a consequence we lost your last spy. I have done my duty."

"Your duty," Viktor Protorov said, "is precisely what I tell you it is. You must read me the papers from the Tenshin Shoden Katori. Your very life depends upon it."

"Then I must surely die, Protorov-san, for I cannot translate this paper. True, it is based on Chinese ideograms on which, also, my own language is based. However, it uses ideograms that *kanji*

443

discarded as being, perhaps, too complex, difficult, or open to misinterpretation." He spread his pudgy-fingered hands. "This might as well be Arabic as far as I am concerned. There is no doubt that this is the *ryu*'s code. If you had allowed me to handle matters at the *rotenburo*, your spy would now be here instead of six feet underground. No doubt he could have translated this." His shoulders lifted, fell. "But now—"

Protorov slammed the tabletop, grabbed up the sheets of paper in his fist. It was so unfair! Here was the secret to *Tenchi* literally in the palm of his hand, the fruition of the most important clandestine operation he had ever mounted, the sword he needed to dazzle the GRU generals, to galvanize the Red Army, to begin his coup, and he could not read it. It was unbelievable!

For a moment he thought he might go mad with frustration. Then he took several deep breaths to calm his racing pulse. One, two, three. Set his mind to working.

"Linnear is ninja," Koten said softly. "He got his training at the Tenshin Shodien Katori. It is conceivable . . ." He allowed his voice to trail off.

Hope exploded like a lightning flash across Protorov's mind. Yes. Linnear was his only hope now. It had been many years since he had lived at the *ryu* but still, traditions in Japan rarely die. Protorov knew that there was at least some chance that the code would be the same. On the surface it seemed a desperate gamble, but he was now working under a severe time element. Mironenko was gathering the generals. In six days' time they would meet and he had to be there to present his plan to them; he had to deliver *Tenchi* to them or lose them forever. With the Neanderthals who inhabited the GRU there could never be another opening; not, at least, for the KGB.

Protorov spun and strode from the small room, calling for the doctor and his magic needle.

"I need to speak with the subject now," he said to the bespectacled physician.

"Now?" The doctor's eyes were round and startled behind his thick lenses. "But you told me you were giving me forty-eight hours for the softening-up process."

"I no longer have the time," Protorov snapped. "The real world, Doctor, is infinitely mutable. You must get used to these sudden changes."

"But I don't know how much I can do on this short a notice," the doctor said, falling into step with Protorov. "I'm getting erratic readings from the cerebral cortex; I can't make head nor tail of them. I can't guarantee how far he's under, if at all."

"Then double the dose," Protorov ordered. "Triple it, I don't care. Just so long as he talks now."

The doctor was frantic. "But that strength will surely kill him in fifteen minutes, twenty at the outside."

Protorov nodded. "That's all the time I'll need, Doctor. Please go to work on him at once."

"His name is Gordon Minck and he came down to Key West every so often to be with me."

"What exactly do you mean by 'be with me.'"

"He loved the way I went down on him," Alix Logan said somewhat nastily. "Does that answer your question?"

"I think it does," Croaker said.

They were in the car, heading through the fumy innards of the Lincoln Tunnel on their way to Matty the Mouth's place.

He considered the nature of her response for a moment. "I'm sorry," he said. "I didn't know that was a sore spot."

Alix put her head back against the seat, closing her eyes. Her thick blond hair spread like sea foam around her cheeks. "What do you think? A guy who's strong and handsome, powerful in an—oh, I don't know—interior sort of way, goes all googley-eyed over me. He's a dangerous man, you can see that on his face like a scar or a ridge of pockmarks.

"'I should have you killed,' he tells me, 'but I can't. I don't ever want to think I'll never see that face again.'"

"Oh, very cute," Croaker cut in. "Why didn't you tell me this before?"

"Shut up," Alix snapped. "I'm telling you now, aren't I?"

Fluorescent light and shadow fell over them in a rhythmic pattern, like notes controlled by a metronome.

"'I don't want to lose you,' he said, 'but I'm in a business where I can't afford to make a mistake.' He looked at me in a way that made my insides go cold. 'Will you be a mistake, Alix?'

"'No, I won't,' I told him. 'Is that a promise?' he asked. 'Yes,' I said, and I meant it." She began to cry. "And now look what I've done." Sobbing fully. "It's all your fault." It was the wail of a lost and confused child.

Croaker didn't think he needed to refute that; it was too irrational. Instead, he changed the subject slightly. "So who's this mystery man Minck."

"Minck," Alix Logan said. "Minck, Minck, Minck." It was like a new toy which she did not want to give up. Then she decided. "Gordon Minck is the man who killed Angela Didion."

Almost drove the car into the side of the tunnel. *"What?"* His

445

head began to ache and there was a fearful red light behind his eyes. "You must be mistaken." His voice was a dry rustle, no more than a whisper. It was all he could muster at the moment. But what if she's right? he asked himself. All these months hiding, living in fear of discovery. He was a pariah at the New York City Police Department; he no longer even existed save as "Tex" Bristol. He had lied, stolen, gone beyond the law he had so many long years ago sworn to uphold and protect. What had happened to him? What madness had possessed him? He felt like a malaria victim who had just awakened from an endless fever through which he had been raving. He had believed so mightily in this truth: that Raphael Tomkin had murdered Angela Didion in cold blood. He had been so sure. All the facts had pointed to it. Now they darted like tiny frightened fish, weaving away from him as he sought again to compile them, to reassure himself that he was right and Alix was wrong.

Alix sniffed, wiped at her nose. "It's like this," she said, ignoring his interruption. "Tomkin made the mistake of talking to Angela about his connection with Minck, and Angela, the bitch, had a memory as deep as the ocean floor. She remembered *everything*. That was part of her scam, how she could get whatever she wanted from almost everyone. She remembered what they did not want known.

"So of course there came a day when she threw this knowledge up at Tomkin. I don't really know why. Perhaps there was a diamond she wanted that he wouldn't give her; maybe he wasn't coming by enough, or maybe he was dropping in *too* much. You could never tell with Angela, she blew so hot and cold.

"Anyway, she could always spot a lever and she knew she had a powerful one with Tomkin. She wanted something from him and if he wouldn't do it, she told him she'd go to the papers with what she had on him. It was S.O.P. with her.

"However, this time I don't think she really understood the nature of the beast she had by the tail. Tomkin shut up immediately, refusing to get into an argument with her; he saw right away that she was intractable.

"So he called Minck and Minck sent out his hounds to snuff Angela. There was no negotiating, no thinking it over. Whatever Minck and Tomkin were into was far too big.

"Of course, Tomkin had to be there when it went down. Angela was so paranoid she wouldn't've opened the door to Minck's people. Tomkin was the front man. But once she unlatched the chain, the three of them came in."

"Was Tomkin actually there when she bought it?" He trembled as he voiced it, knowing how important her answer was to him.

"In the apartment but not in the bedroom. He was at the bar, taking an anesthetic. His hands shook so much he got as much Scotch on the counter as he did in his glass. I had the angle from where I was hiding inside Angela's clothes closet. I was just coming out of the bathroom when she went to answer the door." Her eyes were bleak, almost as if they had lost their rich color. "I heard Angela's high-pitched yelp. It sounded like a dog being whipped." She shrugged. "I don't know why, but I ducked into the closet right away."

"So you were an eyewitness all right."

"There was nothing mean about what they did to her." Her voice, like her eyes, had become washed out. Maybe, Croaker thought, it was her way of protecting herself from something no one should see. He took her hand in his, fingers entwined. "They were very . . . businesslike about what they did to her. It took no time. I remember, just afterwards, being so shocked by that. Such a monstrous thing . . . it should take a long time to undo life." Her eyes closed for a moment. Incipient tears glistened along the lashes. "Afterward, they made it look like something else, of course. Not an execution. Then they went into the living room and thoroughly cleaned up after Tomkin. They didn't find me because I crawled into a secret compartment Angela had built into the back of her closet to store her furs and jewelry; she loved being close to them. I had to curl up into a ball. It was stifling and I couldn't hear anything. I was terrified that at any moment they'd discover me.

"They didn't then, but they must've known about my relationship with Angela because they found me a week after I flew down to Key West. In the meantime, they'd done their homework. They knew where I was that night; they knew I'd seen it all. Minck's men are professionals."

"So I've come to learn," Croaker said distantly. He put both hands on the wheel. So the truth was close . . . but not close enough. His inner laugh was ironic and bitter. The truth was nothing so clearcut as black and white. Tomkin *hadn't* killed Angela; he had only set her up. He didn't order it, didn't execute that order. He merely went along with it, stood by, a wall away, while it was happening. Guilty as charged, your honor. The voice echoed hollowly in Croaker's mind. But what was the charge? Not murder in the second degree; not even manslaughter. Instead, Tomkin had been an accessory to murder. It had not been he who had put pressure on the Commissioner to sweep the Didion murder under the police blotter. That had come all the way from Washington, D.C. From Minck himself.

Cloak-and-dagger Minck, Croaker thought bitterly. How many murders could he be held accountable for? Angela Didion's was just one in a long line. He felt deflated and saddened by the vast gray areas of the world, within one of which he now found himself. It was a bog without form or substance, where direction became hazy before fading out altogether. Where to go now that Angela Didion's murderer was beyond him? For he knew without doubt that he could never touch Minck on this charge or any other. He was defeated.

Sunshine hit them like a fist on the Manhattan side of the tunnel, bouncing off the hood like a starblaze. Croaker headed right, toward Thirty-fourth Street, where he turned left for several long blocks, then right after the light changed, heading downtown on Second Avenue. The city beckoned them with grimy fingers.

Anger bubbled inside him, turned without his knowing on Alix. Women's motivations were so opaque to him. He wished to God she had told him all this days before—although what he would have done differently he did not know. They still had to make the trip out of there. Damn it, damn it, damn it!

She touched his arm and he glanced at her. "I'm sorry for what I said before. I know none of this's your fault." She ran tanned fingers through her hair. "I couldn't stand it down there anymore; it was like prison—worse in some ways. At least in prison I imagine you know where you stand. In Key West, surrounded by those two, I didn't know what to expect next. Would Minck continue to come? Would his feelings fade? Would one of them kill me then?

"It began to feel like there was a balloon inside my head and each day it was being filled with more air. Soon there'd be more balloon than brain and then I wouldn't be able to think at all." She gave a little strangled laugh. "Silly, isn't it?"

"No," Croaker said softly, "it isn't." It was remarkable how she could defuse his rage so utterly. She had only to touch him, to turn those eyes on him, to whisper softly, and all the blackness curled like ash inside him.

She gave a little sigh, as if it had been extremely important that he corroborate her feelings. "I wanted to tell you all of it right away, Lew. It's important that you believe that."

"I do."

Her head was turned sideways toward him. "Not just say it."

"I don't say anything idly, Alix."

She seemed to accept that. "I was in shock; you were such a— oh, I don't know—a bolt out of the blue."

"A knight in shining armor."

448

It was a joke, but she did not take it that way. "Oh, yes. I wanted to believe that very much. But I was afraid to. It was almost like you were too good to be true. I had been involved with this for so long—all this knowledge inside my head like a time bomb with a hair trigger.

"I felt like I had when I was younger, and, you know, I was the prettiest girl in my class by far—oh, don't think me big-headed; you only needed a mirror to see it. Boys buzzing around me like bees. At first I reveled in it. What girl wouldn't?

"But then, as I got to know them, as I went through them one by one, as brief boyfriends, just dating and doing, you know, kid things, I'd always get to a point when I'd suddenly realize why they wanted to date me. They weren't interested in talking, in getting to know me. They loved being seen with me and, after a time, trying to slip a hand underneath my dress. They were hard all the time; it was the only thing they thought of.

"For a while it made me hate my beauty. It was as if I had thick ankles or a long nose or was flatchested."

She put her hand on him. "It was the same with you, Lew. Why were you there, I asked myself? What was it you really wanted from me?" She laughed again. "It even occurred to me that Minck had sent you to test me; but I soon realized that was *really* crazy—you killed both his men."

"Do you care about him?" It wasn't an idle question; in the future it might become a key bit of knowledge for Croaker to have, like an extra shield or a mace held behind his back. Because he had already come to a decision. There was only one thing left for him to do after all.

"How can I answer that?" Alix said as they pulled up outside an apartment house in the Twenties. "The affair has been taking place in limbo or outer space. I don't have any signposts to use as reference points." She turned away. "I wouldn't've gone to bed with him if I hadn't felt . . . something. I'm not at all like Angela was. Yet I haven't a clue what it was I felt. It's almost as if by having sex with him—by establishing a link that was physical as well as, oh, what should I call it, psychic, I suppose?" She shrugged.

"Not emotional?"

"It's possible, but I don't think so. I have some small perspective on it now. I think I felt that by establishing this link with my—well he was my jailor, really, wasn't he—I'd somehow be less of a prisoner."

"But it didn't work out that way."

The curl of a smile. "Do you really think it could have?"

"No."

"Of course not. It was stupid of me, really. I never should have trusted someone like that in the first place. But my God, Lew, I was so desperate. It was just crushing me inside. I felt——"

Alix screamed as the explosive bullet burst through the side window, tore off three-quarters of the top of the sedan. Croaker had already been moving, pulling her toward him, covering her upper torso and head with his bulk.

At the same time his gun was drawn. But another shot rocked the car on its shocks, a great fist reaching out from the void, exploding layers of chrome, steel, aluminum, and plastic. Safety glass webbed and pebbled, fluttering down over them as gently as doves' wings.

Croaker could smell smoke. There was no rear door left on his side, not much top over their heads, either. He leaned forward, making Alix squeal with the pressure, and jerked down the handle of the door on her side. Pushed with the flat of his free hand, rolled her out onto the sidewalk like a sack of potatoes.

He turned off the ignition but the third shot had already hit the car, ripping through metal into the gas tank. There was a dull thud like a dropped bowling ball. Flames licked up, and a curl of oily smoke made him cough.

Croaker turned toward the direction from which the shots were being fired. But he had no vantage point, could move very little, and the smoke was becoming denser. He heard sirens rising and falling, loudening. Coming this way.

He got out the same way Alix had and, taking her hand, began to run. He ignored the entrance to Matty the Mouth's building as if it had no significance for him.

They hurled down Second Avenue, passing a Police Emergency Squad wagon, a fire truck, and a pair of blue-and-whites, all heading the wrong way up Second. Horns blared, traffic snarled. People stood and stared, then began to drift toward the scene. Within moments a good-sized crowd had formed.

Watching the flow of people, Tanya Vladimova cursed herself for firing prematurely. But she had not known how long they were stopped for. Further, just ten minutes ago her beeper had gone off; it was time for the drop into Japan. She had not been ready for that, not when she was so close to her quarry.

Circumstances had conspired against her; they had manipulated her rather than the other way around. Now, as she dismantled the Attlov-Sonigen .385, stowing it in a compartment beneath the carpeting of her car, she resigned herself. Even had she not been on a time allotment she would not have been able to go after Alix Logan and Lewis Croaker. Her link-up with ARRTS had digested

450

the fingerprints she had lifted in Raleigh, had spat out his name. Too many people, too many cops. More coming, more sirens. Detectives' unmarked cars spreading the traffic like Moses heading out across the Red Sea.

Tanya turned her ignition and got out of there, heading uptown, through the Midtown Tunnel, out to the Long Island Expressway and Kennedy Airport.

She cleared her mind of what she had not been able to accomplish here. She accelerated into the left lane. Not more than a mile later she was slowed by traffic that seemed to build up out of thin air. She began to go over what she had to do next and in what order she must do it.

There was a pinpoint of light. It was extremely annoying because it kept pricking into his brain in an odd kind of cadence. *Dum-tee-dum-tee-dum-dum*.

Otherwise he was surrounded by the milky luminescence of *getsumei no michi*. It should have been wholly opalescent and peaceful. It would have been except for the pinpoint of light. *Dum-tee-dum-tee-dum-dum*.

He tried to think of nothing. That, at least, should have been easy. He could not. In vain he reached out for the Void, but each time he sought a clear path to it the pinpoint of light stood directly in his way. He tried to push it aside; he could not. He tried *kiai*; this, too, had no effect. He had no strength left within him because the white pinpoint kept pricking his brain as if with electric shocks. He could not think, could not concentrate, could not center himself. If only he had his *katana*; if only he could remember where he had left *Iss-hōgai*.

Dum-tee-dum-tee-dum-DUM.

"*Iss-hōgai*," Nicholas murmured, strapped and sweating on Protorov's wheel.

"What the hell is that?" Protorov wanted to know. "Koten?"

"It means, 'For life,'" the *sumō* said sullenly. "It sounds to me like a name of a *samurai*'s *katana*." He was not happy. This process was tiresome. He wanted to be left alone with Nicholas Linnear. Five minutes would do nicely, he thought. "Although what a ninja would be doing with a *samurai* sword is beyond me."

"It's his *sword*?" Protorov asked, missing nothing. "Russilov, did you confiscate such a weapon from him?"

"No, sir."

"Did you *see* such a thing?"

"No, sir."

Protorov directed himself back to his client. "Nicholas," he

451

asked in an entirely different tone of voice, "where is your *katana*? Where is *Iss-hōgai*?"

DUM-TEE-DUM-TEE-DUM-DUM.

The pinpoint would not let him go; pincers inside his brain. *"Ro—Rotenburo."*

"That's not good," Koten said. "A *samurai* sword is its master's signature. We don't want anyone picking it up and asking questions about it."

Protorov nodded as if he had already thought of that. "Go and get it, Koten," he said.

"If you bring it back here, there's a chance he'll be able to get his hands on it," the *sumō* warned.

"That won't matter at all." Protorov considered options. "Tell me, is he right- or left-handed?"

Koten moved closer to Nicholas, observing the layers of callus along the bottom edge of either hand. "Right, I would say."

"Break the first three fingers of that hand."

Koten was overjoyed to do it. Almost lovingly he reached out and grasped the index finger of Nicholas' right hand. He undid the strap, then snapped the digit sideways. Nicholas groaned; his body shook. Sweat rolled off him like water scrolling from a swimmer.

Twice more Koten unstrapped a finger and went to work on it. Twice more Nicholas groaned and jerked. He was drenched. His head hung, chin on heaving chest. The doctor stepped in and checked his pulse, his blood pressure.

"Now go and do as I've ordered," Protorov said to Koten. "You will save us the possibility of embarrassment and he will only be able to look at his weapon longingly."

When Koten was gone, Protorov dug out the papers his spy had stolen from the Tenshin Shoden Katori *ryu*. He stared at Nicholas' right hand hanging by the straps at two fingers and wrist. Already the broken digits were swollen like sausages, the flesh was darkening.

"How will the pain affect him?" he asked the doctor.

"It should rouse him a bit."

"Will it interfere with cerebration at all?"

"With him, I would say no, definitely not."

Protorov nodded and, reaching out, took a handful of Nicholas' wet hair. He picked up the head, slapping at the cheeks until the eyelids fluttered open. Then he shoved the first page of coded text in front of the bleary-eyed face.

"Focus," he commanded in a soft voice. "Something here for you to read, Nicholas. Something you'll enjoy."

Nicholas frowned. Deep down he felt a terrible aching, a trident, its tines coated with poison, lancing into him. It seemed very far away, however, as if, even, it might be part of a dream or an hallucination.

It seemed important to focus so he tried to do so. He seemed to be swimming through viscous gas. He could not fathom how he was breathing the stuff because it was obvious that he could not move through it. He flailed and stayed still. Or was it that he only thought he was flailing.

Black and white, breaking up, coalescing, only to dissolve once more.

"Focus," came the command from the bright pinpoint which seemed directly inside his brain. So he thought he would do that. Focus.

Characters swimming by him like schools of fish, like a forest's underbrush, like tongues of fire, like the hissing rain. It was pouring. Pouring letters.

Not letters. *Ideograms*.

He read. And came face to face with that which he had sought for so long. *Tenchi*.

"Three years ago... *Hare Maru* lost at sea in violent typhoon... over fifty lives lost... sailors and civilians... greatest marine disaster in twenty-five years. ... Therefore underwater salvage operations begun immediately the weather cleared at spot of last radio message: Nemuro Straits."

He pushed the dulled pain away from him, sealing it off; he closed an inner door on the white pinpoint: *dum-tee-dum-t...*

Quiet. He moved out of *getsumei no michi*, which had been no shelter at all, and therefore of no use to him. He commenced to still himself, beginning with his fingertips, a number of which, for some reason, he could not feel. Rising inward, the moon lifting into the cloudy heavens, its bright, clear face reflecting in unending undulations.

Thus he began to pull himself together, centering slowly, despite the enormous amount of chemicals inside him. While he began the difficult process of breaking them down into harmless components which would then be flushed out—a *ninjutsu* art known as *Ogawa-no-jutsu*—he did precisely what Protorov was asking him to do: discover the secret of *Tenchi*.

It was not lost on him that what he was reading was in code. The Tenshin Shoden Katori code. He also grasped that if his enemy was showing it to him then he must have no one else to translate it for him. And if Nicholas died, that would be the end, therefore Protorov would have nothing to transmit or to use.

Therefore, Nicholas decided, after he had finished reading this document, he must die. And even as his mind reeled with the fantastic knowledge of just what *Tenchi* was, even as he recalled Sato's wish for Japan to end its childhood of dependence on the rest of the world, to enter the adulthood of self-sufficiency, he began the process.

Just a foot away from him, Protorov could not tell whether Nicholas was just looking or reading. Did he know the code or didn't he?

"Tell me what this says," he repeated over and over, brandishing all four sheets. "Tell me, tell me, tell me." But Nicholas' eyes kept crossing and Protorov noticed that his client's color was fading.

The doctor stepped between them. "That's enough," he said, putting the flat of his stethoscope over Nicholas' heart. Immediately, he ripped the ear plugs off and began to pound on Nicholas' chest, fist against the flat of his hand.

"I warned you against this," he managed between grunts. "We're going to lose him."

"No!" Protorov cried. "You must save him! I order it!"

The doctor gave a grim laugh. "Unlike you, Comrade, I know that I am not a god. I cannot create life out of death." He allowed his hands to drop. He stared at them, then turned around to glare at Protorov. "I cannot undo what you have done, Colonel."

"Rouse him, Doctor!" Protorov was beside himself. "He has told me nothing! Nothing at all!"

"That's always the risk one takes in these neuropharmacological matters. The balance is ever so deli—" He recoiled, bounding off Nicholas' frame, as Protorov hit him with his fist. "That will cost you, Colonel," he said, wiping at his split lip. "Central will hear about this."

"You!" Protorov's voice was a low, guttural growl. "You killed him! It was your doing!" His hands were shaking with the force of his rage. *Tenchi*, the GRU-KGB summit, the great coup, all dust in the wind now, as ephemeral as wishes. "Russilov!" he cried. "Take him into protective custody. If he gives you any trouble at all put a bullet through his head." He grabbed the doctor by his shirtfront, jerking him forward. "You've made your last empty threat," he said, just before he threw the doctor away from him.

Russilov, one hand on his holstered pistol, took the man's arm in a viselike grip.

Watching them depart, Protorov tried vainly to control the rage sweeping through him, shaking him like a tree in a storm. He

454

could not believe it. How could this happen? he thought. It was outrageous, inconceivable. He *would* not believe it.

He turned back to Nicholas' limp body. He looked upon it as one does one's own failings. He despised it with a fierceness that bordered on pain. He remembered striking down an icon once, a Crucifix made of wood, painted in gilt and white, bright red where drops of blood leaked at open palms, crossed ankles, bethorned forehead.

It broke when it fell, and he ground it underfoot with the heel of his polished boot. The agony it had conveyed, which, for the owner, at least, had been transmuted into a constancy of faith, had been incoherent to him.

Yet now the extreme of pain the Crucifixion represented was revealed to him. It was as much a shock to him as if he had woken up in the morning to find that his legs had been amputated. Abruptly the world was not the same anymore, and never would be again. A certain peace—a wholeness not only of flesh but of spirit as well—was gone, and in its stead rose a torment, engulfing and endless.

Up until this moment there had never been any real doubt in his mind that he would achieve his goals. Lofty or not, they would be his. He was clever and he was ruthless. Like Einstein, he was an intuitive thinker who could make great leaps that bypassed plodding logic. That, he knew, was as close as man would ever get to traveling at the speed of light.

Now he had to face the crushing reality that that was not enough. He would not learn the secret of *Tenchi*, he would not make his summit; there would therefore be no coup. No greatness for Viktor Protorov. History would not enthrone him. It would now not even notice him.

Protorov looked at Nicholas Linnear with a murderous glare and saw only his own undoing. He saw how close he had come to ultimate victory . . . and how far away. It was knowledge that he could not tolerate.

A man berserk, he railed at the cool flesh, pounding it over and over again while great gasping grunts emanated from him in such profusion and with such clarion pealing that even Russilov dared not reenter the vault.

But even this physical venting of his rage and pain was not enough. The body was manacled, an absolute prisoner. To strike his late client thus—a man who had caused him to lose everything—both diminished Protorov and increased his agony.

Swiftly, still grunting like a wild boar, he unfastened the leather straps that bound Nicholas to the wheel. First fingers and wrists

455

were freed, then thighs and ankles. Lastly the waist strap came undone, and the form fell onto him with the force of a sack of cement.

Clawing and kicking, Protorov thrust the body away from him while at the same time seeking to follow it to attack it anew now that it had been freed and, in his mind at least, was fair game for him.

What could he think then when, in the midst of his red, red rage, a corpse pronounced deceased by his neuropharmacologica expert reached an arm out and grasped the side of his corded neck?

For the Western mind death is a difficult commodity to come by. Because there is no acceptance of it, because there is no thought as to its confluence with life, human beings are, more often than not, most difficult to kill.

The simple fact is that the organism does not want to die. To this end it will cling tenaciously to life, it will push the body to superhuman, inexplicable feats of strength and endurance. Cars have been moved by quite ordinary people in this kind of situation, extraordinary jumps have been made, exposure to the elements sustained beyond all measure.

Then there is the body itself. A bullet to the head may be turned aside by the skull. Similarly, a knife thrust can be deflected by an intervening rib.

In the East, however, where traditionally death means nothing, it is different. Death comes with the speed of a lightning bolt, giving the spirit of the organism no time to react at all. Ancient teachings, as well, allow an assailant to actually use the human body against itself.

And that was precisely how death came to Viktor Protorov, how Nicholas Linnear did, indeed, become C. Gordon Minck's terrible swift sword. Perhaps he knew to what use he had been put. Certainly he did not care.

Nothing was in his mind—his spirit was as clear as a mountain lake after a strong rain—as he pressed inward with the thumb of his left hand, breaking apart Protorov's collar bone and using it as a sword to sever the vital arteries that rose upward from the heart like a branching tree.

There was nothing to it. It was over in the space of a double heartbeat. It was so simple. Thirty-five years of personal training, perhaps a thousand more before that for the discipline itself, made it so.

Nicholas was slow to rouse after that. The process by which he had withdrawn blood from the surface of his body, by which he had stilled his pulse and his pressure, was an enormously complex and draining one, both physically and mentally.

Slowly, blood returned to all of him and his skin blushed. He was heating up again, a dying sun returning from the embers of dormancy.

Slowly he focused on the grotesquely canted corpse sprawled beside him. Blood drenched them both, binding them in a last attempt to bridge a gap that could never be spanned.

Nicholas felt no remorse. Though there was no fine feeling in snuffing out the life of another human being—or even an animal, for that matter—the elation of life lifted him in its glorious embrace. He was alive and Viktor Protorov was dead. He was flooded with the juices of life. He rode all the air currents of the world, swam in all the seas, lakes, and streams. He padded through the forests and loped across the plains. He stalked the veldts, skittered through the deserts. There was not any place on earth where he was not at that moment. Connected once more to the cosmos, he stood at the Void and was replenished.

"And this is for Third Cousin Tok himself," Nangi said, sliding HK $6000 across the table to Fortuitous Chiu. "I want you to be generous with the *h'eung yau*," he said, knowing that the sowing of fragrant grease brought great face with it. "But also be certain to stress the patriotic elements of this matter. I want it made perfectly clear to Third Cousin Tok just who these people are. In that event there will be genuine pleasure in what they will be doing."

Fortuitous Chiu nodded. "I understand completely."

"Good." Nangi smiled. He had already sown his seeds in the form of anonymous calls to several police sergeants—one in Wan Chai, one in Central, a third in Stanley—who, it was suspected by the Green Pang, were working for the Communists. When Nangi had asked Fortuitous Chiu why they were allowed to operate, the young Chinese had smiled and said, "How do the *quai loh* put it? Better the devil you know than the one you do not."

"You'd do well at the Golden Mountain," Nangi had said, using the Chinese designation for America.

"Perhaps," the young man had said. "But I have no wish to leave the Crown Colony. My fortune will be made here."

Nangi had no doubt about that at all.

Now, as the heavy fog of twilight settled over Hong Kong like a mantle of velvet, he rose and said, "I'm starved. Shall we have dinner?"

Fortuitous Chiu nodded. "Where would you like to go?"

"I want a fine Chinese meal," Nangi said. "I'll leave it in your hands."

The young man looked at him for a moment. Then he bowed slightly and, without making another gesture, said, "This way, please."

Fortuitous Chiu took him into the countryside, north into the New Territories. Gradually, as they approached the border of China itself, the communities became smaller, high rises giving way to two- and three-story housing, strung together by arcs of slapping washing. Naked children ran in the dirt streets. Dogs barked angrily and fought with each other amid the trash heaps.

Parking, they crossed a kind of central square where hawkers abounded, edged down a side street that was impossibly narrow. "This is the restaurant we will be going to," the young man said, using his chin to point. "It's the best of its kind in Hong Kong."

They went past the place and entered an open-air market. Nangi saw that this was built on a long dock. He could see the water, the fishing boats tied up, their crews making ready for the early morning's sail.

As they walked between rows of stalls, Fortuitous Chiu said, "Usually those boats return with holds filled with more than fish. It's a bit too hazy tonight to see, but just across there is Communist China. Refugees are brought in here all the time."

All the stalls sold live fish. Tanks were set up, filled with seaweedy water in which somnolently swam fish big, medium, and small, shellfish such as giant prawn and abalone, conch and crab. Squid with the black button eyes of the dead were much in evidence, as were crayfish as large as lobsters.

"What is your preference?"

"We are in China," Nangi said. "A Chinese should choose."

Fortuitous Chiu took this responsibility quite seriously. As they moved from stall to stall, he would indicate an item here, two there. As they were drawn out of their tanks he would handle them all, sniffing and prodding like an old woman to make certain he was picking the finest specimens of the lots. Then would begin the haggling, a game of endless manipulation and strategy that, like gambling, fascinated and invigorated the Chinese.

At last, carrying his catch in plastic bags made heavy and bulging with sea water, Fortuitous Chiu led Nangi back to the restaurant.

The owner, a fat, sweating Chinese, greeted the young man with the kind of respect one normally accords a visiting lord. Nangi wondered at this but he knew that good manners forbade him from asking Fortuitous Chiu about it.

That evening they dined on no less than nine courses of exquisitely prepared seafood, from succulently sauteed abalone to grilled crayfish, choked with fiery hot chili sauce that made even Nangi's eyes water, made him long for the relative calm of *wasabi*—the traditional Japanese green horseradish—he loved so much.

For more than three hours they feasted and in true Chinese fashion talked of nothing of serious import during that time. The Chinese—as opposed to the Japanese, who were far more fanatic about business—believed that nothing should take away from the savoring of a meal. In that respect they were the French of the Far East.

When, at length, they returned to the hotel, Nangi bade Fortuitous Chiu come with him. Stuffed into the mail box of Nangi's room behind the concierge's desk was a telephone message.

There was no number to call back. Rather, the slip of paper contained an address, a date—tomorrow's, or rather, because it was already after midnight, today's—and an hour, two A.M. Madonna, Nangi thought disconsolately on the elevator ride up, what am I going to do now?

"I'm to meet a man this morning," he told Fortuitous Chiu when they had reached his room. "In just under two hours." He read off the address, which was on Wong Chuk Hang Road.

"That's Ocean Park," Fortuitous Chiu said. "Normally it would be closed this late but this week it's being kept open all day and all night to coincide with the Dragon Boat Festival, which is actually the day after tomorrow, the fifth day of the fifth moon; also to raise money for the amusement park. The tourists, they say, love it."

Nangi went into the closet, rummaging around out of the other's sight for a moment. He returned with two identical manila envelopes. He handed one to Fortuitous Chiu.

"I must take one of these with me tonight," he said. "The copy you have was destined for the Governor. I wanted you with the Governor at the same time my meeting was taking place. I would have felt safer that way. But now—"

"Hold on," Fortuitous Chiu said. "May I use the phone?"

"Of course."

For a little more than five minutes he spoke in a choppy, rapid-fire dialect.

Fortuitous Chiu put down the phone, turned to Nangi. "It's all set now. No sweat."

"What's all set?"

"At two this morning," he said, "I will be sitting opposite the Governor of Hong Kong."

Nangi was nonplussed. "I—I don't understand. How is that possible?"

"My father is taking care of it. Like I said, no sweat."

Nangi recalled the manner in which Fortuitous Chiu had been received at the restaurant in the New Territories. He thought of the power of Third Cousin Tok. He thought of the Green Pang. Lastly he thought of the five Dragons, the five heads of the Hong Kong Triads, the most powerful men in the Colony. Who could Fortuitous Chiu's father be to be able to reach the Governor at this time of the night? How powerful did he have to be? How much clout did he need to possess?

Nangi bowed slightly. "I am in your debt."

"As I am in yours. I have gained great face with my father."

Now, to business. "You will sit with the Governor," Nangi said. "God alone knows what you will converse about."

"My father will do all the talking."

Nangi thought about that. "If I don't call you by three, you must assume the worst. Give the Governor all the evidence against Liu."

"It will cause a sensation," Fortuitous Chiu said. "A scandal of the highest order. The Communists will lose enormous face."

"They will, won't they?" Nangi said, musingly.

"Very bad for them."

Nangi nodded. "Either way, it's very bad for them."

They stood facing each other in the room. There was not much more to say, and time was running short.

Fortuitous Chiu gave a little bow. "Until we meet again . . . Elder Uncle."

Nangi held his breath. The honor which he had just been accorded was vast. "Elder Uncle" was a term used to connote respect and a certain sense of friendship that was not possible to accurately translate into Western concepts.

"May all the gods protect you," Nangi whispered. He was speaking of the myriad Chinese deities, none of whom he, needless to say, believed in, but who were very important to Fortuitous Chiu. Silently, then, he prayed for them both. Godspeed.

Ocean Park, built primarily with funds donated by the Royal Hong Kong Jockey Club, was, Nangi discovered, set on two discrete levels. One entered through turnstiled gates, strolling along paths bordering massive flower gardens, arbors filled with brightly colored parrots who for HK $5 would accommodatingly perch on one's shoulder while a color photo of the occasion was taken by an attendant. Up a short hill was a bonsai collection of awesome proportions. There were tiny pavilions erected by Air New Guinea and other such airlines, featuring local flora.

Farther along in this area was a swan pond, numerous waterfalls and, beyond, an open-air stadium where sea creatures performed. Nangi did not get that far, however. He had been told to buy a ticket on the funicular which ran at an extreme angle from Ocean Park's "lowlands" three thousand feet into the air to the "sky terminus" high atop a rocky promontory jutting out into the South China Sea. There a manmade atoll reef, the world's first "wave-cove," and another, larger stadium waited to entertain visitors.

There were four sets of funiculars—tiny glass-enclosed bubbles within which as many as six people could sit facing inward, hanging by what looked to Nangi to be a slender piece of steel from the cable line. Nangi had been told to take the funicular on the far left. He joined the line, moving forward periodically as the cable cars came back down the mountainside, swung around to make the return journey.

He did not look around; that would have cost him face. But he was nevertheless acutely aware of who stood near him—in front and in back, on either side. He saw tourists from the West and from Japan. He saw Chinese teenagers chattering, no doubt, about the excitement of being at the park so late. Or else, he thought cynically, they were betting on which car would detach itself from the cable and plummet to the craggy slopes far below. He was aware of no one who took the slightest interest in him.

He wondered when contact was going to be made. He was at the front of his line now. Perhaps it would not come until he had landed on the promontory. Would he share the funicular with the Chinese family just behind him?

The car came in empty, swung around. The doors swung open and the uniformed attendant waved him forward. He became aware that the attendant had barred the family behind him from entering his car.

It was so small in there that he experienced some difficulty in sitting. A man swung aboard. Where he had come from Nangi could not say. The doors closed and they were caught in the moving gears.

The funicular shuddered slowly forward. Ahead Nangi could see what was waiting for him. A string of tiny lighted cars, like glass beads strung on a wire, arced ahead and above.

They halted momentarily at the edge of the concrete terminus. It all seemed very solid, safe as a stroll in a garden. Then, with a breathtaking abruptness, they were launched out into space, swinging back and forth giddily, following the path set by the glass beads before them.

Nangi turned his attention to his companion. He was a heavyset Chinese of indeterminate age. He could have been fifty or seventy or anywhere in between. He had a flat nose, brush-cut hair that was so short his sunburned scalp could be seen through it. Against this close scrutiny the Chinese bared his teeth—all gold—in a smile or a grimace, Nangi could not tell which.

"Good morning, Mr. Nangi," the Chinese said, nodding. "I am Lo Whan."

Nangi returned the pleasantry.

"Tell me, have you been to Ocean Park before?"

"Never. But I have been to Hong Kong many times."

"Indeed." Lo Whan's tone of voice indicated that it was of no import to him. He turned in his molded plastic seat, the kind one encountered in hospital waiting rooms. "I myself have been here many times. I never tire of this view. And one rarely gets a chance to see it at this time of the morning."

Indeed the sight of the great flat expanse of the South China Sea, the black humped and hilly shapes of the small islands dotting the space like rocks in a Zen pebble garden, was spectacular. Long ships strung with glowing lights like eyes plowed the depths here and there, dusky jewels set in a dark, rich fabric. Moonlight lent it a metallic aspect, scimitars of cool illumination glancing off the ocean's face as if it were chain mail.

"Consider yourself fortunate," Lo Whan said, and Nangi did not know whether he meant the sight or something more hidden.

The Chinese closed his hand in his lap as they ascended the steep, wooded slope. If they were to drop off the line now, Nangi observed, there would be no chance for either of them, the scree below would batter anything that fell to oblivion.

"It has come to my attention," Lo Whan said, "through sources both far removed from me and devious, that some information is about to be moved." His eyes were bright. "'Vitally important' information was, I think, the particular phrase used. Further, it was passed on to me that this information concerns certain, ah, links to Canton and northward that could, perhaps, be compromised under particular circumstances."

Nangi nodded. "That, in essence, is correct."

"I see."

Nangi produced a copy of the contract that he and Liu had signed. He unfolded it, put it carefully on the empty seat to his right.

Lo Whan, observing what that seat now contained, did nothing but look back at Nangi, though the information that had made its circuitous way to him had included the stipulation that he bring Liu's copy of the document. His eyes were stony.

Nangi handed over the manila envelope. Carefully, as if its contents might be lethal, Lo Whan used one long nail to slit the seal. He slid the contents out one by one and looked at them. They consisted of sixteen 8×10 black and white prints of very high quality and resolution, a mini tape player in which resided an unedited copy of the tape Fortuitous Chiu had made of the proceedings at Succulent Pien's apartment, a twelve-page transcript of the tape recording.

Lo Whan slipped on a pair of gold-rimmed spectacles and for the next ten minutes or so ignored Nangi and his surroundings, engrossed by what he had been given.

By the time he had reviewed all of the material thoroughly, they had alighted at the "sky terminus." They went out, away from the crowds, along the rock promontory.

"Interesting," Lo Whan said, carrying the incriminating evidence under his arm like a business portfolio. "But hardly worth the price you are asking." The Chinese shoulders shrugged. "We can return Liu to the sanctity of his homeland at any time."

"I don't think it will be quite that easy," Nangi said, working hard to avoid the rocks. The path Lo Whan had deliberately chosen was strewn with them. "Liu is a fixture here. He's known by everyone. If you pull him now, in the face of the scandal that I assure you will follow, your country will suffer a great propaganda loss; you will lose all the advantage over England you have gained in the past two and a half years; worst of all, you will lose great face."

The wind blew lightly in their faces, smelling faintly of salt and phosphorus. Lights from the ships far out semaphored unknown messages to unknown recipients. They are like Lo Whan and me, Nangi thought, staring at the low-lying vessels. They may know where they are going but they can't actually see it.

Lo Whan was lost in thought. It seemed to him only just if, in the next several moments, Liu were to slip in the bathtub and break his neck. It would save us all face and I could dismiss this clever ape of a Japanese, sending him back across the sea to his puny island home where he belongs. But he knew none of that would happen or was even possible.

Everything Nangi said was true. It was galling. He could not do away with Liu, not with the information the Japanese had. One word to the Governor and he would be on the phone to Her

Majesty's Government, to one ministry or another. That would be intolerable to Lo Whan and his superiors.

Then an idea hit him. He stared out to sea as if nothing at all had happened. He turned it over, looking at it from every side as if it were a gemstone he was considering purchasing, which, in a way, it was. He did not rush, yet he was acutely aware of the passage of time. He could not make as much use of it as he would wish. To take too long would lose him face in this battle of wits.

But the longer he examined his idea, the more he liked it, and the more he felt that by employing it he would gain the upper hand over this Oriental barbarian.

"It is our considered opinion," he began cautiously, "that we want nothing untoward to happen to Mr. Liu. In fact, we want him precisely where he is, undisturbed." Now he reached into an interior jacket pocket and drew out the mate to Nangi's contract.

"This becomes null and void," he said, "the moment we agree on one point. All evidence amassed against Mr. Liu and, indeed, this Succulent Pien will be destroyed—copies, originals, negatives, everything, will be delivered to an address that I will provide. In addition, you will sign an agreement that from this day forward you will make no move against either of them nor employ, either directly or indirectly, anyone else to do so."

"But I do not want that contract voided," Nangi said. This was a terrible risk, but he judged the potential rewards more than worth it.

Lo Whan stood stock still. It was as if Nangi had slapped him across the face with the document. His surprise cost him face and he did not like that. "What is it you want, then?" he said testily.

"I want us to go back to the original agreement I proposed to Liu. That is, in exchange for a thirty percent interest in the *keiretsu*—a strictly *nonvoting* interest—you agree to provide capital over the next three years in semi-annual payments on January first and July first of each year."

"We already have a great deal of capital invested in you, Mr. Nangi," Lo Whan pointed out. "Thirty-five million dollars worth."

But Nangi was already shaking his head. "That was for the inconvenience your Lieutenant Chin caused the All-Asia Bank. As of now, you have no investment at all."

Lo Whan's eyes locked with Nangi's. He was burning inside with anger and loss of face. He had no intention of being defeated here on his own soil. He had only one last, desperate recourse. "I wonder," he said, "whether you have lost your interest in why we have taken such exquisite pains to acquire a sizable portion of your *keiretsu*."

A vague premonition sprang up inside Nangi but he forced it down. He is bluffing, he thought. Carefully, he said, "Mr. Liu has already delineated the Communist point of view. The Oriental Alliance."

"Yes. We are both familiar with Liu's, er, drawbacks." He cocked his head. "Surely you don't think we've told him everything."

Nangi was silent.

"There are currently in Peking two distinct factions. We have the Maoists on one side and the so-called Capitalist Roaders on the other. In the fifties, as you no doubt know, the Soviets rejected Stalinism. Mao, an avowed Stalinist, bitterly accused the Russians of revisionism. That ideological rift between the two countries has, more or less, stood until the present. However, those currently in power have been clandestinely seeking an accord with the Kremlin for some time now."

Lo Whan shifted his buttocks as if he were uncomfortable. "Others, perhaps not content with the current flow of the river, are seeking to dredge an alternative course. They, it is whispered, seek a propaganda weapon to use against the Soviets and, thus, against those in power in Peking."

Nangi now saw the precarious spot his adversary was in. Lo Whan need not spell out in so many words to which faction he belonged. His masters were not yet fully in power in the north.

His heart beat fast. Did the Communist know about *Tenchi*? "It seems to me," he said, "that there was little good that came out of Mao's reign."

"I will not debate ideology with you," Lo Whan said. "Your *keiretsu* may hold the key to the future of our country. The Oriental Alliance was not a lie. It was simply not the whole of it."

Nangi felt the triumph surging through his veins. I have won! he told himself. There are no more cards for him to play; he is truly defeated now. He may know *Tenchi* exists but he does not know its secret. And now he never will.

"There is nothing more to do," Nangi said, "but to amend the documents."

Lo Whan's back bowed. He felt one hundred years old. "Then you have doomed us and yourselves to a pact that must have diabolical consequences. I dare not contemplate what the outcome of a full alliance between my country and Russia might be."

He spoke, but it was as if Nangi had not heard him. Nangi's own personal triumph had made him drunk; the ancient enmity between these two people impossible to overcome.

It took them almost forty minutes to make all the required

465

changes in the two contracts, to initial the changes and to resign the documents. Lo Whan drew out a pad and commenced to draw up the final clause, which he had verbally outlined to Nangi. At that point Nangi excused himself and went picking his way over the black rocks, to make his call to Fortuitous Chiu. When he returned, both signed the two copies Lo Whan had made. Nangi was now enjoined from interfering with Liu or Succulent Pien.

Both men put their documents away. They stood on the rock promontory, in neat silk suits despite the hour, solemn despite the joyous yelps of people on the other side of the cliff.

Applause came ringing from the ocean theater, where killer whales were jumping through hoops and seals were spinning striped balls on their upraised noses.

With care, Nangi extracted the red envelope that Liu had given him. He presented it to Lo Whan.

"And now," came the electronically amplified voice of the master of ceremonies, ringing through the rocks' faces, "ladies and gentlemen, the thrilling finale!"

Tony Theerson, C. Gordon Minck's Boy Wonder, had one of those beehive minds so sought after in the highest levels of computer technology. Perhaps it was because, when you came right down to it, his mind was tuned more to the binary byways of machines than it was to the ephemeralia of human thought.

It was a rare day, indeed, when the Boy Wonder felt any more complex emotion than hunger, thirst, tiredness, or the mild discomfort of a full bladder. Elation came with the final dissolution of a difficult code—he had ranked them in his mind, giving them names he had made up—into orderly rows of words, sentences, paragraphs, which he then turned over to Tanya Vladimova and Minck himself.

In fact, orderliness to a degree a normal human being would find intolerable was Tony's way of life. The clutter of his office was evidence enough of that. His idea of orderliness resided in his computers' memory banks and in his own genius mind.

For Theerson was aptly nicknamed. No one else on this side of the Atlantic had any chance of deciphering the Soviet Alpha-three ciphers except the Boy Wonder. They were absolute ball-breakers which, not coincidentally, was Tony's designation for the highest difficulty codes he was given to crack.

And like other geniuses of his ilk, Theerson was thrown by factors either unknown to him or inexplicable. His whole life was a crusade to make the unknowable knowable. *Logic rules*! said a brass plaque in his office.

Thus when he finally cracked the most recent of the Alpha-threes, when the English words swam upward onto his terminal screen from the belly of his own private farm of beasts, he assumed that a glitch had sprung up. He cleared the screen and called up the program from scratch.

And got precisely the same message.

That meant no glitch, but he rechecked his functions back down the line until he reached each and every input. The result was still the same: no glitch.

For a long time he sat staring at the message. It was like reading Martian. It made no sense, it had no logic. Just like, he thought, the lyrics to a rock and roll song.

"It's bad," he said after the melody had faded off his lips. "It's very, very bad." He was abruptly aware of how shaken he felt.

With that, he punched for a hard copy. When it clattered out he folded it up and wiped the screen of words. It was time, he thought, to see Minck.

When Theerson found him, Minck was contemplating the end phase of his vendetta against Viktor Protorov. In fact he was enormously pleased with himself. Sending Tanya Vladimova in against his archenemy was a step he had longed to take years ago but could never bring himself to do. The entrance of Nicholas Linnear into his life had changed all that.

In the innermost sanctum of his mind, Minck tended to think of himself much like the god Wotan that Richard Wagner had depicted in the *Ring* cycle—one-eyed and full of pride, and thus flawed; a loving god, and a vengeful one.

It would never have occurred to him to go after Protorov in any direct fashion. It would have been unthinkable, for instance, for him to board a plane for Japan himself, a Webley pistol in hand to hold to his enemy's head and pull the trigger.

That was not at all because Minck was a coward; he was far from that. Battle did not faze him, hardship, both emotional and physical, had been a way of life for him for many years. Rather he saw this kind of personal revenge as being overshadowed by his duty to Red Section, to the people who worked for him and thus depended on his skills to guide them and keep them whole in a world that wished to blow them apart; duty to his country.

Much of this was indeed true; however, it was to Minck's benefit not to dwell too deeply on the other—baser—motivation. He suspected now that he was perhaps closer to feeling like a

god of Wotan's stature than he had realized. The Valh
syndrome afflicted many of his kind throughout the world,
it was Minck's firm conviction that he possessed a power f
as great as the spear Wotan had fashioned out of the World
Tree, the spear by which he controlled all creatures, even
giant Fafnir, the spear by which he need only touch some
to end their life. The agents of Red Section were Minck's sp
they were his power.

Tanya Vladimova was part of that, to be sure, but he lo
her too much to be able to commit her to entering the den c
lion of Protorov's cunning. Oddly, he loved her in just the v
Wotan loved his daughter, Brunnhilde; she was closer to him t
any other human being in the world. With her, he played out
plans, he spun his variegated web. He could not bear the thou
that he might send her to her death at the hands of his enemy.
had held back, waiting as patiently as any Japanese for the ri
moment. Which was now. Already she must be landing in Tok
his weapon against the fall of night.

Abruptly, he looked up, aware that someone was standing
the open doorway to his office. Few had clearance onto this le
of the building, fewer still were allowed to roam unescorted throt
the set.

"Yes, Tony," he said, switching off his train of thought as
would a faucet, "do you have something for me?"

A flicker in the Boy Wonder's manner alerted Minck and
beckoned with his hand. "Come in, come in." All his senses w
questing now.

Theerson came across the bare wood floor and sat in a car
backed chair in front of Minck's desk. "I just cracked the lat
Alpha-three." The paper in his hand wafted back and forth, lifti
and falling in his grasp.

"Are you going to show it to me or just use it as a fan?" Min
saw the Boy Wonder wince and his heart beat fast. What w
wrong? "You'd better let me see that," he said, holding out I
hand.

Almost reluctantly, Theerson passed it over. He sat staring
his hands in his lap. He felt useless and impotent.

Minck's gaze went from him down to the sheet of paper. T
is what he read:

NEWEST PENETRATION VIA LINNEAR, NICHOLAS.
AMATEUR STATUS. WARNING: HIGHLY LETHAL.
OBJECTIVE: TENCHI; YOUR DEATH. SANCTIONED
BY THIS OFFICE. ACCESSED FILE ON LINNEAR FOL-

LOWS. AM LINNEAR'S BACKUP. WILL ADVISE ON
ARRIVAL TOKYO.

VOLK.

Volk, Minck thought. A wolf in the fold. His mind had gone
numb with the thought that Tanya Vladimova, his Tanya, was a
Dig Dug. A Soviet plant. But how? Oh, Christ!

He slammed his fist down on the desk with such force that
Tony Theerson jumped as if struck with a needle. "Get out of
here," Minck growled. "Get out of my sight!"

The Boy Wonder jumped up and retreated across the room.
He had seen Minck in a fury twice before and had no desire to
get in the way of it now.

At the door, Minck stopped him. "Hold it!"

Reluctantly, Theerson turned to face his master. "There's something I don't understand. Tanya knew that you were working on
the Alpha-three codes; she knew you were the best at breaking
them. Why in Christ's name would she use them?"

The Boy Wonder shrugged. "For one thing, I don't think she
had a choice. The Alpha-threes are still by far the most secure
ciphers the Soviets have." He shuddered when he said the word
Soviets; he still could not believe the truth. "She knew that my
success was spotty. In fact, not too long ago we spoke about it.
Now that I think about it, she even asked me how I was coming
on the latest one." He nodded. "That would have been this one
here. I told her it was the worst yet. I didn't think I'd crack it.
Maybe twelve hours after that I got the first breakthrough; it came
like a bolt of lightning. After that it was just a matter of a lot of
donkey work, much of which the computers did."

Minck contemplated the Boy Wonder. He had not even bothered to say something as fatuous as "There must be some mistake!"
He knew Theerson too well; the man just did not make mistakes.
He might not be able to break every Alpha-three but when he did
he knew whereof he spoke.

"You did a fine job, Tony." His voice was as bleak as a winter's
day.

Theerson nodded sadly. "I'm sorry. Really I am."

Minck waved him mutely away. When he was again alone, he
rose and, taking the hideous message with him, went into the now
windowless room next door. Dhzerzinsky Square greeted him, as
ugly as all Russian architecture was to him. Above, the dark,
crepuscular sky. Across the square, Children's World, where gift
wrapped presents were presented. Back across the square, the

black Zil entered the rat's hole of Lubyanka. He had returned, running for his life through the *snyeg*, all sound muffled, all life stifled.

How much information had he unwittingly provided the Russians? How many steps ahead of him was Viktor Protorov? For the message was clear enough: *Volk* reported to him. Tanya and Protorov. How had he done it? *How?*

Minck ground his teeth together. He was having trouble breathing. How the Wolf must have laughed at his idea to send her in to back up Linnear; and how she must have panicked on learning that he had sent Linnear in against her master.

He could see her face clearly at the moment she had learned what he had done, how he had so cleverly improvised. How he had misread her concern! What perspectives the truth lent reality.

He paced the room, Moscow all around him cloaked in winter's dank and frosty grip. He did not want to see the changing of the seasons there; like his burning hatred, he wished only to see the city's immutability.

What to do now? he wondered. How in God's name could he salvage the operation? He had not heard from Linnear. Certainly he could send no other agent in after her; she would be instantly alerted; a call from him, an order home would have the same effect. She knew there was nothing on the boards—there could not be—as important as *Tenchi* and Protorov.

Like a parent at the moment of parting with his child, he felt utterly betrayed. Yet he could not bring himself to hate her. Nothing she could do to him could destroy his love.

There must be an answer, he thought furiously. I have pulled victory from the edge of defeat many times before. Why should this be any different. But he knew the answer to that. Never had he been faced with a disaster of this magnitude.

To have a Dig Dug within his own Red Sector was, for him, intolerable. It was to him other agencies came to ferret out just such dangers within their own hierarchies.

No answer came to him. Tanya, by her very position within Red Section, knew all of its personnel. Individuals from agencies allied with the Family would never get to her. And besides alerting her, there was another danger in going outside his own organization. He'd never live the infiltration down. No one must know of Tanya Vladimova's heinous betrayal.

He was becoming frantic, his mind racing from one possibility to another, discarding each one almost as soon as he had thought of it. Why hadn't Linnear used the access number?

His intercom buzzed. He ignored it but the sound would not

go away. He wanted no interruptions now and reached out for the disconnect button. He hit the on switch instead and the floor receptionist's voice rang in the room.

"Someone here to see you, sir."

"I want to see no one, is that clear?"

"Yes, sir. But the gentleman will not leave. He insists on—"

Oh, for Christ's sake! Minck thought. "Does this 'gentleman' have a name?"

"Yes, sir. He says you know him. His name is Detective Lieutenant Lewis Croaker."

His body was a mass of bruises where Protorov and Koten had beaten him. The first three fingers of his right hand were broken and badly swollen. The pain, however, was no problem; he knew how to control that.

He walked gingerly over to Protorov's desk, turned on the paper shredder, and fed the coded sheets into it. Now the information existed only in his head.

He crawled back to where Protorov lay and continued his deep breathing. He stared down at his bloated fingers and knew there was no help for it; he could not leave them in this condition.

At the Tenshin Shoden Katori he had learned *koppo*, the subspecialization of *ninjutsu* which dealt in the breaking of bones. In fact he had applied some of those techniques when he had gripped Protorov. Now he needed to reverse the process on himself.

Using only thumb and forefinger, he gripped one finger at a time and began to explore. Just as a safe's tumblers will somehow convey to the trained ear when they are about to fall into place, so Nicholas reached a moment in each exploration when his body told him the spot had been found. More investigation revealed to him the precise angle he would need.

A Westerner would grit his teeth, tense his muscles against what his mind told him was coming, thus increasing the pain. Nicholas relaxed his body and mind, decreasing the pain. He floated in *getsumei no michi* as his body healed itself.

When his eyes returned from middle distance he saw that his fingers were set. Ripping off a length of cloth from Protorov's dress blouse, he wound the coarse, heavy material around and around the line of breaks until it was thick enough to act as a temporary splint. He used his teeth to tie it off, mindful of not cutting off local circulation.

Then he took stock. It was not good. He was in a strictly shutended situation. He had been lucky up until now that no one had entered to see what Protorov was up to. That could not last much longer, he knew. He was in the center of a veritable fortress, in a room with one doorway, thick as a bank's vault. He glanced upward. This room, by its very isolated nature, had an oversized ventilation system. It would have been entirely possible for him to get up to one of the vent ports high up near the room's ceiling and exit that way had it not been for his broken fingers and the residue of the drug.

He needed help but he had no allies for many miles around. Therefore he would have to create one.

Using *ichi*, he gave as accurate an approximation of Viktor Protorov's voice as he could summon up, calling out for Russilov. When the lieutenant appeared through the doorway, he heaved Protorov's limp form at him face first.

Russilov's reaction was predictable. The first autonomic reaction of throwing his hands up to protect the body was quickly followed by a stunned cry as he recognized the identity of the corpse.

The combination was enough to paralyze him for the amount of time Nicholas needed to rush him and make him prisoner. He touched Russilov's chest and the Russian felt his heart stutter. He sagged a bit, feeling abruptly faint and unable to breathe. He might just as well have ingested a toxic substance. All color dropped out of his face, and cold sweat appeared on his upper lip and at his hairline.

Still his head whipped around to get another look. "Impossible!" he cried. "You're dead!"

"Then we have just proved that there is life beyond the grave!" Nicholas hissed in his ear.

There was blood on Russilov and, fastidiously, stupidly, he tried to brush it off.

Nicholas took his sidearm, searched him thoroughly for other weapons. He found a knife on the inside of the Russian's left calf. "Now you're going to get me out of here."

"Impossible as well," Russilov said and, when Nicholas tightened his grip, said hurriedly, "No, it is the truth! There is an electronic scanner. Prisoners are stamped with an invisible mark that is renewed every week. If we were to walk or drive out through any gate you would be fried—I along with you if we were in the same vehicle."

"There must be some way to get it off prematurely," Nicholas said.

"There is," Russilov nodded. "Protorov knew how. Only Protorov. You'll never get out of here, with me or without me."

Nicholas did not despair. He had been taught to infiltrate and he knew that there was a way out of every manmade structure, just as there was a way in.

"Quickly," he said, "tell me about this place."

Russilov complied. The building that Protorov had chosen as his base had originally been a barn complex which he had converted to his own uses. There were two exits and, as Russilov had said, they were useless to Nicholas. Stone walls had been erected inside the wooden ones, one extra story had been built, which was where they currently were.

Russilov laughed low in his throat. "There's nowhere for you to go but up, to the parapets. From there you may leap into the dense woods, my friend. Perhaps you will not die; perhaps you will be lucky and the fall will only break your legs!"

Nicholas' mind was racing. It was conceivable that Russilov had described his way out.

"Out now!" he commanded. "And whoever we run across must not become suspicious, is that clear? If you raise your voice, you die; if you make an unaccounted-for move, you die. Clear?"

The lieutenant nodded.

Outside in the hallway, they saw no one. The two lieutenants had taken the doctor downstairs to a detention cell. Russilov led him toward the stairs up to the roof. On the way, they passed a number of bamboo and aluminum poles perhaps fifteen meters in length.

Nicholas stopped him. "What are these for?"

"Bamboo groves all around here," Russilov said sullenly. "Farmers used to store and age these here. The aluminum ones were for anchoring fledgling stands against the winter winds."

"Take two," Nicholas ordered. And when Russilov did so, said, "No, the bamboo poles."

On the roof Nicholas commanded the Russian to strip, ordering him to spread out each item on the stones. In the meantime, employing Russilov's knife, he cut the bamboo poles in half. Then he set about cutting off the arms of the lieutenant's blouse and jacket. He cut his trousers in two, took the laces from the boots.

"What are you doing?" Russilov asked, huddled naked in a corner.

Nicholas said nothing. He sliced the Russian's heavy leather belt into four long strips. Using these and the boot laces, he set to work constructing his scaffolding. Then he attached the pieces of cloth. He worked with the loving concentration of a father constructing his child's first kite.

What in fact he had made was a *hito washi*, what some ninja called "the human eagle." It was a makeshift glider.

When he was finished he walked back to where Russilov knelt. Stripped of his uniform, his rank, he seemed to have shrunk in size. Like many military men, he very nearly had ceased to exist without the armor of his command.

"Good-bye, Russilov," Nicholas said, bending down and touching the *juka*, one of the *kyukon*, the nine organ meridians. This one was just beneath the ears. Russilov immediately collapsed, unconscious.

Then Nicholas mounted the *hito washi*. There was a fair wind blowing from the southwest, gusty and unpredictable. He shrugged mentally. *Karma*. He was enormously tired and he wanted to sleep badly. Soon, he thought. Be careful now.

He mounted the stone parapet. There was no moon and his chronometer had been taken from him. It was deep into the night, the early hours of morning. It was not yet that peculiar time of predawn when a special tinge of nameless color comes into the world, but he did not know how long dawn would be in arriving.

Two good gusts came while he was still working out the vectors. Then, as he set himself, the wind died to a tickle on his face. Come on, he thought. Come on!

His hair began to ruffle, he felt the temperature drop on his bruised and purpled skin. Strengthening. Such an ephemeral thing, you could not even see it. He closed his eyes and felt it.

And when his body told him it was time, he used the powerful muscles in his legs to launch himself into the dark, dark void. Spinning for a moment, plummeting. Then he corrected and caught a substantial updraft.

Soared into the night like a bat.

Akiko picked Koten up at the *rotenburo* and followed him out of there. He had arrived emptyhanded and he left with a long, polished wood case. To Akiko, whose eyes were trained for such things, it appeared to be a weapon's case. Judging by its length it could contain nothing but a *dai-katana*, the longest of all the *samurai* swords.

Deep in the shadows, she stiffened. Koten had passed through a squat ellipse of lantern light and she had gotten a good look at the case. It was the same one she had seen open in the garden between Nicholas and her husband. Koten had Nicholas' sword!

Car followed car. But because there was little traffic this late at night Akiko was forced to douse her headlights, using peripheral illumination, as well as the twin ruby taillights of Koten's car, to aid her. Once or twice, when the road wound up a hillside, she thought she had lost him. But each time as she crested, the lights reappeared.

This was farm country—very rural—and she had to be careful not to be spotted. But the sky's darkness that hindered her also aided her for it made Koten's vision behind him that much more difficult.

Not more than thirty minutes after they left the *rotenburo*, Koten's car abruptly slowed, turning left onto a hardpacked dirt lane that immediately disappeared in underbrush.

Akiko quickly pulled onto the side of the road and got out, following on foot; she could not chance taking her own car in there—the noise alone could alert her quarry.

Because of the narrow, twisting nature of the path she had no difficulty in keeping Koten in sight. In a small clearing bordered by great stands of whispering bamboo, he drew up. Men were all about and she was close enough to hear what they were saying. Nicholas had escaped!

But what of Sato? She had not been at the *rotenburo* for long enough to find out anything of substance other than that a man—apparently a patron—had been killed in a mysterious auto explosion. Who?

She did not know. Koten had come, distracting her; but even so she would not have been able to ask questions without arousing suspicion. Japanese society was extremely clannish. There was a fierce community spirit. She did not belong here; a stranger asking questions about what might easily be a murder—what was in any case an unexplained death—would be noted and the local police notified. Akiko could not afford such scrutiny.

But now she had to wonder. They had spoken only of Nicholas. Not one word was spoken of Sato; his name simply never came up.

To Akiko this led to one inescapable conclusion: Sato was dead. Perhaps it had been he who had died in the car explosion; or again perhaps he had died here at this forested place. It did not matter; part of her revenge had been taken care of for her. That did not make her particularly happy—she would have preferred to exact her own vengeance—but she resigned herself to the reality of the situation.

Nicholas was now her target. She turned away from the edge of the clearing, beginning to quarter the area immediately surrounding the clearing and its central building which looked so much like a barn but which she was certain was not.

At length, to the southwest, she found the remnants of the *hito*

475

washi. She hunkered down, fingering it, admiring the workmanship. She laughed low in her throat. Then she set off after him.

Of course Alix had tried to stop him. She had called him everything from a madman to a moron; she had even cried and, at the end, begged him not to go.

By all this Croaker surmised that she was genuinely afraid for him. But he was not at all sure. After all, she was a consummate actress, making love to the camera every day when she worked. She could turn on or off any emotion as easily as she applied mascara each morning and wiped it away at night.

But then it occurred to him that she had no earthly reason to act in this case. What would she get out of deterring him from flying off to Washington besides seeing him safe? She knew full well who it was who had tried to kill him or at least who had ordered it. The same person who had now contracted for both their deaths, breaking his oath to her.

C. Gordon Minck, the man before whom Croaker now stood.

"Where the hell are we," he said looking around at the leafy patio, "the goddamned African veldt?" He did not like the edge to his voice. But he was frightened, not only of this man and the power he wielded to cut off pursuit, to twist the law to his own design, but also of what he himself was thinking of doing to Minck.

Minck contrived to laugh and Croaker glared at him, his tightly controlled emotions flaring. "I ought to kill you right here with my bare hands," he said low in his throat.

Minck was still trying to recover from seeing a man standing next to him who up until just a moment ago he believed dead and buried at sea. He put one hand tentatively up to his temple, as if with that gesture he could press away the pain that now throbbed there like a traitor.

"You've got to get a grip on yourself, Lieutenant." It was the best he could do for the moment; he needed some time to marshal both his emotions and his thoughts. This day was rapidly turning into one of the worst in his life and he was determined to give his full attention to it lest matters deteriorate even further. He gestured. "Please sit down."

"Which one of these chairs is mined?" Croaker said with a sneer.

"Just what's that supposed to mean?" Minck said despite himself. He had promised himself that he would not vie with Lieutenant Croaker on his own base ground. But the pain in his head was unsettling him.

"You've tried to kill me three times; you've tried to kill Alix

476

Logan twice. What else would you expect me to say walking in here?"

Minck sat heavily down. He groaned inwardly as the pain increased. His heart rate was accelerating. "What are you talking about?" His voice was a trifle shaky; his face pasty beneath his rich tan. It was only now that the true gravity of the situation was beginning to dawn on him. Croaker's expressed threat echoed in his mind like a taunt. How had he managed to miss this tinkering?

Croaker, observing all this, was curious. The edge of his anger had dulled. "Alix and I were pursued out of Key West. Once in Raleigh, North Carolina, and once in New York City, we were attacked. That's attempted murder, Minck."

Minck shook his head. "I don't understand this," he said to no one in particular. "I never sanctioned Alix's death." He looked up, as if abruptly aware of Croaker's presence. "I would never do that. I told her I wouldn't. You must believe me."

Words, as Croaker knew well, were cheap. But there was something in Minck's eyes, a kind of pleading, that caught him. He saw that somehow Minck, who through Alix's eyes he had come to see as a master spider spinning his unbreakable web from the absolute sanctity of the nation's capital, was enmeshed in a gray area just as he himself was. Suddenly they were both lost, both confused as to which direction was up, who was good, who bad. In that moment, their adversary position had somehow been dissipated. For the first time since he had entered Angela Didion's plush apartment and found her naked body as cold as ice, Croaker began to see that there was more here than one model's murder. Much more. "Then who did?" he said gruffly.

And Minck was forced to another inescapable conclusion. To whom had he given over custody of Alix? Who had he entrusted to keep her safe from all harm? Tanya Vladimova, that's who. The same Tanya who had been gone from the building—God only knew where—for the last forty hours or so.

He grabbed up a phone, asked for a trace on Tanya's movements during the last three and a half days. He was immediately patched through to the ARRTS computer. He repeated his question and waited impatiently for the answers. When they came, he stared openly at Croaker.

"Tanya," he said slowly.

"Who the hell's Tanya?" Croaker asked.

"She's the woman who sanctioned both your deaths," he improvised, telling a half truth. Something had begun to spin inside Minck's mind. One dark and tiny satellite that needed some space and time to grow. The germ of an idea. The beginning of a massive salvage job. A kind of miracle, even, if such things actually could be said to exist. Minck did not believe in God so therefore it followed that he could not believe in miracles. Until this moment, perhaps.

In a more normal tone of voice, he said, "About Alix. Is she all right?"

"She's confused, angry, frustrated, and maybe her life's been ruined by all this crap but, yeah, she's essentially okay."

Minck found some genuine solace in that. If he had suspected for any amount of time that he was merely indulging himself by keeping Alix Logan alive, he now dismissed such thoughts entirely. The relief that swept through him went deep indeed.

He took a breath, but before he could continue, Croaker said, "Don't think for a minute I'll tell you where she is, though. If you make any move against me now, she'll go straight to the State's Attorney General with everything she knows. I know you can't afford that. You've gone to great lengths to prove it."

Minck paused for a moment as if weighing Croaker's words. "All right," he said at last. "I'll propose a truce...a kind of bargain, if you wish."

"What kind of bargain?" Despite observing Minck's genuine feelings for Alix, Croaker was a long way from trusting this man.

"What I propose is this. I will not harm you or seek to find Alix's whereabouts, unless she wishes it, of course. In return, you will sit down and listen to what I have to tell you and consider it carefully."

"Then what?"

Oh, good, Minck thought. This man *is* clever in addition to being resourceful. He has killed two of my agents and evaded termination from another—my most deadly, my most traitorous Tanya. Perhaps he can do what none other I can call on could. Perhaps, he thought, as he began to talk of Tanya Vladimova and her ultimate betrayal, of her manipulation of the "Spearfish" ops, which was Alix Logan's detention/protection, this man can destroy that which Protorov and I, jointly, created.

Inside, C. Gordon Minck began to glow. Like a man who has won back his life at the brink of death, he was suffused with an eerie kind of elation that made his fingertips tremble.

It was not difficult to sell Croaker on what he must do. Minck had two powerful motivations which he offered the man sitting across from him and which Minck was quite certain he could not refuse. If the situation were reversed, Minck was aware, he would have been hooked just as much as he perceived Croaker was becoming.

478

Revenge and patriotism. These were the two reasons that Minck suspected Croaker would accept this bargain. Tanya had personally tried to kill him and his charge; that was something Croaker could not tolerate. He wanted her now, and Minck could not blame him at all. They both wanted her, he explained. It was merely that Croaker was in a position to get her while Minck was not.

Then there was the Russian angle. No one liked that, least of all Minck himself. Croaker was right behind him there.

"You'll have full diplomatic immunity," Minck concluded, "a new identity as far as Customs and Immigration are concerned. You'll have full support over there if you need it." He waited a beat. "And you'll be linking up with an old friend of yours, Nicholas Linnear." He had saved what he suspected would be the best for last. The clincher.

And Croaker bit.

But a half hour after the detective lieutenant had been provided with a new passport, birth certificate, business papers, et al; money in the form of American dollars, Japanese yen, and American Express traveler's checks, and delivered to Dulles International to make his flight to Tokyo, Minck abruptly broke down and, for the first time since his long incarceration in Lubyanka, wept bitter tears. He thought of what had been done to him and what, in retaliation, he had been forced to do.

Meanwhile, the object of Minck's love and hate was at the moment debarking at Narita Airport outside smogbound Tokyo. She had not had a pleasant flight. Just after takeoff from Kennedy she had taken two sleeping pills and had fallen into a leaden slumber which had been dominated by visions from her childhood. Protorov stalked her dreams like a sentry, on horseback and on foot, weaponed and booted; wherever she went he was there before her.

Tanya was back in grade school in Rechitsa, the closest town to the rural hamlet where her family lived. Already there was friction at home. Her older brother, Mikhail, did not approve of their father being a policeman. As such her father was in touch with the KGB, whose black-raincoated agents appeared at the house from time to time to remind him to report all unpatriotic activity within his purview.

Within six months Mikhail would leave him, and within a year, at eighteen, would become one of the more militant—and successful—dissidents working inside Russia.

But by that time the headmaster of the school in Rechitsa had journeyed by an old and dilapidated car out to Tanya's house to speak to her parents. She had been offered a scholarship to a fine academy with facilities that, regretfully, the headmaster's school lacked. She was an extremely bright girl, he said, and deserving of this chance. But certain sacrifices had to be made. This new academy was in the Urals, a good 750 kilometers away.

Tanya's mother had cried at the prospect. After all, her son had already gone. But Tanya's father was firm. He was only a country constable, he said, and he wanted at least one of his children to have the benefits he had never had.

So it was settled, much to the relief of the headmaster since a great deal of pressure had been put on him by Protorov himself to bring Tanya to his academy. Quite naturally, her parents and Tanya herself had no idea of the skew of the new school's curriculum.

After she arrived there and discovered where she was and what she would be made into, she dutifully wrote home every week. Never did she hint to her parents or to anyone else, for that matter, as to the academy's true nature, though in truth, perhaps, she longed to tell her father, knowing how proud he would be and how this knowledge might help assuage the terrible ache he felt inside from Mikhail's betrayal.

Protorov. She tried him from the airport while waiting for her one bag to come through, then again when she reached the pulsing overpopulated heart of Tokyo. She used the four-digit access code and received the same answer both times: dead air.

That in itself was not alarming, but Pyotr Alexandrovitch Russilov's presence at her hotel was. She registered, had her bag sent up to her room, then allowed the lieutenant to guide her back outside where they strolled amid jostling throngs of gray-suited men carrying black rolled umbrellas just as if they were Londoners. Many wore white masks over nose and mouth, an increasingly common sight in this city.

Tanya judged that Russilov did not look at all good. His color was pale and he had picked up a nervous habit sometime recently of turning his head to see what was happening behind her. She liked none of this.

But she liked even less what he had come south to tell her.

Her skin was like crepe, the most delicate of rice paper crumpled beneath a powerful fist, translucent still even after seventy-nine years.

"I will be eighty tomorrow," she told him. There was no pride in her voice, merely wonder that life could last so long.

Even now she was one of the most beautiful creatures he had

480

ever seen. As a child he had often compared her beauty to his mother's. He had always found her perfect symmetry losing out to Cheong's more exotic beauty. It was natural, perhaps, for him to be loyal to his mother. But there had been something more: he had hated her for being Saigō's mother, and was blinded.

"Is there anything else I can get you?" Itami asked.

His head was lowered. "No, *Haha-san*." Mother. Much had passed between them for him to be able to call her that, from the time he had come stumbling to the portals of her house.

She lived where she always had ever since he had known her, on the outskirts of Tokyo, to the northwest, not far from the spot where Sato and Akiko had been married. Nicholas had made an arduous journey south from Hokkaido, breaking into a clothing store at night and, armed with fresh clothes and some money, trekking down to Hakodate. He could have stolen a car but did not want to leave such a clear trail to those who might follow or even for the police who would inevitably investigate the break-in at the clothing store. They would pursue their investigation with the assiduousness with which the Japanese approached every task. The less he gave them, the more secure he felt.

He used buses occasionally and, when he was able, hitched rides. He avoided both main highways and railways, however, knowing trails were more easily left there.

At last, at the southern coastal town he took the ferry across Tsugarukaikyō to Aomori on Honshū's rocky nothern tip.

Lacking papers, he could not rent a car, and in any event preferred to utilize buses again, heading roughly south in a zigzag, nonlinear route.

He had been terrified at the thought of seeing his aunt again. It was he who had murdered her only child; it had been Nicholas' father who had garrotted her husband, for which Saigō had in turn poisoned the Colonel and, years later, had pursued Nicholas all the way to New York.

He did not know how she would greet him; he could not imagine what he could possibly say to her. What were words—*any* words— in the face of the finality of death. Nicholas thought that the words "I'm sorry" were perhaps the most inadequate in the English language. But there was nothing much better in Japanese or in any of the world's tongues for that matter.

The house was built by an architect who had been elderly when Itami and her husband, Satsugai, had commissioned him. He revered the old styles of the seventeenth century, which, he had said, were still the best. Time was their proof, had been their victory.

He had designed this house after one in Kyoto called Katsura Rikyu, an imperial villa from four hundred years ago which was still the finest example of the blending of the manmade with the natural to be found in all of Japan.

"What I try to do," the old man had said, "is to impose my spirit upon nature so that it appears to remain natural."

That the result of his handiwork was exquisite in the Japanese sense of the word was without question. Perhaps too many of these details had been too subtle for Nicholas' mind when he was younger for he had not loved the house as a whole but only one room: the one in which the *chano-yu* was performed.

And it was to this room that he was conducted after he had been met at the door by servants, Itami informed of his arrival, bathed, and his hurts attended to by a bent old man who spoke to himself in a constant singsong but who nevertheless knew what he was doing.

Feeling better than he had in many days, Nicholas knelt alone in the room, turned toward the garden outside. The opening was all the length of the room and perhaps six feet high. However, the top half was covered by a rice-paper latticework screen, so that only the bottom part of the garden could be viewed while being immersed in the tea ceremony. It was a peculiarly Zen concept: to have as part of your surroundings the wonders of nature, yet only so much. Beyond that invisible boundary, it was felt, one would have been overwhelmed by the bittersweet delicacy of the cherry blossoms or the flamboyant fan of autumnal foliage and thus the concentration one needed for *chano-yu*—the harmony of this place—would have been broken.

Sunlight, splintered by the trees, splattered against the lattice, turning it the color of newly churned butter, warming the room in tone and temperature. A lone bird strode through the pebbles of the garden, pecking here and there.

A breeze sprang up and rustled the tops of the cryptomeria, making soft shadows move behind the screen, on the polished wood floor. Nicholas shuddered inwardly, remembering the trembling flight on the *hito washi*, the ruffling of his tattered clothes like pinfeathers, the rush of the night against his face, the fear that the inconstant wind might die in midgust, sending him diving hard against stands of bamboo.

Exhilaration and terror mingled within him like liquor, tingling his blood.

He was exhausted again. Physically the drugs had been dissipated, eliminated from his system. Yet their accumulated effect on muscles, tissue, and brain still lingered. Exercise was the only remedy for that.

She came into his sight with a stiff rustle of silk. He rose and bowed, his heart in his throat. He was overcome by the awesome majesty of her beauty. It was not as if time had not touched her, merely that she had somehow made it her friend rather than her enemy. Time followed her about like a tamed animal, present but quite irrelevant.

"Itami-san." His voice was a reedy whisper. "*Oba.*"

"Sit, please, Nicholas-san."

He did so, not wishing to analyze what was in her eyes; what was in her mind.

After tea and rice cakes had been served, after they were alone again, she said, "It is so good that you have returned. My heart is gladdened to see you again, *watashi no musuko.*" My son.

Something broke within him and he bent forward until his forehead touched the glossy wood with the ache inside him. He wept, no longer able to hold all his emotions within him, his Japanese side ashamed even as he did so; but his Western side needed this release and could no longer be denied by any discipline on earth.

"*Watashi no musuko.*" Her voice held such tenderness that she might, indeed, have been his mother. "I knew you would come back. I prayed you would have the courage."

"I was afraid, *Oba.*" His voice, too, was tear streaked. "I was afraid because of what I had done. I did not want to face all the pain I have caused you."

"You never caused me any pain at all, Nicholas," she said softly. "You were always more a son to me than my own blood child ever was. His was a weak spirit, and he belonged body and soul to his father. Satsugai ruled him as the sun does the earth. It was Satsugai who determined Saigō's life path; it was his paranoia which Saigō absorbed."

Nicholas became aware that at no time had she referred to Saigō as "my son." That was quite odd in a mother. His head came up and their eyes met. He found no anger there nor even any sadness. Rather there was a mix of resignation and love . . . love for him.

"He was totally evil," Itami said. "I never before believed such a thing possible in a human being. Complexity, after all, vitiates extremes, or at least one believes that it should." She shook her head. "Not in Saigō's case. There was an uncanny purity to him that might have been admirable if it had been channeled in a proper direction.

"That it was not was a burden I was obliged to live with. I should be shamed to say that I wished him dead, but I am not. How could I be? Everything he came in contact with withered and died. He was a spirit-destroyer."

"Even so," Nicholas said. "I am not proud that I destroyed him."

"Of course not," she said. "You acted with honor. You are your mother's son."

All at once he realized that she was smiling at him. Without thought he did the same, his heart lightening just as the clouds roll back after the thunder of a storm.

For a long time they did nothing but that, basking in the presence of each other's spirit, becoming reacquainted, finding a new, and unexpected, level to their relationship that the heavy baggage of the past had denied to them before.

"I'm glad you came when you did," she said the next day. "We've had one or two earth tremors, nothing major, but uncomfortable enough."

Nicholas recalled the first satellite readout Protorov had shown him that indicated a crescendo of earthquake activity. He said nothing about it, however.

"I did not choose the time, *Oba*; it was chosen for me."

She nodded, smiling slightly. "That is why we must all learn to Cross at a Ford, eh, Nicholas?"

He was slightly surprised. "I did not know that you had read Musashi."

"Read *and* studied him." Now she was laughing outright. "There are many things you do not know about me, though surely in all the world there is no other with whom I have shared so many secrets.

"It was I who guided certain businessmen to Saigō; people whom this Raphael Tomkin had offended; people who wanted him dead."

Nicholas turned to look at her. "I don't understand."

"Do you think for a minute, *watashi no musuko*, that I lost track of you when you left your home? My love is as long as my protection. Whose daughter had you fallen in love with? How long would it take Saigō to find out the same piece of information? How long before the diamondlike precision of merging the two assignments—one professional, the other personal—would dawn on him? Surely it would appeal to his delicate sense of logic; he could not resist it."

Nicholas' mind was reeling. "You . . . It was *you* who sent him after me?" He put his hand to his head; he could scarcely believe what he was hearing.

"My dear," she said softly, "he was like a cape buffalo or one of our giant wild boars who had been wounded. He was dangerous, and becoming more so each day that dawned. I could not in good conscience allow that to continue."

She stopped them in their walk and for the first time touched him, a light but definite gesture, full—as was the case with all Japanese gestures no matter how small—of exquisite meaning.

"Did you think I would send him to harm you? I sent him to his death. Perhaps I murdered him, if one chooses to look at it in a certain light."

"But other people died in the process, *Oba*. You must have thought of that."

She said nothing, moving across the grass dappled in the shadow of a sculpted arbor of boxwood trees. "What would you have me say, *watashi no musuko*? Life is imperfect because we are humans and not gods. Gods by their very definition do not live but rather exist."

They paused and she put her hand against the gnarled back of a tree trunk. "I am sorry for death . . . any death. But often some good tissue must be excised in order to destroy a malignancy."

"It is not fair and it is certainly not to my liking. But it is a time that we must learn to Cross at a Ford. It is not what we choose but rather, as you have said, it chooses us."

That was not precisely what he had said, but he suspected Itami knew that. What she had said was far more apt, in any case. He knew that what had happened between Saigō and himself was really not either of their doing. Rather it had been determined a generation before by the abiding enmity between their fathers. Filial piety bound them, causing them to end what had been begun so long ago.

He could not help but think of those who had perished because of an honor, a code that was not theirs: Eileen Okura, Terry Tanaka, Doc Deerforth, how many cops and others whose names he did not know? and, yes, even Lew Croaker. Nicholas understood the wisdom of his aunt's words, even agreed with them. Yet something inside him recoiled, calling out as if from a distance, *It's too much; even the expunging of one life is too great a price to pay for the extirpation of* giri.

After a time, Itami said, "I have been truthful with you, Nicholas. Now you must return the kindness. Tell me why you have come here. It was not just to see me again after all this time."

"Part of it was that, yes." But she was right again. All the way on the trip south his mind had been rolling the question around. As he had done so it began to increase in size until even in sleep he could not be rid of it.

Akiko.

She was not Yukio, yet she had Yukio's face. Why? Surely she could not have been born with features so precisely akin to his lost love's. Nature simply did not repeat its handiwork in such a manner save perhaps between twins.

And if, as he believed now, her face was manmade, then he was led like a dog on a leash back to the one person who could wish him destroyed; one person who could conceive of such emotional torture.

Itami had been quite correct: he was totally evil. Saigō. So he had instinctively come here, to his cousin's house, in search of answers to the unanswerable.

"But there is another reason, *Oba*; a more urgent one. I recently came across a woman with Yukio's face. She wasn't Yukio and she was. Her name is Akiko."

Itami turned away, her face to the dying sun. "I knew a woman with such a name, once," she said. "I loved her once; she revered me once. As was proper between mother and daughter-in-law."

Nicholas felt his heart constrict. What Itami was suggesting felt monstrous to him, unclean if not unholy. "She was married to Saigō?" he managed to get out.

Itami nodded.

"Was she a student?"

Itami knew very well what kind of student he meant. To them there was only one kind. "Yes." Her voice was a whisper. "They met in Kumamoto. She was there for two years, studying before she left."

"Where did she go?"

"I do not want to talk of it."

"Itami-san—"

"It is a shameful thing." Her voice was cold; old and sad for the first time. "Do not make me utter it."

He moved around in front of her. "I must know. I must! She is your son's—"

"Do not call him that!"

"She is Saigō's last weapon against me, can't you see that? If you do not help me, I am afraid she may succeed where he did not."

Her eyes were clear. "Is this truly so?"

He nodded. *"Hai, Oba."*

"In the alps somewhere to the north lives a *sensei*. His name is Kyōki."

"That is no name," Nicholas said, stunned. "That is a state of being: madness."

"Nevertheless, that is where Akiko went; that is where she learned to mask her *wa*; where she learned *jahō*."

Itami made a face and turned away. "There, I've said it all now, though it makes me ill."

He waited a long time before he spoke again. There were many reasons for this. He wanted, first of all, to allow her to recover her composure. Too, he wanted to drink in this most serene surrounding that gentled his spirit like a mother's caress. Lastly, he did not want this time between them to end.

But at last he was moved to speech. "I must go, *Haha*."

"Yes."

"Will you kiss me good-bye as my father taught Cheong to do?"

Itami turned. Her eyes were brimming and so huge they seemed to encompass the world. Gently her hands held him and, lifting herself lightly on tiptoe, she pressed her lips to his cheek just as she had done it thousands of times before.

"Happy birthday, *Haha*," he whispered.

"Live long, Nicholas," Itami breathed. But she was already alone in the bower, the birds trilling sweetly overhead with the first onrush of twilight.

To Justine, Tokyo was as bewildering as New York City would be to a teenager from Nebraska. It was not what she had expected it to be nor what she had wanted it to be.

It throbbed all around her like a neon hive, its atmosphere as chokingly heavy as that of a coal mine. She entered into it with increasing trepidation and by the time she had been conveyed to the portals of the Okura was prepared to turn right around and go home. The only thing that prevented her was Nicholas or, more accurately, the thought of him.

Craig Allonge was staying at the Okura. She knew him slightly and in desperation she scribbled a note for him and asked the concierge to see that he got it the moment he returned to the hotel.

Then she went up to her room and collapsed on the bed. Her skin felt as if it had been coated with oil and her hair was greasy from the long flight. Groaning, she got up and drew a bath, using water as hot as she could tolerate. She felt she would need that to peel all the layers of grime off her.

She had soaped up and was soaking, her knotted muscles slowly

487

unwinding, when the phone rang. There was an extension within reach and she used it. It was Allonge. He had been set up with a temporary office at Sato Petrochemicals and had returned to the hotel to change for lunch. He was a shirtsleeves man and no one had told him how formal the Japanese could be.

When Justine asked about Nicholas, Allonge did not know what to tell her. He heard the agitation in her voice and did not want to alarm her unduly by telling her he had no idea where his boss might be. Instead he said he would find out and would call her right back. He disconnected and called Sato's office. No, there was no word as yet from Mr. Linnear. Did Allonge-san wish to speak with Nangi-san?

Tanzan Nangi's return from Hong Kong was news to Allonge and he said, "Yes, put me through, please." When the connection was made he told Nangi about Justine.

"Bring her back with you," Nangi said. "I'll talk to the young lady."

Nangi put down the receiver and swung away from his desk. Having just an hour ago deplaned at Narita, his thoughts were still partially back in Hong Kong. He thought of Fortuitous Chiu and his Dragon father. But even more his thoughts were concentrated on the Green Pang Triad. Sometime within the month they would raid the Sun Wa Trading Company on Tai Ping Shan Street. There would be violence, people killed. One of those people would be Mr. Liu; perhaps another would be a young woman by the name of Succulent Pien.

Whatever the outcome, it would have nothing to do with Nangi; it was, rather, Triad warfare; a territorial dispute. Or at least that would be how all the newspapers would write it up; how the populace would see it. That was the accepted way of life in the Crown Colony. Lo Whan would have to accept it as well. *Karma.* Perhaps he should have consulted a *feng shui* man before entering into the agreement with Nangi.

In fact, the raid had been agreed upon by Nangi and Fortuitous Chiu before the meeting with Lo Whan at Ocean Park took place. That had been the reason for all the *h'eung yau* spread around, the patriotic angle that Nangi had asked Fortuitous Chiu to bring up to Third Cousin Tok. Nangi had not abrogated his agreement with Lo Whan; and the disinformation connection with Redman would cease to exist within three weeks time.

But his satisfaction was to be shortlived because in a moment a discreet knock was heard at his door and Nangi swiveled around. He saw Kei Hagura, one of Seiichi's senior vice presidents.

"Enter, Hagura-san." The man looked decidedly unwell, Nangi

thought. Perhaps he needs some time off with his wife and children. There is nothing like being with one's family to restore the spirit.

"Pardon me for intruding, Nangi-san." Hagura was bowing profusely. His face was white and pinched and over his shoulder Nangi became aware of a stir within the hive of offices on the fifty-second floor.

"Come, come, Hagura-san." Nangi's voice was slightly irritated. "What can I do for you?"

Hagura's head was down; his eyes would not meet Nangi's own. "A report has just come over the wire from our Hokkaido office. There has been some kind of ... well ... an accident, perhaps. No one is quite certain as yet."

Nangi sat forward, his pulse accelerated.

"What sort of accident, Hagura-san? How bad was it? Who was involved?"

"I am afraid that it concerns Sato-san." Hagura's voice was faltering just as if he had contracted laryngitis. "There has been some form of automotive accident."

"And Sato-san?" There was a catch to Nangi's voice. "How is he?"

"There was no chance for anyone," Hagura said. He did not want to say the word, as if his reluctance would make all of this mere speculation rather than fact.

"Hagura-san," Nangi commanded.

The senior vice president closed his eyes in acquiescence to the inevitable. "Sato-san is dead, sir."

Nangi was careful to let nothing show. Face was all important now, he knew. This *kobun* was like a *samurai* in the employ of the Shōgun. It was absolutely committed to its course. It could only march forward; never retreat. Even to falter was forbidden. And *Tenchi* could not wait.

"Thank you, Hagura-san. I appreciate how difficult this must have been for you."

Hagura bowed, accepting the compliment. "It was my duty, Nangi-san." Inside he was mightily impressed with Nangi-san's *wa*. He felt the harmony still pervading the room, lending it power. In the face of his tragic and totally unexpected news this was heartening indeed. The news of what had happened in here would spread through the *kobun*, Nangi's heroism and iron determination offsetting some of the void all must feel at Seiichi Sato's passing.

Alone in the office after Hagura's departure, Nangi broke apart. Tears filled his eyes; there was a fist in his throat that made swallowing painful. He stared out through the high panes of glass.

First Gōtarō, he thought. Then Obā-chama, Makita. But not Seiichi, never Seiichi. How many people in one's life were there who one could talk to? How many were there in a lifetime who understood him? One or two, a handful if one were exceptionally fortunate.

Who would he talk to now? Nangi asked himself. Who would he confide in, formulate plans with, gloat over his recent triumph in Hong Kong with? All of this had fallen to Seiichi. Now there was no one.

There was anger as well as a deep and abiding sadness within him now. For this time he turned his love around and hated the God in whom he believed, in whom he put all his trust, and into whose care he had delivered his immortal soul.

How could you do such a thing? he railed inside. Where is the sense of it? There was only a perception of harsh cruelty, of an unfairness so huge as to be overwhelming. They had been like twins, Tanzan and Seiichi, knowing each other's heart, trusting each other's spirit through all their squabbles, arguments, disagreements. And as in every good marriage, those battles had been ironed out in the end to the satisfaction of both of them. No more. Why?

Had Nangi been able to see himself objectively at that moment he would have understood that he had lost more than the friendship he held most dear. He had also lost the Eastern sense of acceptance and resignation, that belief in the course of a cosmic sense of life. He had lost his place in the scheme of things, and that was a serious matter, indeed.

His mask slipped back on his face when Craig Allonge brought Justine into the fiftieth-floor garden where Nangi wished to receive her. The Tomkin Industries executive did not remain long. He made the introductions, then left for his business lunch.

So, Nangi thought, looking her over, this is Raphael Tomkin's daughter. Is she still in love with the *gaijin* Linnear? he wondered. He had heard about their icy demeanor at Tomkin's funeral.

"May I offer my personal condolences, Miss Tomkin?" Nangi said, inclining his head. "I knew your father personally and admired him greatly."

Justine almost said, That's Miss *Tobin*, but already the distinction she had created herself years ago seemed artificial and meaningless.

Instead, she nodded. "Thank you, Nangi-san. Your generous bouquet was most appreciated." She looked around. "It's beautiful here."

He nodded in return. "May I get you a drink?"

"A gin and tonic would be nice," she said, sitting down on one of the chairs near a stand of green bamboo. What's going on here? she asked herself. He seems old and shaken. She knew from Nicholas that she could not ask a direct question.

She sipped at her drink, studiously ignoring Nangi's limp as he went from the bar to a chair near her.

"It is somewhat of a surprise to see you here in Tokyo," he said after he had seated himself. "Is there something specific I can help you with? You have only to ask. I will assign a young lady to take you shopping to all the finest stores. At night, a male escort will take you—"

"I've come here to see Nicholas," she said, stopping him in midsentence. She resented the assumptions he had made about her simply because she was female but she had the presence of mind to show none of this. On the exterior she was cool and calm and thus, in Nangi's eyes, gained enormous face.

He was impressed despite himself. "I see. Well, that is an admirable reason for traveling all this distance."

And as he paused, Justine felt her insides go cold. How she longed to scream out, What's happened? Is he all right?

"Do you know where he is at the moment?" She was quite surprised to find that her voice was steady. Nicholas would be proud of her. But with that thought, tears brimmed her eyes. What has happened? she asked herself again.

"Unfortunately, no," Nangi said. "I myself have just returned from a lengthy business trip. I am being filled in now as to events that have transpired in my absence."

He's so damned calm, Justine thought. How does he do it? She was unaware that she was matching Nangi stride for stride.

Every moment that Nangi sat talking with this *gaijin* his respect for her increased, grudgingly at first, then more freely. Because of her *wa*, he decided to tell her what she would otherwise find out hours from now.

"I am afraid that there has been some sort of mishap, Miss Tomkin. In my absence Sato Seiichi"—he used the Japanese form—"has been killed in an auto crash."

"Oh, my God." Justine's hands gripped each other in her lap, her drink forgotten beside her. "Was he . . . alone?" Her voice had gone quite low.

"I understand your concern," Nangi said. "And, yes, my information is that he was alone in the car at the time of the mishap."

Justine's eyes closed, a muscle tic beginning in one eyelid. *Mishap*, she thought. He uses the word like doctors use the word *expired*, to tidily explain away something dreadful.

"I'm...I'm terribly sorry, Nangi-san," she said. "Please accept my condolences. I have heard many stories of Sato-san's prowess in business and personal life."

Nangi stared openly at her, amazed. Where was the gush of disgusting emotionalism he had expected from this barbarian? Where was the embarrassing reference to Sato and Nangi's closeness that would have humiliated him? Neither had come. Instead she had expressed the proper sentiments in the proper manner, honoring both of them as well as Sato-san.

"I appreciate your thought, Tomkin-san," he said, his voice softened by emotion. "You are welcome to return to your hotel. Or, as I said before, I will assign company personnel to take you about the city, as you wish. In any case, you will be informed the moment we have word of Linnear-san's whereabouts."

"If you don't mind, I'd prefer to stay here," Justine said. "That is, if you don't think I'll be in the way."

"Absolutely not," Nangi said, and rang for Kei Hagura. He had learned his lesson; no woman was summoned.

In the dense forest surrounding Itami's house, Nicholas began his search, employing several of the simple implements he had taken from his aunt's kitchen with her blessing.

He was searching for any of several kinds of holes in the ground, and it took him some time. The forest was thicker than it had been when he had been here as a young boy. But that could only be his imagination, for one is never as alert to one's surroundings when at a place one despises.

The sky, when he could catch a glimpse of it through the arching canopy of branches and leaves, seemed odd and yellow. It was certainly no longer day, yet it was like no twilight he had ever seen before. Too, the atmosphere felt different. It was as heavy as lead, windless, not a blade of grass stirring. Even the insects were quiescent. He saw no birds.

At length he found what he had been searching for and went to work. Most of the time was spent up in a tree, waiting. When he was finished and quite satisfied, he set off.

In little time he found an outcropping of rock and settled down on it to wait.

And that was how Akiko found him, sitting in the lotus position. Darkness was encroaching, long shadows as blue as ice creeping along the woodland carpet, over rocks and toadstools, moss and wildflowers. It was the time of the evening when, normally, the changeover from diurnal to nocturnal was being made. Larks and finch giving way to whippoorwills and owl, boar and rabbits to foxes and weasels. There was little stirring.

She stopped before him. She had emerged out of the dense foliage as just one more shadow, approaching. "I regret that I could not bring you back your *dai-katana*," she said.

"Would you have killed me with it?"

She answered him only in the most oblique fashion. "Come down off your lofty perch," she said, "and we will speak together."

With deliberation, Nicholas descended. He was thinking of Masashigi Kusunoki. Ever since Sato had mentioned that name in connection with the Tenshin Shoden Kaktori *ryu*, it had stuck in his subconscious like a thorn. Although he had been away from Yoshino for quite a long time, still he knew of no *sensei* either in Japan or outside it who went by that name.

Yet he knew that Sato had not lied, and that he had not been lied to. For what possible purpose would either thing have been done? He could think of none. Masashigi Kusunoki existed—or had before he had been murdered—yet he did not exist. Who had he been, and who had killed him?

Had it been Akiko, his pupil, who had sat before him across the *tatami*, speaking of mundane matters, hiding her intent with what Kyōki, the madman, had taught her so that the *sensei* felt only the glow of her *wa*, and was thus put off his guard? Was that what she was about to do with him now?

Grass verge served admirably as their *tatami*. Darkness, stealing in over the hills and treetops, shrouded them, nocturnal creatures that they were, gentling them in its webbed cradle. They were home again in the blackness of the night. The merest trace of starblaze smeared their faces in cold blue highlight.

"I would have found you out even without the tattoos," he said.

"No one but you would have understood their true nature." Her head inclined slightly.

"Yes," he agreed. "I know the legend of Hsing, the shape-changer; the *akuma* he created with *jahō*."

She was laughing at him. "And you believed all of that?"

"I believe in the *Kuji-kiri*," he said. "In the *Kōbudera*, and in the *Wu-Shing*. I knew one *mahō-zukai* . . ." He had kept his inflection up so that she would know that he had not finished. She was no longer laughing. "You knew him too, Akiko-san. Saigō."

He had brought the key in his pocket and now he had offered it to her. He thought that she had taken it but might not yet be ready to use it on herself. He continued.

"Now I know the truth. Your twin dragons spoke to me with tongues of fire. Before he was murdered by his jealous compatriots, Hsing had branded his *akuma*. Hsing was *sensei* to many arts; tattooing was only one of them.

"He did this, so it was said, so that he might be able to identify his pupil for all time, so that they would be inexorably linked on the wheel of *karma*.

"Did you have a *sensei*, Akiko-san, who marked you so with such skilled hands? I cannot think you went to a common parlor off the street." He might, of course, have said more, mentioned Kyōki by name, but in doing so he would give up an enormous advantage.

"So you know about *Wu-Shing*," she said, inserting the key he had given her. She nodded. "Perhaps it is a relief to me that someone else knows. That that someone else is you." And all the while she thought, Amida! I can't believe it. I look upon him and my love for him is so strong that I need to clasp my old hate to me with white fingers; I must concentrate on it every single moment or it threatens to slide away from me like sand.

"Hsing's *akuma* had just cause to enact the age-old vengeance. As do I. My family name is not Ofuda—"

"No," Nicholas interrupted deliberately. "It is Sato. And Satosan, your husband, is dead."

She inclined her head. "I suspected as much. I am sorry." Her eyes blazed in the cruel starlight. "Sorry I could not end his life by my own power, using the fourth state of the *Wu-Shing*."

"*Kung*," Nicholas said, using the Chinese word for "palace," the eunuch's punishment. "You would have castrated him before you killed him."

"He deserved no less," she said with venom. "As does his friend, Tanzan Nangi. He has yet to experience my terrible power. Together they conspired to destroy my real father, Hiroshi Shimada."

Nicholas was truly surprised. "Your father was Vice-Minister Shimada?" He knew the name well and in a quite personal way because Shimada had been one of the Colonel's prime postwar targets. "But his wife bore him only two sons."

"His mistress was my mother," Akiko said proudly. "She was *tayu oiran* in the *Yoshiwara*. She was the best there was."

"Shimada committed *seppuku*. There was a huge scandal—"

"Cleverly concocted by Nangi, Sato, and their mentor, Yoichiro Makita."

Nicholas knew that this was patently untrue. The evidence against Shimada had been overwhelming and incontrovertible.

"They made up lies, half-truths, innuendoes. It was enough"— her face was twisted with her hate—"*more* than enough in an

494

atmosphere that bordered on phobic hysteria when it came to the subject of the war." He felt a gathering of her forces. "But it was your father, Colonel Denis Linnear, who insisted on making these falsehoods public knowledge. Linnear had wanted my father out of the way ever since he had championed a hard line against SCAP's interference into MCI policies."

Nicholas remembered what his father had told him on the day Vice-Minister Shimada was found near his wife in a pool of blood. "Never rejoice over the death of another human being. Rather take satisfaction that a source of evil has been expunged. In this case elements within MCI were perpetuating the power factions begun years ago by members of the prewar *zaibatsu*, in their *kanmin ittai*, control associations. If a man aligns himself with evil, we have our duty before us. We must act. Mankind could not long tolerate life without this weeding-out process."

"There was nothing false in the accusations leveled against your father, Akiko," he said. "You cannot deny the symmetry of crime and punishment." But his words seemed distant to his ears for he found it enormously difficult to disassociate himself from the face so close before him. It seemed to make no difference that he knew that she was not, in fact, Yukio. That was an intellectual response, and what he was feeling was emotional. It bypassed the intellect, the rational completely. What did he see inside her that caused him to react this way?

It did not vitiate in any way the danger he felt himself to be in; it merely clouded the issue, turning the translucent into the opaque.

And he was truly amazed in an entirely different manner as well. Despite what Itami had told him, despite what he already knew of Akiko, plus what he suspected, it came as a shock to probe and feel nothing but the glow of her *wa*. Harmony. Whatever she was actually feeling toward him he could not say. He felt no aggression, no animosity, nothing negative whatsoever. And again he found himself wondering whether this was what the mysterious Masashigi Kusunoki had felt just before Akiko had reached out with her *jahō* and had freed him from life.

"They used the Colonel," she said. "You must see that." Eyes like stones. "They fed him their garbage and he ate it all up."

"Whatever Sato and Nangi deserved had no bearing on the three innocent people you destroyed in the process," he said, ignoring her line.

"Don't talk to me of innocence," she spat. "There is no innocence inside that company at all. Two are guilty; all are equally to blame."

495

Nicholas thought of Miss Yoshida and he was as sad for this woman sitting not a handsbreadth away as he was for her. Look what can become of life, he thought. After this, there is no hope.

But he had accomplished one of his goals; had found out all that he needed to know. By her words he knew that she would not allow him to rise and walk away; that, whatever her personal feelings might be, she had been trained too well, her spirit in the end as weak as her first husband's, the spell of *jahō* taking her over. He could never convince her of the truth. As Akutagawa-san had said, the force of *jahō* was so corrosive to mind and spirit that one always ran the terrible risk of succumbing to it rather than, as one did with all martial arts, harnessing it to one's own needs.

Now he gazed upon her with eyes filled with new knowledge. For at last he saw who it was he was truly facing. She was *miko*, a sorceress who could reach out at any time, masking her true intent, and snuff out his life. It could come in the midst of a kiss or an embrace; he would never know the difference, never feel the flickering of her *wa*, the breakup of harmony by the spitting of aggression. He would never even know that she had reached for the Void.

Her intent was forever beyond his knowing, and he knew that he had been right to wait up in the tree for so long. He knew that he faced death. It did not seem ironic to him that it should come to him in the form of his first true love, only just and fitting. If he should die now, hers would be the last face that he would see. He would go down dreaming of Yukio.

"It is very still," Akiko said softly. "The animals are hiding, the birds are nested, the insects sleep. Even the wind has ceased to blow. All for us."

Her eyes were luminous. He imagined that he could see the moon reflected in their convex surfaces. They had the sheen of finest silk; they reminded him so much of Yukio's eyes.

"For we are lovers, Nicholas. The last two true lovers alive on the face of the world. When we made love it was not just our bodies that were entwined, penetrating and being penetrated. It was our spirits as well.

"The clouds and the rain made our spirits one, Nicholas. Now we have our own tattoos, as indelibly etched as my dragons. We shall know each other for all time. However we may be reincarnated, whatever our *karma* dictates we must be, still will we recognize one another. As human or badger, plover or serpent. The spirit dance we performed will preserve our link."

Had she moved perceptibly closer? Nicholas could not tell. Her words had become as luminous as her eyes, as the starlight that partially enveloped them where broad fans of shadow from the surrounding trees did not.

Was she leaning forward now? Did he feel the hard press of her jutting breasts against his chest? Did he feel her warmth bathing him, her breath like the scent of lilac on his cheek? In all the states he summoned up, both exalted and common, he felt only her *wa*, a glowing beacon, as constant as the sea.

He remembered their fevered night in Sato's garden and thought he wanted that onrush all over again. *Sato*. Felt one of her arms coming around his back, lying along his shoulder, fingertips caressing the side of his neck. Remember Sato, he thought, and how you failed him. Failed in your sacred oath to protect him. There was only one possible way out for him now.

"No!"

His cry echoed into the night. "I cannot allow this! I cannot love you, a *miko*!"

And as he pulled away from her half-embrace, he withdrew the short-bladed knife he had taken from Itami's house. Though it belonged in her kitchen still its blade was finely honed, still it was a weapon of honor.

Without hesitation Nicholas drove the blade to the hilt into his abdomen. Blood flashed out, black in the darkness, glinting on his knees, the grass, Akiko's lap.

Nicholas' face was distorted by agony. His head trembled as he slashed horizontally from left to right across his lower belly. The place where *hara* resided.

Akiko was in shock. Her eyes were open wide. "Amida!" she breathed. There was so much blood! It ran in a torrent from him, from the center of his being, draining him of strength, of life.

So many conflicting emotions strived for dominance inside her. Elation and sorrow, shock and panic. Satisfaction and fear. Was this the end she had been seeking? Was this the culmination of her long thought out vengeance?

She knew that it was, but now she was beginning to suspect that it was not what she wanted. She had struggled all her life, it seemed, to be free of woman's traditional role as servant to man. Her rejection of all that her mother had been, her revulsion for that lofty state of *tayu* had this as its basis. As did her decision to train in the most demanding of the martial arts: man's work. All her life she had fought to take her place beside men as an equal.

But now she was coming to see that that obsession had put her in the position of becoming a pawn to the drives and hatreds of those certain men who she had thought she was closest to: Kyōki, Saigō, and, ultimately, Vice-Minister Shimada. She understood that more than any other person, her father had shaped the direction of her life. Just as Saigō's father had done his. They were the same, then, she and Saigō. Exactly the same. Totally evil.

Too late had she made this discovery. It had taken the death of one she now knew she loved in a way she had loved no other man or woman.

She opened her mouth to speak, she opened her arms to show him her intent, but at that moment the earth beneath them commenced to roll as if it had been transmuted into water by *jahō* beyond even her ken.

Cannonfire crossed them, echoing eerily into the night, the sound bouncing off obstructions that had just a moment before not been there.

For in truth the world was dissolving, had opened up like a pair of gaping jaws. Wildflowers and bushes, trees and grasslands were eaten up, swamped down into the yawning pit that had no end.

Raw gases stung her nostrils, sulphur and the stench of molten metal.

And then she had lost her balance, was falling, rolling end over end, filled with vertigo so that she had no idea of where the sky was and where the earth. All she could do was reach upward, stretching and grabbing at fistfuls of crumbling soil.

Nicholas, too, was tumbling and rolling in the grip of the first earthquake shock, whose epicenter, as the Soviet satellite had accurately predicted, was not more than a kilometer away to the east.

He was sent flying, in fact, away from the spot where he and Akiko had been kneeling, away from the glistening pools of blood which had spurted out when he had knifed into the freshly killed fox he had strapped like a cincture around his abdomen, beneath his kimono. He had suspected, rightly, that only a shock of the first magnitude could deflect the *jahō* for long enough.

He fetched up hard against rocks made sharp by fissures forming in their midst, dividing them, cracking them open like eggs.

Nicholas tried to regain his feet but the earth shudders were still too violent and he tumbled downward again. He had been thrown perhaps ten or fifteen meters from where he had been and now he lifted his head, searching for Akiko. He could not see her, but that was not surprising in all the chaos.

He was in the midst of a world gone mad. Where trees had

been was nothing now but great holes like wounded gums. Those trees now protruded from the agonized earth like arrows shot into it by a giant archer far above his head, their webby root structures shaking themselves free of huge clods of earth.

In a moment, Nicholas began to crawl back the way he had come. It took him some time. He was obliged to make many detours and to stop several times while aftershocks vibrated beneath his hands and knees like the angry shouts of the gods.

He came finally to the fissure, a mighty, jagged rent in the universe. It was awesome to see open space where just moments before solid ground had been. It gave one pause, even one such as he who had been born here and thus was not a stranger to quakes. One never got used to them or ceased to be humbled by their titanic display of force.

In the hollow silence after the grinding of the quake, he thought he could hear a voice. Slowly, he crawled to the edge of the fissure. Its sides were as jagged and irregular as was its face.

He saw her down there. Her tiny oval face leaped up to him through the jumble of debris—rent rocks, split trees, and the like.

"Nicholas."

He saw those eyes, luminous still. Yukio's eyes. He moved forward toward her and felt the earth begin to give way beneath his chest. Dirt crumbled away from him in a torrent and she screamed.

Head cast down into that stygian gloom, he inched carefully backward. His eyes roved for another way down to her. Perhaps that tree just above her. But he could not see its underpinning and if he was wrong, if it would not hold his weight, she would be instantly crushed by its descent.

"Nicholas!"

Something in her voice drew his attention back to her. He peered down. No. It was her voice itself. It seemed to have changed not only pitch but timbre as well.

"Don't move," he cautioned her. "I can't take a chance on coming down myself. There's too much instability within the fissure. I'm going to find vines I can weave into a rope that will hold you."

"No!"

The amount of anguish in her cry froze him.

"Don't leave me, Nicholas. Not again!"

A rumbling had begun, deeper this time as if truly it were emanating from the bowels of the earth. Had he heard right? Nicholas asked himself. Had she said, "Not again"?

"Then I'm coming down after you!" he called.

"No, no! Amida, no!" He saw her face limned by starlight which was somehow stronger now after the quake. It was as if the universe were awakening from a deep slumber. "You'll be killed!" There was movement from down there. He had already lowered himself halfway into the fissure, his bare toes searching for a substantial hold.

He saw Akiko reach for the bottom of the tree substructure, a massive tangle of roots like the Gordian knot. But she had no magic sword and could not unravel it.

The rumbling reached a crescendo and Nicholas heard the awful grinding of the world pulling itself apart. Deep below him, plates shifted, the pressure shooting upward. The fissure walls trembled and slid farther open. Even the sky seemed to judder in pain, the starlight winking out, as the earth heaved in exquisite agony.

Nicholas could hear nothing above the rush of noise that filled his ears to overflowing. He thought their drums might burst with the intensity of the vibration. He saw the tree shifting downward. He opened his mouth to scream, then he was obliged to turn his full attention on raising himself out of the lethal pit before he was cast down.

When he was able to look again, it was as if he gazed upon an entirely different world. There was no tree, no split rocks, none of the rills and valleys that he had recorded in his mind preparatory to his attempted descent.

Like a fragrant, fertile valley re-formed out of sere desert, all that he had first gazed upon was gone. And Akiko with it.

The first familiar person Nicholas saw when he left Toranomon Hospital in Tokyo was Tanya Vladimova. He was not particularly surprised to see her. He had never bothered to call Minck.

She was coming out of an elevator along the same bank in front of which Nicholas stood at the Okura.

"What happened to you?" she said, checking herself in mid-stride.

Nicholas' elevator came and she got in with him. "You look like somebody put you through the meat grinder and forgot to turn the thing off."

"Were you here for the quake?" It was the best he could do at the moment, and was not as inane a question as it seemed on the surface.

"Oh, yes." Her head nodded. "It was quite frightening, I must say. The Japanese took it with just a bit more equanimity." She was evincing a light tone and forcing it. Nicholas wondered why. "How about you?"

"No," he said. "I missed the worst of it."

She waited patiently while he opened the door to his room. "I was in L.A. once when a minor quake hit," she said conversationally. "It was like here, really, though this one, I'm told, was far worse. No one paid the slightest attention to it. It was as if it did not exist."

"That's not at all how the Japanese view it," Nicholas said as he went into the bathroom and turned on the taps, the shower. He was obliged to raise his voice over the sound of all the rushing water. "They accept earthquakes as part of nature. To Californians it's like death: they'd rather not think about it."

Fifteen minutes later, after a long, steaming shower followed by an icy one, he emerged, wreathed in towels. He stripped off the plastic bag used to keep his newly bandaged fingers dry. "I'm glad you're here, actually."

"Oh, good," she said, staring at his hand. "I've come as Minck's messenger girl, really. The focus of our hunt has shifted since your meeting with him last week. Away from Protorov, toward *Tenchi*."

Perhaps it was the fatigue that gripped him or else Akiko was still on his mind: how wholly she had become Yukio or some semblance of Yukio that he still held sacrosanct and pristine in his memory. Perhaps it was only his imagination but it was his decided feeling that the *kami* of his first beloved had somehow taken hold of her lookalike at the end, filling her heart with love and compassion where before there had been only hate and a burning need for revenge. In the end, that might have been foolish of him, but he did not think so. He was too aware of the intertwining of life and death.

In any event, he missed the falseness to her voice that normally he might have picked up. He was not fully attuned to this conversation; his thoughts were elsewhere. Relaxing his overworked muscles he was diffused, without concentration, and therefore vulnerable.

"That's just as well," he said, turning away from her to rummage through his dresser for fresh clothes, "because Protorov has ceased to be a threat to anyone."

"What do you mean?" Tanya said, though she knew very well.

"I mean," Nicholas said, "that I killed him." He turned back in time to see the surprise in her eyes when he said, "I've also broken *Tenchi* wide open."

Tanya felt as if she had been struck by lightning. After Russilov's terrible news, she had lost much of her hope. With Protorov gone, what chance did they now have for the KGB-GRU summit.

She, too, knew Mironenko. In fact, he had been her first lover. Thus had she brought him into Protorov's axis. This had been just before her graduation from the academy in the Urals. Mironenko and several other up-and-coming GRU officers had been given a three-day tour of the premises and facilities.

Of all the visitors, Protorov judged Mironenko to be of the most use to him in the future; that had been the reason for extending him an invitation in the first place.

Protorov had sent Tanya into his room at night. She had been sex-starved, the passion of her emotions mingling with her physical needs. The combination had proved irresistible to Mironenko—as it would have been for almost any man.

Tanya was his first link with Protorov. After the visit he did not want to give her up and, in fact, their affair lasted through the spring and into the summer.

But summer meant Tanya's graduation, and because he had another assignment for her, one far more risky, one that only she could perform, Protorov contrived to have Mironenko's wife become aware of his passion. Chastened, he left Tanya's side. But, partially because Protorov's subsequent intervention saved his marriage—and his career as well—and partially because his own political bent was similar, he moved into Protorov's camp.

In the meantime, Protorov had moved Tanya out of the academy, allowing her to find her own way into the midst of her brother's, Mikhail's dissident apparatus. From his own point of view there was no risk, of course. He knew quite well that Tanya's heart belonged to her father; that she had seen Mikhail's behavior as a betrayal to the family. He had had his instructors work on that angle in oblique manners during her schooling.

Mikhail, for his part, was overjoyed to see her. To him it meant that she had matured. It simply was inconceivable to him that she might be a KGB apparatchik.

Now, as hope returned to Tanya, she automatically abandoned her backup plan to kill Nicholas and, reporting back to Minck in Washington, put a bullet through his brain. With *Tenchi*'s secret safe inside her mind, she would contact Russilov to initiate an escape route for her.

Of course she would not tell him of her discovery. Rather let him think that she was returning to Central a disgrace, having been blown by Linnear. After what had transpired in the safe house in Hokkaido, he'd have no trouble swallowing that.

Then across the frontier, through the Kurile chain, to Mironenko. There was still time to make the summit deadline, and she wished to have no eager ambitious male trying to share her triumph.

No, she alone would address the KGB-GRU summit as Viktor Protorov's handpicked successor. The coup would take place. The dream had not died after all.

Trying with all her will to control the fluttering she felt in her chest, she said, "The sooner you tell me about it, the sooner I can send a signal to Minck and we can put this to bed once and for all."

Dressed, Nicholas was counting out money into a new wallet. "Thankfully, no action will be needed on our part. I'm quite sure of that. But it would have been a full-fledged disaster had the Soviets been successful in penetrating it."

Tanya ground her teeth in anticipation. She could barely contain her anxiety. She moved with him as he walked back into the bathroom to brush his hair, standing just outside the door as he flicked on the hairdryer.

"*Tenchi* is an apt code name," he began. "It means 'heaven and earth.' *Tenchi* is, in fact, a super-robot."

"What?" Tanya cried. "What is this, a science-fiction film?"

"Let me begin at the beginning. Three years ago the *Hare Maru*, a Japanese tanker loaded with radioactive waste, was lost in a typhoon while crossing the Nemuro Straits between Hokkaido and the southernmost tip of the Kuriles.

"It was a disaster of the greatest magnitude, and one which the Japanese Government, as you can imagine, did not want made public.

"Salvage operations were begun as soon as fair weather returned. The radioactive wastes, as it turned out, had not broken through their sealed containers, and the operation proceeded without a hitch.

"But on the third day, divers using an enormously powerful vacuum pump that must be anchored on the ocean floor discovered that the vibrations of the mechanism had opened up a hairline fissure. Out of it a black, viscous substance had begun to leak.

"They had accidentally discovered oil off the coast of Japan where, it had been determined by a host of geologists, none could exist.

"Excitement rose to a fever pitch as the divers rose with their news and the information was transmitted back to the Prime Minister.

"Oceanographers as well as geologists were sent into the area. What they came back with three weeks later was unimaginable. It looked as if this pocket of fossil oil was set very deep. Also, it was vast. If the government could find a way of extracting it, they might never have to buy a barrel of crude again. Japan would be self-sufficient. It was an answer to many prayers.

"But the thorn was getting it out of the rock. Conventional methods of offshore drilling were useless because of the type of rock and its formation. Besides, they were not all that far from a known ocean fault, and they were terrified that any undue activity in the area might cause a major earthquake.

"And so *Tenchi* was born. It has eight articulated arms and legs. It can move over any kind of terrain no matter how rough. It can see, hear, even smell. It can—and will—extract the oil from the bottom of the sea, the first conduit into which billions of barrels of fuel will be pumped on its way up to the surface and a line of waiting tankers via fathoms of pipeline."

"But why all this secrecy?" Tanya asked. "Surely it could have been developed in the light of day."

"Perhaps," Nicholas conceded. "However, the oil reservoir is not only on Japanese soil, though *they* think it is."

"What are you saying?" Tanya said, her heart in her throat.

"The Kuriles are a source of dispute between Russia and Japan. You know that, it's elementary. The real question is, who owns the oil, Japan or Russia? You'll get two different answers depending on whether you speak to a Japanese or a Russian." He turned away from the mirror. "Now you see why Protorov was so anxious to penetrate the operation. The Russians could also have been self-sufficient."

He came out of the bathroom and looked around. But Tanya had already gone.

Moments later he was on his way out to the Shinjuku Suiryū Building, the offices of Sato Petrochemicals, when his phone buzzed. He picked it up. "Yeah?"

"The weather was great in Key West, buddy," the voice said in his ear, "but the company was lousy."

"Croaker!" Like air being let out of a balloon. His knees felt weak and he had to sit down. "Lew, it can't be you!"

"Can, buddy-boy, and is. I'm in the lobby. I didn't want to give you a heart attack by coming to your door unannounced. Can I come up?"

"I'm just on my way out. I'll meet you downstairs." A thousand questions chased each other through his mind. Lew Croaker alive! How was it possible?

"Nah. With what I got, I'd better come on up."

"Okay. Sure."

504

There was a pause. "How you been, anyway?" The voice had gone gruff.

"Nothing's the same," Nicholas said. "But then it never is."

"Hah! Tell me about it. I'll be right there."

He was a bit leaner, certainly tanner, his Robert Mitchum face seemingly far more deeply lined. Still, he looked fine to Nicholas.

They embraced like brothers, and this time Croaker did not mind the contact. He was amazed at just how much he had missed his friend.

He pointed. "What's with the bandages?"

"Later," Nicholas said. "Now tell me all."

And Croaker did, from the moment the mysterious car had rammed him off the road in Key West, to Alix Logan's revelations.

"So Minck sanctioned Angela Didion's death," Nicholas said, wonderingly. "It wasn't Tomkin at all."

"He only knew about it," Croaker sneered. "He only let the killers into her apartment. I suppose that absolves him of guilt."

Nicholas looked at him. He felt a curious ache inside. "I'm sorry he was so weak. He must've been thinking of the leak she represented. National security—"

"He's still a murderer in my book," Croaker cut in. "National security, my ass. Big goddamned deal."

"I disagree, Lew."

Croaker rounded on him. "What d'you mean?"

"You know what I mean," Nicholas said softly. "Why are you here now?"

Croaker thought about that. "National security," he said at last. It was a sigh of defeat. "I'm sorry, Nick."

"Forget it, Lew. It only means we can all be suckered in the name of patriotism."

"Is that what really led Tomkin to let them in?"

Nicholas looked at his friend. "I honestly don't know."

"Well, it sure don't make a bit of difference to Angela. One way or another, she's still six feet under."

"You can't keep torturing yourself over one death, Lew. Be reasonable. You've done everything you could. It's more than anyone else would've done. I think Angela's spirit can rest now."

Croaker sat down heavily, his head in his hands. "I did nothing. I solved nothing, I've gotten nowhere. Just spinning my goddamned wheels in a pile of quicksand. No one's gonna pay for Angela's death, not now, not ever."

Now Nicholas was concerned. "What happened to you down in Key West, my friend? I mean, really."

505

Croaker's voice was muffled. "I don't know, Nick. Damned if I do." Nicholas said nothing, and Croaker was forced to go on to rid himself of the oppressive silence. "My life's come apart. I guess..." He paused, began all over again. "I don't know what's happened to the kid who graduated the Academy in the top five percent of his class. Then I had the law in one hand and my service revolver in the other. I knew what to do with them. I knew that I was on the right side and *they*, the murderers, rapists, addicts, armed robbers, muggers, were on the wrong side.

"That was a long time ago—or so it seems. Somewhere in the interim I seem to have lost the facility to determine the perpetrators from the law officers. I thought sure as I'm sitting here that Tomkin killed Angela. I was wrong... or was I? I don't know anymore. Minck had her killed and I knew I had to confront him. Why, I don't know. Did I want to murder him myself? Become the ultimate anarchist against the law I'm sworn to uphold: a vigilante? I knew when I stood before him that at least part of me wanted to. Even though I know what kind of a bitch Angela was, even though I know that she could—and you're right, *would* have— screwed this whole spook deal Minck had cooking with Tomkin. But the end result is that they took a human life; they played God with her. They *destroyed*, Nick."

His head came up, and Nicholas winced at the bleakness in those red-rimmed eyes. Perhaps he had been crying... for himself, for one lost soul. "No matter what she was, Nick, she had a right to live. I'm right about that, at least, aren't I?"

Nicholas put his arm around his friend as together they sat on the edge of the bed. "She had a right to live, Lew."

Croaker gave a little bark of confused anger. "So instead of taking Minck out myself, I wind up working for him."

"I don't understand."

"Yeah, well you will in a minute, I guarantee you." Croaker stood up, began to pace back and forth like a caged tiger. He was tense and did not mind showing it. "Reason is, see, this Minck bastard's sanctioned someone else. It seems that Tanya Vladimova's a KGB bug planted on him. You ain't seen her skulking around here lately have you?"

Nicholas' mind was on fire. There were too many things hitting him at once. "Tanya," he said, "a Soviet spy? But why didn't Minck contact me himself?"

Croaker pointed to the phone. "Ever think to get your messages, buddy?"

"Actually, no. I've had other things on my mind. I only walked into the hotel a half an hour ago. I ran right into Tanya. She—"

"Yeah? Where the hell's she got to?"

Oh, my God, Nicholas thought. *Tenchi!* I've given her everything I fought so hard to keep from Protorov. Perhaps he's won after all. But that thought, the knowledge of an almost certain war sparked by the territorial incident, was too terrible to contemplate.

"Come on!" Nicholas cried.

"Where we going?"

"To Hamamatsu-chō."

When Tanya left Nicholas' room, she took the fire stairs down the seven floors, not wanting to wait for the elevator or to be seen. In the street she turned north, heading away from the hotel at a rapid pace. She longed to take a taxi but was afraid to leave a trail. In any case, within three blocks she knew that she had made the right choice. Traffic choked the streets and she was far better off on foot, plowing with great power through the crowds like a salmon struggling upstream.

Up the Sakura-dōri, she found the Toranomon station of the Ginza Line. Down into the ground she went, paying her fare, riding one stop to Shimbashi, where she transferred to the J.N.R. Line to Hamamatsu-chō.

There she emerged in the midst of hundreds of other people, mostly tourists, to wait for the monorail to Haneda Airport and a flight to Hokkaido. Now she took time out to wait on line for a phone booth where, when it was her turn, she used a special code to alert Russilov that she was on the run.

"Parachute," she said when the line opened.

It was that time of day in Tokyo, after the noon lunch stampede and before the evening rush hour, when traffic is variable. It can be good or bad according to the whim of the gods.

Nicholas decided to take a calculated risk and grab a cab to Hamamatsu-chō. It was a mistake. Sakura-dōri was jammed, and none of the alternate routes were any better. Near the Onarimon station, he had had enough and, dropping yen like flower petals onto the driver's lap, jumped out, Croaker just behind him.

Onarimon had been on their way along the city streets but now, underground, they found themselves having to change trains twice, once at Mita for the Toei Asakusa Line to Shimbashi, thence to the J.N.R., following Tanya's route to Hamamatsu-chō.

When they came up into the pointillist sunshine they were faced with a massive crowd that flowed down the two staircases on the departing side of the monorail station. A riot of color, voices, jostling bodies. A sea of faces; the rhythm of the heat.

"She could be anywhere here," Croaker said. "Or she could be twenty miles away."

"Stop being so optimistic," Nicholas said dryly, "and go down to the far staircase. In three minutes precisely, we'll both start up, me here, you there. We'll get her someplace in between."

Croaker got serious. "You really are sure she's here, aren't you?"

"You don't know Tokyo, Lew," he said. "She's got to get to Hokkaido as quickly as possible. Haneda Airport's her only means of doing it. This is her best shot for it."

"But there're always a busload of ways out of any major city. What makes you so sure it'll be this one?"

Nicholas could not say really, because it was an intangible. He conjured up Tanya's face at the moment he had told her that he had broken *Tenchi*. That surprise now had added meaning for him. He knew that she had not been prepared for flight. Whatever her plan had been when she had run into him at the Okura, it changed immediately he told her about *Tenchi*.

"Lew," he said earnestly, "she's going home. To Russia. She's running on instinct, and instinct dictates taking the most direct route as well as the fastest. It's a hunch, but an accurate one, I think."

"Okay, buddy," Croaker said with a brief grin. "I've had some experience with your hunches before. See you in the middle up there."

It was hot and getting hotter. So much so that Tanya had begun to sweat. Something was wrong on the monorail line. The unthinkable had occurred: a form of Japanese transportation had broken down.

Moments ago, as she glanced at her watch, she had begun to regret not shooting Nicholas Linnear where he stood in front of his bathroom mirror. But she knew quite well why she had hesitated and then decided against it. She was afraid of him; afraid that she would try it and he would somehow ferret out her intent, and stop her from bringing the secret of *Tenchi* to the summit. She consoled herself with the fact that the meeting was paramount and could not be jeopardized for anything.

She had stayed her hand and was sorry that she had not taken the risk. For she had bolted and was now vulnerable to pursuit. The thought of Nicholas Linnear as hunter filled her with dread.

That was why at the precise instant she saw him moving up the stairs at the near end of the platform she turned away and began to fight her way through the densely packed throng toward the platform's far end.

She had been scanning the bobbing crowd at fifteen-second intervals as she had been taught at Protorov's academy, using reflective surfaces when she could to do much of her work for her.

Her heart turned icy when she saw him rising onto the level of the platform itself. He seemed to slip through the jostling, sweating mob with the greatest of ease. Unlike her, who had to battle for every inch. She felt as if she were in quicksand, her legs frantically pumping but not seeing much result from all that furious effort. Quicksand or a dream.

But it was neither, Tanya knew quite well. So discreetly she drew out her modified Beretta, a flat, powerful weapon for close range.

She was looking over her shoulder as she had seen Russilov do. She had laughed silently at him for it but she found nothing amusing in the gesture now.

And so intent was she on fleeing from her personal hunter that she paid little attention to what was in front of her. To her those people were a quagmire through which she must force herself. They had ceased to be individuals but rather were a part of a maddeningly delaying whole. She wanted to kill them all, spill them pellmell onto the gleaming track that arced away toward Fuji-yama, blued in the industrial haze, and the safety of a plane at Haneda.

Something hit hard against her chest and she pushed back, frantic now, seeing Nicholas gaining on her.

"Stay right where you are, Comrade."

A rough New York accent. Her head spun around, the Beretta coming up automatically, her finger tightening on the trigger.

"Put it down," Lewis Croaker said into her face. "There's nothing you can do with it now. There's no place left for you to go."

She turned for one last look at her oncoming pursuer and felt the lurch of his open hand against her weapon. Instinctively she got off a shot and was preparing for another when a single black eye rose like a tower not six inches in front of her face and erupted with the noise of the death of the world.

Croaker got off the phone and said, "We're to stay right here until Minck's support crew does what it has to." He eyed Nicholas. "The police have already been contacted. No one's going to make a move against us."

Nicholas said nothing. He was staring down at the covered corpse of Tanya Vladimova. Cops were already on the scene, separating the observers from the participants. Moments ago Nicholas had spoken briefly to a young sergeant in rapid Japanese. There were still a battery of formalities to go through.

But he was thinking of other matters. He was thinking again of what his father had said about taking life and eradicating evil from the world. That was the dilemma, he saw now. Why was it that to do the one you had to do the other? Wasn't there any other way? Hadn't there been with Tanya?

There had been no other way with Protorov, he knew; with Akiko as well. *Karma.* He knew that he had still not yet learned to accept life on its own terms. He felt too much for others. Or was it only that he was reluctant to relinquish that degree of control? It was a myth, anyway. Life could never be controlled. And yet he continued to try.

Perhaps it was time to end all that, he thought.

At the Shinjuku Suiryū Building, Nicholas saw Tanzan Nangi first, even though he had been told on his arrival that Justine was there, waiting for him. He did so because he wanted at least one major element in his life settled before he saw her again. He wanted his mind totally free so that he could concentrate fully on whatever it was she intended.

He had spent three hot and sticky hours scouring the city after he left Croaker, and now he carried with him a silk-covered package.

He was shown into Sato's huge office without undue delay. They bowed.

"Linnear-san, please sit down."

"If you don't mind," Nicholas said, "I'd prefer the next room."

Nangi's eyes opened wide and he hesitated a moment as if Nicholas' request had disrupted a pattern set inside him. He nodded, recovering quickly. "Of course," he murmured.

They walked through the narrow passageway housing the *tokonoma*, its slender vase holding one purple peony. Nicholas read the poem on the scroll just above: *"No rain falls/Without bringing life/To blossoms/On mountainside or vale."*

Nangi led him past the small alcove and into another, smaller room that was not an office at all. It was a space that Nicholas had not seen before but had known must be there.

Just before the threshold, the two of them removed their shoes. It was a twelve-*tatami* room. The walls were *shōji* screens, though undoubtedly they covered plaster and lathe. Cool light, indirect and dim, played over the expanse, and from somewhere came the silvery tinkle of water through a streambed.

There was a low lacquer table in the center of the room, several Chinese-red *kansu* chests along the wall, a cedar desk with phone. A hard cedar chair.

They knelt down on opposite sides of the gleaming black table. Nicholas looked away to admire the room as Nangi spent some time and considerable energy in getting his ruined legs to bend beneath him.

"I have come to report my failure, Nangi-san," Nicholas said after a time.

Nangi was curious. "How so, Linnear-san?"

"While you were away, Sato and I struck a bargain. He wished the merger to go through with all good speed; I wished to aid him—and you as well—against the *Wu-Shing*."

"You and Seiichi-san felt that we both had something to fear from these heinous crimes, then?"

"Eventually, yes. We both felt that you and he were to be the final targets."

"Had you any proof?"

"It was Sato-san's belief that something in your past had triggered this vendetta." When Nangi said nothing, Nicholas went on. "I swore to protect him, Nangi-san. It is why I went with him to the *rotenburo* in Hokkaido to find the ninja Phoenix. But Koten betrayed us to the Russians. They killed the ninja; and they killed Sato-san." He went on to relate what had happened next at Protorov's safe house. He said nothing of what had happened after his winged escape.

"Phoenix was from the Tenshin Shoden Katori." Nangi's voice was deliberately calm. "Was anything put into the Soviets' hands?"

"For a moment they had it. But they had no one to translate the *kanji* cipher."

"I see." The relief flooding out of Nangi was palpable.

"I read the document, Nangi-san. I have penetrated to the core of *Tenchi*."

There was no sound in the room now but that of the flowing water, unseen and constant.

Nangi's eyes closed finally. He felt enormously tired, like a long-distance runner who had just expended his last ounce of gallant reserves to embrace the finish line only to be told that the course has been extended another mile.

His dark, avian eyes opened and in a voice like tissue paper he said, "And now that you have the leverage you need, what will you do with this information if I do not accede to your demands regarding the terms of the merger?"

"I have had a call from a man named C. Gordon Minck, Nangi-san. He is in the United States Government. I know him somewhat. I have run a certain errand for him . . . because it suited my purposes. Because I wished to save *Tenchi*."

Nangi nodded. "Save it from the Russians. I understand. You are an American citizen. And now the American secret service establishment knows our deep secret. They can keep us under their thumb forever."

"Nangi-san," Nicholas said softly, "I told Minck that the Soviets had not penetrated *Tenchi* and neither had I. Sato-san once told me that he feared the Americans penetrating *Tenchi* almost as much as the Russians. I did not understand what he meant then, but I know now. America would not wish for Japan to become independent of it. I agree with him."

For Nangi, Nicholas could not have uttered more startling words. "But this is impossible," he said, for once flustered. "You are an American. You are—"

"*Iteki*? Isn't that how you've seen me from the first, Nangi-san? As a barbarian, a half-breed."

Nangi's eyes lowered to the tabletop, but all he saw there was his own reflection. I hate this man, he thought, and I don't know why. He has suffered for this *keiretsu*, has kept its secrets, has almost died for it. He is loyal beyond question. He tried to save Seiichi-san's life. At the thought of his dead friend, a knife went through Nangi's insides and he was shaken anew by his rage against this man. Yet he struggled with himself to understand.

"My spirit is Japanese," Nicholas said softly. "You have only to feel my *wa* to know that. It was not so hard for Sato-san to accept me; to befriend me."

"Sato-san possessed a number of bad habits," Nangi snapped. Immediately, he bowed his head all the way to the lacquer. He was terribly ashamed. "Forgive me, Linnear-san." His voice was a cracked whisper, filled with pain and self-loathing. "You deserve only my abject gratitude for what you have done to protect my *keiretsu* and preserve *Tenchi*."

"I am truly sorry that you cannot give it." Nicholas' face was sad as he rose. "The pledge of merger was with Sato-san. I will not insist that you be bound by it."

"Linnear-san." Nangi's back was rigid. "Please sit down." And, when Nicholas made no move, "I beg of you. Do not add to the disgrace I have already heaped upon myself. If you walk out now, I can never regain face."

Nicholas folded his legs beneath him. "I have no wish to disgrace you," he said softly, remembering all Sato had told him of this man.

"Whatever accord you had with Seiichi-san you have with me. We are one and the same entity. I wish to honor his word." He passed a hand across his eyes. "I was brought up with *kanryōdō*. I hated foreigners as if they were a disease."

"Some—perhaps most—are like that," Nicholas said.

Nangi looked at him curiously. "In truth, I think I never bothered to understand you. I saw what I wanted to see." His eyes slid down again. "And I resented you your easy rapport with my friend."

"He could love you no less for it. But that is obvious." Nicholas raised his cup. "If you wish, we will light incense on Seiichi-san's grave together."

"Yes," Nangi said, and he was no longer ashamed to drape his voice in sadness. His good eye was moist. He raised his glass. "To departed friends, missed and honored for all the days of our lives."

They drank.

"Now what of the *Wu-Shing*?" Nangi asked.

"The threat of the *Wu-Shing* is gone. You have nothing more to fear from that quarter. Vice-Minister Shimada's daughter has been silenced; she has been taken by the earth. Her revenge is incomplete."

Nangi's face seemed to collapse. His voice was a whisper. "Shimada-san had a daughter? I know only of his two sons, who were killed overseas in a plane crash. A *daughter*?"

"By a *tayu oiran* of the *Yoshiwara*."

"Oh, my God!" A tic had begun beneath Nangi's good eye. "I recall some information I amassed on him. There *was* mention of a courtesan mistress. But that she bore him a child!"

"It gets worse, I'm afraid."

"I don't see how."

"Shimada-san's daughter was Akiko Ofuda Sato."

"Oh, Madonna, no! It's impossible." He wiped the sweat off his face. "Did Seiichi-san know?"

"No."

"Thank God for that small blessing. She must have planned it all—the courtship, the wedding. How Seiichi-san loved her!" He watched his hands shake, fascinated that he had lost this much control. He looked up. "She's gone, you say?"

Nicholas nodded. "Swallowed up in the recent earthquake."

"She could have destroyed everything. *Everything!*"

"It was close," Nicholas acknowledged.

"The Russians and the Americans aren't the only ones interested in *Tenchi*," Nangi said after a moment. "Now that we are partners, I have an obligation to tell you why I went to Hong Kong. I deliberately did not speak of it to Seiichi before I left because I had no way of knowing the outcome in advance and I did not want him to worry."

Nicholas listened with growing interest to Nangi's tale of intrigue.

"But I won everything," Nangi concluded.

Nicholas was silent for a time, digesting all that he had heard. "I wonder," he said at last.

"What do you mean, Linnear-san?"

"Would Lo Whan have any reason to lie to you about his motives?"

Nangi shook his head. "No. It cost him too much face. He was begging me for *Tenchi*'s secret."

"I think we should give it to him."

"What?" Nangi exploded. "After all you've said? You must be mad!"

"Oh, I don't mean right away. Within thirty days *Tenchi* will be under way, the oil will be flowing; nothing can stop us then. Tell Lo Whan that he will have what he wants within a month's time."

"But that's treason! The Communists—"

"Would you rather have the Russians link arms with China? What kind of position do you think that would put Japan in? I don't think even America's might could save us then." He spread his hands. "Don't you see, Nangi-san? By providing this faction with a unique kind of ammunition, you will ensure that Russia and China stand apart, *and* you will gain an incredibly direct foothold into Peking, the Forbidden City. Lo Whan's faction will owe us much. And in time they will have to repay that debt. The price will be up to us to negotiate."

"But they are *Chinese*," Nangi protested. "They are Communists."

"They're also Asian."

Nicholas turned and brought up the silk-covered package. This he put on the table. "This is for you," he said. "In light of this discussion I think it doubly apt."

Nangi's good eye opened wide and again he bowed until his gleaming forehead touched the black tabletop.

Carefully he opened the wrapping. An oiled boxwood container was underneath. He lifted the lid and peered inside. Age seemed

514

to dissolve off his face. With great tenderness, he reached inside and took out the two cups. They were of the most exquisite translucent porcelain.

"T'ang Dynasty," he breathed. He watched the light enter them, thinking of Obā-chama. "*Domo arigato*, Linnear-san." It would have been unseemly to have said more.

He looked at his new partner, and perhaps, as he was learning, his friend. "I will consider your suggestion." There was the ghost of a smile on his lips. "I for one would welcome constructive talks leading to an Oriental Alliance."

Slowly, like the cool tendrils of the sea, Nangi felt a return of a certain centrism he had possessed all his life but which had been ripped from him by the news of Seiichi's death. Without thinking, he hugged this core of comfort about him like a robe around a blue-lipped bather. It took him a while to reach the conclusion that this miracle of sorts had come about because he had allowed himself to trust another spirit. Gōtarō, Obā-chama, Makita, Seiichi. And now Nicholas Linnear. With a sharp pang of excitement, he felt the rhythm start up inside him again, a powerful engine roaring in his ears.

When, sometime later, he was about to leave and they were standing side by side at the door, Nicholas said, "This *kobun* no longer manufactures petrochemicals, does it, Nangi-san?"

Nangi laughed. "Ah, Linnear-san, I believe I am going to enjoy our partnership immensely! If only you were going to stay here instead of returning to America. It is here that you belong, truly. Japan is your home, eh. But I tell you nothing that you do not already know in your heart."

He smiled again. "But to give you an answer: no. Sato Petrochemicals was what it was when Seiichi-san began this *kobun*. But after the oil shock of 1973, he perceived that petrochemicals would rapidly become a declining industry in this country.

"The government, in the form of MITI, stepped in. That was me, of course, since I was still vice-minister of the ministry. Before Fujitsu, Matsushita, NEC, and the rest got into artificial intelligence and robotics, Seiichi-san and I spoke of such futuristic concerns.

"Slowly, so as not to bring any attention to our movements, we began to shift goals and priorities from past industry into future ones. We kept the old name as camouflage. And when, years later, the government began the *Tenchi* project, we were in a unique position to help them."

He opened the door. "You must come up to Misawa one day and see *Tenchi* herself. You've earned the right."

* * *

Nicholas found Justine on the fiftieth floor, near the pool where Miss Yoshida had been killed. She had not been told of Nicholas' arrival.

He stopped still when he saw her tan face, his heart fluttering. And he thought, Yukio belongs to my past. Here is my future. "You look well."

"Nick!" She whirled. "My God, I didn't hear you come in!"

He laughed. "You should be used to that by now." He came toward her, his face sobering. "Listen, Justine, there's something I have to tell you."

But she put the flat of her hand against his lips. "No, Nick, please. I've come thirteen thousand miles to tell you I love you. I acted like a spoiled little girl. I took out on you an anger that I felt at myself. That wasn't fair, and I'm sorry. I know I hurt you, and just because I was hurt myself that was no good excuse."

He took her hand away, held it. "Justine—"

"Whatever you have to tell me doesn't matter anymore. Don't you see, there's nothing you could possibly say that could change the way I feel for you. Nothing could diminish my love. So why say it?"

He saw that she was right, after all. He had wanted to tell her about Akiko, about Yukio. He recalled vividly her phone call to him just after Sato's marriage. How wrapped up in his past he had been then! How impossible it had been for him to connect with her. He was sorry for that as well, but he thought that she already knew it.

He drew her into his arms, and she became aware of his maimed right hand.

"What have you been doing?" she said, taking it in both of hers.

He tried to joke. "Made a grab for another woman. She was a black belt in karate."

She looked up at him. "Really," she breathed.

"I stuck my nose in something and got someone mad. Really."

"Will you ever tell me all of it?"

"Justine," he said softly, his face in her hair. "It's not so very important."

She was weeping. "It caused you pain. It's important to me."

He stroked her hair, his eyes closed. "There's no pain now. It's all over."

Together their lips opened, their tongues met, tasting. They felt the heat, passion rising, a cloud of heavy emotion enveloping them.

516

"Oh, Nick," she murmured. "I'm so happy." She was thinking of the couple on the crest of Haleakala crater. Now I have what they have, she thought, contentedly.

Slowly, gently, they began to reexplore each other, both physically and emotionally, two blind people who had suddenly regained their sight. They kissed as teenagers often do, as if this intimacy was the ultimate one, full of emotional complexities and tiny pleasures evolving into a shimmering network of eroticism. The kiss was representative of more than mere lust. Justine had always felt that one gave one's heart in a kiss. The same could not be said for the sex act itself. It was quite possible to penetrate and be penetrated without kissing at all.

Love was waiting on his lips, in the flick of his hot tongue against the inside of her mouth. How long had she waited for this moment? She would never know for certain but she suspected that it had been all her life. She felt alive and free at the same time. The combination was an entirely new sensation for her.

She luxuriated in this pureness, but still there was so much about her that had changed, and she wanted to share it with him.

"Have you been successful so far?" she asked.

"How do you mean?"

"With Tomkin Industries, of course."

He seemed skeptical. "You mean you really care one way or the other?"

"It's my father's company, isn't it? My future husband's running it, isn't he? I think I have a bit of a stake in its success or failure!"

He smiled, surprised at how enormously pleased he was. "Nangi has just agreed to the merger of Sphynx Silicon and Sato's Nippon Memory Chip *kobun*. But there's much more. I think that within eighteen months, two years at the outside, more than just the two divisions will be merged."

"Nick!" she exclaimed. "That's fantastic!" She hugged him. "My father would have been so proud of you."

"I see that's changed, too," he said, grinning.

She nodded. "I've done a lot of thinking about him since the funeral . . . About me. All the hate's gone. I think I'm able to see him more objectively now; as he really was. I can see the bad *and* the good. I'm just sorry that it took his death to allow me to understand all of it. I'd dearly like to tell him all about it; to see his face when I told him."

He stroked her arm. "Your father was an exceedingly strong personality, Justine. He was too much for many adults. It's not particularly surprising that he should have overpowered his children. The important thing is that you realize that he did not dominate you and Gelda deliberately. He didn't know any other way to live."

She nodded and held on to him. "That's another reason I love you so, Nick. You understand me. You understood him."

They kissed again, sliding into it as if they could never get enough of one another. Nicholas, because it was his way, probed inside her with *haragei*. He found to his utter astonishment the flame of *wa*—perfect harmony—ablaze inside her where before had only been darkness and chaos.

He sighed into her mouth and Justine groaned, melting against him. This state was what he perhaps had seen a spark of when first they had met, running into each other on the beach at West Bay Bridge. For both of us now, he thought, the long journey's ended. And it's just begun.

"Dinner tonight," he said softly, after a long time in her arms.

Justine's eyes were hazy with mingled love and lust. "And until then?"

"Go shopping," he said. "Buy a Matsuda dress. Spend a fortune on tonight."

"Yeah? What's the occasion?"

"Can't tell you," he laughed. "It's a surprise."

"Oh, come on, Nick." She had caught his mood, was laughing too. "Tell me."

"Oh, no," he said. "All I can say is that while you're out making yourself even more beautiful, I'll be working out with a friend. It seems he's anxious to learn *aikido* and I've promised to go with him. There's a *dōjō* I've been to quite near the Okura, where we're all staying. I sent him there this afternoon to make an appointment. We'll meet you back at the hotel at about seven."

"Wait a minute. You mean this friend's the surprise?"

Nicholas shrugged, laughing still. "Don't know. Could be."

"Oh, who is he, Nick? This isn't fair!"

"I'll give you a hint. He's an American. Someone you haven't seen in a long time. Someone you thought you'd never see again."

Justine screwed up her face. "I can't think of who it could be."

"You'll meet him soon enough."

"Oh, no!" she cried. "That's all I'll be thinking about all afternoon. I won't be able to concentrate on anything, shopping included."

Nicholas decided to tell her. His face was alight. "Justine, Lew Croaker's alive and well and staying right here in Tokyo!"

"What? You're kidding!" She watched his face. "But the paper..."

518

"The news story was wrong. It's a long involved story, but the gist of it is someone tried to kill him and missed. Lew stayed 'dead' in order to do what he had to."

"Oh, my God!" She gripped him. "But that's wonderful! How fabulous! Oh, I've got to give him a kiss for not getting himself killed!"

Nicholas laughed, delighted that her reaction mirrored his. "At seven," he said, "you can do whatever you want with him—within reason, that is!"

They both laughed at that. Relief and a cessation of tension dissolved them into fits of giggles that did not stop for a long time. Their sides ached with the laughter, but still they did not stop. It felt far too good.

Nicholas met Croaker in the tiny exquisite park in Toranomon-chō's *san-chōme*. They went up the steps to the building on the thirteenth block that overlooked the small temple and Atago Hill.

How long ago it seemed since he had first entered these doors, Nicholas thought. Like another lifetime. He and Justine were both so different now. And Croaker was there beside him.

In the locker room they changed out of their street clothes, Nicholas climbing into his *gi*, Croaker into the simple loose-fitting white cotton trousers and blouse he found neatly folded in the locker he opened.

It was very quiet in the *dōjō*. Classes had been over for some hours. There was no one about, and so they went in search of Kenzo, the *sensei* who had almost defeated Nicholas the first time he was here.

He was telling this to Croaker, who was saying how nervous and naked he felt without his gun. "You know us cops, Nick," he said, "we even take a shower with our piece strapped under our armpits."

They had come through the *dōjō* proper and were now in the *sensei*'s quarters, a series of small, *tatami*'ed rooms separated by rice-paper *shōji*.

"I've been thinking I'm getting too old for this. I'm tired of caring more for my piece than I do for the woman beside me. They pound that into you at the Academy, at least they did in my day. Your piece's the only thing between you and a hole in your chest. Can't say the same about your woman." He tried to smile but could not make it work.

"Does that include Gelda?" Nicholas asked.

"Gelda. I don't know. But it seems to me that if she can't make it on her own we won't make it together. I'm just no good as a crutch. It won't be long before I come to hate her." At that moment he had a piercing image of Alix in the safe house, Matty the Mouth's apartment. She was sitting with her hands clasped between her knees, staring into the darkness. Traffic hissed by outside, uncaring. Was it a true image? he wondered. Was she really waiting there for him to come back? Or was she gone from his life, a puff of smoke he had once felt beside him and nothing more? On the covers of *Vogue* and *Bazaar* she bore an unattainable demeanor. But he had felt her head on his chest, had seen the despair opaquing her caged eyes. He had taken her hand and in its trembling had been privy to her vulnerability. He was astounded by the depth of his hope that she had not fled Matty's into the endless night. Away from him.

"Then you're through being a cop."

"If only I knew what that meant," Croaker said. "But I don't."

"You knew it well enough with Tanya," Nicholas observed.

"Yah," Croaker said, "I did at that."

There was a shadow beyond the last *shōji*. It could have been a human figure.

"Sensei?" Nicholas called. There was no answer. He reached out and slid aside the *shōji*.

"Oh, Jesus Christ!" Croaker said, staring.

Kenzo, the *sensei* of this *dōjō*, was strung up from the ceiling, a length of nylon cord lashed around his ankles. His legs were white as bone, his face the color of a ruddy sunset. His blackened tongue protruded from between his engorged lips.

Nicholas saw the slash through Kenzo's heart, neat as an incision, and knew instantly what weapon had been used to kill him.

"Goddamn!" Croaker cried. "I told you I felt naked without my piece!" He turned, running back through the path of the open *shōji* toward the staircase and the locker room where his gun was locked up, thinking, A cop's what I am; it's what I'll always be. The beat of my heart.

"No!" Nicholas cried, spinning. "Lew, stop!" Running after his friend.

But Croaker did not hear him. He was in a foreign land and he felt terribly vulnerable without his gun. He was in the second room. Nicholas increased his speed, lunging forward just as Croaker sprinted through into the first room.

Grabbed at his cotton blouse, pulling backward and down.

But there was already a whirring in the air, a dazzling blur, the brief wind of an insect passing close by.

"Ah, God!" It was Croaker's voice, full of surprise and pain. There was blood and a flurry of bodies rolling. Nicholas was up in a crouch. Only an expertly wielded *katana* could have made that lethal cut in Kenzo, and that was what he had feared. The strike he was trying to protect Croaker from had been meant for him.

He saw his friend kneeling on the *tatami*, his right hand gripping his left. Blood poured out of the wound at the open wrist that had abruptly become a stump. Fearful shades of steel had sliced through flesh and bone alike.

That peculiar silvery tone was in the air, a lethal shimmer, an oncoming rush of wind that would slice him open if he let it. Used *tobi ashi*, the flying step, launching himself upward and over the oncoming strike.

Koten laughed harshly. "All your ninja acrobatics will avail you nothing. I have the *dai-katana*."

And indeed it was as Nicholas had feared the moment he saw the expert incision through Kenzo's heart. Koten was wielding Nicholas' own sword, *Iss-Hōgai*. Fleetingly, Nicholas found himself wondering how a *yokozuna*—a *sumō* grand champion—such as Koten had had time to learn *kenjutsu*.

He was wearing *montsuki* and *hakama* just as if he were about to step into the *dohyo* to begin a match. His gleaming black hair was immaculately coiffed in *ichomage*. Even the *dai-katana* with its thirty-inch blade appeared thin and puny so near his great girth. He was an enormously powerful man, and Nicholas had to be constantly aware of the discipline in which he was *sensei*.

Sumō was a bit more limited in range than many other martial arts. Perhaps just over two hundred combinations were possible, stemming from thirty-two key techniques based on pushing with the hands—*tsuki*; with the entire body—*oshi*; and clinching—*yori*.

But Koten was also a *sumai sensei*. All contact with such a *sumō* could be instantaneously dangerous since their size combined with their huge *hara* gave them leverage normally unheard of for a human being unaided by mechanical means. Unarmed, Koten was decidedly lethal.

Koten extended the blade and moved forward in quick crablike steps. He was close to the ground—almost squatting—where he was most comfortable and the strongest.

Nicholas burst backward through the last of the *shōji*, found himself in the *dōjō* proper. He looked for the *katana*, but their ceremonial spot was empty.

Koten slashed downward in an oblique strike, the *dai-katana* piercing wood and rice paper, ripping up the *shōji* only centimeters from Nicholas' retreating leg.

"I'll cut into your ankles first," Koten said, "and make you scream." He came crashing through the rent *shōji* like a wild boar. "I made *sumō* scream, too. In the *dohyo*." Iss-Hōgai swept through the air left to right, then abruptly reversing course, swiping at Nicholas' feet. "You thought *ozeki* made no noise during a match. The audience figures they grunt like territorial animals." Blur of blade again. "That is the secret of *sumō*'s popularity. Beneath the formal rituals, the veneer of dignity and civilization, the audience is excited by what they believe they are seeing. Antlered stag going at it with instantaneous savagery."

Koten's bead eyes were bright as his massive legs powered him forward, as his bare soles beat the floor in a thunderous tattoo. "But within that space of time—thirty seconds, no more—I learned to make my opponents scream. The thunder of the crowd was such that only I heard, locked against his sweating body."

Nicholas feinted right, then came in beneath Koten's guard. But the *sumō* let go of the blade with his left hand, slamming the forearm into Nicholas' chest. Nicholas hit the floor hard.

Koten laughed again. "I didn't hear you scream that time, barbarian, but you will soon." The *dai-katana* swooped down, its finely honed tip splintering the polished wooden boards at Nicholas' feet.

Nicholas knew what all this bantering was in aid of. It was Koten's aim to make Nicholas come against him, to make Nicholas use whatever he might know of *oshi*, drawing Nicholas into his own strength.

I might as well give him what he wants, Nicholas thought. It is time To Pass On to Koten that which he wants most.

Koten laughed as Nicholas came at him, a human mountain attacked by an insect who possibly could sting, but nothing more.

He countered Nicholas' *oshi*, using the hilt of the sword instead of, as Nicholas had expected, returning *oshi* for *oshi*. Nicholas felt the crushing blow on the point of his shoulder, felt the resulting grinding of bone and the audible pop of dislocation. Pain ran like fire down his arm, rendering his right side totally useless.

"This is what Musashi called Injuring the Corners, barbarian," Koten gloated. "I'll beat you down in small strokes. I'll make you scream yet."

He ran at Nicholas, feinting with the long sword, employing *oshi* now to throw Nicholas hard onto the floor. He knelt over him on one knee. The blade sizzled downward, cutting a vicious arc through the air.

Desperately Nicholas twisted, raising his left arm upward so that it broke inside Koten's upraised arm, deflected the blow out and away from him. But because of the injuries to shoulder and fingers he was unable to complete the *suwari waza* move as he would have wanted to.

Instead he was obliged to release Koten's arm prematurely to deliver an *atemi*, a percussive strike, with his left elbow. Heard the answering crack as ribs caved in beneath the blow.

Koten cried out, twisting his body up and away, at the same time slashing back toward Nicholas' body with the *dai-katana*.

Two attacks at once and Nicholas was able to handle only one at a time. The steel blade was his first priority. He made contact with Koten's forearm, gliding his left hand along the flesh. At the point of the bone protrusion along the bottom side of the wrist, he broke inward, twisting with the fingers of his left hand. Because it was *aikido*, he was combining his own strength with that of Koten's own momentum. It was power enough to snap the bone.

Now they were even in a way; Koten was obliged to drop the two-handed grip on the sword, his right arm hanging loose at his side as the broken joint began to swell.

But his second attack could not be stopped, and he used a shoulder throw to Nicholas' right side. This time Nicholas cried out with the pain directed at his dislocated shoulder.

He rolled away, scrambling. He knew that he would be done for if he allowed Koten's bulk to dominate him while he was off his feet. This was the danger with *sumai*, and it was enormous. Their territory was bringing their weight and strength to bear in an area close to the ground.

Nicholas was moving away when he felt the presence of the blade swooping after him. He leaped aside, directly into a powerful *tsuki* that forced all the air from his lungs. His head went down and he began to wheeze reflexively as his lungs tried desperately to regain the oxygen denied them.

A second vicious *tsuki* to his sternum rocked him backward awkwardly so that he sprawled on the floor. In an instant Koten was over him, his weight pressing oppressively on Nicholas' chest, further denying him air. Nicholas began to cough, bile rising into his throat.

Koten brought long, gleaming *Iss-Hōgai* crosswise along Nicholas' chest, drawing a horizontal line, peeling back his black cotton blouse.

"The next stroke will pierce skin, drawing blood," Koten said, his voice silky. "Stupid *iteki* Protorov wouldn't let me at you in Hokkaido. Lucky for you; unlucky for him. But now I have you. Unlucky for you; lucky for me." Koten leaned forward, bringing more pressure down on Nicholas' chest. "Next this *katana* of yours

523

will slice through flesh. Finally, bone and organs." He grinned fiercely. "Tell me, barbarian, how does it feel to know that you are going to die by your own *dai-katana*?"

Beginning the first cut, skin rupturing, peeling back like the rind of a fruit. Blood welling, dark and hot.

Nicholas' mind was screaming for surcease. Reaching back for the "no mind" of the Void, he allowed the organism to work on its own. His left arm shot straight up, the fingers together and as rigid as any swordblade ever forged. Into the soft spot of flesh joining Koten's chin with throat.

Nicholas struck as he had been taught *kenjutsu*, as he would have done a sword strike: with all his muscle, mind, and spirit. He thought not of Koten's flesh but rather of what lay beyond it.

The *kite* struck through flesh and cartilage, ripping through Koten's larynx, his mouth and sinuses.

The *sumō*'s eyes opened wide, more with shock than with fear. There was no time for anything else. He was dead before sensation could reach the brain and register.

Sirens screaming. Inside the ambulance, Lew Croaker lay on a stretcher unconscious, in mild shock. The paramedics had kept the makeshift tourniquet he had fashioned, afraid to remove it lest the bleeding begin again.

Nicholas sat next to him, one shoulder lower than the other. He had refused a shot and now sat staring at his stricken friend and his ruined left hand that was no more than a stump.

Across his lap lay *Iss-Hōgai* in its black lacquer scabbard. He gripped it so hard his left hand was white. *For life.* Its name seemed ironic to him now. *There's magic in a Japanese forged blade*, he had once told Justine. But what use was magic that could do this?

At the hospital he climbed painfully down after Croaker had been wheeled inside the emergency room. Leaning the *dai-katana* against a pale green cinderblock wall, he dug a coin out of his pocket and dialed the hotel.

"Justine," he said wearily when the connection was made, "come and get us. We're at Toranomon Hospital." He put his forehead against the cool wall. An intern was calling urgently to him, coming across the crowded corridor to take him away.

"Everything's all right," he said into the phone. "But I miss you." He put down the phone and began to cry.

TOKYO SUBURBS

SPRING, PRESENT

On a clear day in late spring, three weeks after the incident at the *dōjō*, Nicholas and Justine returned from jampacked Narita, where they had seen Lew Croaker off to America.

His arm was healing well. The operation, an attempt to sew back the hand that had been so cleanly sliced off, had been a failure. Too much time had elapsed. But otherwise the news had been good. No complications, no infections. The tourniquet he had fashioned from strips of cloth blouse had quite possibly saved his life, the surgeon had said. He was very encouraged about the prognosis.

Instead of heading back into the choking riot of Tokyo, Nicholas drove them northwest, skirting the city itself. In the backseat of the Nissan sedan *Iss-Hōgai* lay scabbarded and quiescent, its presence an ever-constant weight.

They went past the lake above which Sato had gotten married, where Akiko had first revealed herself, where Yukio had returned from the grave. Bright sunshine turned the water to gold and glass. Herons rose near the inlet to the stream that fed the lake, their white bodies bright and sharp against the deep translucent blue.

"What a beautiful place!" Justine exclaimed. Nicholas said nothing.

Just outside the gate to Itami's property he stopped the car and they got out. He wanted to walk the rest of the way. It was as if the modern conveyance did not belong there; he felt strongly that he would defile the grounds by driving in.

Together they strolled down the flagstone path, Justine holding lightly to his left hand.

"How are your fingers today?" she asked.

"Better," he said. It was what he always told her.

"Has feeling come back yet?"

"They're better." His voice was gentle. "Just better."

Justine looked at him, wondering what it might take now to set his spirit at rest.

They passed a stone basin in the shape of an old coin. It was round, carved on its top with one character at each cardinal direction. Rock. Rain. Fire. Cloud.

Justine wanted to walk over to it and they went off the path. Water filled its square central well, a handmade bamboo ladle resting on the stone.

"I'm thirsty," she said, and Nicholas took up the ladle. They both drank from it. The water was cold and sweet. For a moment the well was less than full, and as Nicholas bent to return the ladle to its resting place, he saw that there was an ideogram carved into its bottom. *Michi*. A path; also a journey.

Miraculously, the house and grounds had sustained no major damage in the aftermath of the earthquake. One outer wall at the southerly end of the house had collapsed, and several trees nearby had been split. But that was all.

Still, it was hardly the same. Without Itami and her legion of servants the place seemed deserted indeed. She had died sometime during the day and a half he had been at the hospital. The funeral had taken place two days later, when Nicholas was healed sufficiently to attend. She was buried in a plot quite near Cheong's and the Colonel's, as she had wished.

There had been no pain in her dying, the white-haired physician had told Nicholas. He had attended to Itami's medical needs for more than thirty years. "One moment she was there," he said. "The next she was gone." Nicholas was at least grateful for that.

Justine watched him as he wandered the house. Something had come over him the moment he had alit from the car. She had felt it when she had taken his hand, when she had looked at his strong, handsome profile as they had walked the gravel path to the house.

In the small room where only *chano-yu* had been performed, he sank down onto his knees. He winced a bit as pain flicked through his shoulder. Then, by some process that was totally mysterious to Justine, he flicked it off, and his face cleared.

She knelt at his side, bending her head a bit to see more of the beautiful garden than the half-screen permitted. "Why is it like that?" she said. "There's so much more to see out there." But even when he explained it to her, she was not certain that she understood. If it's there, she thought, why not take advantage of it?

"I've met with Nangi several times," he said, his voice drifting. "He's anxious that we stay, at least for a time. There's so much to do." He turned his head. "Would that be okay with you, a month or six weeks? Tokyo's not so bad once you get used to it."

"I don't mind," she said, watching him still. There was a wistful look on his face, and a calmness young boys have after a long day's exertion, when, happily exhausted, they return home to a secure rest.

"Well, really, he'd like us to stay here permanently. I told him that that was out of the question."

"Why did you do that?"

He looked at her quickly. "Why? It's not possible. And you wouldn't like it. You'd miss New York. And your new job."

"I'd miss you more if we went back to the States and I saw you longing to be here. Besides, I think I could talk Rick into letting me start up a branch office in Tokyo. He's fascinated by Japanese ad methods."

"I don't want to be here," he said. "Besides, where would we live?"

She smiled at him. "Why not right here?"

"Oh, no," he said immediately. "There are too many memories here. The past's all around, hanging in every corner like a spider web."

"I like it here," she said, regaining her feet. "I'm sorry that you don't."

On the way back, they stopped by the side of the lake. The birds were trilling sweetly, and the air smelled very fresh.

Justine gently stroked the back of his injured hand. "Why won't you smile, Nick. You've been brooding for weeks. It worries me to see you like this."

Nicholas spread out his hands, palms up. "I look at these, Justine, and wonder what they're for besides inflicting pain and death."

She put one of her hands in his. "They're also gentle hands, Nick. They caress me and I melt inside."

He shook his head. "That's not enough. I can't help thinking what they've done. I don't want to kill." His voice trembled. "I don't believe that I ever could have."

527

"You never sought out death, Nick. You've always killed in self-defense."

"Yet I sought out the training, first *bujutsu*, then *ninjutsu*. Why?" His eyes were pleading.

"What answer do you think will satisfy you?" she said softly.

"That's just it," he cried in anguish. "I don't know!"

"I think that's because there *is* no answer."

His head went down and he said in a muffled voice, "Then I have no answer for how I maimed my friend."

"Oh, Nick," she said, pressing her lips against his cheek, "Lew doesn't blame you; why blame yourself?"

"Because without me he'd still have two hands!"

"No, without you he'd be dead. And he'd never have found out who really murdered Angela Didion." Nicholas had told her as much as he could during their long vigil during Croaker's operation. "You know how obsessed he was over that."

With a little cry Nicholas tore himself away from her loving embrace. He went around the car, reached into an open back window, and took the *dai-katana* up.

He kissed Justine hard on the lips. "I'll be back in a little while. Wait for me; listen to the birds, watch the sunlight drift through the leaves."

He went away from her up the small grassy knoll and down toward the lake. The water sparked and danced as ripples creased its surface. Water lapped softly at his feet, running into his socks. It felt good on his feet, and he waded in up to his thighs, unmindful of his clothes.

There was a pain like a stone in his throat. *Iss-Hōgai* had been the Colonel's gift to him to commemorate his passage from child to man.

But, he thought now, there was another passage he must make that came after that one. He was ready for it now; prepared in every way he could imagine. Yet it would still hurt, he knew. Not as much as his hurt for his friend, but it would be bad enough.

"Thank you, father," he mouthed as he lofted the *dai-katana* high over his head in his good hand and threw it with all his strength out into the middle of the lake.

It hit the surface point on, and there was no splash at all. Soundlessly, it disappeared into the depths.

For a long time after that Nicholas stood thigh deep in the cool water, feeling its life-giving lap surrounding his body. He breathed deeply of the air; heard birds calling behind him. He saw a pair of snowy herons lift off from the water's surface and wheel into

528

the white sky. He watched their flight until they, too, were lost to sight.

He recognized the lightness in his spirit when it came, like a fresh breeze after a humid summer's day. It had been time to put away the lethal toys that had dominated his life for so long. It was time to get on with living.

He turned at last and waded the short distance to shore. Just beyond the small crest of the knoll, Justine waited for him. His heart expanded at the knowledge.

As he went toward her, he thought that she might be right after all, just as Nangi had been right. Japan was his home. Did he really want to leave it now?

For the first time he could feel the real force of the calmness he experienced in Itami's *chano-yu* room. There his spirit was truly at rest. He could imagine *tsukimi*—moon viewing—there; celebrating New Year's with traditional *mochi* rice cakes; *hanami* in April when the cherry blossoms fell rich and radiant, reminders of all that life was: exquisite and fleeting. *Sakura* were, after all, as mortal as men and women.

In Itami's house—*his* house, should he wish it—the modern-day Japan had not yet come. The feudal *kami* still resided there, proud and splendid and eternally victorious. Honor lived there, as well as courage.

Nicholas, taking Justine's hand in his, thought it would be the perfect spot to teach a new spirit what life was all about.

GLOSSARY

aikido—*ai*, harmony; *ki*, energy; *do*, the way. A discipline of hand-to-hand martial arts employing pivoting movements to neutralize an attack.

Aisha seishin—in business, devotion to the company.

aka-i-ninjutsu—literally, "red *ninjutsu*." Used for good.

akuma—an evil spirit: a devil.

akuryo—a battle mask in the shape of an evil demon's face. See *mempo*.

ama-gasa—an umbrella.

anata—the polite form of "you" used by women.

atemi—one of a number of percussive strikes in *aikido*.

baishun—literally, *the selling of spring*; prostitution.

bokken—wooden practice sword used in *kenjutsu* training.

bonbori—paper lanterns traditionally hung during *hanami*.

Boryokudan—a gang of thugs employing extremely violent tactics. Its members are not bound by the code of honor of the *yakuza*.

531

bujutsu—generic heading for all Japanese martial arts.

bushido—*samurai*'s strict and unforgiving code of honor.

-chan—informal suffix to a name indicating love and a certain special closeness.

chano-yu—the tea ceremony.

cho—districts within a city's wards.

chome—subdistricts within a city's *cho*.

chunin—tactical unit leader within a particular *ninja* school or clan.

dai-katana—longest of the *samurai*'s *katana*, or long swords.

daikon—a white radish.

daimyo—a feudal warlord.

dan—any of a number of black belt or highest rankings in *aikido*.

denka no hoto—bureaucratic phraseology for the *katana*, the *samurai* sword.

dohyo—a *sumo* ring, where the wrestling is performed.

dojo—physical school of martial arts, the place of practice.

domo arigato—thank you very much.

ekika—in hand-to-hand combat, a vital spot just beneath the armpits.

feng shui—Cantonese for geomancer: he who reads portents in the cardinal elements of life: earth, air, fire, and water.

fusuma—opaque sliding door in the interior of a Japanese house.

futon—a thick, flexible mattresslike quilt for sleeping.

Fuyajo—literally, "The Castle That Knows No Night," the name of a *geisha* house. See *geisha* and *Yoshiwara*.

gaijin—a foreigner.

gakubatsu—the bond between school classmates that extends on into business life.

geisha—one trained in the arts of entertainment.

genin—a *ninja* agent within a particular school or clan.

geta—wooden clogs.

getsumei no michi—literally, "the moonlit path"; a level of awareness suspended between the conscious and the subconscious.

gi—the costume worn during the practice of martial arts.

giri—the concept of debt, usually moral.

goho-no-kamae—a specific opening stance in spike and chain combat. See *manrikigusari*.

gunsen—a war fan, usually made of iron.

h'eung yau—literally, "fragrant grease"; Cantonese for a bribe.

hachimaki—a cloth wrapped around the forehead of a warrior.

haha—mother, informally or lovingly.

hai—yes.

haiku—a Japanese poem of seventeen syllables which strives to encompass a maximum of content and emotion in a minimum of space. A microcosm of Japanese life.

hakama—a traditional black divided skirt worn by *sensei* in certain forms of martial arts; part of the *gi*.

hanami—three days of cherry blossom viewing.

Hang Seng—the Hong Kong stock exchange.

hara—to be grounded within oneself, to possess force of spirit, inner strength; therefore, to garner respect. Most prized by Japanese. *Hara* resides in the lower belly.

haragei—in the martial arts, a form of sixth sense.

hera-mochi—literally, the one with the right to hold the spoon used to serve rice; the head of the household; the mother.

hinin—the lowest level of Japanese caste society. Traditionally, all *ninja* families originated in the *hinin*.

hiragana—the basic Japanese language, consisting of forty-eight phonetic syllables adopted from Chinese Mandarin.

hito washi—"the human eagle," a makeshift glider *ninja* learn to construct.

iai—the art of drawing a weapon—usually a *katana*—and striking in the same motion. May be effected from a position of seeming unpreparedness.

ichi—literally, "position"; an offshoot of *kiai*, using the voice to influence the enemy's thought or action.

ichomage—the traditional intricate coiffure of the grand champion, or *yokozuna sumo*.

Ikagadesuka—the equivalent of "Hello, how are you?"

ikebana—the art of flower arranging.

irimi—exercise variations of *jo-waza*, stave *aikido*.

Iss-hogai—literally, "for life"; the name of a *katana*.

iteki—a barbarian; a derogatory term devoid of all respect.

jaho—magic.

janomegasa—a rice-paper umbrella.

Jinno Shotoki—one of the great books of teaching in the Shinto religion. It was written in 1339 by Chikafusa Kitabatake.

jit suryoko—superhuman powers. See *akuma*.

jitsu—fullness, as in breathing.

jo-waza—the martial art of stave *aikido*.

jonin—leader of a *ninja* school or clan.

joss—Chinese term used variously for luck, destiny; akin to *karma*.

joss stick—incense.

juka—the organ meridian on the human body just beneath each ear. See *kyukon*.

juku—an elite private study group to aid Japan's best students.

junsuisei—the purity of resolve.

k'ai ho—Mandarin ideogram meaning, variously, a gap, an opportunity to be seized; spies. A term used by Sun Tzu in his *Art of War*.

kabuki—a form of highly stylized Japanese theater employing masked actors.

kamae—one of a number of opening stances in spike and chain combat. See *manrikigusari*.

kami—a spirit, ancestral or otherwise.

kamikaze—literally, "divine wind." Self-destruction in war for the good of the Emperor.

kamiza—the upper seat of the *aikido* practice mat. The place of honor reserved for the *sensei*.

kamuro—a serving girl to *geisha*.

kan—a status of power bestowed upon the bureaucrat by Imperial appointment. Originally from the Mandarin, meaning the home of the man presiding over a city.

Kan-aku na ninjutsu—literally, "black *ninjutsu*." Invariably used for evil, the most virulent sub-discipline of which is *Kuji-kiri*.

kanji—the written Japanese language.

kanryodo—the Way of the samurai-bureaucrat; a modern martial art purely of the mind.

kanzashi—traditional long hairpins, usually made of carved wood, ivory, or tortoiseshell; usually part of a set. See *kushi*.

karma—one's destiny.

karyukai—literally, "the flower and willow world." See *Yoshi-wara*.

katakana—adjunct syllabary in the Japanese language used to introduce colloquialisms and words of foreign origin. See *hiragana*.

katana—the *samurai*'s longsword.

kataribe—professional language memorizers used before the beginning of the Japanese written language (prior to the fifth century A.D.).

katsu—a form of deep resuscitation.

keibatsu—the bond created by blood or marriage into a family.

keiretsu—an industrial conglomerate of companies.

535

Kempeitai—in the present, the military police; during World War II, the secret police.

ken—the standard six-foot unit of house construction.

kendo—the art of the sword from an educational point of view; viz. technique is translated as *do*, meaning a spiritual path. See *kenjutsu*.

kenjutsu—the art (*jutsu*) of the sword (*ken*) in a combative, practical sense. See *kendo*.

ki—inner energy required for any of the martial arts.

kiai—a shout to startle and frighten an enemy.

kimono—a traditional robe, usually of silk or cotton, worn by both men and women.

kin-yu keiretsu—financial linkages. The basis of *keiretsu*.

kite—one of a number of vicious percussive blows using either the edge of the hand or the tips of the fingers in concert.

Kobudera—a form of evil magic employed by the *Kuji-kiri*.

kobun—a company; part of a *keiretsu*.

Kodomo-gunjin—literally, "little soldier." A name as an endearment.

kogen—the Japanese highlands.

kokuhisho—black-skin syndrome caused by the inclusion of a coal tar dye in women's skin cream.

kokyu suru—in certain martial arts, an attack stance; to breathe.

komuso—a wandering ascetic; the ideogram used at the center of the *Kuji-kiri ninja* crest.

konzern—division of a *keiretsu* conglomerate, broken down by industry.

koppo—the martial art of breaking bones.

ku—wards, the broadest area designations, within a city.

Kuji-kiri—literally, "nine-hands cutting"; a form of black *ninjutsu*. See *Kan-aku na ninjutsu*.

kushi—traditional comb used in the hair, usually part of a set. See *kanzashi*.

536

kyo—emptiness, as in breathing.

kyodobatsu—the bond between men born in the same prefecture or town.

Kyoiku mama—an education mother; one who helps her children in their academic studies.

kyudo—a martial art.

kyukon—the nine organ meridians on a human body.

kyusho—vital spots.

mabiki—the weeding-out process used to rid a school or bureau of undesirables.

maho-zukai—a sorceror.

makiotoshi—in spike and chain combat, a move to wind the chain about the opponent's neck. See *manrikigusari*.

manrikigusari—literally, "the chain with the strength of ten thousand men," a martial arts weapon consisting of a steel chain weighted at both ends.

mempo—a battle mask made of hinged steel.

menju fukuhai—literally, "reversing in the belly." Slang phrase used by bureaucrats still under the domination of the American Occupation. It meant carrying out American orders on the face of it while reversing policy after some time had passed.

michi—a path; a journey; duty; the unknown; a stranger.

mie—a stylized pose used in *kabuki*.

miira—a mummy.

miko—a sorceress; a maiden in the service of a shrine.

mochi—traditional rice cakes eaten at New Year's.

montsuki—part of the traditional dress of the *sumo* grand champion.

muhon-nin—a traitor.

musubinawa—an eight-meter coil of rope made of women's hair. See *rokugu*.

naga-hibachi—a kind of stove.

nariyuki no matsu—to wait for the turn of events; to be patient.

nekode—cat's claws made of forged steel. See *rokugu*.

netsuke—carvings of ivory or wood, traditionally used to tie off the strings of an *inro*, a carved box, worn around the waist when dressed in a kimono, in lieu of pockets.

ninja—literally, "in stealth." A Japanese assassin.

ninjutsu—a wide field of subspecies of martial arts studied by *ninja*.

Noh—serious Japanese drama.

oba-chama—grandmother.

Oba—mother, formally.

obi—wide silk sash used to hold kimono in place.

ochugen—in business, a mid-year gift.

Ogawa-no-jutsu—the arcane art of breaking down toxic substances inside the body. Part of *ninjutsu*.

ogi—a folding fan.

oiran—a full-fledged *geisha*. There are three levels, of which *tayu* is the highest.

Okagesamade—the equivalent of "I am fine." See *Ikagadesuka*.

omae—the form of "you" used only by men.

omoya—literally, "mother house," the central section of a Japanese house, reserved for family members only.

oseibo—in business, a year-end gift. Westerners may see this as a bonus but, in fact, it is used to repay the obligations that have accrued during the course of the twelve-month period.

oshi—in *sumo* wrestling, pushing with the entire body.

oyabun—the head of a *yakuza* family; the boss.

ozeki—*sumo* champion.

pachinko—a pinball-like game played on a vertical field.

quai loh—Cantonese for foreign devil.

riakon—a Japanese country inn.

ritsurei—in *aikido*, the ritual bow before the *sensei* of the *dojo*.

rokugu—the *ninja*'s six tools for traveling.

ronin—literally, "wave man." In feudal times, a masterless samurai; today it is employed to describe ministers who have retired from bureaucratic life and have not yet formed a new business affiliation.

rotenburo—an outdoor hot bath.

ryochi—a feudal lord's region of power. See *daimyo*.

ryu—a school or discipline of martial arts.

saika tanden—in martial arts preparedness, a state of "nothingness," where one is ready for all eventualities.

saiminjutsu—an arcane form of martial arts practiced by some *ninja*, involving a particularly potent form of hypnotism.

sake—rice wine, the traditional Japanese drink, served hot or cold.

sakura—a cherry blossom, a national symbol.

samisen—traditional stringed instrument.

samurai—in feudal Japan, the warrior. The *samurai* class was the only one allowed to wear swords in public.

-san—suffix to a name used for respect and politeness.

San Ho Hiu—Three Harmonies Association. The traditional name for the Triads.

sanchome—area designation within a city district.

sankinkotaiseido—in feudal times, the annual pilgrimage of *daimyo* to the capital, seat of the *shogun*'s power.

sashimi—raw sliced fish.

sashimono—an ancient battle standard.

seikotsu—an adjunct to the art of *katsu*, a form of deep resuscitation.

seisan fukko setsu—the theory of economic reconstruction through industrial production.

sempai—in business, an elder champion.

sennin—a *ninja* adept, a *sensei*.

sensei—a master. Generally refers to the martial arts but may be used more broadly.

seppuku—ritual suicide. Traditionally, only samurai were allowed this most honorable form of death.

shiken jigoku—examination hell, rigorous cramming for batteries of school tests and college entrance exams.

shimpu—the divine winds of 1274 and 1281 which drowned the Mongol army intent of invading Japan; in World War II slang, daredevil taxi drivers.

shinki kiitsu—the unity of soul, mind, and body that is the essence of all martial arts.

shinzo—level of apprentice *geisha*. See *geisha*, *oiran*, *tayu*, *kamuro*.

shitahara—in martial arts exercises, the awareness of power located in the lower belly; the force of *hara*.

shitamachi—Tokyo's downtown area.

shogun—the supreme warlord of feudal Japan.

shoji—translucent sliding screen defining rooms in a traditional Japanese house.

shomen uchi—in *aikido*, a punishing blow to the head.

shunga—prints with an erotic content. See *ukiyo-e*.

shuriken—any one of a number of small steel blades employed by *ninja*.

so desu—thank you.

soba—buckwheat noodles.

sobi—sublime beauty.

someiyoshino—an early-blooming variety of cherry blossom. See *hanami* and *sakura*.

sotomawari—literally, "going around the track"; in bureaucratic life, an accelerating series of postings and promotions that puts one on the elite track.

sumai—combat *sumo*.

sumo—the martial art of wrestling; traditional wrestlers of large size and girth because of their extraordinary *hara*.

sushi—raw fish wrapped around sticky rice and green horseradish.

Tai Chi Chuan—a form of martial art that emphasizes balance, muscular control, and contemplation.

tai-pan—head of a number of important trading houses in Hong Kong.

tambo—a hard percussive blow in sword combat and practice. See *kenjutsu* and *bokken*.

tanden—the brain's reflex control center.

tatami—reed mat of a specific size comprising the floor of a traditional Japanese house. Room sizes are measured by *tatami* number.

tayu—the highest level of *oiran geisha*.

Tenchi—literally, Heaven and Earth.

tenno no kanri—literally, "officials of the Emperor." Term used to describe the modern Japanese bureaucrat.

tokonoma—raised praying niche.

tonkatsu—breaded pork cutlet.

torii—traditional gate to a Shinto shrine made of wood lacquered crimson.

tsuchigumo—literally, "bat in the rafters," a *ninja* technique for hanging undetected from the ceiling of a room.

tsuka kaikaku setsu—the control of inflation through a commitment to light rather than heavy industry.

tsuki—in *sumo* wrestling, pushing with the hands.

tsukimi—the moon-viewing ritual.

541

Tsunokakushi—literally, "the horn-hider," a ceremonial white hat traditionally worn by a bride at her wedding ceremony. Its wide brim is said to hide whatever bad points she may possess.

tsusho daiichi-shugi—bureaucratic slogan meaning trade number one-ism.

uchitake—a three-meter length of hollow bamboo. See *rokugu*.

ukiyo-e—woodblock prints created for the pleasure of the rising merchant class in nineteenth-century Japan.

wa—personal aura, magnetism. Strong *wa* indicates harmony of spirit.

wakizashi—samurai's short sword; one of its uses is to commit *seppuku*.

watashi no musuko—my son, informally and endearingly.

Wu-shing—Mandarin term for a series of ritualistic punishments by mutilation.

yakitori—chunks of meat or flesh marinated in a sweet soy-based sauce and grilled on a skewer with fresh vegetables.

yakuza—the Japanese criminal underworld, divided into clans with its own code of honor as strict as *bushido*. See *giri*.

yamabushi—wandering, self-mortifying adherents of a religious sect known as Shugendo that inhabit the slopes of Mt. Omine in Nara Prefecture.

yamato-dama-shii—the indominability of the Japanese spirit.

Yami Doko—literally, "Kite in the Darkness," the name of a castle.

yokozuna—a grand champion *sumo*.

yonkyo—in *aikido*, an immobilization technique.

yori—in *sumo* wrestling, clinching.

yoshitanrei—a beautiful appearance.

Yoshiwara—literally, "reed field" or "happy field." That section of the old capital given over to sensory pleasure; traditionally, home of the *geisha*.

zaibatsu—name given to the great family-run industrial conglomerates pre–World War II.

zarei—the sitting bow in *aikido*.

ABOUT THE AUTHOR

ERIC VAN LUSTBADER was born, raised and educated in Greenwich Village. He graduated Columbia College in 1968, majoring in Sociology. While there, he founded an independent music production company, a move which led to a fifteen-year involvement in the entertainment industry. That involvement encompassed work in journalism, marketing, seeking out new talent, graphic design, and publicity. He has worked for *Cash Box* magazine, Elektra Records, CBS Records, Dick James Music, USA, and has written and field-produced a profile on rock star Elton John for NBC-TV's "Nightly News."

Since 1979 Mr. Lustbader has devoted his full time to writing. He is the author of three previous internationally best selling novels, *The Ninja, Sirens,* and *Black Heart*.

He lives in New York City and Southampton with his wife, free-lance editor Victoria Schochet Lustbader.

A Master of the erotic and terrifying thriller...

ERIC VAN LUSTBADER